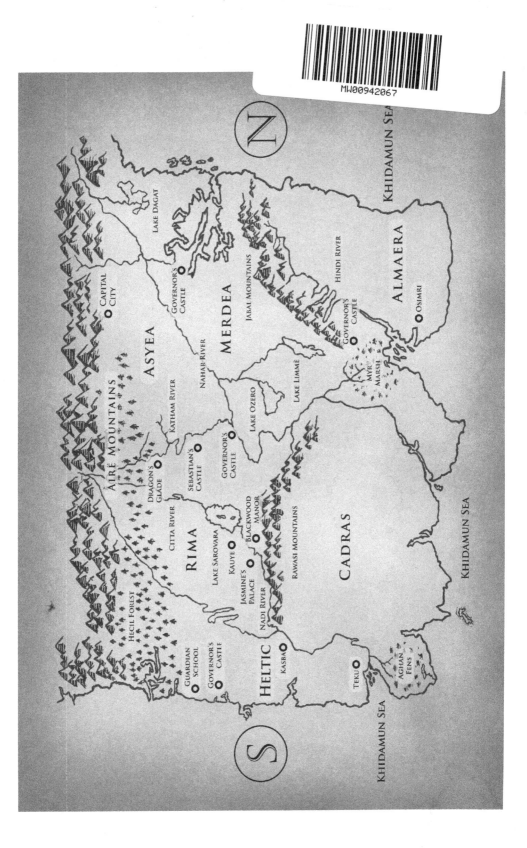

The Chosen
The Guardians of Rima

K.J. Nessly

Dragons: Guardians of Rima

The Chosen

ISBN 978-1512358025

Cover and Interior Design: Isis Sousa.

Dedication

This book is dedicated to Jesus Christ

My Lord and Savior

As the first fruits of my labors

Acknowledgements

There are several people without whom this book would not be possible:

Dad—From start to finish you ingeniously complemented my ideas with your own and braved each new edit, treating each as if it was a new read.

Anna S. —You read the roughest of the rough and told me that you liked it. And you taught me about character.

Dan Murray—You opened my eyes to the real world and always answered my unending questions.

Emily W.—You kept my confidence up and made me believe I could do it.

Kirsten & Mikaela—My humor editors...I've completely lost track of the number of dinners we spent creating harebrained scenes and ridiculous scenarios

Isis Sousa—Your beautiful artwork brought life to the story.

Darkness approaches
Victory after victory it shall win
Death and Sickness reign
Man must search their hearts
To find hope buried within

A false peace shall cover the lands
Never knowing the enemy still commands
Rising upon the chosen power
Like a storm upon an ocean's sands
The innocent and weak, darkness shall devour

Deceit runs rampant
Dishonesty is King
Truth and Light fade from memory
Illusions and tricks shall the evil bring

Sun and Moon in mortal form must rise
And save humanity from the endless tide
Allies and friends they will each advise
Without them, Hope's Victory shall be denied

~Iellwen, Ice Maiden~

Prophesied during the reign of Queen Maira and King Jacen of Cadras four years after the defeat of Daaman Aleksas

Lost several generations before the Great War

Prologue

The sun rose over the occupied fields below, mocking the inhabitants with its golden glow and peaceful approach. Immortal in its duty, its beauty would be forever untouched or marred by the petty wars, schemes, and violence that consumed the inhabitants of the lands below. The horizon turned crimson red as its eternal face entered into the realm of man, portending the struggle that raged continually from the weeks, and years, before. Far beneath the scattered clouds, the sun's rays illuminated a vast sea of warriors treading upon soggy fields saturated with the lifeblood of friends, comrades, allies, and enemies.

A lone eagle soaring high on a thermal gazed down upon the gently moving masses of the two armies and it did not matter which direction the creature looked all that could be seen below even unto the horizon, were tents, cooking fires, horses, war machines, and men.

Men who had not known a moment of peace since the day of their birth. Their whole lives and the lives of those before them for four generations existed to push the invaders, who had wandered into their midst, back across the sea to whence they had come. With one mind they sought to exterminate the invaders who had covered their land like a locust plague consuming, killing, and destroying everything in their path.

Alliances had been renewed and formed as the invaders, or the Wanderers as they were now known, cut a deadly swath across the once peaceful kingdoms. Many had fought, too many had died. Kings fell with frightening regularity and their families disappeared, becoming slaves or human sacrifices to the Wanderers. All too often the standard of the army commander had changed throughout the war. The royal standards which had once numbered six, one for the king of each kingdom, had been reduced to half as royal bloodlines died out. Now, up on a slight rise to the east, the standards of King Dierk, King Calannon, and Chief Einar whipped and snapped in the stiff breeze above the command tent.

Two generations before, King Dierk's forefather, King Darran, had appealed to the Elves for an alliance and through the resulting treaty gained a new class of warriors who became his personal protectors. Exceptionally strong and powerful in magic these warriors, whose ranks were composed of both full blooded elves and half-elves, eventually broadened the scope of their mission to not only protect the king, but also his people. It was through the urging of the high council of Guardians, as the people now called these protectors, that King Dierk sought a second alliance, one with the Marjai of the north.

The Marjai were a hardy desert warrior people, literally digging their kingdom out of the sandstone and rock of the hot desert their people inhabited. Their warriors, with dark skin, stood out amongst the pale Elves and humans. Taller and stockier than the fair Elves, the Marjai were nearly their equal in skill and strength, conditioned by the harsh rigors and demands of the lands where they dwelled, and no mere human warrior could withstand their onslaught in hand to hand combat.

While the Elves favored their bows and fighting knives and the humans favored their double-edged broadswords, the Marjai favored a long curved sword with a single edged blade. The swords were so massive that when the blade's tip stood on stone, the hilt would reach to the heart of its wielder. Their leader, Einar, was a giant even amongst his own people, reaching over three meters from the crown of his head to his toes.

Now these two armies, joined by the army of the Elves, were pushing the Wanderers back; regaining land that had been possessed by the invaders for over a hundred years. During the reign of King Darius, King Dierk's father, the Elves had schooled the ragged human army in tactics and the building of weapons. Together, man and Elf, had worked side by side to strengthen ancient, decrepit strongholds, build machines of war, and improve the techniques used to forge weapons. It was also during this time that King Darius had put together a master plan for the final campaign against the invaders. In this plan he specified a location where the final battle should take place, a site that would benefit the army and cavalry of the Alliance more than those of the Wanderers.

Believing the inhabitants to be cowed, the Wanderers had built their strongholds to impress and frighten. Not until the Alliance had begun its final campaign against them had the Wanderer's generals considered strengthening the imposing, but poorly built structures. And by then it was far too late. Guided by Calannon and the giant Einar, Dierk launched harassing raids at the Wanderers depleting their supply columns and shepherding them to the place chosen years before by King Darius where the final battle would take place. The Wanderer strongholds collapsed as if they had been built out of sticks and river mud. One by one the keeps and fortresses fell until just one remained. One bastion located in the southwestern tip of the old Kingdom of Rima.

To the west stood the Rawasi Mountains, to the south surged the great Eridanus River, and far to the north the Nahar River traced a meandering path across half the continent before finally turning toward the sea. Near the base of the Rawasi Mountains a massive structure stood firm against the elements, a castle with four towers, one for each of the elements the Wanderers worshiped. It was here the Wanderers had gathered for one last stand and it was here that the sun now rose so peacefully above.

Raihji Darktree, the leader of the Wanderers, was a cunning man and widely respected as a brilliant military strategist, even by his enemies. It was at his castle, situated on a small rise above the plains, that his army was now readying themselves for the final battle. For five years the castle, which had been reinforced even as the rest of the Wanderer strongholds had fallen, had stood proud and tall.

Now there was little left but rubble. The golden towers which had once stood so arrogant now lay in crumbling pieces on the ground. Flying boulders from the Alliance's war machines had punched massive holes in the walls, causing them to collapse. The main castle had been reduced to rubble in the bombardment the Alliance had put forth. Raihji's army was encamped amongst the ruins, using the massive blocks and boulders as shields.

As the sun rose higher a band of earth distinguished itself from amongst its surroundings. It was unoccupied land...dead man's land. Scorched black from numerous flaming projectiles that hadn't quite made it to their target with deep furrows running in both directions, dead man's land was desolate and uninhabitable. Any who dared cross was immediately cut down by the opposing side.

Today, however, one army was going to breach dead man's land with the intent of never returning to their side in defeat again. They would succeed or die.

Calannon, Einar, and Dierk stood around a well-worn map with blackened edges, evidence of the close calls it had been in.

One last chance to back out of their plan...

As the sun began to crest over the ruined castle, the Alliance's army began its attack. Hundreds of groups of men-at-arms locked their shields together to form one massive shield covering them on all sides and from above. Each group marched five abreast and one hundred deep directly behind the cavalry who would lead the charge. Off to the right, the Elven army stood ready, row after row after row of warriors with their shields, bows, and pikes. To the left, the Marjai warriors stood ready, their own swords glittering against the sun's rays.

King Dierk rode up to the edge of band of scorched earth. "Raihji!" He called in a voice loud enough to be heard over the shuffling of feet and the jangling of harnesses of his own army, but that was also magically enhanced to be heard by his enemy on the top of the rise a kilometer away. "Your army has lost! Surrender and we will show mercy...although you would deny us the same courtesy."

His message delivered, Dierk rejoined his army and waited.

৪৩·৫৪

High above, sitting in his command tent, Raihji scoffed. "Your army has lost!" He mocked the pagan king's words in a high, whiny tone. "I will show that pagan who has lost. Begin the charge." His lieutenant bowed and moved to carry out his order.

Safe in his tent, Raihji watched as his army raced towards the insufferable foreign army...

The two armies collided in dead man's land.

As far as he could see man fought man, and it gave him immense pleasure. Soldiers were nothing more than a means for conquering others. Many would die, but they would die with honor and their families would be taken care of. Those who did die would continue on to Reingard, the place of heroes and would be given riches according to their purpose in life. Spreading his hands on the ground he prayed, "Oh, Gaelal, Lord of the Earth, accept the sacrifices of our slain enemies and hail our fallen as heroes in Reingard!"

The battle stretched for days. War machines on both sides flung heavy boulders and flaming projectiles towards their opponents. Volleys of arrows streaked across the skies accompanying the barrage hurled by the war machines. The sound of swords clashing was accompanied by the cries of the injured and dying. Wild animals on both sides battled each other.

Raihji listened with glee to reports of their secret weapon, the Nauro, as it ravaged the enemy's troops. Victory was at hand. None could withstand the Nauro, not even the Elves. He watched from his tent and directed his troops with messages to his generals. It was beneath the dignity of the supreme commander to venture onto the battlefield and thus he enjoyed ultimate safety.

Despite how hard Calannon, Dierk, and Einar fought to make their way up to his tent, they would never manage to kill him. His guards were too well armed and were the best of the elite fighters in his army. Even without them he would present a very difficult opponent. Dierk was no expert with a sword and he knew he would have no trouble overcoming the upstart king. Einar and Calannon on the other hand were renowned warriors on both sides of the war. Calannon would bring his two shorter swords to bear, each moving with such speed it would take all of his concentration to stay ahead of the whirling attack. However it was Einar that gave him the most pause. His only chance against the Marjai chieftain was to get in close for a quick strike before the bigger man had a chance to strike with his single edged sword. Raihji knew he could only parry two or three blows before he would succumb to Einar's power, power that could easily cleave a full grown ox in half with one blow. But as supreme commander he would never be expected to face them alone. His subordinates would tire the two warriors before they could reach him and then he would take great pleasure in cutting them down.

And he knew that he would one day face them. It would be an insult for a common soldier to complete a king's mission. He would just have to be patient...perhaps he would present himself as a target, as bait, to try and draw them out at a time when he was prepared for them.

If it would end the war and set him up as victor he might consider such a tactic. Until then, he would let them decimate their own troops until his army could crush them all.

�‮‬ಬ‧ಚ

After sundown on the sixth day Raihji recalled his generals to discuss new tactics. The Alliance was progressing faster, and further, than he had anticipated. The Elves had discovered a way to kill his Nauro and he was furious. Now it was his army that was being slaughtered, not the rebels.

Perhaps now he would present himself as a target. He presented the idea to his generals. Five were in favor, eight were not.

"It is too dangerous," Hajim, his most trusted general argued. "What if, by some twist of fate, they managed to kill you? Then our army would be lost."

"It would not be lost because you would complete our mission," Raihji reminded him harshly. "We have spent two hundred years conquering these pagans. Just because they are now showing a little backbone does not mean they will conquer us!"

Even as he slammed his fist against his pristine map, he became aware of a sharp pain blooming in his chest. It grew until Raihji could stand it no more...just before the darkness took him he registered the shocked looks on his generals' faces, and wondered just what was wrong with him to result in this burning sensation. Then the darkness pulled him into its eternal embrace.

☙·❧

The fourteen archers loosed two more arrows into each of Raihji's commanders, ensuring that the enemy was well and truly dead. Slowly they moved into the tent and dragged the dead bodies to the wall facing the armies. There they hung the bodies of Raihji and his generals, by their wrists, for his entire army to see when day broke.

When the sun's rays shone over the fields the next morning, the common soldiers saw their brilliant leader and his war council hanging dead from the wall. Most ran into the mountains, confused and demoralized. A few were foolish enough to stay behind, fighting for as long as they could...and then surrendered.

The fourteen archers, Dierk's personal Guardians, were dispatched across the now united kingdoms to hunt down and destroy the remaining high ranking army commanders among the Wanderers who had escaped. After honorary negotiations, in which the continued unification of all the kingdoms under Dierk was ratified, the celebrations began. Weeks of merriment and gaiety followed two hundred years of destructive war. Dierk, Einar, and Calannon traveled throughout the kingdom proclaiming the news that the people were free of the Wanderer's oppression and everyone rejoiced. Tired of war and battles, the people quickly threw themselves into creating a long lasting peace. Soldiers became farmers, merchants, bakers, blacksmiths, and scribes. Women returned their attention to creating a home and family instead of instruments of war.

The fourteen archers who had ended the war set up a school so that those blessed with gifts could learn to use them as instruments of peace and justice. They became more famous throughout their lives as the stories of their exploits, both during and after the war, were told over and over again.

Fathers passed these stories on to their sons and grandsons and mothers to their daughters and granddaughters. And so it continued from one generation to another; history became stories, stories became legends, legends became myths, and myths became children's tales. The Great War was all but forgotten and none could remember a time when Guardians had never existed.

The most inescapable prison we can ever find is our past.

The strongest chains,
Our Fears

The thickest walls,
Our Pride

The strongest bars,
Our Memories

The cruelest jailer,
Ourselves

~Princess Maira of Rima~

circa 2500 years before the Great War

Chapter 1

Kathryn knew she was being disobedient but she didn't care, her only goal was to escape from her master and mistress. After fulfilling her duties, she had left the two shouting at each other loud enough to wake the entire region of Rima. It was the second time this morning an argument had erupted between the Lord and Lady of Blackwood Manor and, Kathryn knew from bitter experience, that it wouldn't be the last. There was a legend that said that a great and decisive battle of a two hundred year long war had been fought where Blackwood Manor now stood. If Lord and Lady Blackwood were any indication, the battle had never ceased to end. Some servants whispered that the land had been cursed, so that the fighting would never end.

Kathryn didn't believe in curses. Lord and Lady Blackwood's eruptions, which occurred at least once a radian, were the result of two highly opinionated people living together for far too long. Had she just been an observer in the manor she might have found these explosive arguments amusing in their pettiness, but of course that was not the case. The quarrels always began with either the Lord or his Lady finding something wrong with her or with her actions and then they would begin to punish her *appropriately*. The other would make some snide comment about the touchiness of the other and for the next turn of the radian-glass the manor's corridors would echo with heated voices. Experience had taught Kathryn that if she stayed she'd sorely wish that she hadn't. She'd also learned that if she ever wanted to slip away to be alone, there was no better time than when the argument first began and the Lord and Lady were at each other's throats.

Quietly she slipped through the halls and corridors that made up Blackwood Manor. Small for her ten years, Kathryn had learned to use her lack of stature and ability to blend in to develop the skill of shadow movement. Lady Blackwood had given her innumerable opportunities to practice the acquired talent until she could almost believe she was invisible to the manor residents. Perhaps she was. No one ever seemed to take notice of her—until they wanted something that is.

Reaching the manor's main entryway she waited for the perfect opening. It wasn't long in coming. Silently, she slipped behind a maid burdened down with linens as she opened the door to the courtyard. With a dull *thud*, the heavy wooden doors closed behind her. Slowly, Kathryn let out a breath. The manor was the easy part. Now she had to manage to make it across the various courtyards and down the hillside without being seen.

Normally this wouldn't have been a problem at daybreak, however today was the King's birthday and the entire realm was in celebration.

Including Blackwood Manor.

Spotting an opening she moved forward, using the shade and other various objects littered around the courtyard as cover, being careful not to disturb anything or create any noise. Taking refuge under a wagon she waited as a throng of servants carrying plucked mallard and quail passed before slowly emerging out from under the wagon.

Suddenly, Kathryn felt a tremendous tug on her arm and was pulled into the nearest hut. When she realized where she was, her fear slowly subsided. Claude, the manor's baker, was her only friend and even that had to be kept secret.

"'Ello young miss," he greeted her quietly, kneading a large ball of dough and adding another handful of flour as another group of servants hurried by. His monstrous hands dwarfed the dough he was working with and numerous white scars broke the dark skin with scattered bands and spots of white. "Where be you off to this morn?" As he talked to her, Claude reached up and opened several cabinets, searching for spices above and below the countertop, his large frame making the normally spacious bakery seem inadequate for him.

Kathryn glanced in the direction of the forest. Claude, shaking his head in bewilderment reached into the warming oven. "I'll never understand why ye love that haunted wood," he said as he slipped her a small handful of fresh berry tarts secreted in a linen pouch.

Kathryn nodded a thank you and then soundlessly slipped out of the hut.

Behind the hut was a small crack in the protective wall that surrounded the manor. Over the years, Kathryn had enlarged the aperture slightly so that she might slip through more easily while also taking great pains to disguise the breach. If the manor's contingent of knights and men-at-arms found her secret entrance it would prevent her from leaving until she could locate another one.

Once outside the walls she picked her way down the rocky hillside toward the looming forest just beyond the base of the mound where Blackwood Manor stood. Large boulders and jagged stone littered the steep incline, providing excellent shelter from the sentries above. When it rained the trip was a nerve-wracking slip-and-slide trek through slick mud, but it hadn't rained for several days and the solid ground made finding a sure path effortless.

§ · ∞

The forest was her sanctuary. It was the one place in the kingdom where people weren't yelling, beating, or demanding something of her. Here she could stand up straight and wander slowly through the trees and underbrush without fear. Three years ago she had discovered the tranquility and peace of the forest and had since returned every opportunity she got. As she slipped past the giant evergreens that served as the guardians of the forest gates her senses were assailed with the smell of fresh pine, fragrant flowers, and humble dirt. The dirt and pine needles beneath her feet felt like the silks and satin used to create the gowns Lady Blackwood wore. In the early morning radians, mist shimmered around every tree, bush, and boulder like an elegant cloak, hiding the ordinary beneath. Kathryn moved forward and the mist clung to her like another layer of clothing, as if it was trying to hide the tattered sheath she wore beneath its glittering mantle.

Early in her visits, Kathryn had discovered that while the forest seemed to have a calming effect on her thoughts and feelings, the effect of water went much deeper—soothing as well as calming. Fascinated by water in all its forms, she felt especially drawn toward moving water. She loved to watch

16

it sparkle and shimmer as it fell to the pool below or tumble over rocks in a small creek. Years before she had found a waterfall within walking distance of the manor. Desperate for comfort, she headed there now.

Her waterfall could be heard several minutes before it actually came into view and she paused to listen to the peaceful sound. Water was one of the two things in life that could make her feel alive. When she had trouble sleeping, she would recall the sounds of its gentle rhythms and immediately feel comforted. On her third visit to the waterfall she had discovered that she could sit and watch the water pour over the rocks and lose any sense of time and place. Lady Blackwood had not been pleased that her personal slave had disappeared for four radians without an explanation and Kathryn winced reflexively, feeling the ghosts of that particular beating. Ever since, whenever she ventured near water, Kathryn kept a close eye on the position of the sun so as not to be late again.

When she reached the falls itself, she stopped and gazed at the plummeting water, feeling the spray permeate every fiber of her being, rejuvenating her. On the left side of the falls, a small ledge jutted out from the rock about seven meters above the forest floor. It was her favorite place to sit and listen. Clamping her teeth onto the small bag that Claude had given her, she reached up and began to pull herself up to the ledge. Experienced in the climb, it was only a few moments before she had perched herself on the ledge and was opening the bag. The tarts Claude had given her were her favorite. She never got treats like this in the manor so she savored every bite.

When she had first started slipping off into the forest Claude had been the only one to notice. One day he had grabbed her, just as he had done this morning, and confronted her with it.

Terrified, Kathryn had kept her eyes on the ground, waiting for the blow to come. To her surprise Claude had then handed her a warm biscuit and said, "I won't tell."

From then on, whenever Claude caught her sneaking out, which wasn't often since Kathryn worked hard to make sure no one ever saw her, he made sure she had some sort of treat to take with her. He also made sure that the Mistress of Blackwood Manor didn't suspect her slave was slipping outside the gates, how he managed that Kathryn couldn't comprehend. Lady Blackwood insisted on knowing everything that went on in her manor.

Licking the last of the mixed berry filling off her fingers Kathryn climbed down from her perch. As much she loved the forest, she knew that she couldn't stay long or the Blackwoods would become suspicious. She also had to be more careful climbing down; the climb wasn't as easy going down as it was going up. She'd missed a foothold or handhold once or twice in her early adventures and fallen into the pool below.

 The first time she had fallen she had been more angry than fearful of the water. She'd watched the village children swim for years and that first time she'd hit the water she had immediately began to try and copy their moves. The moves came so quickly and instinctively it was almost as if she and the water were meant to be together. Panicking had been the last thing on her mind, and she was puzzled as to how people could have a fear of drowning.

Swimming turned out to be one of the few activities that she enjoyed, however the Lady of Blackwood Manor did not appreciate her servant returning from her chores dripping wet so Kathryn only had the opportunity to swim if it was raining out.

Once her feet were on the dirt again, she decided that it was time to scout the area to make sure there were no intruders that could stumble upon her unannounced. She carefully made her way across the lea that formed just below the falls and headed for a large rocky crag that overlooked the terrain. Following a game trail that zigzagged amongst the reeds, clusters of typha, and through a copse of evergreen and deciduous trees she quietly approached the mount. After a several minutes of climbing she reached the top and took in the beauty of the forest and the small glen that embraced the tiered pools formed by the falls below. Satisfied that she was alone, she decided to head back for a few more minutes of tranquility. She was halfway down when she heard a small sound. Immediately she stopped and listened.

There it was again!

Unsure, Kathryn slowly finished climbing down and then stood still, the rock's large shadow covering her, offering protection against the unknown. Again she heard it.

It didn't sound human and that was the only reason Kathryn followed the sound to its source. The sound led her to the edge of a clearing and there, at the base of a large oak tree was a baby bird, its gray feathers were caked in mud and it appeared to be soaked through. It let out a pitiful cry as she approached.

As the sound of the cry reached her ears, Kathryn felt something she had never felt before—compassion. She felt sympathy for the little bird, a creature smaller and weaker than herself, and she gently reached out and picked it up. The poor thing was more dead than alive and it seemed all the strength it had was to let out a weak call. Tucking the bird close to her chest Kathryn tried to warm the shivering creature. To her surprise the little bird actually began to worm its head inside her bodice, as if hiding itself away from the world.

The sound of horses and footsteps tore Kathryn's attention from the bird and to the other side of the clearing. People. The knowledge sent Kathryn into a state of panic and she raced back into the cover of the trees, finding temporary shelter in the dark shadow cast by a rocky overhang. *How did I miss hearing them earlier?* she thought to herself.

Lord and Lady Blackwood's argument must have been short if her mistress had had time to send knights after her wayward servant. If they found her, they would drag her back to Blackwood Manor and throw her before her mistress...and she knew what would happen then. The Lady of the Manor was famous for her lack of compassion and mercy. Would she be hauled into the dungeon again or simply given the worst beating of her life? She wasn't sure, and she really didn't want to find out.

The sounds were becoming louder and more distinct and she shrunk back even further into the darkness, desperately trying to become one with the shadows. The bird let out another weak call, briefly drawing her attention away from her own fate. What would the knights do to the little bird currently cupped in her hands?

Even as she asked herself the question, she already knew the answer. They'd kill it. And they'd do it without blinking an eye or feeling one grain of guilt or remorse for taking a life, especially such a small and helpless one. What was the life of a bird compared to the number of times they'd nearly taken *her* life?

Kathryn couldn't let that happen. She would protect the baby bird for the simple reason that no one else in the kingdom would. Voices startled her out of her silent resolve. Angry with herself for letting them get so close without seeking more substantial shelter, Kathryn quickly slipped further into the darkness surrounding the meadow.

Every instinct told her to run, but curiosity won. How had Lady Blackwood managed to order her guards into the forest? Kathryn had never seen anyone venture close to the forest let alone travel into it. Once she had seen Lord Blackwood order a small contingent of knights into the forest to apprehend a thief and every one of the knights had refused to breach the evergreen walls that protected the errant bandit.

As the sounds grew even closer, Kathryn cocked her head and listened closely. She could hear the sounds of horse's hooves, the jangling of saddles and bridles, and the sound of men conversing with one another. What she did not hear was the sound of armor. That could only mean that these men weren't knights, but it didn't necessarily mean that they weren't from the manor. Archers and lowly men-at-arms did not wear any metal armor or chainmail but instead were issued heavily padded clothes.

She waited, curious to see whom Lady Blackwood had sent.

Finally they stepped into view...and Kathryn found herself exhaling in relief. There was no way in the kingdom that the travelers were from Blackwood Manor.

Kathryn had never seen adults like the ones who stood before her. There were three men and a woman. All four wore masks that obscured their facial features. Could they be bandits? The first man was tall with hair the color of the sky on a night when the moons were black, the second man was shorter and had hair the color of fire, the third had hair the color of copper cooking pots and was the shortest of all, half the size of the first, reaching only to his waist. But it was the woman who enchanted Kathryn. She was tall and slim, with hair almost equal to the ebony color of Kathryn's, and skin like newly fallen snow. Their clothing was colored in various shades of green, but the cut was unlike anything Kathryn was familiar with. The men wore shirts that had baggy sleeves and their tunic reached to their knees. The woman wore a dress that was slit in three places up to her knees. Underneath she wore leggings the same color as her dress. All four wore knee-length boots. On the front of each of the men's shirts and on the woman's bodice was an emblem. Too far away to make out the details, Kathryn could see what looked like the vague outline of a dead tree embroidered into their clothing.

Kathryn watched as the group began to walk around the clearing, talking amongst themselves, moving around as if they were looking for something. As they walked around they took off their masks. A few of them wandered past her hiding place and Kathryn was able to study their features. The men had the same look that many of the knights at Blackwood Manor had, a careworn but stony face that told Kathryn that they were extremely dangerous. These were no strangers to killing. Even more surprising was that the woman wore the same expression, only more forlorn as if she regretted all the people she'd killed in her lifetime.

As her eyes scanned the entirety of the meadow a third time Kathryn observed what she thought was a shrub in the middle of the glade. *Strange*, she thought with a frown. *There wasn't a bush there before.* As she stared at the bush she began to notice a sound— a deep guttural moan. Before her eyes, the shrub she had been studying began to grow...and grow...its stem reaching upwards towards the sun, growing thicker with every minute, the silk-thin skin twisting and cracking into rough bark. Fragile saplings grew into sturdy limbs as a fully mature evergreen tree grew high enough to provide shade from the sun. The group began to unpack saddle bags, spreading out items on a blanket that had been placed in the shade of the new tree. Kathryn stifled a gasp and stepped further back into the shadows, the low hanging branches completely obscured her view into the meadow, but also protected her from prying eyes.

These were outcasts—magic workers. The ones who could kill with merely a thought, the ones banished from the rest of the kingdom because they were dangerous. Steeped in the black arts, the outcasts were often possessed by spirits who enjoyed creating pain and suffering. It was said that they were the descendants of the Wanderers.

Turning Kathryn hurried back to her waterfall. Staying low and carefully retracing her previous route to her hideaway, she finally arrived at her destination and sat down on the nearest rock. She had never actually seen an outcast before and something about them both comforted and frightened her. Her mistress had told her horror stories of what they were capable of and what they did. The stories were enough to terrify any child but to Kathryn they held a deeper threat. She could become an outcast.

Years ago she had found she could move water just by thinking about it. When the Lady of Blackwood Manor had discovered Kathryn's previously dormant talent, her mistress had flown into such a rage that Kathryn had yet to witness another like it. Finally it had been explained to Kathryn what such a curse meant. Those who were cursed were banished from the kingdom, those who were foolish enough to return risked certain death. The Guardians protected the kingdom from the cursed and the Wanderers and those who faced a Guardian were rarely heard from again. Kathryn's very life was in danger if anyone found out. Both the Lord and Lady of the manor had made Kathryn promise never to attempt to move water again. It would bring the curse down harder, they explained.

For years Kathryn had kept her promise, but now, for the first time since she promised Lady Blackwood, she felt an irresistible urge to try again. She paused. What harm was there in making a tree grow or water move? As she debated in her mind, the urge grew stronger until it couldn't be ignored. Reaching out with her mind Kathryn tried again.

Staring at the water she tried to make it ripple in the collecting pool. It remained calm. She tried again, concentrating harder this time, the water still remained calm. Taking a deep breath Kathryn cleared her mind of all the warnings and commands Lady Blackwood had given her and imagined the water rippling before her in tiny waves to the sandy shore. Slowly, as if being persuaded to move drop by drop, the water began to move in gentle waves. Elated at the small victory, Kathryn imagined a small splash forming in the middle of the pool. It took a few tries, but she eventually managed to get a small splash to dance around the water. As she played, Kathryn found that it became easier and easier to get the water to do what she imagined.

A sudden thought came to mind and she imagined some of the water leaving the pool and floating in the air. The water reached up to form a long pillar of fluid reaching up towards the sky, but after several a dozen or so centimeters it stopped and Kathryn couldn't make it reach any farther. She paused and considered how to get the water from the pond to her. She decided to try a different tactic. She imagined the water flowing over the edge of the pool in a small river the size of her thumb, curling its way up the side of the boulder like a snake. The concentration it took to perform such a feat was staggering, leaving her muscles trembling and her back soaked in sweat, but a small film of water began pooling on the surface of the rock before Kathryn. Grinning, she imagined the water rolling into a ball and brought it to her hand. For a long time she looked at it, wondering how playing with water in this way was dangerous. Could Lady Blackwood be wrong? Kathryn doubted it, but she also was beginning to wonder why the ability to make a tree grow and water to leave a pool was deadly. Looking up at the sky, she was startled to see that she'd been out for at least two radians. Apparently her ability to work with water hadn't come back as fast as she'd thought. Slowly she returned the water back to the pond, already wincing in anticipation of the beating she would no doubt receive. With any luck the Blackwoods would still be arguing by the time she returned.

She turned to leave—and froze. Standing a few yards away was the woman outcast.

The woman stepped forward and opened her mouth to say something but Kathryn didn't stay to listen. The instant the woman began to move, she bolted. The woman called after her but Kathryn didn't stop. Clutching the little bird to her chest she hurried back to the manor, and to safety.

She managed to get back inside the manor without being seen and stowed away to her small room. Once inside she tucked the little bird on her pillow, opened her top dresser drawer and found a piece of dried venison that she had been saving, tore it into small chunks and offered it to the bird. Without hesitation the bird took it, tilted its head up and drew the morsels down into its craw in a jerking motion. Somewhat surprised as to how quickly the bird took to the food she prayed it would be all right, and then left to find her mistress.

Moving quickly through the numerous halls, she was almost to Lady Blackwood's room when she heard sharp footsteps and a painful yank on her ear. "Where have you been?" Lady Blackwood's shrill voice demanded, her angry face staring down at Kathryn. After a few moments of silence, Lady Blackwood rolled her eyes, and unrolled a leather strap. "Even after five years I keep forgetting you're mute," she muttered as she pulled the little girl into a separate room. Ten minutes later she sent her slave to assist with the preparations. Kathryn didn't let the tears, brought on by the sharp sting of the strap, fall as she hurried to the great hall to begin scrubbing the floor-stones. Her shoulders ached and her back stung as she hunched over to clean the filthy floor. After four radians of steady scouring her muscles felt like they were on fire and her neck wouldn't turn. But there was no respite for her or for any of the servants at the manor. It was the King's birthday and the entire manor was in such an upheaval to be clean that Kathryn wondered if perhaps the King himself was joining them for dinner.

All day long Kathryn worried about the little bird nestled on her pillow, however with the King's birthday celebration she was worked harder than usual and was left no time to check on it.

Eventually she was called to her mistress' room to help her dress for dinner. The Lady of the Manor wasn't exactly beautiful, at least not compared to the outcast woman with hair like the night, but she could still turn the heads of virtually every knight and nobleman in the near vicinity. Aware of her effect on others, she took twice as long to dress and choose jewelry. Her servant couldn't comprehend why. It wasn't as if the Lord and Lady were entertaining visiting nobility and needed to make a statement about themselves and their position within the noble ranks. Finally Kathryn had dressed and adorned her mistress and both were on their way to the dining hall where a feast awaited—or at least awaited the privileged. Kathryn was sent to the kitchens to help the servants prepare and serve the food.

Upon entering the kitchen, Kathryn learned that the manor had guests for dinner, which explained her mistress's need to look her best.

"I swear," the kitchen maid whispered to the cook, "the guests are wizards." The whole room gasped with the exception of Kathryn who didn't have a clue as to what a wizard was.

"Oh, rubbish!" The chef called to the huddled maids. "Wizards ain't been seen in thousands of years. Left with the Elves, they did. Now stop yacking and git yer serving done!"

Before the kitchen gossip could begin and Kathryn could learn what a wizard was, the head manservant entered and announced it was time to serve the feast.

"Kathryn!" The cook bellowed at the small girl.

Immediately Kathryn made her way forward and stood before the cook, waiting patiently for her assignment.

"You look like a village beggar," she sniffed. Moving to the largest linen closet she reached inside and pulled out an overgown that would adequately cover the child and yet would still be large enough to hide her malnourished frame. "Put this on," she ordered.

Immediately Kathryn obeyed and stood quietly while the chef tucked the material in several places. Finally the woman seemed satisfied with the way the fabric lay and reached across the counter to where several pitchers sat.

"You're in charge of the wine." The plump woman handed her a pitcher, and leaned down. "Make sure you give them enough," she hissed.

Kathryn nodded and hurried out the door. She hadn't even taken five steps into the great hall when she caught her first glance of the manor's guests. She froze, and panic threatened to settle in.

There, seated at the table with the Lord and Lady, were the four outcasts from the forest. A poke in her back jolted her feet back into motion. Making her way to the table, she began automatically pouring the wine. The Lord and Lady of Blackwood Manor were in lighthearted conversation with their guests prompting Kathryn to wonder if her mistress knew who exactly it was she was entertaining for dinner.

Throughout the entire meal Kathryn kept her eyes on the floor, hoping against all hope that the strange lady wouldn't recognize her. Unfortunately, all of the guests seemed to take some notice of her, despite her desperate attempts to blend into the background throughout the whole meal. It was the woman who scared Kathryn the most. Throughout the whole meal the dark haired lady kept one eye on Kathryn.

Kathryn was struggling with what to do. If the outcasts were as dangerous as Lady Blackwood had told her, then her mistress deserved to know who she was entertaining. But to expose such a thing would reveal Kathryn's own secrets. Finally Kathryn decided to leave everything alone. Perhaps there was a chance she had been wrong in the forest and these people weren't outcasts. She didn't want to risk losing her small freedom of the forest or the calming power of the water. She would remain silent—as always—she could only pray that the guests would remain silent about what they had seen in the forest.

After the meal was over the privileged retired to a different room and the servants cleaned up the mess. Kathryn felt the guests' eyes on her as they retired to the sitting room, and knew that they were going to ask about her. Her only hope was that the Blackwoods would conduct themselves as they had in the past with other guests; speaking mainly of themselves, their estate, and their ancestors...leaving very little room for their guests to comment themselves.

For the next three radians she was constantly glancing down the hall where her mistress and her guests had gone. Worry making the time feel three times longer than it actually was.

Kathryn's last job was to wash the floor, a chore she looked forward to with great apprehension as the scabs from the last time still hadn't completely healed and her neck was only just regaining its full range of movement. She was halfway done, ready to run back to her room to check on the small bird and hide herself away from the rest of the manor, when a manservant appeared.

"Come with me," he ordered gruffly. Kathryn's heart pounded as she realized he was taking her to her mistress.

The manservant entered the room first, bowing. "Milady."

Kathryn followed, giving her mistress a brief curtsy, before lowering her eyes to the floor.

"Are you sure this is her?" The Lady of Blackwood Manor's voice was suspicious.

Kathryn forced herself to remain still. Lady Blackwood's tone left no doubt in her mind that her actions in the forest had been the most recent topic of conversation amongst the Blackwoods and their guests.

"Yes, Lady Blackwood. I am sure." The woman's voice was light and musical, but still firm, nothing at all like Lady Blackwood's stern, cold voice. And not at all what Kathryn had imagined an outcast's voice to sound like.

"Kathryn, look at me," The Lady of Blackwood Manor commanded. Slowly Kathryn raised her head and looked her mistress in the face.

Satisfied at the response Lady Blackwood continued. "These people say you were using your..." Kathryn caught the brief glimpse towards her guests, "...talents. Is it true?" Her tone of voice was dispassionate, suggesting that she didn't care one way or the other what Kathryn's response would be, but her eyes were cold, and it was the coldness that frightened Kathryn. She had seen it before and the events that followed still gave her nightmares.

But what could she do? She couldn't lie. Not with the outcast woman in the same room. There was nothing to do but tell the truth.

Bracing herself for a blow, Kathryn reluctantly nodded.

Lady Blackwood let out a horrified gasp, as if she had been struck. Fury and indignation burned in her eyes and Kathryn winced at the sight, quickly lowering her eyes back to the floor.

"What am I going to do with you Kathryn?" Lady Blackwood may have phrased it as a question, but her tone left little doubt to Kathryn as to what she planned to do. She resigned herself to more pain and nightmares.

"You will turn her over to me." The strange Lady spoke this with such authority as to startle everyone in the room.

Lady Blackwood looked in astonishment at the speaker. "And why would I turn my servant over to you, Lady Jasmine?" She asked incredulously, some of the anger she felt at Kathryn seeping into her words.

"Because this girl has a gift and she cannot learn to use it if she's a servant," The dark haired lady said severely.

Listening intently, Kathryn thought to herself—*gift? What gift?*

"Kathryn has been with us for six years, I have come to depend on her. You cannot take her from me. And no local sheriff will support your demand that I simply hand over my servant to you without reparation. So how, pray tell, will you abscond with my servant?"

"I will involve the Guardians."

Lady Blackwood sniffed disdainfully. "They are far too busy keeping the peace between villages and farms to be bothered with the fate of a simple servant. Besides, how would you call them? Only their vaunted Council knows the locations of their homes."

"There are ways," one of the visiting men commented slowly.

"Perhaps, but until then you are no longer welcome in my castle or on my properties. If you wish to involve the Guardians than by all means, involve them. But until you ride up to my gates with them behind you, take your leave of my estate."

"And have the child disappear in the time it takes to fetch the nearest Guardians?" The vertically challenged visitor asked sarcastically. "Not likely."

Lady Blackwood stood. "I don't give one wit about your feelings in this matter. Kathryn is *my* servant. My property. Without a legal dispensation from the King giving you the right to take her from me, she belongs to *me*. You can threaten all you like, but not even the Guardians have the right to take a child from her home without the consent of her custodians."

"They can if she's gifted or if she's in danger," the fire-haired man argued.

"Kathryn is hardly in danger here," his host replied haughtily. "In fact, if my Lord and I hadn't taken up her guardianship, the local townspeople would have hung her years ago."

Even though she tried not to, Kathryn couldn't help but cringe at Lady Blackwood's accurate recount of the villagers' hatred of her.

"She is a child," Lady Jasmine protested in dismay. "Who would hang a child?"

"She's a murderer and a sorceress," Lord Blackwood interjected oily. "Or at least that's what the townspeople believe," he added after a moment.

"Maybe you have protected her from the village people," another of the visiting men spoke up, the light haired one this time. "But you cannot deny that she is gifted. At the very least the Guardian Council will want to examine her gifts."

"Kathryn's powers are weak," Lady Blackwood said dismissively. "Hardly worth entrance into the Guardians."

The guests of the Manor all exchanged significant looks. Lady's Jasmine's eyes hardened. "You would deny the child her birthright?"

"She has not used her *birthright* as you call it since she was seven. Now she is ten, years past the admittance age for the school," Lady Blackwood returned sharply, looking pleased with her victory.

The dark-haired lady's jaw tightened. "Are you telling me you knew this child was gifted and deliberately didn't report it?"

Her words were cold and there was a fire burning in her eyes, in all of the visitors' eyes. It should have been warning enough, but Lady Blackwood was too far gone in her anger over such mistreatment within her own walls to notice or heed it. "And have the *Guardians* take my servant from me?" Lady Blackwood let out a cold laugh. "You must be delirious."

"My dear," Lord Blackwood interjected nervously, uncomfortably aware of the crime his wife had just implicated them in. "I think you've said enough."

"Yes. I do believe you have," The black haired man said coldly. All four stood abruptly.

"The child is coming with us and if you continue to object I *will* take the matter to the king." The fire haired guest said and turned to Kathryn who had not moved since the conversation began. "Come child."

Lady Blackwood leapt between the man and her slave. "Take one step out of this manor with my servant, *Sir* Landen, and I will have the entire contingent of knights at this manor throw you and your companions into our dungeons."

Sir Landen's jaw worked as he clenched and unclenched his jaw. "You will do no such thing," he replied calmly after a couple heartbeats.

"I most certainly will! I will not be ordered about in my own home," she said emphatically.

"If you make any move to detain anyone in this party, you will be guilty of treason against the crown," the dark haired man said slowly.

Lady Blackwood eyed him skeptically. "Who are you to make such a claim?"

Lady Jasmine stepped forward. "You may not recognize my companions, but you will recognize me." When Lord and Lady Blackwood looked at her in confusion and anger the woman continued, "I am Dowager Princess Jasmine. The king's *sister*," she added this last bit as if emphasizing a point that Kathryn was unable to comprehend.

For a few moments there was utter silence in the room, and then, "You expect us to believe that the Dowager Princess travels without a retinue due to her station...with only three men to guard and protect her and no ladies to attend her?" Lady Blackwood asked scornfully. "Whoever you may be, you most certainly are *not* the Princess Jasmine and I demand that you leave our residence before we detain you in our dungeon."

The woman reached into her sleeve and pulled out an object that glittered in the dull light of the torches. "My signet ring," she said simply as she handed it to the manservant. Kathryn watched Lady Blackwood receive the ring, an air of impatience and irritation surrounding her. That aura rapidly changed as she studied the ring. Her face paled visibly and she held the ring out to her husband with a trembling hand.

"Are you satisfied that I *am* Princess Jasmine?" The woman asked.

Mutely, Lord and Lady Blackwood nodded and fell to their knees. "Forgive us, Princess. We did not know you."

Princess Jasmine ignored them and walked over to where Kathryn stood, her eyes still on the floor.

"You cannot take Kathryn!" Lady Blackwood cried. "She...she is like a daughter to me." There was no hiding the desperation in Lady Blackwood's voice. Everyone but Kathryn knew the punishment for failing to report a gifted child. And the slight that the Blackwoods had just delivered to a member of the royal family guaranteed that the punishment would not be overlooked.

Turning to face her, Jasmine spoke severely. "First you claim Kathryn is your servant and property, and now you claim she is like a daughter to you. Which is she, your daughter or your servant?" When Lady Blackwood gave her no answer, she turned back to the trembling girl. "Look at me child," she commanded gently.

Kathryn raised her eyes to look at the princess, who smiled down at her.

"Would you like to come with me, Kathryn?" Her voice was gentle and calm, so unlike Lady Blackwood's.

Looking into her eyes, Kathryn sensed something, not pity or sorrow or hatred, but kindness, genuine kindness. It was an emotion that was so rarely directed at her that she was confused. Unsure of what to do, she glanced over at her mistress, who glared at her. Looking back at the Princess, Kathryn shook her head.

Mystified at the unexpected, Jasmine turned to look at Lord and Lady Blackwood. All it took was a look at Lady Blackwood's face. She returned her gaze to Kathryn. "I think you do. Go and pack your things. You are leaving with me tonight."

"Kathryn doesn't have any possessions," Lady Blackwood interrupted.

Jasmine turned to Kathryn. "Is this true?"

Kathryn started to nod, but then stopped. What about her bird?

Without a word she turned and hurried off to her room, scooped up the fragile creature, and hurried back to the stunned adults.

Jasmine, seeing that the girl had something pressed close to her chest knelt down to take a look. "May I see?"

Hesitantly, Kathryn held out the tiny bird for the Princess to see.

"Well we can't leave your friend behind can we?" Jasmine asked after taking a close look at the tiny animal. Kathryn shook her head slowly. "Very well, then we're ready to leave."

"Wait."

Jasmine turned and looked at Lady Blackwood. "Yes?"

Moving towards an oak desk, Lady Blackwood opened a drawer and pulled out an object. "I've been saving this until Kathryn was older, but if she's leaving with you it belongs to her." She held out a small pendant hanging from a gold chain.

"I thought you said she had no possessions," Jasmine reminded her as she took the necklace.

Lady Blackwood gave no answer. Jasmine, perceiving Lady Blackwood's apparent act of kindness as one of self-preservation, albeit a very strange act as the little girl gave no sign of recognition of the jewelry, secured the chain around the little girl's neck.

"Very well then. Come Kathryn." Princess Jasmine led the way out of the Manor. In the courtyard servants stopped what they were doing and stared at the procession, they began whispering among each other. Neither the threats of the Master nor the icy looks from the Mistress could silence their words.

Claude came out to see what was going on, immediately assessed the situation and held out his arms to Kathryn. As he crouched down on one knee, she ran into his gentle embrace and hugged him. "I'll ne'er forget you little miss," he whispered to her, she responded with a quick kiss on his cheek.

"Wait here?" he asked looking at Kathryn, who nodded. He disappeared into his bakery and returned his hands clutching something. Fighting tears he knelt down and handed her a bag of berry tarts. "Here, a couple of your favorite treats for the road."

Kathryn took the bag and hugged him again.

"Go on young miss," He said softly. "They've tarried long enough and won't wait forever."

Kathryn nodded then rejoined the Princess and her companions who were waiting patiently and followed the Princess out of the gates of Blackwood Manor and into her new life.

Chapter 2

Throughout the whole ride to the palace Princess Jasmine tried to make conversation with the silent girl sitting before her. "How old are you Kathryn?" For a moment it seemed like the little girl wouldn't answer, then she slowly held up ten fingers.

"Ten years old?"

Kathryn nodded briefly.

"You don't need to be afraid of me, Kathryn," the Princess told her gently, yet the little girl refused to speak or even to look at her.

Jasmine's heart went out to the small child whose malnourished arms were wrapped around the little bird nestled on her skirt. Shortly into the ride the little girl had opened the bag the baker had given her and had pulled out a single tart. Jasmine found it strange how quickly the bird gobbled up the small flakes of pastry Kathryn offered it, even more surprising was the fact that Kathryn seemed to understand that pastry wasn't a suitable meal for her charge and kept the morsels she fed it small. Turning her thoughts to the little girl, she could only imagine what Kathryn had endured at Blackwood Manor. She had seen the looks Lady Blackwood had aimed in the little girl's direction and seen the barely visible flinches given in response.

Earlier, when they had left Blackwood Manor, Jasmine had taken Kathryn up on her horse and the small group had ridden toward the Rawasi Mountains. They rode into the forest that covered the base of the mountains and as they were riding a large house suddenly appeared out thin air before them. Kathryn jerked at its sudden appearance, but Jasmine had spoken quietly and calmly, assuring her that everything was alright. At the large house they had changed clothes and transferred into a carriage and set off once again.

The carriage they were riding in was equipped with messenger birds and Jasmine called for one. Quickly she penned a message and sent the small bird ahead. By the time they arrived at her estate, Jasmine knew there would be a few surprises for Kathryn.

The ride to the palace was a long one, several times they had to stop and wait for a herd of cattle to move or an inept merchant's dithering to replace a wheel on his disabled pushcart or wagon. "Who moves their herd at this time of night?" Jasmine muttered to herself after the third herd of cattle was safely on the other side of the road and they were on their way again. As the time of night registered, Jasmine's eyes flew to her silent companion, hoping that she was asleep.

But no, Kathryn was still awake and looking out the window, glancing away constantly to check on the small bird. Jasmine slept for a few radians around midday and woke to find her companion as alert as before.

As the first rays of sunset began to dance upon the earth and bathe the sky crimson red, they arrived at Jasmine's home. Two guards quickly advanced on the carriage and one opened the princess's door and helped her out. "Welcome back my lady, I trust you had a safe and pleasant journey"

Although she had much on her mind, she smiled and replied that the trip had been most profitable and that she had a special guest that would be staying for some time. Turning and motioning with her eyes she said, "Regalde, this is Kathryn."

Regalde, his rough and pockmarked face puzzled slightly as he gazed at the little girl, and with a raspy voice greeted her formally. "Welcome, Miss Kathryn."

After Jasmine smoothed her dress she turned and held out a hand to help Kathryn down. The little girl's eyes were wide and she took in the huge windows, towers, and gardens. As Jasmine approached the main entrance her arrival was announced by the chief manservant. As they entered, Kathryn was awed by the size and majesty of the atrium, easily ten times the grandeur of Blackwood Manor. Knowing that the girl had to be exhausted despite the fact that she looked wide awake, Jasmine quickly led her to an apartment next to her own.

"This is where you will stay," she told Kathryn as she opened the door. Dutifully Kathryn entered the room, but stopped short upon seeing the interior.

The apartment before her bordered on regal and was more elegant than Lady Blackwood's. In contrast to the dark stone that entombed Lady Blackwood's apartments, the walls before her were hewn from a light and airy crème marble with gold vines and leaves etched into the walls and ceiling. Forest green furniture with gold filigree sat in a sunken sitting room before her. Gauze curtains that matched the furniture adorned the generous windows set back into the walls. Gold and crème colored tiles covered the floor in an alternating pattern.

"What do you think?" Jasmine asked. The little girl looked up at her, eyes wide with astonishment. Smiling, Jasmine continued, "Come and see the rest of it."

Kathryn couldn't believe there was more to this wonderful room, but she obediently followed the princess.

The bathing room was done in the same color scheme as the sitting room, sporting a huge sunken soaking pool for bathing and glittering mirrors for dressing. Hesitantly, Kathryn leaned over and peered down into the marble pool. Not even Lady Blackwood had this luxury, relying instead on large copper tubs that servants filled with steaming jars of water for her baths. Inside the bedchamber was the largest bed Kathryn had ever laid eyes on. It was topped with so many blankets, quilts, and pillows she wondered if anyone could even fit on it. Slowly, when the princess wasn't looking, she ran her hand over the bedspread, feeling the silk and satin fabrics slide like water beneath her fingers. The walls were done the same way as the sitting room and bathing room, the gold etching smoothly transitioning into the new room. Large windows were present on three of the walls, each sporting a very comfortable looking furnished window seat. Everything in this room was done in gold or crème.

A middle-aged serving woman stood next to the foot of the bed and at the princess' signal she came forward. Kathryn tried to study her discreetly. She was tall, taller than the princess, and had black hair almost as dark as Kathryn's, but unlike Kathryn's or Princess Jasmine's, hers was streaked with silver. Her simple dress and unassuming manners told Kathryn that she was a servant of the palace.

"Kathryn, this is Arianna." Jasmine knelt down and nodded towards the woman as she introduced her. Arianna stepped forward as the princess said her name, bringing her within an arm's reach of Kathryn. The instinctive step back was barely visible, but both women had sharp eyes. Turning her eyes slightly, Jasmine studied Arianna's reaction. The servant was already backing up a few paces to ease the child's discomfort. Turning back to Kathryn she continued gently, "Arianna will assist you while you are here with us. Arianna, this is Kathryn."

Arianna followed Jasmine's example and knelt down to reach eye level with the little girl.

"Hello Miss Kathryn." Her voice was soft and gentle like the princess', but Kathryn still refused to look her in the eye. She paused, taking in her new charge's condition, and asked, "Would you like a bath?"

Wondering if she'd misheard the question, Kathryn glanced up. There was nothing but open honesty in Arianna's warm green eyes and the smile on her lips told her that she had heard correctly. She shifted her gaze to the princess, hardly daring to wish for something so wonderful.

"That's a wonderful idea, Arianna," Jasmine answered for Kathryn and stood slowly. "A hot bath and a hot meal do wonders for a good night's sleep."

"I'll draw the bath while you show Miss Kathryn the rest." Arianna rose gracefully and moved through the door and soon Kathryn could hear the sound of running water. She wondered how that was possible. If one wished to bathe, one must first heat water in the kitchens before it could be brought up to the bathing chamber. She hadn't seen a fireplace in the bathing room that would allow for such a brief interlude between Arianna's departure and the running water.

"Come Kathryn, there is more to see," Jasmine instructed, tearing her mind from the mystery.

What else could there be? Kathryn wondered. Already she was staying in a room that would have had Lady Blackwood consumed with envy, she would be taking the first bath she'd had in months in a bathtub that resembled a pool more than a tub and would probably be getting the first decent hot meal she'd had in years. What more could there be?

Jasmine led the way to an armoire opposite the bed and opened it. Reaching inside she pulled out a small nightgown that looked like it had been created specifically for the room's color scheme. Turing around, she smiled at Kathryn. "I think this is about your size, why don't you try it on?"

Slowly, Kathryn began to step forward and then stopped. She looked down at the small bird still nestled against her chest. Jasmine noticed the movement.

31

"Let me hold your bird while you dress," she said kneeling down, then, seeing the panicked look that flickered across the girl's face hurried to promise, "I'll give it right back when you're done." She knelt down and held out her hand for the baby animal, watching as the first signs of indecision swept across the little girl's face.

All her life it had been drilled into Kathryn to obey every order without pause, but for the first time she hesitated. What if Jasmine didn't give the bird back? Her training won and she slowly surrendered the bird to the Princess, and took the nightgown.

Jasmine held the little bird and watched as Kathryn slipped out of her old clothes. As she did, Jasmine noticed something. She laid a restraining hand on Kathryn's shoulder. The little girl had only partway pulled on the nightgown and her back was still mostly bare. Jasmine couldn't believe what she saw. Multiple thin scars raced up, down, and across her small back. Parts of skin were still bright red, indicating fresh bruises that would soon darken. There were more bruises, each in various stages of healing from a dark blackish-purple to others fading to yellowish-green. Her arms and legs bore the same types of scars and bruises. The only part of her body that seemingly hadn't been touched was her face. Jasmine felt sick and angry. What had this poor girl been through? Had the vengeful villagers done this? She didn't believe Lord Blackwood's claim that the child before her had murdered someone, and she certainly didn't believe that she was a sorceress. But she'd heard of places in the kingdom where some villagers still held to the ancient beliefs and superstitions, had seen some of the victims of those villagers. She couldn't recall a single occurrence that had ended in favor of the condemned. Superstition and fear, she knew from experience, overrode common sense and rational judgment.

Kneeling down she held Kathryn's face with her free hand. This time she studied the girl intensely. Her black hair, matted with dirt and tangled so badly that Jasmine doubted even someone with Arianna's patience would be able to comb it out, hung loosely about her face. Near the edges of Kathryn's face she could see faint marks that indicated faded bruises. Whoever had done this to her had taken great care not to make the abuse obvious so that no one would give Kathryn anything more than a passing glance. Superstitious villagers wouldn't care about something like that. "Who did this to you?" she asked quietly.

The child didn't respond, didn't even raise her eyes from the floor, but Jasmine had instinctively known the answer even as she had asked the question. She vowed to make them pay dearly for their actions.

"It was Lord and Lady Blackwood, wasn't it?"

Kathryn didn't know what to say. She didn't want to lie but neither did she want to tell the truth. Finally she nodded. For a long time Jasmine didn't say anything. The silence unnerved Kathryn more so than one of Lady Blackwood's silences, but she did not make eye contact.

The silence was broken when Arianna returned, announcing that the bath was ready.

"Kathryn, look at me," Jasmine ordered gently and waited for the little girl to look at her. "I'm going to put the bird right here," she moved to one of

32

the chairs situated next to the bed and gently nestled the little bird into the pillow. Kathryn followed her like a shadow, and Jasmine continued, "I want you to take your bath and get ready for bed." Her tone was gentle, but it brooked no argument.

Kathryn nodded and Arianna led her out the door and into the bathroom, glancing back only once towards the chair where the little bird lay. Arianna helped Kathryn out of the nightgown and draped it over a rod next to a fluffy towel. There was a long moment of silence when Arianna saw Kathryn's bare back. Afterwards her hands trembled as she gently removed the golden chain from around the little girl's neck and helped her into the bath, her eyes shining with tears. The emotional response puzzled Kathryn, no one had ever cried after seeing her scars before, but the hot water felt so good that she soon banished all other thoughts from her mind.

Never before in her life had Kathryn been assisted in bathing or dressing, but tonight Arianna wouldn't let Kathryn do anything herself. From washing and combing her hair to tucking her into bed the gentle servant was always there.

A meal arrived while Arianna was still struggling to comb out the tangles in Kathryn's hair. The servant allowed Kathryn to eat while she continued to doggedly finish the task she had started. Her belly warm from the hot soup and bread, Kathryn began to feel the first signs of weariness. The cook had even sent up a meal of kitchen scraps for the bird, which Arianna helped Kathryn feed.

The little bird had a ravenous appetite for something so small and it eagerly gobbled up every morsel Kathryn offered it. As she removed the empty serving tray Arianna quipped, "Well one thing is certain. Your bird is not a picky eater and has an appetite that would put a woodsman to shame."

For the first time, Kathryn looked into Arianna eyes and then nodded in agreement.

Kathryn was tiring quickly. She had had a long day and she hadn't slept in the carriage ride to the palace. Arianna noticed the little girl's exhaustion and as soon as the bird was fed put Kathryn to bed, tucking her in gently and softly humming a tune Kathryn didn't recognize. Within minutes she was fast asleep.

⁊⋅ℭ

She woke to someone gently calling her name. Panic seized her as she realized she'd slept late. Lady Blackwood would be furious. Shocked upright, Kathryn came awake prepared to leap out of bed but a hand on her shoulder stopped her.

"Calm down, little one." The calming voice was neither Lady Blackwood nor Claude. Slowly the events of the last night came back to Kathryn and she realized Arianna was the one waking her and not one of the other servants in the manor. Sunlight was streaming in through the windows, dazzling her vision.

"Would you like some breakfast Kathryn?" Arianna asked as she pulled the blankets back and helped Kathryn sit up.

Rubbing her eyes to clear her vision and unable to ignore the clenching pains in her stomach, which were just beginning to assert themselves,

33

Kathryn nodded. She had eaten little in the days before her departure from Blackwood Manor and while she had survived on less she had learned long ago never to refuse food that was willingly offered.

Arianna smiled. "Good, because breakfast will be here soon. Come and get dressed." Going to the closet Arianna selected a blue dress and held it up for Kathryn to see, only Kathryn was no longer on the bed. Looking around she finally saw her kneeling next to the baby bird.

Carrying the dress, Arianna knelt beside Kathryn. "This little one will be fine," She promised. "Now let's get you dressed."

The dress Arianna had chosen was too big for Kathryn's frame. She frowned as she studied the other dresses in the armoire. Finally she shrugged. "Either we are just going to have to get new dresses made for you or we're going to having to fatten you up a little," she said as she helped Kathryn into the blue dress, spending a few minutes tucking and rearranging the fabric in several places to achieve a better fit. "It's about thirty years out of date fashion-wise," she said with a wry smile as she finished lacing up the back and turning the little girl around for a better look. "But it looks perfect on you." She gave Kathryn another grin and began hunting around for stockings and shoes in the bottom of a chest next to the armoire. "Maybe," she mused quietly, "we can ask the Queen if she has any of the princess' old dresses that she would be willing to give you."

Unsure if she was expected to respond to the question, Kathryn kept her focus on the little bird and studying the dress she was currently wearing.

By the time breakfast arrived Arianna had Kathryn dressed and her hair arranged in two braids coiled around her head. "There," Arianna smiled, admiring her handiwork. "Now you look very pretty."

To her joy, the little girl gave the first ghost of a smile since she had arrived, it was only in her eyes, but it was there. She finished by reverently securing the chain with the flying eagle around Kathryn's neck. Standing she crossed the room and accepted a breakfast tray from a servant who had just arrived. As she returned, Kathryn thought she saw tears in Arianna's eyes again, but as the woman approached, she saw nothing.

Princess Jasmine joined them as the two were just finishing breakfast, an older man accompanied her.

"Good morning Milady," Arianna greeted the princess with a curtsy. Kathryn also curtsied, keeping her gaze tied to the floor.

"Good morning Arianna. Good morning Kathryn. I hope you slept well."

Without looking up Kathryn nodded, it was the best sleep she'd had since she could remember.

"Good." Jasmine smiled at her, then turned to the man standing next to her. "Kathryn this is Lord Mora, he's a close friend of mine."

Lord Mora was a tall thin man with graying hair and a clean-shaven face. Smiling he knelt down and looked at Kathryn.

The little girl still refused to raise her eyes from the floor.

Arianna bent down and whispered softly in Kathryn's ear. The little girl slowly raised her eyes and glanced at Mora's face...without looking at his eyes.

Mora smiled and held out his hand. "Hello Kathryn."

Kathryn looked at his hand curiously for a moment and then curtsied. Lord Mora looked at Princess Jasmine who was desperately searching for a way to get Kathryn to place her hand on Lord Mora's. She needed to know if her suspicion about Kathryn's gift was correct. Once again Arianna leaned over and whispered something in Kathryn's ear.

The little girl's eyes widened fearfully but she tentatively reached out her small hand and placed it in Lord Mora's large paw. Lord Mora smiled at her before turning his gaze toward Jasmine and nodding. Jasmine turned to Kathryn who had already reclaimed her hand from Mora's. "Would you like to see my gardens?" she asked.

Kathryn nodded.

"Arianna, would you be willing to take Kathryn? Lord Mora and I have some unfinished business."

"Of course, milady." Arianna led Kathryn out of the room, but before they left Kathryn picked up the baby bird, taking it with them.

Jasmine turned to face Mora. "What do you think?"

Mora nodded slowly. "She has the power you say she has. I can feel it within her. But there's something keeping her from even touching it. It's like she's built this wall around it that can't be breached."

Jasmine rubbed her forehead in frustration. "I have a feeling Lord and Lady Blackwood told her the outcasts story to keep her power hidden."

"Still, for such a young girl to keep such a deep potential hidden for so long, and even now still be able to resist, no... ignore its call..." Lord Mora paused in his deliberations. "She is obviously an extraordinary girl."

"You should have seen the look on Lady Blackwood's face when Kathryn admitted to using her power in the woods. I thought she would reach out and strangle the girl."

"And you're sure that Kathryn has only used her gift twice, first when she was seven and then again yesterday?"

"I'm almost positive," Jasmine told him confidently. "Lady Blackwood claimed that Kathryn hadn't used her gift since she was seven and was clearly shocked when I told her what I'd observed. With the potential Kathryn has the only way to explain the number of times it took her to master a small movement is if she'd never done it before."

"She obviously fears something."

"I think it is people in general. When she caught me watching her she bolted like a startled deer. It took all my tracking skills to find her. She's very adept at moving unnoticed. She's still afraid of me, although she seems to be warming to Arianna."

Mora chuckled. "Arianna does seem to have that gift. I remember a young princess who was afraid of many things before Arianna became her lady-in-waiting."

Jasmine blushed. "That was a long time ago Mora."

He nodded. "Yes it was. You've come a long way since then. You are no longer the timid girl you once were." He paused, and then asked, "Is Kathryn mute?"

"I've wondered that too," Jasmine admitted. "She doesn't speak... What should I do?"

Mora thought for several moments. "She has obviously bonded with the bird—

"I noticed that as well. She won't let it out of her sight for a minute. It's almost like it's her only friend."

"I have a feeling that's a pretty accurate description," Mora said gravely. "I think an introduction to Lord Jasse may be beneficial. He is quite adept in these matters and might be able to bring her out of her shell."

Jasmine smiled. "What would I do without you old friend?"

Lord Mora chuckled. "Since you had already come to the same conclusion, I have no doubts that you would manage just as well without me." They had moved to the balcony and were watching Arianna and Kathryn work their way through the gardens. At the moment, Arianna was showing the little girl a camalie bush with bright pink and orange blossoms covering every inch of space.

"I will speak to the Guardian Council regarding Kathryn," Lord Mora said as he turned to leave. "They will be hesitant at first and may even demand a demonstration of Kathryn's abilities, but I have no doubt that once they see what you and I see they will have no reservations about admitting her late."

"Thank you, old friend."

Chapter 3

Lord Jasse arrived at Jasmine's palace one week later. She greeted him at the doorway, a smile on her face as she welcomed her old friend. "It is good to see you, Jasse."

Lord Jasse threw her a grin, his green eyes twinkling. "Anything for an old schoolmate, milady."

Jasmine frowned. "How many times do I have to tell you—

"That you hate being called that by me? Only about ten times a day," Jasse finished for her. It was a familiar conversation, one they'd had since they were teenagers. He followed Jasmine through the numerous sitting rooms and toward the private apartments. "So tell me about this little girl who Lord Mora claims is so special."

Normally his presence could manage to tease a smile out Jasmine, no matter how depressed or miserable she was feeling, but this time she let out a heavy sigh. "I'm at a loss Jasse," she admitted. "Kathryn is smart, quick, obedient, and terrified." She turned to look out the broad window that allowed for an expansive view of her gardens, her despair threatening to consume her. She'd issued orders for the punishment of the Blackwoods, but while it gave her a sense of satisfaction to inflict pain on those who had mistreated a child so horribly, it did nothing to help Kathryn now.

"Interesting choice of words," Jasse commented thoughtfully, leaning against the stone wall.

Jasmine turned to face him, her heart heavy with seriousness and despair. Opening up her mental walls, she let him in to feel just how affected she was by the little girl. "Kathryn is undeniably smart, I can see it in her eyes and trying to keep up with her energy is trying, even for Arianna. She obeys every command given to her like she's never experienced any free will," she sighed again. "But terror is the only word that comes close to accurately describing her reaction to people. Lord Mora believes her only friend is a baby bird which she won't let out of her sight."

"Which is why I'm here." Jasse hadn't moved from his position against the wall, but he softened his facial features and voice. He knew how jaded she had become over the years, had striven to balance her cynical outlook on life with his playful one. Over the years he had perfected the techniques taught to telepathic individuals and tried to use his gift to encourage others where they needed it most. She had gifted him with a few mental peeks into just how much of a boon that had been to her during their time in the Guardians.

"Yes, Mora feels that in order to get close to Kathryn we have to go through the bird." Jasmine turned to look at her old friend. "I've never seen anything like it. Kathryn won't look at you unless commanded to, she hasn't spoken a word since I laid eyes on her in the forest, and her body is covered with horrible scars and bruises."

Seeing the distress in his friend's eyes, Jasse paused, and then asked, "Who were her parents?"

The Dowager Princess spread her hands helplessly. "I think she's an orphan. When I asked her the same question, she looked confused and then shrugged."

"An orphan would definitely make an excellent servant to mistreat seeing as the parents aren't around to protest." They'd both seen it many times during their service.

"I reached the same conclusion."

"Where is Kathryn?"

"In the gardens with Arianna and the bird."

Jasse grinned. "How is Kathryn taking to Arianna?"

"Other than the bird, Arianna is the only one who's managed to entice a smile out of her and it was only once." Jasmine smiled at the memory. "Ever since that first night, Arianna hasn't left the little girl's side and seems to know exactly what Kathryn needs most when she needs it most. Arianna seems to be the only one she doesn't constantly flinch around. It's like they've connected on a level so deep neither of them knows it's there."

"Interesting theory, I have noticed that more often than not it's the servants who have stronger ties to noble children rather than the child's parents."

"Something I feel should be corrected. However I believe that is beyond the familiar relationship servants have with their charges. It's...." she struggled to find an adequate description. "It's more like the bond between a mother and child but it isn't." As she finished, she couldn't help the small huff of exasperation that escaped over her vague description.

He chuckled. "I remember back in school when you would rant and rave, spending radians writing numerous letters to your parents, and who knows what else." *Back before you became hardened by the daily horrors people subjected others to.*

"And still nothing has come of it," Jasmine remarked sorrowfully.

"All it takes is one to break the mold before others begin to follow suit. It may not happen right away but it will eventually. Look at your brother's family. His children are close to him and his wife, perhaps the rest of nobility will follow the king's example."

"If they are, they're sure taking it slow. I could crawl faster."

Jasse shook his head. "That was always your stumbling point, Jasmine, you weren't patient enough. That isn't something you can change overnight. Neither is Kathryn. Both will take time and loving care."

"Speaking of Kathryn you should probably go find her and begin your loving care," she smiled and pointed towards the door at the end of the corridor.

Laughing, Jasse moved towards the gardens. "Yes, I suppose you're right," he called out over his shoulder as he left her. Choosing to enter through the back gate, he wandered slowly through the foliage, taking in the beauty around him.

Ten minutes later he spotted Kathryn and Arianna. He stopped a moment and watched the two as they explored the gardens.

Arianna would point something out to Kathryn who stood silently by her side and Kathryn would hesitantly step forward and investigate. She would then turn back to Arianna who would say a few sentences, no doubt explaining what type of plant they were looking at, and lead Kathryn on to the next plant.

After a few moments Jasse decided he had observed enough and moved to join them. "Good morning, ladies," he greeted cheerfully.

Arianna smiled and dipped a quick curtsy in greeting, but Kathryn recoiled in surprise, immediately lowering her eyes.

Perhaps Jasmine wasn't exaggerating after all, Jasse thought as he joined them. As much as he loved Jasmine, he knew from years of experience that she tended to overstate situations on occasion. "Hello, Arianna. How are you this beautiful morning?"

"Very well, Lord Jasse, and yourself?"

"It is always a good morning when I'm invited over to the princess' home," he replied with a quick grin. Turning he looked at the little girl standing mute beside the servant. "And this must be Kathryn."

Arianna smiled gently. "Yes."

Jasse knelt down so that he would be at eye level if the little girl ever decided to look at him. "Jasmine tells me that you have a special friend."

Slowly she nodded without lifting her eyes from the ground. Gently he reached out with his mind and sought her emotions, trying to use his gift to understand her terror, or at least discover a way to ease her anxiety. It didn't do him any good. Kathryn had an astonishingly tight grip on her emotions. He could feel the fear, but nothing below. Even more astonishing, was that after a few seconds she drew her feelings in even deeper, as if withdrawing from his touch. It was definitely something he would have to investigate. Was her second gift the ability to sense emotions?

Until then he would have to do this the old fashioned way. He nodded towards the small bulge in her skirt pocket. "May I meet your friend?"

Jasse noticed the way Kathryn looked to Arianna who nodded and smiled. "It's okay, Kathryn," she encouraged. "Go ahead."

Slowly Kathryn reached into the pocket and pulled out a scrawny baby bird. As the sun touched the soft feathers it let out a small cry. Immediately, a worried look flashed across the little girl's face.

"It's okay," Jasse hurried to assure her. "It's telling you good morning."

Her gaze flew to Jasse, looking him in the eye for the first time; her blue eyes filled with a mixture of hesitancy and curiosity. Wondering which would win, he held out his hand for the bird. "May I?"

With Arianna's persuasion she slowly surrendered the bird and waited.

Jasse held the small bundle of feathers with care and made sure she could clearly see what he was doing, only to become confused. "I think this is a baby eagle, did you know that?" He held out his hand to indicate she could move closer.

The little girl shook her head, briefly skittering backwards out of his reach, but returned to her previous position almost immediately. He wasn't naïve enough to believe that her terror was gone. She merely didn't want to leave her bird in his clutches.

Terrified is a kind term to her reaction to people. If I ever meet this Lord and Lady Blackwood they're likely never to see another sunrise, he thought darkly. Jasse continued cautiously, careful to keep his emotions concealed from her. "It looks like it's about two weeks old, and it's a she." When he looked back at Kathryn he could tell he had more of her attention. "In about two months she'll be able to fly, but it will take a lot of care before she can get to that stage. Do you know how to care for her?"

Kathryn shook her head.

"Would you like me to show you?"

She hesitated for a long moment, and then nodded. Jasse smiled at her, which only appeared to close her down even more.

"Why don't we go to the waterfall and Lord Jasse can begin telling you how to care for your friend?" Arianna suggested gently.

A brief light flickered in Kathryn's eyes but she extinguished it quickly, as if she was afraid that, seeing her excitement, they would decide not to go. Jasse glanced at Arianna, whose sorrowful gaze told him she had seen it as well.

Together the three moved towards Jasmine's waterfall. As they reached the falls, Jasse watched some of the tension ease from Kathryn's shoulders.

Jasmine had been right. Kathryn definitely had the gift of water.

Arianna sat down on the soft grass next to the pool and motioned for Kathryn to sit next to her. Jasse positioned himself next to Arianna so that Kathryn wouldn't feel threatened. For the next several radians Jasse told Kathryn and Arianna everything he knew about birds, eagles in particular.

ↄ·Ↄ

Up on the balcony, Jasmine watched as the three moved off toward the waterfall. She had mentioned Kathryn's attachment to water to Arianna late that first night, and was pleased to see the servant maneuver the little girl into a location where she could find some peace.

Later that night she asked Kathryn. "Do you like Lord Jasse?"

Kathryn didn't say anything, but she did look down at her bird and gently stroked the top of its head.

Every morning Jasse would take Arianna and Kathryn out in the gardens and they would spend time caring for the little eagle. The little girl was a quick learner and, despite her skittishness, always eager to learn new things.

ↄ·Ↄ

The next three months were the most difficult times Jasse had ever dealt with. In his years as a Guardian he had thought he had seen it all. Death. Torture. Abuse. Sickness. Hunger. Anger. Spite. Jasmine hadn't been the only one to rely on his dry wit and always ready jokes to keep from being overwhelmed by the things they had dealt with. They had been his coping mechanism as well.

He had thought he had seen everything people could and would do to each other. But Kathryn's case hit him like an unexpected blow to the midriff. She flinched at everything, refused to look anyone in the eye, and acted like she expected everyone to stop playing this cruel joke and send her back to the Blackwoods.

40

It took those three months for Jasse to convince Kathryn to use her gift in front of him, and when she did it was the smallest possible act she could get away with, but during those three months he noticed something else. Kathryn not only had a gift for working with water, but also a strong potential for working with plants. *Unusually* strong.

Knowing how sensitive Kathryn was about her gifts he didn't mention it around her, instead, one night after Kathryn had gone to bed, he sought out Jasmine. He found her in the library. She smiled as he entered.

"It's pretty late for you to still be up," she commented as he sat down across from her. Jasse grimaced. Kathryn woke with the sun, something that he had not even done as a Guardian and for a person who preferred to wake at noon like Jasse did, it was torture to try and be cheerful at such an unearthly radian. By dusk he was ready to collapse in bed, Kathryn managed much better than he did but still began to flag after the first few radians of darkness.

"Someone has got to tell that girl that getting up at dawn is not required anymore." He reached for the pitcher of wine sitting on the table and poured himself a glass.

Jasmine grinned. "You just don't like dragging yourself out of bed before the noon meal."

"No one should like getting up at such an absurd radian," he returned downing his drink.

"How is Kathryn doing?"

Raising an amused eyebrow at her he replied, "As you know, she's an extremely bright and a quick pupil and I'm having to do more and more research to keep up with her demand for information." *Especially concerning her feathered friend,* he mused as he poured himself another glass. As he sipped his drink a sudden thought sprang into his head.

It couldn't be! ...Could it?

"Has she spoken yet?"

Jasmine's question brought him back to their discussion. He shook his head. "No, but I still don't believe she's mute." After the second month with Kathryn Jasse had come to the conclusion that the girl wasn't mute, just that she had never had a need to talk. He wasn't sure how he knew, he just knew. Jasmine and Mora didn't completely believe him but respected his opinion.

"Has she used her gift yet for you?"

Here Jasse paused. "Yes, this morning I managed to convince her that I truly wanted to see her work with water. Still, she would only make the water ripple, nothing else. And afterwards her body tensed up, as if she was expecting me to beat her for using her gift." He would never forget the memory of the stoic expression she'd plastered on her face as she'd turned her back to him for punishment. Her shoulders had hunched themselves, arms wrapping around her midsection, instinctively protecting her vital organs.

"Jasse if she's still sensitive toward using her gift, what will enrolling her in school do to her?" Jasmine's voice was pained and her gaze never left the flickering flames. "Time is fleeing before us. Surely her fears should have lessened by now." Pausing, she went on, "what else are we to do?"

41

"We have another problem to worry about."

The seriousness of his tone drew her gaze. "Problem? What problem?"

"I have reason to believe that both of Kathryn's gifts are dominate."

Jasmine stared at him for a long time, unable to say anything. Finally she asked, "How? Why? Isn't that impossible?"

Jasse shook his head. "I don't know how or why. And while it's not impossible, the ways it is possible are almost unbelievable. All I can say is that Kathryn seems to have two dominate powers and that she can push aside the urge to use them." He still hadn't figured out how she had known to withdraw her emotions during that first meeting, but it wasn't the last time she had done it. Perhaps she was just reacting to his own body language? He would have to test that theory later.

Jasmine was silent again for a long time. "What is the other gift?"

Jasse brought himself back to the conversation at hand. "She can work with plants."

"How can she resist the urge to use them?" Jasmine exclaimed. "I *still* can't resist my urges and Kathryn is only ten!"

"Neither can any Guardian in the kingdom," Jasse reminded her. "I don't know how she resists the water urge," he shook his head in disbelief. "It takes years upon years of training and meditation to learn to begin to control the urges and yet Kathryn went for years without using them. Her self-control must be unbelievable. Why it doesn't kill her, I can't fathom. As to her second gift I don't think she realizes the effect she has on plants...although she probably feels *something* around them."

"How can a person not know?" Jasmine demanded.

Jasse shrugged. "I really don't know."

"The next potential member of the Guardian Council doesn't know?" she teased, half serious.

He grinned at her. "As I recall we both spent a lot of time passing notes during theory class. Anyway, what I do know is that when Kathryn touches a flower or a leaf the color brightens and it seems to be given new life. I doubt she'll realize it until she makes something grow."

"Which will terrify her even more," Jasmine slumped against the couch. "Oh, Jasse, what am I going to do?"

"The only thing you can do. Give her time and let her know that using her gifts is not wrong."

Jasmine nodded, knowing already that Jasse was right. Kathryn was a conundrum—a conundrum that needed to figure itself out. The two friends talked a few minutes more before Jasse retired.

☜·☞

A month later the little eagle had finally taken to flight, and Jasse and Arianna spent most of their days trying to keep up with Kathryn who seemed to find great pleasure in simply running after her bird, slightly put out at having to remain stuck to the ground while her bird could soar. Radian after radian, Kathryn would spend running around Jasmine's extensive property while the eagle soared just above the girl's head. Sometimes the eagle would perch herself high in the treetops of an evergreen, and despite Jasse's and

Arianna's cautionary comments, Kathryn would rapidly haul herself up to be with the bird.

Jasse had begun to help Kathryn teach her bird to hunt and obey commands, unspoken ones since Kathryn still hadn't said a word. However he began to suspect that Kathryn was speaking to the bird when no one else was around, because the bird began to show an understanding of spoken commands as well.

One day he asked permission to hold the growing bird and after a bit of silent coaxing, Kathryn persuaded her friend to perch herself on Jasse's well-muscled forearm. As soon as the bird had positioned herself on his arm, Jasse found himself shocked at the weight...a bird as small as her should not have weighed as much as she did. He voiced his thoughts, saying, "It's amazing this bird can even get off the ground weighing what she does." Peering at her curiously, he was unsettled to find the bird staring back at him with mirrored curiosity. There was a change in the bird's eyes as though she was scowling which further unnerved Jasse. Suddenly she let out a screech and opened her wings, one of which caught him on the back of his head.

Jasse stared at the bird in complete disbelief. Had she really just delivered a slap to the back of his head? He was still staring when the bird, apparently deciding to dislike him, unexpectedly tightened her grip on his arm. Despite the thick leather gauntlet sheathing his arm, Jasse ground his teeth together to keep from making a sound against the pain. "You can have her back," he gasped as he held the eagle out to the little girl. The bird needed no coaxing; she hopped from Jasse's arm to Kathryn's and settled herself with a very satisfied look in her eyes.

Grimacing, Jasse eased the vambrace off his arm and studied the damage. The eagle's talons had punched through the leather and he could feel the bruises forming on his arm. He looked quickly to Kathryn, worried that the bird was subjecting her to similar treatment, but all he found was Kathryn looking at him curiously. He shook his head and grinned. "You have one bizarre bird," he told the little girl.

80·CB

None of the adults could deny that while the slavery had done some horrible things to Kathryn, it had kept her in great shape and she had more energy than any ten-year-old should have been allowed. Now that she was getting used to the idea of being freed from slavery, Kathryn was slowly warming to the three adults. Arianna had the strongest foundation in the girl's feelings and on more than one occasion, Kathryn had fallen asleep in Arianna's lap while Jasse or Jasmine told a story.

Yet, despite all of their joint efforts, Kathryn never truly bonded with any of them. As the seasons passed she learned to befriend them and accept their help but she did not fully trust them. Especially not after the demonstration for Guardian Council, a year after her rescue from the Blackwoods, in which it had taken all of Arianna's cajoling to convince Kathryn to move the water. Jasmine and Jasse learned just how much independence the little girl had claimed when, after listening to Arianna, she bent down and raced her hand through the pool of water before her. In response the water heaped up causing giant ripples and waves to spread out to the edges of the pool spraying some of the Council members with droplets of water. Kathryn had turned back to Jasmine, her eyes saying, *I moved the water, happy now?*

Jasse had spent the next few moments trying desperately not to laugh. Even Jasmine, though a little disappointed, was heartened by this show of independence from her. Some of the Council members looked furious, but a quiet motion from Lord Mora prevented any outbursts. Arianna bent down and did some more cajoling and finally Kathryn acquiesced. Her frustration and anger at being forced to use something she obviously hated about herself was taken out on the pool of water.

Kathryn turned to leave the gathering, but after turning her back she paused. Suddenly, the grand arboretum filled with the distinctive crackling sound of water freezing drawing the attention of everyone as they watched the pool slowly freeze from top to bottom. As the water froze, the temperature increased dramatically as heat left the water and entered the air. Kathryn left the garden without looking back.

Jasmine stared at the pool in near disbelief.

"She's been practicing," Jasse commented as he tested the firmness of the water with his finger. It was solid all the way through.

Arianna shook her head. "Not unless she's been doing it in her sleep. I've been with her every waking moment for nearly a year now and she's never used her gifts."

Jasse sent her a look. *You can't be with her all of the time; she's too good at disappearing.* Another of Kathryn's seemingly hidden talents. The girl was like a wraith. Disappearing within heartbeats and reappearing just as quickly. He'd lost count of the number of near heart attacks those sudden appearances and departures had caused.

This seemed to impress the Council, who had found Kathryn's unheard of display of attitude distasteful, and after only a few moments of debate, informed Jasmine that Kathryn should be sent to school in a month.

Jasmine protested that a month was not nearly enough time for Kathryn to prepare for such a move, but the Council remained adamant and Jasmine was forced to comply with their demands. When she told the little girl that she would have to leave Jasmine's house and go to a special school, they all noticed a change immediately. Kathryn became stiff and cold again. Jasmine and Arianna repeatedly told Kathryn that they weren't sending her away because they didn't like her or because she had used her gift, which was partly a lie, but because it would help Kathryn as she grew up. It did no good.

Three days before she was supposed to leave, Jasse found Kathryn curled up on one of the balconies overlooking the waterfall. Her eagle sat next to her, preening.

"I know you aren't looking forward to going to school," he told her quietly as he took a seat opposite her. "But it won't be all that bad."

She refused to acknowledge him.

He tried offering the only good news he had. "I'll be at school with you, Kathryn." The Council's message informing him of his appointment to the school had arrived only a few radians ago, otherwise he would have told the girl as soon as she learned she was leaving Jasmine.

She finally turned to face him, suspicion written on her features.

"It's true," he said earnestly. "I just found out this morning otherwise I would have told you sooner."

Kathryn reached out and stroked the eagle's head. The bird tolerated it for a moment before launching herself off the balcony railing and into the evening sky.

"You are going to have to name her," Jasse said softly.

Kathryn watched her soar, and then said softly, "Her name is Destiny."

ℰↄ·ℭↃ

Two weeks later Kathryn was standing at the bridgework and archway that led to the new school. The school was surrounded by a stone wall that made the entire complex look like an impenetrable fortress. Destiny perched on her shoulder, eyes alert. Jasmine and Arianna stood next to a stony Kathryn. The three said their goodbyes and Kathryn walked stiffly through the gate and into a strange new world. Lord Jasse met her inside, his ready smile waiting for her.

He led her through the compound, a maze of tall imposing stone buildings, scattered courtyards, training arenas, and gardens. They walked over a wooden bridge that spanned a small pond, finally arriving at an ancient ivy-laden one story building with several massive wood-hewn doors. Walking over well-worn cobblestones Jasse approached a set of double doors inset into the structure. The doors had ornate carvings of battle scenes against the backdrop of a large tree. Despite its immense size it opened easily as he tugged on one of the door's handles. Standing in front of her on a green tiled floor, Kathryn noticed a girl about her own age smiling shyly back at her. "Welcome to school," Jasse told her, and then motioned to the girl. "This is your roommate, Amy."

Chapter 4

Five Years Later

Kathryn waited for Destiny's signal, her arm muscles burning and her legs on the verge of collapse. A birdcall six inches above her right shoulder sent her right hand flying up to find the break in the rock that would prevent her from falling to her death. Another call two inches above her left leg had her shifting position. Straightening, she listened again. Again the call came and this time when Kathryn moved her hand, the reaching fingers met rough grass. Digging her fingers into the firm dirt she paused and waited. Another call and she moved her left hand, another call and she moved her left leg. Finally, Kathryn pulled herself up over the edge and wearily sat down.

Pulling off her blindfold she stroked Destiny who hopped alongside her. "That's my girl," Kathryn praised as she looked down the cliff she and Destiny had just climbed. It had taken six years to form the friendship and partnership they shared, but every day had been worth it. With Destiny flying above her, Kathryn felt like she could accomplish anything, including free climbing a two hundred foot cliff blindfolded.

After resting a few moments Kathryn stood and began the long walk back to the school.

"It's against the rules to free climb alone."

Startled by the unexpected noise, Destiny screeched and took off. To anyone else it may have looked like the bird had fled the scene, but one signal from Kathryn would unleash seven kilograms of deadly feathers and talons. Kathryn turned to face the newcomer, her hand falling to rest on the hilt of the dagger attached to her belt. Lord Jasse stepped from the shadows, frowning at her. Kathryn, however, wasn't fooled. Lord Jasse's mouth may have been frowning but his eyes were twinkling.

"I wasn't alone," she said, coming to stand before him. Even at sixteen she barely reached to his chest, his head towered above her and she resisted the urge to tilt back to look at him.

Lord Jasse gestured grandiosely about with his hand. "I don't see anybody else here."

Kathryn also looked around. "Well considering it is sunrise, I wouldn't expect anyone to be here."

"Yet you claim you aren't alone," Jasse reminded her.

Grinning, Kathryn pointed up to where Destiny sat perched on a tree.

"I'm afraid Destiny doesn't count," he informed her.

"Why not? She's as good a companion as anyone in the school," Kathryn protested.

"But can she guide you while climbing, or run for help if needed?" he asked pointedly.

Again she grinned. "Why don't you meet me out here tomorrow morning just before daybreak and see for yourself?"

Jasse's face became serious. "Kathryn, you've been at this school for five years and you know the rules. You *cannot* go free climbing without a companion, let alone by yourself in the dark. You aren't even supposed to be out of your room right now."

Kathryn faced him. "I'm not alone," she insisted. "Destiny guides me and I know that she's a faster flier than any runner we have here, so getting help is no problem. As to the darkness I wear a blindfold so that doesn't matter," he cringed at this new bit of information but she continued, "And I do have permission to come out here every morning."

"Who gave you permission to be out here?" Jasse asked, attempting to call the younger woman's bluff.

"Lord Mora," she returned confidently.

He looked at her for a long while, finally he asked, "Destiny *guides* you?" He didn't sound convinced.

"Come tomorrow morning," she repeated, waiting until Jasse nodded.

80·03

The next morning Jasse watched as a feat of daring and friendship was performed before his very eyes. Kathryn hadn't been joking. She would wait for Destiny's signal, while Destiny looked around for safe supports for her feet and hands. The eagle would then land on the spot she deemed safe and would call out. Kathryn would track her voice and put her hand or foot exactly where Destiny had told her. If Kathryn missed the support Destiny called, the eagle would peck her hand or foot until Kathryn found the correct one. They did this the entire way up the cliff.

"If I hadn't seen it with my own eyes I wouldn't have believed it!" Jasse exclaimed when Kathryn reached the top.

Kathryn just smiled at him and praised Destiny. Once she had rested a moment she stood and together the three headed back along the ridge towards the school.

"You know," Jasse said as they walked. "I never told you but you should know that Destiny is no ordinary eagle."

Kathryn snorted. "You mean other than the fact she doesn't look like any eagle I've ever seen?"

"You noticed?"

"How could I not?" she replied. "You claimed Destiny was an eagle when we first met but now that she's full grown she doesn't look like one." She turned to look at her bird feeling a telltale coiling in the bird's muscles. Compared to other eagles, Destiny was only slightly larger than a hawk plumed with gray and white feathers and a black head, not exactly standard issue for eagles. A strong breeze tickled Kathryn's face and Destiny leapt off her arm. Catching the gust perfectly, she began to fly rapidly toward the sea.

"You doubted me?" He asked, somewhat amused.

"I didn't know what to think."

Jasse's amusement increased at her attempt at neutrality. "In other words you doubted me." He stopped and looked at her. "Did you ever discover her species?"

She sighed. "No, none of the books had a description that matched hers."

"I doubt any in the school would," he replied. "Destiny's breed hasn't been seen in several centuries."

Kathryn looked at him, shock plainly visible on her usually impassive face. "What?"

"Destiny is a Merial eagle."

Kathryn considered Jasse's revelation for a time while looking off towards the valley below. "What's so special about a Merial eagle?"

Jasse resumed walking. "Merial eagles supposedly died out when the Elves left so the information we have on them is extremely old but it was said that they were highly intelligent and were able to effectively communicate without spoken words. They were also used as assassins."

"*Assassins*?"

"Yes. Have you ever noticed how heavy she is for her size? The added weight multiplies her striking force and is more than enough power to break a grown man's neck."

"I always thought she was heavy because she ate like a starving boar," Kathryn mused.

Jasse turned to look at his companion to find Kathryn shaking her head smiling. "That certainly explains some things," she laughed. They continued on toward the school, Jasse knowing that he needed to bring up a topic, but knowing it wouldn't go over very well.

After a few moments he spoke, his words slow and deliberate. "I'm worried about you Kathryn."

Surprised she turned to look at him. "Why?"

"When I first met you, you were a loner, caring only for Destiny and trusting no one. Now, six years later you still hold true to that." He looked at her waiting for her response.

"That's not true!" she protested. "I trust and care about you, Princess Jasmine, Arianna, and Amy."

Jasse ticked off everyone on his fingers. "Princess Jasmine rescued you from the Blackwoods, Arianna took care of you, I taught you how to work with Destiny, and Amy's been your only roommate for five years. You haven't taken the initiative to make new friends by yourself."

Kathryn looked away. "That's not exactly true," she said, her voice taking on a hard edge.

He raised his eyebrows. "Oh?"

"My third year at school I attempted to make friends with another girl my age who smiled at me during a lesson."

"What happened?"

Kathryn shrugged. "Her friends didn't like it and she couldn't stand Destiny. Not to mention all she wanted to do was talk, especially about her family."

Jasse cleared his throat. "You are sixteen now, Kathryn, not thirteen."

"I know."

"And you also know what must happen within the next two years."

Kathryn nodded. Within the walls of the school children who possessed gifts were taught to use their special abilities and become Guardians. For several years the students were not only taught how to utilize their powers, but also to engage in mortal combat, attend court, and engage in diplomatic negotiations. Once the students reached fifteen years of age they were eligible to be placed in a family. The unbelievable speed, enhanced by their gifts, with which the students were able to grasp such an education made it possible for them to be placed at such a young age...that and the relatively short average life expectancy of Guardians. A Guardian's natural life expectancy was actually several times that of normal humans. Most of their lives; however, were cut short, not from disease or the ravages of old age, but rather from arrows, swords, poisons, wild beasts, falls, or other violent means while enforcing justice as stewards of the kingdom.

These families were not made up of parents and siblings, but of fourteen Guardians, who lived, worked, and if necessary, died together. They defended the kingdom and protected the weak. Once you were placed in a family you were a Guardian of the Realm.

Kathryn had reached the age where she was eligible for placement in such a family and she was dreading it.

"Why do you fear the change, little one?" Jasse asked gently.

Kathryn sighed, mentally clamping down on the brief fond memory of Claude that came from being called *little one*, wishing Jasse's power wasn't mind reading. Her control over her thoughts was too strong for him know exactly what she was thinking, but over the years he'd become close enough to her to recognize when her emotions shifted. She contemplated not telling him, but realized he should know. In case it didn't turn out well. Turning to face him, she strove for a tone of voice that would discourage questions later. "I lived with an aunt and uncle until I was five, then I belonged to the Blackwoods until I was ten. Princess Jasmine rescued me and I've been here ever since. This is the longest I've had a home, and now I have to pull up the roots I've managed to put down and start over."

ℵ·℺

Jasse didn't say anything right away, he couldn't. This was the most Kathryn had revealed about her past in six years. Over the years everyone seemed to have given up on getting Kathryn to talk about her past. Her cold, hard manner and vague replies were enough to discourage anyone, even Jasmine and Arianna had eventually given up. Only Jasse and her friend Amy kept doggedly asking a question or two.

They walked in silence for several more moments. "It would be the last time." Jasse said quietly.

"What would be?"

"Being placed in a new family. Once a family is formed it isn't broken for any reason."

Kathryn sighed. "I know. I just don't know if I have the energy or conviction to start again."

Jasse was surprised at her answer. "You wouldn't open yourself up to the family you were placed into?"

Kathryn stopped and looked at him, when she spoke her voice had once again taken on the cold, hard tone she used when people tried to pry into her past. "I never knew my parents or their love. My aunt and uncle thought of me as an extra mouth to feed. The Blackwoods regarded me as a slave. By the time Princess Jasmine found me I was ten years old and had been completely unwanted except as additional help."

"But what about now?" Jasse pressed. "Surely Jasmine has taken care of you like a daughter?"

Kathryn nodded slowly. "Yes she has," she agreed. "But I rarely get to see her and feel more like a project than a daughter," then, seeing that he was about to comment, quickly added, "I know I'm not. I know she loves me like a daughter, but as much as I try, I can't view her as my mother. I don't know what it's like to be part of a family."

Jasse could hear defeat behind Kathryn's dispassionate tone, and wondered at its origin. Kathryn never spoke of her childhood ordeals, nor had she ever expressed any interest in learning the identity of her birth parents. But somewhere, deep down inside, did Kathryn desire answers?

By now they had walked far enough to be standing on the cliff that towered over the school. Kathryn walked to the edge and stared down upon the still sleeping school. Destiny swooped down over her shoulder letting out a victorious call.

Understanding hit Jasse like a bolt of lightning. Kathryn had grown up unwanted and *unloved*. She'd never been part of a family and had never experienced the kind of unconditional love it entailed. *That* was why she was so distant and impersonal. She couldn't relate to anyone else she'd ever met and hearing others talk about their families must have seared her heart, knowing that there wasn't anyone like that in her own life.

He had never truly considered the absence of love to be the reason for Kathryn's reclusiveness. Originally he had blamed it on the pressure. Kathryn had entered the school four years later than most and she had had to work extremely hard to catch up. As it was she had caught up and exceeded the expectations of the school. She excelled in nearly all her studies, diplomacy being one of the few skills she'd failed to master. There had even been talk of making her a family leader, the highest honor that could be given. Her inability to form relationships had kept her from being given that honor.

Jasse felt that that was a little unscrupulous of the Council to hold her small number of personal friendships against her when it was partially their fault. Yes, Kathryn had been brought to the school and had sat through a number of classes with students. But those classes had been few and far between and swung from a level near mastery to basic control at the drop of a feather. Most of her time at the school had been spent in one-on-one sessions with instructors or Councilmembers themselves who had struggled to force the stubborn trainee to cultivate her powers. Jasse doubted that a fourth of the students who were ready to graduate would recognize her, let alone know her name and powers.

Not that he could ever reveal any of that to her. Jasse sensed now that Kathryn was becoming uncomfortable by his silence. She hated baring her soul to anyone and his silence made it worse. Quickly he changed subjects.

"You will be at the funeral tonight?"

A retired Guardian had recently died and his funeral was to be that night. Every student was invited to attend, but only after the importance of the ceremony and respect for his memory was stressed. Jasse knew Kathryn had formed a very deep reverence for the actively serving Guardians, those who had fought their whole lives and been relieved of their duties by a younger generation of Guardians, or by an adversary. It was rumored that there was once a time when the Guardians were powerful enough to serve for generations before retiring, but the strength of the gifts was significantly weaker now than it had once been, still making the Guardians more powerful than a knight, yet not nearly as powerful as many believed. Those who managed to live long enough to retire were granted places to live by the King and were provided for.

"Of course," Kathryn replied.

Jasse smiled. "You sound very confident."

Kathryn hesitated then said, "I have been asked to be a torch-bearer."

"That is an honor indeed," Jasse said, trying to hide his smile. He himself had suggested Kathryn when it became known that another torchbearer was needed.

"Yes, it is," Kathryn agreed.

Jasse smiled inwardly. Kathryn was obviously trying to understand why she had been chosen for an honor that only serving Guardians usually claimed. He knew the reason; as of tonight Kathryn would be regarded as an active Guardian, not a trainee. He couldn't wait until tomorrow afternoon when she would be told. To see the look on her face would be worth every trial she had put him through these last six years.

℘ · ℘

"Are you ready yet?"

David looked over at Luke who was fully dressed and had been for the last fifteen minutes. "I'm almost done. Remember, patience is a virtue."

"So is time management," Luke returned quickly.

David grinned. "I'll have to remember that." He turned towards his roommate. "Okay, I'm done."

"Then let's go." Luke practically ran out of the room.

Together the two made their way down to the central courtyard where many had already gathered. Like Luke and David, those present were dressed in the black formal trainee uniform, indicating the somber mood of the event to come. Up ahead was a huge wooden pyre that the deceased Guardian would be placed on while four Guardians set fire to the wood beneath him. Once the entire structure was gone and the ground cold, a tree would be planted on the very spot where the pyre had stood, a testimony to the Guardian's lifelong dedication to his duty.

The ceremony would begin in less than fifteen minutes and the two boys hurried to find a good seat.

Just after the sun set the body was brought out and put upon the pyre. Four torchbearers followed the body and each took up a position on each corner of the pyre.

As the torchbearers waited for the eulogy to end David noticed one in particular. She was standing close to him. Her black hair pulled back into a loose bun, her blue eyes expressionless except for one: reverence. She also looked young, very young; younger than his seventeen years. He had thought he had met every active Guardian. Obviously he had been wrong.

An eagle called from somewhere nearby and David found it strange that one should be out this late. As it was he could have sworn the torchbearer flinched when the cry was uttered.

Finally the eulogy ended and the four torch bearers stepped forward and ignited the pyre. As the body was engulfed in fire, David wondered if he would ever become a full Guardian. He was seventeen and had yet to be placed in a family. Did this mean he hadn't been chosen? Those trained by the Guardians but not chosen for Guardian service usually ended up working as royal protectors. He didn't want to end up as a bodyguard for royalty— he wanted to be a Guardian. With every fiber of his being he wanted to be a Guardian.

After the body was consumed there was a small reception, David's thoughts turned back to the young torch bearer and he looked around, but she had disappeared. That night, as he lay in his bed, his thoughts turned to his destiny. David didn't think he could go through life not being chosen as a Guardian, but it was not his decision. His tortured thoughts kept him awake much longer than usual and his dreams, restless.

Chapter 5

Early the next morning David was summoned to appear before the Guardian Council.

"You'd think they'd pick a better time," Luke grumbled as David stumbled around in the dark getting dressed.

David had to agree with his friend on this one. Daybreak was not normal rising time—for anybody. However the Council had called and he *must* answer. As he made his way to the council room, David couldn't stop the aerial gymnastics his stomach was currently participating in. There were only four reasons a trainee was summoned to the council room, punishment, promotion, expulsion, or family emergencies.

The last time David had been summoned before the Council was when his grandfather had died. He had been released from training for one week for the funeral and to spend time with his family.

Now, as he walked down the halls, David couldn't help but wonder if someone else in his family had died. Several couriers had arrived late in the evening the night before. Perhaps one had brought bad news. At last he reached the doors to the council room. An elderly woman asked his name, and then disappeared into the room. For several tense moments David was left alone before she came back out.

"They are expecting you," she said as she waved him in.

The council room was a circle inscribed inside another circle. Between the outer edge of the first and second circles, fourteen stone chairs sat on a slightly raised platform. Inside the inner circle was an etching of the kingdom. Each of the six realms were subdivided into the regions patrolled by Guardians. The fourteen chairs were occupied by fourteen Guardians who had been chosen by the Council before them.

"Welcome David," Lord Mora greeted him. Lord Jasse also issued a welcome to the now alert teenager.

"My Lords." David gave a bow of acknowledgement to the Council, keeping his eye on Lord Mora and Lord Jasse. Of all the Council members Lord Jasse was friendliest with the trainees and the least intimidating. His face was not sorrowful or carefully controlled, which made it unlikely that David was about to receive condolences.

"Have you any idea why you have been called here David?" Lord Lyrion asked.

David shook his head. "No, sir, I do not."

Lyrion smiled. "Then let us tell you."

Lady Teresë, one of the oldest councilmembers, spoke up. "David, you are being appointed to Guardian status."

David looked at the Council in complete surprise. This was not a possibility he had entertained and the knowledge that he would not end up as a palace guard brought unspeakable joy. But just as quickly that joy was replaced with doubt. "I am honored, but I do not feel ready," he protested quietly.

Lord Jasse looked at him. "It is for that reason you are."

"There is another reason you have been called," Lord Geral, the head of the Council said gravely.

David looked at the Council member, forcing himself to wait patiently for their explanation. What other reason was there for him to be here? They'd already told him he was one of the Chosen, what else could there be? Lord Geral's tone of voice suggested that the news wasn't good.

Lord Jasse spoke up. "You have been chosen to be a leader."

David couldn't believe his ears. "A leader sir?" he asked, trying to make sure he heard right.

Jasse smiled at him. "Yes, David, a family leader."

David couldn't think of anything to say, in the whole history of his family none had ever been awarded this placement. "I am honored," he finally managed.

The Council members nodded at him and Lord Jasse continued. "Your family is being assembled as we speak. You are to return at midday to meet them and be assigned your region."

"Yes, my Lord," David replied.

"We expect," another Council member spoke up, "that you know the responsibilities of a leader."

"Yes Council Member," David replied.

"And that you know if you disregard these responsibilities you will be expelled from the Guardians."

"Yes Milady."

Lord Jasse spoke up again. "We have faith in your abilities David, we would not have chosen you otherwise."

"Thank you sir." David's replies were starting to feel automatic now.

"You are dismissed. Return to us at midday." Lord Mora waved his hand and David left the room.

His world spinning, David tried to process everything that had just happened.

A Guardian!

A Family Leader!

He couldn't even fathom the honor he had been given. Being made full Guardian was the equivalent a commoner being raised to nobility and being made a leader was comparable of a commoner being declared king. He sobered slightly, knowing full well the chances of him falling to an adversary's blade in the next few years were high. Extremely high. A family rarely served more than twenty years and by the end of those twenty years only about a third of those originally assigned to his family would still be living. Those who survived became instructors at the school or entered into the King's service as an elite warrior. Lately the Council had simply added new members to a family to replace ones that fell in the line of duty, but that was a relatively new course of action. Historically they had simply retired the surviving members and assigned a new family to replace them.

He leaned against a wall and tried to imagine his family's reaction—if he could ever tell them. His father and mother would be proud of him. His sisters would probably dance around the room, but what about his brothers?

His second brother was already a Guardian, and had already served for eight years, but wasn't a leader, he wasn't even second in command of his family. Would there be jealousy between the two of them? David prayed there wouldn't be. He loved his brother dearly, but would he understand? His oldest brother would understand his responsibility, and very possibly, be proud of him.

Deciding he needed some air, David left the compound and ran. Often it seemed that running was the only thing that calmed him and today he needed to remain calm. He could not afford to be anxious when he returned to the Council to meet his family. Passing trees and boulders he made his way to the top of one of the various cliffs surrounding the school. Turning he ran alongside the edge for several kilometers. As he ran the reality of the honor he had been granted set in.

As a family leader he was ultimately responsible for everything the rest of his family accomplished, or failed in. While he would listen and take advice from his family, he would ultimately be responsible to make the hard decisions. He would be responsible for sending his new family members to face the unknown every day, to face death, and have to live with whatever result played out. His decisions would govern their duty to serve and to some extent their everyday lives.

Trees and shrubs flew by as he increased his speed, pushing himself to the limits of his endurance. His lungs began to ache as his thoughts raced his feet. As a leader he was responsible to ensure the basic needs of his family; that they were adequately equipped and trained to face the enemy, and ultimately to keep them in line—to prevent radical forms of justice from being executed. If the Council felt that his family needed to be disciplined or brought back in line, while the others in his family would share in some of the punishment, he would take the brunt of it. He was their leader, their protector, and peacekeeper in the family.

Suddenly he was sure beyond all doubt that he wasn't ready for this. How could he keep fourteen very powerful and sometimes headstrong teenagers, most of them complete strangers to each other, from antagonizing each other, or worse yet squabbling, while learning to live together? Even worse, how could he manage to keep exclusionary circles from forming? He'd heard stories of families where the members had not managed to learn to live together and the Council had been forced to intervene. *That* was a situation he wanted to avoid like the deadly Vespine fever. His lungs and legs began to burn as he turned further up the cliff.

His second-in-command would be responsible to keep the family dynamics stable. Even if someone in their family was hesitant to bring a problem to him, they most likely wouldn't have any compunction about bringing it to the second-in-command. He knew, that as the family settled into their new lives, they would choose someone to be their representative to him and act as his lieutenant. David could only hope that he and the family's chosen second-in-command could learn to respect each other and value each other's opinions.

The amount of responsibility he was about to take on was so staggering to David's mind that he actually stumbled in his stride. As he corrected himself, he reminded himself that while it was okay to show some nervousness at the job of becoming a leader, David could not allow it to interfere with the first impression he made to his family—an impression he was determined to make a good one. His lungs and legs felt like they were on fire and yet he pushed himself harder for a few more strides.

Finally, completely out of breath, he collapsed onto the damp grass.

He lay there for several minutes, listening to the blood pounding in his ears, oblivious to every other sound but his own heartbeat.

The cry of an eagle was the first thing he became aware of. Sitting up he tried to locate the bird. Eagles were the emblem of the kingdom and were therefore protected by law from hunting. This one had sounded close.

There it was again. David stood up and peered into the dim light of early morning. There wasn't an eagle in sight.

Another call.

"Ouch!"

David stopped, that had been a woman's voice, yet he didn't see anyone around.

The eagle called again, and again, and again. "Ouch! Oh, call again." The feminine voice sounded agitated. It also sounded like it was coming from the cliffs.

Slowly David moved towards the edge and peered down. There, three meters below his boots, were an eagle and a young woman. He couldn't believe what he was seeing. The woman was free climbing and the eagle, to David's complete astonishment, was guiding her.

David opened his mouth to call down to her, but then thought better of it. He didn't want to startle her and cause her to fall. Instead he sat down on the grass and waited for her to appear.

As the top arc of the sun crested over the ocean horizon a hand appeared over the edge, then another. The woman pulled herself up onto her elbows and waited. David was shocked to notice she was blindfolded, not to mention she was much younger than he had originally thought. He also noticed the emblem on her tunic—she was a Guardian trainee.

Finally the girl pulled herself up completely and sat down on the grass, the eagle hopped alongside her.

Finally David deemed it safe to talk. "That was a pretty impressive stunt you just pulled."

Hearing his voice, the girl jumped to her feet, ripped off the blindfold, and stared at him. He realized he probably should have waited for her to take the blindfold off before speaking to her. She regarded him warily, giving him the impression of a startled deer, frozen but ready to flee at the earliest opportunity.

"I'm sorry if I startled you," he said, rising quickly. "It's just that I've never seen something like that." While brushing the loose grass off of his trousers he attempted to reach out to her with a friendly smile.

She still didn't speak and as David studied her recognition dawned. She was the torchbearer from last night. Surprised he stared at her for a few moments, then realizing she was getting even more uncomfortable asked, "Weren't you a torchbearer at the funeral last night?"

56

She looked at him long and hard before slowly nodding.

David tried again. "Your friend here is amazing," he said gesturing towards the eagle now perched on her shoulder and who was eyeing him with the same distrust as her human friend. "How long did it take to teach him how to do that?"

"She."

Finally, progress, David thought as she uttered the tense word. "I'm sorry?"

"Her name is Destiny."

"Sorry."

She just nodded tersely.

"Is she friendly?" David asked, trying to make conversation.

The girl nodded. "Most of the time."

"Can I pet her?"

"If she lets you, you can pet her." She turned to the bird on her shoulder and nodded towards David.

To David's surprise, and apparently the girl's, Destiny let out a loud screech and then flew away.

"I'll take that as a no," David commented dryly as they both watched the bird fly to a large evergreen tree and land.

The girl didn't comment, but glanced several times between him and where her feathered companion now perched, a ruminating look on her face. He had a feeling that Destiny's opinion mattered highly to her human friend.

David studied her. She was very small and slender; he doubted her head would reach his shoulders if they stood side by side, but like all Guardian trainees was in excellent physical condition—her free climbing skills attested to that. Her black hair was pulled back into the same bun she had worn the night before but it was her eyes that captured his attention, or rather, the experience in her eyes. She noticed his scrutiny and her eyes narrowed, icing over like a pond in a deep freeze.

Suddenly David remembered exactly where he was and what time it was. "Isn't it against the rules to be out here this early?" he asked her pointedly.

"I have permission," she answered in a curt tone. Her eyes constricted into a challenging glare as she took in the trainee emblem embroidered on his own tunic. "What about you?"

"I have permission," he replied, echoing her words.

They stood there for a few tense minutes; finally she spoke. "I need to return to the school."

"I'll walk with you," David said turning towards her. She appeared uncomfortable at the idea.

"There's no need. I'll climb down."

"Then I'll climb with you."

"There's no need for you to do that," she replied as she moved towards the edge.

"You aren't allowed to free climb alone," he reminded her.

"Destiny has been approved as my companion," she informed him tersely.

"By whom?" David couldn't believe any of the Council members would allow a girl to free climb with just an eagle for company, even if they were good together.

"Lord Jasse and Lord Mora." The annoyance in her voice began to grate on his own nerves. She turned and lowered herself over the edge and started down before he could even reply.

Destiny soared down from the tree, screeching in his ear before diving over the cliff's edge. Shaking his head to dispel the ringing, David ran to the edge and watched the two. "Is she climbing or falling?" he asked himself as she sped down the cliff at an impossible speed.

He waited until she reached the bottom and started running back to the school before he too turned and headed back that way, he was halfway back before he realized that he hadn't asked her name. He mentally shook his head. The only reason he'd want to know her name was so that he could avoid her when he returned to school.

David ran hard, pushing himself to the limit once again. By the time he got back to his room it was nearly time for breakfast. He took a quick shower, grabbed some fruit and jerky, and then went for a walk in the gardens.

Pausing to look at a waterfall he heard someone call his name. Turning, he saw Lord Jasse hurrying towards him. He slowed his pace so that the older man wouldn't have to continue jogging to catch up to him.

"Hello David," Lord Jasse said as he came closer.

"Good morning, sir." David noticed Lord Jasse's uncharacteristic anxiety and wondered what this was about.

"You disappeared too quickly earlier," Lord Jasse explained, obviously aware as to his appearance. "I have some information for you that you need to be familiar with before the meeting." He led David to a secluded bench and sat down.

"What do I need to know?" David asked, taking a seat beside him.

"I need to talk to you about someone who will be a part of your family."

David frowned. "I thought we all meet at the same time."

"That still holds true," Lord Jasse agreed. "But this is a special case and I feel you warrant some advice before the meeting."

That didn't sound good. "May I ask who it is?"

Lord Jasse paused. "I'm not sure you know her—

"Her?" David asked, then realizing that he had interrupted apologized.

"That's quite alright David." The Council member assured him. "Yes, she's a sixteen-year-old girl."

David's thoughts turned to the disagreeable girl from earlier that morning. Quickly he pushed them aside. She was not someone he would want in his family. In fact, he pitied the family that she was placed into. "What do I need to know? "

Lord Jasse spoke slowly, as if revealing an ancient secret that could turn the tide in a devastating war. "She's an orphan who became a slave and was abused horribly. She doesn't trust others easily."

David's brow furrowed. "I thought slavery had been outlawed."

"It was," Lord Jasse affirmed. "She was a servant in name, but a slave in reality."

"How did she find her way here?" David wondered.

Jasse hesitated. "A friend of mine found her and rescued her when she was ten years old. I brought her to school a year later."

"I thought you couldn't be any older than six to start here," David said curiously.

Jasse nodded. "In most cases yes, but both my friend and Lord Mora felt there was something different about this girl and they were right."

Now David was interested. "What was different about her? Does she possess an unknown gift?" That was the only reason he could think of for late admittance, then as another thought came to him asked, "What's her name?"

Again Lord Jasse hesitated. "Her name is Kathryn. When I first met her, this girl trusted no one and feared everyone. Even after she had been rescued it took her a year to speak to us. Most people thought she was mute."

David stared at him. "She didn't speak for a year?"

Jasse nodded. "Yes. I was the first person whom she spoke to." His gaze took on a slightly distant look and David guessed that he was back in that moment, hearing the little girl that no one believed could talk, speak for the first time. Realizing that David was waiting he continued. "I brought her to the school soon afterwards and she began her studies. Kathryn faced several barriers when she started here. By entering the school at the age of eleven she was already seriously behind and had to work extremely hard to catch up to her class, and since she had never really used her powers before she had to work with a special mentor to speed up her development."

David didn't believe that. It was unheard of for gifted children to avoid using their powers. Many couldn't learn to control their gifts until attending the school. Even more dangerous, the urges all Guardians faced to use their power could kill them if ignored. "That's impossible," he said flatly.

"That's what so intriguing," Jasse told him. "I've witnessed it myself. Kathryn can go weeks and months, possibly even years, without using her power."

"But why wouldn't she use it?" David asked, his mind reeling with this new revelation.

Jasse's expression darkened. "When she was a slave, her mistress told her horror stories about people who had powers like hers. She told Kathryn that the soldiers would take her away and do awful things to her if they ever found out."

"And she believed them?"

Jasse looked at David. "She was only six years old when she discovered her powers. Someone so young and scared is an easy target for lies and deception. We also suspect that she was beaten anytime she attempted to use her gifts"

David looked at the ground, struggling to contain the distaste that had risen like bile in his throat. He looked back at Jasse, "How could people treat a child like that?"

"I don't know," Jasse admitted. "If you had seen her your heart would have broken for her—so small and scared."

"But she's better now, right? She's been here for five years, surely that's enough time for her to get over the lies."

"The lies, yes. But that kind of conditioning doesn't always disappear. She may no longer be fearful over the use of her abilities, but for her, using them is an anathema," Jasse confessed. "She will always carry the physical scars of her enslavement, but I thought she was past the emotional and mental trauma that had accompanied it."

David felt his heart sinking. "She isn't?"

"She claims she is, but I don't believe it." Jasse looked up at the sky, and then looked into the water. "She's afraid of being placed in a family."

David couldn't believe what he was hearing; trainees usually looked forward to being placed, feared being not placed. "She's afraid of being placed into a family?" he echoed.

Jasse nodded. "All her childhood she never had a family who loved her or cared for her. By the time..." he paused ever-so-slightly before continuing, "we found her she was afraid of making strong bonds with other people."

"But she has made friends, right?"

"She has three."

"Only three?"

"Yes, that is why I'm telling you this; going from three to fourteen in one sudden move is going to overwhelm her."

"But surely she knows that once you've been placed in a family you never get pulled from it?"

"Her mind knows, but her heart refuses to let the mind debate the matter."

"Does she know she's been placed?" David asked cautiously.

Jasse shook his head. "No. I was going to tell her yesterday but I had to focus on the trusting problem."

Dave let out a breath. "Thank you for telling me this. It will make it much easier to understand."

Jasse turned to look at him. "Oh, there's more you should know."

"More?"

"This isn't sad it's more—intriguing."

David waited for Jasse to continue.

"Remember how I told you that both my friend and Mora sensed something different about the child?"

"Yes."

"Well they were right and it's the main reason she was admitted late. You actually came pretty close when you asked me if she had an unknown gift," Jasse paused, trying to figure out how to word his next bit of information, finally he said, "She has two powers."

David looked at him curiously. "Why is that special? Everybody here has two powers."

Jasse shook his head. "You have one dominant and one recessive. One of your gifts is stronger than the other."

David nodded. "That's the way it always is. My main gift is wind, but I can also use the gift of light."

"Both of Kathryn's gifts are dominant."

David stared at him. "B—but that's unheard of!" he protested.

"Not entirely," Jasse said shaking his head. "When a child with gifts is born he has his own power as dominant and the last known power in his family as recessive correct?"

David nodded.

"There are four ways a person can gain two dominant powers," Jasse began. He pursed his lips, as if debating whether or not to continue. "One way is to kill a person with powers and as they die hold them in your arms."

"What good does that do?"

"It transfers the power from the dying soul to the healthy one." Jasse explained.

David looked at him, wide-eyed. "Can just anybody accomplish that?"

"No. Only people who already have power can strip another person of his power. The second way you can gain two dominate powers is if the mother sacrifices her life to save her child."

Jasse paused and looked at David who suddenly felt like he was back in the classroom and had been asked an important question by a teacher. "It's similar to the first isn't it?" he said slowly, trying to order his thoughts. "The mother holds her infant in her arms and gives her life and power to her child."

Jasse nodded approvingly. "Yes it is similar but there is a difference. A power willingly given is stronger than one that has been stolen."

"Is that what you think happened to Kathryn?"

"Either that or the third way."

"Which is?" David prompted.

"She has an Elf parent."

Dave eyed Lord Jasse. "An Elf parent?" He didn't bother to hide the doubt in his tone.

Jasse smiled. "I know it sounds completely farfetched but with Elves the power of the mother shares dominance with the power of her child."

"But the Elves don't associate with us. What would make you think that was how Kathryn gained her power?"

"Each way I've talked about has differing degrees of strength. The first is the weakest, the second stronger than the first, and the third strongest of all."

"Why exactly is there a difference?"

Jasse resettled himself on the bench and David got the distinct feeling that this was a topic not normally discussed among Guardians. "A power stolen loses a good portion of its strength as it's ripped from the body. A power given loses much less strength but still loses a small portion. A power that lives in you is strongest yet. If you are born with a power it is the strongest it will ever be."

"But how does that apply to Kathryn?"

Jasse hesitated here. "When I first met Kathryn, her gift was control of water. As she grew and matured I noticed that the plants also responded to her. The influence she exerts over plants isn't subtle or diminished in power like a recessive gift. I've seen plants respond to her in ways that even some of the most powerful guardians cannot invoke." Slowly shaking his head Jasse went on, "she doesn't even realize the plants are doing this. She knows that her second gift is the ability to work with plants, but I've never told her how... abnormal her second gift is. Because of her unique view on her gifts I've never been able to do a study on her second power. All I know is it definitely did not come from killing another being."

"But it also seems too strong for a mother's sacrifice, right?" David guessed.

Jasse nodded. "Like I've said, I have my suspicions but no proof."

"Can't you just ask Kathryn to show you?"

Jasse laughed. "Remember when I said that Kathryn views using her gifts as an abhorrence? She only uses her power when absolutely necessary. If she can do something without using her gifts, she will choose that path over her power every time. She cringes each time she's required to use it in the classroom."

David was having a hard time picturing this girl. Everything Jasse was telling him, contradicted everything he knew about the trainees. Suddenly he remembered something. "You said there were four ways."

Jasse nodded. "There is the possibility that both of Kathryn's parents were powerful Guardians. If they were both killed while on duty it would explain some of her mysterious past."

"How strong would her powers be in that situation?"

Lord Jasse sighed. "I can't honestly say. For Guardians to marry is an extremely rare occurrence and there's no guarantee that the child will have powers."

"There isn't?"

"No. There are records of powerful Guardians marrying and having children without gifts and there are records of Guardians having children with gifts. All with varying degrees of strength, it's impossible to predict the result."

David hesitated before slowly saying, "Her having Guardian parents feels more plausible in my mind than her having an Elf parent."

"That's the theory that most of the Council is holding to as well," Jasse told him. "But there are a few problems with that theory. The year Kathryn was born, if she truly is sixteen, we didn't lose a single Guardian. By her own admittance, Kathryn never knew her parents. If her parents were Guardians, they would have sent her to the school immediately if they felt that she was in danger. So why didn't they?"

"Couldn't she simply have been separated from them a few years after her birth?"

"Again, that's what many on the Council believe. I just don't feel that it's right."

"You're basing this on a feeling?"

"Instinct and intuition if you will," the older man replied. "When I was an active Guardian, I learned that my instincts were usually right. And they're telling me that Kathryn's parents weren't Guardians."

David absorbed that information. "So what do you suggest?" he asked finally.

Jasse hesitated before speaking. "With Kathryn there's no sure way to make her trust you, at least not that I'm aware of. I've known her for six years and I get the feeling she still doesn't trust me." He exhaled heavily and went on, "From what I've gone through in dealing with her I only have a few suggestions. First and foremost don't push her. She's a shy girl, but she has many talents and abilities that even you would benefit from. Many on the Council consider her to be the most powerful guardian of this era."

David sobered at that thought. Many of the widely acknowledged "most powerful" Guardians he had met were nice enough, but had carried a sense of self-importance he found repulsive. If this Kathryn also had this inflated notion of her importance, it was going to be a very rough start. He was determined not to rely on only the most warrior-like Guardians of his family. Everyone had their value, no matter who they were or how powerful they claimed to be.

Jasse smiled sadly at him. "Kathryn may be powerful," he said gently. "But you have nothing to fear about her opinion of her gifts. If anything, you'll have to order her to use them," he reminded the younger man.

David felt some chagrin at his negative thoughts towards a girl he had never met, but whom Jasse obviously cared about...especially since Jasse could read thoughts. "Somehow I have a feeling that ordering her to use them will alienate her from me and the rest of the family."

"It might at first," Jasse conceded. "The girl can display quite an attitude if she feels threatened, but be gently persistent. Be understanding, it will take her a while to adjust, but even as you are doing those two things, envelop her into the family. Show her that she's done pulling up her roots and that she can trust you."

"Thank you Lord Jasse," David said gratefully.

Jasse stood. "If you ever need me David, I'll help you... both of you,"

"On more question," David said quickly. "Why is none of this taught in school? It seems to me like it should be an important part of the curriculum...especially the ways powers can be obtained."

Lord Jasse sat back down. "Thousands of years ago, when the school was first formed and the Elves associated with us, knowledge like this was taught. But unlike the Elves, humans, even gifted ones, are fallible. A Wanderer named Raihji managed to learn of the procedure, took this knowledge and used it to further his power until it took the combined might of every kingdom, the Guardians, and an army of Elves to stop him—

—and the Council won't take the chance of it happening again," David finished.

Lord Jasse nodded and stood. "We can't take the chance now that the Elves are gone." He stood and prepared to leave, but not before revealing one last piece of information. "And David, one more thing..."

"Yes?"

"Kathryn's been chosen to be your second in command."

"What?!"

Chapter 6

Kathryn stood straight as a statue, motionless in the shadows outside the door to the council room. Twelve other nervous trainees milled around, talking nervously amongst each other. She felt sick to her stomach, although she never would have admitted it. She had been chosen and placed into a family. The very thought was enough to make her blood run cold. Everything she had been dreading was unfolding before her eyes.

Deep inside she felt cold rage. Jasse had to have known she had been placed when he had talked with her the morning of her climb, and yet he hadn't said anything. The betrayal cut deep, she had thought she could trust him. Yet here she was, having been taken completely by surprise. She hated surprises. Once she was done here she was going to need some serious time on the training mats...she wondered if she could convince Jasse to spar with her and then mentally shook her head. The last time he'd been the source of her ire, which wasn't that uncommon an occurrence, he'd learned not to agree to spar with her when she was angry. Kathryn didn't believe in letting her anger get the better of her in a fight like some of the trainees, instead she turned it into a cold, unrelenting, and controlled attack that was rarely overcome by her opponent. Jasse had learned the hard way that Kathryn was more powerful than the image her diminutive form projected.

Gritting her teeth at the distraction that had allowed her mind to wander, Kathryn refocused on the situation at hand.

Inside the council room their family leader was being given some last minute advice before the rest would be ushered in. She remembered with stark clarity her first and subsequent visits before the Council, the retired Guardians staring down at her with faces so impassive that they could give her lessons in chilling stares. It was one of her deepest secrets that she had modeled her own icy glares and cold looks which had kept so many overly curious trainees at bay during her years at school after the ones the Council had thrown her way when she had hesitated when ordered to use her gift. Their solemn and serious moods did nothing to put a nervous trainee at ease and the way they had constantly called Kathryn before them during the five years she had been at the school only served to set her apart even more.

It wasn't often a single trainee was called before the Council and it was usually only done for punishment. From what she'd heard around the school, most of her classmates, at least those who knew she existed, believed her to be a troublemaker and just as many believed that she wouldn't be chosen for active Guardian status. Yet not once had she been disciplined, if anything Kathryn had yet to comprehend just what the Council had been doing, or trying to do, during those sessions.

She wished Destiny was with her, at least she would have had some comfort as she faced the Council. As it was she felt a small comfort in knowing Amy had been assigned to the same family. She knew without having to look that her friend was conversing with another girl named Jenna whom Kathryn had met once before and whom, surprisingly, she had genuinely liked.

Finally, after what seemed like radians, the doors opened and the thirteen trainees went in to face the Council.

Kathryn entered last, taking in everything before focusing on her new leader. Shock coursed through her as she recognized the boy from earlier that morning. The arrogant, self-centered rockhead was going to be her family's leader. He hadn't appeared to notice her and she slipped behind an older boy with blond hair to keep out of his line of sight. She wondered what the Council would think if she announced her resignation just seconds after they informed her she had been made a Guardian.

Probably nothing that could be uttered in polite company.

"Welcome trainees," Lord Geral, the council leader greeted as he stood, he was the oldest Council member and by far the most intimidating. There were few trainees who didn't fear him, and Kathryn happened to be one of them. "Today is a special day for you as you are about become active Guardians."

The trainees remained silent, although many smiled broadly. This was the day they had been anticipating for years.

Lord Geral continued. "Take a look at those around you. They are your new family."

Quickly Kathryn glanced around—five boys and nine girls whose ages appeared to range from fifteen to eighteen. It never ceased to amaze her how immature some of the trainees, or Guardians as the case would be now, could seem. She recognized many of them from various classes and wanted to groan. Aside from Jenna and Amy, most were people she'd avoided contact with.

"David will be your leader." Lord Geral was speaking again and Kathryn returned her attention to him. "We expect you to respect him and support him. He carries the weight of your lives on his shoulders."

Kathryn thought she saw a fleeting glimpse of nervousness flash in David's eye, but before she tell for certain Lord Geral spoke again, capturing her attention.

"We know it is unorthodox, but we have also chosen your second-in-command. Kathryn, please come forward."

For the third time that morning, Kathryn felt like she'd been slapped hard across the face. Not only had Jasse known she had been placed, but he'd also known she'd been made second-in-command. And yet he hadn't said a word. Not one. So much for ever trusting him again...now she was determined to get him on the mats with her before the day was over. She turned to glare at Jasse, to find him nodding her forward, his grin making her painfully aware just how much he was enjoying this.

Slowly Kathryn made her way from the back of the group to stand before Lord Geral. She kept her eyes on the head of the Council rather than David; she didn't want to see his reaction, although she guessed his mirrored her own. Lord Geral addressed her. "You will be David's right hand. Not only are you to help ease his burden, but in emergencies you will take joint command, or if necessary full command of your family."

Great, Kathryn thought bitterly, *so much for hoping that I would be left alone in the family.* "Yes sir," she replied through clenched teeth.

Geral appeared pleased for he then turned to the rest of the group. "Your ceremony will be tonight at dusk. Until then, we would like for you to take some time to get to know each other a little bit, before you leave us completely." Geral nodded. "You are dismissed."

ೞ·ೞ

The fourteen brand new Guardians filed out of the council hall. Lord Jasse followed them.

"The Council has arranged for the southern garden to be kept clear of other students so that you can take the time to get to know one another. I suggest you head there now," he advised.

David noticed he looked quite a bit at Kathryn when he spoke of getting to know one another. He also noticed the ice cold glare she gave him in return. They must know each other well, he decided. He'd never heard of someone staring down Lord Jasse, let alone glaring at him, especially considering how friendly he was. He was also a Councilmember which tended to intimidate most of the students; friendly personality notwithstanding.

Nothing could have described the shock he felt when he realized that his second-in-command Kathryn was the same girl from the cliffs. Judging by the stiffness in her manner when she had stepped forward after Lord Geral had named her second-in-command, he supposed it was just as big of a shock to her. He had a feeling that it was a position she would not take to willingly—which was probably why they assigned it in this case. Suddenly he remembered his earlier thought about pitying the family she was placed into. Who'd have thought that he'd end up pitying himself?

Life has an annoyingly ironic sense of humor, he thought dryly, the one person he didn't want in his family had been chosen to be his second in command and she did not want to become his second-in-command...in fact she looked as if she'd have preferred to be buried alive than be his second-in-command.

And he hadn't missed the way she'd slipped behind Luke once she'd caught sight of him. Nor the way she'd taken a deep bracing breath before accepting the position as his second. With any luck the two of them would manage to survive the first week without killing each other.

A lot of luck.

It was going to be difficult enough to get along with Kathryn let alone taking command of twelve other overly excited teenagers.

Oh yes. If he had wanted to be miserable for the next few years, he couldn't have planned it better. Being a palace guard was suddenly looking a lot more appealing.

Looking around he noticed everyone glancing every which way and decided it was time to take control.

"Right then," he said cheerfully, and feeling slightly idiotic. "Come on everyone." He led the way to the garden Jasse specified and found a picnic lunch set out for them.

66

Several of his new family members immediately tucked into the food. Kathryn, he noticed, was scanning the landscape and looking very uncomfortable. He walked over to her forcing himself to remember everything Lord Jasse had told him and what he could remember of their interaction on the cliff. Skittish. Distrustful. And not one for small talk.

Time to try and make new friends.

"I'm sure Destiny is nearby," he whispered quietly, then, before a very startled Kathryn could reply, he sat down. When she didn't sit down immediately, he turned to her, smiled, and nodded to the space next to himself. Almost reluctantly she sank down, rather stiffly, next to him, observing him with wariness in her eyes.

Oh yes. They were going to get along just great. Just like old comrades— old comrades with large swords and a several generation blood feud against each other.

He handed her a piece of fruit. From the cautious manner in which she took it, he half expected her to test it for poisons. He took a bite of his own fruit and then addressed the group. "Well since we're supposed to get to know one another and I'm your leader we might was well start with me." Oh stars above. Was that the best he could come up with? He definitely needed to brush up on his public speaking skills. *I should have paid more attention during debate and communication class.*

Well, there was nothing he could do about it now but continue doggedly on. "My name, as Lord Geral told you, is David, my gift is wind control. I dislike dancing, especially the waltz, and I love to run." That didn't come out half as bad as he'd feared he reflected, as he bit into another piece of fruit. As he had hoped his comment about the dreaded waltz, at least in the eyes of the young men, brought some laughs. Turning to Kathryn he said, "Your turn."

Kathryn looked like she would prefer to swallow fire.

Oh yes, David thought, *we're going to have great times.* Who had he insulted on the Council to be saddled with such a second-in-command?

"I'm Kathryn, as Lord Geral already told you," she began in the taut tone already all too familiar to David. "My gift is water control, I'm not a diplomat, and love to climb."

David could only too swiftly agree with her lack of affinity for diplomacy.

Next in their group was a girl named Amy. "Hi, my name's Amy," her voice was light and fun and David decided he liked her already. "My power is fire control. I'm not very good at archery and I love horseback riding and swordplay."

David's old roommate was next. When David had watched his family enter the council room he had been elated to see the blinding blond hair and energetic eyes of Luke come into focus, and if the fist pumped into the air was any indication of Luke's opinion, he was just as happy as David. "My name's Luke, my gift is earth movement, I prefer a sword to diplomacy, and I love fencing."

"I can personally assure all of you of that." David spoke up. Everybody laughed... everybody except Kathryn. David began to wonder if she even had emotions, he had yet to see her smile.

David turned his attention to the next person in line, a small shy girl who shared Luke's brilliant hair color, but whose eyes were gray instead of a vibrant blue. "My name's Jenna," her voice was quiet, but surprisingly strong. "My gift is healing, I'm no good in a battle confrontation, and I love to read," she blushed a little as she admitted her love of books.

Not wanting her to be embarrassed David said, "I love reading. We'll have to compare favorite books some time."

It was not known outside the Guardians, but in truth there were few true "super warriors" as both commoners and nobility referred to them. All Guardians could fight extremely well, but those who could be deemed a "super warrior" were rare, and as the generations passed were becoming rarer still. Many Guardians were several mastery levels above the level of the best trained knights, but some, especially healers or those gifted with the ability to sense emotions, were simply average fighters who used their gifts to heighten their abilities. David intended to make sure that everyone in his family was recognized for values that went beyond their fighting skills.

ౚ·ౚ

Kathryn watched in silent, grudging, surprise as David confidently took charge, making sure everybody felt wanted, needed, and unembarrassed about who they were. *Perhaps he wasn't a bad choice as a leader,* she thought as she took a bite of fruit.

As the group gave a quick description of themselves, Kathryn dedicated herself to memorizing each.

Leia, a tall brunette who appeared to be her own age, could talk to animals but feared water, something Kathryn couldn't understand. *How could anyone fear water?* She asked herself as David assured Leia that having an irrational fear did not make her weak.

Kathryn wondered if that was true, her own irrational fear was so fanatical it sent her, quite literally, into panic mode—a state in which she would prefer it if no one ever saw her in.

"My name's Matt," a cheerful red haired, freckled boy who looked about David's age, piped up. "I enjoy cooking and my gift is the influence of small creatures." Every nuance of his body suggested a beet sugar overdose; he hadn't stopped fidgeting since he sat down, if she didn't know any better she might think that ants had crawled into his tunic.

"What kind of small creatures?" Luke asked.

Matt looked confused. "What do you mean, 'what kind of small creatures'?"

Now it was Luke's turn to frown in confusion. "I mean can you only control small creatures like mice and rabbits or do you mean small creatures like baby animals?"

The redhead shrugged. "Small creatures...ah, um, little, ah small...interpret as you will."

"Never mind, Luke," David interjected with some humor over Matt's bumbling definition. "We'll have plenty of time to get to know the details once we reach our region." He turned to the next girl in their group, an older girl named Cassandra who, judging from the way she kept her arms wrapped around her knees in front of her and hunched her shoulders to make her

68

appear smaller, was going to be the shy one in the family. She did admit that she preferred Cass to Cassandra.

Cass could use telekinesis, but was helpless around fire. Noting that her hair matched Matt's, Kathryn couldn't help but wonder if they were related.

Rachel could also control wind, but wasn't very good at archery. Kathryn didn't need to know Rachel to see that the tall blond was outspoken and vivacious; her mannerisms indicated an experienced public speaker. Her tone was firm, clear, and modulated carefully...as if every inflection had been a study in her mind before it had been spoken.

Elizabeth was a girl in Kathryn's age class who could move the earth, but feared heights. Kathryn had observed Elizabeth in a few mock political situations, noting that she was one of the few trainees who could debate nearly any professor and end the victor, and knew instinctively that Rachel and Elizabeth would end up acting as the diplomats for the family. So far, the people assigned to her family were surprising her in the idea that she might be able to tolerate living with them. That changed the moment the next girl opened her mouth.

Natalie could control fire but hated being alone. As she talked she tossed her perfectly styled blond hair over her shoulders, leaving one lone strand to frame her face which she promptly started twirling around one finger, laughing ridiculously at anything one of the boys said. Kathryn bit back on a groan. She recognized her. Natalie had been the biggest flirt in school. Unfortunately she'd also proved to be exceptionally good at intelligence gathering. Kathryn had worked hard to stay off Natalie's radar at school. Living with her was going be torture.

Daniel could sense emotions, but hated making quick decisions. Noting his tall frame and wavy brown hair, Kathryn guessed that Daniel would make an impressionable nobleman at court, grudgingly, had to include both David and Luke in that assessment as well. Lindsey, a girl who was every inch Natalie's twin in personality but complete opposite in physical appearance, could control light but was also afraid of water. Since the two were already becoming fast friends, Kathryn made a second mental note to avoid both of them as much as possible. The last thing she needed was for Natalie and Lindsey to start trying to get to know her. Tyler, the oldest of the group, was also a healer but hated playing the part of a nobleman, hated any sort of playacting.

At least there's someone in this group I might get along with, Kathryn thought as she remembered the few mock political and social settings that had been put on by the instructors—remembered how much she had hated pretending to be what she wasn't.

After the introductions had been made, small conversations started up as various family members conversed with each other, trying to get to know each other. Kathryn talked minimally, preferring to listen and learn more about the family she would now have to learn to live with. Admittedly, most of them didn't appear too difficult, Natalie and Lindsey were probably the only two she would need to be careful around, but she was all too aware that first appearances and impressions were easily manipulated. She would withhold her final assessment until they'd lived together long enough for everyone to show their true personalities.

High above, a movement caught her eye and Kathryn's heart soared as she recognized Destiny.

Apparently David noticed as well for he suddenly said, "We have one more family member that needs to be introduced." He raised his voice to carry over the several conversations.

Eventually everyone stopped talking and looked at him.

"I thought there were only supposed to be fourteen of us," Natalie said once everyone was quiet.

David nodded. "True, but the Council forgot one member who is very important," he looked over at Kathryn, who was a bit confused until he motioned ever so slightly towards Destiny. Immediately she understood—he wanted her to share Destiny with the group. She glared at him. No way.

"Well, who is it?" Matt asked.

David looked at her and raised an eyebrow, a movement that reminded her so much of Lord Jasse that she relented and reluctantly let out a high whistle. Instantly Destiny leaped from her perch and soared down to her outstretched arm. She picked up a piece of jerky and fed it to Destiny who gulped it down in one swallow.

Astonished gasps and other exclamations of delight rippled around.

"That is so cool!" Natalie gushed as Destiny perched on Kathryn's arm.

David turned to Kathryn. "Would you like to do the honors?" he asked.

Kathryn turned to her friend. "This is Destiny, her gift is her amazing eyesight she stinks at diplomacy and loves to go rock climbing."

"Rock climbing?" Cass asked in confusion.

Both David and Kathryn nodded and David said, "It is the most amazing thing you will ever see."

Kathryn briefly entertained the idea of hitting him. In the face. With a tree branch. Or maybe with the entire tree.

"How on earth does an eagle climb?" Natalie asked.

David looked a Kathryn. "Would you and Destiny be willing to give a demonstration?"

Kathryn looked at Destiny, wanting nothing more than to disappear, but she could feel the eager anticipation of the group. She nodded reluctantly, although she felt like she'd rather jump off the cliff without Destiny than perform.

Amy turned to David. "Do you know what the ceremony tonight will entail?"

Graduations of other Guardians were open affairs that anyone in the school could attend and everyone in the group had attended at least two since coming to the school. But watching the ceremony and participating in it were two completely different scenarios. Especially since they were going to be the first full family to graduate in at least a decade, if not longer. In more recent years, the Council had refrained from retiring entire families and instead began rotating in new members to replace those killed, injured, or otherwise rendered unable to fulfill their duties. The abrupt change from graduations of two or three individuals to a full family made David wonder what had occurred to prompt the Council to commission an entire new family, but he kept his thoughts to himself.

Others added their questions to Amy's, regarding the ceremony. David held up his hand. "I know one thing. We have to choose a name for ourselves."

"A name?" Tyler asked

This time Jenna spoke up. "Each Guardian family takes a name to identify itself. Usually they're names of magical creatures, but more common ones have been used."

"The Council doesn't do that?" Matt asked.

"No, they just like us to think that they do so that we don't spend our days dreaming up fancy names when we should be focused on our studies." Someone snorted derisively at her explanation.

David nodded. "We have to announce our name tonight, or more accurately I have to announce it. Anyone have any suggestions?"

"How about Phoenix?" Cass suggested.

Matt shook his head, "There's already a family named Phoenix in Merdea."

"What about Griffin? Luke called out.

Soon everybody was talking at once, until finally, Jenna suggested a name that brought everyone to standstill.

David looked at her. "I like it, how about the rest of you?"

"There has *got* to be a family with that name already in service," Tyler protested.

Elizabeth shook her head. "No," she replied firmly. "The last family with that name was retired seven years ago."

Matt squinted at her. "Did you swallow the clerical records or something?"

Elizabeth shot him an affronted look. He gave her an innocent look in return. At least that was what he probably attempted. To David it appeared more like a "do not trust me with anything having to do with fire or sharp objects" grin. So that was a check in the "probably going to burn the house down" and a check in the "will probably kill you in your sleep if you offend her" categories. Oh, and the "outrageous flirt" category. Natalie was the *second* to last person he'd wanted in his family. He was completely missing the target today for people he wanted in his family. He could only hope Matt and Kathryn would prove his initial impressions wrong. He didn't have any hope for Natalie.

Clearing his throat before things went too far between Elizabeth and Matt, he looked pointedly at everyone. "Yay or Nay?"

It was unanimous.

Luke spoke up. "Are you sure you don't know anything else about the ceremony? As our family leader, shouldn't the Council have given you an in-depth lecture on what's expected for our graduation since it's going to be different from the ones we've attended?"

As near as David could figure, the change in policy had come about because there simply weren't as many gifted students as there had been a hundred, or even fifty, years ago and the Council was hesitant to throw fourteen new and inexperienced Guardians into the fray when they could be placed in more experienced families where their chances of survival were significantly higher. It wasn't a horrible policy, in fact he was willing to bet that it significantly reduced the number of lethal mistakes a new Guardian might make if he was mentored by seasoned and experienced warriors. Still, he couldn't quite ignore the niggling thought at the back of his mind that there was *something* prompting this change to a full family graduation.

Before David could reply Elizabeth cleared her throat. "It's a two part ceremony," she began. "First they will present us with new uniforms and announce our region of service to the rest of the school. The second half of the ceremony takes longer. During this part we will each be presented with new weapons to be worn with our new uniforms. After we have been presented with our weapons we will each be masked in the ways of the Guardians and handed a torch. Each of us will then place our torch on a special metal tree, eventually lighting up the whole."

"Where did you learn that?" Luke asked.

Elizabeth gave him a funny look. "The library of course. Where else?"

Luke raised an eyebrow at her. "Why would you be looking *that* information up?"

"Aren't you ever curious?"

"Sometimes," David put in dryly. "But he usually hits it over the head to get it to stop harassing him."

"Hey!" Luke protested.

"What is so important about a tree?" Tyler asked suddenly. "It's on our uniforms and part of the ceremony, but I can't remember any of the instructors ever explaining what the tree meant other than the fact that the symbol has been handed down through the generations since the Guardians' inception."

Before Elizabeth could answer, Rachel spoke up. "A tree is the symbol of family. You will each have a specific place for your torch; which you will be shown earlier. Some of you will represent the roots taking the form of all that holds the tree standing. Others will represent the branches, the ones that nourish the rest of the tree. Kathryn's torch will end up being the trunk of the tree and David's the top. Our flames represent all that holds the tree together."

Everyone stared at her in amazement. Luke grinned broadly. "Do you spend your afternoons in the library too?"

Rachel shrugged. "Actually, I figured it out during tactics instruction."

Luke stared at her in bewilderment.

"Right," Matt piped up dryly. "Because that makes perfect sense. You must have had a different instructor than I did."

Rachel rolled her eyes. "It makes sense if you think about the progression."

The two boys exchanged a look. "Progression?" Luke finally ventured.

Holding up one hand, Rachel began to tick her points off on her fingers. "First class of the day is history where we learned about the legend of the first family of Guardians. The second class of the day is science where we, on that day, learned about botany and how plants live. The third class was tactics where we discussed the legend of the Great War and how the fabled first Guardians broke tradition and killed the Wanderer leader together, as a team." She spread her hands and gave a smile. "After that I kind of just...I don't know...understood."

Luke and Matt were staring at her, eyes wide. "That settles it," Matt said firmly. "You *definitely* had different instructors than I did."

From the looks traveling around the circle, David could see that a few people doubted Rachel's explanation. He himself wasn't completely sure of the history behind the emblem, but in his mind her explanation made sense. The one to champion Rachel and her explanation was the last person he expected through. "Rachel's correct," Kathryn spoke up.

Everyone's eyes flew to her and while she didn't shift or fidget under their gaze, he got the distinct impression that she was uncomfortable with the scrutiny.

"How do you know that?" Lindsey asked.

Kathryn was still for a moment, as if debating how much of her knowledge to reveal. "Lord Jasse told me," she eventually.

David blinked. He had once asked Lord Jasse for an explanation and the older man had just laughed and said "if you think about it you will figure it out".

"Lord Jasse?" Luke asked in surprise. "He's one of the hardest instructors to get information like that out of."

Kathryn gave a brisk shrug. "Well, he told me."

David suspected that there was a lot more to what Kathryn had told them but decided that here and now was not the place to pursue it. "In any case," he said quickly before Luke could add anything else. "We'll finish the family histories later—

He ignored the look that flashed in Kathryn's eyes.

"... Right now we need to get ready for the ceremony."

The group disbanded and each went to their own rooms to prepare for the ceremony.

℘·℃ß

Kathryn went to her room, knowing it would be the last time she would spend radians reading in the privacy it promised her, knowing it would be the last time she would sleep peacefully for several months. She packed her few meager belongings and went in search of Jasse.

She found him on the training mats, a ridiculous grin on his face.

℘·℃ß

The courtyard was completely full as the sun began to sink behind the horizon. The moon Firea was at it its apex clothing the grounds in a purple hue. The shadowy edges cast by the battlements were more pronounced with the vibrant color giving a sense of regal importance to the ceremony. The trainees were eager to see their friends become Guardians and dream about the day when they would be up there instead of in the audience.

A huge platform had been set up and on it sat the fourteen council members. The King and Queen were present. Off to the right stood a huge metal tree, fourteen torches burning beneath it. The tree had four roots, and eight branches.

73

Off to the left were fourteen unoccupied chairs. The graduating trainees would take their places once the ceremony began.

Finally the King stood. It was time to begin the ceremony. As he strode to the center of the platform the trainees quieted down, waiting for him to speak.

"Good evening," King Darin began, smiling at the audience before him. "As you know tonight is a special night."

He waved his arm around, gesturing towards them. "Tonight we honor those who have completed their training and stand ready to take their place as Guardians of this realm."

He paused as the trainees clapped and cheered. King Darin held up his hand for quiet. "As I am sure you are all quite aware, being chosen to actively serve is a huge responsibility." He grinned at the crowd. "I am sure your teachers and mentors remind you of this constantly, but I will also take the time to remind you exactly what a Guardian is.

"A Guardian faces life and death situations every day. I will not lie to you when I tell you this realm has had more than its fair share of Guardian deaths." A murmur began to pass through the younger trainees and the King held up his hand once again for silence. "Yes," he agreed, "It is dangerous work, but the rewards are immense. Not only does a Guardian serve as a warrior in times of war, but during the times of peace, they keep the order within this realm."

"A Guardian will willingly give his, or her, life to defend and protect this realm. And tonight we honor those who are entering into that commitment."

As he said this, the fourteen graduates, led by David and Kathryn walked down the center aisle of the chairs. They received a standing ovation by the trainees, even the council members stood and bowed as the group approached.

David led his new family to the waiting chairs and took his place before the head chair. The others followed his example. They waited until the King told them to be seated.

King Darin spent a few more minutes speaking of the honor a Guardian served, then relinquished the floor to Lord Geral.

"Tonight," Lord Geral began in a loud voice. "We have heard the honor it is to serve as Guardians. Now we honor those who have made that commitment." He motioned with his hand and the council members stood.

Starting with David, Lord Geral called the new Guardians up to receive their new uniforms. They were much different than the basic trainee tunic. These uniforms were black, rather than the tan color of a trainee, and embroidered with the emblem of the Guardians on the front. The uniform consisted of three parts, a bodysuit, a shirt, and an over-tunic.

The bodysuit was made of a special material called Cirin, woven into a fabric that a sword could not easily cut. It would cover their entire body from just under their chins to the tops their feet. The shirt had a rigid neck to protect against sword-thrusts and its sleeves were slit at the elbow, to provide flexibility in sword fighting and archery. Both the bodysuit and the shirt were slit at the elbow but it had been done in such a way that the slits overlapped so that the Guardians would not be without protection. The lower arm was protected by vambraces or gauntlets, while the upper arm was protected by conforming strips of Cirin. The over-tunic was sleeveless and bore the embroidery of the Guardian emblem on its front. The tunic, unlike the ones Kathryn had seen Princess Jasmine and her companions wearing on the day she was rescued, which had different hem lines for men and women, reached to the knees for both sexes and were slit along the side up to the hip to allow freedom of movement when fighting. Its hem was weighted for battle. The boots were knee-high and also made of Cirin. Gloves for the hands reached to the elbow and could be laced to the sleeves of the shirt.

Besides being extremely light and flexible, Cirin had a unique and mysterious property that caused it to be one of the most closely guarded secrets of the realm. Cirin fabric was not merely just fabric, it was a living substance harvested from the thin bark layer that rested on the heart of the Sebacus tree, trees that only Guardians who had the gift to influence plant life could cultivate and only after years and years of intense training and dedicated practice.

When Cirin fibers were woven together using a technique originally developed by the Elves it would repel all sword thrusts, except those made by a sword forged of the metal helcë, and when damaged it would repair itself. It would also provide protection from fire as it did not absorb heat or burn easily. Although extremely tough, Cirin was very soft to the touch and felt like a shirt made of the finest silk to its wearer.

Cirin's most fascinating property was that it was symbiotic. It drew minute amounts of life energy from the Guardian and forged an eternal bond after the Guardian wore the garment for two weeks. Cirin could sense the Guardian's physical needs and would wipe away sweat and body heat to cool during periods of strenuous activity or return heat to ward off frostbite or hypothermia during the coldest of winters.

If a Guardian were to be injured, Cirin would bind itself around the wound to prevent extreme blood loss and secrete a natural fluid-like sap to stave off infection. Cirin also naturally repelled most insects, although the nature of that particular ability was not fully understood.

Because of the symbiotic bond between Cirin and Guardian, it would reject any other who attempted to wear it. On more than one occasion, young Guardians had failed to keep their uniforms segregated and mistakenly donned their roommate's uniform resulting in a very ugly skin rash that the victims couldn't stop scratching for weeks. To prevent reoccurrence an edict was issued from the Council of Tëlban nearly two centuries ago requiring separate rooms for each Guardian.

Rumors and legends reported that Cirin had actually killed adversaries who had been brazen enough to remove the garment from a fallen Guardian and attempted to make it their own. The usurper suffered a slow and agonizing death as the Cirin constricted the victim as if surrounded by a large serpent. Together, these properties resulted in a uniform that would last a Guardian's lifetime.

The uniform was to be worn while in battle or on patrol. It was designed to make it difficult for an aggressor to injure a Guardian, while giving the

Guardian an edge. The only others in the realm to wear Cirin reinforced uniforms were the Royal Guards.

The Guardian emblem consisted of two parts. Similar to the ceremonial torch tree, an eight branched tree stood on a hill surrounded by darkness, its four roots diving deep into the earth. The tree represented the intimacy of the families, each part doing its own, but needing the rest of the parts to do their own work for theirs to succeed. Fourteen stars surrounded the tree representing the number of guardians that made up a family, the stars representing their life-long dedication to justice and peace. It was all done in dark red cirin on a black backdrop. The Royal Guards wore the opposite color scheme, making them easy to spot in the palace. As well as differentiate them from the Guardians—never mind the fact that the Palace Guards never ventured outside the capitol city without the King, or royal family, in tow.

Once the uniforms had been dispersed, David led his new family off the stage and into a low building off to the right, out of sight of the spectators. Quickly, each new Guardian found an empty classroom and changed into their uniforms.

David struggled to squeeze his well-toned body into the uniform he had been given. Across the room, Luke appeared to be having similar difficulties.

"I think they gave me the wrong size," his roommate grunted as he struggled to pull the bodytunic up his torso. He gave David a wry grin. "Do you think I'd win any awards for being the first Guardian to break his armor on the first day?"

"Probably not," David said as he forced his arms into the sleeves that felt like they'd barely fit Kathryn or Leia. Digging two fingers beneath the neck, David adjusted the fabric so that it didn't feel like it was strangling him. His motions severely hindered by the tightness of the bodytunic, David began to pull the shirt over his head. From across the room he could hear Luke's muffled grunts and the occasional stomping sound that told him his friend was having as much fun with this as he was. *And we're supposed to do this every morning for the rest of our lives?* The thought was unappealing.

Finally, both boys had their overtunics on and belted. The gloves and boots were as tight as the bodytunic and David winced every time he took a step.

Someone knocked on their door. "Come in," David called.

Tyler and Daniel entered the room followed by Matt. All three looked as miserable as David felt.

"Is your armor—" Daniel began.

—Tighter than a snake's embrace? Yep," Luke grumbled as he took a step. "I think we got the girl's uniforms."

"But think!" Matt interjected cheerfully. "Right now the tightness of our uniforms really enhances our toned muscles."

David couldn't help it, the whole situation was so ridiculous he burst out laughing. "I guess that's one way to look at it, Matt."

"You both are crazy," Luke muttered.

"Come on," Daniel said moving to the door. "I think the speeches are winding down.

The girls were already waiting. "There they are!" Amy exclaimed quietly as they approached. "What took you so long?"

"We got your uniforms," Luke replied sourly.

Someone giggled. Cass, David guessed. Looking around, he could see that the girls' uniforms were far too big for their frames.

Natalie looked exceptionally unhappy. "There is no way in the kingdom that I'm going out there like this!" she said emphatically.

"We have to, Natalie," Lindsey told her quietly. "They're getting ready to announce us again."

"I look like a cow! I'm not going!"

David resisted the urge to tug at fabric that seemed intent on choking the life out of him. "Yes, you are. We're all going out, even though I'm sure we all feel uncomfortable."

Natalie opened her mouth to retort, but David's attention was yanked away by a tingling sensation running across his entire body.

"David?" Luke's wary tone suggested that he was feeling the same thing David was.

Glancing around, it looked like everyone was feeling it. The tingling changed to a brushing sensation as the cirin armor began to warp and bend around his body in minute waves. After a few seconds, David found himself wearing a comfortably form fitting uniform that fit so perfectly he could have been sewn into it.

"That's more like it," Tyler grunted in satisfaction.

"Are we going to have to go through that every morning?" Elizabeth asked, running a hand down the front of her tunic experimentally.

"I hope not," Cass said quietly. "I only need to experience that once."

"We ready?" David asked as applause began to sound.

"I am now," Natalie chirped happily.

The spectators gave them a standing ovation while they retook their places on stage. The council members stepped forward, each bearing a large tray with the Guardian's weapons carefully arranged on top.

The weapons presentation was one of the most important parts of the ceremony. The weapons given to the graduates today would be their companions for life. Nowhere else in the kingdom could weapons such as the ones the Guardians wore be found. The metal used in forging the sword was helcë, its origins kept secret, but the fascinating phenomenon's resulting from the mysterious metal were well known throughout the entire kingdom. The cold steel used in the heart of the sword slowly evolved into a crystalline blade that resembled frosted ice, even a faint blue tint at the blade's edge was visible. Harder than any known substance the blade would never nick or crack and its blade was so sharp a court lady could drop a silk scarf onto it and it would be sliced in half. A special scabbard for each blade was required due to another wonder. When heated by fire the blade would glow like a torch, holding the light for radians.

The bows were made out of a wood from an unidentified tree. The wood itself was white-gray in color and sturdy. A Guardian could leave his bow strung for weeks and it would not lose any of its power. An arrow shot from a

Guardian bow by a Guardian archer could reach over four hundred yards, five hundred fifty yards if shot by a master bowman.

Only the King knew who made the weapons and he would never reveal the secret, although many had tried to pull it from him. It was the King's honor to hand out the weapons to the new Guardians. David went first. He was presented with two daggers, two throwing knives—

to be worn either on the back or tucked into his boots, two fighting knives, a new bow and quiver, new arrows, and a new sword. Every guardian received the exact same supply of weapons. Finally after each guardian was armed with his new weapons it was time to be masked. Each council member stood behind a graduate and one by one masked them. Now the graduates stood fully armed, fully dressed, and fully masked before the audience.

The king stood and faced them. "You have been assigned to serve in region of Rima, but who are the Guardians of Rima?"

David unsheathed his sword and held it high, his team following suit. "The Dragons are the Guardians of Rima."

Chapter 7

Welcome to your new home," Lord Jasse announced. Behind him rode fourteen very tired teenagers who looked very much in need of some sleep. Jasse had once heard that growing teenagers needed at least nine radians of sleep to function. At the school they received between seven and eight. Since the ceremony a fortnight before the Dragons had spent all their time traveling to their new post, getting maybe five or six radians of sleep each day. Jasse had been chosen to guide the Dragons to their new home. They had been forced to travel during the darkness of night, using the forest routes by morning and evening, sleeping during the afternoon to avoid word spreading of a large party of traveling Guardians and sending villagers and their governors into an unnecessary panic. Now they had arrived. And the fourteen bedraggled teenagers looked immensely relieved.

"I don't see anything," Natalie groused wearily as they all looked around. They stood at the edge of a meadow. A meadow with absolutely nothing in it.

"You don't see anything now, but you will," Jasse assured her as he urged his horse forward and then completely disappeared.

Before the Dragons could react he reappeared, but with only the front half of his horse. Just behind the cantle, the horse's belly shimmered and appeared to be sheared off. "It's perfectly safe," he called as he disappeared again.

Several of the Dragons shrugged their heads to one side, and blinked several times not trusting what their eyes had just seen. Natalie gasped and stared with her mouth open searching for words to express her astonishment.

Matt eyes lit up and with a big grin he exclaimed, "Woo hoo! What are we waiting for? Let's go!" Slowly the Dragons moved their horses forward and tugged on the reins of their pack mules to prod them along. As if a veil was lifted a house, a barn, several out-buildings, and a garden materialized before their eyes.

The house stood out from its surroundings simply for its sheer size. From their particular vantage point it appeared to be a perfect square with several stories rising above the first two stories in each of the corners. Windows dotted the exterior, covered with heavy wooden shutters that would no doubt weather the harshest storms. A multitude of chimneys also grew from the roof, lending credence to the theory that the house wouldn't be icy in winter.

"What in the world?" Tyler sputtered.

Lord Jasse rode back to them. "It's your camouflage," He explained as he waved his hand around, "This entire meadow is protected by Elven Magic."

Lindsey looked at him dubiously. "I thought the Elves didn't associate with humans. Why would they create such a place for us?"

Jasse nodded slowly. "That is very true, the Elves prefer not to associate with humans, but Guardians are not mere humans."

"How can we not be human?" Amy asked.

"I said *mere* human, not human."

"Are you trying to say that there's a difference?"

"Mere humans don't have the gifts you do. In order for you to have any powers at all, there must be an Elf in your lineage somewhere."

"But there is no record of an Elf in my family line," Cassandra objected.

Jasse smiled at her. "There wouldn't be. If an Elf marries a human they reject the ways of their people. In a sense they almost become human. They retain their power but they lose their immortality."

"How far back can the Elf be in your lineage?" Luke asked.

"He, or she, could be your first ancestor."

"If the Elf is that far back, how come I am the first in my line to exhibit gifts?" Rachel asked.

"Elf traits are dominant, but they won't surface unless the personality of their progeny is compatible with the gift they carry," Jasse explained. "The longer it waits the more potency it loses, although it takes thousands of years for it to degrade enough to be worthless."

"So in a sense," David said slowly. "The gift chooses you?"

"You could put it that way, yes."

Natalie piped up. "You said that the power slowly degrades over time, but what would happen if your mother or father was an Elf?"

"Then your powers would be among the strongest ever seen, you also might have two dominate powers," Jasse replied slowly. "Although such a case has not been seen since the foundation of the Guardians."

David knew that if Jasse's suspicions about Kathryn were true, his last comment was a lie, but remained silent and instead asked, "What if *both* of your parents were Elves?"

"You wouldn't be here," Jasse replied without pause, then, realizing David meant in relation to power-strength said, "You would definitely have two dominate powers and both would be incredibly strong." He gave David an intense look, motioning ever so slightly with his eyes to where Kathryn sat a few horses to his right. Fortunately for both of them, the object of their attention was focused on the treeline and missed the byplay between them.

David understood the message: befriend Kathryn and learn the extent of her powers. Who knew, they could have a half-Elf among them. Perhaps Kathryn knew who her parents were and just wasn't at liberty to reveal her heritage.

"Enough questions!" Jasse exclaimed as Tyler opened his mouth to ask another. "Come, explore your new home."

"I knew they weren't telling us everything at school," Tyler muttered as they moved forward.

The group dismounted and moved in different directions. Cassandra, Lindsey, and Natalie moved towards the house, the boys headed for the barn, Rachel, Elizabeth, and Leia went behind the house, while Jenna, Amy and Kathryn headed for the garden.

$\mathcal{SO}\cdot\mathcal{CB}$

Inside the house the three girls were in heaven.

Natalie immediately shot up one of the curving wooden staircases in the southern corner of the house. It led first to a small alcove landing on the second floor that opened up onto long hallway with multiple doors on either side. Opening the first door revealed an armory filled to capacity with every weapon she'd ever trained with at school; as well as a few she wasn't familiar with. Sufficiently bored, she returned to the spiral staircase. It ended at the second floor, but two smaller staircases were quietly tucked away into small niches in the far corners of the house. She picked one and continued her journey upward.

The stairway continued upward past a small landing with a wooden door which, after Natalie's rampant curiosity got the better of her, led to a small, but comfortably appointed room with windows on two of the walls. A quick glance inside was all she needed to take the measure of the room and in another heartbeat she'd shut the door and hurried upward, pausing on the second and third landings to peer inside each room, hoping fervently that there would be something to distinguish each room from its predecessor. She was to be disappointed. Each room was exactly alike. With a pout, she flounced back down to the second floor and resumed her exploration. Opposite the door she'd originally opened was another bedroom. And this one garnered her attention. It differed from the other three she'd explored for two reasons. One, it was bigger. Not by a massive amount of space, but enough that it was noticeable. And secondly, this room possessed a desk and chair along with small niches in the walls for scrolls and other items that could be stored there. Two important details that none of the other rooms possessed.

In that instant, Natalie made up her mind. This room was to be *her* room. She didn't care who she had to fight for it. Further along the hallway she discovered four bathing rooms, two on either side of the hall, another armory, an empty room, and another bedroom identical to the other on the same floor.

Satisfied that she'd sufficiently explored the upstairs, and found a room that would be perfect for her, she returned to the ground floor and gave her report to the other girls upon entering the kitchen. "The second floor has two bedrooms, the bathing rooms, and armories," she said briskly. "The corners each have three levels of bedrooms. Which means that we all get our own rooms," she squealed excitedly. "Unfortunately they're all identical." After sharing a room with another student for over a decade, the appeal of having her own room was intoxicating. Even if it was barely fit for a peasant. Her excited exclamation fell on deaf ears without an audience, in her excitement she hadn't noticed that the kitchen was empty, and with a huff she turned on her heel to find someone to relay her news to. Her target was just entering the kitchen on her heels.

Lord Jasse had followed them into the house and, having heard her exclamation, said, "Early on the Guardians learned that they needed a room apart from the others to spend some time alone and in peace," he explained to her, "Your bedroom is your sanctuary, and no one may enter unless you give them permission. As to your claim that they're identical, your own personal tastes and preferences will set it apart from the others."

"And we can decorate it any way we want?" Natalie asked hopefully.

Lord Jasse threw back his head and laughed. "Yes, Natalie, you may decorate it any way you like."

"Look at this kitchen!" Cassandra shrieked as she entered the kitchen, her eyes wide with enthusiasm. Natalie turned around, arms flung wide as she spun in a circle to take in the kitchen that should have belonged in a castle.

Cass raced by her, her arms outstretched to open one of the cabinets. "Look at this!" she giggled happily as she quickly busied herself opening every door she could reach. "I could feed an entire army with this kitchen!" The kitchen was indeed large enough to feed an army, comprised of two sinks, two fireplaces for cooking, two brick ovens on either side of each fireplace, and about thirty cupboards—several of which had multiple drawers and sections. It was a kitchen that many manor cooks would have been jealous of. As she spoke she opened every one and peered inside, taking inventory of the dishes and cutlery.

"You may arrange the kitchen in any way you wish," Lord Jasse smiled as Cass frowned thoughtfully into one particular cabinet. "You aren't required to keep it the same way as those before you."

"Oh good!" Cassandra said as she rushed back to one of the first cupboards she had looked inside. "It's more logical to keep the bowls by the plates instead of the cooking pans. I'm not sure what the last cook was thinking organizing the kitchen like this," she muttered as she proceeded to begin removing every bowl from the shelving, stacking them in neat piles on the countertops. She paused, running her hand over the wood noting the deep slices and gouges that would need to be filled in to prevent contamination. "This is going to need refinishing," she said aloud, making a mental note to get it taken care of soon.

"As I said earlier," Jasse reiterated. "You are free to do anything you like to the kitchen."

Cass tipped her head to one side, considering. "You wouldn't happen to know which of the boys are really good at woodwork would you?"

The older man thought for a moment. "Daniel might be a good choice, so would Tyler," he suggested.

She nodded appreciatively and went back to her task of rearranging the various utensils, bowls, plates, and cutting boards.

Natalie, who had since finished exploring the kitchen and had moved on to bigger and better surprises, burst back into the room. "The sitting room will need to be redone," she announced with a dramatic sigh. "All those dark colors. It's so drab and dreary." Flouncing to the other side of the kitchen she surveyed the landscape. "Oh! A warming oven! That's going to come in handy."

"And that's not all." Jasse pointed to a small door in the wall. "That door leads to the cellar—

Before he could finish his sentence, Cassandra and Natalie had raced down the steps that led below. Deciding not to follow, Jasse listened to Cassandra's delighted cries as she discovered the hidden treasures in the cellar. Finally he heard them coming back up.

Breathless with excitement Cassandra looked at him, her eyes shining with delight. "It's even better than I imagined it."

"I'm glad you like it," Jasse smiled.

Natalie looked around. "Where's Lindsey?"

Before Jasse could reply, the two girls raced off through the house, calling for Lindsey. Knowing that they would find her in the parlor, looking through the library, he moved outside toward the barn.

℘·℅

In the barn the boys couldn't believe their eyes. "We have livestock?" Tyler asked in surprise as he looked around.

David chuckled as he nodded towards the three dairy cows. "It would appear so."

Luke frowned. "I don't know how to milk a cow," he admitted.

"I'll teach you," Matt promised a wicked grin on his face. "In fact I'll teach all of you."

David grinned back. "No need to teach me. I know how."

"Hey guys!" Daniel called from further back, "We have beef cattle back here."

Baaaah.

"And goats it would appear," David said dryly as the bleating of a very annoyed goat reached his ears.

Luke looked at David. "What do we use goats for?"

Matt stared at him, stunned. "You mean to tell me you don't know what a goat is used for?"

Luke turned to face him. "I was too busy practicing my swordplay to worry about how to use a goat," he returned slightly flustered.

David fought a grin. Luke was an excellent warrior, one might even say his friend was on the cusp of being considered a "super warrior". At court Luke could manage to charm the shoes off a noblewoman, but put him on a farm, despite all the training, and the charming warrior would be totally and completely lost.

Matt grinned. "This is going to be fun. I get to teach the warrior here how to live on a farm."

David chuckled, grinning at Luke. "I'd say you are in trouble."

"Nice of you to notice," Luke muttered. "I see you aren't offering to rescue me."

"The last time I tried to "rescue" you, you smacked me upside my head."

Luke grinned broadly, remembering. "Oh yeah. I forgot about that."

Daniel rejoined them before David could reply. "We've got three dairy cows, eight beef cows, one bull, six goats, and some sheep...somewhere," he said, brushing off pieces hay that had attached themselves to his clothing and were, at the moment, proving impossible to remove.

"What do you mean somewhere?" Tyler asked.

Daniel brushed harder at the straw before finally giving up with a noise of exasperation. "Meaning I hear them, but I can't see them.

The door opened and David turned to see Lord Jasse join them. "Have you checked out the loft yet?" he asked casually, pointing to the almost invisible ladder in one corner of the barn.

83

Immediately Daniel and Tyler raced up the ladder and pulled themselves up into the loft.

"We have now," David replied.

Jasse shook his head in amazement. "If I didn't know any better I'd say they were mountain migpens."

"You and me both," Luke agreed.

Laughing Jasse nodded up to where large golden squares sat near the edge of the loft. "Have you ever pitched hay?"

"No."

Grinning at Luke's mournful tone Jasse nodded towards a pitchfork standing upright against the wall, "It definitely gives your muscles a work out and it's excellent for conditioning muscles for swordplay."

"Don't tell Matt that or he'll have me pitching hay all day," Luke groaned.

Jasse left David laughing at his friend and left the barn, heading behind the house.

℘·ℭ

Meanwhile Rachel, Elizabeth, and Leia were discovering a river behind the house. For a moment they stood stunned, then Rachel, tired and extremely hot from their journey, not bothering to change her clothes, leapt into the water, Elizabeth and Leia following quickly. For a few moments they laughed and shrieked as they splashed each other with the cold water. Then, reluctantly, they climbed out and stood on the bank, the warm sun quickly began to dry their clothes.

The river, they observed, was about thirty feet wide and, at least where they had been, and over a meter deep in the middle. The water was clear and cool with smooth stones littering the bottom.

"This is amazing," Leia laughed as she wrung the water from her hair. "Fresh water every day, and we didn't have to dig a well."

"Not to mention a quick way to cool down in the heat of the day," Rachel added bouncing up and down, her head pulled to one side, trying to get water out of her ears.

Elizabeth started to comment when then noticed something. "Look!" she cried, pointing across the river. "A training field."

Rachel and Leia noticed what they had been too excited to see while immersing themselves in the river, a fact that would have earned them a slap to the head by one of their instructors for their inattention had they still been at school. Beyond the river was a fully functional training field. Together they crossed the river to the other side to get a closer look.

There were seven archery positions, each with four group targets. Each group of targets had different sizes, positioned at different angles. The target groups were positioned about fifty paces apart.

On the other side of the field was a jousting fence and in between the archery targets and jousting fence was a large space for swordplay or hand-to-hand combat practice. Just beyond the fencing field was a tall masonry wall that resembled a castle keep. It looked as though someone had started to build a castle and stopped when the archer's towers and infantry gate were finished. There were several like it at the school and they were used for mock sieges and tactical planning sessions.

84

Rachel remembered one particular time where her "teammates" during one such siege had shot arrows into the mortar for her to use as handholds while another "team" had worked hard to protect their "keep". Too bad she had slipped and fallen on her backside halfway up causing her team to lose the fight.

Elizabeth spotted Lord Jasse moving to join them and waved.

When he reached them, Rachel looked him up and down. "How did you cross the river without getting wet?" she demanded.

Grinning, Jasse pointed to a small bridge they hadn't noticed, adding a second phantom headslap to their growing repertoire for the day, and then asked, "What do you think?"

"How in the world did they manage to locate a place like this and claim it before the nobles did?" Elizabeth asked.

Jasse laughed. "Because the nobles don't know about it."

"Let me guess," Rachel said quickly. "Elf magic."

"Good guess."

Suddenly Leia was struck with a thought. "What do we do for water in the winter?" She asked. "We're south enough for this area to receive a lot of snow in the winter."

"Good question, but you needn't worry, the river won't freeze over. At least, not unless you experience a deep freeze."

"Why not?"

Rachel intervened before Jasse could reply. "Elf Magic."

"You catch on quick."

Leaving them to return to their water-play, their dripping clothes and hair had been the first thing he'd noticed upon catching up to them, he went searching for the last group of Dragons.

ᔢ·ᔡ

Kathryn, Amy, and Jenna opened the gate that led to the spacious garden. Destiny flew down and perched on the fence as the three girls knelt down to inspect the growth that was just beginning to appear.

"I think this is cermia," Jenna observed, referring to a sweet seed that grew in bundles, as she pulled out some weeds that had taken root.

"This is definitely sirime and ahrea," Amy called from the other end of the garden. "Fresh sallat greens directly from our garden, any time we desire them! Oh, I can't wait!"

"I've got reghire and shcein," Kathryn called quietly as she ran her hands over fresh growth sprouting up from the ground. The red and green roots were a basic staple of sallats and were delicious when stewed. The smell alone was strong enough to permeate the air and rarely was a dinner gong needed when the two ingredients were included in that night's meal.

Jenna found hermea, a thick bulbous root that was blue and tasted good in stews, artise, a thin round tubular root that was used to add flavor to nearly every recipe, and verisce a few rows down from the cermia. "I hope everyone likes verisce," she commented sticking her hands into the dirt, feeling the thick, brown tubular root that would produce a fluffy yellow center when cooked that was excellent when paired with butter from cow's milk and schein.

Amy looked up from the plant she had been inspecting. "Why do you say that?"

"Because there looks to be about six rows of them!" Jenna laughed.

"Hey I've got melons down here!" Amy announced excitedly. Both Jenna and Kathryn hurried over to see for themselves.

"This is redine," Jenna said as she turned the growth over, the red rind glinted off the sunlight where she pointed over two rows. "That's breceia and further down is lemine."

Amy looked at her. "How do you know all of this?"

"I'm an herbalist as well as a healer," Jenna explained. "I've spent years learning about different plants and their uses. I spent radians in my parent's garden growing up."

"So are plants your second gift?"

Jenna nodded. "Yes. We actually knew about my gift with plants before my healing gift."

Amy stood and noticed an orchard at the other end of the garden. Another small gate led to the entrance. Passing through she noted what kind of fruit the trees bore. "We've got amere and orchere growing next to each other!" she cried looking at the red and orange fruits. "How is that possible."

Kathryn and Jenna hurried over, then Jenna grinned. "I'll bet a Guardian with the gift of plants put it here. After all, a plant Guardian can make just about anything grow anywhere."

Kathryn thought back six years to when she saw an oak-like tree grow before her very eyes and considered it very likely and quite possible Jenna was right.

"Ooh, pumera!" Amy called after a few more minutes. "I love pumera!"

"How about liera and menei?" Jenna called back. "I've got a tree full of them." Liera and

Menei were often used to lessen the sweet flavor of certain drinks or add flavor to fish.

"Both?"

"Yes!"

Amy raced over to see the tree that had two different kinds of fruit. "That is remarkable!"

Kathryn, by now, was on the opposite side of the orchard. She leaned against the fence that surrounded the trees and looked out. "Come look at this!"

Directly in front of her, perhaps twenty feet, stood another fence. Inside were eight pigs, all fully mature, one very possibly pregnant.

Beyond the pigs perhaps thirty sheep roamed the grass inside another pen. Their white coats in need of a shave and the bells around their necks tinkling like wind chimes.

Next to the pigs was a chicken pen with more chickens than Kathryn wanted to count.

Jenna pointed, fingering over the chickens. "What are those?" Beyond in a separate pen were several dozen large chicken-like birds with legs nearly as long as hers. They were cloaked in feathers dappled with different shades of gray and a bright yellow strike on the underside of the plumage. They had immense pale green eyes set in a flat-billed elongated head that was strikingly similar to a gooses'.

"I have no idea," responded Kathryn. "But if they are good eating one will feed all of us with plenty of leftovers the next day. Pausing she added, "Or a week for that matter."

It wasn't long before the birds had displayed their annoying habit of baying like a troop of bellows horns and stomping their feet when alarmed. However, they were quite gentle and particularly enjoyed the company of people, sheep, and goats. It was their dullness of mind that persuaded the Dragons to name them pribbles.

"Nice," Amy commented as she stood next to her friend. "All the amenities without having to go into town for the market."

"That's the idea."

The girls turned at Jasse's voice. He smiled at them from his position midway through the garden. "Come on back to the house. I've got some things to tell you before I leave."

He turned and they followed. "What do you think of the garden?" He asked.

Jenna smiled broadly. "It's astonishing. I would never have expected to see such variety or such spaciousness."

"I'm glad you like it."

Destiny called to Kathryn, who whistled a reply. Jasse looked at her curiously.

"She's wondering why we left her alone," Kathryn explained as Destiny came towards them at full speed.

Jasse laughed, "So much for the ever vigilant eagle."

Destiny perched on Kathryn's outstretched arm and clicked a reply to Jasse's comment.

He sighed. "You're a bad influence on her, you know that right?"

80·03

Once Jasse had corralled all of the Dragons around the kitchen table at the same time, a feat of no small measure by any means, he addressed them.

"As I'm sure you've noticed this place has everything you need to sustain yourselves without going into town," he began and they nodded. "It will continue to supply you for the rest of your lives *if* you live on what you have."

"What does that mean?" Lindsey asked.

"Basically it means you don't eat huge meals and don't have a huge wardrobe." He looked at Natalie when he spoke about the wardrobe.

"Why are you looking at me?" she protested.

Matt laughed. "Come on Natalie. You'd shear all those sheep down to their skins and still not have enough fabric for your extensive wardrobe." The girl had brought no less than twenty satchels with her to their new home. And all had been near to bursting their seams.

She pouted and Jasse continued. "This meadow is your sanctuary. Only Guardians can enter and only you can see it."

"How is that possible?" David asked. "We couldn't see it until we entered it."

87

"The magic of the Elves distorts the forest around the meadow to make it appear to be a sheer cliff, a large mound of rock, or not even to exist at all. It's never the same thing twice in a row. The magic now knows that you have been assigned here and will grant you the ability to see it when you are close enough"

Kathryn's mind was sent back in time to the day Jasmine had taken her from the Blackwoods and remembered the house that had appeared out of nowhere. At least *that* mystery was now solved.

"Won't that make people suspicious?" Tyler asked.

"Normally it might, but the magic also distorts their perceptions so that they believe that they've traveled different distances."

"So," David said slowly. "Only we can see it, but other Guardians can enter?"

"Exactly. You can see out and observe travelers around, but they can't see in. You can make as much noise as you want to and they still won't notice you're here. Smoke from your cooking fires won't be seen or smelled."

"That is awesome!" Natalie exclaimed.

"That doesn't mean you can be totally reckless when returning to the meadow. You must make every effort to keep from being followed," Jasse said sternly. "There are those who have gifts, those who were not fit to be Guardians, and out of bitterness use their gifts for malevolence. They can move through the barrier," he warned.

"Can the shield ever be removed?" Tyler asked suddenly.

Jasse hesitated. "It is possible to remove the shield, but it would take the combined power of two or more Elves, therefore it is highly unlikely that an enemy could remove it." He paused, then continued, "It is required of the Guardians to patrol every radian there is daylight. How you choose to do it is up to you."

"No night patrols?" David asked quickly, "None at all?"

Jasse winked at him. "Oh you could throw a couple in here and there, you know, keep the locals guessing. There's also one other...organizational issue, if you will."

"Oh?" Matt lifted an eyebrow. "I can't wait to hear what this new rule is. Is it any like the crazy ones back at school that were utterly useless and ridiculous?"

Jasse lifted his own brow in response. "Contrary to what Matt believes," he said, amused, "Every rule we imposed on you had a reason. You just never took the time to postulate what that reason might be?"

"What possible reason could there be to telling us to 'pick up our sword' and then immediately 'put down our sword' over and over a million times?" Matt demanded.

"Keeping to the original discussion topic," Jasse said smoothly, ignoring the redhead, "this may seem a bit detail managed, but when it comes to room assignments there are two rooms that are specifically set aside for the family leader and his lieutenant." At his words, Natalie's face took on a pout which only soured more as he continued, "David and Kathryn's rooms will be on the second floor. Everyone can pick whichever other room they would like, but the rooms on the second floor must be reserved for the family leader and the lieutenant."

When he finished, Natalie wasn't the only one upset. "How can a room be reserved for the lieutenant when most families don't know who that will be until after they've lived together for several months?" Kathryn asked, speaking for the first time.

"Most families get a general sense on the journey to their new homes," Jasse replied. "And the room assignments can always be flexible...so long as the lieutenant is in that particular room." He eyed Kathryn for a moment before adding, "and don't even think of trying to switch rooms once I leave. The Council chose you and David to lead this family," he took a moment to look David in the eye. "That means you two will have additional duties and responsibilities. The rooms are furnished to serve those needs."

"Understood," David said calmly before Kathryn could try to argue her way into a room on the fifth floor.

That discussion ended, they began the arduous task of assigning rooms. Natalie insisted on sharing a tower with Lindsey while Amy wanted to be close to Kathryn's room. Tyler refused to be in the same wing as Matt and then came the inevitable discussion of which guy would share a tower with two girls. Finally it was decided that Natalie, Lindsey, and Rachel would share the southwest tower; Jenna, Cass, and Amy would share the northeast; Daniel, Tyler, and Luke would take the southeast; and Matt, Leia, and Elizabeth would live in the northwest tower.

"Good luck," Tyler muttered to Leia and Elizabeth. "If you smell smoke, get out as fast as you can."

Elizabeth stared at him. "What does *that* mean?"

"*He*," Tyler pointed to where Matt was in a lively discussion over school regulations with Daniel, "is a pyromaniac. Be careful."

Elizabeth and Leia exchanged worried looks.

Jasse stayed until sunset, advising the new Guardians as to how to meet the expectations of the council, as well as the nobles, then he was off, bidding them farewell as he rode away.

"We might as well turn in," David said as he closed the door. "We've got a lot to do tomorrow."

The family said goodnight to each other and each went and claimed their bedrooms.

෩·ౘ

Kathryn entered her room cautiously, half expecting something lurking within the flickering shadows brought to life by her candle's small flame to leap out and attack her. Or maybe that was just the aftermath of feeling Natalie's enraged glare on her for the entire evening. It had started when Jasse had announced the two rooms reserved for the family leader and his lieutenant and had gotten worse throughout the evening. She'd been careful about training it on Kathryn when others were looking, but Kathryn would swear that she still felt it burning between her shoulder blades.

Granted it had taken her a few minutes to figure out *why* Natalie had been giving her glares that she hadn't seen since the Black—*No*, she told herself sternly *Don't go there*. Thinking about it would only make the

89

nightmares stronger. Squaring her shoulders she stepped further into the room. It wasn't *her* fault that she'd been permanently assigned to the room Natalie had wanted.

Although, why Natalie had wanted this room was a mystery to her. It was plain and sparsely furnished. A bed and a wooden chest at its feet sat against one wall with a desk and chair positioned opposite it. Bracing the door on either side were an armoire and a washbasin. The last wall was dominated by a large window with shutters, currently open to catch the last ray of the dying sun. There was nothing within the four walls that gave it any sort of character and the furniture, while sturdy, was as plain as the walls themselves.

Setting her own meager belongings on the floor, she began a methodical inspection of every nook and cranny. A few floorboards were loose, creaking under her feet as she walked, those would have to be repaired. Opening the chest at the foot of the bed, she lowered her candle to inspect the interior. The polished cedar gleamed from years of use and loving care. At first glance it appeared empty, but closer inspection gave hints at what had been stored within. The smell of oil and weapon polish suggested smaller weapons had been kept in the chest. Nestled in the corners were piles of what appeared to be dust, but when Kathryn raced her fingers through were revealed to be small animal hairs.

Confused, she closed the lid. Crossing the small expanse she took a closer look at the desk.

And found herself staring at a note.

I highly recommend cold weather furs, boots, and cloaks.

Beneath was a sketch of what Kathryn vaguely recognized as the landscape in front of the house…only covered in meters of snow. Included in the drawing were caricatures of people, whom she could only assume were the previous family, struggling valiantly through the cold and wet snow. The courtesy of the previous occupant, as well as the humorous faces carefully inked onto the paper surprised a soft laugh from her. At least that explained the animal furs in the chest.

Setting the paper down, she sat down on the floor and began the process of organizing her belongings. It was a short task, she carried very little with her, and Destiny had already claimed a bedpost for the night, her head tucked quietly under a wing. Following her companion's example, she crawled beneath the foreign sheets.

Before the moons had fully risen all fourteen were fast asleep.

Chapter 8

The next morning Kathryn woke early as was her habit. Letting Destiny out, she dressed quickly and threw her hair back into a bun. Quietly, so as not to disturb anyone, she slipped downstairs to the kitchen and made herself some herbal tea. She sat quietly for several minutes, contemplating all that had happened in the last week before she was joined by David.

"Good morning." He ran a hand over his sleep tousled hair and down his face as he pulled out a chair and sat down. Slightly annoyed at having her peace and quiet disturbed, Kathryn masked her displeasure by pouring him a cup of tea.

Before Jasse had left, he had reserved a few words for her; asking, no *begging*, her to try and accept this group of strangers as her new family...as well as cautioning her that being cold and distant would not assist in forming relationships.

As she handed David his cup she was determined to try and follow Jasse's advice. "Did I wake you?" she asked quietly, while the rest of her mind tried to convince her that the words that just come out of her mouth had been inane and utterly ridiculous.

"No. For some reason I just woke early today." He took a sip of the tea, thankfully unable to hear her mental war. "Thanks."

Kathryn nodded an acknowledgement before returning to her own cup. Now came the difficult part. Never one for small talk, Kathryn was comfortable sitting in complete silence however she had noticed that very few shared her preference. Unfortunately when it came to initiating a conversation she had little to no experience. As the silence lingered she studied him out of the corner of her eye. If she didn't know any better she would have thought David was Jasse's son, they both had the same black hair, green eyes, and build. She shook her head mentally. He even had some of Jasse's mannerisms down perfectly, like the raised eyebrow Jasse would give her when he expected something of her.

"Did you sleep well?" His unexpected question felt like a thunderclap in the tiny room.

Kathryn nodded. "Yes, thank you," she paused a moment and then asked, "You?" That was what normal people asked, wasn't it?

David shook his head. "I felt like I was up all night trying to figure out how to manage to cover an entire day without exhausting everyone."

"And did you?" She sipped at her tea. *Why can't you just enjoy the peace and quiet of the early morning?*

"I've got a rough idea. I would appreciate it if you would listen and give me some feedback."

Kathryn put down her cup, prepared to listen. He wanted to talk about work—that she could handle. However the minute he, or anyone, brought up personal issues, and inevitably they would, she was *out of there*. There was only so much conversation she was willing to play a part of.

"I'll want your honest opinion," David warned.

"You'll get it," she assured him, wondering if she had ever *not* given an honest opinion since joining the Guardians. The days of silence for her were long over.

"I was thinking of dividing up the family into four teams of three. Each would have an equal shift."

Kathryn frowned slightly. "That's only twelve members, what about the other two?"

"That's you and me. We would each take two teams a day, alternating rotations. This enables each team to have either you or me present in case an executive decision needs to be made."

Kathryn nodded slowly, thinking his logic through thoroughly. "It could work," she said finally.

"The first team would begin at dawn and the last team would return at nightfall," he explained.

"What do you plan to do when the seasons change and the daylight lasts longer?" Kathryn was finding work to be an easy conversation topic. As long as David stayed on this topic, she could handle it without feeling inept.

Taken aback, David paused. He obviously hadn't considered that. "Good point," he conceded. "I didn't even think about that." He paused, thinking carefully. "I guess we could add half a radian, or whatever amount is needed, to each shift to compensate for the extra daylight."

"Who do you have on each shift?" she asked, standing. Moving to the kitchen, she rummaged through the cupboards until she found some nuts and dried berries. Grabbing a bowl she scooped two handfuls of the snack into the wooden dish and brought it back out to the table.

David ran a hand through his hair. She was beginning to suspect that it was his tell for when he was hesitant or uncomfortable. "I've got a preliminary idea, but it's not solid yet." He eyed the food as well as Kathryn. To take his attention off of her, she pushed the bowl more within his reach. He grabbed a handful, but didn't raise his hand to his mouth.

Kathryn waited for him to explain.

"The first shift would go from dawn to the fourth radian of the morning. I noticed that you're an early riser so I put you down as well as Matt, Jenna, and Rachel." He nodded toward the large clock that hung on the wall, thirteen radians visible on its face. He dropped a few of the nuts and berries into his mouth.

She nodded. "Sounds like a workable arrangement." *Keep him moving,* she ordered herself, *move his observations away from you.*

"I put you guys together because during the last couple days you were always the first ones up."

"Keen observation," she murmured and then said, "You don't have to justify every decision to me." She wasn't interested in hearing all of his observations on her personal habits. Then again, maybe she did so she would know which ones to make note of and change. It was an idea worth contemplating later.

"Yes I do if I want to make sure I'm making decisions that are mutually beneficial," he replied.

She tipped her head in acknowledgement, and then continued. "Who do you have down for the second shift?"

"That would be Cassandra, Lindsey, Elizabeth, and myself."

"And why did you choose them?" If he felt the need to explain, then least she could do would be to prompt him. And if she prompted him, then just maybe she could keep the conversation away from her.

"They were hard to place, not exactly morning people, neither night owls. I gambled and placed them in the moderate morning."

"I take it then that each shift is four radians?" she asked since he hadn't bothered to clarify that detail.

He nodded. "Approximately, yes. With thirteen radians during the day split over four shifts, it doesn't exactly come out in whole radians."

She nodded, which David took as an agreement and continued. "Third shift would be you, Amy, Daniel, and Leia. Leia and Daniel seemed to be more afternoon people and Amy's your friend. I thought you might prefer a known face in the coming days."

Kathryn looked at her cup. "Thank you," she said stiffly. *Perhaps a little too observant?*

David found her reaction surprising, was or wasn't she pleased to have Amy on her team? Perhaps she didn't like that he'd picked up on their friendship so quickly, in either case he continued quickly. "Fourth shift has me, Tyler, Luke, and Natalie."

Looking up quickly, she asked, "Any particular reason you put Natalie on a team with all guys?" *...Although better him than me.* Kathryn contemplated the idea of being stuck on a shift with Natalie for four radians and considered herself fortunate at such a lucky escape.

"That was a hard decision," he admitted. "In the end I decided that the three of us guys would have a much better chance of overpowering her or protecting her in case something goes wrong."

"Natalie does seem the least mature of the group," Kathryn muttered softly. So softly that David barely heard her.

He nodded, paused and then asked, "What do you think?"

She took another sip of her tea. "I think it's a workable arrangement, at least for now. Once we get the lay of the land immediately around our new home the excursions by the teams will probably extend into days. There are a lot of outlying villages and farms that can't be reached in four radians."

David mulled this new thought over in his mind and nodded in agreement.

Kathryn continued, trying her hand at some humor, "now we just get to tell the rest of the team the plan and hope we don't have a mutiny on our hands."

David chuckled softly and the two sat quietly until the first rays of the sun streamed in through the windows. In small groups the rest of the Dragons joined them, Amy and Jenna being among the first, Natalie and Lindsey the last.

As soon as they were all up, or at least showing signs of being awake, Cassandra ran into the kitchen and began preparing breakfast.

By the time Natalie and Lindsey joined the rest of them, the sun was up and breakfast was on the table.

Breakfast was a friendly, if a bit formal affair. Very few of the family knew each other well enough to truly relax in each other's presence and it showed. David hoped that after a month or so they would be laughing and joking around the table like a large extended family.

After breakfast was over and the dishes cleared David told the rest what he had informed Kathryn earlier. To his immense pleasure the rest of the Dragons accepted his plan almost immediately. *So far everything seems to be running smoothly*, he thought happily, *even Kathryn seems to be warming up. I would never have considered her capable of making a joke before this morning.*

"Well," David commented after the conversation had died down. "I wasn't expecting that discussion to be over so soon, but since it is we have another group/team effort to discuss."

"What's that?" Cassandra asked.

"Chore assignments."

Natalie, Lindsey, and Luke moaned theatrically. "Already?" Lindsey asked petulantly.

David grinned at them. "We can't wait until next week or even until tomorrow if we want to sustain ourselves. Does anyone have any preferences?"

"Can I cook?" Cassandra asked timidly.

He smiled at her. "If you continue to cook the way you did this morning, consider the job yours, the biscuits were delicious."

Cassandra blushed, but smiled in delight.

"I think we need more than one cook," Luke spoke up. "As much as Cass loves to cook, we're going to need someone else who can prepare meals, especially in the early mornings and later evenings."

David nodded. "Good point. Anyone else like to cook?"

"I can do it," Matt volunteered, surprising everyone.

David didn't know a single man who would willingly put himself in the kitchen. Most noblemen considered it beneath their station and the common men preferred to believe that it was the woman's duty to feed the family. "Great. You two can work out your own schedule plan. Now, I'm going to assume that we all know how to milk a cow," he looked at the rest of the group and when no one bothered to correct him, not even Luke, he continued, "we need milk every day and since the cows and some of the goats need to be milked twice a day we'll assign two people to a day. One will milk first thing in the morning; the second will milk in the afternoon."

No one seemed to have a serious problem with that arrangement and the days and times were quickly distributed.

By mid-morning they had the rest of the chores divvied up. Kathryn, Amy, Leia, and Jenna would manage the garden, Daniel, Elizabeth, and Rachel would tend the sheep, pribbles, and goats. Natalie and Lindsey would collect the eggs and tend to the fowl, Matt and Cass would take care of everything related to the kitchen. Tyler, Luke, and David would handle the butchering or skinning of any meat caught or slaughtered as well as tend the beef cattle and the pigs. The boys would take care of the barn work and the girls would maintain the house. However each Guardian would tend to their own horse. The mounts were chosen by the rider soon after birth and trained together so that by the time the trainee was ready to be placed into a family, the rider and horse thought, rode, and fought as one. The horses themselves were descended from the Elven herds, how the bloodline refused to die out no one was sure, but a Guardian's horse lived nearly as long a natural life as a Guardian would, provided it wasn't killed in battle.

"Does anyone else have anything to add?" David asked.

"I think we need nicknames," Natalie exclaimed loudly from the far end of the table.

Tyler, taking a sip of water, choked on his drink. "What?" he gasped between coughs. David, who had barely escaped a similar display, arched a brow to echo the older boy's dismayed question.

Natalie turned on him. "When we're out on patrol we can't just call each other by our regular names, what if someone overhears us?"

"Our identities would be revealed!" Lindsey exclaimed catching on to her friend's idea.

"Exactly!" Natalie cried triumphantly.

David looked at Kathryn, but she remained motionless—neither encouraging nor discouraging the proposal. He turned back to Natalie. "Okay, what have you got in mind?

"Well your name isn't hard, we would probably just call you Dave, you know shorten it. Kathryn I was thinking Kate or Kathy."

Kathryn didn't even blink at the suggestions, but Natalie didn't seem to notice as she continued. "Amy could be Mia—

Amy choked on her water, coughing hard, adding to Tyler's sputtering, but Natalie took no notice. "Tyler can be Ty, Rachel could become Rae, Cassandra we could call you Cassie, or Cass depending on which you prefer."

She looked around the table, "Elizabeth we could call you Beth or Lizzy, Daniel would just be Dan," she looked at him then shrugged. "Leia could be Lei. Jenna we could change to Jen, or Nan if we wanted to."

Here Jenna interrupted her. "Jen is just fine." she said quickly.

Natalie looked surprised at being interrupted but took it in stride. "Well at least we've got one settled. Lindsey could be Lin, and I could be Nat."

"What about Matt or Luke?" David asked her.

Natalie shrugged. "I couldn't come up with anything."

Luke jumped in quickly. "That's quite alright, you can leave my name just the way it is."

"Mine too," Matt agreed.

"You guys are no fun what-so-ever," Natalie pouted, slumping back against the chair's backrest, arms crossed over her chest. She certainly had the petulant spoiled noble girl charade down. Too bad he suspected it wasn't an act.

David turned to Kathryn. "What do you think?"

95

She sighed. "I guess so. There's just one problem. The nicknames Natalie suggested aren't much different than our given names. It wouldn't be that hard to put two and two together."

Across the table, Natalie's excited smile turned into a scowl, a scowl aimed directly at the younger woman. However, before she could say anything, Tyler surprised everyone by jumping into the conversation.

"You have a good point, Kathryn, however we also need to consider the chance that a nobleman, or woman, is going to be traipsing around in a country village or wild forest, or a villager attending a court tourney. Add to the fact that while at court we'll be assuming our court names, and not our day to day ones, we'll already have added protection against our identities being discovered." He grimaced. "I don't see why Natalie's nicknames couldn't work."

Upon hearing this Natalie practically jumped out of her seat, barely able to contain her enthusiasm. "You guys are great!"

"I just hope we don't live to regret it," Amy grumbled, muttering under her breath, "*Mia?*"

The meeting done, the group got up to disperse when David remembered something. "Wait a second, everyone."

They paused and waited for him to continue.

"Lord Jasse suggested that when we go to town we go in groups of mainly girls and one or two guys."

Tyler snorted, "What for?"

"Safety and protection for one, you never know what drunk is looking for a good time."

"Point taken," Natalie said quickly. "If we want to go into town, grab a couple more girls and drag one of you guys along." That said she picked up her skirts and herded the other girls out the door saying something about linens.

The boys watched them go. "I think we're in trouble," Daniel observed.

Cassandra raced back into the room. "Daniel, Tyler, are either of you good at woodworking?"

The two boys looked at each other. "Sort of," they replied in unison.

Cass beamed. "Oh good! The kitchen counters desperately need to be refinished. Do you guys think you could do that for me?"

Tyler looked at Daniel who shrugged. "We can try."

Cass's smile widened. "Thanks, guys."

She was about to say something else when Natalie's voice echoed through the house. "Cass? Cass where are you?"

Cass turned on her heel and fled back the way she had come.

"Actually, I think it's the house that's in trouble." Tyler corrected.

"Come on guys," David laughed. "We have chores to do."

Inside the sitting room Natalie had the girls' complete attention. "Since we'll be living here for the rest of our lives," she was saying, "There's no reason we can't make it look nice." She waved her hand around the room and began to give a running commentary on the depressing color scheme and tacky furniture.

Kathryn was only half listening, her eyes roaming the walls, taking in a detail that she hadn't noticed earlier. The walls of the sitting room were covered from floor to ceiling with small box-like shelving units filled with scrolls. Kathryn was willing to bet that the scrolls contained histories and reports of the lives of the Guardians who had lived here before them. There were some empty shelving units that Kathryn suspected were for the Dragon's to fill with their own reports. With a jolt she realized her mind was wandering and, chastising herself, forced her attention back to the issues at hand.

"It already is nice." Cassandra protested.

"Yes it is," Natalie agreed. "But why can't we make it nicer?"

"She means with pictures and stuff," Lindsey explained.

"What kind of pictures?" Elizabeth asked.

Natalie shrugged. "Nothing too fancy, probably just paintings or drawings we've done."

Lindsey squealed with delight. "Oh I love painting!" she gushed, then turned to each, "I've absolutely got to do a portrait of each of you." Her enthusiasm faltered a little when it encountered Kathryn's stony face, but when she imagined what the older girl would look like with a smile on her face her excitement jumped a few more notches.

"What else do you have in mind?" Rachel asked.

Natalie grinned. "I thought it would be nice to make quilts for our beds, you know, to kind of give it a more homey feel."

Jen smiled. "I like that idea. Quilting is something I enjoy."

"Where would we get fabric?" Leia asked.

Natalie gave her a sly grin. "You don't think all those bags I lugged here are full of clothes do you?"

The girls looked at each other. "Well, yes, we did," Rachel admitted.

"Nope," Natalie laughed. "More than half of them were full with fabric."

"Fabric?" Amy asked doubtfully. "You mean out of the twenty bags you lugged here, at least ten are just filled with bolts of fabric?"

"Yes!" Natalie cried triumphantly.

Amy looked at her for a moment. "Well if you give me some fabric, I can make curtains if you like," she offered slowly.

"That would be wonderful," Natalie gushed. She looked around. "Amy's going to do our curtains, Lindsey can paint for us, but Jenna's going to need help working on the quilts who wants to help her?"

"I can," Leia volunteered. She turned to Jenna. "Just keep in mind I'm not very good at it."

Jen smiled. "That's okay. We don't need anything fancy."

Natalie was grinning broadly now. "Anyone else want to help?"

"I guess I can try," Rachel said slowly. "Although I'm going to need a lot of help."

Elizabeth piped up. "I can spin wool and other materials."

"That's brilliant," Natalie exclaimed, "I wasn't sure if anyone other than myself could spin but having another spinner is going to be great. Can anyone weave?"

Kathryn had been sitting quietly through the whole exchange, watching in surprise as the girls pooled their talents to make this building a home for everyone, unable to offer her talents because she could neither, sew, nor quilt, nor spin. However now she could offer something. "I can weave," she interjected quietly. And then immediately wanted to kick herself for getting involved.

Natalie appeared stunned, but as usual quickly recovered. "That's great. Have you seen the loom yet?"

Kathryn shook her head. All she'd seen of the house was her bedroom, the kitchen, the dining room, and now the sitting room.

Shrugging Natalie turned to the next item. "Can anyone here sew dresses or other clothing items?"

Since most of the girls were from noble families they could adequately handle a needle and thread, only Kathryn and Leia admitted to having absolutely no skill with a needle.

"I can mend, but that's about it," Leia confessed. Kathryn nodded, silently admitting that her own skill could barely manage even that. Jasmine had tried to teach her needlecrafts, but she had not been interested in spending the day gossiping over thread and fabric whilst stabbing one's fingers with a blasted needle.

Suddenly Lindsey started giggling. She was standing in front of a large bay window with her hand covering her mouth laughing to the point where tears were beginning to form.

Elizabeth stood up and hurried over beside her. "What's so funny? she asked.

"Its... its Daniel" she gasped between giggles. "He's being chased by the pribbles," her voice rising and cracking at the word pribbles.

All of the girls rushed to the window to view the spectacle. On the far side of the pribble pen, Matt was standing with one foot on the outer bottom rung and the other resting on the middle stave. Both of his arms were draped over the top rung as he deftly worked a long piece of straw protruding out of the corner of his mouth while cheering the activities in front of him. It was hard to determine if he was cheering for the pribbles or Daniel. Daniel was running as fast as he legs could take him to escape an apparent pribble riot. He was followed closely by three angry pribbles. The first had its head and neck protruding straight out targeting his backside as though it was in the throws of a jousting match. The other two were running erect, wings flapping, tail feathers fully flared, honking and bellowing in the manner that was unique to the strange birds. The remaining troop followed less enthusiastically behind, but still contributing to the noisy uproar.

By this time Daniel was running flat out. Building up speed he timed his strides so that he just cleared the fence as he hurdled over the top railing. Unfortunately, the toe of his trailing leg caught causing him to tumble and land flat on his back in the sheep pen. Before he could gather his dignity he had to quickly roll away to avoid being pecked by several birds that had poked their heads through the fencing. In a strange and almost mesmerizing dance, all of the birds stomped their feet in unison, creating a large dust cloud while bellowing and hissing in perfect rhythm. Two curious sheep sauntered over and sniffed Daniel's face as he pulled in deep breaths while curled around a rather large mound of dung. Meanwhile Matt, had entered the pen, pushed his way through the gang of birds, and was peering down at him with a big grin on his face. To add insult to injury, one of the pribbles rubbed his head against Matt's neck, rested it on his shoulder and gazed back lovingly into his eyes. Matt said something to Daniel, but the girls couldn't make out what he said.

"Looks like he's getting his exercise in for the day," Cass snickered. All of the girls laughed except for Lindsey.

"Do you think he's all right, is he hurt?"

"He's ok," Jenna replied. "Look, he's getting up"

"He's definitely ok, but his manhood may have suffered a mortal wound." Amy's eyes sparkled as she said it to no one in particular. This time everyone laughed.

After a few moments, the girls returned to their seats and continued to discuss their planned activities for nearly a half a radian.

Finally Natalie seemed content that enough projects had been taken on and asked, "Is there anything anyone else would like to add?"

Kathryn spoke up as she stood. "Before you make monumental changes or completely cover the walls and beds with projects, you might want to let the boys know so they have at least some say in this," she advised, then seeing that Natalie wanted to protest added, "It's their home too."

The girls watched as she turned and left the room. Once she was gone Natalie huffed, "What's her problem?"

Amy shot her a look. "Kathryn has plenty of her own problems to deal with, you just make sure you don't add to them," she said fiercely.

Natalie stuck out her lip. "Just because she's second in command doesn't mean she has to be so bossy," she complained.

Elizabeth spoke up. "She wasn't trying to be bossy, Nat," she replied gently. "She listened to your ideas and offered her weaving skills. Her advice to you was sound. The boys live here too."

"Whatever," Natalie huffed. "I'm just glad I'm not on any of her shifts."

∽·∾

Kathryn escaped from the house as soon as she could. Destiny flew after her, ecstatic to be free of the confines of the building. Never in her life had Kathryn revealed to anyone her fear of close quarters, especially close quarters involving other people.

She slipped into the forest and made her way through the underbrush. As she walked she wasn't sure where she was headed but of one thing she was sure, it was better than being back at the house. It was taking all of her self-control to try and be civil to Natalie and Lindsey. Lindsey was sweet enough but far too impressionable. She followed Natalie around like a lost puppy, hanging on her every word. Kathryn had sworn to herself that she would never, ever put herself into such a state of dependency. Dependency makes you vulnerable and being vulnerable can make you an easy victim. She'd been victimized enough in this lifetime already.

She had been on the move for several radians when Destiny let out a hunter's call, the call Kathryn had trained her to use when they weren't alone.

Already as silent as the dead, Kathryn went into stealth mode, picking every step carefully, taking care not to leave a discernible trail. As she traveled forward, she heard the sound of voices, which steadily increased as she grew closer until she could discern the conversation.

"What's the news?"

From her position behind a large boulder, Kathryn couldn't see how many figures were in the small clearing, but the owner of this voice sounded like he'd spent his life inhaling smoke—probably a blacksmith.

"Damaan has granted the Violet Stag membership." This man's voice was smoother, more like that of a nobleman used to talking his way out of trouble.

The first man grunted. "Was that wise?"

"Damaan does not act unless he thinks it is wise." To Kathryn it almost seemed as if the second man was reminding the first of who exactly their leader was and where the power lay.

"So when do we act?" The first man sounded anxious, possibly even excited. Kathryn would have to keep an eye out for him once they started patrolling the towns.

"Patience," the second placated. "We cannot move until we are ready."

"I say we are!" The first hissed.

"Damaan does not agree," his companion returned harshly.

"I am tired of all this secrecy! I am ready to fight!"

"You will have your chance, friend," the second returned. "And when we do, not even the Guardians will be able to help."

Stunned at his words, Kathryn was taken aback and struggled with the thought of apprehending them, but realized that these two were only part of a larger organization. It would do no good to arrest only two. The second would never talk, and the first would fight until he was dead.

They began to move away and Kathryn made her decision. She would let them go, for now. She knew their voices. While patrolling the villages she would listen for them and once she found them, she would pay special attention to keeping track of them.

Chapter 9

Sunrise the next morning heralded the beginning of the Dragon's new role as Guardians of Rima. This first shift would be different from the following shifts as it would include only two members and last all day.

"Kathryn, are you ready?" David pulled his mask on and checked to make sure he had everything in place.

"I've been ready for ten minutes." Her annoyed tone clearly spoke that she'd been the one waiting for him. He briefly wondered if she was annoyed because he was taking forever to get ready or was annoyed because she had to spend the day with him. Well he could look on the bright side, at least he wasn't spending the whole day with Natalie. The woman was starting to annoy him. And it had only been two days. He was not looking forward to a lifetime of her whining.

"Here's your lunch and dinner." Cass handed both of them a small satchel about to burst its seams.

David took his, looked at it, and then raised an eyebrow at Cass. "Are you sure you put enough food in here?"

"Just get going," Cass laughed as she shooed him out the door. David chuckled as he headed towards the stables. He saddled his horse then joined Kathryn who had already finished and was waiting out front.

The first thing he noticed was the absence of her sword. "Where's your sword?"

"I wasn't planning on bringing it today."

He paused. The sword was the preferred method of defense by nobles and thieves alike, although he knew some preferred the mace or club. Unless you were several paces away a bow was not the best choice for defense and using fighting knives to defend against a sword required different techniques, excellent timing, and a lot practice. "Are you sure?"

Even with her face obscured by the mask, David could tell she was giving him The Look. The Look was one he had gotten every day of their trip to Rima from the school as he had tried to engage his second-in-command in conversation. She had rebuffed his every attempt at friendship and remained cold and distant from the group. When he had mentioned his frustration with her to Jasse one night, the older man had sighed and promised to talk with her as well as warned David not to expect to gain her friendship right away. "I've known her for six years and she still doesn't trust me," Jasse had reminded him. Even at the time, David hadn't found that particular information very heartening. On the other side of the coin, Natalie had hounded him every waking moment, wanting his opinion on *this* or his thoughts on *that*. She'd listen with rapt attention to his every word...as if what he said was keeping her alive. Most noblemen would have been flattered by the attentions of a beautiful woman. David found it irritating.

"I think I know what I'm doing," Kathryn replied, somewhat stiffly, jerking him out of his thoughts.

He wasn't in the mood to argue. If she wanted to leave the karcing sword behind, he would let her leave it behind. This time. "Okay, let's go."

Together they rode out of the glade, Destiny leading the way as she soared through the clear blue sky.

"Do you have any suggestions on where to start?" David asked, wondering what had put his companion in such a dark mood. It wasn't as if she was up late at nights, worrying about making a mistake that led to the death of one of his family members...or worse, bringing the Council down on his family. No, those were *his* nightmares.

"No."

"Do you mind if we start near Leneal?" he asked, referring to the town only twenty-eight kilometers east from their current position. He'd spent hours the night before, pouring over the local maps and reading reports from the family before them, trying to decide on a good location to start their new lives. He'd settled on Leneal because all previous reports had indicated that it was a mildly prosperous town with a friendly and accommodating populace.

"No."

David gave up any attempt at conversation. She wasn't in a talkative mood and he wasn't in the mood to hit his head against a wall all day. Ten minutes out of the clearing, David shifted slightly in his saddle, angling his left knee into his horse's shoulder. His horse responded to the trained motion and quickly broke into a gallop. David had missed feeling the wind in his hair and the rhythm of the horse's hooves beneath him and judging by the tightness he could feel radiating from Rumer's muscles, his horse was angling for a good hard run.

He'd been told by his instructors that he was one of the best horsemen they had ever seen, almost becoming one with his mount. Not once had he been out-ridden by any of his classmates, anyone who challenged him to a race quickly fell behind. Obstacle courses presented no challenge for him...or for Rumer.

He pushed Rumer, knowing the horse was as desperate to release the stress of adjusting to a new home just as badly as he was. David really wished he could run for kilometers, but riding Rumer was just as good.

It was a full quarter of a radian before he remembered that Kathryn was with him, he turned to look over his shoulder, wondering how far behind him she was.

He was startled to find her shoulder to shoulder with him, for all appearances looking as if she were simply walking her horse. Reining Rumer down to a gentle trot, he noticed that Kathryn reacted almost instantly, matching his move.

"You're very good," David commented, studying her form. His love of riding had been a gift from his mother at a young age. They had ridden together every chance they'd had. From Jasse's story, he hadn't expected Kathryn, an ex-slave who had probably never touched a horse let alone ridden one before six years ago, to ride as well as someone born in the saddle.

She looked at him, a confused look on her face. "Good at what?"

"Riding. Not even Luke can keep up with me."

He watched her jaw twitch but noticed she didn't say anything. "Were you always this good?" Maybe she'd been taught to ride before she'd become a slave? Jasse had never mentioned how long she was a slave for...

She shrugged. Wealth of information she was. Was she always this obstinate or was it just him?

He tried again. "What's your horse's name?"

"Lerina"

The name sounded familiar. David paused a moment, searching his memory. "That's an old Elvish word for freedom, isn't it?"

She nodded.

If his memory was serving him correctly, Lerina could be translated as freedom in the sense of not being guarded or owned. He wondered if she chose the name as a testimony to others of who she was, or at least, had been. If that was the case he suspected she had never lived life as a free woman before the Guardians. Freedom and Destiny, she certainly knew how to choose interesting names. "I like it."

She didn't comment.

They reached the village without uttering another word to each other.

Dismounting in the forest on one side of the village they left the horses grazing, entering the village on foot.

"I'll take the south end, you can start in the north."

Kathryn nodded and quickly moved away. David watched her go, wondering what type of a girl she would have been had she not been forced to live the life she had. At the very least, he supposed, she would have been easier to live and get along with. Shaking his head slightly, he moved south and aimed to enter the village next to the blacksmith's shop. As he walked he began to wish that he'd brought along a heavy cloak. A brisk fall wind was blowing and it had that sharp bite that indicated that winter was fast approaching and his cirin armor wasn't quite blocking the chill from seeping into his body. He suppressed an involuntary shiver. He knew that the two weeks needed for the cirin to form the symbiotic bond hadn't elapsed yet, but he also knew that it couldn't be much longer. Mentally he counted backward. No, it had. Yesterday.

He sighed, at least the cirin blocked most of the chill, and ambled into the village.

Part of a Guardian's job was to form a sense of trust and reliance with the people they protected so David paused to spend a few minutes chatting with the blacksmith and his two apprentices. "Good morning."

The blacksmith looked up and gave him a smile. "Good morning, sir. I take it you're here about the thefts."

"I've heard a few things. What can you tell me about them?" Of course, being so new to the region, David knew as much about the thefts as he did about Kathryn's past, but one of the lessons that had been driven into the potential Guardians was, *never let the people know you're clueless. The people like to talk, let them inform you.*

"Two horses have been stolen in the past few weeks and travelers are reporting bandits along the road stealing their purses." The old blacksmith waved his rough hand around. "You'd think you Guardians would have stopped this by now."

"Rima is a large province," David replied calmly. "We cannot be everywhere at once and investigations do take time," he reminded the man.

The old man *humphed* as he turned back to his work.

"Have there been any strangers or locals acting suspiciously?"

The blacksmith shook his head. "Not that I know of," he said emphatically. "Not that anyone would tell *me* if there was," he added under his breath. It was a rare town or village that would hand over life-long locals, even if they were acting a little odd, to sheriffs or Guardians without some coaxing. David admired their dedication and solidarity, but knew that someday it would end up being an exasperation.

One of the apprentices, a younger lad with red hair, and two front teeth missing, spoke up. "There were a minstrel. He come through about a fortnight ago. He stayed about two week and move on."

"Was he of a suspicious character?"

The boy paused, as if trying to translate what David had just asked. "He ask lot of questions," and after a few moments as if he were in deep thought he finished with, "when he weren't performin, but we're all thought he was just curious about our village."

"Most of them are," David assured him, no sense in making the locals paranoid. "Thank you for the information."

"Always a pleasure to help a Guardian," the old man said as he hammered a horseshoe, "Just doesn't forget." The boy grinned widely at David and made a grunting laugh-like sound.

Promising to look into it, David moved on. An elderly woman was sitting out front of the healer's shop and he greeted her warmly. "Good morning, grandmother. I think it's going to be a beautiful day."

"Good morning, young sir. I believe you are correct." She paused, peering at him as if she was studying a master painting. "You are new here, aren't you?"

"Just to the village," David assured her. Another important part of Guardian training was never let anyone know just how inexperienced you were...that kind of information would lead to increased difficulties in not only getting people to trust you, but also in convincing lawbreakers to surrender.

The grandmother *humphed* and sat back in her chair. David wasn't sure if it was the wood creaking or her bones.

"Are there any problems that concern you grandmother?" he asked politely.

"Just the missing horses and the outrageous price of bread at the southern bakery," She replied, turning to help a young mother and her irritable child who had just arrived.

David nodded towards the women and moved on. As the grandmother had predicted, the baker's prices were extravagant and David managed to talk him down a little, and even bought two rolls to help win the baker's confidence, all the while praising the workmanship of the admittedly delicious rolls. He visited with several more shop owners and the local washerwoman, listening to their concerns and complaints. As he walked about, continuing to make small talk with the villagers and note the ones who looked prone to trouble, he noticed that he couldn't feel the wind any more. Nor did he feel the slight stinging chill that was indicative of numbness. He fought down a grin. So the cirin *did* block the cold, it just wasn't instantaneous as he had originally believed. Feeling much happier, he headed toward the largest hostelry to have a chat with the proprietor about the thefts and to see if he could learn who the usual troublemakers were.

When he met up with Kathryn a radian later, she too had learned about the thefts, although how she had learned about them David wasn't sure. Kathryn wasn't exactly the type to invite someone to confide in her. However her information suggested an exit vector the thieves might have taken so he trusted that she knew what she was doing.

Retrieving their horses they continued onto the next village, stopping at various farms along the way.

The two Guardians stopped for a midday meal in a quiet forest meadow. The sun had reached its apex and was sending welcome rays of warmth down onto David's head and body. As the sun had climbed in the sky, the wind had lessened until the cirin was working to suppress the sweat his body was giving off. David knew, however, that due to where Rima was located in the kingdom, by tonight the wind would return and the temperature would drop drastically.

The wide range in temperatures during the fall months seemed to be the only exciting occurrence happening in Rima. As he had wandered through Leneal, David had learned that Rima was a relatively quiet province with only small thefts and nothing serious to investigate—

something that both relieved and disappointed him. Relief because he wasn't ready to lead his family into a huge manhunt or investigation, disappointment because he was already getting a little tired of listening to gossip.

He shared his thoughts with Kathryn as they sat down for lunch. Of course, she had a completely different opinion.

She gave him a long look. "Not only is your logic flawed because you're basing this off of one morning in one village," she said coolly. "But we do have a manhunt ahead of us." She bit into a piece of fruit Cass had packed. "We have to locate the minstrel."

"Today?"

"Why not?"

"Because we have other villages and farms to visit." The Guardians were not local sheriffs, responsible for the safety and security of each and every villager and farmer in their assigned region. Each town had its own sheriff who paid visits to the local farms, dealing with small disputes that arose within their assigned villages and farms.

The Guardians took up what the local sheriffs could not. Serving as a justice force higher than the sheriffs, the Guardians were responsible for the farms and villages as a whole. If any disputes between farms or towns erupted the Guardians were called in as impartial negotiators and judges. In cases of multiple thefts, murders, or arsons, the Guardians acted as the investigating body and issued sentences that every village and farm must abide by.

Kathryn shrugged, "We should visit the villages and farms that are on the path a minstrel would take, if we find more evidence of thefts along the way we can be pretty sure we're on the right track." She stood and ambled over to Lerina and ran her hand along the muzzle and rubbed her mount's cheek. She reached into her pack and pulled out a sweet red amere which the horse accepted greedily. She quickly mounted and announced, "let's go."

Knowing her logic was sound, David acquiesced. By late afternoon they had visited two more villages, both of which reported thefts and a traveling minstrel.

"You were right," David acknowledged as they rode on to the next village. "Perhaps the minstrel is in on the thefts."

"Perhaps," Kathryn echoed.

David looked at her. "You don't sound too sure."

"There's always the possibility that another traveler is using the minstrel as cover for his thefts."

"True," David agreed.

"...Although only one of the villages reported having other travelers on the day of the thefts."

"The thief could always be a native of one of the villages who steals when a traveler comes through," he added.

"But then he has the added problem of stealing horses from his own village and runs the risk of the owner recognizing his lost property," she countered.

They rode in silence for a few more minutes before reaching the third village on their route. David was noticing that the deeper they fell into the task they had chosen to dedicate themselves to, the less tense his companion became. She'd graduated from single word to single sentence replies.

They could smell smoke before they rounded the curve that led to their next stop. The village was in an uproar. Streets were choked with people, carts, and animals. All were shouting and screaming at the top of their lungs. When they noticed Guardians amongst them they swarmed Kathryn and David.

"You must help us!"

"Justice cannot be perverted!"

"Catch the thieves!"

"We've been robbed!"

David raised his hands, calling for quiet. *Perhaps Rima isn't so quiet after all*, he thought as he waited for the noise to drop. "Who is an authority here I can speak to?"

An elderly woman slowly made her way forward until she stood before the two horses. "Our treasury and storehouses have been emptied," her voice was calm and steady despite the roiling emotions of the crowd surrounding her. "We trusted a traveling minstrel and his companions and they stole our livelihood."

Kathryn forcefully restrained herself from shaking her head in disgust. *Who trusts traveling minstrels and would allow one to get anywhere near a village treasury?* David was still talking and she forced herself to pay attention.

"In which direction did they head?"

The old woman pointed towards a series of hills that led to the mountains. "When we rose this morning we saw them riding hard towards those mountains."

"And you didn't send anyone after them?"

The old woman shrugged. "By the time our fastest riders could catch up with them, they had disappeared. We're farmers, not trackers."

David nodded and turned his horse towards the hills and let Rumer run. He had chosen Rumer as his horse for his endurance and his speed, now both would be put to the test.

In a radian they had reached the hills, David reined Rumer in and stifled a curse. Tracking was not his strong suit. Kathryn rode up beside him. "They turned east," she said, already driving her horse back into a gallop.

Perhaps Kathryn is a good person to have along, David thought as he rode behind her, *I can't track nearly so well, and neither can Luke.*

As they traveled further, David had to admit that he had never seen anyone track so quickly, not even his professor. No wonder Jasse had spoken so highly of her. Only twice did Kathryn need to dismount to study the ground for tracks, and even then it had taken her less than a minute to find them. They reached the forest where the thieves had camped by mid-afternoon, or at least according to Kathryn's tracking they had.

Dismounting they left their horses near the edge of the forest and quietly moved in. David moved to the south while Kathryn moved to the north. None of the villages had been able to give them an accurate count of how many thieves there were so David wanted to catch them between himself and Kathryn.

The call of an eagle broke the silence of the forest and David could hear startled movement ahead of him.

Loud guffaws reached his ears and he could only imagine the thieves laughing at a few of their companions for jumping at nothing.

As he drew closer he slowed his advance, rounding a large boulder he spotted a clearing directly ahead, the thieves were camped inside, laughing, drinking, and having a good time.

A good time which was just about to come to an end. He spotted the stolen horses and other goods lying about fifty paces from where the men sat around a fire, looking for all appearances to be slightly drunk. However appearances were deceiving and he was willing to bet that the men weren't intoxicated enough to prevent them from being able to hold their own in a fight.

There were five of them, all big men with shaved heads and extremely foul mouths. David watched as one of them put on a blond wig and began to play a lyre and sing in a ridiculously high pitched tone.

Oh what merry men we are
We come from so afar
The people feed and bed us
They don't even suspect us

His companions encouraged him on with loud catcalls and cheers. They joined him for the second verse:

We plunder their horses, money, and grain
Those poor peasants shall experience pain
When in the morning they wake and see
That all their riches with us did flee

David didn't wait to hear what the third verse was. He stepped from the shadows and pointed his sword at the back of the biggest thief's head. The singer, already beginning the third felt the tip of the sword and his voice broke out of his jolly tune with a strangled cry.

"So sorry to interrupt this party," David said his voice cold. "But your winning streak has just ended.

He didn't see Kathryn yet and wondered what she was doing, but he did notice the slight movement of a rather ugly man, one with a huge earring in his right ear. He was sitting on a moss covered boulder next to the thief David's sword was holding motionless. Quickly he brought his sword up to parry and blocked the thrust of the thief's sword. Sparks jumped from the collision point, startling David. *That block should have cleaved his sword in two!*

In that instant the entire camp erupted into motion. All five thieves were on their feet, weapons in hand. David had no doubts that he would have no trouble disarming the two bearing swords, it was the mace and two bows pointed at him that gave him second thoughts.

"He's mine," The earring thief shouted to the rest of group as he lunged at David. The power behind his blow was staggering. Even drunk the man could manage to win this fight if David wasn't careful. Blast it all, where was Kathryn! He couldn't fight five alone.

Interestingly enough the thief didn't aim his thrusts anywhere near David's head, a typical style preferred by bandits. Instead he worked to get David's defenses into a low position that would take to long for him to bring his sword back up to protect his head. David leaped over the fire and quickly exchanged his sword for his fighting knives briefly wondering if Kathryn would give him grief for abandoning his sword after he so blatantly put down her preference for knives. The bandit was stronger than he was and David knew that his best defense would be to attack with rapid strikes and in more than one place, something he couldn't achieve with his sword, the second knife would also double as an added guard against an attack at his head that the first couldn't block. As he blocked, parried, and jabbed David was aware of squeals and shouts from the rest of the thieves, *no doubt urging their leader on,* David thought as he ducked beneath a swing that could have easily taken his head off.

As he fought, David realized something that was enough to shake his confidence even more. Normal bandits used old, beat up swords that a Guardian sword could tear through in a few strokes. This thief's sword was unlike any sword he had come into contact with—it refused to be destroyed under David's own blade. Only a Guardian's blade could remain pure and unspoiled under the attack of a sister blade.

After giving ground for several minutes, David decided that he had had enough. Sword or no sword, he was going to win this fight. Switching from defense to offense he attacked with a series of sudden thrusts that, with carefully timed flicks of the wrist, changed direction at the last minute or added a second strike immediately behind the first. His first swing headed for the thief's head and was deflected downward at the last second towards his shoulder. The thief managed to deflect most of the blow, but not before David drew blood.

His second thrust aimed for the legs, but changed directions to attack his opponent's midsection. The third thrust aimed for the shoulder, but moved upwards to aim for the head. By the fourth maneuver David had to admit his opponent was skilled, or at least skilled enough to deflect or block his blows. He could still hear the calls of his opponent's companions but paid them no heed, his concentration needed to be focused on the thief in front of him.

The man suddenly lunged for David, who dropped to the ground and rolled away, quickly jumping to his feet. His opponent wasn't quite as quick and David brought his right hand around and down for a resounding blow to the man's sword hand. Reflex opened the man's grasp and he dropped his weapon.

Before he could retrieve it, David quickly brought his knives in front of him, crossing below the thief's neck. Then, before the thief could do anything but glare at him, David brought his right hand up and brought the hilt of his knife down on the back of the thief's skull. The man's eyes rolled back into his head and he collapsed on the ground.

Quickly David turned to face the other thieves—only to find them all sitting quietly subdued, their hands tied behind their backs, grimaces of pain visible on their faces and in the stiffness of their limbs.

Now that he looked closer, David could see spots of blood in various places on each of the prisoners.

Kathryn stepped forward, a length of rope in her hands and began tying up the unconscious thief.

"And here I thought you'd abandoned me," David commented as she finished tying the last knot.

She let out an un-ladylike snort. "Hardly. That one there," she nodded to the man who David had originally held at sword point, "aimed to put an arrow in your back, unfortunately for him I couldn't let that happen."

"So you shot him?"

She looked at him, something akin to amusement in her eyes. "I shot them all."

"All of them?"

"Just in their shoulders or legs," Kathryn said matter-of-factly. "I didn't hit anything vital—besides, I couldn't very well come to your aid if I had to deal with the rest of them now could I?"

Somewhat baffled by the turn of events, David went on, "Now what are we going to do with them?"

"That's the easy part, we take them back to the villages and let the villagers handle it." Kathryn brought out another long length of rope and began tying the thieves together. The singing thief, tried to resist, but Kathryn quickly subdued him with a well-placed handhold and a forceful smack to the back of his head. David remembered the time when Luke had delivered such a blow to his own head and covered a wince. Kathryn had hit much harder than Luke had.

David revived the one he had defeated and soon all five stood in a line. He held up the defeated man's sword and demanded, "Where did you get this sword?"

The man glared at him, refusing to answer. David was deciding whether to just ask again or whack the bandit and try again when Kathryn came up from behind him and grabbed his shoulder in a pinching grip.

"The Guardian asked you a question, I suggest you answer it."

If David had ever entertained doubts that Kathryn's voice could get colder and more intimidating he had just been proved wrong. Compared to the tone she had just used, the tone she used at home was warm and friendly.

"I found it," the prisoner mumbled. "In the forest."

David looked at Kathryn who returned his frustrated glance with a raised eyebrow and a look that made him glad he wasn't this particular bandit. "Then you won't mind if the Guardian maintains custody over the sword until its rightful owner can be found," she said as she quickly finished tethering the bandits together.

The bandit glared at her, but gave no reply. Their tether strung between Rumer and Lerina, the bandits were forced to walk back to the villages. It was a long ride back and both David and Kathryn ate their meal on the way since they hadn't had time to stop and eat.

The villagers were overjoyed to have their property returned and the thieves spending the next four weeks alternating between the stocks during the day and prison at night.

David and Kathryn rode back the way they came, returning the stolen property to its rightful owners in the various villages.

As they reached the meadow it was dark, but as soon as they crossed the barrier the lights from their home lit the way. They tended to their horses and then headed inside.

℘·℃

Kathryn followed David inside and immediately headed for her room. They had decided that David would debrief the rest of the team so that Kathryn could retire and get some sleep since she headed the first shift the next morning.

When she opened the door she found Destiny waiting for her. Kathryn fed her, undressed quickly, slipped into her sleeping shift, and let down her hair. She stood at the window for several moments, watching the moonrise cast a red hue over the river and contemplating the day.

As she prepared to climb into bed she noticed a scent on the wind—rain was coming. She took some comfort in knowing the sound would help her sleep. She closed the window which squealed on the tight fitting hinges as she pulled it to its landing and noted that they should be oiled.

Jasse's warning that anyone with gifts could cross the magical barrier, including those who were expelled from the Guardians, came to mind. "Maybe not," she quietly mused to herself. The noise might provide a good warning should some uninvited interloper attempt to steal entry into her room as she slept.

After closing the barrel latch to her window she climbed under the blankets, letting her body heat warm them until she felt like she was sleeping next to the fireplace.

Closing her eyes she let herself drift off to sleep, preparing her mind for the next day's assignment.

80·03

David climbed into bed later that night. The rest of the Dragons had been told of the encounter with the five thieves and warned that any fights that they participated in from now on weren't training sessions. As he lay there, listening to the falling rain he felt confident in leaving the other two shifts in Kathryn's hands.

She may not be much of a people person, he thought as he drifted off to sleep, *but she's definitely the type of person who will get the job done.*

His thoughts turned back to the mystery sword lying under his bed. It was made similarly to the Guardians. But, instead of having a smooth, barely discernible curve to the blade, this blade was straight with red veins mimicking fire scars traversing the cold metal. It was a mystery that he did not feel would have a pleasant ending.

Chapter 10

Kathryn woke at daybreak to prepare for the day's shift. Matt was already in the kitchen and Kathryn moved away, not willing to be drawn into conversation so early in the morning. Instead she made her way to the back porch where she sat down. She reached up and pulled out one of her fighting knives from its scabbard on her back. She'd already inspected the blade the night before, but she did it again...just in case. She could still see the doubt in David's eyes from the day before when she had told him that she wasn't bringing her sword along and had resisted the urge to make an admittedly derogatory comment about his choice to abandon his sword in his fight with the bandit. It had been, she admitted, a very wise decision on his part. That particular bandit had simply been too powerful to meet force on force.

It wasn't common practice, she knew, to leave your sword behind. After all, Guardian trainees spent most of their time training with a sword so that when they faced sword masters they wouldn't easily be overwhelmed. To the majority, the sword became an extension of their arms when faced with a fight.

However, Kathryn wasn't one of them. She disliked fighting with a sword. Despite six years of intense practice with one, she had never come to feel like the weapon was a logical extension of her mind and arm. Her weapon of choice was the bow. She was one of the few experts whose arrow could easily span over five hundred meters and make its mark in one shot. In a tight situation she preferred one, or both, or her knives. If she couldn't take out an opponent from a distance then she wanted to be up close and personal with them; crowding their space so that they didn't have room to swing their sword or stationing herself so close it couldn't reach her physically. Meanwhile, a few stabs with her knife, already positioned next to her opponent's body, and the fight was over. Simple. Easy. Uncomplicated.

When fighting an untrained opponent her method rarely required more than a few large swings before she was in a position to end the fight. Trained fighters, like knights, who had been drilled to circle while fighting required a little more creativity. But even they, with their highly structured drilling regimens, were relatively easy to predict.

She continued to sit and listen to the soothing sound of the river as she heard the others of her shift waking up. Destiny swooped over the training field toward her and landed gracefully on the porch's railing, her breakfast clutched in her talons.

Kathryn moved inside as she heard Matt announcing her own breakfast. Rachel and Jenna, she was glad to see, were both fully dressed and ready to go.

"Morning Kathryn," Matt greeted as he ladled hot porridge into her bowl.

Knowing that she'd been extremely short with David the day before, Kathryn had once again promised herself that she would try to remember

Jasse's request and try to be more approachable. "Morning, Matt, Jenna, Rachel," she nodded at each one in turn.

The two girls quickly added their "good mornings" to Matt's and Kathryn's, making short work of their breakfast.

ℰℴ · ℭℬ

As soon as she was done eating, Kathryn went to saddle Lerina and call Destiny. Her horse gave her a slightly annoyed look at having such a loud, piercing whistle originate so close to her ear, but Kathryn figured that after all these years the look was probably just habit.

Jenna and Rachel followed quickly, saddling their horses and performing one last check that everything was in place. Matt trotted in after them with small satchels of dried meat, fruit, and nuts.

Kathryn eyed the food. "Matt, what is all this food for? We'll be back in four radians."

Matt gave what she supposed was an attempt at a nonchalant shrug but instead gave off a mischievous vibe. "You never know when you might need to bribe a hungry person or animal for information, or who knows you might just get hungry again." While he didn't physically perform the act, she could practically see him rubbing his hands together with glee as he imagined scenario after scenario where he might have to save the group by offering up food as recompense.

Kathryn nodded, a small grin appearing on her face. As much as she hated to admit it, Matt's humor was catching. And despite what most people believed, she did find humor in some things. Matt's flippant personality would apparently be one of them. "Okay then, let's go." She swung into her saddle, glad that once again she had left the cumbersome sword behind in her room.

They rode south, instead of east like Kathryn and David had the day before, visiting with farmers and townsfolk alike. Or at least, Matt, Jenna, and Rachel visited; Kathryn preferred to stay in the shadows and eavesdrop.

Old habits are hard to break, she thought ruefully as she listened to two old women gossiping about the mysterious deaths of cattle that were beginning to appear in the outlying farms. *I listened, melding into the shadows when I was a child, invisible and beyond the senses of those I observed and I still do it as a Guardian.* She had seen the surprise in David's face when she revealed that she too had learned of the thefts. Honestly, she thought darkly, there were other ways to gather information besides actually talking to people. At least with her way they didn't outright lie to you.

When she caught up with Matt she learned that along with the cattle deaths, wells were becoming bitter and crops failing for no good reason.

So much for David's conclusion that Rima is a peaceful province, she thought as she and Matt decided to remain in the immediate vicinity to investigate. What she really wanted to do was to send Rachel and Jenna out individually to other towns to cultivate a Guardian presence, but knew that she couldn't send them out this early in their assignments, best to wait until they had a dozen or more shifts for experience, and then split her shifts up even further.

113

Rachel and Jenna agreed that the situation warranted further investigation and they split up into two groups. Jenna and Matt would maintain a presence in the town while Kathryn and Rachel would visit the outlying farms.

Kathryn sent Rachel to talk with the farmers, getting as much information that she could while Kathryn investigated the wells and crops.

Hauling a bucket of well water up out of the ground, Kathryn tasted it...and immediately spit it back out. *Those old women weren't kidding, however I think they downplayed the actual taste.* The small trickle of water that hadn't been spit out made its way down her throat, scratching and cauterizing as it went. *No wonder the locals are upset, this stuff tastes awful!* She frowned down at the water far below, *and it definitely isn't natural.*

I wish Jenna was here, she thought, her mood now matching the taste of the water, *as a healer she might be able to neutralize whatever it was that had contaminated the water.* She stopped short.

Water.

Her gift.

She scowled at herself. Moving back to the bucket she dipped one of her hands into the remaining liquid. She focused on the water, noting the familiar feel of the water and picking out the element that didn't belong. She forced her mind to focus only on the strange element, learning what it felt like.

Confident that she could now separate the element from water she dropped the film back into the bucket. Taking a deep breath she closed her eyes and imagined a filter forming at the bottom of the well, a filter that would allow nothing but water to flow through it. Slowly she raised the filter through the water, removing the contamination from each water drop, one by one, until the strange element, unable to go through, formed a thin layer that grew thicker the farther up she brought it.

Finally it reached the surface where she paused. Water was her gift, not telekinesis. How could she bring the element to her?

She solved this problem by wrapping the element in a ball of water and urging the water to flow up the side of the well and into her hand where she slowly let it drain away. At her feet now lay a large pile of what looked like grains of sand.

"Impressive."

Momentarily startled, Kathryn relaxed as she recognized Rachel's voice. That was another reason she hated using her gift. It took all of her concentration to work with water and left her vulnerable to outside attacks. Scooping up some of the contamination she studied it.

Rachel moved to join her. "Is that what's been poisoning the wells?"

"Yes. Do you recognize it?"

Rachel bent down and retrieved a handful of her own. She studied it and after a moment shook her head. "No, I don't."

Kathryn pulled out a handkerchief from her satchel and piled some of the unknown material on it. She tied the fabric together and placed it back into her satchel. "Burn the rest of that, would you?" she asked, nodding to the rest of the pile.

Rachel grinned. "With pleasure."

The element that was causing the crops to fail turned out to be simply salt, but Kathryn still took a sample in case it contained other contaminates. Because her gift was water and not earth, and Rachel's were wind and fire, neither were able to cleanse the soil the way Kathryn had purified the water.

However the family living there was simply grateful for the clean water and did not hold the fact that their land was still contaminated against the two Guardians. Four more farms were located on the outskirts of the town and the two Guardians visited them all. For each, Kathryn cleaned the water while Rachel took samples of the contaminates in the soil.

They met up with Matt and Jenna at the edge of the village and Kathryn handed the samples they had taken to Jenna, asking if she would be able to identify the source and find a counteragent to neutralize it. Jenna readily agreed to give it a try. Since they still had two radians to go, they decided to move on to the next village to see if they were having the same problems.

Along the way they found a farmer whose cart had lost a wheel, toppled, and dumped a good portion of his load on the path.

Unfortunately the load he was carrying turned out to be manure. Kathryn and Matt offered to shovel the spilled mess back into the cart while Jenna and Rachel gave the farmer a ride into the nearest village so he could get a replacement wheel.

It didn't take Kathryn and Matt very long to shovel the manure back into the cart and as they waited for the farmer to return Kathryn began to get restless.

Matt noticed. "Why don't you take a look around those woods," he suggested, pointing to the ones about a kilometer before them. "Looks like a great place for bandits to hide."

Kathryn tossed him an, I-*know-what-you're-doing-but-I'll-humor-you-anyway* look before remounting and moving in that direction. Matt was right, it was the perfect place for troublemakers to hide, and it was probably the only reason she was willing to leave Matt alone.

As she rode toward the forest she realized that she didn't have any idea as to what the individual combat capabilities of her shift were. She pursed her lips thoughtfully. Before she considered splitting up her shifts further she would have to examine that aspect. Maybe tomorrow she would take the lunch break to spar with each.

She left Lerina at the edge of the forest, knowing that she could travel faster, and quieter, on foot.

As she moved through the forest she was aware that many of the normal sounds, birds singing, deer prancing, and squirrel chatter, were missing, which was as good an indication as any that *something* else was in this forest, something that animals feared—something human.

Silently, she removed her knives from their scabbard. As much as she preferred to use her bow in a fight—keeping well out of range of any of her opponents or attackers—safety dictated that she keep close combat weapons at hand in case the fight didn't start out at that way.

Her only warning of an attack was the abrupt *snap* of a twig to her right. She was already spinning, bringing her blades up to parry, when the muttered curse reached her ears. A giant of a man leapt out from behind a large oak tree, his blade caught between hers.

By the stars, he's strong! Kathryn thought as she whipped her left knife around to parry his side thrust, *and fast too!*

A second sword appeared in her peripheral vision, aiming for her neck. Kathryn dropped to the earth and somersaulted between the first's legs. She heard his grunt of confusion. Unfortunately, however, the second man wasn't fooled. He nudged his companion aside and brought his sword down in the classic execution's chop.

Rolling to her knees, Kathryn brought both blades up in a block. The power behind the blow was enough to stagger her and she knew she was in a very compromising position—something she was about to change.

She shifted her weight onto her left leg and pivoted, rising up and kicking outwards as she did, catching her second attacker in the stomach while turning to face the first, who had managed by now to pick himself up off the ground after his companion had pushed him aside.

He charged at her, his sword held high above his head, cursing at her with a string of very creative words. However he had failed to notice that as she pivoted she had thrust one of her knives into the ground and stood facing him with just one knife. Or so it appeared.

She feinted left and he moved to block her, still cursing. He failed to notice that as she moved left her right hand had slipped behind her back and even still he hadn't noticed the small throwing dagger concealed in her hand. His companion, still gasping for breath— and no doubt feeling the broken ribs resulting from her kick— shouted at him to finish her off.

He charged again and she threw the knife while throwing herself into a somersault to the right, leaping to her feet to face him. This attacker, however, would no longer be a factor in the fight. Her blade had hit its mark.

She turned, ready to face her original attacker, however he had already abandoned the fight and she caught sight of him fleeing through the trees.

She followed, but lost him after he mounted a horse waiting in a glade and sped off.

Slowly, she made her way back the way she came, carefully observing the trail to see if he had dropped anything. He hadn't.

When Kathryn reached the attacker she had killed she quickly retrieved her knife. As she was cleaning it she realized something she hadn't noticed earlier. Those voices were familiar. But why? She retrieved the dead man's weapon and noticed that the broad sword had the same striations and color as the one David had recovered from yesterday's fight. There were no nicks or damage of any sort on the blade.

Great, she thought bleakly, *with two bizarre swords within two days, Rima is already proving itself to be problematic.*

Making her way back to where she had left Lerina she managed to place the voices. Her two attackers were the same men whom she had overheard in the glade two nights ago!

The knowledge did nothing to improve her mood. One of them had gotten away. Kathryn counted that as a personal failure.

Even Matt noticed her mood when she made it back to where she had left him.

"I take it, it didn't go well?"

She told him about the attack, but not about recognizing the voices.

"They must have been pretty desperate if they attacked a Guardian," he commented as Jenna, Rachel, and the farmer appeared on the road.

Kathryn was forced to agree. They had attacked first, not many bandits would. Most would attempt to flee first before standing and fighting, yet these two had attacked.

She didn't like the implications.

ℴ·Ↄ

When the group returned, Kathryn briefed David on what had happened. He agreed that bandits actually attacking a Guardian was out of the ordinary and promised to keep a look out for the one who had gotten away. He mentioned notifying Lord Mora about the two swords and their ability to deflect Guardian swords but Kathryn didn't pay attention since that was his job and not hers. He asked if she was alright and she, somewhat icily even to her ears, assured him she was.

She had failed. Kathryn didn't like failure and she liked it even less when others tried to make her feel better.

Chapter 11

As the shifts traded out, Kathryn went out into the garden to do some weeding. Destiny hopped alongside catching the occasional worm that Kathryn would toss her.

"That is so gross."

Kathryn glanced up to see Natalie and Lindsey leaning against the fence, a look of disgust etched into their faces. "Is there something you two need?" she asked, striving for a neutral tone that she probably failed to achieve.

"More like something you need," Lindsey said, holding her nose between two fingers.

"A bath," Natalie sniffed.

Kathryn raised an eyebrow and turned back to weeding, shooing away two pribbles that had come to investigate her work. "You'd stink too if you had to rake up manure," she told them calmly. At that moment the larger pribble relieved itself creating a pile nearly as big as a dinner tray.

"Ewwww!" Natalie shrieked.

"Gross!" Lindsey added, her face turning a little green.

Kathryn didn't bother acknowledging them. As far as she was concerned both Natalie and Lindsey had some growing up to do. Just yesterday Natalie had wanted to appropriate three of the four bathrooms for the girls, leaving one for the boys. Kathryn had told her, in no uncertain terms, that the bathrooms would remain open for everyone. In any case, all that was in the bathrooms was a bathtub, a full length mirror, and lots of shelf space for towels and soaps. And it was not a sunken stone bathtub like the one in Kathryn's apartment in Jasmine's palace. It was nothing more than a raised metal tub barely big enough to sit in. Natalie was still simmering. She didn't like having to wait to take her daily bath, and the idea of sharing a bathing tub with one of the boys repulsed her even more.

They reminded Kathryn, a bit too vividly for comfort, of two serving girls back at Blackwood Manor. Linisse and Marite had been very pretty girls, had thought of themselves much higher than their situation allowed, and had often taken great pains to keep themselves looking nice. Many times their efforts had included blaming Kathryn for "undoing all their hard work" on chores they couldn't have been bothered to complete. Of course once they had blamed it on Kathryn, she had been forced to complete their chores on top of her own...plus any extras that had been added on as punishment for making Linisse and Marite look bad. Of course the two girls had found it humorous to watch her do the chores they hadn't done and had taunted her constantly throughout her time at the Manor.

"What would your parents think if they saw you like this?" Natalie asked, apparently horrified at the amount of dirt Kathryn had on her clothes and skin.

Jolted back to the present, Kathryn felt herself slightly confused by the question. "What do you mean 'if my parents saw me like this'?" She asked as she tugged on one particularly stubborn weed. Scowling at it, she dug her fingers down into the dirt to try and pull it out by the root.

"I mean if they saw you digging around in the dirt smelling like excrement."

The root refused to budge. She'd had less trouble with some of the decade-old tarnished silver pieces she'd polished in the manor. Kathryn let out a huff. "Somehow I don't think they would mind," she muttered, working to keep the bitterness out of her tone, she didn't need Natalie to start an inquiry into her past. If her parents could abandon her to a life of slavery, she didn't think they would have any problem seeing her get a little dirty. Finally the root popped free. As she fell back onto her heels, her hand came out of the dirt with a long taproot dangling from her fingers. She could feel Natalie's eyes on her as she tried to carelessly toss the offending plant aside.

"Are you trying to tell me that you're a *peasant*?" Natalie asked disdainfully, her gaze automatically following the arc the weed made through the air.

Kathryn watched as a rather large green worm with blue striations worked its way through the turned up soil. As it inched along it grew longer and thinner until it was nearly twice the length of her foot. After regarding the creature for a few moments she imagined setting overflowing bowls of them in front of her two antagonists and ordering them to eat them.

Well, are you? Natalie insisted.

Kathryn looked up, her eyes narrowing. "Considering we're supposed to be protecting the *peasants* as you call them, you're displaying a pretty narrow minded opinion of them."

Natalie's jaw tightened. "I come from a noble family—

"So do half of the dragons," Kathryn interrupted. She pointed a dirt encrusted finger at the two girls. "As Guardians we give up our status, whether noble or common, to protect the people, whether they are noble or common." Before today she'd never thought she'd parrot the lessons monotonously given by Guardian Liliha, an overly pompous recently appointed Guardian Councilmember who had droned on for hours on said topic. At least Guardian Geral had made their history seem interesting, Guardian Liliha had tempted Kathryn to cut off her own arm to escape the lectures.

Lindsey pouted. "You sound like Guardian Geral."

Well, the comparison could have been worse. Kathryn didn't comment but turned back to her weeding.

"You know what I think you are?" Natalie asked suddenly, her voice smooth as honey but her eyes glinted icily. Kathryn, having experienced the same inflections and rhetorical questions from Lady Blackwood, knew better than to respond. As predicted, it didn't stop the older girl from continuing. "I think you're a child of the Wanderers. An outcast."

Even Lindsey gasped. The Wanderers were an occult sect that wandered through the kingdom offering human sacrifices and praying to the sun and moons. They had been outlawed thousands of years ago but it was said that some communities still lived hidden throughout the kingdom.

It took all of her training from Blackwood Manor not to react to the old fear that her old tormenters had used to enslave her. Kathryn's head came up slowly. "What makes you say that?" she asked coldly.

"Look at you," Natalie laughed, pointing her finger at Kathryn. "Your hair is black as night, your skin is pale even though you spend radians out in the sun, and your eyes are the color of the sea. Not to mention you have a heart of stone and a mind of ice."

How could a person be so shallow as to name Kathryn a Wanderer due to her pale skin and dark hair? "And that makes me a Wanderer?" In that moment she could see Natalie's mind spinning, practically convincing the older girl on the spot of her suppositions.

"Why not?" Natalie blustered, giving a stiff shrug. "You don't fit the profile of any other culture... you certainly aren't an Elf with their fair skin and hair and I've never seen a human that is as unfeeling as you. Why not the Wanderers? You like to be left alone, no doubt through much practice of hiding with your arcane foibles. You speak little and when you do it's hard and cold—"

Kathryn interrupted her before she could continue. "Before you convince yourself, Natalie, you should remember one thing. The Wanderers haven't been seen for over two thousand years, they keep to themselves because others persecute them, so how could you know what they look like?" She maintained eye contact, making sure to modulate a slow, quite tone, that most people would have understood as a threat. "I suggest you keep your prejudices to yourself—"

Natalie opened her mouth to argue, but Kathryn cut her off. "You are a Guardian now and are required to rise above petty prejudices. If you cannot I will report it to David. Do you have any other questions?"

Natalie's eyes blazed, but Lindsey, after studying Kathryn's face, obviously caught on to the cold danger lurking in her eyes. "No, there's nothing else," she said quickly, pulling Natalie away from the fence.

"If you're so adamant you're not a Wanderer, then why don't you just prove you're not!" Natalie called over her shoulder as the two left.

Kathryn sat in the dirt for a long time. She wished she could rebuff Natalie's charge with certainty. But she couldn't deny she was a child of Wanderers because she didn't know who her parents were. It was a futile pursuit she had sworn she would never undertake. Her parents had abandoned her and Kathryn wanted nothing to do with them.

₭·℟

Natalie was furious. "How dare she speak to me that way!" she cried angrily as she and Lindsey sat in her room. "She had no right!"

"What are you going to do about it?" Lindsey muttered as she brushed her long hair.

"She's obviously hiding something," Natalie abruptly stood up and paced the room several times. Reaching back into her memories, she tried to find one of Kathryn back at school. She found a few instances where she remembered seeing the younger girl, but in all of them she had remained quietly out of the way, doing her best to hide from the notice of others. At the time, Natalie had been too busy to truly notice the younger woman, hadn't cared that she'd done her best to become one with the shadows. In all honesty, the girl hadn't been visible enough for Natalie to even consider looking twice at. Now, though, she would discover what it meant to be the object of one of Natalie's investigations. "I'm going to uncover the truth about Kathryn," she announced. "There wasn't a secret I couldn't discover back at school. I'm going to find out the truth about our second-in-command and when I do I'm going to share it with everyone I meet."

℘·CЗ

The next day Natalie put her plan into action. She rose early and pounced on Kathryn when she arrived back at the clearing.

"Who were your parents?" The object of her attention ignored her and continued to unsaddle her horse.

Natalie tried again. "Where did you grow up?"

Kathryn didn't so much as look at her.

"Do you have any siblings?"

No response.

"Any uncles or aunts? Who was your best friend growing up?"

Kathryn finally looked at her, her own face void of any emotion. "Don't you have chores to do Natalie?"

Natalie waved her hand dismissively. "I completed them early because I wanted to get to know you. What's your opinion of the royal family?" Now that would be a revealing topic should Kathryn respond. While the Guardians technically served the Royal Family, Natalie knew that many of the older Guardians were very vocal as to their opinions of the King and his isolationist policies.

Kathryn merely stared at her for a moment before turning to return to the house.

"Oh, come on Kathryn," Natalie said, slightly frustrated. "You have to have an opinion of some kind." Everyone else she'd ever encountered had been more than willing to share their opinions and life stories if it meant that they could be the center of attention for a few moments.

To her annoyance Kathryn ignored her. She didn't answer a single question and refused to acknowledge her. By the time Kathryn's second shift had arrived, Natalie hadn't learned anything but how incredibly tightlipped Kathryn was. "She may be stubborn, but I'll figure it out," Natalie vowed as she watched the third shift ride off. "I always figure it out."

The next morning she tried again, only to receive the same results. Kathryn would stare at her for a few moments before stabling her horse and then go on to complete her chores. Natalie had never worked so hard for anything in her life. Week after week, she attempted to pry information out of Kathryn. Nothing worked. They fell into an insipid routine of Natalie postulating her questions to a rock.

And she hated the *routine* of it all. When Kathryn returned from her shift she would immediately unsaddle her horse and change out of her uniform into a green tunic and leggings. After changing clothes she would do her chores and then spend about two radians shooting arrows and throwing knives into various targets. Once she'd emptied her quiver to her heart's content she would free climb the stone wall. Everything was the same, every day, down to the clothing the Dragon's lieutenant wore when off duty. Natalie *hated* routine.

A week into their new life, Kathryn began to use the remaining radian before her second shift to train with others in her shifts. Usually Jenna. The healer was decent with weapons but apparently wasn't up to Kathryn's standards. Watching, day after day, as Kathryn drilled Jenna in various exercises, Natalie began to feel angry at Kathryn for singling Jenna out like she had. Jenna was obviously a daughter of a noble heritage and should not have been forced to spend day after day constantly picking herself up out of the dirt and grass. After a month, the remainder of the first shift and the others from the third, and eventually the fourth, shifts joined in. All except Natalie.

ℰꝏ · ℭℬ

One day as she watched Kathryn weed in the garden she asked, "Where'd you grow up?" As she had come to expect, Kathryn didn't answer. Natalie suppressed a sigh as she tried to come up with a question that she felt Kathryn just might answer. "What's your opinion of slavery?" She finally asked, remembering a topic that had been debated in one of her classes. It wasn't one Natalie had considered important at the time. After all, slavery had been outlawed in Archaea for several hundred years. What was the point in discussing a topic where the practice was already dead?

That got a reaction.

Kathryn's hands faltered in her weeding and her gaze took on a distant look. Immediately Natalie pushed some more, only her words seemed to break the spell and Kathryn continued weeding as if nothing had happened. But it was as if the world had been illuminated for Natalie.

Later, as she watched Kathryn's shift ride off Natalie felt a small surge of victory. Slavery was a touchy subject with Kathryn, now it was up to her to discover why. The only problem was that Kathryn was so silent. If she hadn't known that Kathryn could speak, Natalie would have sworn she was mute.

Except for the slavery question she brushed off every question without any reaction. However by the third week Natalie could tell that her persistence was starting to work. Kathryn would finish her chores, give a short training session to the others— forgoing one for herself, and then return to her room and close the door until her next shift. Natalie would not be dissuaded. She stood outside the door and continued to ask questions, with Lindsey keeping watch on the stairs in case someone came upstairs.

ℰꝏ · ℭℬ

Four days after she had started taking refuge in her room, Kathryn had had enough. Natalie was not going to leave her alone. She decided that taking sanctuary in her room wasn't enough. Dismounting she stabled her horse, finished her chores, ignored Natalie's numerous questions, and then set off towards the forest. She passed through the barrier, with Natalie chatting away behind her.

There! The perfect spot for her to disappear was straight ahead. Shifting her pack ever so slightly she moved through the forest silently, Natalie falling farther behind with every step until she could hear Natalie calling for her. "Kathryn? Kathryn where did you go? Where are you?"

122

Kathryn wasn't about to stop, she continued on at a running pace, letting her gift guide her to a place where she could find peace. Destiny followed overhead, her flight guiding Kathryn through the trees and around boulders until they reached the place that called to her.

A magnificent waterfall tumbled over the rocks and into a calm pool below. Hot and sweaty, and grateful for the unseasonably warm late fall temperatures, Kathryn stripped off her work clothes, slipped into a bathing tunic and jumped into the water.

The water invaded every pore and dissolved all of the frustration and anger Kathryn had been harboring against Natalie. Diving down she explored the bottom of the pool, swimming over rocks and sandy areas until she was directly beneath the falls itself. She surfaced, feeling the power of the water as it crashed upon her head, neck, and shoulders massaging and soothing her tense muscles. The pounding outside her skull made her forget the pounding and throbbing within.

Reluctantly she pulled herself out of the water and sat down on the grassy bank letting the sun dry her off. Deciding to return every day to the waterfall she sank back into the soft grass, feeling every soft blade brush against her skin. She dozed pleasantly, letting the sound of the falling water block out every other thought.

When she woke she dressed quickly and returned to the clearing with fifteen minutes to spare of her shift. Natalie was nearby as always and quickly made her way towards her.

"Where did you hide?" she hissed as Kathryn saddled Lerina, when Kathryn remained silent she added, "You can't hide forever, sooner or later I'll find your hiding place."

Kathryn mounted and looked down at the older girl. "I've seen you track Natalie, I have no worries about you finding my hiding place." She nudged Lerina into a trot and left the barn, leaving Natalie speechless.

Ⅎ·℃

Natalie trembled with rage. *Fine*, she thought coldly, *if a war is what you want, then a war is what you'll get.*

"Natalie? Are you alright?"

Natalie turned to find Lindsey standing behind her, a worried look on her face. "Come on, we have plans to make." She hurried back to her room.

Closing the door she began to pace again. "How else can we get to Kathryn?"

Lindsey sat down on her bed. "What do you mean?"

"I mean, annoy her, upset her, get an emotional reaction from her!" Natalie shouted. "The girl is stone and I want to make the stone bleed."

"Well," Lindsey said slowly. "Continually asking questions didn't help, she just locked herself in her room, and when she'd had enough of that she sought refuge in the forest."

"Thank you for reminding me," Natalie grumped. "Could you track her?"

Lindsey shook her head. "Tracking is not one of my strong skills."

"We'll just have to make her miserable another way."

"How?"

"We'll figure out something."

Natalie thought for a long time about what she could do to annoy Kathryn. For a long time she could think of nothing, finally, at a loss for any other ideas she moved toward Kathryn's room. Her fury grew as she approached the nondescript door on the coveted second floor. *This* should have been *her* room. And it would have been, if the Council hadn't assigned the position of family lieutenant to a girl who *obviously* didn't want it.

Jasse's warning of 'everyone's room being their sanctuary' didn't even enter her mind as Natalie opened the door to Kathryn's room. Looking around in disgust, Natalie could see nothing that would help her get under her nemesis' skin. The girl hadn't even bothered to decorate her own room. It was as plain as when they had first moved in.

Decorate her room?

Natalie raced back to her room and pulled out bolts of pink and red fabric and other decorating supplies. Hurrying back to Kathryn's room she began to work. She worked until twenty minutes before her shift. Taking one last look at her handiwork, Natalie closed the door and prepared for her shift, wishing she could see the look on Kathryn's face when she saw her room.

She moved to the kitchens where Matt was fixing dinner. When they had first moved in, Matt had made it a rule that no one was allowed in the kitchen while he was creating, however she needed a new water gourd to replace the old one she had lost and he would just have to live with her intrusion.

She opened the door and stepped inside. "Matt I need—

Coming to a dead stop just inside the doorway she stared in horror at the scene before her.

Hundreds upon hundreds of bugs covered the room from floor to ceiling. Suji bugs, large oblong shaped creatures with a hard black and green veined shell covering their backs and sporting a distinctive yellow half-moon on the thorax paced back and forth along the countertops, dragging pieces of meat. Merici, little bugs with six legs and an antenna on top of their heads, paraded across the floor, dragging noodles and sallat greenery behind them. Spiders of every size and species hung from the cupboards lowering spices and other small items into a large cooking pot simmering on the stove.

Mendemire roaches were pulling bread dough every which way, flies were constantly diving downwards over the pot and bees were shaking what appeared to be honey off their legs.

"Natalie!" Matt exclaimed as he exited the cellar, a large jar of spice in his hands and two dozen firebugs flying around his head. "What are you doing here?" Suddenly all of the bugs stopped what they were doing. Slowly each one turned in unison to face towards Natalie. Those with antennae pointed their long slender appendages directly at her face to capture as much information as their tiny sensors allowed. As if of one mind they all waited patiently on what the girl would do next.

Natalie opened her mouth to speak but all that came out was a strangled yelp. She watched as a spider the size of her hand dumped some merchan spice into the pot. Gulping and gasping she finally found her voice. Letting out a piercing scream she turned on her heel and raced out of the room.

Flinging open the front door she sprinted outside in a blind panic and straight into David and Luke, sending her and David both flying.

"Natalie! What in blazes is wrong with you?" David exclaimed as he picked himself up off the ground. Luke was doubled over, hooting in laughter.

"Thekitcheniscoveredinbugs!" she shrieked as she accepted David's hand to regain an upright position.

Both David and Luke stared at her. "What?" Luke asked slowly.

"Iwenttothekitchentogetanewgourdandfounditcoveredinbugswhowereco okingourdinner!"

"Did you understand any of that?" Luke asked, canting his head to one side.

David shook his head. "Natalie, you're hyperventilating," he told her calmly, "take a deep breath," David watched while she did so, "good. Now, tell us what happened."

"I...went...to...the...kitchen...to...get...a...new...gourd...and...found...it...co vered...in... bugs...who...were...cooking...our...dinner." Natalie drug out each word, partly because she was highly irritated at the boys for making her repeat it and also because she needed to catch her breath in between each word...perhaps she really was hyperventilating...whatever that meant.

The two boys exchanged a concerned look before racing to the kitchen to see for themselves. Natalie waited for the shouting to begin but when a few minutes had passed and no one had raised their voice she slowly ventured back inside.

The kitchen was spotless, not a bug in sight and Matt stood stirring the pot with a large wooden spoon with David and Luke laughing beside him.

Spotting her in the doorway Luke called out, "Where are your bugs Natalie?"

She scowled at Matt. "They were right here a minute ago."

David chuckled. "I don't see any now. In fact this kitchen's spotless." Seeing Natalie's angry glare he quickly changed the subject, "Dinner smells great Matt, the rest of the Dragons will enjoy it. Come on Natalie, Luke, we have a shift to start." He pulled Natalie out of the kitchen, missing Matt's smirk.

The story of Natalie's imaginary bugs spread through the Dragons like wildfire and by the time supper started everyone had heard it.

Natalie, usually a girl who loved being in the center of attention, resented both Matt and the Dragons. Matt because he obviously knew the truth but was letting the rest of the Dragons tease her about it— and the family because they *were* teasing her about it.

But what really irritated her was that Matt had made her look like a fool in front of David. The first time she'd laid eyes on her new leader Natalie had taken careful note of his extreme good looks and calm confident demeanor. The way he had skillfully taken control of the introductions had proven to her that he was of a noble family, peasants simply did not possess such tact— Kathryn certainly didn't. He was a perfect match for her and she had decided that she would do everything in her power to get him to notice her.

She wanted him, his attention, and she always got what she wanted. However David was proving to be difficult, hardly taking any notice of her. Instead he seemed to be preoccupied with making sure the Dragons became a smoothly functioning family, the mark of a true leader, but it was definitely running him opposite of Natalie and her ambitions. If she could get close to David, perhaps she could eventually replace Kathryn as second-in-command. The goal was a delicious one to contemplate, one that would be even sweeter due to her irritation over the younger girl.

However instead of getting closer to her, he seemed to take more of an interest in Kathryn. Natalie had caught him staring hard at her adversary more than once and it made her furious. Now, the one time she'd had his undivided attention, she'd looked like an idiot. Briefly she considered retaliating at Matt, but then decided she couldn't handle both Kathryn and Matt, especially if Matt could call on some of his little *friends* for help.

℘·℃

Kathryn unsaddled her horse, grateful that Natalie wasn't around to irritate her with ridiculous questions. She still couldn't forgive herself for reacting the way she did when Natalie asked her about slavery. The older girl had obviously noticed and took it as a sign that she was on the right track.

Sighing, Kathryn climbed the stairs and opened the door to her room—and stared. Pink and red fabric hung from the ceiling and walls. Candles matching the fabric sat ready to be lit and little red and pink hearts had been cut from parchment and strewn about the room.

Natalie. It could only be Natalie.

Sighing deeply, Kathryn bent over and began picking up the tacky hearts and pulling the fabric off the walls. She deposited the pile in Natalie's room.

℘·℃

When Natalie returned from her shift and spotted the pink pile on her bed she smiled. "Well, at least she had the decency to return it," she muttered to herself as she undressed. "That way I can reuse it all tomorrow." She crawled into her bed and snuggled under the blankets wondering just how long Kathryn would tolerate her room being decorated before lashing out at her. It would be interesting to see how long it took for Kathryn to snap.

℘·℃

On the fourth day Kathryn returned from her last shift to find her room once again a collage of pink and red she felt her anger rise.

Fine, she thought angrily as she surveyed the disaster that was her room, *if Natalie won't stop, then the least I can do is make sure she suffers for it.* Gathering up all of the decorations, she stuffed them into her satchel and made her way out of the house and into the woods. On the outskirts of the magical boundary that protected the Dragon's glade she dumped the colorful ensemble out of her bag and quickly set it on fire using her flint and steel. An enormous feeling of satisfaction welled within her as she watched the bright fabrics wither away into pieces of black ash. Her nose wrinkled in distaste as the wind shifted direction, blowing the smoke into her face. Once she was satisfied that there was nothing left for Natalie to salvage she returned to the

126

house, Destiny swopped down over her shoulder screeching victoriously. Kathryn couldn't help but agree with her.

That night, Natalie was puzzled to discover the absence of the fabric and other decorating materials; however, she wasn't worried. "I have a whole closet full of fabrics," she told Lindsey as she theatrically waved her hand toward the colorful stacks. "She can hide them all she wants...She'll *snap* before I run out of fabric."

Chapter 12

The Dragons had settled into their new home and new routine. The first month on patrol had led to numerous small fights with an annoying number of bandits and thieves that had decided to give Rima some trouble. But after that first month, the excitement seemed to die down. Whoever had been poisoning the wells and crops seemed to have disappeared, leaving the Dragons gifted with mastery over water and earth to clean up the contaminated farms. The only trouble the new Guardians faced on a daily basis was that of the weather. The warm late fall weather had given way to the colder winter weather with startling speed.

Jenna and Tyler had been called upon to deal with a few injuries. Luke and Matt had tangled with an outlaw who enjoyed throwing tree trunks into the homes of people who annoyed him. Both had been so black and blue after the adventure that Natalie had begun teasing them that they had rolled on Lindsey's paint palate. Amy and Leia ran into a particularly nasty drunk that had left them with scraped knuckles and huge welts on their heads. A few other cuts and pulled muscles were seen but nothing as serious as a broken leg so much as plagued the family.

After two months in their new home, the snows had come, blanketing the terrain in uniform whiteness. Despite the school's southwesterly location it had been built within a league of the Khidamun Sea making snow in the winter months unheard of. Several of the Dragons had never seen the winter phenomenon before and had found adapting to the decreased temperature challenging. Now it was well into the month of Yavannië and outside the magical barrier surrounding their glade, ice and snow storms ravaged the countryside. The snow still fell within their glade, but unless they were on patrol the Dragons were spared the bone-biting chill of the winds and the blinding whiteness of the blizzards that erased every landmark the Guardians had begun to learn. Not even the cirin could completely protect the Guardians against a winter as bad as the one the Dragons were faced with.

Matt and Cass learned to keep hot broth and drinks ready as the patrols switched out. The boys took turns making sure that the fires in the lower rooms were constantly burning so that the returning patrol had a place to warm up and dry out their uniforms. Jenna and Tyler dug into Jenna's supply of herbs to keep the family from developing chills and fever from the exposure to the cold. A nightly routine was developed as the family gathered around the large fireplace in the sitting room to talk or play various games.

However the animosity between Natalie and Kathryn grew to such an astounding level that it succeeded in making anyone else in the same vicinity uncomfortable. In order to avoid Natalie and Lindsey, Kathryn, who was still conducting training sessions regardless of the snow and cold, took to holding a brief training session between her two shifts and a more extensive session once the fourth shift had left. When Matt inquired about the change,

Kathryn had claimed that practicing in dim light would help them later on, refusing to expand further on her explanation. When Matt remarked that Luke, Tyler, and Natalie, who had participated in the afternoon sessions would be excluded since it was not taking place during their shift, she'd replied that Luke and Tyler were capable of holding their own and that Natalie had never participated in the lessons to begin with. She'd also suggested that the rest of the Dragons should use the afternoons to practice before the evening session.

But simply changing the times of the training sessions did not relieve her of Natalie's extensive irritations. Lindsey, who followed Natalie's every lead, had joined the battle on her friend's side. Natalie was always trying to make monumental changes and more often than not; Kathryn vetoed her plans, for that reason Natalie began to hate the younger girl even more than she had originally.

At every opportunity the two girls made Kathryn's life harder and much more difficult than it ever should have been. At every meal Natalie and Lindsey asked pointed questions about Kathryn's past and continued to pursue the matter until someone else changed topics. Eventually, Kathryn began to eat her meal separately. Natalie never took anything to Kathryn that she felt needed to be addressed. In the beginning she had taken her complaints to David, but he had begun to question Natalie as to why she didn't approach Kathryn with her concerns. For a while, Natalie had come up with fabricated excuses; "Kathryn was busy training with Matt", "Kathryn was lying down in her room and I didn't want to bother her", "Kathryn was..." her list of reasons were endless, but as her frustration against Kathryn grew she finally just began to overtly complain about her to anyone who would listen.

David had been a wonderful listener, sympathetic to her woes, even tactfully voicing his own frustration with their vexing second-in-command, but one day David stopped sympathizing with her and began to brush off her irritation. At one point he even reprimanded her for not attempting to work out her differences with the younger girl. Natalie was shocked...and angry. She didn't know what had happened to change David's attitude toward Kathryn, but she was furious because now David resented her attitude and her standing in his eyes had dropped. Natalie decided to take matters into her own hands. If she deemed that something needed fixing, and there was at least one thing each day, she fixed it herself—without discussing it with anyone. More often than not, Kathryn would quietly observe the new changes and then order Natalie to change everything back. Natalie would change everything back simply out of fear that the younger girl would call her out onto the training fields and humiliate her even further in a combat exercise.

On one particular day, Natalie had decided that the living room was too drab and plain for her tastes so she, and Lindsey, had begun to redecorate the entire room in bright feminine colors. Once Kathryn had learned about the project she confronted Natalie, asking if she had asked any of the boys, or even the other girls, and if they had agreed with her decision.

Natalie, knowing very well that she hadn't even bothered to hint to the others what she had been planning, tried to sweet talk her way out of it. Kathryn didn't so much as blink when she ordered Natalie to remove the purple, yellow, and deep pink fabrics from the numerous chairs and couches, remove the heart doilies from the tables, and throw out the heavily scented flowers that had been placed about the room.

Natalie was furious beyond words. She stared at the younger girl who kept impinging on her freedom. "I can decorate any way I want to! Lord Jasse said so!" she exclaimed, for once not moving to comply with Kathryn's orders.

The younger woman narrowed her eyes at her. "You can decorate your own space any way you wish," she agreed. "You *cannot* decorate to your own tastes and desires any place that is shared by this family," she said coldly, her tone brooking no argument. "There are thirteen other people in this house, Natalie; you cannot dictate their tastes and preferences."

However Natalie, tired of Kathryn's imperious attitude over something as simple as decorating, wasn't about to stand for this correction. "What would *you* know about family?" she hissed angrily. "Especially this one! You don't spend any time around the rest of us, going off all the time to that forest with only *animals* for company. You spend all your time alone. You're a freak!" she paused, waiting for a reaction, but to her disappointment got none.

Fine. She would try harder. She had personally learned long ago that words were far more damaging than any physical wound and since she didn't have the skills to out spar Kathryn she was going to wound her where she knew she could. "You're a rock without emotions. You don't feel. I'll bet you aren't even human," she saw the muscles around Kathryn's eyes twitch and kept going. "No one here likes you. No one wants to be around you. We hate you! Everyone else is too afraid of you to say it but I'm not! Why were you even placed in this family? Why were you even made a Guardian? You're a freak, a wanderer, an outcast!" She practically spit the words at her enemy, who still had not said anything, and aside from the twitch around her eyes, hadn't reacted.

Kathryn stared at her for a few long moments, her face impassive, finally she spoke in a calm voice, "If you want to make any changes in this house you consult with David and the rest of the family *before* you make those changes. Am I clear?" Her voice had taken on a deadly tone and Natalie, despite all her rage, felt a moment of fear and nodded, determining deep in her mind to make life even more miserable for the Dragons' second-in-command.

℘·℃

Kathryn left to take her last shift, which seemed to last forever. Blessedly the day was cloudless, the sun shone brightly on the snow, and even more importantly, there was no hint of a breeze. Nothing serious happened and for once Kathryn wished she could have fought someone. Amy seemed to notice how tense her friend was and constantly asked if she was alright and was slightly taken aback when her friend actually snapped at her.

When the shift was done, Kathryn didn't even return the meadow. She sent the others on ahead and instead went to her waterfall. It didn't matter to her that the sun had already set. She knew the way to her sanctuary by heart and today not even darkness would stop her from seeking comfort there. As Lerina, who by now also knew the way by memory, navigated the path Kathryn felt her muscles coiling with stress. For three weeks the weather had been so bad that not even she had dared venture far beyond the boundary. David had even canceled patrols for a whole standard work week, seven days, reasoning that not even the worst troublemaker would risk life and limb venturing out into the storm. Kathryn had cursed the weather vehemently. If it hadn't been for the snow, wind, and ice, she wouldn't have been stuck in the house with Natalie for three weeks. Fortunately Natalie had behaved herself for the seven days that the patrols had been canceled, but as soon as David had reestablished patrols, she had been back to her normal self. When she had, Kathryn had retreated to the barn, nestling down in Lerina's stall for warmth. On the rare occasion that Natalie had ventured out of the house to try and find her, she'd retreated briefly to the loft and rafters until the older girl had left, often shivering violently. Kathryn couldn't comprehend why Natalie insisted on wearing fashionable dresses in the biting cold, but was grateful as they generally confined her to the warmer climate of the house.

They reached the meadow and Kathryn dismounted. She turned to look in the direction where she knew the frozen column of ice that used to be the waterfall lay. Not for the first time she considered walking out onto the frozen pond and breaking the ice. In these temperatures she wouldn't last long dry even with the cirin. If she was plunged in the frozen pond she wouldn't stand a chance even if she got help.

No. She told herself firmly. *That's the coward's way out.*

Her subconscious rebutted, *it would solve all your problems.*

True, it would solve all of her problems, at least where Natalie was concerned. She clenched her teeth. *I am not a coward.*

Then why don't you stand up for yourself? Her subconscious mocked.

Destiny swooped down beside her, but not even her oldest friend could comfort Kathryn now.

Kathryn knelt in the snow, the tears she had held in check for the last four radians poured down her cheeks. For the first time since she was eight, she didn't try to stop them. She let them fall.

She had failed. Failed Jasse, failed David, failed her new family, had failed herself. She had tried to put down roots, to try and befriend the strangers who had become her family. It hadn't been hard to convince everyone to take part in the regular training sessions, and she'd felt some sense of accomplishment knowing that she was helping them sharpen their ability to defend themselves. On a few cold nights, she'd helped Jenna and Tyler with their herbal tinctures and poultices and they'd seemed appreciative. She had thought she was, slowly, succeeding. But Natalie was right. What did she know about family?

Nothing.

Absolutely nothing.

Natalie's words echoed through her mind. *"No one here likes you. No one wants to be around you. We hate you! Everyone else is too afraid of you to say it but I'm not! Why were you even placed in this family? Why were you even made a Guardian? You're a freak, a wanderer, an outcast!"*

Why had she been placed into this family? She had thought that having Amy in her family would make things easier. It hadn't. If anything it was making it harder. Natalie had noticed that Amy had been placed on a shift with Kathryn, while Lindsey wasn't on her shift, and had complained to Kathryn about it. Kathryn had told her to take it up with David, which had done nothing to endear her to the older girl.

The others in the Dragons were nice enough, but even though they were all aware of the tension between the three girls, no one had made any attempt to intervene. Kathryn couldn't truly blame them. Natalie rivaled Lady Blackwood when she was angry. Still, she harbored some resentment for it. She was looking out for the interests of the whole family and when she got burned for it, and Natalie's temper sometimes caused her gift to create small flames at the tips of her fingers, no one was willing to say anything on her behalf. No, it wasn't resentment she felt, although it may have started out as it, it was disgust. She lived in a house of Guardians, protectors of the realm, who were supposed to stand up for the weak and oppressed and not one of them were willing to take a stand in their own house.

It reinforced the one truth Kathryn had learned from an early age. Depend on no one for anything. Fight your own battles and trust no one.

Kathryn shifted so that she was sitting on the ground, hugging her knees to her chest. She could never reveal to Natalie just how much her words had seared her heart. Her accusations were eerily familiar to Lady Blackwood's accusations and had brought back extremely unpleasant memories.

She sighed. Natalie had asked why she was a Guardian. But Kathryn didn't know what she would do if she *wasn't* a Guardian. She hated the society nobles and their superior notions of themselves.

That's not entirely true, she had to admit to herself. *I enjoy spending time with Lord Jasse and Princess Jasmine...although they aren't exactly the typical noble.*

But the others she met reminded her too much of the Blackwoods. The way they carried themselves, how they walked and sat properly and stiffly as they bantered and postured showing who was the cleverest or most knowledgeable about any and every subject. She particularly disliked their treatment of the commons, but neither could she identify with the peasants and farmers. Perhaps the best choice would be to disappear and live a life alone high in the mountains with Destiny and Lerina where no one could find her.

She had the skills to pull it off, she realized. She *could* disappear where no one could find her, not even the Guardians. But she was trained to be a Guardian, and deep down into the very depths of her being she lived and breathed to be a Guardian. If she left, she didn't know what she would do.

No. She was a Guardian. She couldn't abandon her duty. She would stay.

She was a survivor too. She had survived living with her uncle, she had survived living with the Blackwoods, and she had survived the school. She would survive with the Dragons. Once she retired she could live apart from any living person. She just had to survive once more.

Time to revert back to old habits, surviving here won't be that much different than Blackwood Manor and my uncle's house. The same techniques would work here as well.

I will survive.

ℰ·ℬ

So began a contest of wills.

Once a week, Natalie would continue to enter Kathryn's room and redecorate, always in red and pink, or red and black.

For her part, Kathryn continued to burn the decorating supplies and retreat to the waterfall when the weather allowed, enjoying the one time during the day when she could be alone. This continued to irritate and infuriate Natalie to no end, but she wasn't skilled enough to track the Dragon's second-in-command despite the snow, although there were many times she had tried.

Amy and the other Dragons noticed Kathryn's stiffness and increasing silence and wondered how they could possibly intervene? Natalie and Lindsey were driving their lieutenant from them and while Kathryn wasn't the friendliest person they'd ever met, she'd seemed to have their interests at heart. A few had considered bringing up the topic to David, but his occasional frustrated looks at Kathryn hadn't suggested the conversation would be well received. Not to mention they had no physical proof that Natalie and Lindsey were harassing the younger girl. The duo were the picture of perfect innocence whenever David was around, acting hurt when Kathryn was brusque with them. If he hadn't been so distracted with his new position and reporting daily to the Council, he might have noticed the problems brewing.

One day Amy finished stabling her horse early and was returning to her room when she noticed three red hearts under and around Kathryn's door. Opening her friend's door to return them she received the shock of her life. The room was a mind swirling riot of pink and red.

Knowing Kathryn as she did, Amy knew her friend hadn't done this and it didn't take much thinking to point Natalie's incessant questions and famous closet of fabric as the guilty party.

She left Kathryn's room, hoping that her friend would confront Natalie when she came home. She was bitterly disappointed. Kathryn never said a word. Amy tried to find Kathryn to talk to her about it, but, even though she knew her friend hadn't gone into the forest, she was nowhere to be found—unbeknownst to Amy and the rest of the Dragons, late at night Kathryn had taken to seeking solace in the small add-on that Jenna used to store her herbal supplies. There was one bright spot about the whole affair; Amy now had physical proof of Natalie's harassment. And she was determined to put a stop to it all.

The next morning she sought out David. Finding him alone was the best thing she could have hoped for.

"Good morning Amy!" he called from the barn loft, a pitchfork of hay in his hands. "What brings you out here?"

133

Instead of immediately replying, Amy climbed the ladder up to the loft. When she was standing before him she replied, "I need to talk to you about something."

Hearing the seriousness of her tone, David put down the pitchfork and settled onto a hay bale. Amy remained standing.

"What's wrong?"

Amy looked him straight in the eye. "Have you noticed anything going on between Natalie, Lindsey, and Kathryn?"

David looked confused. "No, I can't say that I have," he admitted. "Up until a few weeks ago Natalie used to vent her frustration with Kathryn at me, but she stopped after I suggested she try and work out their differences." He didn't add that for a while he had actually *joined* Natalie in those venting episodes until one day he had realized how wrong it was for him as the Dragon's leader to participate in such activities. To voice his own doubt and frustration in Kathryn, however tactfully he worded it, was as good as condemning her before the whole family. He'd stopped immediately. When Natalie had stopped coming to him, he'd assumed that she'd taken his advice. Amy's presence was starting to suggest otherwise.

She nodded. "I didn't think so."

He frowned. "What's that supposed to mean?"

"You're not here all the time to observe the goings on around here, but let me tell you, this family is not functioning like it should be."

David looked startled. "We seem to get along fine to me."

"Most of us do," Amy replied. "But for some reason Natalie and Lindsey have gotten it into their heads to make life miserable for Kathryn. I happen to know that Natalie recently entered Kathryn's room and decorated the place for her."

"What?" David stood up in disbelief and anger. "Why?"

Amy shrugged helplessly. "I'm not exactly sure. Perhaps Natalie feels that Kathryn curbs her freedom too much."

"Does she?"

Amy paused. "Not that I've seen, but it could be possible, although I doubt it."

"Why do you doubt it?"

Amy fixed her stare on him. "You know Kathryn's past?"

He nodded briefly. "I know in general what happened."

"Then you should know that revenge and retaliation have been hammered out of her. She wouldn't curb someone else's freedom, it's too important to her."

"Even after all our training?"

"Our training teaches us to fight for others. Kathryn's never learned to fight for herself."

David was silent as he thought this over. Finally he said, "The only way Kathryn will ever learn to defend herself is if she takes up the initiative and does it herself."

Amy sat down. "How can she take up the initiative if her way of protecting herself is to hide?"

"Hide?"

"She hides herself away to avoid getting hurt."

He sighed heavily. "I knew this was going to be difficult, I just didn't realize how difficult."

"What are you going to do?"

"For right now? Nothing."

Amy started to protest, but he cut her off. "As much as I would love to just take your word on this, I can't approach Natalie or Lindsey without seeing it myself first."

"You think I'm lying to you?"

David quickly shook his head. "No. I've just got to actually witness this before I make a decision on how to act."

"And just how are you going to notice if you're on shift when this happens?" Amy asked pointedly.

Letting out another sigh David replied, "I don't know."

"Will you at least tell Natalie to stop invading Kathryn's privacy?"

David nodded." That is a serious offense. You're sure it's Natalie?"

"Who else has a million bolts of fabric that she can just cut up and use as decoration?"

ⅎ·℞

That evening David confronted Natalie, who grudgingly admitted the crime. Other than a stern lecture and a warning, David could do very little in the form of punishment or restitution. The girls would have to make their own peace. He just wished he would be around to observe what actually took place between Kathryn and Natalie.

Chapter 13

A week later the opportunity landed in his lap. The streak of storms seemed to have finally passed and by now the Dragons were used to trudging through snow and occasionally slipping on hidden ice patches during their shifts. The nicer weather was still a hazard though. The sun glared off the snow, blinding everyone who wandered about their business. Oftentimes, David felt like light gifted Guardians were practicing their gift in his face. If it weren't for their special masks, the Guardians would have been in danger of going blind. The locals, however, were used to dealing with the severe winters of their region and as soon as the storms passed, they had doggedly cleared the streets and set up a rotating watch of residents at the animal troughs to break the ice that continually formed. They even had their own version of the masks the Guardians wore, wrapping thick scarves around their heads and pulling a thin ladies stocking across their eyes. David had been impressed at their ability to continue on with life when all he wanted to do was sit in front of a roaring fire all day.

As the first shift returned, David led Cass, Elizabeth, and Lindsey south to where Kathryn had been attacked during her second day on duty. He wanted another look at the place where the bandits had been, as well as to make sure that the troublemakers who seemed to enjoy poisoning water and crops hadn't returned. Matt had told him how Kathryn, once they had all had about a dozen shift's experience, had split her shifts up even further to cover more territory and David had quickly implemented the practice into his own shifts. It was a practice that he found worked very well. He had also been impressed, and mildly amused, to learn about the training sessions she held during his last shift. For the first time he began to wonder if the council *had* known what it was doing when they assigned Kathryn to be his lieutenant.

He sent Lindsey and Cass to check out the villages while he and Elizabeth headed towards the forest. Three radians later David honestly admitted to himself that he would never win awards for tracking. That was Kathryn's specialty.

Elizabeth, spotting some churned up snow of interest, headed off to the right. After David dismounted he moved more to the left and nearly impaled himself on a sword that was suddenly thrust at his chest. Reflex already had him taking several steps off the line of attack and past the sword and he couldn't help but wonder if this was the same bandit who had attacked Kathryn and gotten away.

He shifted slightly to position himself for another attack, and finally got a glimpse of his attacker. And just as quickly came to the conclusion that this was not the bandit Kathryn had faced. Or if she had, she had not gotten as good a look at him as she had thought. Kathryn had described a large man with a limp in his left leg with one arm longer than the other.

The man facing him was huge with a smooth walk and even arms. He also had muscles that looked as if he had stuck a couple of Cass's airy loaves beneath his sleeves. David knew that his best defense against such a brute would be to stay out of reach until he came up with a plan to outsmart him. At the moment, David was positioning himself to strike his left thigh and calve figuring that he could win by letting the monster in front of him bleed out by surprising him with a series of rapid leg slashes.

Easier said than done. When the brute's first swing caught David on his shoulder he felt pain and shock. The second strike came while his arm was still numb. Attempting to retreat out of the man's reach, David was only partially successful. The sword grazed his back and David could feel an uncoiling across his other shoulder as the blade sliced muscle. The shock of the impact was compounded by the simple fact that he *was* injured.

The sword had cut right through the Cirin cloth, an act that should have been impossible. He could already feel the biting cold of the air against his exposed skin. He glanced at his opponent's weapon. It was almost identical to the sword he had encountered on his first day on duty.

This is not good. These swords weren't hacked to pieces after a few parries. David had a real fight on his hands and with only one partially usable shoulder to get him through it.

His opponent lunged at him and David rolled. His back connected with various stones and broken twigs that had been hidden beneath the snow. Grimacing against the pain of grit and other forest debris imbedding in the wound he knew that the biggest danger he faced was frostbite. He could almost feel the muscles tearing more in his right shoulder. The Guardian threw one of his daggers at the man, who ducked, but didn't manage to completely avoid the blade.

David decided that just having one ear did nothing to add to the man's rugged looks as his opponent howled in pain and fixed him with a bloodlust glare—a glare that turned glassy eyed before the big man literally fell forward and lay still, Elizabeth's dagger embedded in his back.

Moving slowly, David edged to where the sword now lay. Elizabeth came up behind him and eyed his wounds. "Jenna's going to need to look at that." Her voice sounded as shocked as he felt.

"I know. Let me grab this blasted sword and we can get—*what in blazes?*"

Even as he spoke the mystery sword appeared to be melting before his eyes, turning into a river of red fluid that looked suspiciously like blood, before seeping into the snow. They stared at the spot for a moment longer.

Finally David, the pain in his back starting to become more pronounced, said somewhat haltingly, "I guess we can go now."

They quickly joined up with Lindsey and Cass, both of whom were stunned at his injury. But if they were shocked then Jenna was horrified. Upon seeing his injury she immediately put him to bed and ordered him to stay put.

Kathryn took over his last shift, making David feel a little guilty, but assured that he would be up and around the next day...or so he thought.

Jenna refused to let him out of bed the next day, claiming that it took more than ten radians to heal and David wasn't feeling strong enough to protest. Kathryn took on all of his responsibilities that day, making David feel like a pathetic noble who couldn't handle getting scratched, but Jenna was adamant.

"You are not allowed to move until I tell you," she ordered as she changed his bandages. "Kathryn is strong, she can handle it."

David planned to be back on duty by the next morning. Unfortunately, his wounds got infected and he came down with a high fever.

Jenna was mystified, the Cirin should have prevented infection but their leader was getting worse and worse. To Jenna it looked like the Cirin *itself* had contracted the illness and was passing it on to its wearer...and she was powerless to stop it. Finally she decided to remove the Cirin. While she cared for David, Tyler worked with the infected Cirin. Both healers appropriated an extra back room off the side of the house as an area where Jenna could mix poultices and herbal rubs and Tyler could try to figure out what was wrong with David's armor. At night, after Kathryn finished with the rounds, she would often join them. Before long Jenna had her mixing the poultices and herbal rubs while she and Tyler focused on the Cirin.

Even with the Cirin removed, David was delirious with fever for two days, at one point he scared Jenna out of her wits when she entered and found him not breathing, but she quickly remedied the situation and he began to mend.

Fortunately, the fever broke on the evening on the third day. After a short meal consisting of broth, bread, and pureed fruit he was able to sit up by himself and recounted the events of the ambush with Kathryn, who listened expressionlessly before promising to be on the lookout for bandits with a similar agenda. Everyone was relieved at his recovery and took turns visiting him. After a radian, Jenna had enough of that and had to shoo out several family members while ordering more bed rest for David.

On the morning of the fourth day David tossed his bed sheet and sat on the edge of his bed. This sudden move startled Jenna out of her light doze and she stood up out of her chair.

"And just what do you think you are doing?"

"Jenna, I am ready and fit for work," David announced.

"No you're not, Jenna protested. I will let you know when you are ready."

"Jenna, you need to stop mothering me." And with that said David promptly stood up and made for the door. Before he took a second step, all color drained from his face and he collapsed like a marionette whose strings had just been cut. Jenna managed to catch him before he did a face plant and wrestled him back into bed.

"Mothering," she gasped while crabbing him back under the sheets. "If this is mothering I'm giving you up for adoption!"

Unbeknownst to David, Luke had stepped up to alleviate some of the pressure Kathryn was bearing, leading one team while Kathryn took the other three. It wasn't much, but it helped.

It was during this time that Luke came up with an idea. Hesitantly he shared it with Amy who quickly agreed. Together they hastily spread the plan, asking for approval and having it accepted by the rest of the family.

One week after David was injured he voluntarily took the first and third shifts, giving Kathryn a morning to sleep in. It was only after she'd agreed that he realized that by forcing her to take the later shifts he was altering her sleeping habits. He'd have to find a way to make up for that mistake.

As Kathryn, Tyler, Natalie, and Luke left for the final shift, David found himself confronted by the rest of the Dragons. Amy, obviously the chosen spokesperson, stepped forward. "We have a proposal for you."

℘·℃

Kathryn's head ached abominably as her team made their way home for the night. It was just her luck that she would take a rather severe blow to the head within the first radian from a desperate, and drunk, farmer. Her determination and skull were too thick for the blow to cause serious damage, but it was enough to leave her with a pounding headache.

All she cared about right now was getting home and collapsing into her bed. It was doubly unfortunate that she was with Natalie right now, who was chattering beyond comprehension, apparently oblivious, even though Kathryn knew it was an act, to the agony Kathryn was in. Luke and Tyler had noticed her ever increasing frown and knit brow and tried to still Natalie's endless stream of chatter, but were largely unsuccessful in that endeavor.

To everyone's complete surprise the windows were lit up as they approached the house. Even more surprising was when the door opened to reveal every member of the family, who stood waiting in anxious anticipation.

"What's going on?" Kathryn asked, alert even though she felt like dropping.

David looked at her grimly. "There's been a mutiny while you were away."

Kathryn, too tired to attempt comprehension, merely stared at him. "A what?"

Before David could reply the rest of the group ushered them inside and into the sitting room.

Kathryn waited silently for someone—anyone to continue.

Amy turned to her. "Luke came up with a brilliant plan." Was it Kathryn's imagination or was her friend blushing slightly? Had Amy, who had sworn off men from the day Kathryn had known her, developed a crush? She would have to talk with her friend later.

Luke stood and faced her. "We've decided we don't like David's plan for shifts," he informed her seriously. "We want some changes made."

Kathryn opted for the direct approach, "Such as?"

"You and David get Lumbar and Nénar off."

Kathryn couldn't have been more surprised if they had informed her she was queen. "What?"

Amy stood. "You and David work twice as hard as we do, pulling two shifts a day. In this last week, you've pulled about four times your regular work load alone and that got Luke thinking..."

Luke jumped in. "It's all fine and well that we have a leader and a second-in-command, but who's going to alleviate some of the pressure from the second if the first is indisposed?"

139

"Something we certainly learned this week," Kathryn said slowly, thinking about how Luke had voluntarily stepped up and led his shift in order for her to get some rest. In all honesty, the work hadn't been that stressful, she'd been worked harder at the Blackwoods. The long radians of patrol merely gave her something to focus on as well as an escape from Natalie. When she led the fourth shift, she would split them up into three teams so that she never ended up working with Natalie. It had worked well, except for tonight when they'd all become entangled in the tavern brawl. But apparently the others had felt that she wasn't strong enough to handle so many patrols and after some thought she'd been more than willing to give up the one patrol she'd been sharing with Natalie.

"Well, we've come up with a plan to help lighten the pressure you two carry," Luke explained. "Both you and David will have two consecutive days off each week."

"Two whole days?"

"Yes, those days will be your time to relax."

"It isn't fair that you're giving us two days off and yourselves none—after a few weeks you'll hate it," Kathryn predicted.

Jenna shook her head. "I don't believe that will be case, in any case we don't carry the pressures of responsibility that you do. In order for you to make good and mutually beneficial choices you cannot be constantly worn down to a thread. Besides, we made sure we'll all get a day of rest."

Rachel spoke up. "After what happened this week we decided that you two would need a time to completely relax and have the pressures lifted so you will be fresh when decisions do need to be made."

Kathryn turned back to Jenna. "Explain what you meant when you said everyone will get a day off."

"We worked out a new system for the weekends," Amy explained. "On Lumbar I will take Daniel, Tyler, Cassandra, Lindsey, and Elizabeth for an all day shift. On Nénar Luke, Matt, Rachel, Leia, Jenna, and Natalie will have an all day shift. In the end all of us will get at least one day off. You and David work harder than we do, so we decided you should receive two days off."

Kathryn turned to look at David. "And you agreed to this?"

"At the time it didn't seem like I had much of a choice," he grinned.

"Then I guess I can work with it as well," Kathryn said as she rubbed her aching forehead.

"Then that means," Luke said quickly. "That Amy and her shift had better get to sleep now since tomorrow's Lumbar."

Everybody dispersed and went upstairs, leaving Kathryn and David alone.

"We're starting to live and act like a family," David commented as the last door closed quietly.

Kathryn just nodded her agreement, then after a few moments asked, "Are you sure about this? The whole reason you set up the shifts like you did was so that one of us would always be present."

He nodded. "I did, yes. But Amy and Luke raised a very good point. What happens if both the leader and second-in-command are unreachable or indisposed? I had it set up assuming that either you or myself would always be available. We've just learned it won't always be that way. Luke and Amy have proven themselves responsible enough I trust them to lead."

"I was impressed by Luke's offer to lead his shift," Kathryn replied quietly. And she had been. She would have been more impressed if it hadn't been because he, and the others, hadn't considered her too weak to handle such long hours.

David studied her for a long moment and for once she wished she had Jasse's gift of telepathy. Surely he didn't think her weak as well?

Finally he said, "Another reason I'm allowing this. Luke has leadership qualities, as does Amy. They just need experience to strengthen them."

"What makes you sure they won't challenge your leadership once they've had a taste of it?"

"I don't," David admitted. "But eventually all of us will need to learn to lead. During a war we will all be troop leaders."

"That's true," Kathryn was rubbing her head again. The only problem with his logic was that the last recorded war Archaea had been involved in had occurred several hundred years ago; and it had been more of a brief uprising than an actual war.

"Are you okay?"

"I'm just tired. I guess I'll turn in." Kathryn turned and headed up the stairs to her room.

David watched her go, wondering what it would take to get her to open up to the rest of them.

౸·౬

David rose early the next morning. Even though he wasn't leading the team, he still wanted to be there when they left. Kathryn wasn't up yet, but considering how much her head had been hurting last night he wasn't surprised. Shaking his head he thought back to last night and Kathryn's brush off of his concern. It had been obvious to him, and probably everyone else that Kathryn hadn't been feeling well. The way she kept rubbing her forehead made it clear it was a headache. She seemed to get a lot of them, either that or she just rubbed her head a lot. It wasn't until he'd caught up with Luke that he'd heard about her knock to the head, as well as the cause for it. He was going to have to talk to Natalie about reckless behavior.

Amy was in the kitchen helping Matt pack their midday meal and supper. She looked up when he walked in. "Good morning. What are you doing up?"

"Habit I guess," he admitted as he snatched a roll. "You guys all ready?"

She snorted. "Right, habit. Because you were always up when Kathryn and the others were heading out the door before the break of dawn," she said sarcastically.

He grinned sheepishly. "I was on the first day."

"Only because you were on patrol that day," she countered.

"Point," he sighed.

We're ready and stop worrying, we'll be fine."

It was as if she could read his mind.

"Your face is as open as a book," Amy grunted as she slipped the pack onto her back.

141

David finished his roll. "I'll have to work on that then, I guess."

"Any special plans for today?"

"Nope."

"Beware, Natalie might have a few suggestions."

He laughed. "I'll bear that in mind. Be careful, stay safe."

Amy grinned at him as she joined the others. "Always."

They left the house and he returned to the kitchen to keep Matt company. "What's for breakfast Matt?"

"Eggs, fried venison, biscuits, and fresh juice."

David's mouth watered at the thought. "Sounds delicious."

"I should hope so," Matt laughed. "It'd better be after all the work I put into it!"

"Do you want me to wake everyone else up?"

"It's still early yet, why not let them sleep in?"

Dave grinned. "And miss the look on Natalie's face when I tell her it's not even dawn yet?"

Matt snorted. "It's your funeral friend."

David pulled himself up onto the counter and watched Matt cook. The warmth from the cooking surface invigorated and soothed his back. After a while he asked, "Have you noticed anything going on between Natalie and Kathryn?"

"You mean other than the fact that Natalie hates Kathryn?" Matt asked as he poured some batter into the skillet, it sizzled and snapped as it came into contract with the hot oil.

David paused. "Hate is a strong word, Matt."

"There's really no other word for it," The redhead replied.

"How bad is it really?"

Matt looked at him. "Let's say not good, and leave it at that."

David made a face. "That bad, huh?"

"The midday meal isn't exactly a time for lighthearted conversation in this house," Matt informed him.

"Do you think any trouble will arise this morning?"

His friend paused. "Hard to say, with you around Natalie just might behave herself. She has in the past."

"Why hasn't anyone brought this to my attention before?"

Matt turned and looked at him. "And tell you what? That Natalie and Lindsay were talking Kathryn to death? All we saw was an endless stream of pointed questions and a few sharp comments every day or so. We had no proof that they were doing anything else and a few of us were worried that you'd consider Kathryn's reaction extreme."

Well if that wasn't a testament to their honest opinion of his leadership, David didn't know what it was. And it burned. He'd tried so hard to be a good leader, trying to be fair across the table with everyone in his family. But a small part of him realized that *that* would have been his reaction had he been told. Were his own initial experiences with Kathryn coloring his judgment where she was concerned? As he considered the redhead's words, David slid down from the counter, stood and reached to snatch one of the fresh biscuits out of the basket they had been arranged in.

142

"Hey!" Matt protested. "Those are for later."

David grinned. "You can't expect me to sit here for another radian just looking at them can you?"

As he lifted the still warm biscuit to his mouth he spotted movement around Matt's collar. Curious he peered closer, only to find himself face to face with a green and purple lizard about the size of his hand. It hissed at him and stuck its tongue out at him. Unfortunately for David he had moved close enough, and the forked orange tongue was long enough, for it to hit him squarely on the nose.

He jerked back. "Um, Matt...you do realize that you have a lizard sitting on you, right?"

"Oh, her?" Matt turned his head and stroked the top of the lizard's head. David swore that it began to purr like a contented cat. "That's just Lacey...she's harmless."

David eyed the lizard doubtfully. "Harmless..." he repeated, wiping his nose with the cuff of his sleeve. *Why do all of the Dragon's pets hate me?* He wondered. *First Destiny and now Lacey?* He hoped that it wasn't about to become a pattern.

At a radian after sunrise Luke, Rachel, and Leia joined the two boys in the kitchen.

"I thought I smelled something delicious," Luke commented hungrily, sniffing the air.

"Would you like me to wake Jenna and Natalie?" Rachel asked.

Matt grinned. "Why not? Breakfast is ready... so, by definition, it's time they woke up."

David eyed him. "Whose definition?"

Matt skillfully transferred the eggs from the frying pan to a serving platter. "Mine."

Rachel turned to leave and David said, "Kathryn's still asleep too. You might want to grab her as well."

Rachel looked surprised. "She's still in bed? Usually she's the first one up."

"She had a killer of a headache last night," David explained.

"In that case first I'll see if it's gone, and then I'll let her know breakfast is ready." Rachel hurried upstairs while David helped Leia set the table.

A bellow from the kitchen brought them running. David couldn't stop from laughing as he took in the ridiculous sight. Luke was sprawled on the floor with his legs apart, looking for all the kingdom like he'd just taken a blow from an opponent ten times his size, while Matt was precariously balanced on the countertop standing on his tiptoes, reaching for Lacey who was perched at the topmost corner of the cabinet. "You didn't have to scare her," the redhead was complaining as he attempted to coax the reptile off her perch.

"She *licked* me!" Luke wiped his cheek with his sleeve, which was already red from his earlier scrubbing.

"Lacey doesn't like you either, huh?" David observed through his mirth.

"Like me?" Stuttering and motioning with his finger, he went on, "th, that, that purple thing was tasting me!" Incredulous he demanded a response from Matt, "Does that thing bite?" Before Matt could respond David's words registered and Luke turned an accusing glare on his friend. "You *knew* about this?"

"Sure!" David responded enthusiastically. "I've known about Laney, sorry, *Lacey* for five minutes!"

Luke continued to glare as Leia helped him up. "This isn't funny."

"No it isn't!" Matt agreed emphatically as he finally dismounted from the countertop, Lacey cupped in his hands. "You scared her to death, Luke!"

"A lizard, Matt? Really?" Luke shot back. "Why couldn't you befriend a dog?"

"Because dogs are too common place," Matt returned shortly. "Now get out of the kitchen unless you want ashes for breakfast." His ultimatum delivered, Matt returned his attention to his cooking, occasionally talking calmly to his newfound friend.

Luke stared in amazement for a few moments before David tugged him out of the kitchen. "Come on, Luke. Let's finish setting the table."

Five minutes later Rachel returned. "They're on their way." She announced as she took a seat, and then grinned, "Although Natalie wasn't too happy about it."

Luke grinned. "I'm just glad it was you and not me waking her up."

"What was the commotion I heard a few minutes ago?"

Luke ducked his head. "Don't ask," he muttered sourly.

Rachel sent a questioning look at Leia who motioned *later* with her hand.

Minutes later the three girls appeared in the dining room. As usual Kathryn was completely dressed and her hair pulled back into her usual bun. Destiny, who was riding on her arm, started getting restless until Kathryn finally opened a window and shooed her outside. Jenna had managed to get dressed and was in the midst of brushing her long blond hair. Natalie however was still in her dressing robe, hair tousled, and a deep frown etched into her face. David tried not to correlate their respective morning habits with their maturity. After what he'd just learned about Natalie, he failed in her case.

Cheerfully Matt brought out the breakfast dishes and they all ate heartily. Luke kept glancing suspiciously at Matt, but as far as David could tell, could spot no sign of Lacey.

"Do you have any plans for today, Dave?" Natalie asked after they had eaten.

David noticed she looked more awake now that she had eaten and her frown had mostly disappeared. "Not particularly no, why?"

Natalie shrugged. "I was wondering if we could visit the village today."

Kathryn and Jenna, who had been in the process of clearing the dishes, stopped and stared at her. Even Matt, who had been suspecting something big, was taken aback. All looked at David waiting for his answer.

He thought about for a couple moments. "I guess I don't see why we couldn't go," he finally decided.

Natalie shrieked with delight and ran upstairs to change.

"I hope you know what you've just gotten yourself into," Matt warned.

144

"What we've gotten ourselves into," David corrected. "We're all going."

"I'm not going," Kathryn spoke up, surprising them all.

Dave turned to face her. "Why not?"

She turned to face him, her face expressionless. "I need to exercise Destiny and I can't do that while visiting the village."

"Can't you do that after we get back?"

"No."

He turned to her looking very surprised. "Why not?"

"Because we're going to be gone all day."

David frowned at her. "I don't know if I like the idea of you going out by yourself."

"I'm not going to be alone. Destiny and Lerina will be with me," she reminded him somewhat sharply.

At her words, David was sent back in time to the day he met her on the cliffs—when she had tersely informed him that she wasn't climbing alone and that Lord Jasse had approved Destiny to be her companion. Finally he nodded.

Kathryn stood and without saying another word exited the house.

"Is she always like this?" David asked the remainder of his team.

Jenna nodded slowly. "Kathryn keeps to herself, especially now that Natalie and Lindsey are haranguing her every chance they get."

Luke shook his head sadly. "Now we barely even see her between shifts, she completes her chores, gives about a one radian training session for the rest of us, and then disappears into the forest and doesn't return until her second shift begins."

So Matt had been telling the truth. Everyone had noticed. Except him. "Does anyone know where she goes?"

Matt looked at him in amazement. "Have you ever tried to track her? It's like trying to track the air—impossible." He cocked his head to one side. "Maybe I should ask her for extra lessons..." Mulling over the idea, he retreated back into the kitchen.

Tracking the air, David thought. *I can track the air with my power.*

"I seriously doubt that she'll spend all day exercising with Destiny," Jenna added. "It was probably just an excuse so that she doesn't have to spend all day in Natalie's company."

David frowned. "I guess that's one thing I'll have to work on."

"What do you have to work on?" Natalie asked as she bounded into the room.

Slightly startled David shook his head. "Nothing. Are you ready to go?"

"Yes." She looked around the room. "Where's Kathryn?"

"She decided to spend the day with Destiny."

Natalie nodded happily. "Good, she's boring. I'm glad she's not coming." She turned to ask Jenna a question and missed David's frown.

Chapter 14

After a few more minutes of preparation the group was ready to travel. As they saddled their horses, David caught sight of Kathryn leaving. Hurriedly he put down his bags and rushed toward her. "Kathryn, wait a second."

She paused, turning in her saddle. Destiny sat perched on the horn preening. She wasn't in uniform but wore a white cloak over her similarly colored tunic, jerkin, and tights. Where did she get those clothes? He'd never seen her in anything but black-gray or green.

"Are you sure you won't come with us?"

"I have no interest in seeing a village I've already seen a dozen times while on patrol," she replied tersely.

"And I really do not like the idea of you going off alone, unarmored, and unarmed," he reiterated.

"Something you made abundantly clear at breakfast. And I am armed," she added coldly. Her breath came out in clouds of white frost, giving her the appearance of a snow queen ready to turn him into an icicle.

Even her tone of voice added to the illusion. The ice was warmer than her manner. Oh yes, the distant and cold woman from the cliff was back. "What happens if you get into trouble that you can't handle?" he asked a little impatiently. "How will the rest of us know to come and help you?"

Kathryn pierced him with a look that told him exactly what she thought of *that* idea. "Unlike others in the Dragons," she said coldly. "I don't get into trouble I can't handle."

He had a suspicion he knew exactly who she was referring to. And while he didn't argue with her on that point, he did have another concern. "And what if the situation develops to a point beyond your control? David pointed out. "You can't control every situation."

She looked at him for a long time. Finally she asked, "Do you have a suggestion?"

"Come with us."

"Other than that."

David sighed and thought a moment. His eyes landed on the eagle. "How about using Destiny as a signal?"

Kathryn's eyes flickered towards the bird still perched and preening on her saddle horn, "Destiny as a signal?"

"You train Destiny to fly to me when you're in trouble."

"To you?"

David wished she would drop the condescension in her tone. "Yes to me," he ground out tersely. It was as if she was deliberately trying to make him dislike her. "Train her to come to me and land on my shoulder."

"She won't even let you *pet* her," she reminded him.

"She obeys you. I'm sure you can manage."

"I'll consider it," Kathryn said as she turned to leave.

His irritation overflowed. "One more thing."

146

She turned towards him, impatience flickering across her face for an instant. "Now what?"

"You and Destiny agreed to give a climbing demonstration, when were you planning on showing the rest of the Dragons?"

She gave him a frigid look, reminding him just who exactly had forced her into such an agreement, before she waved her hand around. "Do you see any cliffs around here?" she asked impatiently. "When you see one let me know, otherwise good day."

David watched her ride off before returning to his horse. It had taken tremendous self-control not to remind the agitated woman that there was a training wall in their backyard. He couldn't blame her completely though. He'd let his aggravation dictate his interaction with her. From now on he would put "questioning her competency" first on the topics he should never bring up in her presence. It was a reminder he shouldn't have needed. Logic told him that if he didn't trust her, he would never have let her lead two shifts on her own. So why did every conversation he had with her seem to bring it up?

Exhaling in frustration, this time with himself, he urged Rumer in the direction of the stables. Luke was just exiting, cooing softly to his mount, as he approached.

"Whatever you needed to talk to Kathryn about, I'm guessing it didn't go well," he remarked after taking one look at his friend's face.

David let out a heavy sigh. "I tried to get her to agree to train Destiny to fly to me in case she got into any trouble she couldn't handle."

"I'm pretty sure I can guess how well *that* idea went with her."

David grunted as his friend swung himself up into his saddle. "Luke," he said shaking his head. "For the first time I can understand why Natalie might want to annoy her."

"That bad, huh?"

"I've seen nobles who were nicer."

"Well Kathryn doesn't like feeling boxed in, which I'm sure is what being a part of this family feels like at times."

Throwing a sideways glance at his friend, David asked, "When did you become so wise?"

Luke shrugged. "Guess that's what happens when I spend a lot of time around Amy." He glanced over to where the rest of the group was still saddling and chatting, and then turned back to face his friend speaking in a low tone, "although for being Kathryn's best *human* friend she knows about as much as we do about Kathryn's past."

"Luke," David said as the others began to join them, "I have a feeling only Kathryn knows the truth."

"And she's not telling."

"Who's not telling what?" Natalie demanded as she rode up between them.

David grabbed frantically for an answer that didn't involve Kathryn, but Luke smoothly stepped in. "Where Cass learned her cooking skills. It couldn't have been at the school, they fed us bricks for biscuits."

Natalie rolled her eyes dramatically and shrugged. “Who cares, let’s go shop!”

David fought to keep his head from shaking. Now he understood why Kathryn felt the urge to get away from Natalie.

They rode into the village in groups. David led Natalie, Leia, and Rachel. Luke led Matt and Jenna. Natalie talked the entire way about things David hadn’t thought were worthy to start a conversation, let alone be the subject of one for twenty minutes. Finally they reached Leneal.

Natalie dismounted with a bounce and hurried into the market place, Rachel right behind her.

David and Leia took a slower pace and gently allowed themselves to become one with the villagers.

Leneal was a large village complete with, taverns, pubs, blacksmith, a trading square, market square, apothecary, prison house, and town hall. The trading square was surrounded by variously sized booths that could be closed up and secured at the end of the trading day. The booths sported various and sundry goods ranging from those locally grown and crafted to the exotic and arcane imported from beyond the kingdom. Its cobblestone streets cut down on the dust during the summer months and provided easy access to the residential areas. In truth, the village was more like a large town, but the people preferred to call Leneal a village because of the camaraderie shared by its inhabitants.

Because they didn’t have anything to trade, the Dragons bypassed the trading square and headed to the market. Due to the weather, the market square had been tented with large sailcloth sheets and small fires were burning on the corner of each stand giving off a smoky but warm atmosphere.

Natalie and Rachel immediately gravitated towards a fabric merchant and began perusing the numerous bolts displayed. Leia stopped at a nearby booth that sold books while David stood back and watched them. He had no interests in any of the items displayed, although he needed a new pitchfork since Luke had broken the last one while attempting to throw it like a spear. He smiled at the memory. Luke was excellent in battle but clueless in the barn. Matt was outraged at the abuse the farm tools had been subjected to since Luke had started working in the barn and kept referring to him as the careless high-born.

Leia rejoined him, watching Natalie and Rachel bicker with the merchant over costs. “What is she going to do with all that fabric?” David asked.

Leia shrugged, paging through the small book she had bought, which as far as David could see only contained blank pages. “Who knows, I’ve never understood why the nobles need so many clothes.”

“Me either,” David agreed.

She glanced up from her planned purchase to look at him. “But,” glancing around to make sure no one was listening, she lowered her voice and asked, “don’t you come from a noble family?”

He grinned. “Just because I come from a noble family, doesn’t mean that I fully understand or agree with all the noble practices.”

“Are there any more like you?”

"Sure, we just get sidelined by the majority who like things the way they are."

"Too bad that's something we can't change."

"We?"

Leia looked around cautiously again, making sure that no one was eavesdropping on their conversation. "We as in...you know," she said quietly, unable to voice their profession. "Nobility harbors such deep prejudices that it's hard for them to get along with anybody who's not a noble."

David nodded his agreement, watching as Natalie and the merchant finally settled on a price. "Believe me, Leia. I feel the same way you do. It's almost too bad we are who we are and therefore can't afford to draw attention to ourselves."

Natalie and Rachel joined them, each toting two bolts of fabric. "Shall we continue?" Natalie asked brightly.

"Natalie, what in the kingdom's name are you going to do with all this fabric?" Leia asked as she eyed the four bolts.

Natalie shrugged and tossed her hair over her shoulder, an impressive move for someone whose hands were full. "Save it for a rainy day? Who knows? I just like to have it on hand. What did you get?"

Leia blushed. "Just a small journal for writing and drawing." She nervously slipped it into the front pocket of her dress, as if she was ashamed of it. "I'm trying to work on my drawing skills."

"If you want I could ask Lindsey to give you some lessons, she's an excellent artist and loves to teach."

Leia's eyes grew wide. "Would you?" She asked breathlessly. "I would appreciate it so much. I love to draw—I'm just not good at it."

Natalie graced her with a dazzling smile. "I bet Lindsey could have you drawing like a professional in no time."

They moved on, Natalie stopped at nearly every booth and almost always bought something. By the time they met up with the others halfway though, Natalie had acquired a box full of feminine items that no man would ever be caught dead with let alone know how to use, four bolts of fabric, a harp, needles and thread, two small wooden boxes, tea herbs, fabric dyes, a new spindle for the spinning wheel, and several other items he didn't know how to identify. And since Leia was eyeing some of those items just as curiously, he surmised that they weren't merely items to pander to female pastimes.

David had managed to buy a pitchfork, only to notice that Luke had done the exact same thing.

"Now we have a spare for when I break this one," Luke laughed after seeing the two pitchforks.

"Natalie, what in the region did you buy?" Matt asked incredulously, eying the bulging saddlebags.

She pushed out her lower lip in a sulky pout. "Just items I thought we needed."

Cautiously, Matt poked a finger beneath the flap of the first bag. "A harp? Why do we need a harp?" he asked as the first item revealed itself to him.

"Our house is too quiet. We need some music," Natalie sparkled emphatically.

David laughed out loud. "Do you know how to play the harp, Natalie?"

She turned to smile at him. "No, but Cass does. I'm sure we can get her to play for us."

"I'm sure she would be delighted to play for us," David agreed, "*After* we convince her that we really do want to hear her play and that she really is good enough to play for us."

Everyone laughed at that observation. Cass was talented in several areas but extremely self-conscious about her abilities. She was the only one who would ever think she wasn't good enough to do anything, while being the first one to tell someone else that they had exceptional talent and were good enough.

The group parted and continued on their separate ways. David bought a new feed sack near the end of the marketplace while Natalie continued to buy up nearly everything in sight.

Shortly before mid-day they regrouped and purchased seasoned pork, broiled skimmer fish, goat cheese, black beans, and freshly baked bread. The girls trumped up sandwiches for the group that they devoured and washed down with a light ale. Afterward they fed, watered and loaded the pack horses with Natalie's goods.

As they rode home, the sun reached its zenith but it offered no reprieve from the winter temperatures. The air was as cold as an icehouse and chapped their skin. As his breath came and went in bursts of white fog, David couldn't help but wonder what Kathryn had done all morning and if she would be home when they arrived.

ℴ·⅃

Kathryn rode off struggling to contain her anger. So David wanted her to train Destiny to fly to him in case of an emergency. Hah! That was a laugh. There was no way she was about to train Destiny to respond to him. It was bad enough having Jasse able to instruct her bird, but David too? Absolutely not!

Kathryn shooed Destiny off her perch and nudged Lerina into a gallop. Destiny let out an annoyed call and took off overhead. As she rode Kathryn's anger mounted.

To think that David had had the nerve to insinuate that she got herself into trouble. It wasn't like she was Natalie. Just last night it had been Natalie who had gotten herself into trouble right at the beginning of the shift and the rest of the Dragons had had to get her out of trouble. Kathryn could still feel the echoes of the headache resulting from that particular adventure. Natalie had insisted on intervening in a small argument that had needed no Guardian intervention and the result had sent the entire tavern into a huge brawl—and that was only the beginning of the night. For the next four radians Natalie and found multiple ways to make trouble. Even Luke and Tyler had been on the verge of strangling her.

No, Kathryn decided, *Natalie is the type who needs an emergency signal, not me.* She rode hard for the entire morning, exploring the forest and the surrounding areas—pushing Lerina, Destiny, and herself to the limit.

By mid-afternoon she was hot, tired, and sweaty. She led Lerina back to the glade where her waterfall sat frozen and dismounted. Removing the halter and loosening the saddle straps she patted her horse's neck and opened her palm to reveal a treat. Lerina eagerly went for the orange calby tuber and Kathryn smiled.

She climbed up onto the rocks next to the falls and sat down on one of the rocks, the cold seeping past her unprotected clothing. The sweat that she had worked up began to freeze on her skin. Shivering, she pulled her cloak tighter around her shoulders but didn't stand up, reveling in the sensation of being able to feel, even if it was unpleasant. Pulling her hair out of its bun she let it tumble down her back, shaking it out to release the stiffness of being pulled back all day in the cold weather. She would never admit it to anyone, but there were many days where putting her hair up gave her a headache. Letting it down, something she never did back at the house, was a relief.

Standing she paused a moment on the edge of the rock she had been sitting on before she leapt into the snow pile below. It was what she imagined jumping onto a cloud would have been like. The snow immediately gave way before her weight and she dropped straight to the frozen ground. The snow had been piled higher than she had originally estimated and as she crouched on the ground, she craned her neck to look up. Surrounding her on all sides was a cave of snow except at the top where a large hole gaped.

She heard Destiny call, muffled by the effects of the snow, and then her bird was diving through the opening, spreading her wings to come to an abrupt halt just above Kathryn's right shoulder.

"Did you miss me?" She asked, amused, as Destiny perched herself on Kathryn's shoulder. Her bird replied with a *squawk*. Outside, she heard Lerina's questioning nicker, followed by several hard hoof beats. Pulling back her left arm, Kathryn punched through the wall of snow before her. It was like being in a blizzard again.

The snow collapsed around her, pummeling her and Destiny and covering them in fine powered snow. Several larger chunks landed on her head and shoulder and she ducked her right shoulder, throwing up her left arm to protect Destiny from being injured from them.

And then it was over.

Kathryn could see the glade and her puzzled horse standing before her. Snow was piled around her, burying her up to her thighs. Destiny let out a loud screech in Kathryn's ear, informing her human of her displeasure at being pounded by the snow.

"Really?!" Kathryn exclaimed, rubbing her ear, trying to dispel the ringing. A thought occurred to her and she grinned. Perfect. David would get what he requested, plus a little something extra.

Destiny shook herself to rid her wings of the snow and took off. Kathryn spent the next few radians playing in the snow and practicing her tracking skills. Finally, she could ignore the growling of her stomach no longer. Destiny landed on Lerina's saddle and called as Kathryn approached.

Smiling, Kathryn reached into her bag and pulled out her meal. She tossed the eagle meat scraps as she munched on fruits, venison, and cheese. As she was finishing her last bite, Destiny hopped over, no doubt looking for more. Lerina had settled down on the ground and Kathryn was now resting comfortably against her back.

"Go on you scamp!" Kathryn laughed. "You can hunt for your own food now."

Destiny gave her one last mournful look before taking flight.

Feeling extremely satisfied Kathryn settled herself more against the warm body of her horse. All earlier annoyance at David and the rest of the Dragons was gone and as she thought about it, she reluctantly admitted that David had had a good point. She couldn't control every situation, Natalie was a good example of how true that was. She probably did need to train Destiny to fly for help. What David really wanted from her was to open up and become part of the family. She wondered how long it would take for him to realize how impossible that was on many levels.

Her jaw tightened when she thought about what Jasse and David wanted from her. What everyone wanted from her.

Her trust.

Trust was the one thing they wanted but it was the one thing she could not give. She'd given others her trust before, she'd given Quint her trust before, and each time the trust she had given had been betrayed. Quint had taught her to trust in no one but herself. After all, how could someone betray their own trust? Arianna was probably the only person in the kingdom who hadn't betrayed her. Jasmine had betrayed her, willing or not, by abandoning her to the school, Amy had accidentally betrayed her when she'd reported Kathryn's nightmares to the Guardian council…who had then spent months trying to force Kathryn to remember them. Jasse had betrayed her by knowing she'd been assigned to the Dragons and blatantly refusing to tell her when he'd had the chance. People she had known for years, people she had come to genuinely like, had willingly or unwillingly betrayed her.

David wanted her to trust him enough to call for help if she needed it. It was far less than anyone else had ever asked of her, and as near as she could remember he was the only one who hadn't yet asked about her past. But of David she knew little to almost nothing about him. He reminded her too much of Quint…his calm and steady — gentle even, manner reminded her so much of Quint it hurt. No. She could never give him her trust. Not when she knew the betrayal would come later.

And it always did.

Still she could not shake the feeling that David had a good point. For once her instincts were warring with her internal desires to hold herself apart. *Later*, she decided. *I'll deal with all that later.* For now she brought out her sketchbook and pencil, wondering what she should sketch. Wondering if she should sketch at all. The last thing she needed was for her fingers to get frostbitten. She looked down at the blank page before her and then back at the waterfall. Her mind went back to when Jasmine had found her and how that waterfall had looked, very similar to the one before her.

As she thought about it she could clearly see every rock, tree, shrub, and curve in the pool. She imagined the pool before her, noting how certain spots were darker in color than others and began to draw. Keeping her eyes closed she recalled the falls and the way the water fell. The right side had more volume than the left, but the left looked like a delicate curtain of water. She saw the twisted, stunted tree that grew up at the top of the falls and the small vines that clung to the rocks alongside. Her ledge came into view and path she used to climb it. She could see herself climbing up to it, reaching for handholds and pulling herself up, carefully protecting whatever treat Claude had given her.

Kathryn came out of the memory with a start, trembling all over, and sweating despite the cold. What had just happened? She had never once thought about her life before Jasmine had rescued her, she had vowed not to. So what had persuaded her to think about it now?

As if the memory couldn't be stopped, her mind continued on to Blackwood Manor and she thought about Claude and wondered how he was faring? What had happened to the residents of Blackwood Manor? Were the Lord and Lady of Blackwood Manor still the same two who had made her life a living hell? Probably not, Princess Jasmine had been furious with them.

"Enough!" Kathryn shouted to herself, pounding her fist. Snow exploded in tiny poofs as her hand punched through it to the solid ground below. She did not want to relieve her past, it was bad enough in her dreams every night, but not here next to her waterfall—

Waterfall. That was what had brought this flashback on, thinking about her waterfall. Well, enough of that. Kathryn gripped the page in her hand, prepared to tear it out and throw it away when she looked down—

What in the kingdom?

She stared at the page before her in shock and bewilderment. While she had been remembering the waterfall at Blackwood Manor she had assumed she had been drawing it. Instead she was looking at a drawing of something she had never seen or heard of.

She had drawn a village, but it was a strange village. The houses were situated in the trees instead of on the ground. Suspended bridges connected the houses to each other and they all led to a huge house that was the centerpiece of her drawing. The huge house encompassed several large trees and had soaring rooflines and arched openings. Every house in the drawing was done in same style, woody yet elegant, primitive yet advanced.

Peering at her drawing, Kathryn attempted to determine the type of trees in the drawing— they weren't a species she recognized.

"How did I do this?" she asked herself. Was it possible to imagine one thing and draw something else...something you'd never seen before? She wasn't sure but she doubted it. She supposed that she could always write to Jasmine or Jasse about had happened, but then they'd become worried and send some council member out to interrogate her. That was the last thing she needed.

Still confused she put the sketchbook away and lay back against Lerina, her mind whirling with questions. Soon however, the warmth of the sun on her face and Lerina's warm body at her back lulled her into a peaceful doze and eventually into a dangerous slumber.

Chapter 15

When David and the others returned to the clearing the first thing David noticed was that Lerina was not in her stall or the corral. Apparently Kathryn hadn't been exaggerating when she said all day. He wondered if the council had known they were giving him such an uncooperative second-in-command. Probably. Supposedly they matched leaders and their family's personalities to complement each other in order to work well together.

Well, the council was human, so was it possible they had made a mistake. This morning was as close to an argument as he and Kathryn had come. He could only wonder what form a real argument between them would take. Would they shoot heated words at each other like sharp arrows intending to wound or maim, or would they take the argument onto the physical world of the training mats? Jasse had once warned him to *never ever* fight Kathryn when she was mad. It was the way the older man had winced and rubbed his shoulders and neck when he'd given the advice right after their first night of traveling, rather than his tone, that had cautioned David to heed his words.

He desperately needed to talk with Kathryn about the situation with Natalie. He wanted, no needed, her opinion of the situation before he went to Natalie. Whatever the situation, it needed to be resolved...and quickly. Perhaps he could talk with her tomorrow.

Resolving to do just that, he finished his chores and challenged Luke to a fencing match. His friend readily agreed. They were joined by Jenna and Leia who had decided to practice some archery.

"Where are the rest of the girls and Matt?" David asked as he carefully crossed the bridge to the field. The bridge was notorious for the ice sheets that covered it and several of the Dragons had slipped on the causeway, slid over the edge and into the icy waters of the river. Jenna and Tyler had kept those unlucky enough to take the plunge near the fires and constantly sipping hot broth for six radians before allowing them back on duty.

Jenna laughed. "Rachel and Natalie are playing with fabric and Matt is getting dinner ready."

"But it's still several radians until dinner!"

"Surely you've noticed that Matt likes to spend radians planning and cooking a marvelous dinner for us."

"I thought he just came up with them a few minutes before we ate, cooking a meal can't be that daunting a task," David replied.

Both Jenna and Leia laughed. "Have you ever made bread? Or noodles?"

"No."

"Those are projects that take all day."

"All day? What on earth takes so long?"

By now Jenna and Leia were laughing so hard it was difficult to understand them. "The dough has to rise."

"Seems silly to me," David muttered as he moved to the sparring field where Luke was waiting.

"What seems silly?"

"Nothing, let's spar."

The two boys sparred until Matt came out to watch. "I think he's going to beat you, Luke," he teased as David did a quick reverse attack.

"Tell me something I don't know," Luke grunted as he blocked the attack.

"You aren't making it easy," David countered, breathing heavily, his breath frosting painfully on his face. "You've improved, Luke."

"Thank Kathryn's sparring sessions."

From the sidelines, Matt laughed. "I just thought I'd come out here and let you know dinner's at the eighteenth radian."

"Thanks, Matt, can't wait to see what you made." Luke lunged at David, who blocked the thrust.

"Hey, Matt, did Kathryn ever come back?"

"Not to my knowledge."

"Okay, thanks." David did a quick wrist thrust and twist, knocking Luke's sword out of his hand. He turned to face Matt, "How about a go?"

"No thanks. I have dinner to prepare, he turned to leave, "besides," he added, "Kathryn gives me plenty of sparring practice when I'm with her."

"Kathryn spars?"

Matt looked at him like David had just grown antlers. "Yes," he said slowly. "You do know about the training sessions every night, right?" He turned to Luke. "Are we sure his fever's gone?"

Luke shrugged before David could answer. "Pretty sure."

"Very funny, Luke. And yes, Matt, I've heard about these training sessions, but I've never seen her carry her sword, let alone use it." He paused before asking, "Is she any good?"

Matt laughed. "Haven't beat her yet, and I haven't seen her use a sword yet either. However I can tell you that she's wickedly fast with those knives of hers," he called over his shoulder as he went back inside.

As Matt walked away, David spotted a green and purple head pop over the edge of Matt's collar. Lacey stared at David for a few moments before flicking her long tongue at him and diving back out of sight. David suppressed a shudder. *He* certainly wouldn't find it comfortable to have a strange creature crawling around inside his shirt.

He corralled his thoughts and turned to look at Luke. "Have you ever seen her use a sword?"

"No, but I wouldn't want to be at the other end of her bow. She shoots like a maniac. It's like she doesn't even aim she releases it so fast."

David nodded in agreement. "She also hits whatever she aims or for that matter doesn't aim at," he said thinking about how carefully placed her arrows were when they apprehended the five thieves on their first shift.

"Like everyone knows, angering Kathryn may be the last thing you ever do, so be careful."

"Guess I'll have to watch myself when I make suggestions to her," David said, grinning. "I wonder where she is?"

"Probably out with Destiny forgetting we exist."

"Probably. Come on, let's go warm up by the fire. My fingers are freezing!" They made their way back across the bridge and into the sitting room. Natalie and Rachel were sitting in the chairs nearest the flames but as soon as she saw the boys with their red faces and fingers, Rachel stood up and ordered David into her chair. Natalie did the same for Luke after a brief hesitation. After a few minutes, Leia and Jenna joined them and they began a game of reverse dervish until Matt called them all to dinner.

"But I was winning!" Luke complained as they all headed into the dining room.

℘·℧

Kathryn felt like she was floating. All around her the trees grew so tall that they blocked out all sunlight on the ground. Looking up she didn't recognize the tree species, nor could she remember any story of a forest where the trees were as big around as a house—or of a forest where the trees appeared blue in color.

Glancing around, she noticed that the ground was sparse, with no grass and very little foliage covering the dirt. What did cover the ground were pine needles, millions upon millions of pine needles that were blue in hue. They formed a carpet that hid the dirt and gave the ground the appearance of being habitable.

Taking a step she clearly felt the needles under her feet and looked down. They were soft and it felt as those she was walking on a thick carpet of moss. Barefoot in a strange forest. How often did she go barefoot?

Never.

Whenever she moved it felt like she was walking underwater, every motion slow and requiring a lot of energy.

She brought her hands to mouth to call out when she noticed her sleeves. She was not dressed in her Guardian uniform or her off duty tunic. Instead she was wearing an exotic dress with narrow sleeves, split at the elbows, which hung down to brush the ground. The bodice was off the shoulder and, from the feel of it, laced up the back. Even though everything she saw was tinted in various shades of blue, as if she was looking at the forest through a piece of blue glass, she somehow knew that the dress itself really was blue. She scowled. Who, or what, had put her into a dress?

She began to walk, not knowing what she was walking towards, just knowing that she had to walk. As she moved she felt hundreds of eyes upon her, but when she glanced around she saw no one. The forest seemed endless and deserted. She walked for what felt like radians, eventually coming to a tree so large four houses could fit inside.

As she approached the base of the tree, root-like tendrils began to snake their way out of the trunk, twisting and writhing amongst each other until they formed a solid wriggling mass. When she came within a few meters of the tree, another mass grew out of the trunk. Without hesitating she put her foot on the first mass of roots. Instantly the mass seemed to solidify into a misshapen, but solid, step. As she climbed upward more steps grew around and up the trunk of the tree with an alarming growth rate. Looking behind her she noticed with a start that the steps behind her were receding and

156

growing back into the trunk, leaving her nowhere to go but up. She climbed until she reached a wooden platform. After stepping onto the platform she turned around and watched the last step retreat back into the trunk.

Trapped high in the air she turned her attention to the platform and where it led. It led to the door of an unimaginable palace suspended high in the trees. Unable to resist its draw, Kathryn approached the wide granite-like steps that led to the heavily ornate doors. The doors appeared to disappear into the mist above and Kathryn had no way of guessing their height. They were white with translucent etchings of vines and leaves that, somehow, Kathryn knew was done in gold.

As she approached the last step the opulently wrought doors opened smoothly on large ancient and elaborate wooden hinges that bid Kathryn enter. She did and the doors closed behind her. Before her was a magnificent hall with a pool for collecting rainwater. The ceiling was airy with large round holes cut into it and loomed high above her. Several large ornate wooden doors were placed at intervals along the walls. Directly in front of her was a dais with four seats, two of which were higher than the other two. A door behind the dais opened and Kathryn began to walk across the hall.

Even though she was barefoot there should have been some sound from her feet hitting the stone floor, but everything was silent, even the opening and closing of the doors was soundless.

The door led to another stairway that rose still higher. Kathryn followed and came to a set of doors with the same etchings as the main entrance. Again the doors opened noiselessly and of their own violation. Inside was a sunken sitting room with lounging couches and low tables. The floor was overlain with green stone that was veined with crème-colored striations. It reminded Kathryn of her room back at Jasmine's palace.

However it was what was in the sitting room that surprised her, or rather who. Eight people were occupying the couches when she entered. They stood as one as she stepped down into the sitting room.

There were five men and three women. They all had pale skin and black hair, and they were all dressed in exotic clothing as she was.

One of the women, wearing a circlet, stood and held out her arms to Kathryn. "Here she is," her voice was low and comforting with a hint of an accent Kathryn couldn't place. "Come to me child."

Kathryn moved forward slowly.

"We have been waiting for this day for a long time," the woman said as she embraced Kathryn.

"What have you been waiting for?" Kathryn asked, her own voice matching the strange woman's.

A younger looking woman stepped forward, placing her own arms around Kathryn. "You were once chosen, but now you have come back to us."

"Chosen for what? Come back where?" Kathryn's confusion was rising.

This time of the men, a boy about her age, spoke. "You have come back to us, Estelwen, your family."

157

Kathryn stepped back, "Wh... what are you talking about? I don't have a family."

The younger woman stepped forward, "We are your family, you were chosen at birth to be the one."

"The one to do what?"

"To lead us to victory against those who would seek to destroy us," the eldest man stepped forward, his gaze piercing. "You were chosen to deliver us."

"Deliver you from who?" Kathryn asked looking around for an escape.

"Those who fear us and seek to eliminate us from existence."

The younger boy spoke again, "You will help us return to power so that we do not need to wander again."

Kathryn's heart sank faster than a stone in water. "Wander?"

The last woman spoke. "We must constantly wander to keep our enemies from finding us, Our cities used to be great, you stand in what was once our great palace, but now we are nomads."

"No!" Kathryn cried desperately. "I won't help you."

"You have no choice my child. It is your destiny to help us."

"No! I will not be a slave to anyone else again," Kathryn fought the panic that was rising rapidly within her. Those claiming to be her family were closing in on her, blocking off every escape route, all talking at once:

"You were chosen."

"You cannot escape your destiny."

"You will deliver us."

"We have waited for thousands of years, do not fail us."

Kathryn woke with a start, trembling so badly that at first she thought the ground was shaking. She was so cold it felt like someone was sticking Natalie's needles into her skin. Horror spread through her as she realized that she'd fallen asleep.

Fool! Stupid! Carless! Of all the stupid things she could have done, she had to pick the most dangerous one. Falling asleep! In this weather! She was lucky she had even woken up. Experimentally she tried moving her feet. She couldn't feel them, or her hands. She needed to get warm. Immediately. It was only after she recognized her need that she realized a fire was burning off to her right. A man sat on the other side, his cloak pulled low over his face, obscuring his features. She jerked violently, but her body refused to obey any commands to move to safety.

"Easy now, child," the stranger spoke softly. "The numbness will pass in time. Pull those blankets back around you and move closer to the fire if you can." His voice was calm and gentle, but behind it there was an air of authority of one who was used to being obeyed when an order was given.

Kathryn stared at him, her sluggish mind struggling to process what he had just told her. *Blankets?* Glancing down she saw for the first time that she was lying on fur pelts, with several more covering her. Lerina had provided heat on one side, the fire on the other. Her own cloak was hanging on a tree branch near the fire, water dripping from its hem. Destiny was sitting on her feet, a curious look on her face.

158

"You are lucky, child," the stranger continued. "You were almost dead when I found you. Tell me," he said, leaning forward. "Was there a reason you wandered into the forest alone, without a fire or other means to keep warm?"

Kathryn struggled to a sitting position. "Wh—who are you?"

"Most people," the stranger continued as if she hadn't spoken, "might have come to the wrong conclusion seeing a young girl sleeping in the snow with only a woolen cloak to keep her warm, and a water soaked cloak at that I might add, with darkness only a few radians away." He lowered his cowl and stared across the fire at her. His face was not what she had expected. Dark skinned with shoulder length black hair he looked like a farmer who spent all of his time working under the hot sun, it was a face that his voice didn't match. It was far too cultured for a simple farmer's.

Realizing that he was waiting for an answer she replied, "I didn't mean to fall asleep."

"And yet, if I hadn't found you, you never would have woken," the stranger replied calmly.

It was the confidence with which he uttered the simple phrase, combined with her own knowledge of deadly temperatures that sent shivers up Kathryn's spine. "Thank you," she said finally, thinking that that was what he was waiting for.

He chuckled. "Anyone who could not be bothered to stop and help another from freezing to death in this weather doesn't deserve to be called a human being," he replied.

Now Kathryn was confused. What was he trying to say? "I'm sorry?" she ventured finally.

He smiled at her. "Thanks are not necessary, child. You would have done the same for another."

As he rummaged in his pack Kathryn studied him some more, trying to make sense of him. Her experience with others was that they would have continued past someone freezing to death without so much as a second glance. His words seemed to suggest otherwise. Her rescuer pulled a small pot and metal stand from his pack. He noticed her scrutiny and grinned.

"You do not agree?" he asked as he anchored the metal stand in the ground.

"My experience says otherwise," she replied as he filled the pot with snow and hung it from the stand over the fire.

He regarded her with a twinkle in his eye. "You are so young to rely solely on your experiences."

Kathryn felt her jaw clench. "I've lived through events most adults can't even dream of," she returned sharply.

"Indeed?" he returned mildly. "Such as?"

She gaped at him. Did he actually expect her to share? "They aren't experiences I care to disclose."

He stared at her for a long moment before shrugging. "That is your decision," he replied softly, turning his attention to the fire.

"You don't approve."

His eyes met hers. "In my experience, when a person refuses to discuss events that have caused them significant pain, their wounds fester and spread like a fever through the body until that person is consumed."

Kathryn felt her gut clench as his words brought back a memory of the sickness that ravaged the village where she had lived as a child. The nauseating images threatened her control over her own body and it took an extreme effort not to lose what little she had left in her stomach in the snow. Exhausted, she lay back down on the pelts.

Her companion wisely did not comment, but busied himself adding herbs and various spices to the pot. After a few minutes a mouthwatering aroma consumed the glen. The stranger brought out two animal hide flasks and filled them with the tea from the pot. He passed one to Kathryn saying, "Drink. It will make you feel better."

Wary, Kathryn accepted the offering, but waited until he had taken several large sips before bringing the flask to her face and sniffing it. It smelled like one of the teas Jenna had given David when he had been injured, but gave off more of a tangy scent. She took a sip. The warmth spread from her mouth all the way down to her core where it began to melt the ice that had taken over her body. Tilting her head back, she took a long gulp. The heat felt marvelous.

Glancing across the fire, she noticed that the stranger was watching her, an approving look on his face.

"I have to say that I'm surprised," he said after a moment. "You are cautious, but not to the point where it would kill you," he nodded toward the flask in her hand. "And yet you were careless enough to fall asleep in the snow."

"I told you," she reiterated. "I didn't mean to fall asleep. It was an accident."

"Kathryn, you control everything in your life. You don't let accidents happen."

She jerked upright and stared at him in open mouthed astonishment. "Who are you!?" She demanded. "How do you know who I am?"

The stranger spread his hands. "I am Elyon and I am an...advisor of sorts to your King Darin."

"An advisor of sorts," she repeated coolly. "What does that mean?"

Elyon cocked his head to the side, considering his words. "I advise your king on certain matters," he said finally.

She stared at him in incredulous disbelief. Had he truly answered her question in such an insipid manner? Finally, the rest of his words penetrated. "My king? Isn't he your king as well?"

Elyon shook his head. "No, child. This kingdom is not my home. I am just passing through."

"And you expect me to believe that someone just *passing through* has the ear of my king above all his other advisors on *certain matters?*"

"On foreign affairs, yes."

Kathryn found that she couldn't argue with him. To her knowledge, no one from the kingdom of Archaea had left in several hundred years. No one knew what truly lay beyond their own borders of the Khidamun Sea and the Airë Mountains. "So," she ventured slowly. "Where do you come from?"

"A place of great distance from here."

She scowled. "I am not a child, there is no need to speak to me as such."

He regarded her carefully. "You are not ready for such knowledge," he told her firmly. As she opened her mouth to protest, he held up a hand to forestall any other questions she may have had. "The radian grows late and night soon approaches. If you are to return to your glade safely you must leave now."

Kathryn stopped breathing. "What?!"

He frowned at her. "Your home, where you live with the others, you must return soon, before they come looking for you."

It took all of her self-control to maintain a dismissive manner. "I don't know what you're talking about."

"Your identity is safe with me Kathryn," he said standing. "Next time we see each other, I hope that you'll trust me enough to tell me about your experiences."

She stared at him in shock as he packed the tea pot and its stand away in his pack. Shouldering the bag he gave her a smile. "Keep the furs— Just in case you decide to venture out on your own again."

And with that last word, he walked out of the glade and disappeared.

Kathryn stood staring at the spot where he had disappeared for several minutes. Shocked beyond words, she only came to her senses when Destiny let out a call. Quickly she packed away the furs and mounted Lerina.

&)·G3

David was whittling in the front room when he heard the faint sound of hooves. He looked up; it was too early for the rest of the family to be home so that must mean it was Kathryn. It was. She rode into the meadow and directly into the barn.

Stamping down his urge to follow her in, David stayed by the window and concentrated on his project. Half a radian later, when she still hadn't exited the barn, David was seriously considering going in after her. He was still making up his mind when she appeared at the entrance.

Relieved he leaned back in his chair, only to sit up straight again. Something was off. Kathryn appeared...edgy. Her normally unwavering walk was jerky, as if she was constantly being caught off guard. He opened the door and stepped outside to meet her.

"How was your day?" David asked as she stepped up onto the porch.

He expected a reaction from her, probably a cold, terse, "fine". What he did not expect to see was the way she jumped and the fear that flickered across her face. He spoke quickly. "I'm sorry, I didn't mean to startle you." Now that he thought about it she looked frozen. Her face was deathly pale and her lips were tinged blue. Her hair was down and disheveled. He was seriously considering calling for Jenna when she finally answered him.

"It's my fault. I should have been paying attention."

Her quiet reply sent up warning flags. "Are you okay, Kathryn?"

She didn't seem to hear him, instead she was gazing out over the clearing a faraway look in her eyes.

"Kathryn?"

"Hmm?" She turned back to face him a confused look on her face. "I'm sorry, did you say something?"

The hair on David's neck went up, something had definitely happened today. He should have insisted that she go with them. "Are you okay?" he asked again.

"I'm fine."

The amount of distractedness in her manner told him otherwise.

"Would you like something to eat? I think there's some leftover soup from dinner in the kitchen."

"I'm not hungry."

"Were you gone all day?"

She nodded, still looking across the clearing.

"Kathryn, are you sure you're okay?"

"I'm just tired. I guess I'll turn in early." She went inside and David followed. Natalie was in the foyer and immediately 'welcomed' Kathryn home with her numerous questions. But Kathryn didn't seem to notice her. In fact she didn't seem to notice anyone. She climbed the stairs and entered her room without saying another word to anyone.

"What's with her?" Natalie huffed. "She couldn't even say hello?"

David continued to stare at the door to her room. "I honestly have no idea, Nat. I've never seen her like this."

"Rude?" Natalie asked sweetly

"No, not rude, just the opposite. When we were outside she apologized to me for not hearing a question I asked her."

Natalie stared at him in disbelief. "Are you serious? I don't think she's said a kind word to anyone, let alone apologize."

David shrugged. "Maybe it's the start of a new Kathryn."

Natalie let out an un-ladylike snort. "Don't count on it. Tomorrow she'll be back to her normal self," she predicted as she flounced back toward the sitting room. David shook his head sadly. He was beginning to wonder if his new family would survive Natalie's vendetta.

He was on his way to the kitchen when a scream erupted from the direction of the sitting room. As he entered the room, followed closely by Matt and Luke, David caught sight of Natalie standing on the couch, a pillow raised high above her head. Lacey stood at the foot of the couch, her head cocked at Natalie as if she was confused.

"STOP!" Matt shouted. Darting forward he ducked under the pillow as Natalie swung it downward and scooped up his pet. "She's harmless, Natalie!"

"SHE?" Natalie demanded. "You mean to tell me that this...this *thing* is yours?"

"Her name is Lacey," Matt replied sourly.

"LACEY?"

"Natalie," David said calmly. "Could you please stop shouting?"

By now the rest of the family had joined them, even Kathryn and Destiny to David's surprise. A brief glance at his lieutenant told him that she'd returned to her normal self even if she was still very pale. He also noticed

Jenna studying her with what he had come to know as her *Healer's Look*. Before the night was over he was positive that Jenna would have Kathryn drinking something hot and getting her into a warm bed. That matter settled, he returned his attention to the events at hand.

Gingerly, Natalie climbed down from the couch. She turned an appealing eye to David. "Can you *please* tell Matt that he can't keep that *thing* here?"

As Matt opened his mouth to protest, no doubt angrily, David held up his hand to silence them both.

"If I do that, then I'd have to tell Kathryn that she isn't allowed to keep Destiny anymore," he replied calmly. "An action that I strongly suspect would *not* be advantageous to my heath. And none of the other Dragons could ever decide to have a pet either," he added. He shook his head. "Matt has the right to choose any pet he wants so long as he takes care of it and sees to it that it doesn't wreak havoc on the family."

"Well, it's wreaking havoc on *me*!" Natalie returned hotly.

"She's not dangerous, Natalie," Matt said quietly.

"She's a lizard!"

"So? What difference does her being a lizard make?"

Natalie wrinkled her nose. "She's ugly...and unclean...and purple!"

Jenna stepped forward, surprising everyone. "On the contrary, Natalie," she spoke gently, taking care not to anger the older girl. "Lacey is very beautiful. Just look at her coloring," she gestured toward Matt who slowly relaxed his grip on his pet. David gave the lizard a more in-depth study than he had in the kitchen a few radians earlier. Jenna was right. Lacey's bright green skin was contrasted with a royal purple that swirled over her back and sides in a way that reminded him of an ocean current. Her eyes were a dark blue, almost black, and her sleek head had a purple diamond on its crown.

He flicked his gaze to Natalie and saw that the older girl was starting to calm down.

Jenna continued to talk, "as to your charge that she's filthy...look at her, Natalie," she instructed. "She's far cleaner than any of our horses or even Destiny."

Finally Natalie relented. "Oh, all right!" She huffed. "But," she added ominously, pointing a finger at Matt. "If I *ever* find her in my room, I'm squishing first and asking questions later."

Matt bowed his head in acknowledgement. Natalie brushed past everyone and marched out of the room.

"Nicely done you two," Rachel commended David and Jenna. "I couldn't have done better myself."

Matt was nodding his head vigorously. "Yeah, thanks!" He turned to leave but stopped dead in his tracks.

Surprised, David turned to find the redhead glaring at Kathryn. David was surprised. Matt had always appeared to respect Kathryn. So why was he glaring at her?

"Don't you even think about it!" Matt ordered in a low tone.

David was utterly confused until he glanced at Kathryn who was looking at Destiny. For her part, Destiny was eyeing Lacey with a savage gleam that only a hunter who had spotted her prey would employ.

This could be trouble, he thought to himself as Matt pushed by Destiny, shielding Lacey in his hands, and left the room. After giving Matt a few minutes head start, Kathryn followed and disappeared upstairs.

"I don't know about you," Rachel commented dryly. "But Destiny looked like she'd just found her midnight snack."

"Kathryn keeps her locked in her room at night," Jenna replied firmly. "She won't let her hurt Lacey."

Rachel turned a wicked smile on Jenna and David. "I don't know about you, but I can't wait to see what happens between Lacey and Natalie."

David groaned. "Please don't encourage them, Rachel. My life is already hectic enough as it is."

഑·ോ

A few radians later the rest of the team returned. After they had debriefed David on their activities for the day, he pulled Amy aside.

"What's wrong?" she asked as she sipped the tea Matt had made for them.

"It's Kathryn."

"She's not hurt is she?"

"No, not at all," David hurried to assure her. "Or if she was it wasn't something I noticed. I actually don't know what to think. But today the rest of us went into Leneal whereas Kathryn spent the day with Destiny."

"What's so wrong about that?"

"Nothing," David agreed. "It's the state she came back in that has me worried."

"What state?"

"Confused, disoriented, distracted, and fearful are a few accurate descriptions. She actually apologized to me because she wasn't paying attention when I asked her if she was alright."

Amy was silent for a moment, fingering the rim of her mug, then said quietly. "I've only seen her like that once before and it was years ago."

"What happened?"

"It was a dream."

"A dream?" David echoed.

"Yes, one night, years ago, Kathryn experienced a dream, nightmare really, that left her completely shaken. I got to see the real Kathryn that night and it wasn't pretty."

"What was the dream about?"

Amy shook her head. "We don't know. As soon as Kathryn woke up she couldn't remember and nothing any of the professors or healers did could help her remember. Not that I think she wanted to remember." She looked out the window into the inky blackness outside. "I'd never seen Kathryn lose her composure the way she did that night. It terrified me." She gave David a smile. "I depended on Kathryn's coolness and calm exterior many times in our early days as roommates. You probably wouldn't believe this, but when I was eleven a lot of the kids in my classes would pick on me because I wasn't very good with weapons. When Kathryn became my roommate she became my wall. Anyone who wanted to tease me had to go through Kathryn and no one tried for very long."

164

David shook his head. "I don't know if I can see her like that considering she won't stand up for herself."

Amy smiled, "Kathryn saw someone who was suffering and took it upon herself to end the suffering. I lost count of the bullies Kathryn stared down. When she became more vocal, all it would take was about a sentence to send them scurrying away."

"Why?"

"They knew Kathryn was different, she had been admitted to the school late and had been personally brought by... Lord Jasse." David noticed a slight hesitation in Amy's speech when she mentioned Jasse. There was something about Kathryn's arrival at school that no one was telling him. "Then there were the extra classes, numerous visits to the council, and tutoring sessions that set her apart. There were rumors that Kathryn had special powers that had never been seen before and that the council was testing the extent of those powers," she laughed, "I can't begin to describe the relief some of the students our age displayed when they saw that her power was water control."

"So why was she admitted late?" David asked carefully.

Amy shrugged. "I don't know. Perhaps because Lord Jasse personally showed up and asked? Who knows? All I know is that I'm grateful because she helped me learn how to handle a sword and a bow better than anyone in my class, or at least until she joined my class."

There was no pause at the mention of Lord Jasse's name this time. Definitely a mystery he would have to work on later. David grinned at her. "A great friend to have."

"I owe her several times over," Amy admitted.

There was silence for a few moments, and then Amy asked, "Do you have any plans for tomorrow?"

David grimaced. "I was going to try to talk to Kathryn about this problem with Natalie, but now I think I'll wait until she's back on her feet."

Amy flashed him a smile. "You're going to wait until the wounds of the dragon have completely healed before attacking it again? You are a strange knight."

David chuckled. "No, just an honorable one. Besides I'm not attacking, I'm inquiring."

Amy waved her hand at him as she mounted the stairs to her room, "It'll be the same thing to Kathryn."

"Good night Amy."

"Good night."

David waited until Amy was in her room before climbing the stairs to his own room. As he lay in bed he couldn't help but wish that Lord Jasse was here to help him understand Kathryn. She wasn't going to let him, or any of the Dragons, in until something drastic happened and he wasn't sure if that would open her up or send her back further into her shell.

Chapter 16

Kathryn woke abruptly from a restless sleep. Groaning she sat up and glanced out her window—it wasn't even sunrise yet. Sighing she pulled herself out of bed and dressed, but since no one else was up yet she left her hair down. The sun's rays had yet to fracture the darkness as she slipped downstairs with Destiny perched on her shoulder. She made herself a cup of hot cirena, a sweet drink considered a delicacy among the nobles. Jasmine had sent her some sachets of the spice before she had moved with the rest of the Dragons to take up residency as the Guardians of Rima. The smell was intoxicating and Kathryn breathed in the delicious scent, letting the mug warm her hands. Her body still hadn't purged the remaining vestiges of bone penetrating cold, even after Jenna's hot tea and extra blankets, and she was grateful for the added warmth this morning.

She hadn't slept well thanks to small replays of the dream she had at the waterfall. She wondered if she would ever again find peace there after what had happened. Destiny let out a sharp cry, indicating she wanted to go out.

Quietly, and attempting to shush the bird Kathryn stood and opened a window, shooing the noisy animal outside. Sitting back down Kathryn considered the other reason she hadn't slept well. The dream she'd had at the waterfall was the exact same one she'd had at the school years ago. Only she hadn't remembered it after she'd woken up then, she did now—all too clearly for her preference. Thankfully she'd managed to put Elyon out of her mind, hopefully forever. Picking up the sketch book she had brought down with her, she opened it up to the page she had used at the waterfall.

Her drawing was a perfect artist's rendition of the mysterious palace from her dream. Picking up a pencil she turned to a fresh page and began drawing what she could remember from her dream. She drew the tree whose steps grew out of the trunk, the magnificent doors, the raised dais, and the sunken sitting room. Once she was done with those she started to draw the forest from different angles as best as she could remember, but quickly gave that endeavor up as each drawing looked almost identical to the one before it.

By the time she finished the forest, the sun was beginning to rise and soon the rest of the Dragons would follow. Quickly, before anyone could come downstairs, she placed her mug next to the sink and returned to her room.

Every room in the house was identical except for hers and David's— a bed, a writing desk and chair, a washbasin and chest for clothing. Kathryn's room looked pretty much the same way it had when she had first moved in with the addition of a perch for Destiny, a nondescript layer of blankets on the bed, and clothes in the trunk.

Upon moving in she had discovered that one of last occupants had left the tools needed for hooking a rug near the loom. Since then she had considered making herself a rug, but hadn't found the time.

In fact she hadn't taken the time to personalize her room in any way, at least not compared to Amy and Jenna who had sketches and drawings of family and friends on their walls and personal items strewn about the room.

Perhaps now she should. Tearing out her sketches from the book she tacked them up on the wall. Maybe one day she would add color, maybe when the dream was in color other than shades of blue. At least Natalie had stopped decorating her room for her, for the time being anyway. Until she got frustrated again. She knew that they only reason Natalie had invaded her privacy was because she hadn't been getting anywhere with her barrage of questions. Kathryn smiled grimly. Natalie had no idea what she was up against. It was one thing to get information from people who liked to talk. Getting it from someone who had been conditioned not to make a sound while being beaten into unconsciousness was something else entirely.

She heard Amy stirring in the next room and immediately exited her own room and hurried downstairs. Passing the kitchen she moved to the small alcove, just off the sitting room, that held the spinning wheel and weaving loom. For a moment she stopped and stared at the loom.

For a moment indecision halted her idea, but it quickly passed. Before she realized it, she had snaked dozens of colored threads through the heddle and attached them to the front beam. After preparing the loom she sat on the wooden stool and closed her eyes. She hadn't woven anything in a few months and hoped that the mindless activity, mindless at least compared to staying ahead of Natalie, would calm her disquiet. After a few minutes of sitting in contemplative silence, she began working the device. In the beginning she was a little rusty but soon she had fallen back into the repetitive patterns and in a matter of several minutes she was weaving. She didn't know what she was weaving, instead she let her fingers move of their own violation, just like when she had drawn the first sketch.

As she wove she could heard the shift of Dragons rise and greet each other, she heard them prepare to leave and heard the silence that followed the closing of the door. For a long time all she heard was the sound of the shuttle as she wove, then she heard Cass rising to make breakfast a good radian later. After about another radian she heard the others begin to stir rising to the smell of fresh biscuits and bacon.

Lowering her hands from the loom she brushed her hair out of her face, she hadn't put it back yet, something she quickly remedied as she gazed at her work. In less than three radians she had managed to complete a good sized wall hanging...a tapestry that looked exactly like her first sketch.

Tying off the ends she carried it upstairs, bumping into Amy.

"Good morning, Kathryn," her friend yawned sleepily.

"Good morning."

"Have you had breakfast yet?"

"Only if you count smelling it as having breakfast."

"In that case, would you care to join me?"

Kathryn offered her friend a smile. "Sure, just let me put this in my room," she lifted up the rolled up tapestry for Amy to see.

"Did you make that this morning?"

Kathryn allowed herself a smile. "Yes. It's probably my best one yet," she said as she opened the door to her room and deposited the object inside.

"How long have you been up?"

"Long enough to weave that."

Amy scowled at her. "Gee, that's informative."

"What's informative?" David asked coming up behind them. Amy jumped a little but Kathryn, having noticed his approach, didn't twitch.

She was mildly disgusted with how easily her family members were startled. While they were on patrol they were a little more observant, but within the safety of their own glade they let their guard down completely. It was a practice she found dangerous and foolhardy. Attacking someone where they felt safest was one of the best tactics to start and win a battle in moments. People didn't like to prepare for trouble where they felt safe for the simple reason that it would suggest that their safety zone wasn't actually safe. Kathryn believed that safety was a lie. True safety didn't exist, it was all relative.

Oblivious to her friend's mental lecture that she wished she could give to the Dragons, Amy tossed her head in Kathryn's direction. "I asked her how long she's been up and she said long enough to weave a wall tapestry."

David looked at Amy, then at Kathryn, and then returned his gaze to Amy. "I have no idea how long something like that would take."

Amy's scowl deepened. "I don't either, which is why she stated it that way. She does it on purpose just to annoy me."

David looked at Kathryn who shrugged. "Well in any case," he said changing the subject, "let's go down and see what kind of breakfast Cass cooked up for us."

The three entered the kitchen together to find a sumptuous feast laid out for them as well as a very unexpected surprise.

"Lord Jasse!" David exclaimed. "Welcome!" After a moment's hesitation he added, "Why are you here? Is something wrong?"

Kathryn, meanwhile was trying to determine just how Jasse had come to be in the house without her hearing his arrival. Apparently weaving had made her just as oblivious to the events around her as using her gift. It was a realization that did not sit well.

Jasse rose from the chair he had been occupying and came over to greet the young leader. "Good morning David," he said as he embraced the younger man. "And no, nothing's wrong. Consider this visit a three month plus review. How are things faring in Rima?"

80·03

Sitting down, David gave him a very brief outline of their adventures thus far.

"Well, except for these mystery swords, it seems like you're doing very well for yourselves," Jasse commented after David had finished. "Are you all settling in?"

David pretended not to notice that Jasse glanced at Kathryn, who was steadfastly ignoring him for the moment, when he asked this. "Fairly well," he replied. "We had a few rough spots near the beginning, but I suppose that's to be expected when fourteen strangers start living together." He knew

168

that Lord Jasse probably wasn't looking for a diplomatic answer, but that's all that he was willing to provide until it was just the two of them.

"Yes," Jasse agreed. "In fact the council would be suspicious if you didn't have a few hiccups in the beginning."

Cass set down a plate full of hot biscuits. "Why is that?" As she released the tray, she grimaced slightly. The abrasions on her knuckles from her last fight hadn't completely healed and were still making her fingers stiff. David sympathized. He was missing a large patch of skin on his right arm from a fight where the tree he'd been chasing a bandit up decided to retract its roots from the ground and had toppled. David had come out of the encounter with just some skin missing, the bandit hadn't been so lucky.

Jasse grimaced. "My guess would be because of the old saying. 'If something's too good to be true, then there's something rotten at the core', but that's just my guess."

"You don't know?" Amy asked in disbelief. "How can you be on the council and not know?" She wore her long hair down today and it hid the long scrape that ran along the length of her chin bone from her ear to her jaw. They were all learning the hard way that life outside the school was not as forgiving of small mistakes. Virtually everyone around the breakfast table was sporting small injuries, Kathryn being the only exception. Much to the annoyance of several.

"There are separate sub-councils within the council," Jasse explained. "I'm not on the one that chooses the family members."

"Which one are you on?" Lindsey asked.

He smiled at her. "Sorry, can't say." He laughed at Amy and Cass's stunned faces. "Come on now," he chided. "The council has to have some secrets from you youngsters!"

They finished breakfast in a pleasant fashion and afterwards Jasse leaned back in his chair. "Tell me Cassandra, where did you learn to cook like that?" he asked. "It certainly couldn't be at the school because the biscuits there are bricks."

David laughed. "We said the exact same thing, and she still won't tell."

"Well in any case, I think this should be considered your third gift. Your cooking is marvelous."

Cassandra blushed. "Thank you."

It wasn't long before the others joined the reunion over the meal table. After about a radian, Amy and Kathryn cleared the breakfast dishes and the rest of the family scattered. Lord Jasse motioned for David to follow him.

His curiosity building, David followed Jasse to the training field where Jasse handed him a bow, "How is you archery these days?"

"Good enough." David wished that there had been enough time to grab a cloak before exiting the house. He was already fighting shivers.

Jasse gave him a knowing smile. "We'll see about that." His first shot hit the farthest target dead center. Turning to David he grinned. "Your turn."

David's shot hit the bull's eye, but wasn't dead center like Jasse's.

"Not bad," Jasse acknowledged as he studied the marksmanship. "At least, not bad for a swordsman."

His fingers were already frozen and David fought the urge to glare at them. He was from a northern region where snow was never seen and he was still struggling to adapt to the cold. "Somehow I don't think you brought me out here to discuss my archery skills."

"No," the older man agreed. "But we have other things to discuss before we reach the real reason for my visit."

"Such as?" David asked as he released another arrow.

"Oh," Jasse began as he took aim. "I thought we might discuss the hiccups you encountered so far." The arrow leapt from the bow and buried itself deep in the heart of his second target.

David shrugged. "We reorganized my shifts to give Luke and Amy a chance at leadership as well as to give Kathryn and I some rest."

"Who came up with the idea?" Another arrow hit the target dead center.

David released another arrow. "Luke, but Amy contributed to it."

"What brought this on?"

"We learned early on that two leaders may not be enough. We needed...sub-commanders, if you will, to relieve the pressure put on the leader or the second in case someone was injured."

"Has it worked?"

David grinned as he finished his last volley. "I'll let you know. This is our first week on the new system."

"I'm pleased to see that the Dragons are taking the initiative to look after each other already. There were many families where it took nearly a year to forge such relationships."

"We were fortunate. Luke was my best friend at the school and Amy was Kathryn's. They noticed the problem and decided to do something about it."

"How's Kathryn settling in?"

"She hasn't."

Jasse appeared startled by his blunt reply so David hurried to explain. "For a while it appeared like she was fine but suddenly she closed up even further than before. Recently I've found out that there's a bit of animosity between Kathryn and two other girls. Apparently it's gotten so bad that Kathryn will disappear into the forest to get some peace. I'm guessing that this is probably the reason for her withdrawal."

Jasse was frowning into the distance. "What have you done about it?"

"Nothing yet. I heard about this through Amy, and while I trust her I wanted to try and see it for myself before I approached anyone."

"Wise decision. Have you seen what Amy has?"

David shook his head. "No. The two girls behave themselves around me for the most part and yesterday when we had the opportunity to go into the village, Kathryn bowed out and disappeared for most of the day."

"So what are you going to do about it?"

David hesitated. "While I haven't personally seen it, everyone I've talked to has so I'm confident that I can intervene. I was going to talk to Kathryn yesterday when she got home but—

"But what?"

"She was distracted when she returned late that night, she didn't even notice me standing in the doorway until I spoke. I decided to wait until whatever was bothering her was resolved."

Jasse nodded slowly, "That was probably a good idea since Kathryn tends to just react, with force, when startled. She has...excellent reflexes." David noticed that Jasse absentmindedly rubbed his right shoulder as he spoke. "Will you talk to her today?"

"We'll see. First I have to find her."

"Find her?"

"By now Kathryn's long gone into the forest. No one's been able to successfully follow her and tracking her is impossible so we just wait for her to return."

"Water," Jasse said suddenly.

David looked at him curiously. "Water?"

"Yes," Jasse nodded. "Water is the one thing that gives Kathryn peace. If there's a waterfall or river nearby you can bet that's where she goes."

"Thank you for the information, I guess I'm going waterfall hunting later."

"Have you been able to confirm my theory?"

He shook his head, "I haven't even seen her use her gift of water control let alone plants. No, I cannot confirm your theory yet, but give it time, we're all still adjusting."

Jasse nodded slowly in acquiescence.

"So why did you really come here?" David asked quickly.

The older man smiled at him. "You don't waste time do you?"

"It's not mine to waste."

Jasse looked at him for a long time before finally saying, "You have a new assignment."

℘·℃

After briefing David on the Dragon's new assignment, one which entailed determining the location of the hideout of one particularly nasty outlaw band, Jasse went looking for Kathryn. In any other location he would have followed his own advice to David and followed the sound of falling water until he found a glade with a waterfall and pool. However, this was the dead middle of winter in Rima and Jasse knew better than to think that there was any body of water, running or otherwise, that remained unfrozen.

But there was another reason he didn't need to listen for water to know where the closest waterfall was. He wasn't sure if he could ever tell the Dragons, but he and Jasmine's family had been assigned to this very region over thirty years ago. The Dragon's house had been theirs as well. He knew the immediate layout of the forest surrounding the glade intimately. And he was almost positive he knew where Kathryn spent most of her time.

Focusing on his gift, he searched for her distinctive emotions. He found her, several kilometers away. Exactly where he'd predicted. Sighing he began the long walk to her location. He was short on time, but Jasmine had given him orders not to return without seeing Kathryn first.

He found her in the small glade he remembered fondly. He had Jasmine had wiled away a few afternoons playing in the water and enjoying picnics in

171

this very location. The small frozen waterfall the centerpiece of a winter masterpiece, ice hung everywhere in the glade, and Kathryn and Destiny were enjoying themselves. She was throwing snowballs at Destiny who was easily avoiding them.

"What did she do now?" Jasse asked dryly.

Kathryn turned to look at him and grinned. "Nothing. It's our new game: Avoid getting hit."

Jasse glanced at the eagle who was lazily sliding out of the way of each snowball that Kathryn lobbed at her. "I think she's showing off," he said finally.

She laughed. "I think so too, but for some reason Destiny likes it."

"We'll examine the mystery that is your bird some other time," he said. "I don't believe you even said hello to me this morning," Jasse chided.

She rolled her eyes, but smiled and said hello. Jasse laughed and embraced her, despite the fact she was dripping large drops of water from her clothes and hair. She'd obviously been playing in the snow for a while. "You'll never change, will you?"

"That depends on the sort of change that's expected of me," She replied as she searched in her bag for a treat for Destiny.

Jasse cut to the chase. "I've just come from talking with David."

"I know," she replied. "You're archery isn't half bad." She found a small piece of jerky and tossed it at Destiny who swooped down to catch it.

"He told me some interesting things," he said slowly.

"I'll bet he did," she muttered running her hair through some cloth to dry the ends.

He waited for her to elaborate and when she didn't asked, "Care to talk about it?"

"What's there to talk about?" She finished drying her hair and searched for a brush to tame it.

Jasse sighed. "Kathryn, you can't be as unfeeling as you make yourself out to be."

"Why not?"

"Because you are not a rock."

"Natalie would disagree with you on that," Kathryn replied softly, remembering the older girl's tirade.

"Have you made any attempt to get to know the rest of the Dragons?"

"I know them as well as I care to," she replied.

"Blast it, Kathryn!" Jasse exclaimed angrily. "You can't go through life alone. You need help."

Surprised as she was by this uncharacteristic outburst, she replied quickly...and forcefully. "I tried!" She returned hotly. "And all I got for my attempts was more trouble."

"Have you told David?"

"No."

"Why not?"

Kathryn was silent for a moment, finally she said softly, "I'm sorry I failed you."

Jasse started. "Failed me?" He brushed some snow off a stump, sat down, and worked his shoulder muscles to ease some of the kinks that settled in from his long walk. He returned his eyes to Kathryn with a questioning look.

"I couldn't handle learning to live in a family. I've failed everybody."

Jasse could hear the defeat in her voice and he relented a bit. He knew that what he had asked of Kathryn went against everything she believed in and that reaching out first went against every survival instinct she had. "No, I'm the one who's sorry. I asked a lot of you and had impossible expectations. I will still say that you need to ask for help in this."

Kathryn frowned slightly. "What is it with people telling me that?"

"Telling you what?"

"That I need their help."

"Who's told you that?"

She threw her brush back into her bag, "You, Jasmine, Arianna, David to some extent, some stranger who called himself Elyon—

Jasse sat up straight. "*Elyon!*"

Kathryn paused. "You've heard of him?" she asked slowly.

"Only in whispers," Jasse replied. "But what I have heard says that he's a powerful king, an ally of our King Darin...a miracle worker," he added the last two words in a whisper. "Some say that he's the last great sorcerer left alive."

"So, I guess he's not some crazy lost soul wandering the woods?"

Jasse looked at her in shock. "Please tell me that you didn't call him that to his face."

"Of course not."

They were silent a few moments before Jasse stood. "I have to leave," he told her reluctantly, wishing they could finish this conversation. "But if Elyon ever appears to you again—

"Alert the council?" Kathryn asked dryly.

Jasse shook his head. "No, Kathryn— *trust* him. Listen to him."

80·03

Kathryn watched Jasse disappear into the forest, thinking over all he had said. Wonderful. Today she'd managed to anger Lord Jasse, something she'd never seen happen before, and learn that she'd practically insulted a visiting king, or wizard, to his face. Oh, yes. Life was just wonderful.

As she packed up the rest of her stuff she became aware that she wasn't alone...again. No doubt David had followed Jasse to discover where she went every day. Why couldn't anyone in this blasted kingdom leave her alone? She was tired of pretending.

She turned to face David, accusations ready but they died before they were spoken.

Seeing her startled face, Elyon smiled. "I told you we would meet again."

"I didn't think it would be this soon," she managed after a few moments of awkward silence.

"You didn't think it would be ever," he corrected with a twinkle in his eye.

Kathryn began to feel uncomfortable. "I really wasn't sure what to think."

173

"Don't try to lie to yourself, Kathryn," Elyon admonished. "You understood exactly what you wanted to see, not what you did see."

"There's a difference?" she asked stiffly.

"There's a great difference. As a Guardian, you know this to be true."

Unfortunately she did. As she'd lain in bed last night, she'd come to the conclusion that Elyon had been one of the gifted, but not chosen to be a Guardian, individuals she'd heard about. Yes, she owed him her life, but had believed that she would never see him again. There were a few more moments of silence as Elyon walked over to a snow covered log and sat down. "Will you join me?" he asked as he motioned to the log.

She didn't budge. "I heard something very interesting about you this morning."

Elyon smiled and looked towards the waterfall. "Really?"

"I was told that you are a king."

"Partially."

She waited expectantly for his reply but he gave her none. "Are you?" she prompted finally.

"Am I what?"

Was he playing difficult or was he honestly not paying attention to her words? His gaze was locked on the frozen majesty of the waterfall, as if he could see something she couldn't. "Are you a king?"

"Of a sort. Among my people I am a Dūta."

Kathryn felt her brow furrow at the unfamiliar term. "And what, pray tell, is a dūta exactly?"

"A Dūta is many things," he explained calmly. "I protect my people in times of trouble and give them guidance when they lose their path or need direction. I am an executioner as well as a giver of mercy. But most importantly, I reveal to the people the will of the Ancient One."

Throughout his speech, Kathryn fought the urge to roll her eyes. "In simpler, and less extravagant terms," she summarized, "you are a king." Just wonderful. And one who claimed to be able to contact the world of the spirits. If their history instructors were to be believed, leaders who led at the so-called *calling* of some spiritual deity were the most disruptive. David was going to love learning the kingdom had another crazy cultic leader wandering around. Even worse, it was someone who had the ear of the king and the Guardian Council.

"Partially," he agreed.

"Partially?" Now she was sure he was being difficult on purpose. "How can one only be a partial king or sorcerer?"

"I am not only a king, but a servant as well. Which is true of any king."

"I would love to see you address King Darin as a *servant*," she replied sarcastically. "He is most definitely not a servant." It didn't escape her notice that he failed to address the second rumor of his identity. "A king is the ruler of his people, he cannot be a servant as well."

"A king cannot rule his people without putting their needs before his own. In this way, he is their servant," Elyon told her seriously. He must have seen the confusion on her face for he added. "If you're willing to trust me and become my friend, there will come a time when it will make sense."

Where in the kingdom had that come from?! She stared at him in bewilderment. Become his friend? She'd only met the man once before and even then she hadn't wanted to see him again. And to top it off he was some pious fanatic. Or at least played one for his people. The last thing she needed in her life was someone trying to convince her to believe in a spiritual entity. Kathryn believed in one person, and one person only. Herself.

Then anger and disgust blazed through her veins as the first of his words hit her. Was there some competition throughout the kingdom with a grand prize awaiting the first person to gain her trust? Deciding not to dance around the issue with Elyon like she did with Jasse and David she replied coolly, "I don't give others my trust."

"I have noticed." He turned his gaze on her and motioned towards the log, his eyes not demanding, but asking her to sit. Well that was a first. A king who didn't command her to obey his every order.

Grudgingly, she moved forward but did not sit, crossing her arms across her chest. Unable to meet his gaze she glanced towards the column of ice that glinted in the sunlight, and he continued. "Your past is a painful one—

His words whipped her head around to pierce his fiery gaze with her frigid one. "How could you know my past?" she demanded sarcastically. "We've never met before."

"No, we haven't met before," he agreed patiently, and then he smiled gently. "But I have been watching you for a long time." Kathryn felt chills spread throughout her body, but Elyon wasn't finished. "I know what you endured before you were rescued by Princess Jasmine."

Kathryn narrowed her eyes. "I doubt that," she said stonily. "No one knows." *And I've worked hard to keep it that way.*

Then Elyon began to speak. He spoke quietly of her life with her aunt and uncle before the Blackwoods and the sickness that had killed over half of the village just before she'd become a slave. "Stop!" Kathryn ordered heatedly before he could continue her story after she had been taken to live at Blackwood Manor. The ones of her aunt and uncle's village were bad enough but it was the Blackwoods that haunted her nightmares nightly. But that may have been because her young mind had blocked out much of what she'd experienced in that village. Now that he had oh-so-kindly ripped the tapestry from the window into those experiences she found herself remembering more than she wanted to.

Surprisingly he did and he waited patiently for her to regain control of her memories. Once they were no longer crowding in and threatening to suffocate her she turned and glared at him. "If you *ever* tell anyone—"she threatened ominously.

Elyon looked at her kindly. "No, child. Your past is not my story to tell, it is yours...and it *must* be told," he said firmly.

She turned and stared at the frozen water. "Why?" she asked harshly. "It is in the past. It doesn't matter anymore."

"Because until you face your past, you cannot face your future."

King or not, her patience with his oblique responses snapped. "You speak in riddles!"

"You are a prisoner of your past," Elyon explained. "Your dreams are plagued by memories and you struggle with your identity. There are trials quickly approaching where you must be sure of yourself, of who you are."

"And how do you suggest I learn to be sure of myself?" She demanded.

"Embrace your past, learn from it—

"Oh, I've learned plenty," she spat bitterly.

"Learn *new* lessons and move on."

"What new lessons?"

Elyon laughed softly. "That is something only you can determine, Kathryn." He stood and prepared to leave. "One last thing," he told her as he raised his cowl. "You must learn to embrace your gift fully. It is a part of you, and you cannot find yourself by ignoring it."

Watching Elyon leave, Kathryn couldn't help but feel a small sense of unease and relief. Elyon's statement, that he'd been watching her for a long time, she had to admit that it had been more than a little unnerving. All her life she'd been a shadow child and now, to learn that someone had been watching her, practically from the day she was born...he needed a new hobby. It certainly didn't seem to Kathryn like the kind of activity a king should be involved in. Crazy sorcerer's? Maybe. King's? No. She hadn't had the courage to challenge Jasse's claim that he was a powerful sorcerer, which only made her mood fouler.

But there was also some release in her spirit as well. At first when Elyon and begun to tell her about her past Kathryn had felt the punch of those memories more than she'd ever felt the beatings and the sharp sting that had lingered with the heavy weight in her chest had burned terribly. But afterwards, knowing that someone else knew and understood, her pain had eased. It wasn't completely gone, her chest was still heavy and the burn was still there, but it had lessened slightly.

His gaze was a new experience for her. Never before had she met someone whose gaze could communicate so many things. Power. Wisdom. Authority. Love. There was something unsettling in his eyes, like he was able to penetrate every layer of her being, walk through every wall she had erected, to see her inner spirit—eyes that could not only see, but also discern thoughts and inner fears and that, despite everything, it didn't matter to him.

Or it's just that he already knew and I didn't actually have to relive it myself, she thought bitterly then realized that that particular observation wasn't accurate. She *had* relived it. As his words had pierced her heart, her mind had taken her back in time to relive events she'd never wanted to remember. Making a mental note to slap him for that the next time she saw him, she sighed and looked for Destiny.

Her bird was perched high above, and at her whistle launched herself from the tree top to soar down to Kathryn's position. Destiny clicked her beak a few times in greeting before crawling up her arm and settling on her shoulder. Tipping her head slightly, Kathryn let it rest gently against Destiny's feathered head.

Comforted, her thoughts returned to Elyon's words, especially about embracing her gift. It was common knowledge to her teachers that she shied away from using her talents. Many thought it was because she was insecure about starting late, but that wasn't it at all. Not even Lady Blackwood's stories about the cursed and wanderers held any power over her anymore. They might bring the horrors of her past to mind, but they didn't control her as they had once done.

When she used her gifts, Kathryn felt different. Not more powerful different, but a different person completely. She didn't think the same way when she used her gifts and it terrified her. She prided herself on her control and when she used her gifts she felt like she lost some of that control...no she felt like she lost *all* of her control.

Still, Jasse said I should trust him, she mused.

Trust.

How did a girl who had never depended on anyone, who had sworn not to, learn to trust a stranger when she couldn't even trust the people who were supposed to be her family?

For a few long moments she stared at the ice... debating, arguing with herself until, finally, she summoned the courage to try something she had only ever done once before.

Moving to stand next to the pool she let go of every fear, insecurity, fact, and common sense she possessed and opened herself fully to the gift she had been given. It rushed free of the confines she usually captured it within and in a heartbeat Kathryn's gift began working its magic of its own accord. Ruthlessly controlled on a daily basis, it snatched at the freedom she offered it with breathtaking swiftness. When she tried to bend it back to her iron will, it reared and bucked as if it were a wild horse she was attempting to break. Gingerly she backed off slightly, allowing the churning magic within her to settle. Instead of trying to control her magic's actions, she guided it, pushing it in a slightly different direction or nudging it to an alternate action. She had a vision in her mind and was curious to see if she could bring it into the waking world. It was an exercise in patience and calm...tenderness. Her magic sought to tame the kingdom now that she'd released it and she had to gently, but firmly, herd it back to smaller and more reasonable heroics.

After what felt like years she sat back down into the snow, completely out of breath and drenched in sweat. Sharp cracks and moaning slowly ebbed and echoed through the quiet as her creation settled. Her gaze swept across the clearing and she couldn't stop her mouth from opening in astonishment. Massive ice arches had grown out of the pool on either side of the waterfall, curving around the glade in gently curving sweeps. The base of each arch was enveloped by large fern-like flora. The fern's stems were bluish green and as large around as a man's waist. Each stem supported a network of what appeared to be massive yet delicate leaves that were spider-webbed together and veined with light blue ice crystals. The land encircled by the arches was covered in a solid sheet of ice that gleamed brighter than any polished ballroom floor. From the tops of the arches, additional sheets of ice had grown inward and upward until they formed a sort of roof with a circular hole in the very center. From the floor corkscrewing ice columns had grown, branching outward as they reached the roof, giving Kathryn the impression of tree branches spiraling out from a trunk. White ivy-leaved plants trailed and coiled around the rising columns reaching up and forming elaborate patterns across the massive roof structure glistening and reflecting sun light as though they were lit from within. Intertwined within the matrix of ivy were clusters of bulbous flowers of various sizes hued in various shades of blue and green at their base with the petals themselves of pure white.

Destiny swooped down and landed on the only snow pile remaining in the ice room beside her.

"What did you think, girl?" Kathryn asked as she stroked the bird lovingly.

The look in the eagle's eyes seemed to ask, *what took you so long?*

Chapter 17

Four Months Later

Destiny's hungry call startled Kathryn out of a light doze. Groaning she sat up and rubbed her eyes. Spring had come to Rima and the melting of the ice and snow was accompanied by an explosion of colors as the wildflowers and grass reclaimed the landscape. The sun remained in the sky for longer radians and the patrols had been increased in length. And of course with the warm and pleasant weather, the nastier side of life had decided to crawl out of their filth ridden boroughs and hideouts to practice their illegal trades and offenses.

Both she and David had been taking turns working extra radians, running extra patrols late at night to deal with the increase in brawls, tavern fights, and thefts. Injuries had increased as the family dealt with longer hours and sharp words could be heard echoing through the house as everyone began taking their frustration out on each other. Natalie was becoming increasingly difficult to live with, for everyone, and Kathryn wondered how long it would be before they either destroyed each other or learned to work out their differences.

She had returned late again last night and slept restlessly. The outlaw band that Lord Jasse and the Council had tasked them with finding had covered their tracks well…it had taken her two months to find their hiding place.

But they had been two months she'd actually enjoyed. She'd taken the opportunity to spend days at a time alone in the forest, tracking with just Lerina and Destiny for company. David had complained loudly at her adventures, but whenever she'd been back she'd taken all day shifts with the others so he could only yell at her for disappearing alone, not for completely shirking her duty to her family. Once, Natalie had complained that Kathryn was getting a holiday from actually working, but Tyler, who had accompanied Kathryn on one of her jaunts, at David's order, quickly shut her up with the description of how they'd traveled.

When she tracked, Kathryn carried as little as possible with her. Water skeins, a thick cloak, her weapons, rope, and her flint and helcë were all that weighed her and Lerina down. Her food she could trap, hunt, or forage on her own. And she slept for a few scant radians each night, preferring to make use of all the life in the forest to guide her to her intended destination. Add to the facts that it was still winter, although slowly beginning to warm up, after Tyler had finished describing the *horrendous* and *tedious* way she traveled through the forest, David didn't force anyone else to accompany her. She had almost been disappointed when she'd found the hideout.

Even so, once it had been found, the Council had sent word that the Dragons were to deal with the outlaws themselves. It hadn't been a fun task. David had taken two weeks, despite Kathryn, Luke and Tyler's protests that the outlaws could very well relocate in those two weeks, to come up with a plan of attack.

Admittedly his plan had been well thought out and, had everything gone perfectly, it might even have been considered brilliant. Of course not everything had gone according to plan. Kathryn had personally tracked three of the leaders to the edge of Katham River where they had refused to surrender to her and Amy. They paid the ultimate price for their stubbornness. Later, after Kathryn had given David a short debrief and coldly received his assurances that she and Amy had done the right thing, she had attempted to fall asleep. Unable to calm her mind, she had wandered back to her waterfall and simply stared at the melting ice hued ombre red in the moonlight of Niena. She'd stay there for radians before she began to feel tired enough for sleep. She hadn't tried any similar feats with her powers since that day Elyon had visited her but the memory of the structure she created would overlay reality every time she returned.

Returning to the waterfall had become a recurring habit since then, especially with Lacey popping up all over the house. It was driving Natalie to distraction, which meant that she had less time to worry about antagonizing Kathryn as she constantly triple checked where she walked and where she sat down. After the first month the family learned not to run at full tilt toward the sound of Natalie's piercing screams.

Kathryn couldn't help but feel sorry for Matt. Over the past four months, Lacey had crossed paths with Natalie numerous times and poor Matt had been getting an earful from the older girl. She suppressed a smile thinking about the events of last night.

Natalie had been enjoying her nightly bath when she'd suddenly found Lacey sitting on the edge of the bathtub. Her shrieks were heard throughout the whole house. By the time Kathryn had gone to bed, Natalie still hadn't finished ranting at Matt. When she had finished with the poor cook, she had ranted to Lindsey about the unfairness of her life. The racket had kept her up for radians. *Honestly*, she thought darkly, *after all this time Natalie should be used to Lacey's presence by now.*

Reluctantly, she had pulled herself up and left her refuge. It wouldn't be long until dawn as the sun started to rise behind the hills to the east. Sunlight was just starting to bathe the forest canopy in its warm embrace, but at ground level it was dark and poorly lit from a combination of moonlight and the scattered rays of the sun's first light. As they headed back to the compound Destiny swooped down and pitched upward several times just missing Kathryn by inches as she darted back and forth navigating the dense foliage with relative ease. Occasionally, she would land in front of Kathryn and hop from side to side attempting to engage her in some kind of play.

Kathryn smiled. "Sorry girl, my heart just isn't in it. Besides it's getting late and we need to get home." When they arrived the sun was just beginning to burn off the dew and she managed to trudge upstairs without being noticed.

She looked wistfully out her bedroom window and thought of her sanctuary. Oh well. She'd sleep well tonight. Hopefully. She stood, bent over the hand basin, and splashed cold water across her face, letting the shock bring her to full awareness. She quickly changed, but paused on her way out the door to look at her sketches, absently wondering if the dream was true. It had been months since that winter afternoon when she'd experienced the dream…and so far it hadn't returned. Destiny called again and Kathryn crossed the room, unlatched the sash's barrel lock and let her out.

Kathryn stood for several minutes at the window, letting the cool breeze brush across her face. Sighing she turned back to her room, no sense in wasting the morning. She pulled her boots back on and twisted her hair back into its usual bun, wondering where she wanted to patrol today.

She had just decided to tell David that she wanted to do an overnight patrol to spend more time in the western part of Rima, down by Lake Sarovara, when a knock sounded on her door. Curiously she glanced at it. It was unheard of for anyone in the Dragons to rise this early. Opening it she was taken completely by surprise to find David standing there, a very serious look on his face.

"What's wrong?" she asked, stepping out and closing the door behind her.

"I've called a family council."

Surprised Kathryn looked at him inquisitively. In the seven months the Dragons had been a family David had never called a family council before and it was only to be done in extreme situations, "Care to tell me why?" She hated surprises and hoped he would indulge her instead of waiting for the entire family.

He nodded slowly then said, "I received a missive from the King by messenger bird. His daughter, Princess Roseanna, was abducted yesterday morning."

Kathryn didn't say anything. If the King sent a messenger bird to a Guardian family, then whatever problem that letter contained was one he expected them to fix. She could only hope that there was some more detailed information in the missive or it was going to be very difficult to locate the princess in a timely manner. When they entered the sitting room they found the rest of the Dragons present and waiting anxiously.

"I've received a letter from the King," David said without ceremony as he took his seat. "Someone abducted Princess Roseanna yesterday morning."

"Oh the poor girl!" Natalie cried and Kathryn resisted the urge to roll her eyes at Natalie's theatrics. If Natalie put that much effort into the dramatics of a simple kidnapping, she'd pass out from hyperventilation if she ever heard Kathryn's story.

David nodded. "The King wants us to get her back."

"He asked for us specifically?" Elizabeth asked. "Why not a more experienced family? We haven't even had a year on patrol."

Again he nodded. "The King wishes for me to lead a small team composed of no more than six members to rescue the princess. As to the experience issue, I can honestly say I have no idea."

"Do they know where she's being held?" Rachel asked.

"They have a guess but they aren't positive." David paged through the letter until he found the paragraph he was looking for and passed it around, summarizing it as it was handed from family member to family member. "They suspect Duke Sebastian abducted Roseanna out of spite because the King wouldn't permit a marriage between them."

"Why not?" Natalie asked curiously.

"Apparently the duke is thirty years older than the princess."

Natalie made a face at this announcement. She opened her mouth to comment, but was, mercifully, cut off by Luke.

"Who did you have in mind for the task?" David's old roommate asked.

David looked around and sighed, he'd obviously been dreading this part. "I was wondering when you'd ask that. I'm taking Kathryn, Jenna, Daniel, Matt, and Natalie." He looked at them all. "It wasn't an easy choice. I would have preferred to take all of you."

Kathryn cringed inwardly at the news that Natalie would be joining them. While Natalie's antics had lessened over the last four months thanks to Lacey, she was still a nuisance to Kathryn's peace of mind.

"Why didn't you take Amy or Luke?" Cassandra asked curiously. "After all, not to slight the rest of us, they are two of our top five warriors."

"I thought about it." David admitted, "But if I took Kathryn as well as Luke and Amy it would leave the rest of you without someone with leadership experience."

Suddenly Natalie piped up. "Why me? I'll be the first to admit I'm probably the worst of us all at swordplay or using a bow."

Kathryn forced herself to breathe calmly as Natalie fluttered her eyelashes at their leader. For some reason Natalie acted like a love-struck serving maid whenever David was near. David, she noticed with some humor, didn't seem to notice which only served make the older girl try harder.

David smiled slightly. "I have it on good authority that Princess Roseanna loves fashion and parties and figured she might like to have someone who could keep her company without boring her to death."

Kathryn fought the urge to strangle him. If that was the only reason he was bringing the ditzy blond along, then the princess could survive a few days of boredom in order to make room for a more seasoned and capable fighter to join their party.

"How long will you be gone?" Amy asked.

"I wish I knew. It's a good ten day ride to Duke Sebastian's castle and it will take at least a day or two to get an idea of defenses and plan an attack, from there, we would take the Princess to the capitol and then ride back."

"So at the very least a month," Amy surmised, doing the calculations in her head.

"Probably more like a month and a half. We just learned the hard way that things don't always go according to plan."

Luke jumped up. "What in the kingdom's name are you guys still doing here?" he demanded. "You go pack, Tyler you and Matt can go saddle their horses."

"What are you going to be doing?" Tyler asked grumpily as he picked himself up off the couch and began to head towards the stables.

"I've got some meals to prepare," Matt said as he bounded into the kitchen, leaving Luke to help Tyler. Eventually everyone regained their senses and the whole house was soon a study in controlled chaos. Fueling it all was the energized excitement that the King had chosen *them*, the least senior Guardian family, to accomplish a rescue mission for his family. Kathryn, however, couldn't help but wonder if the assignment was some kind of test or evaluation of their capabilities as Guardians.

Two radians later David was leading his team through the forest and out of their glade. The mood was serious and even Natalie seemed to sense the danger of the mission they were on for she hardly said a few sentences at a time. Eventually however, Natalie regained her voice and chatted on with Jenna who rode beside her. David and Kathryn rode in front while Daniel took up the rear. Matt seemed content to bounce between Daniel and the two girls.

While Natalie and Jenna talked fashions and who knows what else, Matt and Daniel mulled over how they each might use their gifts during the rescue. David and Kathryn concentrated on tactics.

"Do you have a plan?" Kathryn asked, initiating the conversation.

Doing his best to hide his surprise, in the seven months they'd been working together he'd never known her to initiate *anything*, David replied, "I've got a very general plan. When I was seven I visited the duke's castle but my memory of its layout is sketchy at best."

"What do you remember?"

"It's situated on the plains, however it buts up against some sheer cliffs. An attack from behind would be almost impossible."

"But not entirely," Kathryn added, finishing the basic rule that had been drilled into them during their training. And considering her free climbing skills, might actually be something to contemplate. The rest of the team might not be able to enter from that direction, but if they could get Kathryn up there with her bow to pick off the sentries it might be worth investigating.

"Exactly. The castle itself has three large towers and four walls."

"Four walls?" Kathryn arched an eyebrow in surprise. "I've never heard of castle with such defenses."

"It was supposedly built three thousand years ago, when the regions were still fighting amongst themselves." He shook his head in disbelief. "It's hard to believe anything in this kingdom could last that long." After a moment he returned to the original topic. "I'd guess that Sebastian would keep the princess in one of the towers, rather than in the dungeons."

"What makes you guess that?"

David smiled bitterly. "Normally, one would expect a captive to be kept in the dungeon with the rest. But the princess is no ordinary captive. Sebastian will keep her locked high in a tower to make rescue difficult."

"You wouldn't happen to have an idea of which one?"

"There's a strong possibility she's being kept in the central tower," David replied easily.

Kathryn eyed him suspiciously. "I thought your memory of this place was sketchy."

"It is. I remember nothing about guard placements or any other tactical advantages the castle has." The central tower was also the strongest and more well-kept tower of the whole fortress. It made sense to keep the princess in a location that central and easily defended.

"Just as well," she replied. "They've probably been changed." She paused and then asked, "What were you doing there anyway?"

This time he was sure he failed at hiding his surprise. Kathryn, curious about personal details? It was unheard of. David hesitated. "My family is of nobility and it's...customary to travel to other nobles homes."

Kathryn wrinkled her nose. "Sounds awful," she said dryly.

"Oh Kathryn!" Natalie called from behind.

Sighing, Kathryn turned to look behind her and replied in a moderately agreeable tone, "Yes, Natalie?"

"I was just wondering if you could tell me how you and Destiny got so close?" Natalie cooed.

David tensed then immediately relaxed, not wanting Natalie to see his reaction, waiting to see what Kathryn came up with for an answer. If she would answer.

"I suppose it's the same way you develop a bond with horses or dogs," she replied calmly, although David noticed her eyes were hard. "You just have to spend time with them."

"But how did you get her to even let you care for her?" Natalie purred. David didn't have to turn around to hear the victory in her voice. He guessed that this was the first time Kathryn had ever replied to any of her questions and he was willing to bet it was only because *he* was present.

Kathryn's jaw hardened, recognizing that answering at the risk of appearing too unsocial in front of him had opened the floodgates to Natalie's inquisition. "I suppose it's because I saved her life," she replied, obviously forcing her tone to remain neutral.

"How did you save her life?"

Kathryn lost the battle with neutrality. "Destiny was abandoned," she replied in a clipped tone.

David couldn't blame her. He'd known Natalie by reputation at school. In fact, he doubted that there was a single person at school who hadn't at least known her by that reputation. When she'd been assigned to his family he'd been cautiously optimistic at the idea of having someone experienced in intelligence gathering as a part of the team. But after seven months of working with her, he'd discovered that her methods of gathering information left much to be desired. She wasn't subtle about it and because of her approach the reports she gave him often contradicted each other. Interrogations? Yes, she was good at those, mainly because whoever she was interrogating cowered at her temper when they refused to answer her.

But overall the single reports he got from Kathryn, Luke, and Amy were more complete and accurate than all ten of the ones he received from Natalie. Someone was going to have to explain to her the difference between quantity and quality. And since she and Kathryn were not getting along, it was going to have to be him.

"You don't have to get all snippy," Natalie's voice took on a hurt tone. "I'm only trying to get to know you."

Right, David thought darkly, *by making yourself look good and at the same time making Kathryn look even worse in front of your latest love interest*. Kathryn turned back to David. "You were saying?"

He hurried to continue their conversation. "In any case I want to spend a night or two in the village to glean as much information as we can. The information that we have could be wrong. Sebastian may not even have Roseanna."

Hearing the doubt in his voice she asked, "Just how much do you doubt the information?"

His reply was quick. "None at all."

"Kathryn who were your parents?" Natalie asked riding up between them before Kathryn could question the reason for David's certainty.

Kathryn actually looked startled. "What do you mean who were my parents?"

Natalie looked at her funny. "I mean, like who were they? Names, titles... all that stuff."

David felt powerless to stop the interrogation without making things worse. Natalie was more stubborn than a mule when she wanted something. And right now she wanted to antagonize Kathryn. It was part of her method for obtaining information. She simply irritated her intended victim until they told her what she wanted to know so that she would leave them alone. He wanted to help ease Kathryn's discomfort but he couldn't do or say anything right now that wouldn't draw Natalie's attention.

Kathryn held the older girl's gaze. "I never knew my parents. I learned everything I know from Jasmine and Lord Jasse."

Natalie practically jumped out of her saddle, "How in the kingdom did you make such an intimate acquaintance with Lord Jasse? And who is Jasmine?"

David noticed that she took no notice about Kathryn being an orphan. If Kathryn's clenched jaw was any indication, he suspected that she had noticed as well.

"Jasmine found me when I was ten years old and Lord Jasse was one of my instructors." Kathryn's tone was forced but Natalie was taking no notice.

The older girl snorted. "Lord Jasse probably instructed all of us," she argued. "How come he took a shine to you?"

Kathryn's jaw moved from side to side before answering. "Turns out, Lord Jasse likes birds and he was interested in Destiny."

Natalie paused, then after doing some mental math asked. "Who took care of you between your birth and tenth birthday?"

"I bounced from place to place."

"Oh, gee, that's informative," Natalie replied sarcastically before moving back to join Jenna.

"Does she do this often?" David asked, trying to get a feel of the situation from Kathryn's point of view.

"Every day," Kathryn answered through clenched teeth. "Although she's behaving herself right now. So you don't have any idea of how we want to do this?"

This was Natalie behaving herself? He was surprised that she hadn't killed the older girl already. Why hadn't anyone brought this to his attention sooner? He shook his head. "Nothing that would help us during the attack. I'd like to send one of us to scope out the castle but none of us have the talent to do that without being seen."

Jenna, who had by now tuned out Natalie's endless chatter, heard David's last comment. This time it was she who nudged her horse forward, only instead of splitting the two riders she came up next to David. "Kathryn could do it," she told him softly, hoping Natalie wasn't listening.

David looked at Kathryn in surprise. "You can?"

Natalie's abominably cheerful voice called out, "Kathryn can do what?" She rode up on the other side of Kathryn, looking at her expectantly.

Both Kathryn and David sighed, which Natalie noticed. "What did I say?" she demanded.

David waved his hand dismissively. "Nothing." He turned to Kathryn, "Can you really do it?"

"I can," she admitted slowly.

"Can do what?" Natalie demanded again.

"Gather information without being seen," David replied, realizing she wouldn't leave them alone until they told her, as well as realizing that this was probably how Kathryn gathered all her information while on patrol. It minimized human contact and was often times more reliable.

Natalie turned to Kathryn. "Where in the kingdom did you learn a trick like that? They don't teach us techniques like that at Guardian School." Then her face scrunched up into a frown. "Is it anything like those disappearing acts you do every day?"

"No, they don't teach hidden movement at school," Kathryn agreed, declining to comment on Natalie's second question.

"You know," David added thoughtfully. "Hidden movement would be an excellent technique for the Guardians to learn. It would certainly help on reconnaissance missions. Why don't they teach it?"

Daniel and Matt, who by now were tired of being left out of the conversation, rode up. "How could we possibly convince the Guardian Council to add another technique to an already packed program?" Daniel asked.

"Why don't we have Kathryn teach us how to master hidden movement," Jenna suggested. "Then, before we talk to the council we use it ourselves first, making sure it really does help."

"Like a trial run," David mused.

"Exactly," Jenna smiled glad to have been of help. She and Daniel moved back to their original positions.

Destiny swooped in and hit Matt on the top of his head with her talons as she landed on Kathryn's arm. "I swear that bird hates me," Matt muttered as he dropped back to join Jenna and Daniel to get of range.

David didn't bother pointing out that the possibility of Lacey's presence around his shoulders probably had more to do with the bird's actions than her feelings toward Matt and turned to Kathryn. "Do you think you could do it?" He asked eagerly.

She appeared to consider the question as she gently stroked Destiny. "You mean teach the rest of you?"

"Yes."

Destiny let out a screech that made David wince. *Why does she always have to do that so close to my ear?*

Reaching inside her cloak, Kathryn pulled out a piece of jerky and tossed it up into the air. Destiny took off like an arrow shot from Kathryn's bow, catching the jerky on its downward spiral, and took off in the direction of the horizon. Kathryn was silent for a moment, and then said, "I guess I could try."

Natalie, her lingering question about the origins of Kathryn's talent forgotten, was eager to get started. "What's the first thing we need to learn?"

David thought he saw a gleam in his second-in-command's eye.

Kathryn turned to Natalie and, keeping a straight face, replied, "The first technique one must master is silence."

Natalie's eager face fell. "Well I've just failed," she announced, and then she turned a suspicious eye on Kathryn. "You aren't just saying that to make me shut up are you?"

Kathryn shook her head. "No. The whole key to hidden movement is silence."

Natalie asked a couple more questions about the method of hidden movement before regaining her original position next to Jenna. Together she and Jenna discussed all they could think of on hidden movement.

"Just between us." David whispered. "Where did you learn the technique?"

Kathryn smiled grimly. "It was one of the many things I learned courtesy of Blackwood Manor."

David was careful not to react. It was the first time Kathryn had ever mentioned something, anything, from her past. Blackwood Manor. He had heard of the place. Apparently the Lord and Lady had broken several laws and were caught by someone who had powerful connections. Now he knew what laws they had broken. It was a serious crime not to report a child with gifts. David suspected that the person who had really found Kathryn was Lord Jasse, not this enigmatic Jasmine whom she refused to give any details about. It would explain a lot about their relationship.

For the next fortnight, David went completely against all their training. Normally, whenever Guardians were on the move, they traveled openly from town to town in full uniform to give the wrongdoers a warning and a chance to repent before the Guardians arrived, however David wasn't about to play by the rules—not when the princess' life was at risk. And especially not with those mysterious swords that could repel a Guardian's. If there were any at Sebastian's castle, the Dragons were going to need the element of surprise in order to recover the princess.

The group traveled in nondescript clothing and avoided every village and town they came close to. There were times the avoidance cost them time, but David considered it worth it. When both Kathryn and Daniel had asked about going against protocol, David had simply given them the rational responses he had already formulated.

They finally arrived at Sebastian's fief fifteen days after they left home. They left their horses and gear hidden in the woods and calmly walked into the village. Up ahead the castle loomed like a dangerous shadow. In the fading light the towers looked like extended claws, poised, waiting to strike those below.

The group found an inn and paid for two rooms for the night.

"You kids planning on staying long?" The ancient innkeeper asked in a wheezing tone as he handed them keys to their rooms.

David smiled. "Just passing through."

Upstairs, he advised his group, "Get a good night's sleep. We have a very long and very busy day tomorrow."

Chapter 18

Clouds hung low in the sky the next morning. Those didn't bother David so much as the ones that hugged the ground. It was so foggy he could barely see three meters in front of him.

"Wonderful," David muttered as he looked out the window. "This is going to make things difficult."

"How so?" Matt asked pulling on his boots.

David reached for his own. "With this fog I won't be able to tell where I am until I'm practically on top of something, which means we'll all be making a lot of noise." He slid one of his feet into his boots only to encounter something alive. He jerked his foot out and peered inside. Lacey hissed back at him. David sighed and held out his boot. "Matt..."

"True," his friend agreed as he retrieved his pet from his leader's boot. "But we can make the best of it."

"We'll have to," David replied grimly. "Any reason you couldn't have left Lacey at home?" he asked irritably.

Matt shrugged. "I couldn't find a volunteer to take care of her," he lamented.

"I see that it's not only the sky that's dark today." Daniel commented dryly from across the room.

"What's that supposed to mean?"

"It means your mood is as dark as those clouds. Usually that's Kathryn's job." He poked his head out the window. "It looks like rain."

David scowled. "Just wonderful."

Downstairs they found the three girls already having breakfast. "I think we should go to the marketplace first," Natalie chirped as soon they sat down.

David seriously considered strangling her for being so cheerful on such an ugly day. He noticed Kathryn frowning slightly at him and realized she was probably picking up on his sour mood like Matt and Daniel had. Sighing he reminded himself that he was their leader and had to set a good example for his family to follow. Swallowing his irritation at the world he refocused on Natalie.

"After all," Natalie continued. "There's so much to learn in a different marketplace." The server came and brought the boys their breakfast

"That's a good idea," David agreed as he eyed his breakfast.

Breakfast was little more than lukewarm porridge and stiff bread, but it was filling and the team ate heartily.

By the time they had finished eating the fog had lifted some, lifting David's own spirits considerably. "Kathryn and Daniel can start at the south end of the market," he decided as they left the inn. "The rest of us will start here." He watched as Kathryn gave Destiny, who was perched on the roof of the inn, a subtle hand motion which sent the bird flying off toward the castle, eventually disappearing over the cliffs behind the stronghold.

Kathryn and Daniel headed for the south end without comment, trusting David's leadership. Matt wandered off on his own, focusing on the apothecary and spice market.

Now the Dragons were in their element. Immediately Natalie began to browse the various shops and vendor's stalls, chattering the whole while. David and Jenna followed a bit more slowly, but making their own conversation and picking up on the slight clues revealed in the body language of the local villagers.

In a radian David learned that Sebastian was a tyrant. Not that any of the villagers would actually come out and say such a thing, but the way they ducked their heads or shifted uncomfortably when face with polite queries about their protector told David all he needed to know.

ဆာ·ർ

Natalie was inspecting a piece of pottery when the sound of thunder reached her ears. At first she looked up, thinking the sky was about to send a torrent of rain down on them, but quickly realized the thunder she as hearing was the sound of horsemen...very excited horsemen.

Turning to the right she caught sight of three fully dressed knights barreling down the center of the marketplace. The villagers were scrambling to get out of the way, throwing their wares and purchases into the air trying to escape the path of the knights. Natalie felt someone grab her arm and pull her further back into the stall just as the three knights rushed past, apparently oblivious to the destruction and havoc they were causing.

When the dust had settled the marketplace began to thrive again. Dusting herself off Natalie asked the stall keeper, "Does that happen often?"

He shrugged. "More and more since the woman arrived."

Natalie's ears perked up, but she kept forced herself to keep her voice calm. "What woman?"

Again the man shrugged. "Some woman arrived here about a fortnight ago."

"Have you ever seen her?"

"Why would a noble lady show her face in a place like this?" The man waved an arm around.

Natalie ducked her head. "Good point." She quickly made her purchase and left to find David.

He and Jenna were further down at a grain stall. Jenna was haggling over some barley and David was there to make sure she got a good price. As she approached, Natalie couldn't ignore how handsome and intimidating David was. He stood just behind Jenna, slightly off to the right, with his hands folded across his chest and a serious expression on his face. His wavy black hair was gently dancing in the wind. Oh, if only she could get him to notice her! He was perfect for her, and the fact that he was of a noble family only made it that much easier. Yet for over seven months he had steadily ignored her, or at least treated her the same way he treated every other Dragon. It was frustrating her to no end.

Gently Natalie pulled David away and slowly walked down street. "Apparently," she said softly and adding in a small flick of her hair to keep his attention, "There's a noble lady staying in the castle who arrived about a fortnight ago."

David nodded. "It seems that Duke Sebastian has heavily stepped up security at the castle. The common people can't even get near the drawbridge."

"What's your next move?"

"I need someone to get inside."

"Didn't you just hear yourself? How can we get inside if we can't get near the drawbridge?"

"I'm hoping Kathryn can manage it."

Just the mention of her nemesis caused Natalie to scowl "What is it with Kathryn and questions?" she asked remembering their ride in, and then remembering something else, she turned on David. "I've been wanting to ask you this since you set up our teams. Why did you put Amy on Kathryn's team when the rest of us had no one we were familiar with? Why the favoritism?" She probably shouldn't be second-guessing his decisions, not while on a mission, and *especially* not when she was trying to get him to notice her in more than a platonic way, but that little bit of information had been niggling at her for *months*.

David looked at her sternly. "What I am about to say goes no further than you and me. Got it?"

She rolled her eyes. "I got it, it's a secret."

"I put Amy on Kathryn's team because she's the only one Kathryn trusts enough to confide in or allow to help her. Also, because you make friends easier than Kathryn, I knew you could handle being alone. Besides, it's not entirely true that Kathryn is the only one who knows someone on the team. Luke was my best friend at the school and he's on my team."

"What's Kathryn's problem with trusting?" Natalie demanded hotly, ignoring David's last comment. "Why can't she learn to trust like the rest of us?"

"Kathryn's past is what caused her to lose the ability to trust," David told her firmly, "Until she decides to reveal it to you or anyone else don't, I repeat, do not push her to answer your questions."

Natalie moved away in a huff. "Fine. But I still don't like it."

David let out an exasperated sigh. He had brought Natalie along hoping that she would end her feud with Kathryn but it was appearing to have been for naught. Praying fervently that the two would make up, David went to find Daniel, Matt and Kathryn, hoping they had learned more than he had.

&)·C3

"Are you sure you can do this?" David whispered.

"I don't think it will be a problem," Kathryn replied calmly as she removed her sword and daggers leaving her armed only with her bow and fighting knives.

David, who had been forced to order her to bring her sword, frowned when he realized she wasn't taking them with her. "You have no worries about the guards?"

When David had caught up with Kathryn and Daniel earlier that day he found they had learned the exact number of guards that were patrolling the castle. An even better show of good fortune was when Daniel found a guard who was mentally weak enough for Natalie to swoop in and distract him enough for him to estimate how much time was left before the evening shifts would begin to see if he had time for a drink. Normally, even a weak minded knight would prove difficult to glean information out of, but Natalie's charms and flirtatious, David might have even considered them suggestive, gestures were very persuasive in turning his thoughts quite blatantly to how much time he had before his watch started. The effort of keeping the thoughts of other knights and patrons in the tavern separate from his target was far more than Daniel had ever attempted since leaving school and took a toll on him but he still managed a very disgusted grimace before saying, "I will *never* get those images out of my head," as they melted away into the crowd.

Now, the team was poised on the cliffs, waiting for the shift to change and Kathryn to penetrate the castle's defenses for reconnaissance.

"I don't like the idea of you going in with just your bow and knives," David admitted.

"The sword will only slow me down," Kathryn protested as he tried to hand it back to her. She didn't want that thing anywhere near her. "Besides," she said as she slipped her bow and quiver off her shoulder and handed it to David, "the fewer encumbrances the better."

"You're not taking your bow?" David asked in disbelief.

Kathryn looked into his protesting face and sighed. "I have a lot of climbing to do in a short amount of time and it will just get in the way"

"Then at least take a dagger," he insisted.

"I don't need it," she hissed back. She lifted Destiny to a perch and said, "Silence."

Destiny bobbed her head up and down a few times and opened her beak wide as if getting ready to let out a victory call. Instead only her tongue appeared in the dark void between her beaks. Not a sound came out.

Matt, who had been watching the strange interaction, muttered quietly to himself, "That is just weird."

Kathryn shot him a wry grin.

"Fifteen minutes," Jenna whispered from above. She and Natalie were keeping an eye on the time as well as watching the guards in case the change happened at a slightly different time. Daniel was further away watching for patrols in the cliffs.

"Got to go." Kathryn slid down from the ledge and disappeared into the darkness before David could protest again.

The leader of the Dragons looked at Matt who was eyeing Destiny with suspicion. "Please tell me that you didn't bring Lacey," he hissed.

Matt looked hurt. "I couldn't just leave her in the room."

David suppressed a curse. "Well make sure she stays hidden," he ordered. "The last thing we need is for Destiny to go after her or Natalie to scream and give away our position."

Matt grimaced. "Good point, I'll see if I can get her to stay in my pocket."

"No," David ground out. "You will make her stay. I've tolerated her terrorizing Natalie Matt, but I won't let her risk our lives."

He waited until Matt acknowledged his ultimatum before moving upward to join the two girls. "Anyone spotted her yet?"

"She just left," Natalie reminded him sourly. "She's hasn't even reached the first wall." She paused and then added. "I still think that *I* should have been the one to go," she complained irritably. "After all, *I'm* the one who distracted the drunk knight so that Daniel could peak into his thoughts. Not to mention I have intelligence training."

"Oh, sure," Matt agreed sarcastically from below. "Let's send the one person who hasn't been participating in the extra training sessions these last seven months, and who doesn't have intrusion skills, over four castle walls we aren't sure she can climb in daylight, let alone the dead of night, so that she can sneak past a castle swarming with trained knights, who are on alert for trouble. We'd end up having to rescue both you *and* the princess," he predicted. "At least we know that Kathryn can do it."

"How do you know that I can't?" she hissed back.

Daniel coughed hard, announcing his return. "Seriously? After seven months, Natalie, we pretty much know what everyone else is capable of in this family."

"And climbing castle walls and becoming a night wraith aren't in your skill set," Jenna added.

"Kathryn isn't trained in intelligence," Natalie protested with a sniff. "She doesn't know what to listen for. I should have gone with her at least."

"So you can distract her with your interrogations like you do at home and get the both of you killed?" Matt suggested mockingly. "Brilliant idea."

Silence fell over the cliffs so abruptly, David wondered if his companions were all still with him or if they'd somehow fallen off the precipice without him knowing.

"If you're going to accuse me of something, Matt," Natalie said stiffly, "just come out and say it."

"Fine," he turned to face her directly, not an easy feat to accomplish since she was sitting five meters above his head in the cliffs. "*You're* the reason Kathryn hasn't been able to settle in to this family. If it wasn't for you haranguing her every chance you got, she might actually want to spend time with us and get to know us."

"How—How dare you!" Natalie sputtered.

"He's right," Jenna spoke up. "Don't bother denying it Natalie, we all know the truth. You hate Kathryn and have been making her life miserable for months."

In any other time and place, David would have been thrilled to have this discussion take place. As usual, fate had decided to time it for the most inappropriate time. "There is a time for everything," he spoke up forcefully before anyone else could say anything. "And this isn't the time for family disputes. We're on a mission. Get your heads back into it,' he ordered.

"He's right," Daniel agreed after a few tense heartbeats. "We can't help Kathryn if we're too busy snapping at each other to notice that she's in trouble."

"*Each other*?" Natalie whispered incredulously. "You all were snapping at *me*."

"Enough." David put the full weight of his position as family leader into his tone.

They waited tensely for the next fifteen minutes to pass. David strained his ears against the night, willing himself to detect any signs of Kathryn's entry, any sign that she'd been discovered. But he came up empty. No alarm calls rose from the castle walls.

"At least there's cloud cover to help mask her movements," Jenna whispered encouragingly as if sensing David's anxiety.

"I still don't like the idea of her going in alone."

Jenna, knowing that nothing she could say would calm their anxious leader, wisely didn't comment.

They kept their eyes glued to the wall and the small patches of light that were illuminated by torches. All tensed when the changing of the guard happened and there was no sign of Kathryn.

"I didn't see her," Matt whispered.

"None of us did," Jenna whispered back.

"Now what?"

"We wait," David said firmly. "Kathryn has two radians to gather information between now and the next changing of the guard. We get to wait."

ଋ·ଔ

Kathryn slipped down from the ledge she had been perched on, moving silently towards the castle walls. When she reached the wall she stretched up and found a handhold. Slowly she began to climb. She wished Destiny was here to help guide her, but she managed to reach the top without any serious problems arising.

Moving slowly she made her way to a section of the wall that wasn't bathed in light before climbing up and over. Cautiously she looked around then moved to the other side and began climbing back down. She was halfway down when two guards appeared below her, torches in hand. Frozen in place she listened to them discuss their sour opinion of the extra security before they moved off.

She descended the rest of the way and moved across the small open area that separated the first wall from the second. Again she scaled the wall with no trouble, but as she prepared to descend she noticed the third and fourth walls.

Pausing in the darkness she considered the obstacle before her. The third wall was different from the first two. Instead of having a patrol space with a three foot wide walking path on top, the third wall came to a point and had spikes about the height of a man protruding from the top.

The sound of shuffling feet sent her flying over the edge of the second wall and she cautiously made her way down. As she crossed the space between the two walls she was forced to move slower, unlike the first, this area was pitted with holes and small rounded bumps in the earth. However Kathryn was naturally surefooted and combined with her training, as long as she moved carefully, had no trouble negotiating the field.

She climbed the third wall more slowly than the first two, trying to come up with a way to get over without impaling herself or leaving anything behind to mark an intruder.

When she reached the top she made a pleasant discovery, the spikes were just barely wide enough for her to squeeze through. That turned out to be a blessing as the upper third of the spikes morphed into a four bladed pike no doubt to prevent infiltrators from clambering over the top. Well, the original builders, or whoever had augmented the decorations on this wall, obviously had not planned on smaller women being part of an infiltration team. Peeking over the top she was grateful to find the three sentries below at ease and definitely not watching the wall.

Effortlessly, she slipped through two of the spikes and made her way down. It was easy getting past the sentries who, she could now tell had had way too much drink earlier in the evening. They were in no condition to stand watch, let alone fight an intruder.

She started on the last wall, taking her time finding secure supports, when she reached the top she noticed that this wall was extremely wide, wide enough for at least two carts to fit side by side. Silently she slipped over the side and moved along the pathway. She was on the ground five minutes later.

For a moment she stopped in the shadows. David had guessed that the princess would be housed in the highest tower. Looking around she spotted it a courtyard over. Moving like an apparition she made her way across the first courtyard. She had just reached the arch that led to the second when a guard suddenly appeared from inside the arch. Kathryn froze as he calmly walked past her and toward the three sentries. Once he passed her, she continued to move through the arch.

Inside the second courtyard were ten sentries. Climbing this tower might be a challenge. Kathryn was still contemplating how to get across and up when a shout echoed across the courtyard— instantly six of the ten guards ran off.

Sparing no second, Kathryn moved to the tower and began to climb. By the time the six guards returned, shaking their heads at the false alarm, she was halfway up. This tower was older than the rest of the castle and the mortar holding the stone blocks together wasn't as strong as the material used in the building of the walls. While the chipped away mortar gave her better hand and footholds, she had to be cautious not to knock the stuff off. The last thing she needed was a guard looking up because a chunk of mortar had landed on his helmet.

Kathryn pulled herself up the rest of the way. Moving around the tower she came across a window with a faint light coming from it. Peering inside Kathryn saw a young woman with long black hair. Princess Roseanna looked exactly as David had described her. The young woman was obviously agitated, pacing from one side of the room and back again, reminding Kathryn of a caged animal.

Kathryn was about to tap gently on the glass when the door opened and an older man stepped into the room. Immediately Kathryn ducked her head away from the glass, listening to the conversation.

"Good evening my dear," the voice that spoke was arrogant and sophisticated with a cold, cruel edge that reminded Kathryn of Lord Blackwood. It could only belong to one person—Duke Sebastian. "I hope these quarters are to your liking."

There was the sound of a slap. "I demand you release me at once!" Princess Roseanna's voice wasn't how Kathryn had imagined it, light and un-intimidating even with her anger giving it a cold edge.

"I'm afraid I can't do that your highness," Duke Sebastian chuckled coldly. "You see if I did release you, your father would have my head."

"Do you really think my father will stand for this? He will send somebody for me."

Sebastian chuckled again. "It has been over a fortnight, princess, your faith in your father is admirable, but face the truth my dear—no one's coming for you. They don't even know you're here."

"The Guardians will come," the princess declared defiantly.

"The Guardians," Sebastian spat. "They're nothing but pompous wizards who have nothing better to do with their time than to meddle in the affairs of others."

"The guardians defend the people of the kingdom," Princess Roseanna replied stiffly. "

It is their business to meddle in the affairs of others, especially murderers and kidnappers."

"Please don't tell me you're still upset with what I had to do to your slave." If Kathryn hadn't heard the sorrow in the princess's voice when she had called Sebastian a murderer, she might have suspected the duke had been commenting on the weather.

"Marina was not my slave!" Roseanna's tone was rising. "She was more than my lady-in-waiting. She was my closest friend and you killed her!"

"Now, now my dear," his voice was calm and cold. "It won't do for you to raise your voice like that. We don't want you mute on the day of your wedding do we?"

There was silence for a moment. "What wedding?" Kathryn could hear the fear in the princess's voice.

"Our wedding, my love!" Sebastian announced it like he expected the whole kingdom to come and celebrate with them. "In just two days' time we shall be man and wife."

"I will not!" Roseanna's voice was firm, but Kathryn could detect the fear underlying her tone.

"You will have no choice in the matter," Sebastian told her harshly.

"No minister of matrimony will marry me to you without the king's consent, for that matter none would marry us without my consent."

"I've found one who will," he informed her calmly. "You will marry me and you will have no say in the matter."

"Why?" Roseanna's voice was broken, and much to Kathryn's disgust, she sounded on the verge of tears, "Why are you doing this? I am fourth in line for the throne with three brothers before me. Becoming king cannot be of interest to you. So why abduct me and force me to marry you?"

Sebastian laughed. "Because I want you," His voice turned to ice, "and I always get what I want. Enjoy your last few days of freedom, my love."

There was the sound of heavy footsteps followed by the sound of a heavy door closing. Kathryn heard the turn of a lock and then silence.

Princess Roseanna began to weep and Kathryn waited a few minutes before peeking into the room again. It was empty except for the princess sitting on the bed, her head in her hands, crying bitterly.

Cautiously Kathryn tapped on the glass.

At the sound of tapping Roseanna's head jerked up and she almost cried out as she spotted a head outside the window. Moving quickly she opened the window and asked quickly, "Who are you?"

"Speak quietly your highness," Kathryn instructed, pitching her voice an octave lower than normal. "Voices travel far in the night and the guards are alert."

Lowering her voice Roseanna repeated her question. "Who are you, for that matter how did you get here?"

"Names are not important your highness and as to how I got here you're better off not knowing."

"But why are you here?"

"Your father sent me."

Roseanna closed her eyes and let out a relieved sigh. "I knew he hadn't forgotten me," she whispered.

"Your faith is admirable, princess."

Roseanna turned back to the window. "Surely I'm not to come out there with you?" she asked hesitantly.

"No princess. You will not come with me tonight."

"What!"

"Please Princess, you must remain quiet." Kathryn fought the urge to scold the woman like a child. "You cannot come with me tonight because I'm trying to find a way in for others."

"You mean you're not alone?"

"No, there are a few others, but we need a way in that doesn't involve climbing like this."

"You must come for me tomorrow night." Roseanna pleaded. "He cannot be allowed to marry me."

"I heard. We will come for you as soon as we can, but until then you must remain patient."

"I will try, but you must know he plans on moving me."

"Do you know where to?"

Roseanna shuddered, "most likely to his room, that's where the ceremony will probably take place."

"Men," Kathryn spat in disgust. Of course, back at Blackwood Manor, the Lady had had just as many clandestine...partners as her husband had. "Do you know where his chambers are?"

Roseanna shook her head. "I was blindfolded and drugged when they brought me here."

Kathryn nodded slowly. "I'll find it." She began to climb down but Roseanna caught her hand.

"Thank you," she whispered. "You've given me hope."

Kathryn looked at her. "You must keep that hope hidden. Sebastian cannot know what happened tonight or what will happen tomorrow."

"I'm a good actress," the princess assured her. Kathryn sincerely doubted it.

Kathryn slipped down the tower the same way she had come up. While she was thrilled to hear that the Duke was going to move Roseanna from the tower, which would make rescuing her that much easier, her next challenge was to locate the Duke's private chambers. And it was going to take time she wasn't willing to spend.

Entering the castle itself proved more difficult than climbing the towers but Kathryn made it without too much loss in time. Once inside she found herself grateful that the halls were dimly lit and virtually empty with the exception of the occasional guard. Apparently all the extra security was confined only to the castle grounds. She supposed she should be grateful for the Duke's overconfidence in his fortifications and drunk knights.

Finding the Duke's quarters turned out to be the most difficult part of the whole mission. The castle was not laid out in a neat and orderly fashion. Kathryn came to the conclusion that it had been built solely for the purpose of driving someone crazy. Dead ends were everywhere and hallways lead to another hallway to another hallway and then back to the original hallway.

Knowing she was running out of time Kathryn sped up her search. Her frustration grew as she found room after room that never ended up being the Duke's room. Suddenly Kathryn felt a gentle breeze brush past her ear. She froze, attempting to determine what had caused the breeze, but she could identify nothing as its source. The breeze returned and curled down her arm and to her wrist. She noticed a torch off to her right and two corridors down flicker. She remained motionless. The breeze returned, stronger this time and repeated its journey from her ear to her hand. Again the torch flickered.

Abruptly Kathryn understood. The breeze was trying to guide her to where she needed to go. But how in the kingdom's name...?

David.

It could only be David. He had used the wind to listen in on her and Roseanna's conversation and was now attempting to help her navigate the castle. Had more time been available, Kathryn would have ignored him and kept looking on her own, but time was short, and while she didn't want the help she grudgingly admitted to herself that she needed it. She followed the breeze and eventually found what she believed to be Sebastian's private rooms.

Inside was such extravagance that it physically shocked her. Heavy gold curtains hung over the windows, push carpets adorned the floors and everywhere around her were golden and jeweled trinkets that took up more space than the bed.

Leaving quickly Kathryn found a route back less extensive then the one she had taken in.

"It's past the changing of the guard," Matt whispered. "Something must have gone wrong."

"It's not that far past," Jenna objected. She looked over at David who, after fifteen initial minutes of anxious pacing, had suddenly sat down and closed his eyes. He hadn't moved yet.

"Twenty minutes?"

"She'll be here." Jenna informed him. "If she'd been caught it would have been obvious."

"Now that's a charming thought." Kathryn's wry comment cut through the darkness.

Matt whirled around to find her standing a few feet above and to the side of him. "How did you do that?"

Kathryn climbed down to join them. "The same way I got inside."

"What did you learn?" Daniel asked.

"We have to rescue the princess tomorrow night."

"Why tomorrow?" Natalie asked sourly. Matt, Jenna, and Daniel all shot her angry looks. Kathryn studied them intently. Something had happened while she'd been gone and whatever it had been, it had set the three against Natalie. Normally she wouldn't complain, but on a mission like this, any division in the team could prove lethal.

And not for their enemies.

"Sebastian plans to marry her in two night's time," David said as he picked himself off the ground and handed Kathryn her bow and quiver. He didn't appear as affected by whatever had taken place, but she didn't miss the 'don't argue, I'm in charge' glare he leveled at Natalie.

"How in blazes do you know that?" Daniel asked.

"He listened in," Kathryn replied stiffly.

David raised his eyebrows at her and after an initial glare she avoided his gaze. While he understood Kathryn's natural inclination to do everything on her own, he at least expected her to admit to herself that she had needed the help. Without his breeze to guide her, she wouldn't have made it out in time. In fact without his breeze to cause the distraction in the courtyard he doubted she would have been able to make it up the tower before another changing of the guard.

Not that he would ever voice his thoughts to her. He wasn't suicidal.

"We go tomorrow," David said firmly.

Together they faded into the night like ghosts.

Chapter 19

The faint moonlight breaking through the cloud cover outlined Sebastian's castle in the darkness. Its cold stone walls stood like silent guardians, the towers with their golden windows appeared like the ever watchful eyes of a deadly predator.

Together the Dragons stood ready in the very spot they had been the night before, dressed as Guardians; their faces completely masked and the hilts of their weapons covered with dark residue to cut down the reflection of the metal, ready to act. They stood, waiting. Waiting and watching for the right moment, and then, moving as one, they started down the cliffs.

When they reached the first wall the rest waited while Kathryn ascended, scampering up the vertical monolith with ease. Her movement was barely noticeable to those on the ground. There was no sound, no heavy breathing, no scraping as her feet found traction in the wall's crevices, no grunting as her arm muscles pulled her ever upward with ease. Moments later, two breaching ropes unfurled themselves as they reached ground. The faint hoot of an owl sounded and the rest joined her on top of the wall. Upon reaching the top they moved the bodies of the guards Kathryn had efficiently disposed of with poisoned darts— which Matt had conveniently concocted out of roots, minerals, and herbs he had bought while wandering the apothecaries and spice market. Like apparitions they disappeared into one of the service doors in the wall that led to the forward extension of the castle gateway.

The guards inside had no opportunity to react. One moment the hallway was empty and they were discussing where to go for a drink once their shift ended, and then there was a sharp sting in their necks followed by rapidly spreading numbness. As his vision went dark one of the guards thought he saw a dark robed figure moving towards him. It was his last living thought.

The outer wall sentries were easily defeated and the first real trouble the team encountered was in the narrow courtyard leading between the second and third wall. Kathryn and Daniel released their poison-tipped projectiles at the same time, but at the last second, Kathryn's target moved slightly and the dart hit the wall instead of the guard. He was able to utter half a startled shout before Kathryn's second dart hit its intended victim.

Alerted, the rest of the guards took up defense positions, two of the guards were foolish enough to attempt to charge their unseen enemy. Matt and David's arrows cut them down before they could move three meters. The remaining four guards huddled together, shouting at the top of their lungs for help, but to the Guardians standing a mere twenty feet away the soldiers looked like fish out of water, mouths opening and closing with no sound coming from them. Poison darts and arrows quickly cleared out any remaining resistance.

"Interesting trick," Kathryn commented quietly as they moved into a deserted corridor.

"Well, we couldn't have them raising the alarm," her leader replied defensively.

"I wasn't saying it was a bad idea," Kathryn muttered as she raised her dart gun and took down another unfortunate guard. "I just said it was an interesting trick."

Moving faster now the Dragons hit three more pockets of guards before they hit the inner courtyards.

Here there were too many guards to handle without making noise or raising the alarm. David had decided earlier that the courtyards would be the likely place where the alarm would spread. He wanted four Dragons fighting in the courtyards and two to slip behind the action and enter the castle keep. As they entered the courtyard Kathryn and Daniel faded back and moved as one with the wall, using the shadows to cover their movement

Everything was easier said than done.

David and Natalie fought as a team, protecting the others' backs. David grunted as he parried one knight whose strength suggested he lifted trees for exercise or perhaps he just did it for fun. It didn't really matter, his days of impressing others with his unquestioned vigor were about to end. Reaching down he released a long thin dagger from his hip and thrust it upwards into his assailant's chest. The knight fell to the ground with a heavy thud, only to be replaced by an even bigger man. *Where does Sebastian get these people?* He dodged a particularly lethal thrust to his midsection. Spinning around he threw his knife at the same time he attacked with his sword. His opponent blocked the sword... he hadn't seen the knife throw. As he avoided another blow, David pulled his knife from the dying knight and prepared to face his next opponent.

Natalie, like all female guardians, had been trained to use the feminine advantage of agility and speed to overcome her opponents. However she was faltering. She had never been in a real battle before and her confidence was wavering. If she had to be honest, it had started failing before the attack had begun. Earlier, when David had gone over the plan, she'd originally been partnered with Matt. Then Matt had shocked her, shocked everyone, by saying that he wasn't comfortable having Natalie at his back. David had looked at him long and hard before asking why. Matt had argued that Natalie hadn't been participating in the extra training sessions, whereas Jenna had and he preferred to have someone at his back who he knew could cover it. Natalie had held her breath as David had considered his words. Their leader hadn't been happy about Matt's argument, but had agreed to take Natalie as his partner for the fight, pairing Jenna and Matt together. It had been humiliating beyond words. Kathryn hadn't said a word throughout the whole exchange, but Natalie hadn't missed her intense gaze as she'd studied the expressions on Jenna, Matt, and Daniel's faces.

Now, despite her vows to prove to Matt that she was just as capable as the rest of them without Kathryn's extra training she had to admit that she was failing miserably. As she fought one particular knight she noticed his thrusts getting closer and closer to her skin. Her training told her not to panic, but adrenaline and experience were telling her that panic was okay. Her own attacks were becoming more and more sloppy. Inexplicably her opponent grunted before falling to the ground—dead. Natalie looked up to see David looking at her, his eyes ordering her to keep her focus, his throwing knife embedded in the knight's neck. She nodded and he spun around to face another opponent.

Ω·℥

Across the courtyard, Jenna and Matt were fighting their own mini-war. Jenna's preferred weapon, like Kathryn's, was the bow. She and Matt had their backs to the wall to prevent anyone coming up behind them. Unfortunately it also meant that they couldn't retreat if they were overwhelmed. Jenna stood behind her partner, using her bow to pick off the knights at the edges. Matt stood in front of her, using his sword to end the life of any knight who dared to challenge him. The arrangement worked nicely. Jenna would funnel the knights towards Matt's whirling blade and Matt would dispose of one or two at a time. After what seemed like radians only one knight stood before Matt. Surprising both Jenna and the knight, Matt put his sword away.

"What are you doing?" Jenna hollered, drawing her bow, an arrow already nocked and ready. Matt signaled for her to lower her bow.

The knight was becoming uneasy. If any other opponent had put away his weapons, he would have attacked immediately. But this opponent was a Guardian and attacking could be a trap. For a moment he hesitated, the second Guardian appeared as confused as he felt and he had a feeling that whatever was about to happen wasn't going to be pleasant. But with the Guardian's weapons away, the knight knew he had the tactical advantage. Several more knights joined him and the first knight felt his courage return.

Even as he made up his mind and began to move forward he felt the ground move beneath him. Startled he glanced down to see a large bulge of dirt growing steadily before his feet.

In a calm voice Matt said, "Come forward."

"Matt, what are you doing?" Jenna hissed from behind him. "They don't need any encouragement!"

The ground exploded without any warning and the stunned knights soon found themselves crawling with insects of every size, shape, and type. The insects burrowed into their armor and began attacking them from inside. Screaming, they dropped their swords and began hitting and pounding on their armor, trying to squash the miniature assailants.

Jenna came up to stand next to Matt. "The influence of small creatures, huh?" she asked, echoing his words from that distant afternoon.

Matt smiled. "You know, I've always wanted to try that."

David and Natalie moved to join them, having cleared their side of the courtyard of knights. "We need to keep moving," David said as he nervously glanced around. There should have been more guards pouring through the courtyard entrance, but there weren't—and that worried him.

Natalie looked down at the now still knights and the long trail of insects leading back to the hole in the ground. "I told you!" She exclaimed looking at David. "I told you there were bugs in the kitchen! Now do you believe me?"

David glanced at the dead knights and motioned his team through the still empty courtyard. "Yeah, I believe you. Now let's find Kathryn and

Daniel." As they entered the second courtyard they found the remains of at least twenty knights spread around, all with arrows sticking out of them... no wonder there hadn't been more guards. Kathryn and Daniel obviously hadn't had the easy entrance they had hoped for. Up ahead David could hear the sounds of battle.

&)·&

When the team of Guardians had stepped into the courtyard it had become chaos. Kathryn and Daniel had only managed to get halfway around the wall before they had been spotted. After a brief moment of hesitation, Kathryn had decided to try to get by without stopping to kill any, leaving that to the others. She and Daniel had run, dodged, and crawled their way through the first courtyard only to enter the second to find twenty knights maintaining a steady line of defense.

Daniel had come to the same conclusion she had at nearly the same time. Twenty knights, standing fifty feet away all armed with swords...this was going to be easy. Sheathing his sword he knocked an arrow on his bow even as he retrieved it from his back. By the time he had released his first arrow, Kathryn had already killed two knights.

It had been poor tactical planning to send twenty knights into the courtyard armed only with swords and no support from archers. By the time the knights began their charge, their numbers were already down by seven, halfway across the courtyard they numbered nine, and when they finally reached close quarters there were only four, who quickly found out that some Guardians can use their bows in close quarters just as easily as from a distance.

Kathryn nodded to a small, almost invisible door in the side of the wall. "This way." They entered the castle, only to find themselves contending with more knights concealed in the corridors.

Steadily pressing forward, Kathryn and Daniel fought the knights. Kathryn still managed to make use of her longbow in the tight hallways, but it was Daniel's sword that was doing most of the damage.

"This is taking too long," Kathryn observed as she dropped another knight. Deftly she switched from her bow to her two knives, quickly downing another two guards.

"Tell me about it," Daniel grunted pulling his sword from a downed enemy only to turn and face a new one.

"We need a way to speed things up."

"Well I'm open to any suggestions." Daniel ducked beneath the blade of another knight while thrusting his own upward, his opponent fell only to be replaced by another. "How many of these guys are there?"

"Sebastian supplemented his security remember?"

"Yeah, but by how much?"

Kathryn didn't have the time to reply. Arrows were beginning to rain down on them from hidden archer enclaves. As she landed a sturdy kick to an attacking knight's head, Kathryn put away her knives and retrieved her bow. Keeping her back to a wall, she focused on an arrow as it sped into the fray and quickly calculated its trajectory. Knocking and drawing an arrow

203

almost simultaneously she aimed and fired. As each new ballistic missile flew towards them, Kathryn sent one of her own back.

The two were still in the corridor when David, Natalie, Matt, and Jenna, joined them. Now the odds were better, six Guardians against the remaining one hundred and fifty nights.

℘·℗

From inside Sebastian's quarters Roseanna could hear the commotion. Her heart leapt with joy, she was going to be rescued.

Suddenly the door opened and the Duke himself hurried in, locking the door behind him. Roseanna jumped up from the chair she had been sitting in, backing as far away as she could get.

Sebastian smiled at her coldly. "We don't have much time princess, at least not as much as I would have liked." He lunged for her saying, "So I guess we'll have to rush this a little."

Roseanna screamed and leaped out of his reach.

Eyes blazing he came at her again. "We don't have time to dance around the issue," he growled lunging at her again. This time he caught her wrist but she kicked him in the shins.

Howling with pain he let go of her wrist and rubbed his leg.

Taking advantage of his momentary distraction Roseanna flew to the other side of the room.

"You will pay for that," he said, his icy voice sending shivers down her spine. Instead of rushing at her he moved slowly and deliberately towards her, blocking off every avenue of escape until he was practically on top of her.

Roseanna desperately tried to slip past him but he grabbed her around the waist and picked her up. Both hands flailing Roseanna barred her nails and scratched as his face as much as she could.

He hollered at the pain but didn't release her, instead he lowered her feet to floor released her waist, but grabbed both hands and twisted them behind her back.

This time is was Roseanna's turn to cry out. He pushed her towards his bed while she desperately tried to break loose.

℘·℗

"This is getting hopeless." David hollered as he bashed in another knight's skull with the hilt of his sword, the knight toppled to the ground unconscious.

"I agree." Daniel shouted back. "At this rate we'll never get to the princess in time."

"Kat!" David yelled above the commotion. "Do you have any ideas on how to speed this up?"

"Just one."

"What is it?"

℘·℗

Sebastian tied Roseanna's hands together and wound a gag across her mouth. "Sorry my, love, it looks like we're going to have to make a fast getaway."

204

Roseanna struggled as much as she could with her arms tied behind her, kicking out at his shins and knees as often as she could. Her courage strengthened with every grunt he let out, letting her know she had hurt him.

When Kathryn didn't immediately answer him, David tried again. "What's your idea Kat?"

"Blind them!" Her arrows whizzed by his head, inches from his ear.

"Watch it! You almost took off my ear!" He yelled as he began to reach inside and tap into his power.

In his mind he imagined the corridor glowing like the surface of the sun and he knew Natalie was doing the same thing.

He sensed the hall growing brighter and brighter. The combined power of two light gifted Guardians made the corridor so bright it seemed like the blazing furnace of the surface of the sun.

"I can't see!" One of them cried, groping for shadows in the bright light.

"My eyes are burning up!"

"Natalie!" Kathryn called. "Finish them!"

"How?" Natalie's question held a slight hit of panic. She'd managed to hold it together in the courtyard but was beyond comprehending what Kathryn was asking of her.

"Burn them, create a fire barrier, or whatever you want, just do something!" Kathryn let another arrow fly as she moved away from a sword thrust aimed at her neck.

Natalie let steams of fire flow from her hands, engulfing the unfortunate soldiers still in the hallway.

The panicked screams of the knights echoed through the halls scared the reinforcements back into the courtyards.

"Okay!" David cried after a few moments. The acrid stench of charred flesh and hair filled the corridors making David's head spin slightly. "Enough. They're out of this fight." *Natalie's going to have to work on control*, he thought as they raced through the halls.

The light dimmed back to normal and the six Guardians hurried through the smoke filled corridor and toward the Duke's bedroom, unchallenged and unmolested. Jenna and Matt lagged slightly behind the other four to maintain a rear guard. Matt paused for a moment while wiping tears from his eyes and hacking smoke residue from his lungs. Bending over with both hands on his knees he rasped between breaths, "That's just nasty, real nasty."

"Of all people, I would have thought you'd be used to a little smoke and the smell of burnt flesh."

Matt straightened with an incredulous look while narrowing his eyes. "You have a problem with my cooking?"

Jenna grinned and headed off in the direction of the rest of the team. Turning she gestured for him to follow. "Come on char-boy they might need some help!"

Matt harrumphed to himself and followed after her with sword in hand.

ଶ·ଓ

Upon finding the door locked David and Daniel broke down the door.

Duke Sebastian was a giant of a man by any standard. Standing at almost seven feet tall, he dominated everyone in the room. He was still attempting to keep a steady hold on the struggling princess, who looked like a small child in his muscled arms. David vaguely remembered hearing that the Duke had been a renowned warrior in his youth and the size of his shoulders and arms convinced David that the Duke kept up on his training. Seeing that he had no other choice Sebastian whipped a dagger out and held it to the princess' throat, intending with every fiber of his being to slit her from ear to ear.

David seeing what he was about to do tried to move quickly enough to prevent it. Before he even took half a step, an arrow flew past him just above his shoulder causing him to twist away. A second arrow whizzed by.

The first arrow hit the Duke in his arm and the second took him in the shoulder and sent him sprawling to the floor.

David turned to Kathryn to see her holding the bow at ready, another arrow already notched and ready to go. "I'm sure glad you're on my side," he said in surprise. "Any particular reason you didn't kill him?"

Kathryn moved to the princess and cut the ropes that bound her. "We need a hostage to get out of here," she replied, helping the sobbing princess to sit up. "He seems like the best choice."

"I didn't think you'd make it," Princess Roseanna cried.

Immediately Natalie ran over and put her arms around her. "We're glad that we did," she soothed.

"Your Highness," David addressed the princess. She stared at him, shock beginning to overwhelm her. "We need to move quickly, can you walk?"

After a few moments, the princess appeared to collect herself and nodded. "I'm ready to run if needed." Roseanna got to her feet, determination written across her face. "Just get me out of here."

"We'd be glad to," Daniel grunted as he hauled the duke to his feet. David crossed the room and used the rope that had bound the princess to secure the duke's hands behind his back.

Roseanna crossed the room and placed herself in front of the seething Duke. "I guess now you're about to find out just how much my father does care." She told him hotly before slapping him across the face.

David chuckled softly. "Princess you stay between Kat and myself. Dan if you think you can handle him, you can walk up front with our hostage. Nat you walk after Dan and Jen you walk after Princess Roseanna."

"Aye, aye Captain!" Daniel called as he moved towards the door. The rest of them formed up and walked out of the chamber.

At first they met up with some resistance but it quickly died when they realized their leader was captive and being led out in his underclothes. Daniel successfully and uneventfully led the group out of the castle and out of its grounds without so much as loosing another shot.

Natalie helped the princess up onto her horse then mounted behind her. David went to the stables and found a horse for the duke to ride. After securing Sebastian they started riding towards the capitol.

For three days everything went smoothly, they tended to the few wounds they had amassed during the fight that first night, and then two days before they were scheduled to reach the palace, the group woke up to find Duke Sebastian gone and Natalie as well.

"What happened?" David demanded furiously.

"The only thing I can figure," Daniel said, looking at the tracks. "Is that somehow Sebastian got loose during the night and took a hostage should we catch up with him."

"And Nat being the least immature of us all..." Jenna said slowly.

"Made her the perfect hostage," Kathryn finished.

"Oh, this is just great." David was frustrated beyond anything he had ever felt before. "Who tied the duke last night after dinner?"

Kathryn sighed. "Nat."

"She was in a hurry." Roseanna spoke up

"And is paying for it." David replied angrily.

There was silence for a few moments then Daniel asked, "Um, shouldn't we be going after them?"

David turned. "You, Matt, and Jen stay here with Roseanna, Kat— David looked around for her and found her missing as well. "Hey! Where did she go!?"

"To find Nat," Roseanna spoke quietly. "She left right after she last spoke."

Spinning on his heel David set out after her. "You guys wait here, if I'm gone more than a radian, continue toward the capitol, we'll catch up." As he followed the trail Kathryn had left behind David told himself that when he caught up with her they were going to have a serious discussion about teamwork.

℘·ℰ

Despite the dense foliage, following the trail was easy. Natalie was smart enough to leave an obvious trail for her rescue, at least obvious for a Guardian, either that or Sebastian wasn't worried about being tracked. Kathryn ran silently through the trees, Destiny flying high above, and her ears and senses alert for any indication that she was approaching the fugitive and his captive.

Finally, near midday, Kathryn heard Natalie's voice.

"You won't get away with this you know."

"Oh shut your mouth!"

"My friends will come for me."

There was the sound of a slap. "I said shut up!" Sebastian bellowed.

Kathryn slowed and approached cautiously. It didn't take a genius to tell that the Duke was desperate and desperate men did desperate and stupid things. Kidnapping Natalie fell into the second category. She was still trying to figure out why the Duke had chosen Natalie as a hostage instead of going for the Princess again.

The sound of water, which had been growing steadily stronger, had graduated into a full-fledged roar. Sebastian had taken Natalie to the Nahar River. Was he expecting a rescue committee? Kathryn pulled an arrow from her quiver and notched it. Destiny landed in the dirt next to her feet. Silently, she tapped three fingers against her hip, commanding Destiny to stay put.

Warily Kathryn rounded a bend and caught sight of the two. Natalie was standing next to a large boulder, her hands bound in front of her, her mask gone. Sebastian paced nervously in front of her.

"This will never work," Natalie informed him defiantly.

Sebastian whirled around his hand ready to slap her. "I told you enough— He brought his hand down in a sweeping motion—

At that moment Kathryn stepped out of the trees pulled the arrow back and fired. It went straight through his hand tearing flesh, muscle, and bone, as she knew it would. Sebastian screamed in pain.

"Give up, Sebastian!" she called.

Natalie began to move toward Kathryn but Sebastian, too desperate to surrender grabbed her around the neck and held her in front of him.

"If you want to kill me, you'll have to kill her," he rasped. Despite the arrow still lodged in his hand, his grip on Natalie was inhumanly strong. Blood poured out of his injured hand, soaking the front of Natalie's overgarment.

Kathryn, who by now had already redrawn her bow considered her options. Natalie was small, much smaller than Sebastian. In fact the girl only came up mid-chest on the man. She had an open shot, but there was a possibility that Sebastian would move and her arrow would fly past him. She might not have another chance to get off another shot before he snapped Natalie's neck.

Another danger was the river directly behind them. From where she stood, Kathryn couldn't see the river between the banks, and from the sound of the water, she guessed that it was a good sized drop to the water. If her arrow did hit its mark there was a possibility that Natalie would be pulled backwards into the river with Sebastian. Still another danger was along with being pulled backwards and down, Sebastian had his arm wrapped around Natalie's neck, if he moved wrong, he could break it.

In each scenario was the possibility that Natalie wouldn't make it, but Kathryn didn't have a choice. Her job was to take Sebastian, dead or alive. And at this point, the man had seen Natalie without her mask. Easy decision. She looked at Natalie and for the first time she saw fear in the girl's eyes.

Kathryn looked Natalie straight in the eye. "Do you trust me?"

Natalie's lip quivered, but just for an instant. She'd also identified each of the scenarios Kathryn had and understood the risks Kathryn was about to take. She also knew that Kathryn didn't like her options, but neither of them had a choice. "I trust you."

In that instant Kathryn loosed her arrow.

Sebastian never imagined that Kathryn would risk her companion's life to capture him. That the Guardian would make the leap from capturing to killing him in a single breath he never even contemplated. The arrow jumped from the bow before he could react.

It took him in the left eye and he slumped backward, pulling Natalie with him.

Kathryn leapt forward but was too slow to cover the distance. Both Natalie and Sebastian disappeared over the side.

Natalie felt the arrow strike Sebastian, could feel his body shudder with the impact. As she felt him drag her backwards she struggled to free herself. His dead weight plunged them both over the side, as they fell Natalie grasped blindly for handholds along the bank. Her hand snagged a root and she held on for dear life.

The sudden stop, brought with her grasp of the root, loosened Sebastian's arm around her neck and he fell into the water.

Natalie gasped as the root began to part from the embankment, causing her to swing in an arc, she needed to find another support. Kathryn's head appeared over the bank.

"Hold on, Natalie!"

"I'm trying!" Natalie called desperately. She could see Kathryn looking around frantically for a vine or stick that she could use to pull her up. The root slid some more. "Hurry Kathryn!" Natalie begged. "The root won't hold much longer."

Kathryn fumbled at her waist for the sash she wore. It wasn't much, but hopefully better than the root Natalie held. She threw the end down and Natalie grabbed at it just as the root gave way. The sudden addition of weight nearly sent Kathryn over the edge.

Desperately Kathryn tried to regain her footing as she began sliding closer to the edge. "Natalie!" she called, "is there any sort of ledge available for you to stand on?"

Natalie looked around, three meters below her was a small outcropping no more than a half a meter wide. "Yes!" she called back. "But I don't know how steady it is." Her foot found a small rock sticking out of the dirt and she braced herself on it.

Kathryn wracked her brain for other options, but they didn't have any. At this rate she'd be over the edge in about a minute. "We don't have a choice, I need you to stand on it."

"It's three meters down," Natalie called back, suddenly the tiny foothold she'd found collapsed and she dropped downward, pulling Kathryn with her.

&)·C8

Kathryn felt the jerk but was powerless to prevent herself from tumbling over along with Natalie. Keeping a death grip on the sash in one hand, Kathryn's other hand frantically sought roots and outcroppings as she plunged down the side of the bank. Her hand snagged a thick root and their combined weight nearly wrenched her arm from its socket, but their fall had been stopped. Natalie was about half a meter below the ledge she had found and managed to pull herself up onto the ledge, where she collapsed, sagging against the wall. "Thank you," She gasped.

Kathryn carefully dropped to the ledge. "You're welcome."

They were silent for a moment, catching their breath, and then Natalie said softly, "It's my fault Sebastian broke free."

Destiny called from somewhere above and Kathryn answered her with a whistle. To Natalie's comment, Kathryn's reply was surprisingly gentle. "We know."

"Then you also know why he chose me as a hostage." Natalie's tone was bitter as she thought of the way he had taunted her as he dragged her through the forest.

Again Kathryn's reply was calm. "We guessed why." Well sort of. The Princess would still have been an easier hostage, but Roseanna had been kept far away from the Duke and within a protective circle of Guardians. Destiny appeared in front of them and perched herself on Kathryn's knees.

Natalie looked at Kathryn in disbelief as she stroked her bird. "What, no lecture on the proper procedure for tying criminals? Or about how a Guardian needs to be attentive at all times?"

Kathryn shook her head. "We all make mistakes," She said quietly, and then looked at Natalie. "The important thing is that we learn from them," she said sternly.

Natalie, who had been expecting a lecture, wished she'd gotten one instead of grace from the person she had hated most. "I don't deserve your mercy," she said miserably. "I've treated you horribly."

"That I won't deny," Kathryn agreed, shifting her arm slightly to relieve some of the pain that was beginning to throb in her wrist. "The question is, what are we going to do about it?"

Natalie paused a moment. "I don't suppose a simple apology will do it for you?"

Her lieutenant snorted. "After what you put me through? I don't think so. But it is a start," she said after a pause.

Natalie swallowed hard. "Did you have something in mind?"

Kathryn thought for a moment. Natalie could almost see the vengeful wheels turning in the younger girl's eyes. *Whatever she decides, I'll bear it*, she vowed. *I deserve it.*

"I'll discuss it with David," Kathryn said finally.

Natalie felt wretched. Instead of taking the opportunity to humiliate and ensure that a strict punishment was enforced, Kathryn was willing to temper her feelings about the situation with David's far more impartial judgment. Natalie knew that she could never have been so gracious. Abruptly she realized just how wrong she had been.

"I truly am sorry," Natalie said quietly.

"Don't worry about it," Kathryn replied, her voice a little brusque, as she gingerly examined her wrist which was beginning to swell slightly.

"No!" Natalie exclaimed. "I won't let you brush it off. I was cruel and insufferable to you, I wouldn't have treated a servant the way I treated you. I hated you. I imagined trying to replace you as the second in command. I even broke the rule against invading privacy. I was even mad at you for being assigned the room *I* wanted."

Kathryn sighed, and shifted uncomfortably against the embankment. "It's alright Natalie, I've been treated worse."

"No it's not alright!" Natalie insisted vehemently, and then added more slowly, "I'm sorry Kathryn, I was wrong to treat you that way. You are the best choice for second in command. This mission proved that to me. The night you went scouting, Matt, Jenna, and Daniel all made it clear that they blamed me for your reclusiveness and that they thought I was a bloody idiot. And then Matt refused to partner with me..." she trailed off. "I hurt my own standing in this family more than yours. You had our best interests at heart when all I wanted was everyone else to look at me."

"I forgive you Natalie, I've never held it against you." Well, maybe a little, but Kathryn felt that it wouldn't do Natalie any good to know that.

Natalie slumped back against the embankment. "Thank you," she said softly.

Unexpectedly, Natalie flung her arms round her old rival in a hug. Kathryn was so startled at the sudden contact that she almost slipped from the ledge. Then Natalie suddenly pulled back. "What did you mean when you said were treated worse? Who would dare mistreat you? Besides me that is..."

Kathryn took a deep breath. She supposed that it couldn't hurt to tell Natalie the bare basics. "I was abused as a little girl, Natalie. Treated like a slave in both my uncle's home as well as the manor I was brought to afterwards."

"Oh Kathryn!" Natalie cried, "I am so sorry! I didn't know."

Kathryn smiled sadly, her gaze locked on the distant horizon. "There are very few who knew."

Natalie paused for a moment. "I envy you, you know."

Kathryn's own low self-esteem couldn't comprehend what Natalie was saying. "What?"

"I envy you," Natalie repeated. "You fight like you were born for it. I've never seen you hesitate in battle, and you never miss. I couldn't even manage to effectively kill one knight back at the castle. Yet you killed probably twenty or thirty men and when Sebastian had Roseanna you didn't even hesitate when you shot him in the arm, and when we went after the outlaws you and Amy killed three of their leaders on your own. All I did was watch from the sidelines...and David was always focused on you, I could never manage to get his attention. No matter how hard I tried," she added.

"Don't envy me, Natalie," Kathryn said quietly. "Confidence in battle and an ease of killing men is not something you should admire."

"In this job it is," Natalie replied firmly.

Kathryn was silent for a moment, then slowly nodded. "In this job, yes, confidence in battle is essential, but killing men should never come easy. And I'm fairly certain that the only reason David was paying so much attention to me was because he was imagining painful ways to kill me for being so uncooperative."

Natalie studied her. "I'm not so sure," she said slowly.

Now Kathryn was confused. "What do you mean?"

Natalie thought back through all of the times she'd studied David, only to find him studying Kathryn—with a look that was only partly with frustration. She suspected that her leader didn't even realize it yet himself. An idea popped into her head...Kathryn was going to kill her for this but it was going to be so much fun. And it would help make up for what she'd put Kathryn through.

Seeing that Kathryn was waiting for a reply, she began to reply but noticed a movement over her companion's shoulder. "There's a spider on your shoulder," she said quietly. The reaction she got was the last one she would have ever expected.

Kathryn turned, almost frantically, to look at her shoulder and came eye to eye with a spider roughly a hand span in size. She shrieked and the sudden, and totally unexpected, noise nearly sent Natalie off the ledge.

Meanwhile Kathryn, whose movements were usually smooth and effortless, was frantically trying to brush the spider off herself and only managed to topple both her, and the spider, over the edge of the ledge.

Natalie grabbed at Kathryn and managed to catch her hand while holding onto a root to keep herself from falling.

"Is it gone yet?"

Natalie looked down and noticed that Kathryn's hysterical movements and fall had indeed managed to dislodge the spider. "Yes," she answered honestly.

Intense relief filled the younger woman's face as they worked together to pull her back up. Once Kathryn was back on the ledge she turned to Natalie, "If you ever tell anyone, I swear I'll kill you."

Natalie grinned and nodded. "Understood."

After a few moments Natalie's shoulders started shaking until she could contain herself no longer. Letting out a snort she started giggling in uncontrolled waves.

Puzzled, Kathryn stared at her. "What's so funny?"

Natalie responded by mimicking Kathryn's frantic arm waving while attempting to dislodge the spider.

"That's not funny," her companion growled.

Natalie recovered her composure and twisted to face her in an attempt to apologize for her insensitivity.

As soon as she made eye contact, she giggled and was soon laughing so hard she could hardly see because of all the tears. Dumbfounded, Kathryn continued staring and finally shook her head while rolling her eyes.

ॐ·ॐ

David followed the trail until he reached the river. He saw the scuffed ground where a small battle had obviously taken place and he saw where Kathryn had shot her arrow, but there was no one to be seen. "Kathryn!" he called out. "Natalie!"

As he neared the bluff, he saw her bow and could hear a bellowing roar reverberating down the canyon from the scene below. He listened intently, but the crashing of the river drowned out all other sounds. If they'd fallen into the river they were going to have a rough time of it, Kathryn's gift notwithstanding. Who knew where they'd manage to escape the current? He knew that if they had fallen in, Kathryn would get them back to the glade. But the idea of leaving them, especially with Natalie's vendetta against the younger girl, made him cringe.

"Kathryn! Natalie!"

Kathryn voice called out, "down here!"

Quickly he crossed to the edge and looked down. There, a good five meters below him, sat Kathryn, Destiny, and Natalie, perched on the smallest outcropping possible. "What in the kingdom are you doing down there?" he asked.

They glanced upward. Kathryn was cradling one of her arms in her lap, David guessed that at the very least she'd sprained it and he was very interested to hear the story of how they'd ended up down there. However it was Natalie who was confusing him the most. Even though he could barely hear it from his location above the noise of the river, Natalie, after glancing from him to Kathryn had started laughing hysterically and from the tear tracks in the dirt on her face, she'd been laughing for quite some time already. Either that or she'd had a good cry before he'd arrived. What had happened?

Natalie paused in her mirth and flashed a smile at him. "What does it look like? We were waiting for you." He was as confused as he'd ever been. Two days ago they'd been enemies. Now they were sitting together like old friends. Women. He would *never* understand them.

David managed to rustle up some thick vines that the two girls could use to climb up the sheer embankment. Tossing the vines over the edge, David ended up pulling both girls up. As he had suspected Kathryn had strained her wrist when she had grabbed the root and Natalie had pulled a muscle in her leg. Climbing was possible—their training demanded that— but it would have been painful. David, unwilling to cause either of them any more pain had argued at length with both girls in order to persuade them to set aside their professional pride and let him help them.

Natalie went first and helped David as he pulled Kathryn up. The entire way up the cliff Destiny refused to move from Kathryn's shoulder making the trip up awkward, but eventually both made it.

"You know," David said as he studied Destiny. "You have one bizarre bird."

As they made their way to rejoin the others, Natalie confessed everything to David. When she'd finished he was quiet for a long time. Finally he turned to Kathryn, but the question he asked wasn't the one Natalie had been expecting. "Why didn't you come to me?"

"Not my style," she replied, hacking at the dense foliage that seemed to have already swallowed their initial path.

Natalie watched his jaw work and wasn't entirely sure whom he was more annoyed with, her or Kathryn.

After another minute, David sighed. "Fine, we'll work on *that* problem later. We still need to figure out what to do about Natalie's actions."

Kathryn was struggling with one particular bush that seemed determined to ensnare them in its thorns. "I figured that I'd leave that up to you." With a grunt she snapped off several of the branches directly in her face.

David couldn't hide his surprise. "You want me to decide the punishment?" He brought out one of his own knives and began hacking at the stubborn bush from the other side. Whatever the thing was, it caught on everything. He could feel the thorns snag in his tunic.

213

"Her actions were against me," Kathryn reminded them as she continued doggedly forward. "I'm not exactly impartial in this case. And you are our leader."

The conversation would have been serious if the two most powerful Guardians in the Dragons hadn't been fighting a losing battle with a plant. Natalie knew that she should have been acting contrite and humble, but she was fighting a losing battle with her laughter.

David must have heard her because he sent a glower her way. "This isn't funny, Natalie."

Oh, but it most certainly was. About thirty or so thorns had been hooked into his clothing on all sides, rendering him essentially motionless. She couldn't help it. She braced her already aching sides as her laughter bubbled out

David struggled to free himself from his captor and only succeeded in hooking more thorns into his clothes.

By this time, Kathryn had stopped her trail blazing and was staring at him, a slight smile raising one corner of her mouth. He turned his glare on her. "Get me out of here."

"Oh, I think you're doing fine on your own."

Natalie was bent over double, her hands wrapped around her waist, she was laughing so hard. "You look so ridiculous!"

"Kathryn, do something!"

The Dragon's lieutenant walked over and inspected the situation. "As far as I see it we have two options. I can cut the branches that are attached to you and you can walk back to the campsite with thirty branches attached to you, or I can saw the branches off at the base of the thorns and you can spend this evening's campfire digging them out of the cirin."

"Can't you just pull them out?" Natalie asked.

Kathryn shook her head. "The thorns are barbed," she explained. Reaching up she snapped a small twig off the bush and walked over to her. She held up the twig for Natalie to observe.

Natalie held the plant between two of her fingers. The thorns appeared to be comprised of several smaller thorns that had grown together and were hooked at both ends with points that reminded Natalie of a ship's anchor. "Yikes."

"If you're done with your examination of the local plant life, I'd like to be on our way...soon!" David called out sourly.

Natalie grinned at Kathryn. "He's grouchy today."

"And bossy," Kathryn agreed.

"Anytime today, ladies!"

Kathryn turned to face him. "I gave you the two options. I haven't heard you pick one!" She returned sharply.

"How about option three?"

"And just what is option three?" She returned sarcastically. "We dig up the bush and you carry it?"

"Convince the plant to let me go."

She stared at him. "How in the kingdom am I supposed to do that?!"

"Your gift!"

"What gif—?" Kathryn began angrily, but then abruptly stopped. "Oh. Right."

David let out an exasperated sound, but wisely didn't comment further. After a few moments, the bush began to retract its branches slowly. Thorn by thorn, David was finally released.

As soon as he was free, he stepped quickly away from his former prison and inspected his uniform. As far as Natalie could tell, there were a few puncture holes, but nothing serious. "Thank you," he said dryly.

"You're welcome," she returned sarcastically.

Natalie forced her smile down. This was the most she had ever seen Kathryn interact with anyone and she had a snarky sense of humor that made Natalie want to grin with every word. She would have to remember this.

They skirted around the thorn bush and continued on toward the campsite. After they'd gone about a kilometer, David continued their earlier conversation. "Natalie, I know that you've apologized to Kathryn and that she's forgiven you, but I can't ignore your actions."

"I understand."

"For seven days I want you in the barn mucking out the stalls."

Natalie felt her shoulders droop. "All the stalls?"

He nodded. "All the stalls."

∞·∞

The others had already left by the time the three arrived back at the campsite, but they didn't have that much of a lead and David, Natalie, and Kathryn quickly caught up with the rest of the group. Later, around the campfire, Kathryn sat down next to Natalie. "Why didn't you fry Sebastian with your gift when he took you?" she asked quietly.

Natalie was silent for a moment, the flames flickering in her emerald eyes. Finally she spoke. "He recognized me," she said quietly.

Kathryn stared at her in disbelief. "He what?"

"After he ripped off my mask he recognized me from a party several years ago. He threatened my family if I didn't cooperate."

For the first time in her life, Kathryn was truly grateful that she didn't have a family that could be held over her as leverage. "Did you try?" she asked finally.

The older girl nodded. "Of course I did. I tried several times. He made me so angry when he threatened my family, but deep down I was terrified for them. I wanted to make sure he could never hurt them, but when I tried..." she took a deep breath. "It was like I'd never had the power. I couldn't find it inside myself. It was like my gift had abandoned me."

Kathryn shook her head. "It didn't abandon you, you simply lost your focus."

"It happened back at the castle too." Natalie said quietly remembering the difficulty she'd had controlling the fire used to demoralize the rest of the knights.

"We can fix that."

Surprised, Natalie turned to look at Kathryn. "We?"

"I'll work with you on improving your battle skills."

"Really?"

"We start tomorrow."

"Thank you!"

Kathryn smirked slightly at Natalie's enthusiastic tone. "You won't be so excited once I get done with you," she warned.

"I can handle it."

"That I seriously doubt."

Chapter 20

David led the group back to the Capitol where Princess Roseanna rejoined her grateful family and, after a heartfelt thanks from the royal family, the group set off for home. During the ride home David noticed that Kathryn and Natalie spent a lot of time together. He had planned on talking to Natalie about what had happened at the Duke's castle, and later with Sebastian, but Kathryn appeared to be covering that for him. His lieutenant spent radians after they had camped each night working with Natalie, utilizing both physical weapons and their gifts. Occasionally Kathryn would enlist someone else's help during those training sessions, usually Matt or Daniel. David had been recruited for one such session and found himself slightly shocked at the degree of ruthlessness that Kathryn employed in her teaching. Gentle was not a word he would be using to describe her anytime soon.

He noticed, with some confusion, that Kathryn spent more time focused on physical training than on Natalie's gift. When he'd asked her about it she'd replied, "Natalie's problem isn't her inability to use her gift, it's her inability to react when facing an opponent who truly means her harm. She panics when faced with something that wasn't covered in school. By increasing her skills that don't involve her gifts, she'll be able to adapt to new situations with confidence and that confidence will help her retain her control over both her physical and gifted abilities."

He hadn't been able to find a flaw in her logic so he let them be. After a few days, he noticed an easiness in the group that hadn't been there before. However brutal and bizarre Kathryn's technique was it appeared to be working.

When they were three days away from home he and Natalie went hunting for dinner together and David asked her about it.

"I notice you've been spending a lot of time with Kathryn lately," he commented as they fought their way through the thick underbrush. "Does that mean you two have ironed out your differences?"

Natalie nodded. "Yes."

"What, no elaboration?" He joked half seriously. Any insight into Kathryn would be appreciated.

"Do you need it?"

"I guess not," he conceded, spying the tracks of a wild pig. "Has Kathryn opened up to you at all?"

"No."

"No?" He found that hard to believe. "All the time you've spent with her and she hasn't mentioned anything?"

"Not a word. And I've done enough prying, so I'm not going to ask."

They followed the tracks to a large growth of dense underbrush. Taking up defensive positions David was preparing to scare the pig out from its burrow when a piercing shriek from above commanded both Guardians' attentions.

A dark blur shot downward into the underbrush. There was the sound of branches breaking followed by the roar of an irate pig and the continued cacophony of squeals and shrieks. Suddenly a large wild boar, weighing in at what looking like about two hundred fifty pounds, burst out from under the bush, bucking and hollering at its attacker.

"It's Destiny!" Natalie cried in amazement.

It was. Kathryn's eagle was dive-bombing the pig with the force of an arrow launched from a powerful longbow or ballista. The pig stomped and charged the bird, but Destiny was far too small and had the advantage of speed and agility. Both Guardians watched in amazement as the ferocious bird completed the task they had set for themselves. After about fifteen minutes the pig was lying dead on the hard ground, dead from massive blood loss. Destiny swooped in and landed on the pig, letting out a victory call.

"That is one impressive bird," David said shaking his head in amazement. But Destiny wasn't done yet. After preening her feathers for a few moments, she thrust her talons into the dead animal and attempted to drag it away.

"I do believe that Destiny's eyes are bigger than her stomach," Natalie laughed.

David threw back his head and laughed as the little bird struggled to move the dead weight. "Come on, Nat, let's get this thing back to camp." David field dressed the animal while Natalie cut and trimmed some staves. They secured the legs to the poles, hefted the poles to their shoulders and headed back.

During dinner, Natalie and David had great fun telling the story of Destiny's great feat. Matt, Jenna, and Daniel were as amazed and stunned as Natalie and David had been. But Kathryn merely sat quietly, feeding Destiny strips of hot pork as she listened, giving David the impression that this was not the first pig Destiny had taken on, nor would it be the last.

৪১·୯৪

As was their custom, the Dragons took a different route each time they returned to the compound. This minimized tracking signs lest they leave an easy route to follow for an adversary or a curious countryman. In this case they took the northern route over a holt that rose several hundred meters from the assault wall. As they reached the summit, Daniel peered through the massive trees.

"As many times as I've seen it I still can't get over it."

"What's that?" Jenna replied as she ambled up next to him.

"The magic." He motioned his hand pointing in the direction they were heading, "It looks like a swamp, even smells like a swamp. There is no sign of the river, no sound at all, no barn or buildings, no smoke or smell from a cooking fire. It just amazes me."

"No honking pribbles either," Jenna replied with a grin.

For the most part the pribbles enjoyed the company of people. But there was something about Daniel that set them on edge. Every time he entered their pen, a troop of them would rush towards him hissing and bellowing until he relented and left. It was a mystery because Daniel couldn't think of anything he could have done to upset them.

Daniel frowned and prodded his horse forward and muttered to himself, "pribbles"

℘·℃ℬ

They reached home without any further incidents and when Luke reported that all had gone smoothly during their absence, David breathed easier. Having been separated for nearly two months, the rest of the Dragons were eager to hear about the rescue, and the rest of the family was only too happy to oblige. When they got to the story of Destiny and the pig the startled bird suddenly found herself at the center of unwanted attention as the rest of the family tried to pet or stroke her. With an indignant ruffle of her feathers she leapt from her perch and flew upstairs, drawing more laughs from the family.

℘·℃ℬ

Midsummer, three months after David and the rest of the Dragons returned home, David received a letter from the Council. As he studied the missive, he smiled. Natalie was going to be thrilled. Kathryn would probably try to get out of it. He was going to enjoy this.

The next morning he woke early and told Matt to prepare enough food for the whole family. Despite Matt's curious glances, he refused to say anything more and instead went upstairs and woke everyone up.

Those who weren't scheduled to be on duty that day weren't all that thrilled to be woken up at the crack of dawn, but David told them that he would make it worth their time. They came, if only to satisfy their curiosity.

He kept the news to himself throughout breakfast and resisted the urge to laugh at the various attempts made to force him to reveal it. Finally, once everyone was practically done, he said, "I'm sure you're all wondering why I dragged you all out of bed this morning. Well, to start, I'm canceling patrols for today."

Immediately the Dragons stopped what they were doing and looked at him, waiting for his explanation. Kathryn shot a frown in his direction and he knew that, as the second-in-command she should have had prior knowledge to something as big as this, and he hurried to continue. "I have an announcement and I wanted the whole family to hear it at the same time."

"Who's in trouble this time?" Tyler asked dryly.

"It's nothing serious, like a rescue or anything," he assured them. "But perhaps something just as exciting. Well for some of us," he amended.

"We don't have to eat rabbit anymore." Natalie piped up dryly.

"No," David told her chuckling. "Although this is something you might enjoy. Last night I received a summons to court for a three-night celebration." He barely got the last words out before Natalie squealed with joy.

"Court!?" Delirious with excitement Natalie pressed David for more information. "What kind of celebration? Will there be balls every night? Will we personally meet the royal family?"

David held up a hand to try to stop her questions. "Hold on, Natalie, let me finish. The celebration is for the Queen's birthday, and yes there will be balls every night for your young ladies delight, and for us gentlemen there will be tournaments during the day, and as to meeting the royal family, that's entirely up to them."

"Don't forget Natalie," Kathryn added seriously. "While at court you cannot reveal that you are a Guardian."

Natalie sighed. "Yes, yes I know that Kathryn, but a ball! This is going to be so much fun!" Suddenly she paused, cocked her head, and then looked straight at Kathryn. "What court dresses did you bring?" she asked. "I don't remember seeing any in your closet."

Kathryn arched an eyebrow at her. Small red spots of embarrassment appeared on Natalie's cheeks. David fought the urge to laugh again. He watched as Natalie kept her focus and didn't back down to Kathryn.

Kathryn's eyebrow rose again, whether in surprise or approval David couldn't tell, before saying, "It's in the back of the closet, you must have missed it."

Natalie stared at her. "It? As in *singular*?"

"Why in the kingdom would I have need for more than one out here?"

Natalie's jaw dropped in disbelief. "You are kidding, right?"

Amy laughed. "Honestly Nat, haven't you figured out by now that if it isn't practical, Kathryn doesn't want anything to do with it?"

Natalie was still staring at the younger girl in disbelief. Finally she turned to look at David. "When do we leave?"

He took a sip of his tea before answering. "To avoid attracting attention, we will be leaving in small groups over the next few days. Your group leaves tomorrow morning."

"Tomorrow morning!" Natalie jumped out of her seat, sending it crashing to the floor. "You mean you're only giving me a couple radians to put together a wardrobe for Kathryn?"

"A what?"

Instead of replying Natalie raced over to Kathryn, grabbed her arm, jerked her out of her chair, and dragged her out of the room. "Come on Kathryn! I need to get your measurements and color choices."

"For what?" Kathryn's reply was almost lost as the rest of the girls hurried after them, eager to help.

David could barely contain his laughter and his curiosity. What in the kingdom could Natalie cook up in a couple radians? At the very least it would be entertaining.

"Who wants to bet that Natalie strangles Kathryn two radians into this project?" Luke asked. The boys burst out laughing.

"I don't know," Matt managed between laughs. "Kathryn looked like she was about to face a hangman's noose. I'd bet that it's Kathryn who strangles Natalie."

David wanted to groan: Natalie's vanity versus Kathryn's stubbornness. He wasn't entirely sure which would win today. "They don't need any encouragement, guys."

Luke grinned at him. "Oh come on, it would be epic."

Tyler rolled his eyes. "Sure, but think about the collateral damage. The house would be gone, destroyed first by fire and then by water and we'd all probably look like pincushions."

Daniel shook his head. "Kathryn doesn't miss with her bow. She'd only need one shot."

Tyler glanced at him. "I wasn't referring to arrows from Kathryn's bow."

Sighing, David shook his head. "Come on guys, we have packing, and in my case buffing and polishing, to do."

A round of groans traveled around those remaining at the table. Luke made a face. "Right now I'm really missing a servant to make sure my clothes are presentable for me."

"You could always ask Natalie or Kathryn to do it for you," Matt suggested teasingly.

"Oh, sure," Luke returned sarcastically. "And after they agree, they'll give me the option of how I want to die."

"By fire or by helcë," Daniel laughed.

Tyler stood, "Ask Kathryn. It would be quicker," he advised as he left.

Matt pondered his words. "I'm not so sure," he said slowly.

David turned to face Matt. "Lacey stays here," he said firmly. When Matt opened his mouth to object, David cut him off. "No arguments Matt, we can't risk her raising eyebrows at court."

Sullenly, Matt nodded his acquiescence.

℗·ℛ

"That's the last of them," Natalie commented as she wrote down the last of Kathryn's measurements.

"Finally," Kathryn groused as she moved to stand near the window.

Natalie laughed. "Oh, it's not that bad. It's not like you have to infiltrate a castle without being seen."

"I'd rather be assaulting the castle," Kathryn grumbled as Natalie picked up her sketchpad and started drawing. While she appreciated that Natalie had dropped her inquisition into her life, she wasn't sure how she felt about the older girl's attempts to treat her like a beloved sister. At best they confused her, at worst she found them just as annoying as her questions about her past.

"Since I don't have time to create these dresses from scratch, we're going to have to alter some of mine." Without looking up Natalie asked, "Who here is really handy with a needle?"

Since all the girls were moderately handy with a needle and thread, except for Kathryn, Natalie simply placed them into three groups.

"Wonderful. Leia, Amy, and Lindsey when I finish this you can start altering," she pointed to a green day dress hanging in the front of her closet, "that dress there. Cass, Rachel, and Elizabeth can work on the second dress," she nodded towards a light blue dress, "and Jenna, Kathryn, and I can work on the third...whichever that will be."

"I don't need three new dresses!" Kathryn protested as Natalie handed her first altered design to Amy.

"Yes you do!" Natalie countered. "While at court, you have to play the part of a noble lady and you can't do that in three dresses. My goal is to get at least six done."

"Six?" Kathryn looked like she was ready to run. "It's only three nights!"

"What about slippers?" Elizabeth asked.

Natalie paused. "Slippers are easy," she finally said. "I'll just buy them in the capitol."

Seconds later she tore a page from her book and handed it to Leia who immediately shared it with the others in her group.

"It's only three nights," Kathryn muttered again, but no one paid her any attention. Sighing she gazed at the drawing; it was far more elegant and lavish than anything she'd ever worn. "Can you at least make them less ornate?" she asked, knowing she could never talk Natalie down in number, but perhaps in style.

Natalie looked at her, and then shrugged, "Okay." She turned to her sewing book and began to make a few corrections.

"Just out of curiosity," Kathryn said. "Do you have enough fabric to complete these dresses?"

Natalie nodded towards her closet, just as Lindsey opened the door. Inside were bolts upon bolts upon bolts of fabric and trimming.

"Where did you get all this?" Kathryn asked, forcing her jaw to remain upright.

"I love to sew and design. My mother collects fabric. She gave me some of her collection, and I've done some collecting of my own since we've settled here," Natalie explained, handing a second design to Cassandra who returned to her group for color choice.

Kathryn glanced at her. "I notice that there's not much pink or red colored fabric in here," she said casually.

Natalie laughed. "What did you do with that stuff anyway?"

Kathryn hesitated before answering. "I got rid of it."

The older girl looked up. "I'm guessing that I'll never get it back."

Thinking of the piles of ash in the woods, Kathryn nodded. "Probably not," she agreed.

For the rest of the day the girls stayed in Natalie's room, sewing furiously. Kathryn had very little expertise sewing so she mainly hemmed the garments. Natalie oversaw all the work and worked on most of the detail herself. Natalie reluctantly complied with Kathryn's request for simplicity, but in the end she realized that heavily elaborate gowns would overwhelm the small raven-haired girl.

At one point during the afternoon, Natalie had Kathryn try on the half-finished dresses so that Natalie could fit them more accurately. While Kathryn had been slipping on one of the dresses, Natalie had caught sight of her bare back.

"Kathryn?" She whispered hoarsely as she dragged one finger gently along the crest of one scar.

Kathryn let out a heavy sigh. "I was abused, Natalie. I already told you that."

Natalie wanted to throw up.

The scars...

The overwhelming number of scars...

Kathryn hadn't been abused, she'd been tortured.

"I am so sorry," she whispered, tears beginning to fall down her cheeks.

"It was years ago," her lieutenant said briskly. "Let's get this over with so I can get out of these dresses."

Natalie took the hint. Kathryn did not want to talk about it. She forced herself to go back to the job at hand.

At sunset, Matt and Daniel graciously brought up a large platter mounded with various meats, a tray filled with fruits, two large loaves of freshly baked bread, as well as an ewer freshly filled with spring water. They took one look at the whirlwind state of Natalie's room, handed Jenna the platter and had quickly retreated, their eyes wide in disbelief. With her mouth half full Natalie continued to bark out the plans for several more dresses. The girls quickly ate and returned to the task at hand.

The girls sewed through the night, sewing in shifts so they might get a few radians sleep, and in the end their diligence paid off. By the next morning Kathryn had eight new gowns in almost every color and style. None were exactly alike.

Suddenly realizing the significance of the morning light, Natalie stood up from the chair she had taken a brief respite in to ease her aching muscles. Quickly she gathered up Kathryn's dresses and handed them to her.

"Here," she yawned. "A wardrobe fit for a lady of the court. Now, get out so that I can pack"

The girls scattered to their own rooms, throwing clothing into their travel satchels.

Since fourteen was a defining number for the Guardians, David opted to split his family into smaller traveling groups so that their identities could be preserved. The Guardian Council, through whom the invitations to the ball had been forwarded, provided several copies of the invitation and David made sure each group had one. The next morning the Dragons departed over a series of three days. Daniel, Elizabeth, Lindsey, Tyler, and Natalie left first, after the sun had risen. Luke, Rachel, Matt, and Cassandra followed the next morning a few radians after breakfast. David, Kathryn, Amy, Jenna, and Leia left on the last day around mid-afternoon.

ജ·ഃ

Finally, after a fortnight of travel, the capitol city appeared on the horizon, the palace standing like a guardian over the city.

Upon their first glance at the city Leia and Amy became anxious with excitement and could barely contain themselves as they rode through the gates. David led the way to the palace gates and showed the guards their invitation. A radian later after their horses were stabled they were being shown to their quarters by several servants.

Kathryn and David's rooms were last.

"Sir Darian you are here and Lady Kathryn you are directly across the hall." The servant opened both doors and then departed. *Darian*, Kathryn quickly memorized David's court name so that she wouldn't be caught off guard with it later. With her warning to Natalie about preserving their anonymity as Guardians, it would be humiliating if she was the one who slipped up.

When Kathryn entered her room she found a wonderful surprise waiting for her. "Jasmine!" she cried in surprise as she closed the door and crossed the room to stand before her mentor.

Jasmine smiled at her and pulled the girl into a hug. "Oh, Kathryn you've grown up so much," she whispered into her hair. Then holding her at arm's length said, "let me get a good look at you."

"How did you know I was here?" Kathryn asked as she spun slowly for Jasmine to see.

"Lord Jasse let me know when you arrived. Come, why don't you change out of your riding habit and walk with me in the gardens?" Jasmine suggested eagerly.

At that moment Arianna stepped forward and Kathryn noticed her. She greeted the servant with just as much pleasure as she had Jasmine. Arianna helped her change, selecting a blue day gown that Natalie had miraculously conjured for her.

Half a radian later, Kathryn had been washed down, put into the new dress, had her hair arranged, and was ready to walk with Jasmine.

"I never took you to court did I?" Jasmine asked as they exited the palace and entered the first garden.

Kathryn shook her head remembering snippets of visits during which she had dug in her heels at the idea of having to wear a fancy gown. Despite the failed attempts at begging, cajoling, and outright bribery at times, they had never worked. Kathryn had dug in her stubborn heels every time. Jasmine had finally just given up and left without her. "You tried, but it never worked out."

"As I recall you were as obstinate as a mule whenever I tried to get you to come," Jasmine replied dryly.

"I still am," Kathryn replied with a laugh. "It took a summons directly from the king to get me here."

Jasmine laughed. Kathryn had changed so much in the last six years Jasmine could hardly reconcile the small, terrified girl with the woman walking next to her.

Kathryn spotted Amy a few yards ahead and called to her. She introduced Jasmine to her friend.

Amy curtsied. "I've always wanted to meet the woman who rescued Kathryn."

Jasmine laughed. "And I've always wanted to meet the woman who befriended such a," she turned towards Kathryn with a smile in her eyes, "obstinate, strong-willed, and most lovely girl. Come, walk with us," she invited.

Amy gladly agreed and the two girls told Jasmine stories from their school days that had the princess laughing.

Suddenly David, accompanied by another man, approached them from the side. Kathryn estimated the second man's age in the late twenties. "Hello what's this?" David's companion asked as he stood before the ladies. "Who has enough wit and humor to make my aunt laugh?"

It took a few moments for the meaning of his words to sink in. *Aunt*?

Kathryn and Amy glanced at each other, unsure how to respond. Finally Amy responded, "I guess we do, Lord Prince," she curtsied.

The prince turned to Jasmine. "Tell me, Aunt Jasmine, would you be willing to introduce your companions to me?"

Jasmine smiled at her nephew. "Of course Derek. This is Lady Kathryn and this is Lady Amira. Girls, allow me to introduce Crown Prince Derek."

Kathryn was taken completely by surprise. *This* was the Crown Prince? As she studied him she had to admit that he definitely looked a lot like the Princess Roseanna. They shared the same black hair and tall stature but the prince's behavior was—well, not what she would have expected from their heir to the throne.

Derek's ears perked up. "Lady Kathryn as in my aunt's ward Lady Kathryn?" he asked quickly.

Kathryn felt a blush spread across her cheeks. "Yes, Lord Prince." She stole a glance at David who looked like someone had hit him with a satchel of rocks. Great, the last thing she needed was for him to learn that she was the ward of royalty. Now she would probably face a million questions about what living in a palace was like. She just hoped that he wouldn't tell Natalie. She'd never hear the end of it from the older girl.

"Well I am honored to meet the young woman my aunt raised," Derek continued. "She has told my family very little about you."

Kathryn found that information very relieving. She glanced back at David, curious to see how he was taking this. To her shock he winked at her. Of course he would have to find this amusing. Setting her face she turned her attention back to the Crown Prince.

"Is this your first time at court ladies?" Derek was asking.

Both girls nodded. "Splendid!" he cried. "Tell me, do either of you have escorts for the balls?"

Kathryn nodded. "I have been claimed for the first and last nights, Lord Prince."

"Then I shall claim the second! The prince exclaimed. He turned to Amy, "And what of you, milady?"

"I have been claimed for the third night, Lord Prince," Amy replied.

"Then may I have the privilege of claiming the first?" Derek asked.

Mute in surprise, Amy nodded a yes.

"Splendid!" Derek exclaimed exuberantly. "For two nights I shall have the two most beautiful women in the realm on my arm."

Both Kathryn and Amy blushed deeply but smiled and curtsied.

However the Crown Prince was not done. "Tell me ladies," Derek continued in a friendly fashion. "Will you be present at the tournament later today?"

"Yes, Lord Prince," Amy replied for both of them.

"Wonderful!" Derek clapped his hands together, "I shall leave orders that the Lady Kathryn and the Lady Amira are to be seated in the royal box along with the royal family."

At his announcement even Princess Jasmine looked startled. "Is that wise my nephew?" she asked cautiously.

"Where else should two beautiful ladies of the court reside?" Derek asked. "Besides, I plan to dedicate a couple jousts to these ladies."

By now both Kathryn and Amy were flushing furiously. David was fighting hard to keep from laughing. He had never seen Kathryn look so uncomfortable and, after all that he had put up with, he found it decidedly satisfying.

"In fact," Derek continued. "I wish for both of you to be seated in the royal box whenever you watch a tournament."

"If it pleases, Your Highness," Amy murmured, her cheeks flaming with embarrassment. Kathryn remained silent, but her normally pale complexion was colored soft pink.

"Wonderful. I shall speak to the Captain of the Guard immediately." He paused then appeared to think of something. "Another thing ladies, I wish you to address me not as Your Highness or Lord Prince but as Derek, nothing more."

"Nephew that is not wise!" Jasmine protested. "Only those highly favored are given such an honor."

"Only those who are highly favored are allowed to sit with the royal family," Derek reminded her calmly. "I wish to get to know these two lovely ladies, and by favoring them I give myself the opportunity to do so."

Startled as he was by the Crown Prince's latest antics, David was about to burst out laughing while Kathryn and Amy looked like they were ready to die of embarrassment.

"We'd best be going," Jasmine announced suddenly, as if she had just taken notice of the two girls' embarrassment. "Good day Lord Prince." She curtsied to Derek, and Kathryn and Amy followed her example before they hurried off.

℘·℃

When they were out of ear shot Derek exclaimed, "Lady Kathryn is the most beautiful creature I ever beheld."

David nodded slowly. Kathryn was beautiful, but in his opinion no more beautiful than the other Dragons. However because he didn't want to get into that particular argument, again, with the Crown Prince, he simply agreed with him. "Yes she is."

Derek wasn't done however. "What I want to know is who in this realm had the audacity to claim her hand for two nights before the Crown Prince?" he asked in mock disbelief.

David grinned. "I did."

Derek looked completely shocked, and then he burst out laughing. Clapping David on the shoulder he exclaimed, "Well you've done it again little brother, stealing the most beautiful woman right out from under me."

"You're too old for her," David laughed.

"Excuses, excuses."

Chapter 21

Is the crown prince always so..." Kathryn struggled to find a word that fit... "friendly?"

Jasmine chuckled softly. "Not always, most of the time yes, but not always." She sighed. "Derek is much too trusting for his own good."

Kathryn nodded in agreement. "I was thinking something similar along those same lines."

"How about forward?" Amy asked suddenly. "Is he always as forward to the ladies as he was back in the garden?"

Jasmine gave a graceful shrug. "It depends on the lady," she said with a glimmer in her eye. "If he's smitten then yes, he's definitely forward with her."

Amy grinned. "I think he was smitten with Kathryn."

"In your dreams," Kathryn muttered as she sipped her drink.

"I've said it before and I'll say it again. When it comes to men, Kathryn is completely and totally blind," Amy laughed as she reached for a piece of fruit from the platter sitting on the table.

When they had returned to Jasmine's apartment the Dowager Princess had ordered a light meal to be sent to her quarters. Kathryn and Amy were delighted at the small spread of food that was ten times more flavorful and delectable than their ordinary fare. Now the three ladies were enjoying a small meal that would, hopefully, last them through the tournaments until the banquet that would be served in the great hall.

Destiny flew in the nearest window and perched herself on the edge of Kathryn's chair, eyeing the food. Kathryn picked up a piece of fruit and tossed it to the bird. It was caught in Destiny's beak almost as soon as it left Kathryn's fingers.

"I'm always amazed at the bond between you and Destiny," Jasmine observed as she took a turn tossing fruit at the hungry bird.

"I must admit," Kathryn said as she slowly stroked the eagle's feathers, "that there are times I marvel at her loyalty to me. I often feel like I don't deserve her friendship."

"You did save her life," Amy pointed out as she reached for more food.

"Yes, but how often does that inspire this kind of loyalty in a bird?" Kathryn asked as Destiny decided to go hunt meatier fare.

The women were silent a moment, each lost in her own thoughts, and then Jasmine suddenly asked, "Kathryn what does your wardrobe look like?"

Kathryn, who had been in the process of taking a bite of a sandwich paused, the small morsel halfway to her mouth. "What?"

"You heard me," Jasmine returned. "What does your wardrobe look like nowadays?"

Frustrated Kathryn put down her sandwich. "What is with everybody asking me about my clothes all of a sudden?"

Confused by Kathryn's outburst, Jasmine looked to Amy for an explanation.

"One of the girls just made Kathryn a whole new wardrobe after learning that Lady Kathryn only had one court dress," Amy offered.

Jasmine turned to look at her ward. "One court dress," she repeated her tone skeptical. "Kathryn you have a whole closet full of formal wear."

"At your palace," Kathryn replied while taking a bite of her sandwich.

"You mean you didn't take them with you?" Jasmine yelped in disbelief.

"Well I didn't exactly have any use for them at school and I didn't have time to get them before we left for our new home," Kathryn explained matter-of-factly.

"What do you mean you didn't have any use for them at school?" Jasmine demanded. "I happen to know that there are dances held at the school and imitation balls where you are supposed to dress formally."

"I took one with me for those occasions," Kathryn reminded her. "I didn't see any wisdom in dragging around an extra closet's worth of dresses that I would rarely use."

Jasmine raised her eyes and hands heavenward. "I tried. I really honestly and truly tried."

Kathryn looked at her. "Tried what?"

"To turn you into a lady," Jasmine explained in exasperation. Quickly she turned to Arianna. "Fetch me all of the dresses Kathryn owns," she ordered. Arianna disappeared from the room.

Amy and Kathryn looked at each other. "What are you doing, Jasmine?" Kathryn asked warily.

"I'm going to take a look at your wardrobe to decide how soon I need to call my seamstress," Jasmine announced. She paused and then changed her mind. "Actually I'm going to summon her now." She sent another of her ladies-in-waiting to fetch Madame Nireta, the palace seamstress.

"What in the kingdom's name do you need a seamstress for?" Kathryn demanded as the serving lady left the room.

"To correct your wardrobe."

"My wardrobe doesn't need to be corrected," Kathryn protested as she moved across the room and sat down gruffly on a rather ornate settee.

"I will not have my ward running around the palace dressed like a common noble woman," Jasmine declared.

"I didn't know there was such a thing," Kathryn muttered as Arianna returned with her clothes.

"No, no, no! This won't do!" Jasmine cried as she looked through the dresses. "You are my ward and I intend to see you dressed as my ward." It took Jasmine less than ten minutes to go through each of Kathryn's dresses and while she admitted that the workmanship was normally something she would have approved of, it would not be suitable for dance attire in the capitol.

"Milady, Madame Nireta is here."

"Thank you, Sira, show her in."

Madame Nireta, a tall graceful woman with graying hair entered the room followed by three of her subordinates. "You sent for me milady."

"Madame Nireta, I don't believe you've met my ward, Lady Kathryn." Jasmine nodded to her ward who looked like she would rather be anywhere than sitting on the couch at the moment.

"It is an honor," Madame curtsied. "Is Lady Kathryn in need of a new wardrobe?"

"Immediately."

Madame flew into action. Her three assistants measured Kathryn while Madame picked through Kathryn's wardrobe. "Not exactly royal made," she commented as she held a dress between two fingers. "Although whoever made this has a sense of fashion." She squinted at the beaded bodice as if it held the secrets of the ancients, before skimming her gaze down the full skirt.

That would be Natalie," Amy told her, trying unsuccessfully to hide her gleeful grin at her friend's obvious discomfort.

"Well, I would like to have this Natalie working for me."

"Sorry, that's not possible."

"Pity." She turned to her assistants. "You have her measurements?"

"Yes, Madame."

Kathryn, resigning herself to her fate, mumbled softly, "It's only three nights!"

"What did you say?" Madame asked

"Nothing," Kathryn sighed.

"Good," she turned to Jasmine. "I shall return tomorrow with several new gowns for your ward, in the meantime this gown," she picked up a deep purple dress, "will suffice."

Kathryn grimaced. She remembered trying on that particular dress back at the glade. It was hot and heavy; not to mention the corset had a loose bone that dug into her ribs every time she took a breath. When Natalie had tried it on, it had looked stunning; the wide, stiff skirt held out by too many petticoats to count appearing to float out from her waist before dropping in light flounces to the floor. The gold embroidery on the bodice and skirt hem had complemented the older girl's skin beautifully whereas Kathryn felt like nothing more than a servant playing dress-up in the gown.

"Thank you, Madame."

Knowing that if she left the design to the older woman she would regret it for her entire stay, Kathryn called out, "Before you go, I have one request."

Madame wrinkled her nose as if expecting Kathryn's one requirement to be a significant breach of fashion. "Yes?"

"I want the style of the dresses to echo what you see here." Seeing that Madame obviously didn't understand she summed it up in one word. "Simple." The last thing she wanted was to be the dragging heavy, ornate gowns currently in vogue through the palace on a hot day. The purple dress would be bad enough, but if Madame added jewels and beading to her new creations...well she could imagine the comments she would later receive on her apparent "crankiness" from the Dragons.

Madame looked to Jasmine, who nodded her approval. "As the Lady wishes," she sighed, sounding as if Kathryn had just asked her to slit her own throat.

After Madame left the three women returned to their luncheon. They ate quietly for a few moments before Jasmine asked, "How have you been settling in Kathryn?"

"Settling into what?"

Jasmine rolled her eyes. "To your new life, what else?"

"Fairly well, I'm still getting used to it."

Before Jasmine could reply, a servant came into the room. "Prince Darcy to see you Milady."

A young man in his mid-twenties strode into the room, a large smile plastered on his face. "Good morning, Aunt Jasmine," he bent down and kissed her cheek. "How are you?"

"Very well, Darcy. How are you?"

"At the moment very curious," he sat down on one of the couches. "You see, Derek came to see me and told me that two angels were staying at the palace and so of course I had to see for myself."

Jasmine smiled at him. "I presume you speak of my companions and not of myself?"

Darcy shook his head. "You are the Queen of Angels," he laughed. "And now you've brought forth your hidden jewels." He laughed, but Kathryn got the impression that he was laughing at himself and his ridiculously poetic reply.

"I see you haven't lost your touch," Jasmine laughed as her nephew kissed her hand.

"Thank you," he said with an amused grin. "Would you care to introduce me to your companions?"

For the second time that morning, Amy and Kathryn were flattered and introduced to royalty.

"Will you ladies be at the tournament this afternoon?"

"They have been invited by Derek to sit in the royal box," Jasmine explained. "Are you jousting today?"

Darcy shook his head. "Not today, but I am fencing. Come and cheer me on."

"We'll see how the afternoon goes," Jasmine said noncommittally.

"Well I shall look for you," Darcy said as he took a seat opposite of his aunt and proceeded to engage the Dowager Princess and her companions in well-educated conversation. Kathryn found herself liking Prince Darcy. Prince Derek was charming but too trusting and exuberant. Prince Darcy on the other hand was learned and confident, although she had to admit he was just as charismatic as Derek—just in a different manner than his elder brother. His blond hair certainly set him apart from his older siblings.

"I'm afraid I must go," he said after half a radian of conversation. "It was an honor ladies." He gave Kathryn and Amy a quick bow before exiting.

"Are all the princes' forward?" Amy asked once the door was safely shut.

Jasmine smiled. "You're fresh blood girls, and on the plus side you're very pretty. All the gentlemen are going to be all over you."

"And we aren't allowed to do anything about it?" Kathryn asked in disgust.

"Don't go getting any ideas," Jasmine warned. "You will behave yourself Kathryn. You're my ward and must now act like it.

"Come," she said picking up her skirts. "We must get ready for the first tournament."

Chapter 22

It is abominably hot, Kathryn thought as she sat in the royal box, waiting for the first day of the jousting tournament to begin. The purple gown that Madame had declared would *suffice* was ridiculously hot and heavy for the blistering summer weather. Why couldn't she have picked the green gown? Kathryn would have settled for the pale yellow dress with blue trim, though Natalie had declared it an "emergency" dress as the colors washed out her complexion. At least both were made of lighter linen and cotton. The satin and velvet currently draped over her body made her feel like she'd been stuffed in an oven.

Beside her, Amy looked far more comfortable in a delicate red dress of lace and cotton. She was seated between Amy and Jasmine at the far right hand corner of the box, allowing an excellent view of the field. At least the canopy above kept the sun from shining down directly onto her. So far she'd managed to pick out the other girls from the Dragons in the crowd around the tournament field. The looks of surprise and disbelief on Natalie and Lindsey's faces when they had spotted her and Amy in the royal box had stirred some feelings of satisfaction deep within her.

As she waited for the games to start she quietly observed the royal family. King Darin she was already familiar with, having seen him at several Guardian graduations, including her own. His silver hair and regal bearing were hard to miss. His two sons had his regal manner and charisma. Briefly she wondered about the last child of the King and Queen, a son if rumors were to be believed. Children of the Royal Family were kept hidden until they were twenty years of age, or unless something tragic occurred, for their safety as well as an attempt to give them a "normal" childhood. If Crown Prince Derek and Prince Darcy were any indication, he would probably end up being a lady charmer, but she wondered if he'd be more like Derek or more like Darcy. In either case he'd be heavily sought after by the court ladies. Kathryn found herself glad that she would never have to interact with any of the royal family on a daily basis.

Queen Estelle was younger than her husband; her red hair still pure, showing no signs of gray. Her daughters had inherited her slight figure and delicate features. Kathryn wondered if Princess Roseanna's and Prince Derek's black hair came from their father. Princess Lillian was younger than Roseanna but still just as beautiful—

A trumpet sounded, announcing the start of the tournament. Kathryn turned her attention to the playing field. Well over one hundred competing knights paraded past as the crowd cheered. After today, only half that number would continue on to tomorrow's event. The third and final day of the tournament would pit the top twenty knights against each other. Kathryn sincerely hoped that Jasmine would not require her to attend all three days of this.

King Darin stood. "Let the games begin." He dropped a red handkerchief and the knights split into two groups. The first pair, drawn by lot, took their places and waited.

The crowd held its breath as they waited for the two knights to move, no one daring to so much as twitch until the competitors did. All that could be heard was the jangling and creaking of armor and the pawing of the ground by the battle horses.

Finally, in a sudden burst of energy, the two knights lowered their lances simultaneously urging their horses forward thundering across the field like two unstoppable forces.

They collided with a crash that resounded across the field and the knight coming from the left, a larger man with a purple stag on his shield, fell to the ground. The victor, a knight with a green falcon's head on his shield, raised his sword in acknowledgement of the king and rode off to begin again.

A smaller replica of his shield was moved from its position along the fence that encircled the field and placed on the tree of arms. The falcon knight had struck his opponent in the center of his chest, winning him two points. A hit to the center of his opponent's shield would have won him a single point. At the end of the day, the knights with the most points would continue on.

The second challenger, a huge knight with a black snake head on his shield took the first's position. The two charged and again the victor was the green falcon, again with a hit directly to the chest of his opponent.

The crowd loved the knight, cheering him on and practically leaping for excitement when he emerged victor. The crowd's second favorite was a knight who bore a shield emblazoned with a white horse's head. Like the green falcon, this knight was uncannily good at unseating his opponents with a hit to the chest. The people cheered him on with as much enthusiasm as the falcon.

To Kathryn, it felt like the jousts went on indefinitely. Unlike Amy, who was perched on the edge of her seat with anticipation for each joust, Kathryn felt that after one match, she had seen them all. After all, it wasn't like they were doing anything new in the later jousts. It was still two grown men trying to knock the other off his horse.

The weather, if at all possible, was becoming even hotter and the humidity was increasing with each radian. Kathryn couldn't imagine how uncomfortable the knights had to be, in their full metal armor and padding. She was wearing a comparatively light dress, sitting in the shade and she felt like melting, what she wouldn't give for a strong breeze to chase away the suffocating heat.

Finally, the contenders had been narrowed down to half, and the fifty-eight knights stood before the king. In an exciting turn of events, the white horse knight had managed to surpass the green falcon in points during the last three matches. Kathryn was surprised to see Crown Prince Derek was the white horse knight, but she was shocked to see David as the green falcon, although he had demonstrated on several occasions his excellent, superior even, horsemanship. She realized that she should have figured it out, or at the very least recognized his horse. She was pleased to see that Matt, Luke,

Daniel, and Tyler had joined David in making it through the first day of challenges.

King Darin stood. "Congratulations to the victors of today's jousts! Choose your Ladies wisely," he advised with a wide smile as the knights dispersed across the field.

This was the part Kathryn dreaded. As victors, the knights were, by custom, to choose a Lady and become her champion in later fights. The Lady would donate a token for the knight to carry as a sign of her favor. If the knight were to win the entire tourney, he and his Lady would be declared Festival King and Queen and would take places of honor at the final feast. The two knights with second and third highest points would become Festival Princes and their ladies Festival Princesses.

The Crown Prince moved toward the far end of the box. *Oh, please no*, Kathryn thought desperately. She remembered all too vividly Amy's earlier teasing about the prince and the thought of possibly becoming a festival *royal* made her stomach clench uncomfortably. That, combined with the stifling heat, was enough to make her nauseous.

Prince Derek approached and bowed. "Lady Amira, would you grant me the honor of becoming your champion?"

Kathryn wanted to wilt with relief, but Amy was too stunned to move or reply. Finally, Kathryn nudged Amy with her elbow, jolting her friend out of her surprise. "I would be honored, Lord Prince," she said standing and allowing him to kiss her hand. Kathryn suppressed a grimace, oh yuck! Amy reached into her sleeve, pulled out a silk scarf, and handed it to her new champion.

"May I have the honor of escorting you off the field, My Lady?" The Prince asked as he received the token.

Amy glanced at Kathryn in surprise and delight. "You may."

Prince Derek grinned happily and led Amy out of the royal box and seated her on his horse.

Kathryn was so focused on Amy that for several moments, her senses failed to register a second figure standing before her. Tearing her gaze from her friend she was surprised to find David standing there.

He looked ridiculous. Where his hair wasn't matted down with perspiration, it stuck up and out at different angles as though he just came out of a windstorm. His faced was streaked in dirty sweat where the dust had stuck during the match. His face reminded her of a court jester, especially the smug look that was currently plastered all over it. *Don't you dare!* Kathryn thought fiercely.

David also moved forward to the royal box. "Lady Kathryn, may I have the honor of becoming your champion?"

Kathryn suppressed a growl. For a brief moment she wondered what would happen if she refused, but sensing Jasmine's gaze on her, as well as remembering her earlier warning, she stood, offered a small, forced, smile and her hand saying, "I would be honored, Sir Darian."

Following the Prince's example David kissed her hand. She fought the urge to wipe her hand on her skirt. Now came the interesting part. Jasmine had been in such a rush to get to the field that Kathryn had nothing on her that she could offer David as a token. Well, she had one thing, but she wasn't sure she wanted to give it away.

She would have to; there was nothing else she could give him. Slowly she reached into her sleeve and pulled out a long feather. It was one Destiny had lost recently and Kathryn had found it on her saddle bags when she had been helping Arianna unpack. Before the tournament she had tucked it into her sleeve for comfort.

Handing the feather to David, she couldn't help but notice how appropriate the feather was considering his shieldcrest. He tucked it into his own sleeve. Wonderful. His crest was a falcon and she offers him a feather in token? That was certain to provide fodder for the court gossips. "May I have the honor of escorting you off the field, My Lady?"

Glancing up, Kathryn saw that many of the knights were escorting their chosen ladies off the field, displaying their patronage to their opponents. She might as well go along with it. "You may."

David helped her out of the box and onto Rumer. It was a trickier feat than she'd imagined it could be. Her dress easily added ten kilos to her normal weight and the numerous petticoats and stiff outer skirt made finding a stable position nearly impossible. Desperately hoping that she'd managed it with some degree of grace, the last thing she needed was the noble women gossiping about her inability to sit a horse, she nodded her readiness to David determinedly ignoring the amused smirk at the corner of his mouth.

Off to her right, the first knight David had fought, the one with the purple stag crest, was helping Princess Lillian out of the royal box. Looking around as David led Rumer off the field, she sought out the other Dragons. The boys had all picked one of the female Dragons to be their ladies and she noted with some satisfaction that the rest of the girls had been asked by other knights to become their patrons. At least no one would harbor any envy or bitterness over not being chosen this trip.

ᏕᏅ·ᏟᏅ

"Well done, Sir Darian!" Prince Derek called as they approached. He already had Amy on the ground and was engaged in cheerful conversation. His two sisters were off to his right, with Darcy looking on to ensure that their knights behaved properly. The other knights were already disbanding, some leading their ladies off to explore or just take a walk. Others parted ways and went off alone. Kathryn didn't see any of the other Dragons and wondered where they had wandered off to.

"I could have sworn I had you on that last joust, Lord Prince," David joked as he assisted Kathryn down from Rumer.

Hearing David answer to his court name still struck Kathryn as a little odd. After seven months of learning to call someone by one name and then having to switch to another, she suspected that she wasn't the only one having trouble with the new names. All the Guardians had official court names that differed from their given names, another measure to protect their identities. All except Kathryn. She lived under her court name on a daily basis. Her special name had been a gift and it was one she kept close to her heart. Only one other person besides herself knew it.

Dismounting, Kathryn was startled to find herself feeling lightheaded, and she placed a hand on Rumer to steady herself. She grit her teeth as world spun slightly and she willed it to right itself.

"Lady Kathryn, are you okay?"

Kathryn forced herself to look at David. "Actually I really don't feel too well."

"Perhaps you should lie down," Amy suggested hurrying over.

"Is everything okay?" Princess Lillian asked as she and her champion, a Lord Tanner, joined them.

"Lady Kathryn isn't feeling too well," Prince Derek explained.

"I think it's the heat, I'm not used to it," Kathryn heard herself admit. "I think I'll go lie down for a while."

Lord Tanner looked her over. "Pardon my observation, Lady Kathryn, but you do look ill. Perhaps you should see a healer. This heat can easily induce fever and fatigue in someone as delicate as yourself."

Someone as delicate as myself?! Kathryn felt anger stirring, pushing away the nausea. "I assure you, Lord Tanner, there is no need for a healer. I am simply tired from my journey and the heat compounded the issue," she told him icily.

Lord Tanner opened his mouth to argue, but apparently thought better of it. He closed his mouth, nodded, and gave a brief bow before walking back to his horse. Kathryn watched him go, fighting the urge to go after him and demonstrate just how delicate she really was.

Someone beside her chuckled in amusement. Turning, Kathryn saw that Prince Darcy had joined them in time to witness the exchange. "I'm afraid that Tanner is still old-fashioned," Darcy observed. "He still believes that a woman's place is to marry young and provide her husband heirs. And they certainly don't have the constitution to watch an event such as this, the blood alone could damage their delicate sensibilities and ability to bear strong children."

His sister wrinkled her nose. "Surely he could get with the times. Women are allowed in the Guardians and even some noble women are trained in swordsmanship."

"Which reminds me," Derek said. "Have you and Roseanna been practicing?"

"Of course," Lillian replied.

"Good. We don't want a repeat of Sebastian's antics." Derek's jaw hardened as he mentioned the kidnapper and for a moment, Kathryn saw something beyond Derek's over-enthusiastic personality.

Lillian hugged her brother. "Roseanna's fine, thanks to the Guardians, and Sebastian would never have tried to kidnap Roseanna if you and Darcy had been around."

For some reason, the exchange between brother and sister left Kathryn feeling hollow inside. No one had ever attempted to protect her as a child, and seeing the Prince do it so naturally for his sister physically hurt.

Forcefully she pushed aside the unwanted feelings. She didn't want or need anyone to look out for her. Trusting others only got you hurt.

David seemed to notice that she was growing uncomfortable. "Would you like me to escort you back to your room, Lady Kathryn?"

Before she could reply, Princess Lillian hurried to her side. "I'll walk with you," She said, linking one of her arms through Kathryn's. "I need to return to the palace anyway."

"That's very kind of you," Kathryn said as they walked off.

Prince Derek turned to Amy. "Perhaps you would allow me to show you around the grounds?"

Amy gave him a shy smile. "Of course."

The two walked off together, Derek already acting as a guide, informing Amy of the history behind the palace.

David, Prince Darcy, and Lord Tanner, who had observed the interaction between the Crown Prince and his Lady, looked at each other and shrugged. "I think he's smitten," Lord Tanner observed.

"I think you're right," David replied, grinning.

80·03

Kathryn closed the door to her room and sagged against the wood. Next chance she got she was going to strangle David. What was he thinking going and asking her to become his Lady? She had seen his skill on Rumer, and he was good enough to become the champion of the tourney which would put her in the spotlight as his Festival Queen. Apparently he hadn't gotten the message that she hated being in the spotlight. Well when she saw him again, she would give him the message in a way he would never be able to misinterpret. She was going to kill him!

Sighing, she pushed up off the door and massaged her temples. Perhaps her lightheadedness came from both the heat and her pounding headache. The hair style that Arianna had created was beautiful but it piled all her hair on top of her head and the extra weight was making her miserable.

She pulled out the pins Arianna had used to tame her hair and shook it down. The lightheadedness that accompanied the motion nearly sent her to the floor.

Perhaps I really should lie down, she thought. Moving to the large windows, she pulled the heavy curtains shut— effectively darkening the room enough for a midday nap. She pulled off the purple dress, struggling a bit with the thrice cursed corset—she was going to have bruises from that stupid loose bone— and hung it in the wardrobe. Grabbing a nightgown she slid into it.

Pulling herself up onto the huge bed she rearranged the pillows and laid her pounding head down.

"Here's your murderer!" The thin lady screeched, pointing at Kathryn who shrank back against the cold stone wall. "She killed them in their sleep she did! Judge her now, and give those poor souls the justice they deserve!"

Silence hung in the room after her declaration. Kathryn heard the frantic beating of her own heart as she waited. No one cared about the truth—they wouldn't have believed her had she told the truth. She had motive and opportunity and best of all she didn't open her mouth to defend herself.

"What justice do you think fits the crime this child committed?" The speaker was a tall thin man with gray hair and even grayer eyes. He was Lord Blackwood of Blackwood Manor, judge, jury, and hangman for the region.

"Hang her!" The fury in the woman's shriek sent Kathryn cowering against the wall again. She didn't understand why the woman was so adamant about the 'crime' that had been committed. She'd hated Kathryn's uncle and his family, always threatening to kill them herself. Yet here she was, blaming Kathryn and insisting the she be hung.

Lord Blackwood looked to Lady Blackwood, a small reed-like woman who sat beside him, she nodded.

"Very well," Lord Blackwood stood. "Take the girl to the dungeons pending her execution."

Two guards grabbed Kathryn's arms and dragged her down the corridors to the gated door that marked the entrance to the dungeons. The door opened silently and she was dragged down the curving staircase that led to the dungeons beneath.

The Master of the Dungeons was an older man with large hands and scars, lots and lots of scars. "What do you have for me, Sir Knights?"

One of the knights tossed Kathryn on the floor. "New prisoner for you Kad, be careful 'round this one, she's a murderer."

Kad looked down at Kathryn who cowered on the floor. "Murderer?" he asked incredulously. "What did she kill? A mouse?"

"Her uncle and his family," the second knight replied. "The whole lot of 'em in one day."

The dungeon Master looked down at Kathryn. He reached down and grabbed one of her arms, dragging her to her feet. "A murderer huh? Well, do you know what we do with murderers down here?"

Kathryn didn't make any move to reply; just stared at him—waiting.

"We punish murderers." He unfurled his whip and let it crack against the floor. "Let's begin."

He tossed her back onto the floor and kicked her severely in the side until she rolled onto her stomach. She heard the sound of the whip traveling through the air, heard its sharp crack and felt the sharp pain travel across her back. The two knights had since left, leaving her alone with Kad.

Whimpering, she heard another crack and braced for the pain, unable to hold in another whimper.

"That's right, murderer," Kad laughed cruelly. "It hurts doesn't it? Go on, cry!" He kept on, bringing each stroke down harder until Kathryn did cry.

She cried not only from her heart, but from her soul, a soul that was being shredded. Her tears ran down her cheeks and into the cracks between the stones. Her fingers gripped the stone until her fingernails were broken and bloody.

Finally, Kad had had enough and threw her in a cell with an older male prisoner who was chained to the wall. As she lay on the rotting straw that littered the cold stone choking back sobs, Kathryn could now hear what she hadn't earlier—the screams of the other prisoners. They echoed throughout the dungeons, the disembodied voices of broken people.

Carefully, Kathryn pulled herself into a sitting position, her back was on fire and she could feel the blood flowing freely down her back. She crawled to the nearest solid wall and pressed her back against it, the pain was unbearable and each labored breath she took sent waves of pain through her small body. She'd tended to enough of her cousin's wounds to know she had to stop the bleeding—but oh! It hurt so much.

"Well," a voice rasped. "You're certainly a clever one aren't you?" Her cellmate peered at her through the darkness, his chains rattling with every slight movement. "Usually takes the new ones three beatings to figure out they need to stop the bleeding."

Kathryn didn't reply.

"You're a young one, how old are you?" When Kathryn didn't reply he persisted, "Come child," he said gently. "How old are you?"

Slowly, Kathryn held up five fingers.

"Five years old," her cellmate repeated in amazement.

Kathryn continued to huddle against the stone wall, she didn't know when she would be hanged, but she vowed she wouldn't cry. She would never cry again—no matter what they did to her.

She didn't sleep that first night, the cries of pain and pleas for mercy kept her awake.

When Kad came for her the next morning, he didn't carry his whip. Instead he brandished a long rod which he took great pleasure using it on her. But Kathryn kept her vow, she did not cry—she whimpered once, but she did not cry.

"Brave little thing," Kad muttered as he tossed her back into her cell.

After he had left, her cellmate shifted slightly. "I've seen a lot of things in my life," he said slowly. "But a five year-old girl who denies the dungeon master her cries and pleas for mercy is not one of them."

Kathryn simply curled her throbbing body up tighter.

"Can you speak, child?"

She simply looked at him.

"My name's Quint. What's yours?"

Here she couldn't answer him. She didn't have a name. Her aunt and uncle had simply referred to her as girl.

Quint tried to make conversation again, but she ignored him and tried to fall asleep.

For four more days Kad beat her daily, however he soon grew tired of a prisoner that didn't cry out or beg for mercy and left her alone. For his part, Quint constantly talked to her. After those first two days, he stopped expecting her to talk back and instead told her stories. They made the time pass and she found herself grateful for them.

The prisoners' food was delivered once in the morning—a loaf of bread, some weak broth, and water.

Two weeks after Kathryn had arrived at the dungeons Quint offered her his bread. "Come on little one, take it. You need it more than I do."

239

When she hesitated he reached it out to her as far as his shackles would allow. "Trust me little one."

Slowly she extended her hand and took it. As soon as she reached her side of the cell, her cellmate began shouting at the top of his lungs, "Dungeon Master! Dungeon Master!"

"What now?" Kad asked annoyed. "Shut up unless you want another beating!" He cracked his whip threateningly.

"But she stole my food!"

Kad peered into the cell. Sure enough he saw the little girl cowering with a loaf of bread in her hands. "Well we can't have that can we?"

He dragged her out of the cell and gave her another sound whipping. Throwing her back into her cell he told her, "Because you stole from Quint, he gets your rations for two days."

For the next two days Quint enjoyed double portions while Kathryn's strength waned dangerously.

A few weeks later Quint offered Kathryn his bread again, "I'm sorry about the last time," he told her, "I didn't think he'd take your food away. Come child," he chided when she shrank away from him. "You need to eat, you're nothing but bones. Take it." He shoved his bread at her, "trust me."

Kathryn didn't know what made her believe him, but she accepted his bread, only to have the exact same thing happen again. Quint hollered at the top of his lungs, Kad came and gave her another beating and Quint got her food for two days.

Never again, Kathryn vowed as she watched Quint devour his food— and hers, never again would she trust another person.

A little over one month after she was sent to the dungeon, Kathryn was brought up to face Lord and Lady Blackwood. Forced to kneel before them with her face touching the floor she listened to them talk.

"You committed a serious crime, child," Lady Blackwood told her, "But you are young and we hope that your time in the dungeons taught you a lesson. Did they?"

They had no idea how many lessons the dungeons had taught her. She nodded.

"Very good," Lord Blackwood intoned, "Because we believe you have learned your lesson we are rescinding our earlier verdict. Instead of being hanged you will stay at Blackwood Manor and serve my wife, your new mistress, as her attendant. Do you understand?"

She nodded.

"No one in the village knows your name," Lady Blackwood told her. "What is it?"

Kathryn remained silent. She heard a huff. "Fine," Lord Blackwood said in disgust. "Since you refuse to tell us your name, you will be given a new one."

Kathryn woke with a start, her heart racing and body trembling. The nightmare had left her damp with sweat and she brushed away wet strands of hair that had fallen into her face. There was more to the memory, so what had caused her to awaken?

A knock at the door startled Kathryn. Scowling Kathryn lay back down, hoping that if she didn't answer, whoever it was would go away.

The knock sounded again followed this time by, "Lady Kathryn, are you okay?"

Her scowl deepened. What could David possibly want? Swinging her legs over the side of the bed she quickly pulled her hair back, she didn't want him seeing her like this but it didn't sound like she had a choice. His knocks were becoming more insistent. Reaching for a dressing robe she hurried to put it on.

Bracing herself and taking a deep breath she opened the door.

℘·℃

David was considering breaking the door down when Kathryn finally opened the door. He was shocked at her appearance; damp hair, askew robe, ragged breathing, and scowl. "Lady Kathryn, are you okay?"

Her scowl deepened. "I'm fine, do you need something?"

His curiosity was overwhelmed by intense irritation at her and he nodded curtly. "I just wanted to let you know that the banquet's starting in a radian." He turned to leave.

"Why did you do that?" she asked suddenly.

Confused he turned back to her. "Why did I do what?"

Her eyes flashed. "Why did you have to make me your Lady? Surely you know by now that I don't like to be at the center of attention?"

David was starting to feel perturbed. Something was wrong. Usually Kathryn guarded her emotions jealously, but now she actually looked ready to start a screaming match, he looked up and down the hall. "May I come in?"

"What?" she asked angrily.

He nodded towards her room. "I'll explain why, but it's not something we want the servants to hear," he said his voice low.

Distrust flickered in her eyes, but she admitted him. When he was inside she simply glared at him, waiting for his explanation. She may have verbally waited for him, but the rest of her body was tense and it suggested to him that if he didn't start talking, and have one seriously good explanation to boot, she was going to start throwing him into the walls.

Abruptly the conversation that he'd had with Lord Jasse so long ago popped into his head—specifically the warning that when agitated Kathryn would react forcefully if she felt threatened. He'd known that her security and anonymity would be threatened by becoming his sponsor, but he'd thought that she'd be able to handle it.

David waited until he was in the middle of the room, out of arm's reach, before he spoke calmly. "Prince Derek wanted to make you his patron. He planned on winning the tournament and making you his Festival Queen and the only way I could talk him out of it was that if I made you my sponsor instead," he explained.

Kathryn sat down hard, her face white. "*What?*"

The speed with which her anger dissipated and the look of incredulity on her face was enough to convince him that his actions were only the tipping point. Something else was going on with her. "I know you hate being at the

241

center of attention," he said quietly. "And when Prince Derek told me his plans I talked him out of it. Took a few radians, but I managed." He didn't tell her that he had convinced Derek that Kathryn had already consented to being David's sponsor earlier in the day. Of course his brother had taken that information as a sign that his little brother was in love and had teased David about it for radians, but at least he had agreed to leave Kathryn alone.

He looked at her for a long moment. "Do you forgive me?"

He watched as emotions rapidly flickered across her face. David had not missed the murderous look in her eye as she had grudgingly accepted his request. He had also noticed that, while she wasn't normally a girl to relax, even at home, the level of her discomfort had seemed to have increased tenfold.

He had hoped that after she and Natalie had ended the animosity between them that Kathryn would once again begin to settle into the Dragons. His hopes had been quickly dashed.

While Kathryn and Natalie were no longer at odds with each other, Kathryn had not made any new attempts at befriending the rest of the Dragons. Her manner, while less chilling than it had been when Natalie and Lindsey had hated her, was still uninviting and cold.

She had grown even less inviting during the ride to the palace. Early on in their journey, Kathryn had preferred to ignore them and kept to herself. However, the closer they had gotten to the palace, the more Kathryn had begun to get short with all of them. Even Amy had noticed and commented on her moods.

Something big was going on that was bringing her to the point where she was going to snap. When Natalie had ceased her interrogations it hadn't prevented Kathryn from shattering, it had merely put it off. He thought back to the day Natalie had talked him into taking the family to the village. The day Kathryn had returned from the woods completely out of character. If Amy was right, she'd experienced a nightmare that day. Later, Amy had also confided that Kathryn used to get nightmares all the time, until they'd gradually stopped.

David was willing to bet that they'd never stopped and that Kathryn had simply become better at hiding them and recovering from them.

Chapter 23

Kathryn was speechless, and for the first time in her life felt a twinge of regret. She had been thinking the worst of David and all he'd done was protect her. Never in her entire life could she remember someone doing that for her...No one except Claude. "There's nothing to forgive," she said woodenly. "The whole affair caught me off guard and I assumed the worst." *There, an apology...well, sort of.*

He actually grinned at her. "So I gathered." He sat down across from her. "Kathryn did you have a nightmare?"

His question startled her. Frantically she sought speech. "What makes you think that?"

"You came to the door with ragged breathing, damp hair, and a rumpled dress, all evidence of a nightmare."

She narrowed her eyes slightly. "You are incredibly observant." Too observant. *Why can't you be like everyone else in the kingdom and leave me alone? The only thing I've ever desired is to be left alone, why can't anyone understand that?*

"Occupational hazard," he assured her. He paused and then asked, "Want to talk about it?"

For the second time in five minutes he left her speechless. "Talk about it?" she echoed finally.

He nodded seriously. "I've always been told that talking about something makes it easier to deal with, easier to move past."

The very idea of reliving the nightmare chilled her to the bone. She looked to the windows. "No."

"No?"

She looked back at him. "Talking doesn't make it easier to move past, to deal with."

He pierced her with a look. "How would you know? According to what I've been told, you've never discussed your past with anyone."

How dare you! Kathryn felt her anger surge like a rapidly rising tide. "So you've been spying on me?" She accused, her voice rising again.

He shook his head. "Not spying, just trying to understand your distantness towards the rest of the family." David looked at her for a long time. "We've been a family for almost a year, Kathryn. I understand your hesitancy to form relationships, but you are going to have to fully trust me and the rest of the Dragons someday and I would prefer it to be soon."

"Oh you would, would you?" she asked sarcastically. "What makes you think I'm going to trust you?"

His gaze was steady as he replied. "Because I'm family."

Her angry retort died before she could vocalize it. His answer wasn't the one she had expected. Then again, David just had to be the one person she had ever encountered that she couldn't seem to predict with any accuracy.

"Why you? Why not Amy or another Dragon?"

"You had all the years at school to tell Amy, you didn't. Besides, I'm our family leader."

"So that automatically makes you trustworthy?"

David sighed. He did not want to have this conversation here, but her uncharacteristic anger and talkativeness convinced him that he needed to address a growing problem. "You are shattering, Kathryn."

"What do you mean by that?" She demanded, coming to her feet.

He remained sitting. "Look at yourself," he said, forcing himself to remain calm. "You're distracted and jumpy. You can't focus on assignments the way you used to. On the ride here you practically tore Amy's head off when she asked you if you were hungry. You didn't even notice I was standing before you today at the end of the tourney."

"I can focus just fine," Kathryn replied through clenched teeth.

David shook his head. "No, you can't," he argued. "You keep others away by your cold manner, refusing to react when someone takes a shot at you. That tactic kept Natalie frustrated for months, and yet here you are, ready to argue with me, something you hate to do."

"Only because it's a waste of time, nobody believes me, *they* didn't believe me."

David remained silent, forcing himself not to react, hoping against all hope that Kathryn would continue in her outburst and help him understand.

It wasn't to be. Kathryn, seeming to realize the importance of what she had just said, moved to the window and stared at the closed drapes. Mute.

"Who's they?" he asked quietly.

"No one I care to discuss." Her tone could have frozen the ocean.

He took a gamble. "It has something to do with Blackwood Manor, doesn't it?"

She stiffened, asking in a tense tone, "Who told you about Blackwood Manor?" He could almost see her mind working, wondering, *how much do you really know?*

"You did, weeks ago."

"I did not," she protested. If anything she looked practically fearful at the prospect of having said the name. Did it hold that much power over her?

"You mentioned it," he reminded her cautiously.

Skepticism crossed her features. "When?" she challenged.

"When we were riding to Duke Sebastian's castle I asked you where you had learned the technique of hidden movement. You told me it was one of the things you had learned, courtesy of Blackwood Manor."

She paused, obviously trying to recall the conversation. He pinpointed the moment she remembered, her face going pale and her shoulders stiffening. "You have a very detailed memory," she said finally.

"It was the first hint of your past, I assure you I wasn't about to forget it."

"You should have." She was quiet for a long moment before asking, "What do you know?"

Her question surprised him. "I know that you were abused but nothing more," he replied slowly.

"Abused?" Kathryn asked incredulous as she turned to face him. "Is that what they're saying?"

David paused before answering, had Lord Jasse been wrong? "That's what Lord Jasse believes, is he wrong?"

For a brief moment, at the mention of Lord Jasse's name, anger flashed across her features. Then it was gone, her expression coolly composed before returning her gaze to the window. "Calling what I went through abuse would be like calling a lethal dose of poison potentially dangerous," she said coldly.

David waited patiently, hoping that she would decide to finally trust him. She turned to look at him and he could tell that today wouldn't be that day. Before she could speak he said quickly, "I'll wait while you dress for the feast. Is there anyone you would like me to call to help?"

She paused, and then shook her head. "No thank you, I'll manage."

"You're supposed to be a lady," he reminded her. "It wouldn't be acceptable for Dowager Princess Jasmine's ward to arrive at the feast dressed like a common noble woman."

The familiar sight of her eyes narrowing at him caught his attention. "What?" he asked in confusion. "What did I say this time?"

"A common noble woman," she repeated slowly. "You are the second person today I've heard say that."

He shrugged. "It's a regularly used phrase around the palace. I'll try and find Amy to help you."

ಬ·೮౩

David left before she could protest. Sighing, Kathryn pulled herself away from the window and moved to her closet, she had a banquet to prepare for. Blasted nobles! Blasted chivalry, she thought bitterly. Blast the King's summons! If only she could have been deathly ill or something, then she could have begged out of the celebration and wouldn't have to deal with this whole ridiculous nonsense of being a lady.

She snorted softly. Her? A courtly lady? She would rather be a milk maid or pig farmer than spend her life at court. All this pomp and ceremony reminded way too much of the Blackwoods and their parties and events—only this time she was one of the airheaded ladies whom Lady Blackwood surrounded herself with instead of a servant.

Lady Blackwood.

Court.

Kathryn dropped the dress she had pulled out of the closet. What if the Blackwoods had been invited to attend the birthday celebration? What if they were here now? What if she was forced to dance with Lord Blackwood?

Stop it! She told herself sternly. *After what they put me through, Jasmine would never allow them to return to court and even if they did, they wouldn't recognize me, I was a mute the last time I saw them.*

As to dancing with Lord Blackwood, it was an easy problem to solve. She'd stomp on his foot and thrust a dagger in his eye.

Now stop being such a weakling and pick out a dress! She turned to her closet and saw the purple dress hanging up front.

There was nothing in the kingdom that could convince her to wear that purple dress again, time to see what she had left now that Jasmine and Madame had gone through her wardrobe.

Madame must have worked overtime, Kathryn thought as she fingered through the six new dresses hanging in front. Even she had to admit they were beautiful. Reverently she brought out a pale blue creation and laid it on the bed.

The workmanship was beyond anything Kathryn had seen. The silver embroidery alone should have taken weeks to complete, yet here it was, lying on her bed. The sleeves were long and split, the sheer fabric flowed like water over her hands. Blue ribbon that matched the color of the dress laced the back of the bodice. The skirt was simple, with only a single underskirt to give it definition and drape. The fabrics were heavy, but she guessed that it they would move like ocean currents every time she moved. It reminded Kathryn of the fashion popular at court a century ago, back when ostentatious displays of wealth had been limited more toward furnishings and architecture.

Kathryn drew in a sharp breath and stepped away as if she'd been burnt. She now knew why the dress seemed so familiar. It was the dress from her dream all those weeks ago, before rescuing the princess, back at the meadow when she had fallen asleep near the waterfall. This was the dress from her dream.

Before she could throw it away Amy burst in, excitement bubbling from her. "Oh, Kathryn!" she called as she rushed over. "Can you believe that Prince Derek asked me to be his Lady?"

Tearing her gaze from the dress, Kathryn smiled at her friend. "Of course I can! He would have been a fool not to ask you."

Amy actually blushed. "Actually," she admitted. "I thought he would choose you." Her gaze fell to the bed and she practically jumped on the bed. "Is this what you're wearing tonight?" she asked excitedly as she snatched the dress and held it up.

"I don't think so," Kathryn said hurriedly, she did not want to wear that dress anywhere.

Amy looked her in disbelief. "Why not? It's a gorgeous dress!" Running her hand over the skirt, she studied it. "I've never seen a style like this before."

Kathryn jumped on the excuse. "Exactly, I don't want to wear something that will stand out."

Her friend took on a determined look. "No."

"No?"

"No. You can't wear anything else. This is the perfect dress for tonight."

Kathryn panicked. "Amy I can't wear that dress!"

"Why not? It's perfect for you?"

Frantically Kathryn sought an excuse and came up empty. "Because I can't," she protested lamely.

"Oh, nonsense! Let me send for my dress and we can dress together." She walked hurriedly to the door, pulled it open and peered out while motioning at someone in the hall. She turned back to Kathryn, "how are you going to do your hair?"

"I hadn't really thought about it."

Amy cocked her head at her, grabbed her gently by the shoulders and turned her. "I think you should let it down," she suggested.

Kathryn looked at her, appalled. "Let it down?" Self-consciously she reached up to brush her hair, only to find it was still pulled back. *I thought I let it down before I fell asleep...*Oh right. She'd pulled it up when David had knocked on her door.

"Well, at least part of the way," Amy proposed as she finished talking to her servant who hurried off to retrieve her dress. "Come on, we can do you first."

Unable to talk her friend out of the blue dress, Kathryn unwillingly submitted to wearing it, although once it was on she had to admit to herself it felt like it belonged there, more than any of the other court dresses she'd ever worn, which only made her want to tear it off even more.

"Wow," Amy exclaimed as she stood back.

"Wow what?" Kathryn turned to look in the mirror but Amy grabbed her hand and kept her from looking.

"Nope, you can't look till I'm done with you."

"Amy..."

"Don't *Amy* me, this is going to be so much fun."

"What is so great about the dress? Why did you say wow?" Kathryn demanded.

Her friend grinned at her. "Let's just say that the dress changes your appearance drastically."

"How?" Kathryn wasn't in the mood for riddles. The servant arrived with Amy's dress and laid it on the bed.

"It makes you look...what's the word? Exotic." Amy jabbed her finger at Kathryn. "That's the only hint you get so stop asking." She sat Kathryn down on a stool and began to do her hair. "I never realized what perfect hair you have."

Kathryn was getting uncomfortable. "Would you stop with the compliments?"

Amy looked up surprised. "Why?"

Kathryn shifted on the stool. "They're embarrassing."

Her friend tossed her a grin. "I guess we'll have to work on that too."

"What is that supposed to mean?"

"You're a lady of the court," Amy explained. "You have to know how to accept compliments from smitten young men." She looked at Kathryn. "Honestly, how did you pass the etiquette courses?"

"I only had one," Kathryn reminded her.

"There," Amy said reaching for one last pin. "Done."

"So I can look?"

"I said your hair was done, we still have make-up to do."

"No make-up," Kathryn said firmly.

Amy, who had been reaching for the cosmetics lying on the table, turned to look at her friend. "Why not?"

"I've never worn the stuff and don't intend on starting."

"Every other lady at court will be wearing some."

"No make-up." Kathryn was adamant.

"It will help hide your identity if you wear make-up."

Scowling Kathryn considered Amy's argument. "Okay fine," she groused. "But just a little!"

Grinning like a little girl, Amy quickly applied the cosmetics. "Okay, now I'm done. Let's do me."

Kathryn helped Amy into her stunning red and gold dress, "Prince Derek will appreciate this," she commented as she laced her friend's corset and tied on her sleeves.

"That's the idea," Amy laughed.

Amy wanted her hair up and curled and it took almost the entire rest of the time to finish the style she had imagined. Since Kathryn didn't know how to apply make-up Amy did her own.

Finally both girls were ready; they didn't have time to look in the mirrors before they heard a knock at the door.

"Our escorts?" Amy asked as she moved towards the door.

Prince Derek and David were standing outside, both admittedly handsome in their fresh tunics. Kathryn felt herself become increasingly uncomfortable as both escorts stared at them for a few moments in shock.

Finally Derek collected himself and offered Amy his arm. "Are you ready for tonight?"

Amy rewarded him with a smile. "Of course."

Together they headed down the hall. Kathryn reluctantly turned to look at David.

Chapter 24

When Amy had first opened the door, David hadn't noticed Kathryn in the background. He noticed her now. In fact it was getting to be exceedingly difficult not to stare at her.

What had Amy done? Kathryn didn't look like the Kathryn he knew. Her hair was styled so that most of it hung down, softening her facial features to such an extent he almost didn't recognize her. The dress she was wearing didn't match any style he had ever seen before, but it enhanced Kathryn's features and unlike the wider skirts that his sisters wore, hers was left to fall naturally, making her look taller.

Earlier he hadn't understood what Derek had seen in her that stood out to him. He did now. Kathryn was stunning.

"Is everything alright?" she asked as she closed the door behind her.

"Everything's perfect," he assured her as he offered her his arm. He could see her hesitation to accept it. "I don't bite," he joked. She took it gingerly.

They met Arianna in the hall and the servant gave Kathryn a peculiar look, followed by one that Kathryn would have sworn was pride, and hurried off.

"What was that about?" David asked curiously.

Kathryn was just as confused as he was. "I have no idea."

When they reached the courtyard where the feast would take place, Kathryn was surprised at the décor. The Royal table was set at the far end of the courtyard. Behind the table a massive mural depicting the four seasons at the castle formed a colorful backdrop. Five long tables were spread out perpendicular to the head table and it was to the head of one of these tables that a servant showed Kathryn and David. Mercifully, across from them sat Natalie and Luke, which would make the dinner conversation easier. At least it would if Natalie remained civil. As it was, the older girl was eyeing her dress with a calculating gleam in her eye.

The King signaled for the feast to begin and within minutes the servants were carrying platters from the kitchen and filling up the tables with delicious foods.

Kathryn ate sparingly. The nightmare had robbed her of her appetite and even spending time with Amy hadn't brought it fully back. To her annoyance, David noticed her lack of enthusiasm and kept urging her to try some new dish. Even Natalie began to notice, asking if she'd tried the smoked fish or jellied fruit.

Despite her lack of hunger she had to admit that the food was very good. Roast mallard, goose, pheasant, and quail dominated the farthest reaches of the table. Baskets of breads, tureens of various soups, and bowls of dipping sauces were scattered between and around the various roasted birds. The center of each table was dominated by three large platters; one a roasted pig, another a smoked deer, and the last was covered with various types of fish.

There were several different types of wines and berry juices present and Kathryn filled her cup with berry juice. Her dislike of wine stemmed from her duties at the Blackwood's and there were nights, especially after a nightmare, when she would swear that she could smell the scent of the sharp wine they had favored in her room.

After dessert, a wide selection of fruits, nuts, berries, and cheeses, the toasts began. If there was any part of a royal, or even noble, party that Kathryn hated the most, it was the toasts. As far as she was concerned, the toasts gave every windbag attending the opportunity to make their presence and perceived importance known to the rest of the poor guests by boring them with long speeches, ridiculously formal phrases, and false nods of acknowledgement to the royal family. This was the one part of the feast she would have given her left leg to be excused from. Blessedly, as a woman, she was excused from having to give a toast.

Prince Derek went first. "Unlike my predecessors," he began with a smile. "I will not bore you with a long dull speech." Laughter and cheers erupted from around the courtyard as the people approved. "Instead I will merely toast to my mother's continued happiness on this special day and to the people for their love."

That was mercifully short, Kathryn thought as she sipped her drink.

She was back in the exotic hall floating high in the trees. Only instead of being empty, it was filled to capacity with strange faces. As she gazed out at the faces, Kathryn was startled to realize she wasn't standing near the doors, but next to the raised dais—facing the crowd. She was wearing the same dress she had worn before and those on and around the dais were those who had been in the room the last time she had come to this place.

"Ei syr!" called one of the men on the dais. "Sai Volaer, Estelwen, thys mi car vaeresaer sai iar!"

It was only then that Kathryn realized they were all raising wine goblets high, "Sai Volaer Estelwen!" The crowd echoed enthusiastically.

"Lady Kathryn?"

David's concerned question brought her out of the vision—she turned to look at him.

"Are you alright?"

She nodded, not trusting her voice to answer confidently. Quickly she turned her attention back to the toasts, pushing back her rising panic.

To her relief the rest of the toasters followed Prince Derek's example and most were no more than a few sentences. There was one toast that lasted for five minutes but the speaker was eloquent and, as far as Kathryn could tell, spoke the truth in all his words. Best of all, there were no more day...what could she call that? A daydream? A day nightmare? A vision? *I hope not.*

The feast concluded and those who were fortunate enough to have received an invitation left to participate in the ball that followed.

Kathryn accepted David's arm and allowed him to lead her to the ballroom. As they walked she was eternally grateful that her escort wasn't pushing to understand what had happened during the toasts—not that she would have had an answer anyway. What—or who— was bringing these...visions, she decided, to mind? She didn't know and wasn't entirely confident that she wanted to know. What she did know was that she wanted the visions to stop. Immediately.

They entered the ballroom and David gracefully transitioned their walk into a waltz as he brought them onto the dance floor.

Kathryn hated waltzes. They were intentionally slow to allow the couple a chance to talk, or in some cases flirt, without becoming out of breath. She especially hated how it was an unspoken requirement that you look into your partner's eyes throughout the dance. She wanted nothing more than walk off the dance floor and get out of sight for a few radians.

"You want to tell me what happened during the toasts?" David asked as he deftly sidestepped a less experienced couple. As much as he had protested to hate the waltz back in the garden at school, he was proving to be an extremely graceful dancer. Kathryn found that this knowledge only served to irritate her even more. When he kept glancing at her expectantly, she forced herself to answer his question.

"Not really." She worked to keep a straight face. If he kept on this topic, she just might be hitting him before the night was over. Maybe she could make it look like he'd insulted her honor and just maybe, she wouldn't have to be his sponsor anymore. It was a possibility to consider.

He glanced down at her and grinned. "I'd say that's progress."

Confused, Kathryn glanced at him. "Excuse me?"

"Not really is not a no, therefore you aren't adamant about not telling me which means we're making progress and you're considering telling me."

She stared at him for a full ten seconds before slowly shaking her head. "I hope that made sense in your head, because I can't follow your logic."

He laughed.

"What's so funny?"

"You sounded exactly like my mother when you said that. She was always telling me that when my curiosity got the better of me."

"Who are your parents?" Kathryn asked, genuinely curious. "Are they here tonight?" She was intensely intrigued when he looked away before answering.

David quickly scanned the dance floor and the head table. "No, they aren't here."

She tipped her head to the side. "Okay. But who are they?"

"No one of consequence," he replied as he turned her expertly.

Interesting. She'd never seen him so closed to questions, or at least she'd never seen him so evasive. Usually he encouraged questions within their family in order to facilitate the formation of close relationships that they would need later in life. "Are they nobility?"

'No."

"So they're commoners," she deliberately used the word nobility used to describe those they believed to be below them.

His reply was calm, unflustered. "No."

"No?"

"No," he confirmed.

"They aren't nobility, but they aren't commoners either," Kathryn repeated. *What else is there to be? Do you enjoy riddles? Is this your way of getting back at me?* "What else could they be?" she asked her first question out loud, she didn't dare voice the last one.

"I told you, no one of consequence."

Another possibility popped into her head, "Are they dead?"

"No."

"So they are alive, but neither noble or common." She mused over the riddle before asking quietly, "Are they Guardians?"

"No."

She let out a heavy sigh in frustration. David chuckled and she glared at him. Her irritation got the better of her. "You're doing this just to annoy me."

He shrugged. "No more so that you refusing to reveal your heritage to me."

She narrowed her gaze. "Somehow I don't think you had quite the childhood I had," she replied stiffly.

"You're right, I didn't," he agreed. "But at least I don't let mine hold me back."

The music ended and he bowed to her. "Thank you for the dance, milady."

Kathryn, still sputtering after his last comment, performed the customary curtsy but before David could escort her off the dance floor, and she could give him a piece of her mind, Prince Derek came to ask her for a dance.

Kathryn acquiesced only to find herself dancing another waltz. She briefly wondered how well the musicians could play if they were soaked completely through. *Jasmine would have my head if I tried such a stunt,* she thought sourly. *Not to mention I'd probably give myself away.*

"Are you enjoying the ball, Lady Kathryn?" Derek asked as he steered her around the room.

"Yes, Your Highness, I am. Are you?"

Derek frowned at her. "I thought I told you to call me Derek?"

Kathryn felt her cheeks redden from embarrassment, something that rarely happened, "Yes, you did, forgive me."

He flashed a grin and winked at her, "No harm done, I just hate being called Your Highness all evening and watching eyes wink at me from behind fluttering fans."

Kathryn frowned. "Somehow I agree with you."

He laughed. "Somehow you don't seem like the type to flirt outrageously with your prince."

"I believe you to be correct."

"Are you always so formal?"

"Only during a waltz," she assured him.

He threw back his head and laughed heartily, drawing the stares of those around them. Kathryn felt exceedingly exposed as she waited for her partner to finish expressing his amusement.

"I like you Lady Kathryn," he informed her as they waltzed around the room. "You aren't afraid to speak frankly. I will confide in you that I hate the waltz as much as you appear to." He bowed to her as the music ended and thanked her for being such a delightful partner.

Matt's cheerful face appeared before her as he asked her to dance. Kathryn, already tired of playing the part of a noblewoman, agreed only because Matt's playful manner was infectious and she couldn't bring herself to say no.

"You seem to be enjoying yourself," Matt said as he led her around the room.

She rolled her eyes at him. "You need to work on your observation skills, Sir Matias."

He grimaced. "I hate that name. Why my mother had to give me such a pompous name, I'll never know."

Smiling, she couldn't hold back a small laugh. "Perhaps she thought you would be destined for great things."

"She was probably hoping that I'd follow my namesake's example and sire fifteen children."

Kathryn choked on a laugh. "That's a lot of kids."

"Don't I know it. Try growing up with over two hundred cousins and having to learn everyone's name. It's a royal pain."

"I have to admit, I don't envy you there."

Leaning in, he placed his cheek next to her own and Kathryn had to force herself not to react. "So what's your court name?" he whispered.

"You already know it," she whispered back.

She laughed at his disappointed look.

Soon the waltz was over and Matt bowed to her, thanking her for the dance and wringing from her the promise of another dance.

Before another eager man could ask her for a dance, Kathryn hurried to the table set up for refreshments. Picking up a pre-filled cup, she slowly sipped the cool liquid. Whenever a hopeful young man approached her and asked for dance she informed them that she wasn't available at the moment and would hold her glass up as proof.

After five potential suitors seeking her affections came and went, Kathryn found a chair and sank down into it. She was smart enough not to grab a seat on a couch—she wasn't in the mood to fight off a knight with less than chivalrous intentions.

Amy came by between dances and chatted for a few minutes before being claimed for another dance.

As she watched her friend dance, Kathryn wished she could be anywhere but here. Give her a crisp morning with a thief or murderer to track down through the woods, anything but a ball. Amy, Natalie, and the others came from families that were used to this sort of thing. Even at school, Kathryn hadn't participated in many of the classes dedicated to teaching court etiquette, she'd only been required to attend the most basic courses before being whisked into classes dedicated to developing her hardly used gift. She had never gone to an imitation ball.

Glancing around Kathryn attempted to locate the rest of the dragons. Amy was dancing with Derek again. Kathryn smiled at the thought of the crown prince being smitten with a woman he could never have. Jenna was dancing with Matt and apparently knee-deep in serious conversation by the looks of their faces. She fought the urge to slap them upside the heads and remind them that they were supposed to look like they were enjoying themselves. Natalie was dancing and flirting with Lord Tanner, who appeared to be immune to her charms.

Lindsey, Rachel, and Elizabeth stood in a circle with other noble ladies, giggling and fluttering their fans.

Leia was dancing with Tyler, who was actually turning out to be a respectable dancer. Luke and Cassandra were talking off to the side near the musicians. Daniel was dancing with a pretty red-head who was flirting outrageously. Kathryn grimaced in disgust at the lady's antics. Didn't she realize how unbecoming and humiliating her actions were? Fortunately Daniel was level headed enough to brush off her advances. David was—where was David? Glancing around, Kathryn failed to spot their family leader.

Oh well. As she watched the rest of her family she took careful note of their appearances and compared them to others dancing or mulling around them.

 She wanted to grimace slightly when she realized that none of them were common looking. Every girl had several characteristics that would have admirers flocking around them. The boys were well muscled and well-tanned, a look that was in style as of late. They stood out in this crowd, noticed by all who glanced in their direction. If they ever needed to put together a clandestine mission within the noble ranks, they were going to run into some serious problems. She would have to think of ways to hide the Dragons in plain sight.

So where did she fit in? She had been told by every love-struck Lord or Sir she had danced with that she was beautiful. She certainly didn't feel beautiful, but then again, beauty was in the eye of the beholder. Perhaps that was her curse. Beauty made one stand out, no matter how much money they had. So, no matter how much she tried to hide, they would always seek her out.

She would have to learn to hide better.

℘·℃℘

David watched Kathryn from the shadows of the balcony where he had taken refuge. Like his second-in-command, he had grown tired of playing the necessary game of subterfuge and chase found at court. He had lasted longer than she had, but he had been born into this, she hadn't. As it was he had only managed to dance with Kathryn, his sisters, Amy, and finally his mother, who returned to the ball after a short absence, before retreating...something his mother would probably lecture him on tomorrow. He wasn't worried. He'd probably heard the lecture ten times by now. Besides, he found watching so much more enjoyable...and entertaining.

Even now, he watched Kathryn glance around the room taking careful note to locate each of the Dragons. He saw her smile as she located Amy and Derek and was impressed at the transformation of her features. After locating the rest of the Dragons, he watched her glance around the room several times, *no doubt looking for me*, he thought with a smirk. She wouldn't find him.

He watched her turn away several potential partners as she continued to watch the rest of the Dragons.

Kathryn is a mother hen! The realization hit him with such a force it took his breath away and made him want to laugh at the same time.

Despite all of Kathryn's cold manners and uninviting gazes, she still looked after the rest of the Dragons like a mother watched out for her children.

I don't believe you're as cold and unfeeling as you make yourself out to be, Kathryn, he told her silently. *And I'm going to prove it— to the Dragons, to the kingdom, but most importantly—to yourself.*

He watched as Derek whisked her out onto the floor for another dance and briefly considered returning to the floor when another one of her partner's hands began a slow uninvited travel during the dance. However Kathryn leaned towards his ear and spoke a few words and afterwards her partner's hands stayed put as etiquette dictated, in her hand and on her waist.

He left the balcony for the last dance and managed to claim Kathryn before any other lords, or either of his brothers.

After the last dance, he escorted her back to her room. Neither of them spoke, Kathryn too exhausted from playing the part of the gentle noblewoman, and David unwilling to upset her again like he had earlier.

Chapter 25

That night the nightmares and flashbacks became worse than Kathryn had experienced in years. Usually she could wake up and shake off the effects within a few minutes. However, while she was still sitting at the window waiting for the restlessness to cease not even the reddening of the sky from Niea and how it transformed the night into a beautiful landscape comforted her.

She knew that she could forget about getting any sleep. She would have to take careful steps to ensure that none of the other Dragons noticed her edginess and lethargy. The last thing she needed was for Amy or David to start badgering her about her sleeping habits.

She desperately wanted to ride Lerina for several radians, but it was far too early for anyone to even be close to waking and going down to the stables now would raise too many questions. Sighing, she pulled out a scroll she had secreted from the royal library earlier and settled in to read for a few radians.

Destiny's sharp peck at the window drew her attention from the book and as Kathryn looked up she saw that the sun was now visible above the Airë Mountains. Quickly she donned a riding habit and slipped through the still sleeping castle. It was only a few radians after daybreak, far too early for any of the party-goers to be even close to stirring. Kathryn hoped that it also meant a secluded ride without any prying eyes.

"Good morning Milady," the stable master greeted her as she stepped into the stables.

"Good morning." Kathryn forced what she hoped was a pleasant smile onto her face and nodded to him.

The toughened horse master looked up at the sky and grinned. "I do believe it's going to be a beautiful day."

Kathryn followed his eyes and nodded in agreement. "I believe you're right,' she continued on, assuring the horse master that she didn't need help saddling her horse.

Lerina snorted a greeting and Kathryn fed her a sugar cube from the stash she kept in her saddlebags—which she kept in her room to keep her greedy horse from nosing through.

Minutes later she was flying across the grassy plains behind the palace—the wind whipping her hair out behind her. *Perhaps I should have tied it back,* she mused as she raced away from the palace. But no, she didn't need a headache this early in the morning, and it was a rare noble, man or woman, who rose early after a ball. No one would be around to see her conduct herself in a manner befitting a peasant.

As she rode, Kathryn felt some the tension and fear drain from her body. With every step Lerina took, she felt a small weight lift from her shoulders. The farther they went, the more relief Kathryn felt. After a radian Kathryn felt more like her old self.

"Come on girl," she urged her mount. "Let's see if we can catch the wind!"

Lerina took off like an arrow shot from a longbow; it was as if she had been waiting for such a command and now rejoiced at the opportunity to race the wind.

Destiny called from high above. Riding a rapidly rising thermal she was but a black speck against the blue cloudless sky. Before them the plain stretched for kilometers before rising sharply to form the Airë Mountains.

According to legends the land beyond the Airë Mountains was the homeland of both the Elves and the remaining Wanderers. It was said that a mystical forest lay beyond the mountains and that both races could perform magic that would make the Guardians look like children with an adult's sword.

Kathryn reigned in Lerina until they stood motionless before the towering mountains.

It is odd that both the Elves and the Wanderer's histories begin beyond the mountains, she ruminated as she shifted in the saddle. *The Elves, with their places of healing, desire for knowledge, and dedication to a mysterious being should not come from the same land that houses the heathen Wanderers who sacrifice their own children and worship the sun and fire.*

According to the ancient scrolls the name Airë originally meant something in an ancient Elvish language, but its meaning had been lost over the countless generations and the ink on the scrolls had faded so badly, the significance was impossible to make out. Interestingly enough, Airë was also the last month of the year, all the other months names had meanings, just not Airë. Kathryn had often wondered if the name wasn't Elvish, but an ancient dialect used by the Wanderers. The Airë Mountains contained the highest peaks in the kingdom and such an altitude could have been considered by the Wanderers to bring them closer to their object of worship, perhaps Airë meant something along the lines of worship.

Not that there was anybody who could confirm or deny any theory that arose. Those who traveled across the mountains never returned. Rumors spread like wildfire throughout the kingdom claiming anything from the supposition that no one ever crossed the mountains alive to the idea that the wild tribes on the other side killed them as soon as they arrived, or that some dark and evil magic sought out and enslaved those who would dare to cross the mountain barrier.

Kathryn believed that it was a combination of the intense cold and thin air at such high altitudes and the hungry mountain predators that kept the questers from ever returning.

Returning. Something she should probably consider since it was likely the castle guests had started to awaken from their slumber. Glancing back at the towering peaks, Kathryn reluctantly turned Lerina back towards the palace—a mere speck on the horizon.

They made it back in just over a radian and as Kathryn rubbed Lerina down she heard male voices enter the stable. It didn't take her long to discover the speakers' identities.

Luke, Tyler, and David walked down the long rows between the stalls. Luke was muttering something about not getting enough sleep, Tyler was complaining about his sore feet, but David wasn't saying anything.

Kathryn retrieved a strand of leather and quickly tied her hair back before stepping out of Lerina's stall. The boys, three stalls ahead, stopped.

"Good morning, Lady Kathryn," Luke called, his voice sounding like he was still half-asleep. Or still suffering from the effects of the wine from last night, he'd sure drunk enough of it. Later she would have to discuss his drinking habits with him. He wasn't helpful to *anyone* in an inebriated state. She sincerely hoped that it had been an act, she didn't want to live with another drunkard.

She frowned at him. "I hope you aren't planning on competing in that state, Sir Lucian."

Luke turned to Tyler. "What is she trying to tell me?"

"She's trying to tell you that you're acting like you're a drunk who hasn't had a good night's sleep in days and that if you try to compete you'll be skewered by your opponent before you can find your balance on your steed," his friend informed him matter-of-factly.

Luke grimaced. "What a lovely image to consider so early in the morning."

David laughed. "It's almost time for brunch. I hardly think it is that early."

Luke frowned again. "All I said was good morning! I hardly think that deserves a lecture. If you guys make this a habit, I'm not going to speak to anyone before noon."

Looking up, David winked at Kathryn. "Make sure you do this every morning," he told her in mock seriousness. "He can't form a coherent sentence before noon so it would save us all the trouble of having to translate his garbled words."

As Luke protested, Kathryn rolled her eyes skyward and quickly moved past them. Men! Couldn't they ever be serious? Well, perhaps Tyler could, he seemed to be the only sensible one in the family. Maybe David too, she added grudgingly.

When she returned to her room, she found a breakfast tray had been delivered with a delicious assortment of fruits and cheeses. As she ate she considered what competitions she wanted to watch.

Thanks to David asking her to be his sponsor, she would have to attend the joust. Javelin throwing held no appeal to her, neither did hand-to-hand combat. Something about half naked men wallowing and grunting in the mud and dirt while slapping each other silly held no appeal for her. Although some of the other noble ladies were convinced that such was the high point of the competition. Archery she would definitely attend as well as the sword fighting. *Of course if I had my way, I'd be competing instead of sitting in the heat wearing a ridiculous dress.*

Now that she had finished breakfast she moved to her closet to pick out a dress. Brushing past the ball gowns, with the dreaded blue gown hanging in front, she picked out a deep green day dress. The light material would keep her cool throughout the tournaments and the color was one she favored.

By the time she finished bathing and dressing it was still early so she decided to visit the palace's massive library.

There were a few brave souls who had risen early and taken refuge in the numerous rooms that made up the library, Kathryn wandered through the rooms until she found an empty nook. The room she found herself in housed books of fantasy and fiction.

Kathryn chose a book called *The Dragon's Call* off the shelf and settled herself in a window seat as she opened the book.

Immediately she was pulled into the story of a kingdom that was undergoing an insurgency—one of the king's own sons had killed his father and declared himself king. His two brothers he kept locked away in the dungeons and mines. His eldest brother, the true heir, was deceived by the usurper's charms and believed everything he was told and remained partially free. The younger brother was not deceived and the false king sent him and his beloved to work the mines. After a month, the dictator called the young prince's beloved away from the mines and to his side for she was a very desirable woman and he wanted her. However the young woman resisted him—until the dictator offered her a way to save the one person she loved. If she married him, and became his wife in every way, he would free his brother from the mines.

"Lady Kathryn?"

The quiet question startled Kathryn out of the fantasy world and back into reality. She looked up to find Natalie and David looking down at her.

"Are you okay?" Natalie asked, settling herself onto the other half of the window seat.

Kathryn looked at her, confused. "Of course I am. Why wouldn't I be?"

"It's just that Sir Darian and I were able to get within three meters of you, talking the whole while and yet we startled you," Natalie explained slowly.

That was a disturbing piece of information. In a place as quiet as the library, she should have been able to hear them *enter*. Kathryn grimaced, nodding toward the book she had placed on the side table. "It's a very intriguing book." And one she wouldn't risk picking up again. She couldn't risk being caught off guard again.

David picked up the book and raised an eyebrow at her. "*The Tales of the Great Wizards of Old*. Normally I give books the benefit of the doubt, but our history instructor read parts of this to my class. He cured everyone's insomnia in about five minutes."

Kathryn quickly reached out for the book. "That isn't the title at all," she exclaimed, looking down to correct him, only to stare at the words, *The Tales of the Great Wizards of Old*. "I don't understand," she whispered slowly. "This wasn't the book I grabbed off the shelf," she opened the book to look inside. "And this certainly wasn't the story I was reading."

"It's okay if you like the book, Lady Kathryn," David told her. "It's just that I personally thought it was boring."

Kathryn shook her head. "No, it's not that at all. This was not the book I was reading." She watched Natalie and David exchange a look and knew that they didn't believe her.

"Oh, never mind." She pushed herself up off the window seat and headed back towards her room.

"Hey!" Natalie and David hurried after her, "Where are you going?" Natalie demanded.

"Back to my room, I need to get ready for the tournaments," Kathryn replied, her voice stiff.

"You look ready to me," Natalie commented eyeing her appearance. "Maybe do a little something with your hair and you're ready to go." After a moment she added in a low tone, "And I can't believe that you didn't tell me that you are the Dowager Princess's ward!"

Kathryn risked a glance at David who was watching her intently. "I didn't think it was important."

"Not important?" Natalie's voice rose a little. "You're practically royalty and you don't think it's worth mentioning?"

"I'm not royalty," Kathryn ground out. "I'm the ward of the Dowager Princess, whom I rarely see, so what's the point of mentioning it?"

"What's the point?" Natalie echoed incredulously. "Kathryn, you're in the perfect position to get to know the princes! Perhaps even be courted by one!"

"I've met both of them and I'm not interested," she retorted sharply.

"Come on, Kathryn, you have to be a little curious about what's underneath their royal exterior. What about the youngest prince?"

"I could care less," Kathryn replied firmly. "I've seen enough and I'm certain that the last prince is going to be just like his brothers—someone I don't wish to associate with."

Natalie threw her hands into the air. "I give up. The youngest prince's identity hasn't even been revealed yet and Kathryn has already decided to hate him just because he's royalty."

"It's not just because he's royalty," Kathryn protested. "It's because the whole royal family's character is all the same and I can't see it changing in the last prince."

Natalie sighed heavily. After a moment she asked, "Do you want me to do your hair for the tournament?"

Taken off guard by Natalie's offer, Kathryn stared at her in bewilderment. "What?"

"Would you like me to style your hair for the tournament?" Natalie reiterated with a roll of her eyes.

"What's wrong with my hair?" Kathryn demanded.

"It's boring," Natalie said candidly. "You never vary your hairstyle, it's always the same bun."

"I like it," Kathryn protested.

"Which is part of the reason I think you're a boring person," Natalie informed her.

David watched Kathryn's entire frame go rigid. Quickly he ushered the two girls outside the library so that they wouldn't disturb the other readers. "Come on," he urged. "We all need to get ready for the tournaments," he fixed his gaze on Natalie.

She shrugged. "See you later," She tossed the phrase over her shoulder as she was leaving. David turned to face an irritated and angry Kathryn.

Chapter 26

David braced for a repeat of yesterday's scene back in her room, instead Kathryn surprised him.

She swallowed hard, closing her eyes tight—as if she was willing her ire to disappear. *Or trying to prove to both me and herself that she is in control.* After a moment she opened them again and looked at him. "I'm going back to my room. Do you know when the archery competition begins?"

Surprised that Kathryn had managed to hold onto her temper, David had to race to collect his thoughts. "I think it starts just after the ninth radian."

She nodded a thank you before abandoning him in the hallway. He watched her go with mixed feelings of annoyance and admiration.

Turning he returned to his room and collected his bow, quiver of arrows, and sword. He had no illusions that he would be the best archer on the field, however he was confident his swordsmanship would put him in the top three. After all, the only person who could out-spar a Guardian was another Guardian.

He spent the radian before the ninth rechecking his equipment and practice weapons. When he got to the archery field he noticed that the crowds had already gathered. Kathryn and Amy were once again seated in the royal box. He grimaced remembering how Kathryn had pursued the truth about his parents and how she'd just told Natalie that she didn't want to associate with royalty. Life had a fine sense of irony,

He didn't know what she'd do if she found out that he was really Prince David, not just an annoying family leader who couldn't leave well enough alone. Come to think of it, he really didn't want to find out what she'd do if she knew the truth. Of course, once he turned twenty she'd find out. He wasn't looking forward to that. Come to think of it, he wasn't sure whose reaction he dreaded more; hers or Natalie's.

The royal family would never speak of it—it was against the rules of the Guardians. As a Guardian, David had forsaken his royal heritage to become someone, and something, else. Only if both his brothers died would he be permitted to leave the Guardians to run the kingdom. There were many reasons that the Guardians did not allow the public release of the fact that royal children often joined the ranks of the Guardians. The most important reason being that there were discontented people who would accuse the royal family of placing their children in positions where they could control the justice the people would receive.

David had never heard of such an event taking place. As it was, royal children technically forfeited their royal status when they entered the school—only under extreme circumstances with approval by the entire Guardian council, could a royal child take place in official sovereign affairs once inducted into the Guardians. The reason for this was simple. A power hungry king was a pain but a manageable one. A power hungry king trained in the ways of the Guardians would be nearly unstoppable. Of course, in reality, royal children were expected to be seen at court. They were expected to be seen with their kin, or at least maintaining their own castles and families. More often than not, any gifted children born to the King and Queen were presented at court once and their continued lack of court presence was covered by carefully selected doubles who would take their place when the Guardian returned with his assigned family to their region. It wasn't a perfect system, but the fact that everyone involved kept their lips tightly shut allowed for nothing more than speculation from the ranks of nobility.

Balls and feasts such as the one David was attending now were a common occurrence in a Guardian's life. They needed to be able to mingle with both the common people and those of the aristocracy.

Royal children and children of nobility came in handy in situations like this because they already have contacts in the form of their own family. Just as in the same way children from the villages and farms came in handy because their biological families served as contacts.

A trumpet signaled the start of the competition. David wondered what the other Dragons would say if they knew he was about to throw the competition.

After all, he thought as he released his first arrow, it hit just outside the bulls-eye, *nobody can excel at everything except a Guardian*. At least that what was generally believed. And that false perception was also what gave those who were gifted the ability to hide in plain sight. The people, common and nobility alike, were fed stories and legends of omnipotent Guardians and warriors. As such that was what they expected to see. When what they saw didn't match their own perceptions, they disregarded it or completely disbelieved it.

He made it to the fifth round before his shooting wasn't good enough to go on. As he left the field he looked towards Luke and the rest of the guys. From their sympathetic faces it didn't appear as though they had picked up that he purposefully lost the match. Amy had the same sympathetic look as the guys. Kathryn's face was set in its usual rigid expression.

Mentally sighing, David found a place on the sidelines and watched the rest of the contestants. Prince Derek hadn't even entered the competition, supposedly to prepare for the swordsmanship contest, but David knew better. His oldest brother's archery skills were pitiful. Prince Darcy was an exemplary archer, so was Lord Tanner. In the end it came down to the two men, with Lord Tanner scoring three points higher in the end.

The sparring tournament was one David was determined to win. When it came his turn to spar he had been able to watch most of the contestants go before him, giving him a chance to analyze the stronger competitors' strengths and weaknesses.

His first opponent was a Lord Grenville, a man he knew to be a pompous windbag in his father's court, but equally well known for his strong arm on the sparring field. However Lord Grenville was not as young as he used to be and he preferred his reputation from his younger years do the fighting for him. He was good, yes, but his style was severely outdated and couldn't account for new maneuvers and techniques that any recent Guardian graduate, or even newly appointed knight, had been thoroughly grounded in.

However he was a very good warm up exercise and David let the man thrust and attack until his own muscles were warm and fluid. Then he struck, not in a quick and rapid form that so many of the newer knights preferred but a slow and steady approach that ensured that he made no mistakes. Each challenger he faced he tackled the same way, giving ground for a few moments into the fight before standing firm and utterly destroying his opponent's defenses.

Darcy was his first opponent in the semi-finals round. David knew his brother's strengths lay in agility and swiftness rather than the heavy handed blows Lord Grenville preferred. Quickly he exchanged his two handed grip for a one handed grip to allow for fast returns and parries.

As the two fought, David had to admit that his older brother was indeed quick, not to mention devious. There were several times during the fight when Darcy had appeared to swipe at David's legs, to change direction at the last second and aim for his shoulders or arm only to change direction halfway through and strike at the legs again. David had often used the double feint attack, aiming at one target and then switching to a different one at the last second, but he had never heard of, let alone seen, a triple feint attack. It took enormous wrist strength and flexibility to change the momentum of a moving sword and to do it twice in a row was a considerable show of control and strength.

Suddenly it was over, a quick side thrust from David and his brother was abruptly disarmed. Surprised, David looked at his brother and saw the answer in his eyes. He threw the match. The truth surprised him, Darcy had always been competitive when it came to swordplay, and yet here he was, throwing the match to his younger brother. David would have to ask him why later.

Finally it was down to Lord Tanner, Derek, and David. *Interesting*, David thought as he faced off Lord Tanner, *The champions from the jousting tournament once again facing off on the field. Only this time, I shall be the winner*, he vowed has he lunged at Lord Tanner.

Tanner was good, David had to admit it. Tanner used the same triple feint attack that that Darcy had used earlier, only Tanner used it with more skill and ease. After the fourth triple feint attack, David understood why Darcy, who wasn't nearly as effective or at ease with the technique, had used it. To prepare him for Tanner.

Finally David had decided he had had enough. A rapid fast series of thrusts and false attacks had Tanner disarmed. David fought to keep a smile off of his face. When it came to sword fighting, he was a fast learner and the technique hadn't been nearly as taxing as he'd expected it to be. Both men stood panting in the hot sun. Because Tanner had been defeated he would face off with Derek and the winner of their match would face David.

Grateful for the respite, David watched his brother fight. Derek had a style that was completely his own that was difficult to predict. David instinctively knew he would end up fighting his brother so he paid close attention to the small signs that signaled his brother's next move, rather than watch Tanner.

His prediction was correct, Derek emerged the victor. The two men bowed to each other, Tanner's a bit begrudging.

After a half radian break, to give Derek a chance to rest, the two brothers faced off.

As their swords clashed, David felt the steely strength behind Derek's blow. Quickly he brought his sword upwards towards his brother's head, only to flick his wrist and send it whipping around at the last second to aim at the ribcage. Derek wasn't fooled by the maneuver and quickly brought his sword around to block David's strike.

The Crown Prince angled his sword for a strike at his opponent's left arm, which David easily blocked, only to feel the Derek's sword sliding up his own sword. Quickly he spun away, dropping his shoulder and pulling his neck away to prevent a strike that would have probably ended the fight. As soon as his back was facing Derek, David raised his sword over his head, the tip pointing downwards, blocking the strike he knew had been coming. Turning your back on an opponent during a fight usually resulted in your death, David knew, but the row of shields that now faced him had provided a makeshift mirror that had only confirmed his prediction of Derek's blow.

Spinning, he went on the offense with rapid fire strikes. His first blow was aimed at the neck—blocked. Thrust at the ribcage—blocked. Thrust back at the head, whipping away at the last second to the right knee—blocked. His fourth thrust touched his brother on his arm, but did not score as a disabling injury.

Derek swung his sword in a wide cut, David jumped back to avoid being caught in its path, only to realize that as he jumped back Derek jumped forward ending the wild cut and changing to a thrust aimed at his middle.

As he turned away from his brother, David brought his sword down, managing to deflect most of the attack. Derek aimed an attack at his feet, instead of leaping backwards; David leapt up and brought his sword around for a side cut.

His sword too low to parry his brother's attack, Derek jumped back and to the side. David's sword missed him by centimeters—but a near miss didn't account for anything in this game.

Derek leaped forward with an attack aimed at his brother's head which David parried, but instead of parrying with a moving block, David held his sword steady. Their blades locked, the brothers looked at each other, each putting all his strength behind his sword, hoping to crush the other's block. Knowing that remaining locked would drain his strength faster than David's, Derek flicked his wrist, releasing his sword and sending it into a wide circle that brought his sword up again in time to block the younger man's cut at his head.

David had had quite enough. He picked a point on the ground and refused to give any ground, weaving right and left, back and forth—always returning to the same spot, while at the same time running through several two and three point feint attacks in rapid succession. Derek barely managed to keep up, and a sharp flick of the wrist brought David's sword clashing down on his brother's near the hilt. The sting from the sudden sharp vibrations loosened Derek's grip on his sword and another rapid strike from his brother's sword disarmed him.

The crowd went wild, but neither brother paid them any mind. David picked up the sword and handed it back to Derek who accepted it with a graceful loser's bow.

℘·ℭ

The second jousting tournament took place three radians after the morning meal the following day. All of the Dragons but Matt made it into the final joust. Lord Tanner, Kathryn was pleased to see, didn't make it through the second qualification round. The final event took place at midmorning on the day of the final ball. Crown Prince Derek was the winner and received the victor's crown and scepter with pleasure from his proud father.

Chapter 27

The third and final ball outshone all the rest. All day long the servants put forth a tremendous effort to make this ball a night to remember. Freshly washed and polished, the mosaic dance floor glittered as if made up of precious gems instead of crystal and colored glass.

The King's Royal Guard, the only other service which employed gifted individuals fully trained in the ways of the Guardians, had used their gifts to transform the ballroom into an enchanted forest. Small planters had been brought in and placed at intervals along the walls. From the planters, the guards gifted with plant control had caused woody trunks to entwine their way up the ballroom walls. When they reached the ceiling, the trunks had splintered into numerous branches which stretched across the expanse of the room to form a canopy of limbs. Light gifted guards had filled glass orbs fitted with wire loops with their light and, with the help of wind and telekinesis gifted guards, had floated the glass lights up into the branches and suspended them above the dance floor.

Behind the far wall opposite the entrance specialized pipes and collecting trenches were crafted to resemble a thick growth of vines extending from rocky pools at the base of the wall, and with a little persuasion from water gifted guards, a steady stream of water poured down the wall creating a delicate sheet waterfall. Behind the water, small glowing pebbles had been inserted into the wall, adding to the illusion. The gardens outside had also been decorated. The paths had been lined with glowing rocks and any water, whether standing or flowing, had glow rocks illuminating the depths below the surface.

As the nobility prepared for the night, the kitchens spent all day busily preparing the delicious feast that would be enjoyed at the twenty-fourth radian that night. The musicians practiced until they could perform the music selections flawlessly and those servants attending the ball as helpers, frequently freshened their uniforms.

Nobody wanted this night to be a failure, nothing was to go wrong— it was to be perfect.

ຂ·ຕ

"Kathryn I think you should wear this dress!" Natalie exclaimed pulling a gown out of the closet.

Kathryn turned to look at Natalie's selection. "I don't know, Natalie, it seems a bit formal," she frowned at the older girl's choice—a two piece ensemble consisting of a shimmering white under-dress with wide off the shoulder straps and an off the shoulder sheer overdress that formed sheer sleeves. It was designed in the same style as the blue gown she had worn the first night but definitely had a more formal...more regal appearance, despite its simplicity.

"I think it's beautiful," Jenna commented from the dressing table where Rachel was doing her hair. "And besides, balls are supposed to be formal.

266

You should wear it." Kathryn frowned remembering her conversation with Jasmine earlier that day.

"Where did you get that beautiful blue gown you wore to the first ball?" The princess asked as she sipped her tea. Kathryn and Jasmine had left after the conclusion of the sparring tournament and were taking a midday meal on Jasmine's balcony.

Kathryn, in the process of reaching for a sandwich, paused. "I thought you had it made for me," she replied slowly, carefully watching Jasmine's reaction.

The older woman shook her head. "I asked Madame and she said that she would never have thought to create a gown like that."

"I have no idea where the gown came from then."

"Whoever it is, I'd like to have them designing my gowns," Jasmine commented as she sipped her tea.

Kathryn however was unsettled by the news—swearing not to wear a single dress whose origin's she didn't know.

As she considered the dress before her, Kathryn couldn't remember seeing that dress earlier. "Where did you get the dress, Natalie?"

Natalie, in the process of holding up the dress to the light, looked at Kathryn like she'd lost her mind. "From your closet, silly. Where else would I find it?"

Kathryn shook her head. "It's just that I've never seen that dress before."

"Probably because I had to dig through all the rest of your dresses before I found this one," Natalie said as she held the dress out to Kathryn. "Come on, put it on. I bet David would appreciate it."

Kathryn stared at her confused. "What in the kingdom does that mean?"

Natalie wrinkled her face in disbelief. "What else is it supposed to mean? He's a man, you're a woman. Men like to see pretty women dressed in pretty things."

"Is that why the women at court wear so many necklaces and rings they look like one feather could tip them over?" Cass giggled. Lindsey and Elizabeth joined her.

"I'd give anything to wear a dress that simple," Rachel sighed wistfully. "Do us all a favor and wear it Kat. At least one of us can be comfortable."

"Hear, hear," Amy agreed. "This corset is going to be the death of me. Why does it have to be laced so tightly?"

"To enhance your figure," Natalie informed her primly.

"My figure is just fine without it," Amy retorted firmly. "Why the dressmakers have to sew court dresses two sizes smaller than everyday wear I will never understand."

"Well, how else are you going to catch a husband?" Leia teased.

"I'm not looking to catch a husband. I catch outlaws."

"You sound like Kathryn," Natalie muttered. "There isn't a romantic idea between the two of you. Now put on that dress!" she ordered, seeing that Kathryn hadn't moved to change.

"It's hard to be romantic when the only men you meet are breaking the laws of the kingdom," Elizabeth commented wryly as Kathryn reluctantly complied with Natalie's edict.

Rachel, who had finished styling Jenna's hair, called Kathryn over. "How do you like your hair done?" she asked as she brushed Kathryn's long locks.

Kathryn scowled at her in the mirror. "No one listens to me when I give my opinion, so why do you ask?"

Natalie breezed over, looking at her jewelry selections. "Nobody listens to you because you don't have an inkling as to what's in style," she explained as she picked out a pair of earrings and put them on. "I'm next," she told Rachel.

"You mean the *style* that you all are griping about wearing?" Kathryn muttered as Natalie moved away with the swish of her skirts.

Rachel gave her a wide grin in the mirror before reaching out to finger Kathryn's hair. "How come you never wear this down?" she asked softly.

I let it down at home. Just not when anyone's around, Kathryn mused. "It still gets in my way."

Rachel smiled and picked up a white jeweled barrette. Deftly she pulled the hair ornament through Kathryn's hair until one side had been pulled away from her face. Snapping the barrette in place, Rachel made a few minor adjustments then smiled. "There, that looks nice." Cass stepped over, stood behind Kathryn and placed her hands gently on her shoulders. While looking at their reflection she beamed, "Oh, Kathryn you look absolutely stunning! The look suits you."

Kathryn shifted uncomfortably in the chair causing some hair to uncoil and fall in front of her left eye. "What do I do when the other side gets in my way?" Kathryn wanted to know as she puffed air out the side of her mouth attempting to move the offending lock.

Rachel laughed and shook her head. "Would you like me to pull both sides back?"

"Please."

Smiling, Rachel redid the style so that the sides of Kathryn's hair was twisted back and anchored with the barrette.

Amy hurried over. "What kind of makeup should I use?" She asked Natalie.

Natalie considered Amy's deep green gown. "I think gold eye shadow would complement the trim on your dress nicely. You could use dark green eyeliner to match your dress."

Kathryn vacated the chair she was sitting in so that Natalie could have her hair done and Amy could use the mirror. She moved over to the bed where all the jewelry had been laid out.

"Kathryn do you remember when we pierced your ears?" Amy asked as she applied blush.

Kathryn frowned at her. "I remember you saying it wouldn't hurt only to find out that it did."

"Just be glad you didn't get an infection," Amy laughed at her in the mirror.

Cass came up to stand beside Kathryn. "Here," she handed Kathryn a pair of teardrop earrings, "these would go better with your dress than with mine."

"I can't take your earrings," Kathryn protested.

"Yes you can," Cass insisted. "Besides, Lindsey already said I could borrow a pair of hers, gold hoops go better with my dress than those." She motioned to her deep green dress with gold embroidery and Kathryn had to agree.

Eventually all the girls were ready to go. Laughing they made their way to the ballroom where their escorts had agreed to meet them.

℘·℃

"Matt, stop fidgeting," David laughed. "They'll get here when they get here." He gave his green and gold tunic one last once-over to make sure everything was in place. His mother had insisted that he wear the new clothing she had commissioned for him. Personally, he felt like it was a little overdone, that it looked too royal, but after his sisters had joined their mother's side he'd surrendered.

"How long does it take to get ready?" His friend complained as he tugged on the collar. David suppressed a smile. How Matt had managed to prevent his hair from clashing with his maroon tunic he couldn't comprehend, but he was impressed. Daniel stood nearby in a white tunic with green embroidery looking dignified. He looked more like a prince than David did at his best. It was a little discouraging.

Tyler huffed. "They're girls, Matt, forever." He was dressed in a red tunic with unique white embroidery. Most nobles David was familiar with preferred gold or black embroidery on a red tunic.

Luke, standing next to him and looking extraordinarily handsome in a deep blue and silver tunic, rolled his eyes as he detected some movement down the long corridor. "However," Luke added returning his gaze as the girls came into sight. "Forever is worth the wait." Quickly he hurried over and took Cass by the arm, "Shall we?"

Cass giggled. "If you like, milord."

David watched the two enter the ballroom with a grin. Luke was a lady charmer and he knew it. One by one the rest of the escorts claimed the arm of their ladies.

David held out his arm to Kathryn. "Shall we, milady?"

"You sound like Luke," she muttered as she took his arm.

David's grin grew, "I didn't realize that that was a bad thing," he said as they made their way down the wide steps.

"I'm just glad that this is the last night," Kathryn said as they took their positions for another dreaded waltz. This time, the waltz required that they literally dance cheek to cheek. It would provide them the opportunity to talk privately, but the close proximity to another person was already making Kathryn uncomfortable.

"Tired of the rich and pompous already?" David asked in mock disbelief.

She tossed him a quick glare. "I was tired of them before I got here."

The musicians began playing and the couples began to dance.

"I do agree that they seem to prefer to let their reputations from their younger days speak for themselves rather than prove it later in life."

She grimaced. "Lord Grenville has the worst form I have seen in years."

David laughed. "Only you would consider commenting on his form."

"I noticed you did rather well during the fight with Prince Derek—

269

"Thank you—

"—considering you threw the archery competition."

He glanced down at her. "You noticed that?"

"I think I was the only one. I've seen you shoot at home and while you might not be a master archer, you aren't that bad."

"You noticed all that from the royal box?" He asked in amazement. "I'm impressed."

"Not really when you consider that archery is my preferred method of fighting."

"I heard that you are good with your knives."

Kathryn shifted to look up at him. "Who told you that?"

"Matt mentioned it."

"Oh."

"Are you any good?" David asked curiously, interested to hear her opinion of her own skills.

"What did Matt say?"

"That he hasn't beaten you yet."

For the first time he could remember, Kathryn laughed, it was a soft laugh, but it was definitely a laugh. "Neither have Daniel or Tyler."

"You've beaten Matt, Daniel, and Tyler?" David asked impressed.

She nodded against his cheek.

"What about Luke?"

She shrugged. "His style is similar to yours. You really should consider adding in some faster strokes. If I'd been your opponent during the sparring tournament I could have ended the session before you'd parried three of my moves."

He was fighting a grin now. She said it so matter-of-factly he doubted she even realized that she was giving him advice on how to stay alive. "Perhaps I should take lessons from you."

She shrugged again. "You aren't too bad. If you were desperate enough you might be able to beat me, although you'd have to come up with some new moves since I just watched them all during the tournament."

"You sound confident, especially since most of those moves were for sword fighting and not knife fighting."

"I have reason to be and besides, your sword fighting style differs only slightly from the style you use when you wield your knives, most of the moves transfer directly over."

"You are very observant." He paused. "You beat all three?" he asked remembering how advanced Tyler was with the sword. Whenever they sparred, David had to work hard to emerge the victor. He was almost as good as Luke.

Smiling with her eyes she added, "And both sword-masters at school."

David almost tripped over his feet. "Both?"

She nodded.

He stared at the young woman in front of him. "In that case, I definitely want lessons from you."

The dance ended and Lord Tanner came over to ask for a dance. Another waltz began and immediately Kathryn noticed several differences between

David and Tanner—the first difference being the placement of their hands. Tanner kept his hands considerably lower than David.

Kathryn wasn't about to put up with a cad on the dance floor, she reached around and replaced his hands, "If they ever drop any lower," she warned. "I'm walking off this dance floor immediately."

Properly chastised, Lord Tanner apologized. "Did you watch the sparring tournament?" he asked as they waltzed.

"Yes." Kathryn had an uneasy feeling about Lord Tanner, his hands may have followed her edict to stay put, but they wouldn't stop moving.

"What did you think of the contestants?"

"Sir Darian is an impressive fighter."

"What did you think of Prince Derek and myself?"

"I noticed that you both lost to Sir Darian, was there something else?"

Lord Tanner's jaw tightened. "I could have beat Sir Darian if I'd tried harder," he informed her tersely.

"Why didn't you?"

"It would have been embarrassing."

Kathryn didn't ask him to elaborate, even though it was obvious that he wanted her to. In fact, for the remainder of the dance her responses were just shy of rude. After the dance she quickly curtsied and hurried off, feeling, for a reason she couldn't identify, distinctly filthy.

For the rest of the night, Kathryn did her best to avoid Lord Tanner. Both Prince Derek and Prince Darcy asked her to dance several times, so did Matt, Daniel, Tyler, and Luke. David constantly appeared when Lord Tanner seemed to approach, asking her to dance. She wasn't sure how she felt about the knowledge that David was playing protector...again.

When her feet began to ache, Kathryn left the ballroom and took shelter in the gardens, following the paths and streams to a small waterfall. The sound of the falling water soothed her nerves.

"It's time to go home," Kathryn muttered to herself as the first rays of dawn appeared on the horizon. Picking up her skirts she hurried back inside where the last strains of a minuet were being played.

"Wasn't that a marvelous party?" Natalie asked dreamily as the girls made their way back to their rooms. "I wish we didn't have to leave."

I'm so glad we do, Kathryn thought as she collapsed on her own bed for a few radians' sleep.

Chapter 28

Dressed as nobility, the Dragons left the palace in the mid-afternoon, Natalie bemoaning the lack of parties the whole way out of the city. David had decided they would travel as nobles until they reached home. "After all," he had reasoned. "A large party of nobility returning from the king's celebration is a lot less conspicuous than a large group of teenage commoners."

Natalie enjoyed traveling as a noble rather than a commoner. "It gives me a chance to ride a lady's way," she had chirped as she seated herself.

The rest of the girls, however, did not share Natalie's opinion of the sidesaddle. "Nothing more than a pain in the butt," Amy had complained as Luke and helped her into the saddle.

Kathryn had to agree, especially since she had only ridden sidesaddle twice before. Jenna, Leia, and Cass endured the discomfort in silence, but Lindsey and Rachel occasionally let out phrases of disgust once they were well on their way.

Luke rode up to where Kathryn and David rode in the front. "I never got a chance to tell you," he said to David. "But your archery stinks."

David smiled. "It stunk on purpose, Luke."

"You...you mean...?" His friend couldn't bring himself to say it.

David laughed. "Yes, I threw the match."

"I can't believe it!" Luke cried. "Why would you do that?"

"Because I intended to win the sparring tournament, which I did."

Luke turned to Kathryn. "Did you know he threw the archery tournament?"

"Yes."

"And you let him?"

"I couldn't exactly call out from the royal box to tell David to get his act together."

Luke suddenly grinned. "Why not? That would have been hilarious!"

Twisting slightly in her saddle to face him, she responded, "I also noticed that you didn't participate in the archery contest, any particular reason why you didn't?"

Here David felt honor bound to protect his friend from making a complete fool of himself in coming up with a believable reason aside from the fact that he wasn't a good shot. "Luke had already distinguished himself in the hand to hand combat and doing well in the javelin tournaments," he said smoothly. "I'm sure he didn't want to risk an appearance of omnipotence by excelling in archery as well."

She tossed both of them a look that clearly displayed her lack of enthusiasm for David's explanation, but she dropped the matter and Luke resumed his position next to Amy.

જી·લ્ક

They followed the Nahar River for over a week, and then planned on tuning east at the convergence and upwards towards their home. It was a long way to return home, but David wanted to ensure that no one would suspect where they really lived. He planned for Kathryn, Amy, and Jenna to visit Princess Jasmine's palace, with Daniel and Matt playing escort, nothing that wouldn't be considered unusual since Kathryn was his aunt's ward.

He mentally shook his head as he remembered his surprise when Derek had told him that their aunt was finally bringing her elusive ward to the celebrations. David's response had been something along the lines of, *what ward*? When his brother had asked Kathryn if she was the ward his aunt had raised he'd thought Derek had suffered a blow to the head. He hadn't been prepared for Kathryn to reply "yes". Natalie could have kissed him at that moment and he probably wouldn't have been able to react.

They were still quite a distance from the place David had selected for Kathryn and company to go their own way when David called a halt. Stopping for a midday meal, David couldn't help but admire the nice weather they'd had on the trip so far. "What a beautiful day."

Kathryn frowned and looked over her shoulder. "Not for long," she informed him.

"Why do you say that?"

"Look at the mountains."

David turned to look. The Rawasi Mountains looked as normal to him as any other mountain range. "What about them?"

Kathryn sighed. "Not at them, look above them," she instructed.

He looked again and noticed what she had, dark boiling clouds were heading towards them—and fast. "That does not look good."

"Can we outrun them?" Luke asked following their gazes.

Kathryn studied the sky for a moment. "I doubt it. Those clouds are moving extremely fast."

"We'll just have to tough it out," David decided. "Get out your rain gear," he called as he remounted. "We're about to get wet."

By evening the storm was upon them. The wind hit first, its intense fury howled all around them flattening the grass before them and ripping at their clothing. The horses kept their heads down and plodded onwards, struggling against the raging storm. Half a radian later the clouds arrived, darkening the landscape and the mood of those beneath. With the clouds came rain, lightning, and thunder.

The powerful wind drove the downpour into every crack and hole in their gear. Despite all their best efforts the Dragons were soaked through in minutes. Lightning lit up the sky in quick bursts of energy, destroying their night vision and their ability to navigate. Rumbling thunder made it impossible to understand each other unless they shouted in one another's ears. Destiny had perched on Kathryn's saddle the moment the storm began and was presently nestled in a special pocket inside Kathryn's cloak.

They plodded on. The lighting flashes and roar of thunder were incessant. Several of the horses were on the verge of bolting, their eyes wide with panic. Daniel, Matt, and Luke bent forward gently thumping their horses necks while reassuring them. David could just make out a few of

Matt's words between the near deafening peals, "...alright girl....make it...won't be much longer."

Leia, Lindsey, and Amy were doing their best to calm the horses using their gifts, but the strength of the storm was overpowering their influence.

"We can't continue on like this!" Luke shouted to David after several radians of blind navigation that was only serving to get the group lost.

"I know!" David shouted back. "We need shelter, but I haven't found a safe place yet!" He was hesitant to use the forest in a storm like this since the lightning, and winds this strong, could easily topple trees.

A rumble of thunder drowned out Luke's next words. "What was that?" David hollered. The wind tore the words from his lips, flinging them across the storm battered plains.

"I said look harder!" Luke shouted back.

Kathryn, huddled on Lerina, looked around for shelter. Another flash of lighting illuminated a tower of rocks.

A tower of rocks that was very familiar.

A feeling of dread washed over Kathryn, penetrating farther than the wind and rain ever could.

No! Anything but that!

"Face your past. Learn new lessons. Until you do, you cannot know yourself." Elyon's words echoed through her mind. Since his last visit she had tossed aside his words like dry leaves in the wind. Now it looked like Elyon just might get his way after all.

"Follow me!" She shouted to David, and turned Lerina towards the rocks. With every step her horse took, the worse Kathryn felt. They passed the rocks and she led them near the edge of a forest.

After a few minutes she stopped and squinted, it should be right—there! The large mound of rock where shelter stood was about eight kilometers away. She felt physically sick.

"What do you see?" David shouted in her ear.

Kathryn pointed northeast. "Do you see that rise?"

"Barely." The lightning flashed again, illuminating a steep incline topped with an odd-shaped rock. "Yes, I see it."

"There's shelter up there."

"I hope you're right!" David hollered as he waved the rest of the group together.

I hope I'm wrong, Kathryn thought miserably. She'd rather take her chances in the forest.

"We go in groups!" David shouted in order to be heard by all. "Jenna and Kathryn will go with me, we're on our way to Deirca," he said, referring to a city on the Rima-Heltic border. "Matt you take Elizabeth and Rachel, you got lost on your way to Heltic, pick some random nobleman's manor as your destination. Amy, Natalie, and Lindsey I want to go with Luke, you were on your way to the governor's palace in Cadras. Leia, Cass, you go with Daniel, you were heading for the city of Taerma. Tyler you're going to come in alone, you were on your way to Frarler. Keep your story true to the basics. You were returning from the King's Ball and got caught by the storm."

Each group quickly assembled and David sent Luke's group up first. After twenty minutes passed, and he picked up no heightened emotions from the wind, he sent Matt, Elizabeth, and Rachel next. He waited what he guessed to be a radian before sending Daniel's group up. Tyler departed half a radian later and after another radian David prodded his own horse forward, followed quickly by Jenna and Kathryn. He felt bad for forcing Jenna to stay out in the bad weather for so long, but he had wanted to make sure that the rest of the Dragons had had time to arrive and settle in before their group made an appearance.

They reached the mound a radian later and prompted their horses up the well-worn, but now muddy and running path. A large manor house with flickering lights in the windows greeted them as they entered the courtyard. They rode to the door and David dismounted and knocked on the heavy door, "Open in the name of the king!" he shouted, hoping that he could be heard above the wind.

After a few moments an older, sour faced woman opened the door, taking in David's bedraggled appearance she asked, "What can I do for you?"

"My companions and I were returning from the king's ball but were caught in the storm," David explained. "We are in desperate need of shelter. Can you accommodate us?"

The woman studied him for a moment then sniffed disdainfully. "Stable your horses in the barn. I shall inform my mistress she has extra guests."

David gave the woman a quick bow. "Thank you."

They stabled their horses and with the help of the stable hands the chore was done quickly. Hurrying to the house, David once again knocked on the door. Kathryn kept Destiny hidden inside her cloak. The same woman opened the door and bid them enter.

She led them to a sparsely furnished room with two large, and mercifully lit, fireplaces which did much to dispel the cold and draftiness of the room. "Once you're dry, I will show you to your rooms," the woman said, closing the door.

Large puddles dotted the stone floor, telling David, that while none of the other Dragons were in the room, they *had* arrived. He helped Jenna out of her soaked cloak, she shivered and moved quickly to the fire. "Oh, this feels so good," she muttered through chattering teeth.

Kathryn joined them, her cloak still hanging from her shoulders.

"You'll dry faster if you remove that," David suggested as he nodded to the soaked material.

He watched her jaw clench and unclench several times before she moved to unclasp the cloak. Destiny flew out of the cape and perched herself high above and out of sight. Kathryn moved stiffly towards the fire, rain water dripping from her hair. The raging wind and driving rain had tangled her hair so badly that David wondered if she'd ever be able to comb it out. Glancing at Jenna he didn't doubt she too was facing a long evening of similar activity.

The sound of large amounts of water splashing on stone drew his attention and he glanced back at Jenna to see her wringing water from her skirt. That, at least, explained where the puddles came from. The healer let out a sigh of disgust. "If only cotton didn't absorb so much water," she moaned. "I feel like I've gained five kilos."

"You probably have," David chuckled.

She threw him a reprimanding glare, the first he'd ever seen cross her face. He hurried to explain. "Like you said, cotton absorbs water and water weighs a lot." Where was Luke to talk him out of trouble when he needed him?

Before she could reply the door to the room opened and a richly dressed couple entered the room. Beside him Kathryn stiffened and drew in a sharp breath. He turned to look at her, but her gaze was locked on the flames.

David stepped forward to greet his host. He sensed Jenna and Kathryn falling into place behind him. "I cannot thank you enough," he said with a bow.

"It is our honor to provide shelter for those of our own class," their host intoned. "Please, you are most welcome to stay until the storm passes."

"My companions and I are grateful for your hospitality."

Their hostess appraised him with practiced eyes. "You are not the first this evening to be caught by the storm," she told him. "Four other groups have also sought shelter here tonight."

"It is not a good night to be traveling," David replied. He bowed again and introduced himself, "I am Sir Darian, and my companions are Lady Jenevieve," Jenna curtsied as he introduced her, "and Lady—

Kathryn interrupted him before he could finish. "Caterina," she said a little stiffly. "Lady Caterina."

David forced his surprise to remain hidden. He'd never heard the name before and wondered where Kathryn had come up with it. And why she was introducing herself with it? Could she know their hosts? Their reaction seemed to disagree with that idea.

Their hostess raised her one of her eyebrows in incredulity and suspicion. "Caterina? What a...unique name."

Kathryn nodded graciously in acknowledgement.

Their host spoke up before his wife could, no doubt, make another degrading remark about the uniqueness of Lady Caterina's name. "We are Lord and Lady Blackwood," he said regally. "Welcome to Blackwood Manor."

David bowed again, only this time it was to hide his surprise and not out of gratefulness. Blackwood Manor. His memory immediately swept back to that first afternoon at the capitol, where Kathryn had gone pale, terror in her eyes, at the very mention of the name. Her fear of this place had been palatable then, and yet despite it she'd brought them here for safety when they'd needed it most. He had a feeling he was going to owe her a massive debt.

Their host and hostess swept them out of the room and down a long hall. "I am afraid that Lady Blackwood and I have already supped," their host said apologetically. "But we can have a light supper sent to your rooms so that you can rest."

David nodded. "My companions and I would appreciate such a gesture."

The Blackwoods departed, leaving the servants to guide their guests to their rooms. David took careful note of where his second-in-command's room was located before retiring to his own.

Kathryn sagged against the heavy door as it closed. Her stomach was still roiling from when she had introduced herself to Lady Blackwood. Oh why hadn't she picked a different name! Why had she given them her name? It had been first time she'd ever spoken her name aloud and she'd given it to the Blackwoods as if it meant nothing. Her name had been the most precious thing she'd ever been given and she'd thrown it away like soiled laundry.

She let her gaze wander the room and felt her spirit sink even lower. A soft cry, barely audible over the storm, sounded outside her door. Destiny flew through the instant the crack between the door and the frame was wide enough. As David and Jenna had followed Lord and Lady Blackwood out of the hall, she had given Destiny a silent command; *follow, quietly*. Now she was just grateful for the comfort of the bird's presence.

She remembered this room with cruel accuracy. Eight-years-old and she had been forced to scrub the stone floor with a rag and a bucket of clear liquid that had smelled awful and stung her hands. The stones had shredded her skin and the cleaning liquid had only served to inflame her wounds. After a few radians her knees suffered the same fate as her hands, yet the Lady of Blackwood Manor had no pity for her slave. She could still hear Lady Blackwood screeching, *"You call this clean? This isn't fit for pigs you wretched child! Clean it again!"*

She could still feel the echoes of the burning sensation as she gingerly put her hands back into the bucket to retrieve the rag, could still feel the aches of her cramping muscles and sore shoulders. Her knees hurt the worst, raw and bleeding, she was forced to kneel on them all day to clean the floor, not once, not twice, but three times until Lady Blackwood was satisfied.

Afterwards she remembered trying to escape to the forest, desperate for peace, if not from the pain, then from Lady Blackwood's demands. She remembered Claude catching her hiding underneath his table as he listened to Lady Blackwood instruct him on what sort of crème she wanted used in the pudding for that night's evening meal. After Lady Blackwood had left he had picked her up and carried her into his small hut above his bakery.

While she was inside his small home, Kathryn had experienced the first tender care in her life. Gently Claude had washed her bleeding hands and knees, apologizing for every wince and small cry she had let escape. He had given her cold, fresh, water to drink and warm broth to sip. Carefully he had smoothed soothing salve over her raw wounds and tenderly bound them with clean bandages. Once he had tended to her outside wounds, he had pulled her into his arms and told her it was okay to cry. She had, slowly at first, but eventually reaching a point where she had had trouble breathing she had been crying so hard. He had simply held her, not saying anything, just held her and let her cry. Aside from the episode with Natalie, it was the only time Kathryn could remember crying after arriving at the manor.

After she had sipped enough broth to satisfy him, he had given her a berry tart and told her to get some sleep. At first Kathryn had been too afraid to sleep, but Claude had assured her, *"I'll take care of Lady Blackwood, little one. You need to sleep."*

She had slept a few peaceful radians and Claude had kept his promise. Lady Blackwood never asked about the bandages nor did she punish Kathryn for disappearing. Kathryn had never asked how Claude had done it, she was simply grateful.

Now she stood and walked over to the window where rivers of rainwater were being propelled across the glass at breakneck speed by the furious wind.

Memory after memory hit her and it was like taking a blow to the midsection from an opponent ten times as big as her.

"Empty the tub as soon as you've finished helping me dress," Lady Blackwood ordered as she stepped out of the tub into the robe Kathryn held out for her. *"And I want you to shine it until it gleams."*

Dutifully Kathryn helped her mistress into a beautiful gown and helped arrange her hair into a style that was popular with the court ladies.

"That's enough," Lady Blackwood waved her away. *"Now empty the bathwater."*

Kathryn backed away and turned back to face the huge copper tub filled with soapy water. She frowned at it and the enormous task before her. It took five servants five trips each to fill the tub, and they were carrying huge buckets of steaming water. At best she could manage a tenth of the load each could carry. If only the tub could empty itself. She glanced at the window above the tub and sighed inwardly. Life would be so much easier if the water would simply climb its way out of the tub and out the window. She wished it would.

A ripple formed in the tub and she backed away in fright as the water began to build upon itself and reach, inexplicably, towards the window. After a few seconds it dropped back into the tub and the water lay still. Hesitantly, Kathryn moved towards the tub. The water remained calm.

How had the water done that?

NO! Kathryn forced herself out of the memory. She was not going to relive it! It was the day she had discovered her power.

It was the day her life had ended.

A knock at the door startled her and she frowned in its direction. Who could possibly be knocking on her door? Neither Blackwood had recognized her, of that she was certain. There was no way in the kingdom that Claude could know she'd returned. Her frown deepened. It was probably David...which meant that he'd keep knocking if she didn't answer. Sighing she moved to the door and opened it.

To her surprise it wasn't David, but a servant bearing a tray. "Lord and Lady Blackwood send with their compliments," the servant told her. Kathryn sincerely doubted that, but she allowed the servant in and waited patiently while the older, sad faced woman placed it on a small table near the very window where she had been standing. "Will that be all?" The servant asked woodenly, standing awkwardly in the middle of the room.

"That will be all," Kathryn assured her. "You are dismissed." The servant hurried out of the room and left Kathryn alone. She crossed to the tray and cautiously lifted the lid, half expecting it to explode. It didn't and a tureen of soup and a small loaf of bread were revealed beneath. Immediately she flashed back to that first night back at Jasmine's and the soup and bread dinner she had eaten. She slammed the lid back onto the tray.

"Enough!" she told herself. *Pull yourself together! You can handle this...it's just another mission.*

But it wasn't. This was her personal hell and she was about to relive every moment of it. Her nightmares, the ones she had dealt with every night of her life, came to the surface in full force. She tried to stop them, but she was just as powerless against them as she had been against the Blackwoods nearly seven ago, and they just kept coming. Memory after memory hit her in wave after wave, pounding her into a mindless oblivion.

The memory of her first beating at Lady Blackwood's hand, the memory of the terror she had felt when they told her lies about her power, the memory of being invisible, being unwanted, until someone had a craving or needed something. By the time Kathryn had revisited the worst memories she felt like she had run for days, her mind and spirit exhausted as well as her body. Flashes of memories sped by, just bits and pieces all jumbled together, and she began to feel dizzy and nauseous.

She blearily recognized that at some point she'd collapsed onto the cold floor, her legs unable to hold her up. Tears were streaming down her cheeks, making her eyesight as blurry as her mind.

Destiny stood next to her, a sympathetic look in her eyes. Kathryn reached out a trembling hand and stroked the bird. "You were the only good thing that happened to me here," she whispered.

Kathryn forced herself to stand, on shockingly wobbly legs, and braced herself on the stone window sill for support. She had no idea how much time had passed...radians? Minutes? She felt more exhausted than she could ever remember. Stripping off her dress she threw herself onto the bed and prayed that she'd simply fall asleep, that her dreams would leave her alone for just one night.

She should have known better.

The dreams woke her continuously throughout the night, usually jerking her awake in a cold sweat. Her nightmares hadn't been this bad since...she couldn't remember a time they had been this bad.

By the time she heard other doors begin to open, a sure sign that the rest of the manor was starting to wake up, she felt like she hadn't gotten any sleep and that she'd spent the entire night running at full speed from a pack of hungry predators. A knock at the door forced her to get up off the bed.

Another servant stood in the doorway. "Breakfast will be in half an radian," she said dully.

There was no way Kathryn would make it through breakfast, not in her present emotional and physical state. "Please inform Lord and Lady Blackwood that I will be unable to attend breakfast as I find myself unwell this morning." She hoped it sounded like something a pampered Lady would say…and that it wouldn't send any of the Dragons racing to her door to confront her.

The servant finally seemed to take note of Kathryn's haggard appearance. "I will inform my Lady," she said in a gentler tone. "Perhaps I could send some servants later to draw you a hot bath?"

Kathryn had been prepared to politely decline anything the servant had offered, but the thought of a hot soak suddenly appealed to her and she nodded. "I appreciate your consideration."

The servant curtsied and moved on to the next door. Kathryn shut the door before she discovered whose room it was. She fell back onto one of the sofas in the room and considered the day ahead. The storm was still raging in full force outside which meant that no one would leave this afternoon or evening. That meant that she had to endure at least another twenty-six radians in the vicinity of Lord and Lady Blackwood. She was determined to find herself in their presence as little as possible.

Sometime later another knock on her door sounded. Too weary to attempt to reason out who it could be she simply opened the door. She was pleasantly surprised to find servants bearing hot water standing in the hallway. Quickly she opened the door and let them in. Her tub wasn't as big as Lady Blackwood's, so it only took three trips instead of five to fill it, but it was enough. She let the soothing presence of water envelop her every sense, blocking out every other thought. Pushing everything else from her mind she focused solely on the water surrounding her in an attempt to give her tortured mind a rest from the memories.

It worked until the water cooled and the chill brought her back to reality. Briefly she considered reheating the water herself but quickly realized that such an action would only arouse the suspicion of the servants, especially if she remained in the water for over a radian after it would have normally cooled.

Sighing she removed herself from the tub and wrapped herself in a robe. A maidservant was waiting in the bedchamber and Kathryn allowed her to comb out and arrange her hair. As her hair was arranged the tub was emptied and soon Kathryn was left alone again. Judging by how much time had passed she guessed that breakfast was almost over and she left her room to avoid running into any of the Dragons. She knew every nook and cranny of this manor and she intended to use that knowledge to hide.

Knowing that David would search every room in the manor for her she decided not to remain in the manor. Instead she wrapped herself in her now dry cloak and, after a quick stop at the library, headed for the stables. Outside, the wind and rain still battered the countryside and Kathryn was sure that when she returned to her room, she'd probably request that the fire be lit. The stables were cold, but not unpleasantly so, and leaning against Lerina's warm body more than made up for the damp chill.

She brought out the book she had chosen from the library and started to read. The words gave her weary mind something to focus on besides the back-flashes and she found herself feeling a modicum of peace. Halfway through, her instincts alerted her to the fact that she was no longer alone.

Glancing up she saw David leaning against the stall door. Scowling at him she asked, "How long have you been there?"

"You weren't at breakfast."

"That doesn't answer my question."

"That doesn't answer mine."

She deepened her scowl. He held her gaze. However she was much more practiced in the art of patience than he was. He backed down first.

Shrugging he said, "Not long. Now why weren't you at breakfast?"

"I wasn't hungry."

"Strange considering how long we rode against the storm," he commented casually.

"Perhaps for pampered nobility," she returned hotly. "I'm accustomed to eating less."

He raised an eyebrow at her. She ignored him and stroked Lerina who was starting to sense the tension in Kathryn's body.

"Is it any good?"

His question confused her. "Is what any good?"

David nodded to the book in her lap. "You were so focused on the story that you didn't even hear me approach. I can only assume that it's a good book."

She glanced half-heartedly at the scroll. It really wasn't that great of a book, just a distraction really. "It's okay, it takes my mind off the...situation."

"Funny, I see a warm bed, hot food, and a strong shelter to reside in during one of the worst storms I've ever seen, a stroke of luck not a situation."

She had to tramp down the urge to blast him with a wall of water. Mockery was not something she tolerated, especially from him. "I just want to be home," she finally said.

Lerina snorted softly, blowing spittle and bits of hay across Kathryn's shoulder. A small grin tweaked the corner of her mouth and she gave the horse an affectionate pat.

He pushed himself off the door and came into the stall. "The maid who did your hair is going to be furious," he chuckled.

"Why?"

"Because you are covered in hay," he reached out to brush some hay off of her cloak, but truncated the motion when she flinched reflexively. His eyes hardened. "It happened here, didn't it?" He asked.

She sent him a confused look, "Did what happen here?"

"The abuse, it happened here."

She stiffened. "We are *not* talking about that. I think I've made that perfectly clear before."

"Yes, but that was before we arrived here. I can see it in your eyes, Kath— Caterina. It happened here. If you were given the option, you would ride straight out into that storm and never come back, wouldn't you?"

"You know nothing."

He raised an eyebrow at her, "If you're so adamant about it, then why don't you come back inside?"

The idea chilled her and unfortunately he somehow noticed. He sat down next to her. "What happened?"

"We aren't discussing it," she told him coldly.

"You need to."

"I don't want to, nor do I need to."

"You can't go through life alone."

"With the...rest of you guys around, I'll never be alone."

He sighed. "That's not what I meant and you know it." He stood and brushed off the hay off of his clothing. "Come back inside. Please," he added, "Amy's worried to death but she can't come looking for you herself. Let her see you and know that you're still alive."

For Amy she would. She reluctantly got up and followed him back into the manor.

Chapter 29

Before they entered the manor, Kathryn took the time to pick out all the bits of straw from her hair. David inspected it and nodded his approval. "It looks alright."

She returned the book she had borrowed to the library, picked out a new one, and made her way back to her room. Soon after her arrival a servant appeared bearing a tray. Savory scents wafted from the tray and Kathryn realized that, after going without dinner last night and skipping breakfast this morning, she was hungry.

Lunch consisted of a small roasted field bird, with two sauces for dipping, fresh bread, and an assortment of seasonal fruits. It was, admittedly, delicious. She kept away from the wine that had been sent with the fare and tossed the glass's contents out of the window and into the storm.

Contentedly full, she relaxed against the couch and enjoyed a few moments of blessed peace. A knock sounded at her door. She frowned. If it was David again she was going to stab him.

She was surprised to find Jenna standing outside her door and she quickly let her in. "We missed you at breakfast," Jenna said gently, but without preamble.

"David mentioned something along those lines," Kathryn said as she retook her place on the couch.

Slowly, Jenna lowered herself onto the settee opposite Kathryn. "Amy was worried about you," she said quietly.

Kathryn suspected David was the one who had really sent her and tried to give a reasonable answer. "I'm not sure why, I've always worked to avoid such situations."

"How did you sleep?" Jenna asked, and then she leaned forward and spoke quietly, "I'm asking you as a healer and a friend, and whatever you say won't leave this room."

Kathryn knew exactly how well she had slept —not at all—but she wasn't comfortable divulging that particular fact. "I slept a little less than I normally do at home, which in a strange environment is to be expected I would guess." Surely that was an answer that would satisfy the healer.

Jenna, however, frowned. "Considering how hard we rode and how roughly the storm battered us, you should have been tired enough to sleep a week."

Kathryn frantically sought an answer. "It was the wind," she said quietly. "I wasn't used to its howling and it kept me up for a while."

That seemed to appease Jenna who nodded, "It certainly sounds terrifying when you're in a strange room all alone. I know I was scared, at least for a little while."

"The lightning and thunder probably didn't help either," Kathryn added, surprised by the sympathy she was starting to feel towards Jenna. The girl was the gentlest soul Kathryn had ever met and had no doubt found this adventure trying. "I wonder why David didn't just," she paused, "you know..."

Jenna shrugged helplessly. "Maybe he didn't feel he was strong enough?"

That was a reasonable conclusion. Usually a Guardian's power wasn't nearly strong enough to compete with a storm the size of the one that was still running rampant across the countryside.

Jenna spoke again. "So can I tell Amy that you're okay and assure her that you aren't dying?"

Kathryn felt a small smile part her lips. "Why don't you just send her by later? She'll still fret and worry after you talk to her until she actually sees me."

The healer stood. "Okay. Will you stay in your room all day?"

"Probably." Kathryn shrugged. "It's not like we can explore the grounds in this weather." *Not that I'd ever want to...*

"True."

Jenna left and Kathryn waited for the inevitable arrival of Amy. To pass the time she started the new book she'd picked out from the library. The first one had become too boring and too political to hold her interest and now that she started reading it she had to admit that the new one wasn't that much better. She'd felt rushed in the library and hadn't taken the time to pick out an engaging book, and she was afraid she'd pay for it with the inescapable arrival of more memories.

She did.

"Girl!" The shrill voice startled a weary Kathryn from a sound sleep. Already rolling out of bed she hurried to the kitchen where her aunt was impatiently waiting. Upon entering the kitchen she lowered her eyes to the floor and waited.

"You call this clean!" her aunt shrieked, shoving a cooking pot beneath Kathryn's face. "It's filthy! Everything is filthy. Clean it again! Clean everything again." The woman threw the pot to the floor and it clattered across the flagstones. "And while you're at it," her aunt declared as she exited the room, "wash the floor too."

Holding back tears, Kathryn knelt down and picked up the pot. It had several new dents in its side that would have to be pounded back into the correct shape...and it would take her radians.

Wearily she glanced toward the collection of cooking pots. It wasn't a large collection, at least not compared to what would be found in a manor or palace, in truth it was a very small collection, but for a five-year-old girl it was a chore that would leave her exhausted. Resigned, Kathryn sat down on the kitchen floor and began to scrub.

Her arms began to ache a radian into the chore and they trembled constantly within the second radian, by the third radian she had finally managed to scour the pots until her own dingy reflection was reflected in the golden red of the metal. Just in case her aunt decided that the chore hadn't taken long enough, Kathryn washed them all once more for good measure.

Then she started on the floor. Heating the water was the easiest part of the chore, but pouring that hot water into a bucket with soap scrapings was the hardest. She already had several burns on her arms and legs from not being able to control the heavy pot. Today was no exception. By the time the bucket was full of hot water, she had new burns on her arms and one on her chest.

Arms trembling and chest burning, Kathryn knelt and began to wash the stones.

A knock on her door brought Kathryn back to reality and she forced herself to move to the doorway.

"Yes?" She called through the heavy wood, vowing not to open the door to anyone but Amy.

"Lady Caterina? It's Lady Amira," Amy's concerned voice came through the door. "Lady Jenevive mentioned that you weren't feeling well."

Sighing, Kathryn opened the door and let her friend in.

Amy took one look at her and her own brow furrowed. "You haven't been sleeping," she stated bluntly. When Kathryn opened her mouth to protest, Amy held up her hand. "Don't bother trying to deny it. I can see it on your face. You may be able to fool Jenna and David, but we've known each other too long for you to be able to hide it from me."

It was a testimony to her fatigue and emotional state that Kathryn realized she wanted to pout. It was humiliating. But Amy was right, she had seen enough of Kathryn's late nights and midnight awakenings to recognize the signs.

"Fine," Kathryn conceded. "I'm not sleeping. Happy?"

"No. Why aren't you sleeping?"

Kathryn felt her eyes narrow. "Did David send you up here?"

"I sent David and Jenna to find you. Where in the kingdom did you disappear to?"

"I went to make sure Lerina was okay." It was a lame excuse and Kathryn knew it, but even she couldn't admit to Amy that she'd been hiding from everybody.

"All morning?"

"I had a bath first."

"So you had a bath and then went to visit the stables...most noblewomen do that the other way around."

Kathryn threw up her hands and turned toward the window. "I'm not like most noblewomen...what's it to you?"

Amy ignored the jab. "You haven't been acting like yourself lately. Are Natalie and Lindsey still bothering you?"

"No, we're fine. I just...I don't know..." She did know, but she didn't want to get into it with Amy, David, Jenna, or anybody.

Her friend sighed. "I can't stay long, but I wanted to make sure you're okay."

"I'm alive, that will suffice until we get home."

"You may be alive, but you don't live," her friend replied softly before exiting the room.

಄·಄

Amy shut the door and, fighting back tears, she moved to Jenna's room. Inside both the healer and David waited, expectation written on their faces.

She shook her head. "She's not in a very cooperative mood," she told them dejectedly.

"We didn't really expect her to be," Jenna reminded her softly.

"It's like she's a different person!" Amy exclaimed in frustration. "She practically took my head off and she's never done that before. Usually she just changes the subject, but today...something is wrong."

"I think this place is the key to Kathryn's past," David stated quietly.

Amy felt lightheaded. "Blackwood Manor?"

He nodded. "She introduced herself as Caterina to the Lord and Lady and hasn't appeared at any meal. Whatever happened to her, it happened here."

Jenna shook her head. "You can't be sure, David. There could be any number of reasons for her to be acting strangely."

"What else could make her act so wounded?" Amy asked tiredly. "She's usually so unflappable."

Jenna shifted uncomfortably. "I can think of one thing that might have caused her to...withdraw so much."

Amy was completely lost. "What?"

"Something that could have happened at court..." Jenna looked like she didn't even want to consider the possibility...like she couldn't even speak it.

Amy was about to beg Jenna just to spit it out when she heard David's quick intake of breath.

"You think she might have been..." he paused, as if searching for a kinder term, "...violated."

Amy sat down on the bed—hard. "No. No way. Kathryn would never permit something like that, she'd kill him first."

Jenna looked apologetic. "Kathryn's very innocent in the ways of a married couple," she replied quietly. "She might not have understood until it was too late."

"No," Amy replied firmly. "Kathryn may be innocent, but she wouldn't let anyone get within three meters of her who would have been thinking about it."

"She might not have realized it until it was too late," Jenna reiterated...she paused and looked down at the floor. "I didn't."

Her words were barely audible but Amy felt a shock run through her. "Jen?" she whispered.

The healer looked up, pain written across her features. "All I'm saying is that you can't always know."

David placed a hand on her shoulder, "I am so sorry that someone put you through that," he said quietly. "But in this case, I believe Amy's right. Kathryn wouldn't let anyone get close to her, she doesn't drink wine so she would have been able to think clearly, and, let's face it, Kathryn would kill anyone who attempted to force her to do something she didn't want to do. And if she couldn't handle it, that crazy bird of hers most certainly would." He paused, remembering Kathryn's conversation with Roseanna while she had been clinging to Sebastian's tower. "And I don't think she's as innocent as we think. She would know."

For a few moments Jenna thought of how Destiny killed the boar and shuddered at what she might be able to do to a man. "It's just a possibility," she said quietly after a few seconds. "You could be right, David. It could be that Kathryn's past is here...but we don't know that for sure. She doesn't talk about it and refuses any overtures we offer."

David smiled grimly. "Actually, she did mention her past once to me. She mentioned learning hidden movement courtesy of Blackwood Manor."

"Well then, I hope you're right and not me, because I don't want anyone else to go through what I did."

"Do you want to talk about it?" David offered gently.

She gave him a weak smile. "Thank you, but no. I've talked about it and moved on. No sense in digging up what's past." The flicker in her eyes gave away her lie, but Amy knew that now was not the time to help their healer.

"If you're sure..."

"Positive."

He smiled at her. "Well then, we have several radians to kill before dinner. As much as I want to shake Kathryn and get her to listen to reason, I suggest we leave her alone for a few radians and let her collect herself for dinner. If I have to order her there I will, but it will raise more than a few eyebrows if she doesn't attend."

"Just make sure you're wearing your arrow-proof armor," Amy said. "If you have to order her to attend, in the mood she's in, she'll probably shoot you."

"At least I can count on her excellent aim to make it a quick death."

Amy snorted. "Don't get your hopes up. With all the abuse she's been through, she probably knows how to cause pain and make sure it lingers."

"Thank you, Amy. I now bestow upon you the job of ordering her to dinner."

"She's a higher rank than me. You're the only one in the family who can order her to do anything."

He sighed. "I knew being a leader was going to be hazardous to my health."

⬥·⬥

Dinnertime finally arrived and David stationed himself outside of Kathryn's room. She had received his order with as much enthusiasm as Amy had predicted, but fortunately her bow had been nowhere in sight and he'd survived the encounter intact. Now he was waiting for her to appear.

Jenna came up beside him. "Still in one piece I see..."

He grinned. "She was tempted, but all of our weapons are in the stables."

"Lucky you."

His reply was cut off by the opening of Kathryn's door. As she stepped into the hall he gave her clothing a cursory glance. She was wearing an elegant green and gold dress simple and light in its design. The style was unique and not as elaborate as the gowns she had worn to the balls at court, but it would suffice in her role as a noblewoman. She wore no jewelry but her hair was up in a fancier style of bun than she usually wore. He'd been prepared to order her to change if she'd been dressed as she preferred to at home but was relieved that he wouldn't have to.

287

"Who did your hair, Lady Caterina?" Jenna asked as she inspected the intricate strands that had been braided and woven into the bun.

"I did," Kathryn replied as she closed her door.

Jenna looked surprised. "Really?"

Kathryn shot her a slightly amused look, a look so out of character for the last twenty-six radians that David thought he was seeing things. "I can do more than one style, you know. I just choose not to."

"Well, it's beautiful. You'll have to teach me."

Kathryn shrugged. "I can if you want me to. It's not hard."

David felt some relief settling in. Whatever had happened in the few radians between Amy's visit and now, Kathryn had clearly found a way back to her old self. Perhaps he was wrong. Perhaps Kathryn's past wasn't connected as solidly to Blackwood Manor as he believed.

They walked down to the dining hall. As David had expected, they were the last to arrive. They took seats at the far end of the table, something that seemed to loosen Kathryn's manner just a little.

The meal was excellent, a little rich for David's tastes, but still skillfully prepared. He did however believe that it had been overdone; in fact everything about the meal was overdone. Lord and Lady Blackwood were wearing ensembles that he would have expected at court, not an evening meal, and the fanfare with which the food was presented was oddly reminiscent of the court celebrations he had just attended. The variety and spread of the food was astonishing, especially for a small manor such as this. It rivaled the banquet of the Queen's birthday celebration and David couldn't help but wonder if it was meant to.

Natalie, Rachel, and Elizabeth complimented their hosts on the meal, comparing it to the banquet at court. David couldn't help but notice how the praise seemed to swell their hosts' sense of importance.

"Ah, but if only I could go to court once more," Lady Blackwood said wistfully. "My happiest memories are from those balls and special events." She looked over at her husband and giggled. "My Lord was one of the best swordsmen those knights ever faced."

Natalie spoke up. "Why can't you go to court? Surely every nobleman and noblewoman, such as yourselves, receives an invitation?"

Their hosts exchanged a sorrowful look. "Unfortunately," Lady Blackwood said solemnly. "We angered the Dowager Princess Jasmine over an accidental oversight and found ourselves banished from court seven years ago."

David sensed Kathryn stiffen beside him. He suddenly remembered how his aunt and the Guardian council had been in an uproar over something that had happened over six years ago...in Southern Rima, the exact location where he learned Blackwood Manor resided. *Nice,* he thought as he sipped his wine, *in one fell swoop she plays the innocent backwater Noblewoman who was preyed upon by the Dowager Princess, effectively making the royal family the wrong doers.*

"I met the Dowager Princess while at the palace," Amy said thoughtfully. "She was a very sweet and kind woman."

Lady Blackwood smiled again. "I'm sure she can be, Lady Amira, but in our experience," she reached out and grasped her husband's hand, which was conveniently located on top of the table, "she's as ruthless as an enraged tiger and flaunts her position. When my husband and I didn't recognize her at first, she used our embarrassment and turned it into humiliation."

Lady Blackwood continued her horrid tale, going into excruciating detail of the Dowager Princess's anger and how the Blackwoods had barely escaped the encounter with their lives. By the time the second course had arrived David thoroughly wished they could be excused. Now that he knew the Blackwoods were the most likely cause of his aunt's and the Council's anger, it wasn't hard to see how manipulative his hosts really were. It took a lot to anger his aunt to action and when she did, she spared no mercy. Whatever his hosts had done, and he was starting to form a very dreadful suspicion, he was positive they'd earned their punishment. Lady Blackwood was a scheming and devious woman. He had no doubt that they put on this exact same show for every visitor they received, noble or common. Kathryn didn't speak a single word throughout the entire meal.

As they finished the last course Luke raised his wine glass and said, "My compliments to your chef."

Lady Blackwood smiled. "Wait till you have dessert, our baker is rivaled nowhere." She picked up a gold dinner bell and rang it. Almost immediately a huge dark man entered the room through the main serving door having to bow his head to keep from hitting it on the lintel. He wore a white apron pulled over his head that provided ample covering for his chest, shoulders, and waist. The garment was almost as tall as Daniel, but only reached partway down to the giant's upper legs. It had one small pocket over his left breast and two large pockets at the waist and fit rather snuggly over his clothes. Surprisingly, he didn't sport a large belly so common among chefs. He was well muscled with arms as large as most men's thighs. He looked and moved with the grace of a warrior and must have been at least two and half meters tall. The Dragons sat in stunned silence as his presence filled the cavernous room. Natalie, Matt, Daniel, and Elizabeth just stared with their mouths gaping wide.

David gathered his wits and asked, "And this is?"

"Claude," she replied; pleased with herself as though she were show-casing some exotic pet.

Dessert was served by Baker Claude himself. It was a crème cake often favored by nobility but normally too rich for David's taste. *Lady Blackwood is right*, he thought as he tasted the dessert, *Claude is an excellent baker.*

"Non' for m'lady?" Claude asked, his heavy accent hard to decipher, when Kathryn politely declined.

"You have no idea what you're missing, Lady Caterina," Lady Blackwood called from the other end of the table. "Not even the king's chef can compete with our Claude."

Was David imagining things, or was Claude suddenly studying Kathryn out of the corner of his eye.

"I'm afraid sweets are not something I enjoy," she apologized, speaking for the first time. David noticed something akin to wistfulness flicker in her eyes and felt his curiosity aroused. He had never, ever seen Kathryn look wistful before, and he would never have thought she would manage the look while appearing miserable.

Claude's eyes lit up. "Den per-aps something else can interest you, ave I," he said as he hurried away, ducking just in time to clear the doorframe.

David turned a curious eye towards Kathryn who shrugged. Claude returned with a small tray of pastries. Beside him he heard Kathryn catch her breath.

Claude set the tray next to her. "Once knew someone who enjoyed dese ave I, per-aps you will as well."

"Claude!" Lady Blackwood scolded, her voice rising. "Lady Caterina does not care for your simple tarts!"

Kathryn held up her hand to silence Lady Blackwood, "On the contrary, Lady Blackwood," she said looking up into Claude's face, "They're perfect. Thank you."

Something passed between Kathryn and Claude that David couldn't identify. He did however notice the quick wink that Claude gave Kathryn before he left.

After a few moments, Kathryn stood. She addressed Lady Blackwood. "Please excuse me, but I find that I am still wearied from our journey through the storm and feel the need to lie down." She waved her hand at her untouched tarts. "I still would very much like to enjoy these later, perhaps after I rest. Could you arrange for them to be sent to my room?"

"Of course, Lady Caterina," Lady Blackwood hurried to assure her. "I will arrange it with Claude," she turned to face the rest of the group. "He refuses to let anyone but himself handle his pastries, claims that no one else can keep them in perfect order."

Kathryn curtsied and left the room, but not before David saw a solitary tear work its way out of her eye and race down her cheek.

For the rest of the evening David's thoughts constantly flew to Kathryn. He was positive now. Kathryn's past was here. Something awful had happened here, no doubt the accidental oversight Lady Blackwood spoke of during dinner.

But apparently not everything was awful. There was a history between Claude and Kathryn, a history that seemed to be the one bright spot in Blackwood Manor. David was determined to find out what it was.

Chapter 30

She couldn't stop crying. No matter how stern a lecture she delivered to herself or how hard she focused on not tearing up, the tears kept coming even half a radian after leaving the dining hall. Kathryn's mind flew to the day she was rescued, especially Claude's parting gift of a bag of strawberry tarts...and then to her second day as Lady Blackwood's slave.

"Well, what 'ave we here?"

The deep baritone startled her and she whirled around only to find herself face to face with a giant.

She must have looked absolutely terrified because the giant knelt down and spoke quietly and calmly. "'Ey, now...it's alright, little one. I'm not goin' to hurt 'ya."

He smiled at her as she calmed down. "Dere now, at's better. Name's Claude. What's your name, little one and how did 'ya get here?"

She lowered her eyes to the floor and looked away. One of the servants passing by overheard Claude's question, "That's Lady Blackwood's new servant," she said with a sniff. "Her name is Margit."

Claude gently studied her as the servant continued on her way. "You remind me of my own little Caterina," he said softly. "I think dat's a better name for you den Margit."

Surprised at his tender manner, she studied him.

"Margit!" Lady Blackwood's piercing call shattered the silence, startling both girl and man. "There you are!"

Claude straightened as Lady Blackwood came around the corner. "Apologies milady," he said quickly. "Twas sayin ello to young Kathryn, ere."

Lady Blackwood opened her mouth to speak and then closed it abruptly. Finally she said, "You know this girl?"

Claude nodded. "Seen er in the village before, ave I."

Lady Blackwood paused. "And her name is Kathryn?"

Again Claude nodded. "Yes, milady. I 'eard several people call her dat, assume at's er name."

Lady Blackwood whirled on the young girl. "Is it your name?"

Deciding that she liked Kathryn better than Margit, she nodded.

The lady of the manor rolled her eyes. "Thank you, Claude. You've solved one mystery for us. Perhaps you know why she refuses to talk as well?"

Claude rubbed his chin thoughtfully. "Think it's cause she's a mute, milady," he said slowly.

"Well that would certainly explain some things. Kathryn report to the kitchen immediately."

As she hurried to the kitchens, Kathryn glanced back in time to see Claude smile and wave at her.

A soft knock at the door roused Kathryn from the memory. Reluctantly she pulled herself up and opened the door.

Claude stood before her, a small tray of fresh tarts in his hands. He turned his head peering up and down the hallway considering those who would be within earshot before he spoke in his deep basal voice, "milady wasn't ungry for deese earlier, thought you might ike em now, I did."

Kathryn waved him inside, closing the door securely behind them. They looked at each other for a long moment, finally she asked, "You know who I am?"

Claude smiled and dropped the ridiculous accent he affected when speaking to anyone but her. "Yes, little one, I know who you are."

She couldn't stop the tears from falling down her cheeks. "How did you know?"

"Oh, Caterina, how could I forget your eyes?" Claude asked, his own eyes glistening.

Kathryn smiled through her tears. "You knew me by my eyes?"

"Well," Claude shrugged. "You were also the only person named Caterina I knew outside my village."

"You named me Kathryn, not Caterina," she reminded him.

He smiled at her. "Ah, but Kathryn and Caterina are the same name. Caterina is my people's way of saying Kathryn."

"What does it mean?"

He brushed a tear from her cheek. "It means pure, or innocent, one."

Kathryn laughed softly. "So you knew me by my eyes and my name."

"No, I suspected. I didn't know until I offered you my berry tarts."

She was crying again. "I didn't think you'd remember me."

"How could I forget you?" You were the bravest little girl I had ever known." Claude reached inside his apron and brought out a handkerchief which he handed to her.

"You were my only friend," she told him, wiping her eyes.

"What about that little bird of yours?"

"You remember that?" Kathryn asked in amazement.

Claude smiled.

"I named her Destiny, she still stays with me." She nodded towards the perch near the fireplace where the eagle had returned to and from where she warily eyed the baker.

"I am happy you have a better life now," Claude said as he moved towards the door. "I have to get back to the kitchens but I want you to know I have never forgotten you, and I never will."

Kathryn pulled his head down and gave him a quick kiss on the cheek, "Thank you, Claude."

His dark skin hid the redness of his blush but Kathryn could see it in his eyes, finally he spoke, "Years ago you were a silent shadow of a girl, now you are a beautiful, confident woman." Claude settled to one knee, reached out, and enveloped her with his arms and she embraced him. After a minute he stood and placed both of his hands on her shoulders smiling at her and she at him.

They bid each other goodbye and Kathryn closed the door behind him. She had given up trying to fight the memories, she simply let them come and flow through her mind. Surrendering required less energy than fighting...at least in the beginning.

Sometime later, another knock sounded at the door. Kathryn considered turning the person away, but thought better of it. Anyone who would be knocking wasn't someone who would give up. Opening the door she found David, once again, standing before her.

"Can I come in?" he asked quietly.

Too tired to refuse him she nodded and opened the door wider. He entered quickly and noticed the tarts sitting on the small dressing table.

"I never knew you liked berry tarts," he commented.

Kathryn looked to the treats, "He remembered," she whispered. "After all this time, I can't believe he remembered."

"The baker?"

She nodded. "Claude was the only one who cared about what happened to me."

"What did happen to you?" David asked quietly, coming to stand behind her.

Kathryn couldn't stop the tears that wouldn't stop flowing no matter how hard she tried, "You wouldn't understand," she whispered.

"Why not?"

All her life she had never said a word and suddenly she was very, very tired. Tired of hiding, tired of hurting, tired of the pain, and tired of being alone. "Because no one can ever understand what I went through!"

Destiny left her perch and flew to the small table that stood next to Kathryn. Emotionally ravaged, Kathryn looked to her old friend for comfort. Reaching out a hand, she gently stroked Destiny's feathers. Her companion let out a soft call and then bobbed her head back and forth several times. Confused, Kathryn studied the bird.

Destiny hopped several times toward the edge of the table and then stretched her neck outward, as if pointing toward something behind Kathryn. Stymied, Kathryn glanced behind her. All she saw was David. Her confusion soared. What was Destiny trying to tell her?

"I don't understand," she whispered.

She may not have understood Destiny's message, but Destiny understood her. The bird hopped up onto Kathryn's shoulder, gave her a quick nuzzle and then stretched her neck out again in David's direction.

"What about David?" She asked quietly.

Destiny crossed the room in a single glide and perched herself on David's shoulder. The surprise in David's face was as great as Kathryn's. Destiny had never let David pet her and suddenly she was sitting on his shoulder? The bird hopped gently for a few seconds and then let out a soft call.

It took Kathryn a few seconds to place the familiar mannerism but when she did she sat down hard on the floor. She stared in shock at the wall.

It was their rock climbing signal. When Destiny found a safe ledge she would hop on it several times before calling out. She'd just done the same thing to David. Kathryn finally understood. Safety. Destiny was telling her that David was a ledge that Kathryn could grasp to keep from falling.

୫·ଓଃ

Destiny's talons gripped David's shoulder and he forced himself not to wince. Destiny was sitting on his shoulder. He was more surprised than when he had learned Kathryn was his aunt's ward. He glanced away from the bird to see the remaining color leech out of Kathryn's face. Already moving as she collapsed, he hurried to her side. "Kathryn?" Destiny had already left his shoulder and was hopping on the floor next to her friend.

Kathryn however, wasn't noticing either of them. Her gaze was locked on the wall, shock and distress plainly visible on her face. "Kathryn." She still didn't reply to him. He took her face in his hands. "Kathryn? Come on Kathryn, say something."

Whatever Destiny had done, it had completely scrambled Kathryn's wits. Panic began to bubble up in his body when she remained unresponsive. He was a heartbeat away from sending for Jenna when she finally stirred.

Her eyes flickered to Destiny who was standing next to her knee. "Safety."

Confused, David looked to the bird who was bobbing her head up and down and cooing. He didn't understand what the bird was trying to convey.

Kathryn apparently did though. "Safety," she whispered again. "That's what you're trying to tell me, aren't you girl?"

Destiny nuzzled Kathryn's knee and pointed toward David again. With a heavy sigh, Kathryn started to get to her feet. She swayed from side to side so badly that David was afraid she'd fall again. He wrapped one of his arms around hers and helped her up.

Gently, David steered her to the small couch and helped her sit down. Destiny followed and settled herself in Kathryn's lap. David sat down next to her, cautious concern in his eyes. Idly, Kathryn began stroking her like his sister would stroke her cat.

Kathryn took a deep breath and finally said. "I've never told anyone what happened." She was staring at the far wall, but her eyes told him she was seeing something beyond the grim gray stone that made up the barrier between them and the storm outside.

He waited patiently. Experience with his sisters had taught him that if he pushed, Kathryn would most likely close up and he'd lose this one chance. When she was still silent after several minutes, he was tempted to prod her, just a little. However Kathryn had taught him something about patience in the months they had been together so he waited her out.

୫·ଓଃ

As she took comfort in the feel of Destiny's feathers and her warm body, Kathryn felt the urge to get up and leave. Forget what she had told David. Up until now, she hadn't told him anything that he hadn't already known or guessed. She could stop now and put this whole episode behind her. Her past could remain in the past, the wounds left half-healed. But Destiny, the only person in the whole kingdom that she trusted, was telling her to confide in David.

And, surprisingly, there was a small part of her that wanted someone else to know. A small part that wanted someone else to feel her pain—so that she wouldn't have to be alone. Kathryn felt that it was time to share her story and she knew that David had been right. He was the right one to hear it.

Taking a deep breath she began, "I never knew my parents. I was raised by a couple who claimed to be my aunt and uncle."

Their faces swam before her vision. Her uncle, the village blacksmith, covered in black soot and his clothes dotted with small burns from embers that had escaped the fires he worked with. As she remembered, she saw in her mind his face – a face twisted and styled into a permanent snarl forged by a life of bitterness and hate. In one hand he held a long fire poker, glowing red at the tip, and in the other, his ever present tankard of strong spirits. As she gazed on his face she could see his lips moving, her mind filled in his voice and the words: *worthless, coward, disgrace.* Those were the kinder terms he had called her.

Her aunt's face swam into focus next. Sapling thin from hard labor, her aunt's forehead was deeply furrowed and creased. Kathryn couldn't remember ever seeing her smile. Her aunt's arms were covered and dotted with long scars. Kathryn remembered far too many nights with her aunt cowering in a corner while her uncle flew into a drunken rage tossing furniture, crockery, and any else he could get his hands on. Stumbling and staggering he would pursue the helpless woman throughout their small hovel spitting curses and accusing her of being lazy, greedy, and disrespectful of him. Pieces of chewed pork and sputum would catch in his greasy beard as he barked out orders and raved at the children. More often than naught he would do more than just ransack the house. Catching her by the hair he would pull her aunt close and with wild eyes he would rave at her through blackened and missing teeth, his rancid breath nearly causing her knees to buckle. Then the beatings would begin. During the day her aunt would nurse her wounds while Kathryn cleaned up the mess. Memories of days and nights of aching hunger caused her stomach to clench.

"I don't know if they were my true aunt and uncle. They never treated me like one of their own children and I didn't resemble them. When it was meal time I had to wait until their family had eaten and survive on what was left.

"It was bad enough having an uncle who was a destructive drunk who enjoyed annihilating every item in the house. As you can imagine money was tight in the home." Her cousins, two boys and a girl, had voracious appetites and had hungrily devoured every meal her aunt had prepared as if they had gone days without food. Her uncle was just as insatiable and by the time they had finished there was very little for both Kathryn and her aunt to survive on. Usually her aunt gave her the last few scraps of food from her plate, but there had been many nights where there had been nothing in Kathryn's belly.

"They insisted I sleep in the barn with the animals, during the snowy months I was allowed inside, but never by the fire and heaven forbid that I should be given more than one blanket." After a short pause she went on. "It wasn't so bad, I was able to sleep next to the animals and use their body heat to keep me warm during the colder nights."

She could still smell the musky scents of the old horse and cow that had been her roommates. Those nights were part of the reason Kathryn often found solace in the stables, reading with her back against Lerina's warm body. On the nights she had slept in the barn, she was often warmer than those nights she had spent in the house. And, by sleeping in the barn with the animals, she could escape from her uncle's inebriated antics.

She'd lost count of the number of days when her aunt had ordered her to sweep up the broken crockery and haul the shattered limbs of chairs and tables out to the woodpile. Her hands and feet began to sting reflexively as she remembered the number of times she'd cut herself while trying make sure she got every piece of pottery. Glancing down, she noticed that her hands were fidgeting, her fingers rubbing against each other and the palms of her hands. They were also covered in sweat. Grimacing, she wiped them on the edges of her skirt. Destiny watched her hands closely.

"My aunt had me doing most of the cleaning. I learned how to shine the pots and pans and scrub the floors and fireplace spotless. The one chore that I proved utterly useless with was mending." The tips of her fingers recoiled into her palms, remembering the sharp pain of the needle burying its tip into the sensitive skin. "I lived with them until I was five." Until a few years ago, Kathryn had never stopped to consider the enormity of the tasks that had been heaped upon her head at such a young age. She'd been completing tasks at two and three years old that children of seven or eight would struggle with. Now, she knew, it was because of her gifts, her increased strength and intelligence, that she had survived. But a small part of her wondered if her "family" had ever suspected her abilities. If anyone in the village had, and everyone had known how her uncle had treated her, they'd kept silent.

Now came the worse part of the nightmare. The Blackwoods. "During the spring months of that year, a sickness unlike any ever seen before ravaged the village. People were dying everywhere. In their homes, in the streets ... I remember a couple who dropped while waiting in line to buy bread at the bakers."

The images of the dead littering the streets forced their way into her mind. Their eyes empty, open and unseeing. Expressions of excruciating pain frozen on their faces. Bodies contorted into unnatural positions. Some had even foamed at the mouth like wild animals. She swallowed hard. "I woke one morning to find my adoptive family all sweating heavily, their skin covered in what resembled blue spider webs. I did what I could for them. I cooked broth and helped them sip it. But they weakened quickly. By that evening they couldn't walk anymore. They could only crawl. I stayed with them all night, wiping the sweat from the faces and trying to get them to sip cold water."

Her cousins' pain wracked faces floated up in her mind, their mouths forming words, begging her to help them. Begging her to stop the pain. She remembered the feeling of utter helplessness that had accompanied her attempts to help her uncle and his family. There had been no cure for the sickness, nothing that she could have done to help them. One by one they had died, her cousins first, her uncle last. Dragging her hand over her face, Kathryn forced the images out of her mind.

"They died quickly, but it wasn't a painless death." She didn't want to relieve their last radians, the way their bodies had jerked violently, wracked with pain. Their necks had swelled, closing off their voices. Throughout that night they had cried out to her silently, their eyes turning blue as the disease took hold of their bodies.

"One of my uncle's customers found them the next morning." The woman had been a customer her uncle had always argued with. Kathryn would never forget the delighted gleam that flashed in the woman's eyes when she had entered the house and spotted the bodies lying haphazard throughout the rooms. And then the woman had spotted her. "She—" Kathryn choked on the words. Clearing her throat she tried again. "She started screaming for the sheriff. At first I didn't understand but when the watchmen arrived she spoke to them outside for a few moments. They came into the house and took me with them to the manor house." The nightmare that had plagued her sleep that first day at the capitol came back in full force.

"Here's your murderer!" The thin lady screeched, pointing at Kathryn who shrank back against the cold stone wall. "She killed them in their sleep she did! Judge her now, and give those poor souls the justice they deserve!"

"What justice do you think fits the crime this child committed?" The speaker turned his attention on Kathryn, his unforgiving eyes pinning her to the wall.

"Hang her! Hang her like the murderer she is!"

She wished she could become invisible, she wished that she could escape from the gray hall and the eyes that condemned her. Her fingers dug into the cracks in the stone wall behind her—desperately searching for any chance to flee.

Lord Blackwood looked to Lady Blackwood, a small reed-like woman who sat beside him, she nodded.

"Very well," Lord Blackwood stood, "Take the girl to the dungeons pending her execution."

Execution. The word echoed in her mind like a bell's chime echoing in an empty tower.

"Hey, Kathryn. You're safe now, relax."

David's calm voice brought her out of the memory. For the first time since she had started speaking she looked at him.

"You're safe here," he reiterated. He reached out and covered one of her hands with his.

Belatedly she became aware of the dull throbbing in her palms. Unclenching her hands she stared at the red crescents that dotted the pads of her palms. The tips of her fingers were stained bright red with blood and she flashed back again.

The stones shredded her hands as she ran the rag over the flagstones, scrubbing them clean of the dirt and dust that had settled on them since the last time she had washed them. Wincing in anticipation of the stinging, she dropped her rag, stained black with the grime and red with her blood, into the pitcher. She watched as the fabric slowly unfolded in the water, removing the signs of her fist from the folds.

With a jerk she came back to the present. Shakily she rubbed her hands on her skirt again, smearing the blood across her palms. She glared at the blood. How could such small indentations bleed so much?

Slowly she became aware as to how dry her throat had become. She swallowed several times, debating whether or not to continue. The flashbacks, the memories, she was beginning to feel nauseous.

Stopping now seemed like such a waste of energy.

She braced herself and took a deep breath. "When the watchmen took me before the Blackwoods, my uncle's customer claimed that I had murdered my uncle and his family. No one seemed to care that there was a sickness spreading through the village and that my family had displayed all of the symptoms when their bodies had been found."

Her throat closed as she remembered the later accusations. "No one who contracted the disease survived and those who attended the sick inevitably fell victim to it as well. In the whole village I was the only person to live in close contact with the illness and survive. There were those in the village who began to believe that I had survived because I was the one who had controlled the disease—that I had created it to destroy my abusive uncle and his family and hadn't cared about the deaths of scores of villagers who it succumbed to it before my family."

Her hands were becoming restless again and no matter how hard she tried to still their movements they managed to twist and rub against each other in her lap. But her hands weren't the only part of her that was restless. Destiny moved to Kathryn's shoulder as she stood and moved to the window.

"The woman who found my uncle and his family didn't just stop with calling me a murderer," she whispered. "She accused me of being a witch. With the sickness ravaging the village, and me being the sole person to survive close contact with it, it didn't take long for the population to convince themselves I was a practitioner of black magic." Then came the flashback of the mob that had demanded her death. "They...they set my uncle's house on fire around me," she could smell the acrid smoke burning in her nostrils from the pitch they'd used as fuel, "but I knew of a loose section of straw and I managed to kick my way through before the fire could claim me." Inhaling deeply she tried to clear her mind of the scent of fire and death from that day. "A few of the crowd saw me escape and captured me before I could reach the forest." The forest that was just beyond the pane of glass in front of her. If only she'd been able to reach it! How much different would her life have been if she'd managed to escape that day? "They dragged me before the Blackwoods, demanding that I be punished for my crimes."

Now that she was older, she could recognize the calculating expression in her memory of the Lord and Lady of the Manor as they'd dispassionately listened to the mob's demands. "The Blackwoods bowed to the wishes of the villagers and sentenced me to execution. They sent me to their dungeons. Their dungeon master introduced me to the world of... unbearable pain." One of her hands reached up to her shoulders, her fingers slipping beneath the edge of the bodice to trace the scars beneath. She could still feel the sensation of her blood pooling on her back and sliding down her sides onto the floor. Her body shivered as it remembered the crushing blows from Kad's cudgel. Her fingers traced the cold stone of the window sill. The dark veins in the gray stone pulled her focus down like a magician mesmerizing his audience.

Gripping the sill, she braced herself and continued. "They locked me in a cell for a month. Several times a day, the dungeon master or his underlings would remove me from the cell for interrogation. I learned a lot about life from these sessions. If I let my tears fall, they would laugh and beat me harder. They were experts on generating excruciating pain just beneath the level which would have robbed me of consciousness. After the first session I swore to myself that I would never let them see my tears." There was still a location in her heart where that vow sat like a hard stone. Impenetrable and unfeeling. "Eventually they got tired of beating a prisoner who didn't beg for mercy and left me alone in my cell."

Oh how she wished the nightmare simply ended there. Her head was beginning to feel like Kad had just used his cudgel on it. *Stop, just stop*, her mind told her. *You've relived it enough.*

But she had come this far, she might as well finish. "I shared a cell with an older man called Quint." She paused, remembering the recent nightmare that recalled Quint's cruelty. "We were given broth and bread in the morning and one day Quint told me to take his bread, claiming that I needed it more than he did, telling...no commanding me to trust him. But the minute his bread was in my hands he shouted for the dungeon master and accused me of stealing his bread. The dungeon master punished me severely and gave Quint my food for two days. He did it twice before I stopped trusting."

Kathryn paused trying to shut out the voices and the screams that still haunted her. "The Blackwoods were not kind to their prisoners," she continued. "I can still hear every whip's crack and the cries of those who bore the stripes. Other prisoners were being beaten with clubs and maces, the sound of wood or metal crushing bone is something you never forget.

"After a month I was brought before Lord and Lady Blackwood. I was forced to kneel before them with my face touching the floor. For several radians they questioned me severely, but I refused to answer them." Her spine began to spasm as it remembered the radians it had spent, bent in that position as the unseen figures had fired question after question at her. She'd wanted to set the record straight. She'd wanted to tell the truth. But as she had listened to the questions and the tone used to deliver them she had realized that no matter what she had said, no one would have believed her. So, as usual, she had held her tongue. Just like she had while living with her uncle's family, just like she had while in the dungeons. Her voice hadn't mattered then, so she'd hidden it away.

"When the Blackwoods first told me that they had decided to rescind their earlier judgment and spare my life, I was relieved. Then they revealed their new judgment. I was to become Lady Blackwood's personal servant. At first, it sounded like a dream come true," she admitted. "My aunt had told stories of her days as a lady-in-waiting to the former Lady Blackwood. I would listen quietly as I cleaned while she described elegant balls, rich clothing, and extravagant food to her children. I quickly learned that the life my aunt had lived in the manor would not be the one I would live." Kathryn rolled one shoulder reflexively, remembering one of the beatings she had received. "My first beating at Lady Blackwood's hand came when I hesitated to hand over the one possession I owned. A pendant shaped like a soaring eagle that hung from a golden chain. My hesitation bought me ten lashes with the whip." It had taken her three years to recall that memory. When Lady Blackwood had given back the jewelry on the day she'd been rescued by Princess Jasmine, Kathryn had not recognized the pendant. Only after she'd been at school for a year had she remembered.

The object of her memories, which she never took off, suddenly became ice cold against her chest. She brought it out and held it in her hand. She stared at it for a long time. *A soaring eagle, the ultimate symbol of freedom. The one thing in my entire life that I have been continually denied.*

She closed her hand around the metal and returned her gaze to the window. "I was whipped on average of once a week, sometimes more. Lord and Lady Blackwood argued every morning and I was the one they took their anger out on. Lord Blackwood may have hit harder, but Lady Blackwood induced injuries that stung for radians."

The reasons for the Blackwood's arguments came to mind and she wanted to curse at the pettiness of them. She still couldn't believe that they were able to be in the same room together after all this time since she doubted the arguments had ceased after she had left. "I quickly learned to leave Lady Blackwood's bedchamber as soon as she was dressed. They would argue soon after she was dressed and I learned it was much better to endure one severe beating after they were done then to endure their argument and a severe beating afterwards. Lady Blackwood would blame me for the arguments, saying that I needed to be punished for bringing discord into their lives."

In the window she could see the outrage and disbelief on David's face. She shrugged. "I didn't understand what I had done but I believed her, believed her in the same way I believed I had to earn my keep with my aunt and uncle. As I grew the beating became harsher and more prolonged. I never spoke to them, which in the beginning infuriated Lady Blackwood and inspired numerous beatings, but eventually they... came to the conclusion I was mute and enjoyed having a servant who wouldn't talk back." It was only after Claude had casually suggested that she was mute that the beatings for that particular infraction had stopped.

"When I was seven I learned that the forest that surrounded the manor was a peaceful place where I could be alone and not listen to Lady Blackwood shrieking at everyone. I was eight when I discovered I could move water with my mind..." her voice broke and she closed her eyes willing herself not to fall into that memory.

"I made the mistake of discovering my ability within Lady Blackwood's sight. She flew into a rage unlike anything I had ever witnessed before. I received a beating to rival all the ones I had ever experienced." Kathryn felt tears choking her throat as she remembered that beating. Not even Kad's beatings could have competed. "They whipped me so badly I lost consciousness for a time. After a while Lady Blackwood told me horror stories about people who had powers like the one I showed her. She told me that if others knew I could move water with my mind they'd take me away and try me for black magic and perform awful experiments on me, she called it a curse. She made me vow never to use it again."

Kathryn closed her eyes, desperately wanting to stop talking. She wished she'd never started, reliving everything as a memory was difficult enough, but reliving while telling someone...the nausea was becoming worse and it was taking all of her concentration to force it away.

"But you did."

At David's quiet statement, she realized that she couldn't stop, not yet. Taking a deep breath to fight the roiling in her stomach she said, "Yes, although I wish I never had. Even after..." she paused, "... Lord Jasse rescued me my power has proven to be nothing more than a curse. At the school I was treated differently by the Council which alienated me from the rest of the students."

David moved so that he was standing behind her. Placing his hands on her shoulders he turned her away from the window to face him. When her gaze slid to the side out of habit he spoke. "Kathryn, look at me."

When she didn't immediately raise her head he repeated his command. "Look at me, Kathryn."

It was a command, not a harsh command, but definitely a command. Slowly she raised her face to look him in the eye.

"Your gift is not a curse." He spoke slowly and deliberately. "It never has been and never will be. Lady Blackwood was wrong to tell you those stories. The reason the Council paid you deference was because of your troublesome history. They wanted to make sure you transitioned peacefully, after that it became a habit for them to keep an eye on you."

"Maybe my gift isn't a curse," she said bitterly. "But I am cursed. Cursed with surviving."

"Being a survivor isn't a curse."

"It is for me," she returned sharply. Now that she was done reliving her past, she felt anger and resentment toward everyone in it. "It would have been far better for me to die with my uncle and his family then to endure everything that has happened since."

"But if you had died with your uncle's family, then you wouldn't be one of us. You would never have found Destiny and Amy and you would have never learned to make new friends of the Dragons."

"Because I've done such a good job at that," she returned sarcastically.

"You have Kathryn, you just have to see it," he told her calmly. "You took it upon yourself to continue training the others so that they wouldn't fall as easily to an opponent's sword. While at the capitol you kept a close eye on every Dragon, ready to play the protector if they found themselves in trouble. You prevented Natalie from forcing her personal tastes on all of us. You worked out your differences with Natalie, without forcing your own resentment into her punishment, and you worked with Tyler and Jenna to help me when I was sick," he reminded her.

Kathryn stared at him in disbelief. "I never told anyone about helping Jenna and Tyler," she said quietly.

"Being the family leader has its advantages," he said with a smile. "There are very few secrets that I don't know about."

"And the capitol? How could you possibly know...?"

"While you were watching the Dragons, I was watching you." He held up a hand to forestall her angry reply. "And before you take my head off, it didn't start out that way. The Dragons are my responsibility and it's my duty to look after them. When I realized that you already had that corridor covered for me, I decided that while you were watching our family, someone should be watching your back."

She stared at him again, a million thoughts flying through her mind. Finally she said, "You're wrong."

"Wrong?"

"I don't deserve to have anyone watching my back," she replied dully. "I don't even belong in the Guardians." The memory of being an outcast at school, the other students afraid of her because of the close attention the Council paid her came rushing back. "I don't know how to live with others. I don't...I don't even know who I am."

"You're a Dragon," he returned firmly.

"And how can you know that for certain? How do you know that I shouldn't be an outcast or village beggar? How do you know that the Council didn't make a mistake?"

℘·℃

David chose his words carefully, he could see that she was almost at the end of her endurance and didn't want to say anything that might upset her even more. "Because you're here with the rest of the Dragons, serving as a Guardian, and not as an outcast struggling for survival in the forests or streets. While it is possible that the Council can make mistakes, they didn't make one with you."

She looked up at him, her eyes deader than he had ever seen before. "Natalie called me a Wanderer."

"She what?!" David asked horrified.

"Months ago, when we were first stationed in Rima, Natalie accused me of being a Wanderer."

No wonder Kathryn had identity issues. "How did you handle it?"

"The accusation stung, but what was far worse is that I couldn't deny it. I have no proof that what she said is false," Kathryn admitted slowly.

"I think I need to have a talk with Natalie," David muttered angrily. *A very long, very overdue talk.*

"No, she's sorry now. She said it out of anger and frustration. She didn't truly mean it." He noticed that she didn't say it with much conviction...either that or she was too tired to care how anything sounded.

Perhaps now would be a good time to move her focus to something positive. "Out of curiosity," David said, "How do Destiny and Claude fit into all this?"

Kathryn gave a ghost of a smile as Destiny let out a soft call at the sound of her name. "On the day the Lord Jasse rescued me I found an abandoned baby bird in the forest. For some reason I felt a connection with it. I smuggled her into the manor and brought her with me when I left."

"Kind of like kindred spirits?" David asked.

"I guess so. Anyway, for the first couple months I never let her out of my sight. The first time I spoke was when I named Destiny."

"That's a powerful memory."

"Yes it is, and Destiny's been with me ever since."

"So in a sense, you both rescued each other."

Kathryn paused, considering what he had just said. "I never thought about it like that before," she admitted. "But you're right. We did kind of rescue each other."

"And Claude?"

A tiny spark of life appeared in her eyes. "When I first arrived here, I refused to speak. Because of this, and the fact that my uncle and his family never bothered to give me a name, I was nameless in more ways than one. The Blackwoods gave me the name Margit. On the second day, Claude came across me in the hall and told me that I reminded him of his little Caterina."

David smiled. "The name you used to introduce yourself to the Blackwoods."

"Yes. Lady Blackwood came looking for me and Claude pretended to think that she was looking for him and called me Kathryn." She paused. "I liked it better than Margit so when Lady Blackwood asked, I confirmed it and I became Kathryn."

David couldn't help but feel admiration for the baker who'd gone out of his way to ease some of the pain a six-year-old Kathryn had been feeling. He guessed that Claude's small acts of kindness hadn't stopped with giving Kathryn a beautiful name as well as making her feel like his own child.

He looked over at Kathryn. She was silent now, her eyes staring out the window, her body trembled with exhaustion. Standing, he moved to the doorway and called for a servant. One quickly appeared.

"Lady Caterina requests a sleeping draught for tonight, please see that one is delivered immediately.

The servant hurried away.

"I don't need a sleeping draught, David," Kathryn protested as he closed the door.

"I disagree," he replied quietly. "You've been through a lot in the last day and while you're exhausted now the dreams will come again, and you won't sleep."

She turned her head away. "They make the nightmares worse," she told him quietly.

He was startled that she actually admitted to the dreams since she hadn't spoken of them while telling her story and even more surprised that she'd admitted to what she could only consider a weakness with the sleeping draught. With a shake of his head he said, "Not this time. If you take the draught while you're still physically and emotionally as tired as you are now, the draught will calm your mind enough to bypass the dreams and give you peaceful sleep."

She eyed him doubtfully. "If you say so."

The next few minutes passed in silence, Kathryn continued to watch the rain fall against the window pane, although not as forcefully as the night before. David processed everything she had told him. His own body was simmering with rage, but instinct told him if he let her see any of his fury, it would chase her away. She needed someone to act as a pillar for her to lean on, a root to keep her from blowing away in the wind...not the fiery whirlwind of an avenging spirit

A knock sounded on the door and David retrieved the sleeping draught from the servant. He held it out to his second-in-command. She eyed it suspiciously.

"I'm not leaving until you drink it," he told her.

Grimacing she took it and held gamely onto it.

Amused, David crossed his arms over his chest. "It won't explode."

She shot him a look that told him she was not finding the situation as amusing as he was, but drank the draught.

Satisfied, David nodded and turned to leave. "I'll leave you to get some sleep. If the weather is clear, we'll leave as soon as everyone's awake."

He'd barely taken a step before she reached out and grabbed his wrist. Amazed at the swiftness of her reflexes in her exhausted state he turned to face her.

"Please," she begged. "Don't tell anyone what I just told you."

David looked into her eyes. "They're going to have to learn eventually."

She bit her lip. "I know, but I'm not ready to tell them yet. You're the first person I've ever told and I need time to get used to the idea of someone else knowing."

"You're going to need to learn to trust them one of these days."

"I trusted you, didn't I?"

℘·℃

David stepped out into the hall and closed the door behind him. The anger he had felt as Kathryn had told her story finally got the better of him and he slammed the butt of his fist against the stone.

A voice came out of the darkness to his right. "If you want to go after our hosts, I'll join you."

Startled, David peered into the gloom. Daniel stepped out of the shadows and into the light of a low burning torch. The look on his face was probably identical to the one on David's. "I'm tempted," David admitted.

Daniel grimaced. "I never thought it could have been that bad."

David motioned for Daniel to follow him and quickly returned to his own room. Closing the door he asked. "How much did you learn?"

The younger boy glanced down at the floor. "Most of it. Probably all of it."

"Eavesdropping?"

Daniel looked up hurriedly. "Not on purpose!" he said earnestly. "I was trying to gauge the mood of the manor, you know, reach out and see if they suspected who we really are."

Impressed with Daniel's initiative, David asked, "Do they?"

"I don't think so," Daniel said slowly. "But before I could do a more thorough investigation...I kind of got hit."

304

David raised an eyebrow. "Hit?"

Daniel nodded. "I don't really know how else to describe it. One minute I was working through the threads that make up Lady Blackwood's tangled mind and the next it felt like I'd been broadsided by a siege ram."

"Kathryn?" David guessed.

His companion nodded. "I was so focused on getting into the intricacies of our hosts minds, looking for the smallest of suspicions, then Kathryn's emotions overwhelmed me and it was like getting sat on by a horse."

"It got your attention," David said dryly.

"It didn't just get my attention, it took over." Daniel paused, trying to collect his thoughts. "It was weird," he said finally. "I've been trying for almost a year now to get a glimpse into Kathryn's mind, to understand her or help her. But the amount of emotion she just let loose was paralyzing. I literally couldn't move and I couldn't block it out."

Curious, David asked. "Were you privy to her words or just her emotions?"

"A little of both. They melded together, sometimes the images would drown out her voice, muting it like it was coming from behind a stone wall or under water, other times the images would fade and her voice would come through clearly against a black backdrop." Daniel shuddered. "Some of those images...I'm going to have nightmares for weeks."

"Do I want to ask?"

Daniel shook his head. "Two words: Vespine Fever."

Now David suppressed an involuntarily shudder. He'd seen paintings in classes of what happened to the victims who had fallen to the deadly plague and if that had been what Kathryn had survived, he would have nightmares too.

"There's something else, David," Daniel said slowly.

Alerted by the wariness in the other's tone, David motioned for him to go ahead.

"Kathryn...lied. Not about her past," he added quickly. "Well, only about a small part."

"Go on."

"Lord Jasse wasn't the one who found her."

David nodded. He'd already figured that much out by himself. "Let me guess. Dowager Princess Jasmine?"

Daniel nodded. "Yeah. I can understand why she might lie, but I figured you should probably know, the Dowager Princess being your aunt and all."

It was said so matter-of-factly that for a brief moment, David didn't process what Daniel had just told him. When his overwhelmed brain finally made the connection he struggled to find a way to refute it. Finally he managed, "I think your head is still rattled from your experience."

"Can't lie to a mind reader," Daniel replied simply.

If David's interactions with Lord Jasse were any indication, Daniel was probably right. Sighing, he leaned against the stone wall. "I thought you were able to sense emotions, not thoughts."

Daniel scratched his head. "It used to be just a sense, but lately it's been developing into actual thoughts. I'm not entirely sure what's happening. Maybe all mind readers start out sensing thoughts?"

"We could always ask the Council," David suggested.

Daniel shrugged. "Why bother? They have more important things to be doing. In any case, you don't have to worry. Your secret's safe with me."

"Thanks...I think." David sighed and ran a hand through his hair. "I remember an episode six years ago at school that had the Council and my family in an uproar. I pieced together some of it at dinner tonight when Lady Blackwood mentioned angering the Dowager Princess. But I didn't even begin to imagine..."

Daniel nodded. "Well, with any luck by tomorrow we can leave this place and be done with them."

"Hopefully. I don't think Kathryn could handle another day here."

Daniel chuckled softly. "At least no one would ever have to worry about the Blackwood's again."

"Don't give her any ideas."

"Oh, she already has them," Daniel told him. "But her desire to remain out of their presence trumps her desire to kill them at the moment."

"Pray it stays that way. I don't want to have to explain a double murder by my second-in-command to the Council. No matter how justified it may have been."

"Now that you mention it, I am severely tempted to go downstairs and remove the heads of the Lord and Lady myself."

"Well said," David responded. "Let's get out of here as soon as possible before things get out of hand."

Chapter 31

The next morning dawned clear and bright. There would be nothing to keep the Guardians from leaving Blackwood Manor. When Kathryn opened the window for Destiny the bird simply ruffled her feathers and refused to leave. *You are a strange bird,* Kathryn thought as she dressed and carefully packed up the rest of her possessions. It was strange, Kathryn mused, to be leaving Blackwood Manor a second time. However this time there was a difference. The first time she had left she had been facing the unknown with only Destiny to love. This time she knew exactly where she was going and felt a confidence she normally only experienced in the midst of a fight.

Perhaps Lord Jasse, Jasmine, and David had been right all along. She'd refused to talk about her past because of the intense pain that came with the memories. And yes, when she had told her story last night, the emotional pain had been severe—however now it was as if talking about it had smoothed a salve over all her wounds. A salve that had burned as it destroyed infection, but was now cool and soothing.

For the first time in her life, Kathryn felt free—as if it was only just now that she was leaving Blackwood Manor for the first time.

She was glad David had decided not to remain for the morning meal. Despite the fact that she felt free, she still couldn't stand to stay another morning in this place. As she shouldered her pack she remembered David's words from the night before. *"They're going to have to learn eventually."*

That was something she didn't look forward to. David would never react out of pity for her, but there was a strong chance the others would. Kathryn hated pity. She would rather be scorned than pitied.

Perhaps the rest of the Dragons didn't need to hear the full story? Maybe she could just give them small glimpses into her past? David probably wouldn't approve, but really—did the rest of the family have to know the *whole* story?

As she descended the stairs with Destiny perched on her shoulder she discovered the rest of the family gathered in the foyer. That was odd. She would have thought that David would have had them leaving at separate times. Of course, after what she'd told him last night, maybe he just wanted to make sure that they all got out of the Manor at once. He could easily have them all riding in different directions to hide their familiarity. *Blast*, she thought, spotting her hosts at the door, *of course they have to play the perfect host.* As she drew closer she overheard something that put a chill through her veins.

Natalie was promising to put in a good word for them at court, perhaps even send a letter to the king. Lady Blackwood was oozing polite gratefulness.

The thought of meeting Lord and Lady Blackwood at court after what they had done to her snapped something inside of Kathryn. As she joined the group she spoke loudly, "No, Lady Natalia, you will not."

Everyone turned to look at her in astonishment. Lady Blackwood struggled to keep the air of gentility on her face. "Is there a problem Lady Caterina?"

Kathryn didn't stop moving until she stood before her old mistress. Lady Blackwood was taller than her by several inches, but for once, Kathryn didn't feel intimidated. "Under no circumstances will anyone ever speak well of you at court." On her shoulder, Destiny let out a cat-like hiss. Kathryn wasn't sure if the appalled look on Lady Blackwood's face stemmed from her words or Destiny's presence on her shoulder.

"But, Lady Caterina!" Natalie protested.

Kathryn held up a hand for silence. "No, Lady Natalia!" she snapped, her voice filled with cold anger. Natalie flinched, but relaxed slightly when she realized that Kathryn wasn't angry at her. "Do not promise them anything until you know the truth of their *accidental oversight.*"

Lady Blackwood was struggling to keep her temper, Kathryn recognized the signs—stiff jaw, the clenching and unclenching of her hands, her bone-breaking rigidness. "And just how would you know—

The question died on her lips as she spied the golden pendant hanging around Kathryn's neck. An expression of disbelief and horror flickered across her face. "Impossible!" she whispered hoarsely. "You can't be her. She was mute."

"Impossible?" Kathryn asked in a dangerously calm voice. "I was never mute, Lady Blackwood, I just never learned to speak up. But now I will and I will tell everyone the truth about this horrid place."

Lady Blackwood laughed nervously. "You were too young to remember everything."

Kathryn narrowed her eyes at the woman before her. "Too young to remember every day I spent wallowing in your dungeon?" she asked icily. "Too young to remember every crack of the whip before it ripped into my flesh?" She stepped closer. Intimidated, Lady Blackwood took a step back. "Too young to still feel every slap of your hand against my face and body?" Kathryn continued, keeping her voice calm and controlled. Her words were not loud with anger, but they held the entire room as captive as she had once been.

"Too young to remember your anger and hatred? Too young to remember every beating you gave me? Too young to remember torn and bleeding hands and knees when the floor wasn't clean enough to suit your needs?" Kathryn felt resentment building and quickly quashed it. If she gave in to her urge to scream at her past tormentors they would win. She had to remain in control. "Too young to remember every story you told me about the outcasts? Too young to remember your fury when you discovered I had the gift of water?

"Too young to remember how you and your husband laughed and joked that you had the perfect slave? Too young to remember the beatings you gave me when I refused to talk or cry?" Kathryn stepped back, eyes narrowed. "How can I forget these things when I still carry the scars on my back and shoulders? How can I forget when my dreams are plagued by memories?"

The entire room had gone silent. Lord and Lady Blackwood stood, cowering before the young woman as the rest of the Dragons watched in complete shock and horror—shock and horror not directed at Kathryn, but at their hosts. Hosts who had spun silky tales of misunderstanding and prejudice against them only to have everything revealed as lies. Kathryn could feel disgust and anger roiling off the Dragons like the whitecaps of an ocean tormented by a winter storm. Matt actually looked ready to start in on his hosts with his fists. Even gentle Jenna had taken on a fighting stance.

Finally David broke the silence, disbelief lacing his words. "You're gifted, Lady Caterina?"

For a moment Kathryn didn't understand, and then she realized that she'd made a grave error. She'd mentioned her gift in front of everyone in the manor—an error that could result in her expulsion from the Guardians. Thinking quickly she shot a murderous glare at the Blackwoods. "I was, but thanks to these two I was unable to be admitted to the school for the gifted...I was too old," she bit out the last word as if it was a curse. "I was forced to learn to control my power on my own, in the end ..." she paused as if remembering a difficult decision, "...in the end I gave it away."

"Gave it away?" Lord Blackwood yelped in disbelief.

Kathryn clenched her jaw. "I was unable to become a Guardian and people avoided my presence because they feared my untrained power. So in a special ceremony I gave it away to a member of the Council. The power you feared," she spat at her old tormentors, "is gone. However I still possess the power of being the Dowager Princess' ward."

She took a step forward, her hand falling to rest on the ornamental dagger that sat at her waist. "If I ever receive word that you have been spinning tales and telling lies about the truth of this whole matter, trust me when I say, you'll live to regret it. You will regret it for every miserable day left of your lives. The judge who handled your case should be removed from office. For what you did to me you should not have just been banished from court. You deserved to have every rank and title pulled out from beneath you. This manor should have been placed into the care of others and you," she spat the word, "should be wallowing in your own dungeon. Lie about this whole affair again and I promise you that's what will happen."

Lord and Lady Blackwood could only nod numbly and watch the Dragons depart from their home. In the courtyard, Kathryn stopped to say goodbye to Claude.

"Thank you for remembering, old friend," she whispered as she gave him a kiss on the cheek.

"Did she just kiss him?" Natalie whispered to Tyler who elbowed her in the side. "Oww," she complained petulantly.

Claude chuckled. "I will always remember, little one." He handed her a basket, "These are for the road."

Kathryn took the basket smiling. "I may have to come back, just to have some."

Claude shook his head. "Don't come back here little one, you're done with this place. Don't look back."

She looked at him a long moment before nodding.

"I do however attend markets on Lumbar in the nearby towns." He winked as she laughed.

"Goodbye, Claude."

"Goodbye, Caterina."

℘·☙

When Blackwood Manor was no longer visible the Dragons, who had initially ridden off in different directions to keep their secret safe, reunited. David turned to Kathryn. She hadn't spoken a word since she said goodbye to the baker and neither he nor Jenna had been keen to interrupt her thoughts. They were all in shock of what they had just learned. When the others had rejoined, he'd seen several of them glance toward Kathryn, questions in their eyes. He'd waved them off with a warning look and a quiet shake of his head.

Fortunately the others were smart enough to heed his silent advice.

But now, David decided it was probably safe to bring up the last encounter. As they rode alongside a river at a comfortable pace he said with some humor, "When I said you needed to tell the rest of the family soon, I didn't mean it had to be the next morning."

"I hadn't planned on it," she said quietly. "But I guess in the end it worked out best. Now I don't have to repeat it again. Thanks for the save, by the way."

"That's what family does," he replied easily. "I was impressed with the way you handled yourself and the Blackwood's—I do believe they were actually afraid of you."

"Cold, restrained anger is often more intimidating, and deadly, than a loud, violent outburst."

He nodded slowly. "I think it depends on the type of personality you're dealing with, but in the general sense I agree with that assessment."

She slanted him a sideways glance. "Trust me. Calmness is more frightening than aggressiveness."

"Why?"

"If you know how, you can manipulate someone who's angry into making mistakes. It's much harder to do that to someone who's in control of their emotions."

"But anger can fuel an attack so vicious no technique in the kingdom can save you," he argued.

"That's when you manipulate the anger. Get them to react to what you're saying or doing. Make the violence predictable. Uncontrollable rage is exactly that. Uncontrollable. It's almost entirely offensive. They can't think on the defensive side of the spectrum because they're only thinking about hacking you into tiny pieces. The ability to reason flies out the front gate. If you can get ahead of them, mentally, you can beat it. Once you know the secret, it's not that difficult."

"Oh, not difficult at all," he said dryly. "Where did you learn this?"

"The same place you should have, school."

He stopped talking, trying to recollect a lesson that even vaguely resembled what she had just lectured him on. Unfortunately, he came up empty. Shaking his head in disgust at himself, he vowed to go back over all of

310

the material they'd been taught back at school. His second-in-command was making him feel extraordinarily inadequate as a leader.

∽⊙·∾

They rode for another eight days before finally arriving home. After everything that had happened, Kathryn had decided she had no desire to visit Jasmine and would return to the glade with the rest of the Dragons. David was suddenly relieved that he hadn't mentioned the possibility of Kathryn's visit to his aunt, only to have it cancelled at the last moment. His aunt would have never forgiven him. Destiny let out a joyful call as the meadow came into view.

"Someone's happy to be home," Luke commented as he dismounted and then rubbed his legs. "Remind me again why we had to spend the last three days at a steady trot?"

"So that we could get home in time for Matt and Cass to cook us a marvelous dinner," Natalie laughed as she brushed her horse.

Luke looked at the two cooks who were just beginning to unsaddle their horses. "Tell you what," he called over to them. "We'll finish the horses, if you run straight to the house and start cooking."

Laughing, Matt and Cass handed their horses over to the rest of the family and returned to the house.

Kathryn remained quiet as she rubbed down Lerina, she may have felt more at peace with herself and her past but she still wasn't in the mood to join in the gaiety. Destiny flew in and landed on the rafters overhead, a dead rat clutched in her talons.

"Kathryn if your bird drops that thing on me, you're picking it up!" Natalie called from two stalls over.

"Come on, Nat!" Luke called. "It's just a dead mouse."

"It's not a mouse it's a rat!" Natalie argued. "And it's huge!"

"Probably diseased," Tyler added.

"Tyler!" Leia called from across the stable.

"Well it probably is," he protested.

"Lighten up!" Several voices expressed the opinion at the same time, leading into laughter that filled the entire building.

Why did Destiny settle for just a rat?" Daniel's voice asked suddenly from the stall next to Kathryn's. "She took down an entire wild boar, and tried to drag it away. Surely she could do better for herself than a rat?"

"Must be just a snack," David's voice laughed.

Kathryn smiled, but didn't join in. She finished rubbing down Lerina, exited the stable and headed toward the house. Destiny followed, her dinner still clutched in her talons.

Dinner was a delicious meal of roast pheasant, warm biscuits, cold water, and fresh fruit.

Several of the Dragons took turns tossing Destiny scraps of meat which she eagerly devoured while still refusing to release the dead rodent from her talons.

Natalie squirmed in her seat. "Does she have to bring that thing in with her?"

Ignoring Natalie, Daniel quipped, "that bird can really pack it away," to which Luke agreed, "I'll second that." Responding to his voice, Destiny turned toward him, spread her wings, opened her mouth wide, and made cooing sounds.

"She's begging for more?" Amy said in disbelief.

All at once Matt, Tyler, Luke, and Elizabeth made a grab for the remaining scraps on the serving platters. Giggling and laughing they showered Destiny with the leftover fragments. After swallowing several chunks, she made a huffing sound.

Daniel leaned over and nudged Kathryn, "I didn't know that birds belched."

Kathryn smiled briefly. "This one definitely belches."

Afterwards the group split up into their own preferred activities. Natalie picked up a sewing project she had left behind. Lindsey brought out her pencils and paper and began to draw. Rachel and Leia managed to convince Cass to play the harp for them. The boys brought out knives and began to whittle. Matt was joyfully reunited with Lacey who sat contentedly on his shoulder and watched him carve a miniature of her.

Luke came in with a smile and said triumphantly, "It worked!" He held up two full pails of milk.

"Looking up from her latest creation Lindsey asked, "What worked?"

"Just before we left Leia did something to the cows, for that matter all of the livestock, and now they look as though we were just gone for a day. It's like they were dormant or something."

Leia smiled. "I asked all the animals to retreat and sleep, like a hibernation of sorts, till I woke them."

"That's amazing," Natalie gasped. She thought for a moment. "Can you do that with people?

Shaking her head as she responded, Leia said, "no, just animals--at least so far."

Kathryn watched as the rest of the family settled into a night routine that would have anyone believe they did it every night. But despite the events at Blackwood Manor, Kathryn still didn't feel like she belonged, she almost felt like she was still intruding on someone else's happy family. Climbing the stairs to her room, she couldn't wait for the morning patrols. She desperately needed something to take her mind off everything and working seemed like a good option.

౮ᐧ೮ౠ

It was Lumbar, four days since the Dragons had returned home and Kathryn desperately needed a break. Ever since the rest of the family had learned about her past it had been nothing but problems. It was as if the entire family had decided to check up on her at every waking moment.

"Kathryn do you need something?"

"Kathryn are you alright?"

"Do you want to talk about it?"

"How are you holding up?"

She was ready to tear her hair out! She just wanted to be alone to sort out her own feelings but the Dragons weren't giving her the opportunity to do

312

that. This morning she had slipped away to find some peace. Only David, Amy and, surprise of surprise, Matt, weren't pushing her, they seemed to understand her need to be alone. If only they could convince the rest of the Dragons.

There had to be a way to convince the rest of her mothering family that she was still Kathryn. She was still self-sufficient and didn't need their help—didn't want it. Natalie and Lindsey had already crossed the line into pity, something Kathryn resented. Others, like Cass, Daniel, and Rachel, were on the border.

When she reached the waterfall she stopped and listened. It took a moment to realize that the water wasn't having the soothing effect it normally had. She frowned, was something wrong? Water had always been a source of comfort to her.

She dipped her hand into the cool pond and felt the water respond to her touch, living, breathing water, welcoming her home. *Okay, so I haven't lost my gift, why can't I respond back?*

Gazing into the water she saw her own reflection. *Who am I? Am I merely an ex-slave who lived by virtue of a miracle? Am I an abused child who was simply rescued and given another chance at life?* She reached up and fingered the scars that covered her shoulders and back. *Am I the child of a race who sacrifices infants?* She shuddered at the memory of the dream she had experienced here. *Am I the deliverer of an oppressed race?*

Who am I?

She remembered what Claude had said to her, how her name meant pure. Frustration welled up inside of her and she raced her hand through the pool. She didn't feel pure. She felt like unclean laundry that had been trampled in a pigsty.

A figure appeared behind her in the pool's reflection. She recognized him immediately and her loneliness and emptiness boiled into anger.

"Are you satisfied?" she demanded, turning to face Elyon. "I've faced my past now and all it's done is cause me more grief."

Elyon moved closer until he was standing beside her. "Facing your past is only part of the challenge," he told her gently. "Now you must embrace it."

"And just how am I supposed to do that?" she asked bitterly.

Elyon smiled. "By moving past it. Stop dwelling on the memories and move onwards."

"But I never dwelt on my memories," she argued. "I never thought back to what my life was like before I became a Guardian."

Elyon sat down on a rock near the edge of the pool and let his fingertips brush the water, "You ignored your past," he said quietly. "By ignoring your past in your waking life you gave it leave to torment you at night. Because you refused to face your memories during the light they became monsters that slowly ate away at your soul in the darkness."

"How poetic," she replied acerbically.

"But true," he replied firmly.

"What do you want from me now?" Kathryn demanded.

He smiled at her. "It is not your turn to give, child, but mine. I am here to help you."

313

She eyed him skeptically. "Why would you want to help me?"

He moved to stand beside her. "Because I know who you are."

Shock coursed through her system so fast it made her lightheaded. "What!?" She looked at Elyon in shock. "What do you mean?"

A gentle smile curved his lips upward. "I mean exactly what it sounds like. I know you who are."

"You...you know who my family was?" The question burned in her chest as she asked it, but she had to know!

"Is," he corrected softly.

She blinked at him, unable to comprehend.

"I know who your family is."

The air left her lungs in a rush. "They're *alive?*" she whispered.

He nodded slowly.

Cold numbness crawled up her limbs, stealing her strength, and she sat down hard on the ground. After a moment, fury replaced the shock. "*They're alive!*" she exclaimed heatedly.

"Yes."

Indignation consumed her. "They're alive and *they*, and *you*, left me to die in that hellhole?!"

"They've spent the last sixteen years believing that you were dead," he responded mildly. "Well, all but one."

"But they know I'm alive now?"

"Yes, I told them."

"*You* told them?!"

"Yes."

"And why aren't they here with you? They must be as cold as the Blackwoods if they aren't trying to reunite with the daughter they thought dead."

"It is too soon."

"What's too soon?"

"You would reject them, just as you've done with the Dragons."

Surprise opened and closed her mouth several times. At first she thought that he was fishing for confirmation of who, and what, she was. But looking into his eyes, she could see marble conviction. He *knew*. "Who are you?!" she demanded. "Only the King and Guardian Council claim to have the omniscience you appear to be demonstrating."

"I told you, an advisor of sorts to your King."

"No mere *advisor* would have such knowledge," she countered.

"Very well then, an ally of your King."

"An ally from where? And for what? We aren't at war."

"War comes eventually, it always does. Is it not better to be prepared than to be caught off-guard?"

"If the legends are true, the last war was over two millenia ago. That's a karcking long time to prepare."

"Then your people should have no problem winning the next one, should you?"

Kathryn got an unsettling feeling that there was more to this than simple philosophy. "You know something, don't you?"

"Know what?"

"War is coming to Archaea, isn't it?"

"It's possible," he replied with a shrug. "It depends on certain events."

"What events?"

He smiled at her. "That knowledge rests between me and your King."

She glowered at him. "You would condemn us? That hardly sounds like the actions of an ally."

"An ally comes in many forms. Instructors are allies to their students, but their method of helping can involve allowing the students to fail before they can succeed."

"That prolongs the process."

"But it makes the student stronger and more confident in the final outcome. Look at you. The torture you endured at the hands of the Blackwoods and your uncle should have broken you. Any other person would have shattered, but not you. You came away stronger. Battered, but stronger."

"So is that my failure," she asked sarcastically.

"No, child. That was the equivalent of the lecture hall. If events play out, the final test is still coming."

She felt the blood rush from her face, numbing her. "What are you saying?" she asked in horror.

"There are two paths open to your kingdom. One leads to peace, the other to war. If the path of war is chosen ancient, dark secrets will consume the light. Others will rely on your strength to survive it. And without your past, *you* would not survive it."

Staring at him in mute dismay, she struggled to comprehend what he was telling her. "How will we know?" she asked finally.

"Know what?"

"That the path of war has been chosen versus the path of peace."

Sadness clouded his features. "Trust me, child. When darkness begins to overtake the light, you will know."

"Why are you telling me this?"

"Because you will play a pivotal role in the fate of your kingdom. Decisions you make in the future will affect the outcome, be it peace or death."

"Surely the fate of Archaea does not rest solely on my decisions!?" she exclaimed, panicking at the idea of so many lives riding on decisions she had yet to make.

"Not just yours, no. There are others who are just as instrumental as you, but the path of the kingdom is determined by the decisions of the majority. If you chose peace, but the majority chose war, war would come. However," he added gently, "if war does come, there is the possibility changing the path."

She stared at him. "No," she said flatly. "You have me confused with someone else."

"I am not mistaken. I know who you are, remember?"

His reminder of her family chased away the terror in her body and replaced it with resentment. "I don't suppose you could *tell* me who my family is? Surely that is harmless enough?"

With a shake of his head he replied, "That knowledge could change the path of the kingdom. It could change *you*."

He cut off her protest with a quick wave of his hand. "You are not your parents, Kathryn. You must learn to discover yourself before you learn of your heritage. You are conflicted, I can see it within your eyes. Telling you who your sires are will not solve that. There are issues in your life you must come to peace with before such knowledge is revealed to you."

"Such as?" she demanded angrily.

"Trust for one. You must learn to trust others, rely on their strength instead of your own."

She stiffened. "No one, in my entire life, has proven worthy of my trust, and anyone I have ever trusted has betrayed me."

"Then perhaps you have trusted the wrong people too much and the right people too little?"

"And just who is right and who is wrong?" she countered.

Elyon spread his hands. "That is not for me to determine."

"Then how are your words of wisdom helpful?"

"By making you think."

"I already think."

"Not on this matter you don't. You made a decision as a child and have not revisited or revised it since that day in the Blackwood's dungeon," he rebuked her.

"Why should I revisit and revise it if no one has ever given me reason to?"

"Because you do not allow them the opportunity to give you cause to do so." His eyes softened as he asked, "where is your faith, child?"

"Back in the Blackwood's dungeon with my innocence and trust," she retorted sharply.

"Not everyone is like Quint, Kathryn," Elyon told her quietly. "Not everyone has a secret agenda."

"My experience suggests otherwise," she shot back, suppressing a shiver at the name that had haunted her as a child; the face that still haunted her.

"Jasmine? Jasse? David? Amy? Claude?" Elyon listed them on his fingers. "Surely they all don't have hidden motives every time they deal with you?"

"They all have at one point or another," she replied firmly. *Except maybe Claude.*

Elyon shook his head. "That is the way of people, Kathryn. They are not perfect. You need to accept that at some time or another, they will desire something of you. But you can't hold those few times against them for the rest of their lives."

"I don't."

"Yes, you do. It's how you rationalize your actions toward even the friendliest of people. By assuming that they want something from you, you give yourself the right to treat them coldly."

"People are selfish, they *always* want something from someone else."

"But sometimes that selfishness can lead to purer actions. Have you ever considered the possibility that all they desire from you is your friendship and companionship?"

"So that they can pry into my personal life? Force me to relive memories I would rather forget?"

"How can you make friends without sharing a part of yourself with others? Until they know your story, how can they know when they are getting close to your wounds? If they reach out blindly they are more likely to stick their finger in an open wound than if you give them an idea of where you're injured and where they should tread cautiously."

"They shouldn't be poking around in the first place!"

"How can a healer gage the extent of a wound without first examining it? A little poking and prodding is necessary to determine the depth and severity of the wound before a treatment can be devised."

She glared at him, unwilling to admit that in that point he was correct. She'd seen Jenna and Tyler in action enough times to know how a wound was treated.

"Think on what I've said," Elyon said finally. "You've set one foot on the path of healing, I can help you with the second step but the third is up to you."

"What is the second step?" She tried to remember how Jenna and Tyler treated injuries, but couldn't manage to draw any similarities between her case and theirs.

"The first step in healing is to treat the injury," Elyon told her softly. "The second is to prevent further injury by infection from setting in. Lastly, the victim must overcome the physical and psychological restrictions that injury placed on them.

"You have already done the first. You've faced your past. By facing the Blackwoods and your darkest secrets you've acknowledged and treated your injury. But a resentful fever still burns in your body over what happened to you. And it's a fever you feed every time you touch your scars."

"So what's the cure for the fever?" she asked sarcastically. "Remove the scars?"

"Yes," he replied calmly.

"Good luck," she returned derisively. "The most gifted healers of the Guardians tried to remove them and couldn't. What makes you think you can?"

"My gift of healing is stronger than that of the Council Guardians. I have the power to remove them."

Kathryn reached up and fingered her shoulder, hardly daring to believe such a thing was possible...Could he live up to his claim?

"How?"

"What do you mean?"

"How do you have the power to remove them? The Council employs the strongest healers in the Kingdom. How can you surpass their power?"

"The Guardians rely on their natural gifts to supply their power. Not only is my power stronger than theirs, but I possess techniques long lost to the Guardians."

"What kind of techniques?" she asked hesitantly.

"The Elves and Guardians were not the only ones with the power to heal," he replied with a smile. "There was another group of people who were given healing powers."

Kathryn felt her brow furrow as she tried to think. The answer hit her like a rock. "Wizards?"

He nodded.

"You know wizard magic?"

He nodded again.

"That's impossible! They died out several millenia ago."

"Just because they can no longer be found within the borders of Archaea, it doesn't mean that they died out," he said with a twinkle in his eye.

And if the legends were true, wizard magic *could* remove scars. "You can really use wizard's magic?" she asked again, slowly.

Elyon nodded. "Yes."

"And what would you demand in return?"

"Nothing, child, it is a gift I will gladly give you."

That raised alarm bells in the back of her mind. "Nothing in this world is free."

"My child, a gift is free to all. If something is asked for in return then it is not a gift."

Kathryn hesitated only a moment. "Then, please, I ask you to remove them."

He placed one hand on her shoulder. "Do you that believe I can?"

His question made Kathryn pause. Did she believe that he, a stranger whom she'd only met twice before, could remove her scars? He radiated power and confidence that surpassed even that of King Darin. He was gifted, of that she was sure. And his calm responses to her questions told her that he was completely confident in everything he had revealed to her. It was his eyes, something in his eyes that prompted her response. She was surprised to discover, that yes, she did believe that he could. "I do."

Elyon laughed, it was a pleasant sound, nothing like the cold hard laugh of the Blackwood's, but the warm comforting laugh of a father. It reminded her of Lord Jasse's laugh. "Then reach up child, and see that you are healed."

Kathryn immediately reached up and felt nothing but smooth skin. "But...but how?"

He smiled down at her. "I am a leader of men, this is true, but the one I serve is even stronger and it is his power that I call upon. It is by his authority that I am given the power to heal." He cupped her chin in his hands and Kathryn could feel the intense power and calm that radiated from his touch. "I am not a king in the sense of your King Darin," he said calmly. "I am a Dūta. I *serve* a King, much like you serve yours. My services are free to those within his kingdom."

"But I'm not in his kingdom," she protested. *And how can you call a kingdom yours if you aren't a king?*

He smiled again. "You are, child. You have been since you were born. All that is left is for you to realize it."

"But how can a King give another magic? Magic is born not given," she whispered, trying to sort through his confusing words.

Elyon smiled. "It is both," he said with a light laugh.

"I have watched over you since your birth and will continue to do so," Elyon promised her. "Remember that, child, for your next test has yet to begin."

"What next test?" she asked warily as she stood, her mind returning to his warnings of the two paths her kingdom faced. She wasn't ready to face those decisions yet.

"The trial that will tell you who you are," Elyon put his hand on her shoulder and gazed into her eyes. "I fear it will not be an easy test for you, but you must have faith."

"Faith? Faith in what?"

"Faith in yourself, faith in your family, but mostly faith in my king."

Why would I have faith in a stranger? "Why should I have faith in a king I've never met?" She demanded.

"Because my magic is that of a child compared to his."

Now that was a disturbing thought. He'd already demonstrated abilities that would throw the Council into a tizzy, but the knowledge that someone *more* powerful than he existed...it would cause a full-blown panic. Time to change topics and return to the second most disturbing thing he'd said. "Will you be there during the trial?" Was it to be like the tests back at the school where a panel of instructors observed and graded each student's abilities?

"I will be watching over you," he reminded her. "Even though you cannot see me, I will be there."

"How can you be there if I can't see you?"

"You must trust me."

"I already told you that I don't trust others," she replied a little heatedly. He may have just performed a miracle she'd never let herself dream of, but that didn't give him the right to become presumptuous.

Elyon smiled. "You believed that I could heal you."

"Trusting and believing aren't the same thing."

"I know child, which is why what I am about to ask you will be difficult for you."

She arched an eyebrow. "What are you going to ask me?"

"To put all your trust in me and the one I serve and to believe me when I say I will never leave or abandon you. Even when it seems like everything and everyone else has."

Kathryn stared at him a moment before shaking her head. "You ask too much," she replied. "I don't even know you. How can I trust you?"

Elyon chuckled. "You know me, Kathryn. Search your heart and you will find you know me." He reached out to her and pulled her into an embrace.

Stunned and surprised by his sudden movement, she instinctively stiffened, but then another emotion took over and Kathryn finally knew what it was like to feel protected. She knew, deep down, she knew he was the one who would never betray her. How she knew she couldn't say, but somehow she knew.

When Elyon let her go she nodded at him. It wasn't a nod of trust, but one of a promise to try. It was all she could offer.

He smiled and laid his hand back on her shoulder. "Then go Kathryn, and know that you have been given a second chance."

Chapter 32

As suddenly as he had appeared, Elyon disappeared. For a moment Kathryn stood motionless, then, fearing what she had seen and heard was a dream, she quickly reached her hands up towards her shoulder blades. Where there had been rough skin and long narrow scars there was now only smoothness, not even tenderness. The tautness and dull ache that permeated her back and shoulders for years was gone.

"A path that leads to war and another to peace," she mused over his words, turning them over and over in her mind, trying to make sense of it. *What in the stars is that supposed to mean?*

"Kathryn!"

She turned to find David hurrying up behind her. "Who was that?" He demanded.

"You saw him too?"

"Of course I saw him, what did he say to you?" He peered at her. "Is everything okay? You look a little...I don't know."

She arched an eyebrow at him. "I look a little what?"

He blinked hard several times before saying, "Never mind, I must have imagined it."

"Imagined what?"

He shook his head emphatically. "Nothing. Who was that man?"

Kathryn debated how much to tell him. "A man I've met before," she hedged.

"You willingly took part in a conversation with a strange man in the middle of the forest?" He was looking at her like she'd lost her mind. She was beginning to wonder the same thing.

Rolling her eyes she replied. "He's not dangerous...just a little odd."

"I don't like it."

"Lord Jasse knows him. In fact, he asked me to get to know him." *Sort of.*

He hadn't been expecting that reply. She could see the wheels turning in his head before he finally spoke. "Okay, fine. Lord Jasse is as good a reference as you can get, but you still haven't told me his name or why he was here."

Turning to look back at the spot where the stranger had disappeared she said, "His name was Elyon, he told me...he said... he said...things that didn't make sense," she didn't want to set him off with Elyon's talk of war, "and he took away my scars."

"He took away your what?" David didn't look, or sound, convinced.

She nodded. "My scars. He told me I had carried them long enough."

David moved closer to view the miracle, but her tunic completely covered her back and shoulders. "And what was his price for removing them?"

"Nothing."

One of his eyebrows shot upward toward his hairline. "Nothing is free."

"That's what I told him. He said that it was a gift." *Or maybe I would just owe him one...*

"I don't like it."

Kathryn turned and frowned at him. "I can take care of myself David."

"I know you can, I just don't like the idea of strangers approaching young women alone in the forest."

"He wasn't dangerous," Kathryn insisted.

"How would you know that?"

As she sought an answer, she realized that she didn't have any—just an indescribable knowledge that this man had truly wanted to help her. And it probably wouldn't be wise to admit that he'd saved her life the previous winter. "He isn't dangerous," she said finally. Thinking about his words she added, "He may bring danger, but he himself isn't dangerous."

David opened his mouth with some prepared retort, but it died when her words reached him. "What? How can someone bring danger but not be dangerous?"

She shrugged. "I can't explain it any other way."

"What else did he want?"

She struggled with her reply. *Oh, we just talked about the fact that my family is still alive and that they thought I was dead all these years. And how our kingdom is probably headed for war, but good news there, I may be able to stop it if the special majority I'm a part of choses the path of peace.* Oh yeah, that would go over well. "He just wanted to talk."

"And you obliged him?!"

She sort of understood his incredulity, after all, why would she talk to a stranger in the woods when there were fourteen of them living in her house? "I didn't say that he wanted to get to know me," she replied sourly. If Elyon was to be believed, there was no need for him to get to know her, he already did. "Just that he wanted to talk."

"Talk about what?" David pushed.

"Random topics." She figured that her family, her past, war, and the other myriad of topics they had covered during their whirlwind conversation counted as random. "I think he was lonely and just wanted someone to talk to."

"So you just sat around and listened to him talk your ear off?"

She sighed. "Are you going to stand here and argue with me or was there a reason you tracked me down?"

He raised an eyebrow at her. It was blatantly obvious that he wanted to continue his interrogation, but she put some ice into her eyes and he backed down. "The rest of us are going into the village, Natalie wanted to know if you wanted to come too."

Kathryn looked back at the waterfall, then, realizing she had already found her peace, turned back to David and said, "Sure."

He looked genuinely surprised. "Really?"

"Why not?"

"You never have before."

"So I can't now?" she quirked an eyebrow at him.

"That's not what I meant."

They left the falls and walked back by the way of the meadow without commenting anymore about Elyon.

Natalie talked the entire way to the village, reminding David about his promise to stay the entire day. Kathryn thought David looked like he regretted making that promise, but wisely didn't comment. Immediately upon entering the village, Natalie and the rest of the girls headed toward the marketplace. Kathryn had no desire to see the market. Instead she wandered the streets aimlessly until she found herself standing before the village poorhouse.

She could hear children crying and the sound drew her to the source inside. Once her eyes adjusted to the dark interior she could make out about twenty children sitting on cots or scattered on the floor. Several bassinets stood nearby, their tiny occupants sleeping despite the clamor inside.

"We don't got no room for any others!"

Kathryn turned at the harsh voice and found herself face to face with the elderly matron in charge of the children. "I'm not here to drop anyone off," she quietly reassured the woman, "I'm here to help."

"Elp?" the old woman scoffed. "An why would the likes of you elp dis brood not worth a bordar's spittle?"

Kathryn, a little taken back looked around. "Surely not all these children were unwanted by their parents," she exclaimed quietly.

The matron nodded to a small girl curled on a cot at the far end of the room, "That 'un there, Pa beat 'er 'cause she weren't a boy," she nodded to twin boys at the far end of the room, "those were numbers nine and ten. Their pa decided he couldn't wait till they were biggen enough to till the ground. Ten is to many mouths to feed." She turned a sorrowful eye towards Kathryn, "most here got the same story—nobody wants em til they big enough to do a days work--then they want em."

Kathryn moved slowly to where the small girl cowered on the bed. Gently she sat down and looked into the frightened child's eyes. "Hello," she said softly. She avoided staring at the child's numerous scars that were visible all over her small body; scars that, until that morning, were similar to the very ones Kathryn had carried.

The child looked at her, but didn't make a move to answer her.

"My name's Caterina, do you have a name?"

The little girl nodded slowly.

Kathryn grinned. "Shall I try to guess it?" When the little girl nodded again, Kathryn pretended to think a moment, and then asked, "Is your name Evelyn?" As the little girl shook her head, Kathryn said, "Hmm...is it Elise?"

A tiny glimmer of a smile made its way to the corner of the child's eyes. "Is it Magda? No? How about Gertrude? Wrong again? What about Marlee?"

The little girl let out a soft giggle. "Dawn."

Kathryn smiled. "That's a very pretty name."

"Mum named me after her happy time of day," the little girl told her proudly.

"Where is your mother?"

Casting her eyes to the floor she pursed her lips. "She died. Taken in the great sickness—last year," Dawn told her quietly. "After she gone, pa don't want me round no more."

"Do you like to play games?" Kathryn asked quickly, trying to distract the little girl.

"Mum made me a doll when I was this many," she indicated by holding up three fingers. "Her name's Starla."

"That's a very interesting name," Kathryn said quietly. "Did you pick it for any special reason?"

Dawn nodded seriously. "I like stars, mum said it was a good name."

"It is a good name," Kathryn told her. "Can I meet Starla?"

Dawn hesitated for less than a second. "She's sleeping, but she's napped enough." She hopped down from the bed and hurried into a back room.

"Well now," the matron huffed behind Kathryn. "You ne'er told me you was a miracle worker."

Kathryn looked up at her in surprise. "What do you mean?"

"Tha' little en ain't spoken a word since she showed last year. Thought her a mute, I did."

"Do you know how old she is?"

"Her pa said she was four, but who knows." The matron shrugged as she walked away.

Kathryn couldn't stop from drawing similarities between Dawn and herself. Five, maybe six years old, abused by authority figures, and silent.

Dawn came hurrying back, carrying a well-worn doll. "Dis is Starla," she announced as she crawled into Kathryn's lap.

Kathryn stayed at the orphanage for the rest of the day, spending time with the children. It wasn't often someone visited the orphanage and the children welcomed her presence. The girls invited her to play dolls and the boys asked her to judge their running games.

Later in the evening, as the sun sunk below the horizon Kathryn and Dawn sat on the steps outside and watched the greater light slowly disappear.

"Do you still hurt?" Dawn asked suddenly.

Startled, Kathryn looked down at the little girl who sat comfortably in her lap. "What do you mean?"

"Where dey hit you," the little girl said. "Does it still hurt? Mine do."

"What makes you think I was hit as a little girl?" Kathryn asked quietly.

"I watched your face when you said ello to me. You saw me scars but didn't stare or say I was bad like errbody else." The little girl sat up straighter, "When you said ello, your eyes said I know—I hurt too."

It's funny how the ones discarded by society end up learning the most about it. I didn't even need to say anything, but she knew. She smiled down at the expectant little girl. "No, they don't hurt anymore. Although up until a few days ago they did."

Tears filled the little girl's eyes. "Will mine ever stop hurting?"

Kathryn closed her eyes and hugged her close. How often had she felt like Dawn after she had first been rescued? She had lost count. When the hurt had refused to leave, Kathryn had buried it deep, refusing to acknowledge it. Recent experience had only just vividly shown her that that hadn't been the right solution. "I don't know, Dawn. I hope so."

Eventually David caught sight of the orphanage. When he and the others had started getting ready to leave, he had been surprised to learn that no one knew where Kathryn was. It was only after Jenna had mentioned seeing an orphanage that David knew where to find his second-in-command. His heart turned over at the sight of Kathryn still holding a little girl in her arms. He approached slowly, not wanting to be heard nor wanting to disturb them.

The little girl was sniffling, big tears rolling down her cheeks. Kathryn held her close to her chest like a mother would hold her child. He stood in the shadows, watching and waiting. He had never seen such tenderness from Kathryn and it surprised him.

After a while the little girl quieted and grew still, David guessed she had fallen asleep, but Kathryn refused to let go.

Slowly David approached, but for once Kathryn's training seemed to be pushed aside for she startled when he sat down beside her.

"Who is she?" he asked softly.

"Her name is Dawn," Kathryn replied softly. "She's almost six years old."

David didn't know what to say. Looking down he got a closer look at the scars that covered the little girl's body. Some leapt over her legs like flames; others were rounded and thin like a rod. Beneath the scars her skin was purple and yellow tinted from the bruises. Her arms resembled her legs and on the left side of her face a jagged scar ran from above her eyebrow to below her neck.

Carefully David brushed back the flame colored hair that had fallen across the little girl's face, it was dirty and matted like it was rarely washed. He also noticed that her bottom lip had a scar and the top looked like it had been split multiple times.

"Who could do this to an innocent child?" he asked in disgust. Then, realizing that Kathryn had probably borne similar marks when she had been rescued, tried to send her an apologetic look.

Her eyes were trained on the setting sun, but the absent look in them told him that she was looking into the past. Finally, she broke herself away from the memories and refocused on him. "It was her father," she explained quietly. "He wanted a boy and got a girl so he took his frustration out on her."

They sat there for several minutes; both studying Dawn until an older woman came out and told Kathryn that Dawn needed to come inside with her.

Hesitantly Kathryn surrendered the child and the woman thanked her before carrying the still sleeping girl inside.

For a long time Kathryn was still, not moving, just staring directly in front of her.

Finally David stood and held out his hand to Kathryn. "Come on. The rest of us are ready to go."

Kathryn nodded, but stood on her own. "I'm coming back tomorrow."

He faced her. "Is that wise?" he asked slowly. "You still struggle with your own past, should you get involved with another abused child?"

"Dawn knew I was abused before I even mentioned it. I'll help her through her grief, and she can help me through mine."

₧·₳

For the next six weeks, on her days off, Kathryn visited the orphanage and spent time with the children. According to the matron, they so looked forward to her visits that they would constantly ask if it was Lumbar yet, even if it was only Ambar.

The days fell into a routine. Early in the morning she and the girls would play with dolls, have tea parties, and play house. After a small lunch, everyone would pile outside to watch, and judge, the various races the boys held.

Playing with dolls was a completely new experience for the Guardian. Growing up, she'd never been allowed to touch one and she struggled to play along with some of the girls' stories. But the children were patient and enjoying teaching her how to play 'pretend'. After a few weeks, Kathryn discovered that she could slip into a different character easily. She enjoyed creating new obstacle courses and games for the boys to play and the children loved running them.

Except for that first night, David didn't try to talk her out of going to the orphanage again. He understood what many of the others didn't. Kathryn was using her time with the children to make up for her nonexistent childhood. No one else accompanied her, which was fine with Kathryn. The children were pleasant enough company. Besides, she would never have had so much fun if one of the Dragons was around to keep her company.

Destiny was always nearby, soaring high above or roosting on the tops of roofs.

Everything was perfect until one Lumbar evening when a voice called out to her just as she was leaving, "Lady Kathryn, what in the kingdom's name are you doing here?"

Startled, Kathryn turned and caught sight of four fully armored knights, their leader none other than Lord Tanner.

Chapter 33

While Kathryn executed a curtsy, Lord Tanner swung down from his horse. "Good evening, Lord Tanner."

"I must say," Lord Tanner exclaimed as he approached. "This is the last place I would have expected to see you." He eyed her clothing. "Not exactly dressed for a ball are you?"

Kathryn knew very well what she must look like. Her simple gray and brown dress was splattered at the hem with mud and grass, her hands were filthy and her hair was beginning to escape its bun. At least she was wearing a dress today instead of the tunic and leggings she preferred around the glade. "Forgive my appearance, Lord Tanner," she apologized. "I did not expect to run into any of our class here."

"What were you expecting to run into here?"

Kathryn forced herself to remain civil. *What is it with people needed to know my business?* She waved her hand at the orphanage. "I'm spending time with the orphans in the various villages," she replied. "I've found that court attire intimidates the children and since my goal is to draw them out I've traded my ball gowns for more practical clothing."

Surprise followed by suspicion flickered in his eyes. "And why would a gentlewoman, such as yourself, be interested in orphans?"

"I presume you know I was adopted as Dowager Princess Jasmine's ward?" Kathryn raised her eyebrows, forcing herself to play the part of a courtly lady when every survival instinct she had was screaming at her to run.

"Of course. As such I cannot help but wonder if she sent you here to spy on me."

Spy on him? Of all the stupid, self-centered, moronic— "I assure you, milord. I was not sent here by Princess Jasmine. Before I was adopted by her I was an orphan myself." She nodded to the orphanage, still barely visible in the waning light. "I find it brings the children, as well as myself, some comfort to spend time there."

A cold smile spread across Lord Tanner's face. "A likely story," he said coldly. "But not one I'm likely to believe."

Kathryn raised her eyebrows at him. "Well I'm sorry I can't offer you another you might more readily believe. I'm afraid the children drained my supply of stories earlier today."

She moved to leave but Lord Tanner blocked her path. "Really, Lord Tanner," she exclaimed, her anger rising. "It is late and the children have exhausted me."

"Where are you staying?"

Who does this troglodyte think he is? "I'm not comfortable having you know," she informed him, knowing it was one hundred percent the truth.

"Are you staying in the village?"

If I just say yes maybe he'll leave me alone. "Yes."

His face clouded. "There's only one inn in this village and it's not worthy of cattle. You will lodge with me in the governor's castle."

"That is hardly necessary," Kathryn protested. There was no way she was going to willingly spend a radian, let alone the night, in his residence...especially with Lord Merlae presently at court. "Besides, it would take a whole day's ride to reach the governor's castle."

With reflexes that startled her, Lord Tanner reached out and grabbed her arm and began pulling her towards his horse. "No, I insist."

"Unhand me!" she ordered, struggling. *If only I wasn't supposed to be playing the part of a noblewoman*, she thought in disgust.

He ignored her protests and kept on. *He's much stronger than he looks*, she realized, *I couldn't break his hold easily even if I was utilizing my training as a Guardian instead of acting like a lady.*

Lord Tanner lifted her, still struggling, onto his horse and quickly mounted afterwards. As soon as he settled into the saddle, they were off at a steady gallop with the village and the forest slowly shrinking into a tiny speck.

They rode through the night and most of the day before the surreal reality that she was being kidnapped dawned on Kathryn. They stopped for a meal in the middle of a barren plain with nothing but grass covered hills for as far as the eye could see. Now that they were outside the range of prying eyes, Tanner had ordered Kathryn's hands tightly bound and kept the strongest of his two men nearby to prevent her escape. After a radian of rest, Lord Tanner gave the order to remount and the rode well into the night until lights of a castle began to distinguish themselves from the numerous stars that dotted the night sky.

As they clattered into the courtyard, Kathryn could hear the sound of a closing portcullis and drawbridge. *Blast*, she thought, *he has a moat. That complicates things.* Knowing the kind of person Lord Tanner was, he'd probably had the moat equipped with sharp spikes and ropes attached to hooks, intended to grab hold and drown its victims, hidden just below the surface lurking in his moat. It would make escape difficult, especially if she had to swim a moat filled with unknown obstacles. Of course, she could always try walking on the putrid water. She hadn't tried that before— but definitely better than being immersed in it, she mused. Although the threat of becoming impaled on a spike or caught in a net of fish hooks probably wasn't the best incentive for trying a brand new technique...or was it?

Just before he dismounted, Tanner surreptitiously sliced through her restraints, then, as if to preserve his façade of chivalry, he offered Kathryn his hand.

She glared at him. "I do not appreciate being kidnapped," she informed him icily.

He chuckled. "Come now, Lady Kathryn. I haven't kidnapped you, I've rescued you!" He pulled her off his horse.

Righting herself, she yanked her arm from his. "You've saved me from what exactly, Lord Tanner?"

"From having to spend the night in a beastly inn," he exclaimed "Instead you can warm yourself by my fire, dine on my fine food, and sleep in a soft bed without worry of rats, sucking bugs and insects, and whatever vermin patronizes those hovels."

"I would rather have the inn," she informed him coldly.

"Now I know you're a little upset with me," he said in a calming tone as two serving ladies approached. "But you are overreacting and have no right—

"You know I have every right to be angry at you!" she exclaimed angrily.

— but once you rest I'm sure you'll thank me in the morning." He turned to address the two serving women. "Lady Kathryn will be staying with us. Help her bathe and dress before sending her down to supper." He looked over at Kathryn. "Choose a dress that is more befitting of her station."

"How dare you!" Kathryn seethed as the two women attempted to draw her inside.

"Please, milady," the younger of the two maids whispered when they had no luck bringing her inside. "He'll beat us if you don't come with us."

Kathryn looked at the young woman. The young maid was hardly older than herself and looked genuinely afraid of her lord and master. Stifling a curse, Kathryn allowed herself to be dragged inside.

The two women led her through a maze of corridors and long halls until they stepped inside a large room.

"I'll see to your bath," the older woman wheezed as she hurried back out the door.

Kathryn remained standing stiffly in the center of the room as the younger maid hurried to a closet filled with gorgeous gowns.

She pulled out gown after gown. From what Kathryn could tell they were all ridiculously adorned and looked extremely heavy. With all those meters of fabric, she wouldn't be able to fight efficiently if the two women managed to stuff her into one of the dresses.

Servants began filing in and filling the marble soaking tub in the adjoining room.

"Is milady ready for her bath?" the older woman asked stiffly once the tub was full.

Kathryn narrowed her eyes at her. "I'll take the bath, but I'll bathe myself."

Both serving women looked at her, horrified expressions on their faces. 'But...but that is not how it is done."

"I have bathed myself my entire life," Kathryn informed them, "even when I reside with Princess Jasmine I bathe myself." *Except for those first few times*, she thought wistfully, remembering Arianna's gentle touch.

"But Lord Tanner—

"I will deal with Lord Tanner, now leave me!" Kathryn put the full force of a demanding noblewoman's tone behind her words.

The two women scurried away, busying themselves laying out gowns and jewelry.

Kathryn sighed as she lowered herself into the steaming water. At least she had won that particular battle, she wasn't sure how many more she was going to win. As soon as dinner was over she was coming back up here and escaping. She didn't know how she'd do it, but she was going to.

After scrubbing herself raw she stepped from the tub and dried herself. The younger maid had already lain out clean undergarments and Kathryn quickly put them on. Her thoughts momentarily flew to David and the rest of the Dragons. When she hadn't returned on Nénar, they would start to worry and would eventually break out into panic when she didn't take her shift tomorrow. It would take at least five days to walk back, or at least to travel in a way that Lord Tanner couldn't track or observe her. Perhaps she could steal a horse...but no. Lord Tanner probably had them trained to stampede if someone other than himself tried to mount...something a lot of nobles were doing nowadays. It was supposed to be an anti-thief measure, one that was going to make her escape twice as hard as it should have been.

She momentarily considered sending the Dragons some sort of message, but how would she get it to them and what would she say: *Help, I've been kidnapped?* It was hardly the type of message for an independent, self-sufficient, Guardian to send.

No. She could figure a way out of this on her own. She didn't need anyone's help. She just had to make sure she did it in a way that didn't lead Lord Tanner to suspect she was a Guardian. Despite the gravity of her situation she would never break the cardinal rule of her order—protect your identity at all costs, even at the cost of your life.

The younger serving maid held up a deep purple gown with gold trim. It made the gown she'd worn to the first jousting tournament at the Queen's birthday tournay look like a homespun rag.

"No," Kathryn said flatly.

"But it would look wonderful on you!" The girl protested.

"I don't want to look wonderful for Lord Tanner."

"Please Milady, if you won't do it for the master, than do it for us. For he'll have our necks if you don't," the serving girl pleaded.

"Oh, shut your trap!" the older woman hissed as she rushed over and began running a comb roughly through Kathryn's hair. "The Lady doesn't want to hear about our problems."

In truth, Kathryn very much did want to hear about their problems, any insight into Tanner's ruling methods would aid her escape, but a noblewoman would not so she held her tongue. Finally she nodded and allowed herself to be laced into the purple dress.

The older woman styled her hair in an elaborate style that already had her head aching from the weight and pricks of the pins.

She refused any jewelry, threating to rip it off her body and hurl it into the wall if they attempted to put any on her, and slowly made her way downstairs to the dining hall.

Chapter 34

Kathryn was escorted by one of the servants and Lord Tanner rose as she entered the dining hall.

"Much better," he commented as she stood at the far end of the table.

She glared at him, refusing to say anything.

"Come now, Lady Kathryn," he said as he motioned to a servant to hold out a chair for her. "You aren't still mad at me, are you?"

Kathryn fought down a sudden urge to strangle him. "Oh, I'm no longer mad, Lord Tanner," she replied icily. "I'm furious with you."

He chuckled. "I love a woman with spirit." Before Kathryn could respond he motioned to her, "please sit down."

The servant holding her chair looked to her with pleading eyes and for his sake she acquiesced.

"You are mad if you think you can keep me here against my will."

"And where would you go?" he laughed. "Darkness has fallen and there isn't a town or village for leagues."

"Let me assure you when I say I would rather walk all night than spend one night here with you," she returned frostily.

"Tut, tut," he tsked. "You aren't a very grateful guest."

"Quite right," she agreed as the servants brought out wine. "I'm an unwilling guest."

"I'm sure if you give me a chance you would find me quite charming," he replied with the best smile he could fashion and spoken in a tone that was so popular with the kingdom's elite.

Kathryn calculated in her mind the nuances of placing an arrow between the small gap separating his two front teeth. "I seriously doubt it," she returned.

By now the wine steward and waiting servants were observing the banter with interest as this young woman stood her ground. Their eyes followed the debate much like a pfilour exchange between two contestants in a bloudar match.

"Princess Lillian found my company to be quite entertaining."

"Obviously Princess Lillian hasn't spent much time around cads."

He laughed. "Is that what you think I am, Lady Kathryn? A cad?"

"I have no doubt of it."

"Tell me," he said, leaning forward as if waiting to hear the final chapter of a gripping suspense story. "Is this another trick Princess Jasmine taught you? To identify miscreants and evil-doers?" There was humor in his eyes, but Kathryn found no humor in any of it.

She huffed. "Realizing that you are a blackguard hardly takes any skill," she informed him. "And no, Princess Jasmine didn't teach me how to identify one—I taught myself."

"Ah," he said as he leaned back in his chair, his wineglass in hand. "A self-sufficient woman, I admire that."

"I learned to be self-sufficient when I was young, Lord Tanner. It's a habit that's hard to break."

"Yes," he mused quietly. "So I've noticed."

"You will return me in the morning." She purposefully phrased it as a demand and not a question.

"We'll see."

"You'll see?" she began furiously while standing and knocking her chair backwards to the floor with a resounding clatter that seemed to echo in the large room.

He cut her off. "Would you care to dance, Lady Kathryn?"

"What? No, I would not!" she exclaimed hotly. Every muscle in her body was taught and her fists were balled so tightly they began to lose color. "Now will you or will you not return me to the village in the morning?"

"We'll see," he reiterated. "It would hardly do to send you back to the village if the weather isn't cooperating. After all, what would the people say if their new governor sent a Lady away in the rain."

Kathryn's fury subsided slightly in the light of this new information. She frowned. "I thought Lord Merlae was the Governor of this province."

Tanner waved his hand, "He was. I was only recently assigned. Lord Merlae has serious health issues that impede his ability to govern."

Won't David be interested to hear this, Kathryn thought. *That is, if I ever get back.*

"Are you sure you wouldn't like to dance, milady?" he asked mildly. "My musicians are some of the best in the kingdom."

"I hate dancing." *Well, not really. Just with you.*

"You seemed to enjoy yourself at the Queen's ball."

"If that was your conclusion, then you can't read me very well at all. Prince Derek and the king himself noticed and commented on my lack of enthusiasm for the waltzes."

"Ah, but that is only one form of dance," he replied smoothly. "There are many others."

Kathryn was ready to wrench the life out of him and drown everyone else in the castle with the foul water from the moat, "Lord Tanner—

"I would prefer it if we could dispense with the titles," he told her as he sipped his wine. "I hate the formality they represent."

"What a pity for you," she replied sarcastically, "I shall be addressing you by your title for the remainder of my stay and you shall address me by mine."

Lord Tanner nodded to a tall and gangly servant who promptly set Kathryn's chair back in order. She turned and the servant glanced a brief look with fear in his eyes. She relented and sat down abruptly.

"You are a very demanding woman," he commented as the servants brought forth their supper.

"Merely keeping everything in its proper order," she replied angrily.

She saw rage flicker through his eyes and felt a twinge of unease before he stood abruptly. "Proper order?" he demanded angrily. "I'll show you proper order." Whirling he brought out a small dagger that had been concealed on his right arm and thrust it into the side of the unfortunate server who had been placing his master's supper on the table. The poor servant let out a mangled gasp, his eyes mirroring the disbelief in his mind. He collapsed to the floor, taking the tray of food with him. The clatter of the metal dishes on the stone floor echoed ominously in the room.

Without a glance towards the injured man, Lord Tanner snapped his fingers and two new servants appeared instantly. "Clean up the mess...and bring me a new napkin."

Horrified by what she had just seen, Kathryn leapt to her feet. "What have you done?" she cried in dismay. She watched in shock as the unfortunate server was hurriedly carried downstairs by the remainder of the servants.

"Do not concern yourself with his fate, he's a mere servant," Lord Tanner replied coldly as he retook his seat.

Kathryn tore her eyes away from the archway that the unconscious server had been taken through. "Merely a servant?" she asked letting cold fury seep into her words. "You killed an innocent man because he was merely a servant?"

Lord Tanner waved his hand at her. "Sit down, Lady Kathryn. You can rest assured I didn't kill him." He gave her a cruel smile. "The physician employed by this castle has become proficient in sewing up knife wounds. In a few days he will be back to serving."

Kathryn felt sick with horror and disgust. There was no possible way she was going to spend another minute in the presence of Lord Tanner. She looked around for any possible escape routes, only to find them all guarded by at least two fully armed knights.

"Don't try it," Lord Tanner warned casually as he took a sip of his soup.

"Don't try what?" she demanded.

"You're thinking of trying to run," he told her calmly as he dapped at the corner of his mouth with a napkin. "I wouldn't try it. I have every entrance guarded by exceptional guards who would render you unconscious before you could try to leave."

Unsure of what to do, Kathryn stood in a quandary. She desperately wanted to teach Lord Tanner a lesson or two, but couldn't do so without bringing down the wrath of his guards—it didn't matter how good a swordsman or archer she was, she couldn't take them all.

"Sit down," Lord Tanner commanded.

Slowly, she lowered herself back into her seat. "You are a tyrant," she bit out.

His cruel laugh echoed throughout the hall. "Really? And here I thought I was nothing but a local Governor doing his bit for the kingdom."

"What do you want with me?" she asked stiffly.

He looked up. "You haven't touched your supper," he said nodding towards her plate. "Eat, it will make you feel better."

"After what I just witnessed, nothing could make me feel better!" she exclaimed.

His eyes turned cold. "Eat," he commanded, "or I will be forced to do it again...and again until you do eat."

She looked at him, numbed. Not even the Blackwoods had demonstrated such cold ruthlessness. "You would attack another servant simply because your atrocities make me too sick to eat?"

He tore a piece of bread in half and buttered it. "Perhaps you haven't noticed, Lady Kathryn. I like to have my way."

Slowly she picked up her fork and began to pick at the roasted quail on her plate. She had no appetite but did not wish a replay of his earlier wrath.

He watched her for a few seconds before nodding, "good," and turning back to his own meal.

They ate in silence for the remainder of the meal. Lord Tanner ate heartily, often calling for more wine. Kathryn ate only enough to appease him, barely touching her own drink.

Finally the dishes had been cleared and the servants were getting ready to bring out dessert. Lord Tanner called for another glass of wine and settled back in his chair. "It is a pity," he said gazing at her. "That you did not wear any jewelry with that gown."

Kathryn refused to speak to him, choosing to take a sip from her wine goblet. She had never learned to like the taste of wine and tonight was no exception to her preference. Whatever was being served had a bitter taste that held no appeal whatsoever.

"Still angry at me?"

Kathryn's patience wore thin. "What do you think, Lord Tanner?" she exclaimed angrily, "You kidnap me, hold me here against my will, decide what I will wear, stab servants in my presence, and then pretend nothing's wrong! What possible reason could I have to be angry with you?"

"So," he said slowly, swirling his wine. "You do not approve of my actions towards my servants."

"Your actions are inhumane and deplorable. No servant should ever be treated the way you treat yours."

The servants returned with their dessert, a sweet cake with a berry filling. They quickly cut the cake, served it, and hurried out of the room for fear of being the next to have a knife shoved into their sides.

"I find it interesting," Lord Tanner continued. "That you would have such feelings for servants."

"It helps that I was a slave until I was ten," she replied sarcastically, surprising herself with the ease that declaration was made.

He paused mid-sip. "Really?" he asked in amazement. "I did not know that."

"Not many people do." Kathryn was beginning to feel unwell. Her stomach was dancing and her head hurt.

"Tell me Lady Kathryn," he said slowly. "What hand contained the concealed dagger?"

She frowned at him. "Your right hand. But what does that have to do with anything?" she asked.

"Perhaps nothing, perhaps everything."

"Do you enjoy speaking in riddles?"

"I find it keeps me alert."

"Well, I find it extremely vexing."

"I have it on good authority that women enjoy being vexed," he replied taking a bite of his dessert.

"Not this woman," she returned coldly.

"Do you enjoy being a Guardian?"

Kathryn jerked. *There's no possible way he could know!* "What?"

He downed the rest of his wine. "You correctly identified which arm the concealed weapon came from and it wasn't a guess. No other person, except a Guardian, has ever correctly identified the arm."

"I have very good eyes," she assured him. "And why would you suppose that only someone with a Guardian's skill could identify which arm you pulled your knife? Any trained knight in the kingdom could identify which hand it was. It seems a rather puerile standard to me. Besides, Guardians guard their identities with their lives. How would you know that the man who identified the arm was a Guardian?"

"There are some who, let's just say, are less discreet about what they say in public than others. And while you are correct that any trained knight in the kingdom could determine which hand I used, *you* are not a knight."

Kathryn was struggling to keep her panic from showing. If Lord Tanner did indeed discover for certain that she was a Guardian—she didn't want to think about the consequences. "I was raised in a situation where my observation skills determined whether or not I was punished," she told him icily. "After I became the ward of Princess Jasmine she had the Royal Guard instruct me in basic swordplay and archery so that I would never suffer as a slave again. And if I was a Guardian, trust me when I say this, you would not be sitting so smugly in your chair right now."

He stood and shrugged, "Perhaps what you say is true, but it could also be true that you know that if your identity is discovered you will be forced to retire and go into hiding."

"And how would you have such firsthand information about Guardian procedure?" she asked hotly. "The Guardians guard their secrets jealously. How would you come across such information?" Her head was really beginning to pound now and her vision was turning the room into a kaleidoscope of colors.

He laughed at her. "Is that the question of a curious woman or a frantic Guardian? A hard question to ask. A harder one to answer."

The world suddenly spun and Kathryn had to grip her chair. What on earth was wrong with her? She looked up and saw the smug smile on his face.

The wine! The extra bitter taste had not simply been the flavor of the wine but a drug!

"I see you've figured it out," he said, ringing the bell for the servants. "Another point in favor of your being a Guardian."

"I. Am. Not. A. Guardian," she said through clenched teeth, trying to stop her vision from going completely black.

"Perhaps not, but hear this," he said as he stood and walked over to her end of the table. He leaned close to her with his lips close to her ear and grasped her elbow, "If you aren't in that room tomorrow morning," he warned, pointing with his free hand toward the staircase, "I will announce

335

that you are a Guardian to every nobleman and woman I meet. In the end it won't matter whether or not you are a Guardian because they'll put you into protective custody and you can forget about ever showing your face again."

The two serving maids arrived. "Help Lady Kathryn back to her room," he commanded. "She's fallen ill and needs to rest."

I should have shoved my dagger into his ribs the minute I laid eyes on him in the village, she thought miserably.

As the two women helped her to her room, Kathryn considered her options. She couldn't escape now. Being a Guardian was all she had. Nothing could jeopardize it. But she couldn't stay here forever either.

The two women tucked her into bed and closed the heavy drapes, turning the room into an unfamiliar cave with threatening shadows.

She had no choice. She had to get a message to the rest of the Dragons. How she was going to do it she had no idea. But she didn't have a choice.

Lord Tanner had brought her here for a reason and she had a feeling that the reason was going to be an unpleasant one. As she drifted off into oblivion her thoughts briefly returned to Elyon. He had told her that her next test was coming and that it would be difficult. She had a feeling she had entered it; after all, there was no worse feeling to her than being helpless. And she was helpless—and would remain so until she was rescued, by someone other than herself.

"Elyon," she whispered as the darkness enveloped her mind. "If you're truly here, then please help me."

Chapter 35

The delicious smell and sound of sizzling slabs of pork, cooking eggs, and warm biscuits roused David from a deep sleep. Groggily he sat up and squinted out the window. Sunlight was streaming in, painting odd shaped squares and rectangles on his floor and walls. Quickly he threw back the blankets, washed, and hurried to get dressed.

He entered the warmth of the kitchen moments later, still shaking the water out of his hair. Why couldn't he have the power to heat the water that stood in the washbasin? Every morning it felt like melted ice, he was beginning to wonder if Kathryn froze the water during the night just to annoy him in the morning. Cass was the only one in the kitchen and she was pulling out fresh biscuits.

"Morning, Cass." He took a seat on the counter and poured himself a glass of water. "Breakfast smells good."

"You're up early," the cook commented as she tossed a hot biscuit in his direction.

David caught it with ease. "Ouch!" he exclaimed as he dropped the biscuit to the counter, "I think I'll wait a minute to eat it."

Cass giggled and continued to rescue the warm biscuits from the hot oven. They sat in silence for a few minutes, David enjoying the quiet of the early morning, Cass concentrating on keeping the rest of breakfast from burning.

"Shall I wake the others?" David asked once Cass had placed the food on the table.

"If they want a hot breakfast you probably should," Cass called over her shoulder as she went to clean the flour out of her shirt.

Assuming that those still remaining probably would want a hot breakfast, David quickly roused the others. Lindsey groused a bit over being woken up so early but the news of a hot breakfast quickly endeared her to the idea.

David didn't bother knocking on Kathryn's door. It was a rare morning for anyone to rise before Kathryn. He hadn't seen her yet, but she was probably out with Destiny enjoying the early morning quiet. No doubt she would be waiting downstairs when he returned.

"Morning, David," Amy called softly as she exited her room. "What's for breakfast?"

"Bacon, eggs, and biscuits."

"Don't ever tell Matt," she whispered as she approached. "But I prefer Cass's biscuits to his."

David grinned and whispered back, "My lips are sealed." Matt was an excellent cook but when it came to pastries or bread-like substances he tended to burn them.

"Have you seen Kathryn this morning?" Amy asked as she entered the kitchen.

"Not yet." Out of the corner of his eye he glimpsed Amy biting her lip and glancing back upstairs, he stopped and faced her, "Is something wrong?" It was rare to see someone worried about their self-sufficient lieutenant.

Amy hesitated. "It's just that...well...I didn't see her come home last night and I usually hear Destiny's let-me-outside call in the morning."

"And you didn't hear it this morning?"

She shook her head. "I haven't heard anything this morning."

David shrugged. "Well, she has been spending all her time at the village orphanage. She probably didn't stay for breakfast this morning and instead went straight there."

Amy cocked her head as she considered his words. "You're probably right. I'm overreacting, there's nothing to worry about."

Satisfied that Amy was no longer ready to organize a search party to look for her missing friend, David nodded and returned to the kitchen where he thoroughly enjoyed Cass's airy biscuits, flavorful eggs, and the crispy strips from the boar that Tyler slew the week before. After breakfast he transitioned to the barn where he and Tyler spent the morning cleaning out the horses stables and pitching hay.

"A far cry from a lavish suite in the palace isn't it?" Tyler asked as they took a brief break around midday.

David chuckled. "I prefer the hard work to lounging around all day in a palace, I think I'd go crazy."

Daniel, who had been honing his archery skills across the river crossed the bridge and ambled over to join them. "What was Amy anxious about this morning?" He asked taking a seat on one of the hay bales.

David shrugged. "She was worried because Kathryn wasn't around this morning. She isn't even sure if she came home last night."

Tyler grunted. "You know, for someone as talented as Kathryn is, she doesn't see things that are right in front of her."

"She knows," Daniel said. "She just doesn't know what to do with it."

"Where is Amy now?" Tyler asked.

"I'm not sure, probably on her way to the village to make sure Kathryn's at the orphanage," David guessed.

Daniel laughed. "Kathryn could take on the palace guards blindfolded and Amy's worried because she didn't come home last night?"

David shrugged. "Friendship and family aren't always rational, Daniel."

Neither Tyler or Daniel could refute him. After a few more minutes David declared the rest break over and returned to pitching hay and tending to the barn while Tyler and Daniel set out to cut and split firewood.

℘·℃℞

As soon as she reached the edge of the forest, Amy coaxed her horse and broke into a run and she didn't stop running until she reached the front of the house. She dismounted, raced up the steps to the house and burst through the door. "Where's David?" She demanded to a very startled Cass and Elizabeth who were in the midst of a discussion.

"Uh," Elizabeth began. "He's with Tyler. They were cutting up some logs they floated down the river." Reaching out she touched Amy's arm before she made it out the door. "No wait, I think he's in the barn. Why?"

338

Amy didn't stop to answer, racing out of the house before Elizabeth had even finished asking the question.

"David!" She hollered as soon as she was inside the barn. "David!"

Both David and Daniel came running from the back.

"What is it?" David asked hurriedly, "What's going on?"

Panting, Amy sat down hard on a bale of hay. Daniel hurried off to get her some water, "I...just came...from the...village," she gasped between lungfuls of air.

"Easy," David urged, pressing her head lower to keep her from passing out. "Get your wind back and then tell me what's wrong."

Daniel returned with a large skin of water, which Amy downed.

"Okay," David said, sitting down on an opposite bale of hay from hers. "What's wrong? What happened in the village?"

"I went to the village to find Kathryn," Amy began, "When you suggested the orphanage I knew that was the first place to look—only she wasn't there."

"Maybe she hadn't planned on going today?" Daniel suggested.

Amy shook her head. "I asked the matron and she said that Kathryn had planned on returning today, but never showed."

David looked at Daniel.

"I've never known Kathryn to go back on her word," the younger boy told him.

Amy continued. "I also asked the matron when Kathryn had left the night before—sometime just before nightfall." She looked at David, worry etching her features. "I think something's happened to her," she said quickly. "I don't think she came home last night."

"Amy," David said calmly. "Kathryn can take care of herself—

"Something she tells us every day," Daniel muttered.

David ignored him. "I'm sure she's fine. Maybe she spent the night in the village so she wouldn't have to walk as far to see the children and then overslept."

"It's past noon," Amy said shaking her head. "There's no way Kathryn would have waited this long to visit the children."

"Kathryn knows that she has a shift to lead tomorrow," David replied calmly. "You know as well as I do that she doesn't shirk responsibility."

Amy still didn't look convinced. "Could you look for her please?"

David failed to hide his surprise. "Look for her?"

"With the wind. Surely it could tell you if she's nearby."

Seeing that Amy wasn't going to leave him alone until he did something, anything, he agreed to do a quick search of the surrounding woods and village.

Somewhat placated, Amy returned to the house, leaving the boys alone in the barn. Daniel shifted uncomfortably a couple times before speaking. "She's really worried David."

"I would never have guessed," he replied dryly.

"More than usual," Daniel continued. "I'm getting the sense that this isn't normal behavior for Kathryn."

"Kathryn likes to hide," David replied shortly. "I'm certain that that's what she's doing now."

"And yet in the back of your mind you can't ignore the fact that Amy's panicking," his friend said.

"Reading my mind, Daniel?"

Daniel shrugged. "Maybe a little."

Shaking his head, David left the barn and headed for Kathryn's waterfall. He was immensely surprised to find it utterly deserted. *Well*, he reasoned, *perhaps Kathryn feels that she can't come here anymore because I followed her here two months ago.* Sighing in disappointment that this wasn't going to be as easy as he'd expected, he sent a handful of breezes out to search the surrounding countryside for his vexing lieutenant.

ℰ·ℭ

Pound. Pound. Pound.

David groaned and rolled over. Whoever was knocking on his door at such an absurd radian could wait until it was light out.

Pound. Pound. Pound.

Pound. Pound. Pound.

Resigning himself to the knowledge that whoever was beating on his door wasn't going to go away, David hauled himself out of his warm bed and forced himself to cross to the door and open it.

Matt, Rachel, and Jenna were standing in the hallway. "We have a problem," Matt said seriously.

ℰ·ℭ

Kathryn woke slowly. Her head felt like it weighed forty-five kilograms, no doubt the lasting effects of the drug Lord Tanner had used last night.

"Good morning, Milady."

Kathryn rolled onto her side and forced her eyes open. It was the younger maid. She was across the room opening the heavy drapes, the bright sunlight hurt Kathryn's eyes and she turned her face away saying, "It is hardly a good morning."

The young woman came over to the bed. "Is Milady still feeling ill? Did you not sleep well?"

Kathryn turned to face her and glared. "I think you know how well I slept. Tell me, does Lord Tanner often drug his guests?"

The serving girl's face reddened as she sought an answer.

"Oh, never mind," Kathryn growled as she threw the heavy blankets back and sat up. She turned and faced the nervous young woman before her. "What's your name?"

"My name Milady?"

Kathryn rolled her eyes and snapped, "Yes, your name. How else am I supposed to address you?"

"Lea, Milady."

Pushing herself off the bed, Kathryn strolled to one of the great windows. "Well, Lea. What am I going to do?"

"Do, Milady?"

"Enough with the milady," Kathryn barked. Her patience was running as thin as a court lady's silk scarf. "I hate that form of address."

Lea looked positively lost. "Then how should I address you?"

"I have a name as well, use it."

340

"But the master will stick his knife into me if he hears me addressing you by just your name!" The poor serving girl exclaimed.

Kathryn sighed heavily, "Fine, you can address me as Lady Kathryn, but nothing else." She felt her patience run even thinner as she remembered what day it was. Ambar. Which meant that by now her whole family would know something was wrong and she was positive that no one would think to look for her here—which meant that somehow she'd have to find a way to tell them.

Movement outside her window caught her attention. Perfect. Slowly, so as not to arouse suspicion she turned to Lea. "Fetch me some cold water from the kitchens," she ordered irritably moving away from the window. "My head is killing me."

If Lea suspected anything she didn't comment as she quickly curtsied and left the room. As soon as she was gone, Kathryn raced back to the window and opened it. She let out a quick whistle, hoping it wouldn't draw the attention of the guards below.

Destiny, who had perched on the rooflines all night long, flew to her immediately. As glad as she was to see her friend, Kathryn didn't waste time. Quickly she rushed to the writing table and tore a scrap of parchment from a scroll.

Dipping the quill in the ink, she paused. What would she write? She couldn't risk blatantly stating the truth in case Lord Tanner's men somehow managed to shoot Destiny down. She wracked her brains, willing herself to come up with a message before Lea returned.

Suddenly the image of a purple stag's head painted on a shield flickered before her eyes. It would have to do. All the boys had fought against that shield at one time or another during the tournaments. Quickly she penned the phrase and then rolled up the small message.

Crossing back to the window she gave Destiny the note, which the bird held tightly in her beak and then gave her one command. "Fly to David."

The magnificent bird took off just as the bedroom door swung open and Lord Tanner himself strode in.

"What are you doing?" he demanded hurrying over. Spotting the fleeing eagle he turned to face Kathryn, delivering a sound slap to her face as he did. "Playing with animals are we? That's another talent used by the Guardians."

Face burning, she turned to face him, struggling to contain her irritation and the urge to throw him out the window. "I hardly think that admiring our kingdom's emblem constitutes playing with them. That magnificent creature was perched on your rooflines when I woke this morning."

"What were you doing leaning out the window, looking like you had just shooed it away."

"I did just shoo it away," she informed him tartly. She narrowed her eyes at him. "I saw those trophies in your halls. There was no way I was about to let you or your men kill such a beautiful bird."

He looked at her for a long time and Kathryn refused to back down from his gaze. Finally he shrugged. "It is no matter," he said indifferently. "My castle is too well guarded for even the Guardians to stage a rescue."

"Then what do you plan to do with me?"

"You will remain here until I am certain that you are not a Guardian, and then we'll discuss it."

"And just how do you intend to determine whether or not I am a Guardian?" she demanded hotly.

He turned his cool gaze toward her, "I know that those with gifts, as the Guardians call them, cannot go forty-eight radians without using them or they'll severely injure or kill themselves. We'll just wait until two days have passed and go from there."

"You seriously believe that Princess Jasmine will wait that long to send a rescue?" Kathryn asked, trying to bluff her way through the situation. She'd never heard of such a thing, although come to think of it the rest of the Dragons did seem to use their powers a lot...even when it wasn't needed. If that was Lord Tanner's test then she would pass it easily. She went *years* without using her gifts. Two days would be a snap.

Lord Tanner shrugged. "If she does there's no way anyone can reach here in time, and as I've said before, my castle is well guarded. Will you join me for breakfast?"

"I'm not hungry," she replied stiffly.

He looked at her coldly and for a long moment, she thought he was going to order her to join him, but he shrugged again, said, "As you wish," and walked out of the room.

Ha, she thought bitterly, *as you wish, my foot.* She moved back to the window, Destiny was nothing but a small blot against the blue sky. *I thank the stars that David was wise enough to suggest such a signal,* she thought as she watched the small dot grow smaller and smaller, *and that I finally relented to his urging.* It would take several radians for Destiny to reach the meadow and even then she didn't know how long it would take for the Dragon's to decipher her message. She would have to be patient, and she hated being patient. Briefly her thoughts returned to Elyon and his words, "I fear it will not be an easy test for you, but you must have faith."

If this is what you mean, Elyon, she thought glumly, *then you were right, this will not be easy for me.*

ℬ·ℭ

David forced himself to focus on the wind and all of the voices within. Ever since Matt and the girls had woken him up before daybreak to inform him that Kathryn was still missing, he'd been using his gift to try and locate her. It was proving both difficult and frustrating. He'd even stationed himself in the glade where the waterfall she frequented was located, hoping that her familiarity with the location would help him discern her from the whirlwind that was carried to him. The control that he had to utilize to accomplish this was a feat he'd never attempted before, not even at the school. Not only was he listening to the air around him as new breezes entered the glade, but he was exerting his control far beyond his location. Winds as far away as his aunt Jasmine's palace were under his, albeit weak, control. Now it was nearly dusk and he was as empty handed now as he had been that morning.

"Any luck?"

342

David opened his eyes to find Luke crouched next to him. Releasing his grip on his gift he let himself recover from the strain. He shook his head. "Absolutely nothing."

"Amy will be thrilled to hear that," his friend said. "David, what is going on here?"

"I have no idea. Something's up, I just can't figure out what it is."

Luke pursed his lips. "You don't think that there's even a small chance that this is all a false alarm?"

"Kathryn wouldn't forget about her shift and if she's not here I can only assume that she's injured so badly that she isn't mobile or that she's being prevented from returning."

"And what about the possibility that facing the Blackwoods completely unhinged her and now she's looking to live out a life of solitude?"

David hesitated. "I considered it," he admitted finally. "But it just doesn't seem to fit the situation. Maybe while she was being hounded by Natalie...but now? She hasn't exactly been the warmest person to live with, but she never once shirked her responsibilities. It just doesn't fit."

"I had to ask."

"I know."

Luke unsheathed one of his daggers and started fidgeting with it. "So what do we do now?"

David sighed heavily. "That is the question. We'll have to wait until the others get back from the villages and farms but I'm going to bet that they haven't had any more luck that I've had."

Mounting their horses, they left the glade and returned to the house. Leia was sitting in the middle of the training field when they arrived, various forest creatures surrounding her.

"Any word?" Luke called as they approached. The small brunette stood and the multitude of animals retreated in various directions to the forest. She shook her head. "If Kathryn's in the forest, the animals have no memories of her."

"The wind can't find her either," David told her. "It's like she's completely disappeared."

The sound of a door slamming captured their attentions and they watched as Matt raced out of the house and joined them. "Nothing," Matt panted as he joined them. "I don't think she's in the forest."

"We've already reached that conclusion," Luke said sourly. "How about giving us some good news." Despite his question about Kathryn willingly leaving them, Luke was just as worried over her disappearance as the rest of his family.

"Hey, it's not my fault!" Matt protested.

"Enough," David interceded. "We're all frustrated. Taking it out on each other won't help us find Kathryn."

"Has Jenna been able to get the plants to commune with her?" Leia asked quickly.

"She's working on it." Matt grimaced, "I'm not sure that it's going so well, though."

"We knew it was a long shot," David said tiredly. "None of us have a primary gift of plant influence."

"If she's not in the forest, then she has to be somewhere in town, right?" Luke asked.

David sighed. "Luke, I'm not even sure she's in Rima anymore."

Leia looked dumbfounded. "If she's not in Rima then how are we going to find her? She can't have gotten that far!"

Matt shook his head. He'd already made the calculations in his head. "She went missing on Lumbar and there was no sign of her on Nénar. Now today's Ambar. That's a good two days that could easily have her in Asyea or Heltic if she was moving at a fast and steady pace on a horse."

"Right now we have to hope that someone in the village saw something," David said. "It's our only lead to her disappearance."

The sound of horse's hooves drew David's attention. "The others are back." Quickly he moved around the house to meet the returning search party. Jenna stood on the front porch and from the look on her face David knew that her search had come up empty as well.

He jogged over to where Amy and Tyler, leading the rest of the family, were just entering the glade. "Tell me you found something."

Amy could barely meet his gaze, shaking her head sadly. Tyler dismounted. "Nothing. It's like the whole kingdom went blind when...whatever it was happened."

"Did the orphanage matron confirm that Kathryn was at the orphanage on Lumbar?"

"Yes. And according to her, Kathryn had planned to return the next day. She seemed genuinely surprised that Kathryn hadn't. At least," Tyler jerked a thumb toward Daniel who was dismounting, "according to our resident mind reader she was. I still say she could have been faking."

"It takes years of intense practice to disguise your thoughts," Daniel grumbled from behind him. "It takes even longer to manipulate your feelings to the point that they feel real when someone like me is looking at them."

"So you don't think that she was faking."

Daniel shook his head. "She was honest with us. However the tricky part of mind reading isn't reading someone's mind, it's asking the right questions. As long as we don't ask questions that could cause any doubt in her mind, I won't pick up on it."

David turned to Lindsey. "How about you? Light is everywhere, surely you found some trace of her."

She shrugged helplessly. "Light is...unpredictable at best. With my gift I can really only influence its intensity. I've never pulled an image out of light."

"I was afraid that would be the case."

"And since I can't find her," Luke added. "She's not on the ground. Or in it," he added encouragingly to Amy.

"Could this be any more frustrating?" Natalie exclaimed heatedly. "We need to do something, but without a clue there's nothing we can do!"

"What about you, Cass? Kathryn's drawn to water. Surely you can pick up something from it?"

Cass was shaking her head before David finished. "It's not my dominate gift...and it's not one I've worked hard to cultivate." She looked apologetically at Amy. "It was hard enough to learn to levitate and move things. I didn't want to try to learn to influence water too."

"It's alright," David replied. "We've all done everything we can to try and find her using our gifts. It looks like we're going to have to do this the old fashioned way."

"We have been!" Rachel protested. "And we've gotten nowhere."

"So you want to just give up?" David asked calmly.

"I didn't say that!" She replied, frustration lacing her words. "I just don't know what else we can do."

"We do what we have been doing," David replied firmly. "Eventually we'll ask the right question or someone will remember something." He looked at the disheartened faces around him and knew that they all needed a break. "In the meantime, I need Cass and Matt in the kitchen making supper."

"Supper!" Amy cried. "How can you think about food during a time like this?"

"Amy, we're all tired and we can't help Kathryn if we can't think straight," he said, trying to reason with her. "We need a break before we go back out again."

For a moment it looked like she wanted to argue with him. Eventually however, her shoulders sagged and she reluctantly nodded. "I know."

"Come on," he encouraged, holding up a hand to help her dismount. "We'll find her, Amy," he promised once she was on the ground. "No one messes with our family and gets away with it."

Cass and Matt retreated inside to make a late supper and David ordered the rest of his family to do something that would help their minds relax. "I don't care what it is," he said as the moved into the house. "So long as you aren't directly thinking about Kathryn's disappearance."

Supper was a relatively simple affair. Matt and Cass used some leftover noodles to make a venison stew chock full of verisce, artise, schien, and cermia. It was delicious and had the situation been different it would have inspired friendly banter and creative discussions at the table. As it was, there was very little talk throughout the meal.

$\wp \cdot \wp$

Once the soup bowls had been cleared, Cass brought out a surprise dessert. "Pudding!" Elizabeth exclaimed with delight. The response from the others was less than enthusiastic as everyone just continued staring at either their plates or some spot on the table.

"I thought we needed a treat," Cass explained meekly.

As David dug his spoon into the delicious delicacy a black and white blur suddenly sped through the window, landed painfully on his shoulder and let out a loud call right into his eardrums that startled him off his chair. "What in the kingdom?" he exclaimed, rubbing the ear that had been blasted.

"It's Destiny!" Amy exclaimed hurrying over.

David felt a cold feeling of dread knot in his stomach. The signal he had asked Kathryn to teach Destiny if she was ever in trouble, the one she had scorned, had just played out.

Chapter 36

David looked warily at Destiny and rubbed his ear, "this is not good, Kathryn is in serious trouble."

Amy looked at him darkly. "Did Destiny squawking in your ear have anything to do with clarifying that for you?"

Continuing to rub his ear, David replied, "Months ago I asked Kathryn to train Destiny to fly to me in case she ever found herself in a situation she couldn't control," he stared at the bird who fidgeted nervously on the back of his chair. "When I mentioned it she scorned the idea. I didn't think she would do it."

"Apparently she did," Cassandra said slowly.

"And if it took Destiny this long to get to us, I can only imagine where Kathryn is now," Leia said slowly.

David held up his hand, shaking his head. "We don't know for certain where Destiny started from. For all we know, she might have just started flying this afternoon."

"Look!" Amy cried pointing to the floor where a small scrap of parchment lay partially under David's chair. "I bet Destiny dropped that when she screeched in your ear."

"Thanks for the reminder," David muttered as he bent down and retrieved the paper. He glanced at the words penned on the parchment, and frowned. *Kathryn now is not the time to be cryptic!*

"What does it say?" Cassandra asked.

David motioned Amy near him. "I want to make sure that this note is really from Kathryn first. Does this look like her handwriting to you?"

Amy studied the note for a minute. "Yes. That's her handwriting."

"Well what does it say?" Luke demanded.

"The lavender deer is enslaved to his new province."

"What kind of a message is that?" Natalie cried.

"The kind she sends in case the messenger got shot down," Tyler said quietly.

David considered Tyler's words and nodded. "I think you're right, whatever she wrote is a clue but not an obvious one in case it made it back into the hands of whoever, or whatever, has her."

"What makes you so sure someone has her?" Elizabeth asked. "A deer is an animal."

"But why in the kingdom is it lavender?" Cass asked.

"There's no such thing as a lavender deer," Elizabeth said confused, "So why would she say that?"

"What about the rest of her note?" Amy asked. "The part about being enslaved?"

David read that part again."...enslaved to his province?"

Daniel spoke up. "If someone's enslaved to something it usually means it's his duty. Could Kathryn mean someone who's nobility and trusted with high levels of responsibility?"

"...and a governor rules a province," David muttered. He turned to Daniel, "I think you might be right. But Lord Merlae is presently at the King's Palace, so it couldn't be him."

"But notice the word new in front of province," Amy pointed out. "I think she's saying it isn't Merlae but someone who is a governor."

"So she's not even in Rima anymore," Tyler shook his head. "I have to hand it to her, when she gets into trouble, she really gets into trouble."

"Tyler that isn't helping!" Amy snapped.

"I've got it," David exclaimed, interrupting them. "The lavender deer, it's not an animal at all. It's a crest."

Tyler nodded, "Now that makes sense. She sent the crest instead of the name."

"But whose crest is it?" Lindsey asked.

The team was silent for a moment each thinking hard. Suddenly Daniel spoke up, "At the tournament Lord Tanner's shield had the head of a purple stag painted on it."

"He's right," Tyler agreed. "Lord Tanner's crest was a purple stag. Lavender deer, purple stag, it's the same idea but different words."

"But what's he doing out here?" Amy asked. "Doesn't he own a manor in Echel Province over in Heltic?"

"Once we find Kathryn, I'm sure we'll learn the answer to that question," David said moving towards the door. "For now we need to head into town and get information. Only this time, instead of asking about Kathryn we're going to ask about Lord Tanner."

"Are we going as Guardians or villagers?" Tyler asked.

David made his decision in an instant. "We're going to do it the same way we did it with Duke Sebastian. Lord Tanner is reckless and cold and we have no idea what kind of messenger system he has. If he learns that Guardians are on the move, he may just kill Kathryn before we discover where he's holding her."

Amy paled at his words. He wished there were some words of comfort he could give her, but if Kathryn was in enough trouble that she was calling for help...there weren't any.

80·03

As the evening dragged on, David began to wonder if they'd interpreted Kathryn's message correctly. None of the villagers had heard of a Lord Tanner, nor had there been any visiting knights recently.

The orphanage matron mentioned hearing Kathryn speaking to someone at the edge of the village but had been too busy with the children to step outside and look.

He had just left the orphanage when he heard a small voice call, "wait!"

Turning, he caught sight of little Dawn hurrying after him, a small doll in her arms. "Can I help you, Dawn?" he asked, tramping down the urgency he felt telling him to keep going.

I saw Miss Caterina. With big men and - and dey were mean to her," the little girl said quietly.

Instantly David dropped to his knees to look at the little girl. "What did you see?" he asked quickly.

Dawn pointed to the end of the street. "Miss Caterina had just left to go home when dis many," she held up her hand to indicate five, "big horses rode up. One of the men called Miss Caterina Lady Kathryn," she turned to look at David, "Is Miss Caterina a Lady?"

"When she wants to be," David replied. "What else happened?"

"She was surprised-to see dem—she call one of de men," the little girl frowned in concentration, "...Lord Tan..Tanter. Dey quarrel. I don tink Miss Caterina was appy to see em. Affer a little while e..e grabbed er arm and..and e trew er up on is orse. E mounted behind er and dey rode off." The little girl sniffed and wiped her eyes. "Will she be kay?"

"She will be now that you've told me this," he assured her. "Which way did they ride?"

Dawn bit her lip pointed at the road that left the village. "Straight I tink. It was really dark by dat time. Lord Tanter say someting about being a gov..gov.." she searched for the right word, "govenernor I tink."

David reached out and pulled the little girl into a hug. "Thank you, Dawn. You've been a big help."

"When you find er, will you tell er dat Starla misses er?"

"Of course."

The little girl ran back to the orphanage and David hurried to find the rest of the Dragons. "A little girl confirmed that it was Lord Tanner who kidnapped Kathryn," he told them quietly. "She also pointed out the general direction they fled in."

"What are we waiting for?" Amy demanded. "Let's go."

"For once, I agree with Amy," Tyler said. "We need to hurry. If Lord Tanner is as cold as you say he is, we need to move quickly."

David nodded. "Apparently Lord Tanner told Kathryn that he was staying at the Governor's castle."

"Lord Merlae didn't mention any visiting Lords or caretakers in his letter, to the Gryffons," Cassandra said slowly, referring to the Guardian family closest to the Governor's castle in Rima.

When a governor or noble left his castle for an extended period of time, he sent a letter to the Guardian council who would forward the letter to the family closest to the fortress so that they could keep an eye on it. Once the closest family had seen the letter, it was distributed to the rest of the Guardians in the region. The letter often detailed if the Governor was expecting guests who might arrive before he returned or if he had engaged some other Lord or Lady as a caretaker.

The Dragons were quiet for a time, finally Elizabeth asked, "Could Lord Tanner be planning a coup of some kind?"

"It's beginning to look that way," Daniel replied. "Why else would he take over the castle?"

"We don't know for sure that he did take over the castle, Daniel," Lindsey argued. "We just know he's staying there."

"We're wasting time," Tyler inserted gruffly. "We can ask Lord Tanner these questions after we rescue Kathryn."

"I agree," David said quickly. "But we need to clearly think this through before we break into the castle. It's a fortress."

"And this time, Kathryn's not here to pave the way," Amy pointed out.

Nodding slowly, David said. "I know, which is why we're going to try for the night after tomorrow."

"That late?" Cass cried, "I thought you said we needed to move quickly!"

"We do," Daniel assured her. "But David's right. This is going to be a tricky mission and it takes at least a day and a half, maybe two hard day's ride to get there. If we're going to be riding that fast, our horses will be exhausted and there's a good chance that we will be as well so an assault on David's timeline isn't even a guarantee, more like a best case scenario."

Amy bit her lip and nodded. "Daniel's right. We can't rush this. Not if we want to be assured of success."

"And while we won't be attacking for a few days," David said quickly. "We won't be idle. I want us to spend as much time in the area as possible around the castle so that we can do some reconnaissance."

"Could we send a message to the Gryffons and ask them for assistance?" Lindsey suggested.

Amy, Daniel, and Cass quickly voiced their support at the idea, but David shook his head. "The Gryffons are several days ride to the south on a mission for the Council," he informed the rest of his team. "And the Sphinx's are in the process of ridding the western edge of an occult group. We're on our own."

His grim declaration silenced any other suggestions that may have been offered up.

℘·℘

While the Dragons prepared to leave David asked Luke what he remembered about the governor's castle.

"It's a fortress," Luke replied.

"We know. Anything else you can remember?"

Luke thought a moment. "There are some cliffs behind the castle where we might be able to regroup before an attack, but I'm going to guess they're patrolled since the rest of the land surrounding the castle is pretty flat."

"If I remember correctly there are some hills just past the castle."

Luke nodded. "Yes, about two or three kilometers past it, but what has that got to do with anything."

David looked at his friend, "They just may be of some use to us." He turned to the rest of the group. "We're leaving in the morning and I hope to reach the governor's castle by noon the next day. Hopefully we'll be rested enough to attack that night. If not we'll try for the next."

The other Dragons reluctantly moved to their rooms to try and sleep. David knew that he should probably get some sleep as well, but he was too disturbed to be able to rest.

The next morning he decided that he, Luke, Amy, and Jenna would travel on horseback in the open. The rest of the Dragons would stick to the trees where they would have less chance of being spotted. That night they would meet up to camp and go over and revise the plan if necessary.

"Luke, Amy, Jenna, and I will ride beyond the castle until we pass the hills three kilometers beyond. We'll leave our horses and use the cliffs for cover as we approach the castle," David explained, pointing to the map spread out before him as he pointed out specific landmarks. "The rest of you will use the forest, exit beyond the hills and leave your horses with ours. We'll meet up here," he placed his finger next to a small stream indicated on the map, "and wait for darkness."

The ride to the castle was long and painful. Glancing over, David noted that Amy looked like she was facing an army alone, which is probably how he'd feel if it had been Luke in trouble and not Kathryn. He wished he could think of something comforting to say, but all he could think about was that he should have listened to Amy. She knew Kathryn the best and if something smelled off to her than he should have paid more attention, instead he had let Kathryn convince him that she was invincible...he would never make that same mistake again.

They reached a boggy marsh late that evening and pitched camp. Destiny alighted on the top of a dead crabus tree and made short work of a small ferret-like animal. Content that they were alone, David sent Luke to guide the rest of the Dragons to the campsite.

"Matt, can you please do something about these bugs that are intent on drinking my blood!" Natalie complained after the tents had been set up, slapping at the bugs that attempted to land on her body.

"It's that scent you're wearing. It's a bug magnet. I really don't understand why you bother, as soon as you put on your armor the cirin will neutralize it anyway"

"I like to smell pretty," she replied with as much dignity as she could muster.

"Complain to David," the cook grunted. "A steady wind works better than me trying to control all ten thousand of them."

"David..."

Her leader, engaged in a discussion on tactics with Luke and Amy didn't hear her.

Natalie focused on a spot that was in the center of their little circle. A small flame burst into existence.

Quickly David stamped it out. "Natalie, I told you no fire!"

"I'll stop playing with fire as soon as you do something to get rid of these infernal bugs!" She returned hotly. "They're after my blood and nothing's dissuading them, especially since you said we can't put on our armor yet."

He sighed and called a stiff breeze. "Happy now?"

"Very."

80·03

Four days without food and very little water were taking their toll on Kathryn. There was no way she could attempt an escape on her own now. She had avoided eating, drinking the bare minimum to prevent Lord Tanner from drugging her again, but now she felt just as weak as she had when she'd been under the influence of the drug.

So far Lord Tanner had visited her only during meal times, each time asking her to join him. She kept refusing him, although she had a feeling that if she kept refusing for much longer he'd order her force fed to keep her from starving herself to death.

To top it all off, she kept having nightmares that jolted her awake in the middle of the night covered in sweat. The events varied but the general storyline stayed true in each dream. Somehow the Dragons managed to decode her message and arrived to try and breach the castle. Each time they failed and died in the attempt. The dreams scared her far worse than Lord Tanner ever could. The revelation startled her and she realized that, while she resented many of the things the Dragons did and often wished that they'd simply leave her alone, she had already begun to consider them her family--more so than Jasmine, Jasse, or even Arianna had ever been to her.

Her anger rose and Kathryn found herself wishing that she could reach out and throttle all of the guards and Lord Tanner to ensure that none of the Dragons lost their lives trying to rescue her. However there were so many questions she needed answered from Lord Tanner that she couldn't afford to kill him, at least not yet.

Lea stayed close by. Kathryn could tell that the young serving girl believed that she was going to die.

"Lea," she said quietly.

The young woman hurried over. "Do you need something, Lady Kathryn?" she asked quickly.

"How did you get here?"

Lea frowned. "I'm afraid I don't understand."

Kathryn waved her hand around the room. "How did you come to serve Lord Tanner?"

"My family was in debt, and he took me as payment," Lea said after a moment.

"I'm sorry." Kathryn paused, and then asked, "Do you miss your family?"

"I don't even know if they're alive." Lea stared out the window for a long moment, suddenly she turned and gripped Kathryn's hand. "Are you sure that there's no one you can call for help? No one at all?"

Kathryn thought about her note to David and wondered if they'd figured it out yet. "Not anymore," she said quietly.

Lea appeared on the verge of tears.

"Lea, what's wrong?"

"You can't stay here. You must escape!"

"I'm in no condition to escape," Kathryn told her softly, this was not a conversation she wanted other servants to overhear.

Lea pressed harder, "You don't understand Milady. Lord Tanner was ordered to kidnap you for someone else, but now he wants you for himself. You have to get away."

"Who ordered Lord Tanner to kidnap me?" Kathryn asked quickly.

"I don't know," Lea said shaking her head. "Probably someone higher up in the Brotherhood."

"The Brotherhood?"

"I don't know anything other than that Lord Tanner is a new member of something called the Brotherhood. I do know that the Brotherhood hates the Guardians."

"Probably because they're all criminals," Kathryn reasoned quietly, noticing that her vision was beginning to swim…

"We need some ideas," Luke said. "That place is a fortress."

"What we need is a way in that doesn't involve shooting the guards," David replied, "and it's going to take a miracle to get a miracle."

The two boys were lying on the sharp gray rocks that made up the cliffs behind the castle. Slowly they inched their way back down the steep incline and dropped to the dry bed of a stream where the rest of the Dragons waited.

"Well?" Amy demanded.

"This is not going to be easy," David told her.

"Lady Kathryn!"

Lea's frantic voice brought Kathryn out of the vision. Quickly Kathryn grabbed her arms, hardly daring to hope. Maybe this was a way to ensure that the Dragons succeeded. If not, it would certainly be their doom. "Lea is there a dry creek bed in those cliffs?" She nodded out the window to the gray cliffs made even darker by the clouds.

"How did you know that?" Lea asked in amazement.

"It's better if you don't know." Kathryn looked into the young woman's eyes. "I need you to do something for me Lea."

"Anything, Lady Kathryn."

"Can you get out of the castle without being seen?"

Lea nodded. "Yes, ma'am. I'm very good at moving without being seen."

Kathryn swallowed hard. She wasn't even sure that she could trust Lea, but she had no other options. David would need help getting in, all of her dreams attested to that, she just hoped that she was sending the right person. "I need you to go to the creek bed. There will be Guardians there. Ask to speak to David. Tell him everything you know."

"Guardians?" Lea whispered. "Are you sure?"

"I'm positive." Kathryn took a deep breath. "I need you to deliver a message." Quickly she relayed the message she wished to get to David and had Lea repeat it. "Now go!"

Lea hurried out of the room and Kathryn prayed that she had made the right choice.

𝕤𝕠·𝕔𝕤

Lea walked slowly down the stairs towards the kitchens. "Where are you going?" The harsh voice of her master brought her to a standstill. Quickly Lea lowered her eyes.

"Lady Kathryn asked me to fetch some cool water," she said quietly.

"Humph, well take your time," Lord Tanner ordered. "I don't want her thinking she runs this castle."

"Yes, milord."

Lea hurried down to the kitchens grabbed a bucket and slipped outside. She hurried to the well and began to fill it. After a few moments she moved away from the well and began to head towards the cliffs that towered behind her. Because the cliffs provided such a perfect natural defense there was no castle wall or gate to contend with and that suited Lea perfectly.

Quickly she found the small trail that led up into the cliffs. She hurried, even though it increased the chances of her being spotted. As she stumbled over rocks and old gnarled roots she sincerely hoped that Lady Kathryn was right.

The creek bed had just entered her line of sight when strong arms grabbed her from behind, the hand across her mouth stifling her startled scream.

"Easy," the low voice commanded. "What's a servant girl doing way out here?"

The hand covering her mouth dropped slightly allowing her to ask, "Are you a Guardian?"

"What makes you say that?"

"Because I was sent to find Guardians."

"By who?"

"Lady Kathryn,"

The hands holding her spun her around and she found herself facing an entire team of Guardians. She almost fell over in surprise. How had an entire family arrived without anyone knowing about it? "What do you know of Lady Kathryn?"

"She told me to go to the creek and ask to speak to the Guardian named David."

The Guardians exchanged looks. "She specifically told you to speak to the Guardian named David?" A female Guardian asked doubtfully.

Lea nodded quickly. "Yes! I swear I'm telling the truth!"

One of the Guardians glanced at another who was gazing intently at her. Finally he seemed to come to a conclusion and looked to his companions. "She's telling the truth," he said firmly. "At least as much as she knows it. Lady Kathryn did tell her to come out here and asked her to deliver a message."

Lea gaped at him. "Y...yes," she stammered. "How did you know?"

The Guardian ignored her and continued. "Lady Kathryn's message is that if we attempt to storm the castle we guarantee our deaths and her own. Lord Tanner chose his guards because they had all faced Guardians before and as such she recommends that we use unconventional tactics when dealing with them."

Lea's mouth dropped open.

The original Guardian who'd grabbed her rubbed his masked chin. "Well at least that settles our discussions on attempting to take the castle by force. Now things get complicated." He faced Lea. "Tell me everything about Lord Tanner and the castle itself."

Quickly Lea told the Guardian what she knew, ending with, "Please hurry. Lady Kathryn has grown weak and I fear my master will try to take her for his own rather than follow orders."

"We're rescuing Lady Kathryn tonight," the first Guardian assured her. "But we need your help."

"Anything."

"We need to get inside without being spotted. Can you help us?"

Lea considered his request. "The servants' entrance on the southern side," she decided. "It's used rarely by most servants and the guards avoid it because it smells bad."

One of the other Guardians made a disgusted noise but the first Guardian, whom Lea suspected was the one named David Lady Kathryn had sent her to speak with, cut her off with a wave of his hand. "Where is Lady Kathryn being held?"

"On the fourth floor in the south wing. Her room has the deer's head crest and two guards stationed outside."

"What about the other servants?"

"What about them?"

"When they see Guardians storming through the castle how will they react?"

"Lord Tanner keeps those of unquestioned loyalty close to him," Lea told them. "The rest he sent to work in the kitchens or other various jobs."

The Guardian leader nodded. "Very well. When the first stars come out, we will attack."

℘·℃

After Lea had left, Tyler turned to David. "Are you sure about this?" he questioned. "How do you know that we can trust her?"

"We can," Daniel assured him.

Tyler scowled at him. "You can't get a full reading of someone's true intentions in a few minutes."

Daniel nodded in agreement. "True, but Kathryn did send her and the message was from her." He turned to look at David. "Lea has secrets, don't get me wrong, but she's on our side...at least for this battle."

"What I want to know is how Kathryn knew to send her here," Elizabeth said in bewilderment. "It's not like we sent her a message telling we'd arrived."

"A puzzle for a later time," David decided. "For now we have to trust that Daniel's reading of Lea is correct. If we attempt an obvious approach, we all die."

"And I really want to know how Kathryn knows that," Tyler muttered.

"She's in the castle, Tyler," Amy replied tartly. "She's in the perfect position to gauge the possibility of success of such an attempt."

"Right, and she came to the same conclusion we'd pretty much already come to," he argued. "So why did she risk all of our lives to warn us against a plan that'd we'd practically already discarded."

"She didn't want us to risk our lives," Jenna said slowly. "Even with all of our planning we were still holding such a plan in reserve in case we couldn't come up with anything better," she reminded them.

"So why warn us?" Tyler persisted.

"Because she knows us," Amy sighed. "We've spent the last year learning to live together and I spent years as her roommate. She knows how we think, how we react." She looked to David. "Even after just one year I already know that if one of us ever gets into trouble you wouldn't hesitate to do whatever it costs to get us out."

David nodded. "Of course I would, this family is my responsibility. You're all family to me now. Even Kathryn."

Amy nodded. "Exactly. And Kathryn knows it. She knows that you'll risk your life on a rash plan even if it only has a scant chance of success. Same as me. She's seen me do foolhardy things in the past for friends back at school." She turned back to face the rest of the Dragons. "Kathryn's warning us against acting rashly because she knows what course we would take if no other option presented itself."

"And when she felt like there weren't any viable options, she came up with one of her own," Luke surmised.

Matt couldn't stop from grinning slightly. "She can protest all she wants. She loves us."

Chapter 37

As the first stars appeared in the night sky and the last of the sun's light disappeared from the land, the Dragons carefully crept toward the southern servant's entrance. David left his sword sheathed, but kept one hand on the hilt in case Tyler's suspicions had been right and Lea had betrayed them.

When the door opened, revealing a lone Lea standing in the shadows, David let out a breath that he hadn't realized he'd been holding. Silently the Dragons entered the castle.

"Lord Tanner is on the fifth floor," Lea whispered as she closed the door.

David nodded his thanks. "You might want to get out of sight," he advised. "If Lord Tanner's guards get jumpy they might just kill you and the other servants."

Lea's face paled. "Can I warn the others?"

"Only after our presence has become obvious to the guards," he ordered sternly. "Any sooner and you risk revealing our presence too soon."

While Lea clearly wasn't happy she agreed and disappeared down the corridor after pointing them in the correct direction.

David led the way as they made their way through the silent castle.

"Lea wasn't kidding about the smell," Natalie gagged. "What could possibly smell this bad?"

"You really want to know?" Tyler muttered in disbelief.

"Quiet," David growled. The cobbled floor was looking more worn and he suspected that the area they were entering was more commonly used. "Stay alert," he ordered quietly. He drew his sword and heard the quiet *wisps* that indicated that the others had followed his example.

They passed through the servant's passages into one of the main corridors and the sudden brightness of the large number of torches along the wall temporarily blinded David. After a brief moment his eyes and mask readjusted for the brighter light and he glanced around. So far there was nothing to indicate that any living person, guard or servant, was anywhere in the vicinity.

David wondered if, that in staffing the castle with people loyal to him, Lord Tanner had been forced to reduce the number of servants and guards that would normally be found in a castle this size. It was one possible explanation for the lack of servants and guards in such a well-used hallway, but so was the time of the night. He put the thought out of his mind. Guardians were trained to expect worst case scenarios so that's what he mentally prepared himself for.

While crossing the first floor the Guardians leapfrogged in teams of two or three from one niche or alcove to another rather than marching directly in formation. The overly cautious movement mimicked those of assassins rather than an assault force. After the rescue of Princess Roseanna, Kathryn had begun to work in siege exercises and ambush scenarios into her training sessions. It had been the family's first introduction to the concept of hidden movement and Kathryn had taken to drilling the basics of the methods and techniques as an integral part of their training. Fortunately, after three months, the basics were second nature to them. They reached the first set of stairs.

Wide and straight they were made out of a blue veined stone with a bright purple carpet running down the middle. "We go in pairs up each side." David nodded for Luke and Natalie to take one side and motioned for Amy to join him. He'd known going in that keeping Amy from the forefront of the fighting was going to be impossible so he might as well keep her at his side. He signaled the remaining Guardians to wait and blend into the shadows.

Taking each step one at a time, and keeping his back to the railing while keeping Luke and Natalie directly opposite him and Amy, David cautiously made his way up the stairs. It wasn't a long staircase, but the slow speed that David led them up made them seem infinitely long.

Warily, David eased his head above the last stair. Still no guards or servants. Looking back to where the rest of the Dragons waited he motioned them forward. He waited until they were all on the landing before proceeding again. As much as he hated to keep them grouped together, he felt that it would be safer in the long run...at least until they ran into trouble. Both the wind and Daniel's gift would alert him if they were walking into an ambush or a patrol.

The second floor proceeded much like the first. They were halfway to the second staircase when David felt a sudden touch on his arm. At the same time he felt the breeze warn him about an approaching servant. Glancing back he nodded at Daniel who released his hand from David's elbow. Silently David waved his hand, motioning the Dragons to find cover. Luke, Cassandra, Elizabeth, Tyler, Rachel, and Leia were on the other side of the corridor and he watched as they melted into the shadows of the door frames.

David pressed his own back against the frame of one such door and waited. Footsteps sounded in the hallway and for a moment his heartbeat quickened. He forced himself to relax as his ears recognized the sound of a single pair of light footsteps. *Most likely a female servant*, he reasoned. He relaxed even further as the footsteps began to fade. Slowly he eased out of the shadows and began to proceed forward again. The others noiselessly followed his lead.

They met the first real resistance on the third floor. As David and Amy were waiting for the rest of the Dragons to finish climbing the stairs an eddy in the air gave David a brief warning.

"Patrol!" he hissed, barely making it behind an ornate statue before he heard the sounds of feet walking in unison. The unity surprised him. Most people who had fought Guardians before were criminals with no discipline. Perhaps Lord Tanner had taken it upon himself to instill order in those under his command.

"What do we do?" Amy whispered from her position on the stairs. Behind her the rest of the group had fallen into crouched positions that still enabled them to move quickly if needed.

David thought hard and fast. They were already halfway to Kathryn's room and while he wished that he could have made it to the fourth floor before running into trouble, he knew that they had been extremely fortunate to have come as far as they had without running into a patrol. He felt his grip tighten on the hilt of his sword and forced himself to relax. He smiled at Amy. "I think it is time we announced ourselves."

Her eyes widened in surprise but after a moment she grinned at him. "We'll wait for your signal."

"What signal?" Luke whispered as the sound of the patrol grew louder. He had taken up the same position as David, using a large statue for cover.

"Don't worry," David assured him. "You won't be able to miss it."

Closing his eyes, David listened intently. The patrol was close enough that he could make out the sounds of the guards voices.

Closer, he urged them.

The voices grew louder still.

Come on, he encouraged them in his mind, *just a little closer*.

Stretching out with his senses, he listened to the breeze as it relayed the patrol's progress to him. He waited until they were within a few meters of the stairs. If they got too close they would see the rest of the Dragons crouched on the steps and then surprise would be lost.

"She's sure a pretty thing don't you think, Jorg?" One of the guards was saying.

Releasing his breath, David stepped around the statue and into the light. In one smooth motion he crossed to the nearest guard and swung his sword. In his periphery he could see Luke, mere seconds behind him, doing the same thing.

The first two guards never recognized the danger. The second two were caught off guard by Natalie and Amy as the two girls leapt up from the stairs and came at them, knives whirling. The last two guards were fortunate enough to have been a meter or two back from their companions and watched in horror as their patrol was cut down in a moment of time.

David cursed as they drew their swords, raising the alarm at the same time. He and Luke quickly cut off their shouts but the damage had been done. David could hear the sounds of doors opening and the pounding of feet.

Quiet the castle may have been, but now on high alert the noise was approaching that of a rathskeller on a holiday weekend. The rest of the Dragons had made it to the landing. "What now?" Daniel asked, elevating his voice to be heard over the sound or rushing feet.

David had already made up his mind. "Luke, Jenna, you're with me. We're going to find Kathryn. The rest of you keep the guards busy."

He could tell that Amy wanted to protest but he didn't give her the option. With Luke and Jenna behind him he moved quickly along the length of the hall. When the breeze warned him that a large wave of guards was approaching he opened the nearest door and stepped inside.

ജ·ൽ

Tyler took command as soon as David, Luke, and Jenna left. He split the group in two. "Matt, Cass, Leia, Amy, and Natalie I want you to flank us," he nodded to the rest of the Dragons. "I'm certain that Lord Tanner will have stationed guards on every floor so we can expect resistance from both directions."

The groups divided up as directed and prepared themselves for a two front assault.

They didn't have long to wait.

Lord Tanner may have been a lot of things, but sloppy in his security wasn't one of them. A wave of twenty or so guards appeared at the end of the corridor and stopped short.

So we still have the element of surprise, Tyler thought grimly. *At least that's something.* "Release!"

At his command Daniel, Rachel, Lindsey, and Elizabeth released the arrows that they had drawn. Behind him, he could hear Amy order the others in her group to release their own arrows.

So it begins, Tyler thought as he signaled for another wave of arrows to be released. *Time to show these people what happens when you mess with a Guardian family.*

The knights' advance faltered at the sudden barrage of arrows that came at them. But they didn't stop. Quickly regrouping, they doggedly made their way down the corridor using their shields to protect themselves from the arrows. Tyler commanded loudly, "Legs!"— and within seconds the Dragon's arrows began tearing into calves, knees, and feet. The throng quickly realized their vulnerability and crouched while advancing so that their bucklers and shields covered their entire body. Tyler finally called a halt to the arrow barrage and brandished his sword. He sensed Daniel come up behind him to stand at his shoulder.

Seeing that the bows had been put away, the knights charged.

Tyler and Daniel raced forward to meet them, putting as much distance between them and the girls as possible. In such close quarters Tyler and Daniel could rely on brute strength to overcome the knights but Rachel, Lindsey, and Elizabeth, as women, would need to rely on agility and speed. By spreading out as far as possible, the two boys gave them the room they would need to deal with the knights in their own way.

Dropping his knees and center of balance at the last second, Tyler rammed his shoulder into the first knight's stomach. They collided with a bone jarring smack. Tyler heard a loud whoosh as all the air left the knight's lungs. The Guardian didn't waste another second. Bringing up his free hand he thrust the dagger he had pulled from his belt up under the knight's armor and into his chest. With a grunt that knight fell to the ground, completely out of the fight.

A second knight was in the process of bringing his sword down in a devastating chop. Shifting all of his weight to his left foot, Tyler sprang forward and upward, catching the knight's blow on his sword before it had reached its apex, lessening the power behind it. Shifting to the right, Tyler used his dagger to force the knight's right arm into his own body. In a sweeping motion he switched the positions of both hands and brought the dagger up under the knight's helmet, severing his throat. Turning he braced himself and allowed his training to take over as the small army of knights overwhelmed the Dragons.

Let your anger inspire you, but don't let it control you. Kathryn's advice was in the forefront of Amy's mind as she faced the first knight to make it up the stairs. He glared down at her as he raised his sword. She let a seductive smile break across her face.

Utter confusion crossed his face and his strike faltered long enough for Amy to dart forward and draw her dagger across his throat.

Smiling at your enemy, especially as a woman, can confuse them. Kathryn had encouraged Amy, and later Jenna and the rest of the girls, to use their femininity to confuse and distract their opponents. Amy smiled grimly as the next knight appeared in her line of vision. Men's minds tended to go blank when a beautiful woman smiled suggestively at them. Of course it was something taught at Guardian school, but Kathryn had encouraged Amy to take the practice to a whole new level. *You can't just smile at them,* she had told Amy once. *You have to look like you mean it. Most men can tell when you're forcing yourself to look like that. You have to make sure that they're stopped in their tracks otherwise you'll be taken off guard when your ploy doesn't work. It doesn't matter if you're masked or not. They can see your eyes and they can see your mouth, their minds will imagine the rest.*

The second knight didn't even make it to the top of the landing before Matt leapt forward and engaged him. Amy turned her attention to where Tyler and his group were facing a horde of knights and were threatening to be overwhelmed. Taking a deep breath she concentrated her focus on where the line of Dragons stopped.

Before she could do anything, however, Destiny swooped over her head and barreled into the neck of one of the knights attacking Daniel. The knight's helmet went flying and the man dropped like a rock to the floor, his sword clattering lamely from his grip-less hand. Soaring upward into the gallery, Destiny let out a victorious call before diving down into the fray again. Another helmet went flying and crashed against the wall as a second knight succumbed to the bird's fury.

ℬ·ℭ

David waited until he heard the rest of the Dragons engage the first wave of knights before leaving the room and hurrying to the end of the corridor. They didn't get far. A second battalion of knights appeared in the hallway, halted for a brief second before brandishing their swords, and charged.

Irritated at the possibility of a delay, David tapped deep into his power and gathered a large orb of compressed air in his left hand. *Everything in order tries to sink into chaos,* his mentor's words echoed in his mind. With a grunt, he threw his hand forward and released the energy. The tapestries on the walls were torn from their hangings as David's self-created wind vortex flung itself down the hall in an attempt to release the pressure and order David had created while keeping it captive in his hand.

The knights either suspected something, or the whirling tapestries gave them enough warning, that they dropped to their knees and braced their shields before them. The wind hit them like a heard of stampeding horses, knocking several knights flat on their backs. Unfortunately it only served to slow them down and make them angry.

"Blast them!" David cursed as he readied his sword and moved forward. The knights had recovered from his attack and raced toward him. The Guardian met the first knight's strike with a sweeping block that allowed him to completely bypass the startled knight. Leaving the knight alone, David focused instead on the second knight, knowing that Luke would handle the one he had ignored. The second knight swung at David's ribcage, he blocked and returned with a strike at the man's knee, aiming for the joint in his armor. Leaping back, the knight avoided his blow and brought his own sword down for cleaving strike at David's collarbone.

Stupid, David thought as he swept the blow aside. *Steel and bone doesn't mix and only damages your own sword.* One of eighty drill rubrics from his basic training, he recalled. Its meaning was all too simple. Aim for flesh, not for bone. As he easily swept his opponent's sword to the side, he flicked his wrist in an upward circle and brought his own sword across his opponent's lower abdomen. He felt the sudden resistance that the man's chainmail and flesh presented to his blade, but he also felt the momentum that carried his sword all the way through. The knight dropped and David turned his attention to the next enemy that wished to challenge him.

There were plenty. Ten knights were arrayed around the three Guardians. David felt his eyes narrowing and his gut clenching. The number wasn't a problem, but the time that they would need to dispatch them was frustrating. Not wasting another second, David attacked the knight closest to him. Methodically he and Luke worked their way from one end of the knights to the middle while Jenna used her bow to shoot at the gaps in the knights' armor and helmets. Three of the knights dropped before either Luke or David could reach them, blood running out of their eyes from the arrow that had made it through the eye slits.

As Luke dealt with the last knight, David was already sprinting up the spiral staircase that led to the fourth floor. Most stairwells in a castle turret rotated to the right making the defenders more effective since most men are right handed. A right-handed attacker moving upwards would be forced to expose more of his body to wield his sword than the defenders would. Trained as a Guardian, David was just as proficient with his left hand as his right. Switching his sword to his left hand he ascended quickly. After only a few strides up the stairs he ran into another contingent of guards.

These guards were well armed and trained compared to the earlier knights. These were the guards who clearly had experience in dealing with Guardians. And they had learned those lessons well, David had to admit that. But he was more stubborn and wiser than he had been a few months ago and unlike that first patrol almost a year ago where he had been surprised when the bandits hadn't fought like bandits, David was prepared for the techniques the guards used. He once again took the brunt of the attack, leaving Luke to deal with anyone, or weapon, that managed to get past him. Jenna maintained a rear guard and protected their backs with her knives and bow.

As to the knights, they had been warned to expect swordsmen whose skills appeared almost unnatural coupled together with the speed and agility that made the guardians famous. The women, they were warned, were faster and more agile than a cat, and the men strong as a battle horse. Their own previous experience with Guardians had seemingly made this warning unnecessary. However the knights had previously fought Guardians who were on the verge of retiring, not fresh, young warriors whose attacks were fueled by an ice-cold determination to rescue their friend.

The inhuman strength David put behind his blows, jarring them down their spines, convinced the knights that they were severely outmatched. Nor were they completely prepared for the extent of the damage that the guardian weapons would do to their own. Each attack they parried left deep gouges in the hardened steel until the sword was altogether useless. The knights had fought older Guardians in brief skirmishes, not a full-blown battle. The guards barely managed to slow the advance of the Guardians by a few moments.

Together the three Guardians quickly managed to kill or severely injure each wave of knights arrayed against them and followed on the heels of those that retreated up to the fourth floor.

80·03

"Milord! The Guardians are here!"

Shock propelled Lord Tanner to his feet. "What? How is that possible?" he demanded as cold fear began to settle in the pit of his stomach like a hard stone.

"I do not know milord," the young soldier said quickly. "We were patrolling through the corridors when they suddenly appeared.

"But how could they suddenly arrive here?" Lord Tanner demanded, working hard to keep his fear from entering into his tone. "There was no news of traveling Guardians throughout any of the surrounding towns! ...You must be mistaken!"

"No, Milord," the young knight shook his head. "They are Guardians and they are advancing quickly."

Lord Tanner rushed past the knight and hurried to Lady Kathryn's room. He could hear his captains yelling orders and the fighting in the hallways and knew that the knight had not been mistaken. Entering the room he raced to where Lady Kathryn sat. "It's time to go, Milady," he grunted as he pulled her out of the chair she had been sitting in.

"Unhand me!" she ordered, scratching at his face with her free hand.

"Not on your life," he grunted as dragged her out of the room When the Guardians caught up to him, he might need to use her as a bargaining chip. Despite the fact that she wasn't one of their own, she was still a Lady, and the Dowager Princess' ward, and they would have to do whatever he demanded to save her life.

Kathryn fought him with everything she had. She reached for his face and ripped her nails across the sensitive skin. He howled at the pain, but didn't let go. She tried again, but he anticipated her move and captured her wrist, twisting it painfully behind her back. Throwing her body against his, she tried to run him into the wall, but only ended up jarring her own shoulder. He was unstoppable, dragging her past several doors until he came to one reinforced with iron. He opened it and raced up the stairs into the tower. He tossed her inside, followed quickly, and locked the door behind him.

Striding over to her, he grabbed her hair and yanked her to her feet, the pain in her shoulder increased as if a blacksmith's red hot iron had been stabbed in the wound—she let out a small cry. "How did you do it?" he demanded, slapping her hard across the face. "How did you get the Guardians here?" He hit her again, feeling satisfaction in seeing blood begin to trickle from her split lip.

She kicked him hard and low. Howling with the pain he let go of her hair and she scrambled out of his reach, ignoring the pain that hammered through her body in disorienting waves.

"You will pay for that," he hissed advancing towards her.

80·03

"The room's empty!" Jenna cried as the boys fought two guards who had chosen to engage the Guardians rather than run away.

"Find her!" David grunted as he thrust his sword into his opponent.

Jenna raced down the hall, looking for possible escape routes, a long stairway led upwards and she remembered the way Duke Sebastian had imprisoned Princess Roseanna. "This way!" She hurried up the stairs that led to a high tower room. When she tried the door she found it locked. Inside she could hear the sounds of a fight. "Hurry!" she called down to David and Luke.

David finished off his opponent and hurried in Jenna's direction, only to find himself facing the largest group of knights they had yet encountered. He cursed again. They didn't have time for this.

Luke stepped in front of him and opened his hand. A torrent of white and blue flames exploded into existence, overwhelming the knights. The first two gasped in surprise as the fireball seared their lungs and their flesh quickly charred. The remnant turned and ran, leaving several lagging behind rolling on the floor in an attempt to extinguish the flames from their tunics and woolen cloaks. The corridor filled with smoke and the acrid stench of burning skin, hair, tapestries, and wool.

"You couldn't have done that earlier?" David ground out as he used the wind to fan the flames.

"Not with you insisting on leading the charge each time we encountered resistance," Luke countered. "I couldn't risk hitting you too."

"You could have told me to stand down," David growled as they raced up the stairs that Jenna had already taken.

Luke snorted, "Not likely."

"Come on!" Jenna urged from above them. "I can hear a fight going on inside!"

Chapter 38

Natalie felt like her arms were about to fall off. She wished that she had spent more time on the training fields like Kathryn and Amy. Even Jenna, the gentle healer, spent more time sparring with Kathryn and Matt than she did. Still, she was better off in this battle than she had been when they had rescued Princess Roseanna. Her movement was more fluid, her reflexes sharper, and her parries and thrusts were precise and deadly. Kathryn's lessons during the trip back had seemed grueling at the time but compared to the unending fight she was participating in now they seemed like ideal situations. *Focus is everything*, Kathryn had told her. *If you let your mind wander, even for a second it will kill you, maybe not the first time, but eventually it will kill you.* It was advice Natalie had heard many times before at school, but for some reason Kathryn made it stick in her mind...as well as her warning. *Be focused on your opponent, but don't allow yourself to see only him. Broaden your focus to include the entire battlefield so that you aren't taken by surprise.*

Natalie had been surprised by her words. The school had taught them to focus directly on their opponent and yet Kathryn was the best fighter that the family had, perhaps that was part of her secret.

A knight came at her, a battle axe in his hands. Natalie felt her courage die a little bit. Swords she could handle, knives she could handle, even maces weren't that bad. But battle axes were a whole different story...and this guy looked like he knew how to use one.

The knight swung his weapon in a stroke strong enough to rend her in half. Natalie stepped backward and to the left. Air whistled as the axe passed close to her body—too close. She knew that the cirin armor she wore would protect her against the sharp blade, but it couldn't change the basic laws of the earth. The cirin would protect her from being cut to ribbons, but it didn't help much when it came to a good hard pounding by an opponent twice as big as her. Even if the axe merely grazed her, she would most likely end up with several bruised or cracked ribs, and quite possibly, some internal bleeding.

She was still trying to decide what to do when a gray blur shot over her shoulder and hit the axe-man full force. His cursing was loud enough to be heard above the sounds of the battle going on all around them.

Destiny shot back around at what seemed an impossible speed and stretched out her talons toward her opponent's face. Still recovering from her first attack, the man didn't see her until it was too late. As accustomed to gore and blood as she was, Natalie still fought the urge to lose her last meal at the sight of the man's shredded face and ripped throat. Tearing her focus away from the dying man and the expanding pool of blood, she quickly scanned the fight for another opponent.

There was no need. Tyler and Daniel were dispatching the last two knights while the others verified that the knights on the ground were truly dead.

In the distance she could hear the sounds of another fight still raging.

හ·ිෂ

Kathryn heard Jenna's voice outside the door and fought with renewed determination, she only needed to hold out for another minute. Lord Tanner came at her in a fury. He managed to grab one of her flailing arms and twisted it painfully behind her back. She kicked him hard in the shins. He grunted, but didn't release his grip. He gripped her already injured shoulder and pushed on the joint.

Dragging one of her feet behind her she locked it behind one of his and yanked. Unprepared and slightly off balance, Tanner failed to recover. They fell together with a resounding crash that Kathryn was sure dislocated her shoulder.

Now she could hear others outside the door, hacking at the wood, trying to get through. She just had to hold on a little while longer.

Tanner grabbed her injured shoulder and yanked her to her feet, twisting it behind her back again. She couldn't stop the scream that resulted from the pain.

"I was supposed to deliver you to my mentor," he hissed in her ear as she fought the waves of pain that caused the room to spin.

The door let out a resounding crack indicating that whoever was on the other side was coming through.

She felt Lord Tanner shift. "But now it's too late," he told her, breathing heavily. "If I can't have you—no one will...and you're too much trouble as a hostage."

At the same time the door flew open, Kathryn felt an explosion of sharp pain radiating out from her stomach. She looked down to see only the hilt of the knife Tanner had stabbed her with.

It was the last thing she saw.

හ·ිෂ

Jenna heard scuffling and Lord Tanner grunt in pain as Luke and David joined her. Luke began to hack at the door with his sword, trying to break it down.

A scream echoed through the room and down the stairs.

Jenna felt her heart rate triple.

"That's not going to be fast enough," David said as he concentrated, gathering air in his hands, compressing it tight.

"You could help," Luke grunted, throwing himself against the door. It cracked against his weight. "Two of us would be faster than one."

"So would this." David threw the ball of air at the lock. The pressure expanded inside the lock's mechanisms, breaking it. The two boys threw the door open—and watched in horror as Lord Tanner plunge his dagger into their friend. When he saw the Guardians, Tanner dropped Kathryn. She hit the floor and didn't move, a red tide already beginning to seep outward from her wound.

365

"Jen, Go!" David ordered as he rushed Tanner, trusting the healer to understand.

Tanner brought out his own sword and the two men engaged. Luke was half a second behind his leader. Tanner had no delusions of getting out of the situation alive, but he refused to give up. Instead he fought like a maniac. The power behind his blows was impressive and David realized that this wasn't some simple duel on a tournament green. This was for real and Tanner really did want to kill him. Abandoning all thoughts of old camaraderie with Tanner, David focused on not just winning the fight, but staying alive and in one piece. His opponent lunged at him, his sword aiming for David's neck. David parried while Luke attacked from behind Tanner. Impressively, Tanner seemed to sense Luke behind him ducked slightly and managed to parry his thrust with another dagger. Sparks were flying whenever blades connected, but unlike the knight's swords below, Tanner's weapons appeared to sustain no damage from David's or Luke's sword.

How many of these blasted swords are there? David thought in frustration as he swung his sword in a swipe at Tanner's knees while Luke swung for his neck. Tanner swept his sword downward deflecting David's sword while blocking Luke's attack by smacking his sword's hilt with his gauntlet, sweeping up and out. David began a strike aimed at Tanner's right shoulder, but as Tanner moved to block he flicked his wrist and brought his sword down at Tanner's left leg, aiming for the gap between his armor plates. Luke followed his lead and faked Tanner into blocking a shot to his head while a last second flick of the wrist reversed the sword's direction and ended up at Tanner's right leg. Tanner managed to deflect Luke's blow but David's sword found flesh.

Tanner let out a cry of rage and attacked wildly. For several moments both Luke and David were forced to go on the defensive while Tanner hacked at them with all his strength. David felt sharp contact with his left arm and Luke took a blow to his forehead. Emboldened, Tanner stepped forward for another wild round but as his sword swung at David's neck, his target dropped to the ground and rolled toward his legs. Tanner quickly jumped backwards to avoid David's flashing sword...and impaled himself on Luke's.

Coming to his feet, David hurried over only to watch a mortally wounded Tanner still put up an impressive fight against Luke's sword. David was done playing games. His left hand swung behind his back and grabbed his hunting knife. In one smooth motion, as he was still hurrying to his friend's aid, he threw the knife towards Tanner, where it sliced through his brigandine and chainmail, burying itself into his back.

Tanner collapsed, bleeding profusely from wounds in his chest, legs, and back. David moved to stand over him. "You have won...this round," Tanner gasped, blood pouring from his mouth. "But the...Brotherhood shall...prevail." He gave David a cold, cruel smile. "Soon... the Guardians...will...be...nothing more...than...a memory," he gasped the last two words as his last breath rattled from his now lifeless body.

David didn't stay by his side another second. Tanner was dead, he didn't know about Kathryn.

He hurried over to where Jenna knelt by Kathryn's still form. Luke was already there, kneeling beside them; his knees surrounded by blood. "Is she alive?" he asked quickly.

Jenna nodded. "She's still alive, but it's not good. Tanner's dagger did a lot of damage internally." She turned a sorrowful face at David. "He didn't just stab her, David. He twisted the blade while it was inside her. The odds are against her with this type of wound...I...I don't know if she'll make it through the night."

The honesty in those simple words and the brutality of Tanner's attack tore at David. The Dragons were a family and he was responsible for them. Now it looked like one of their own was going to leave them—permanently. "I should have listened to Amy," he muttered darkly. "If I had, none of this would have happened."

Luke stood up and put a hand on his shoulder. "You can't know that," he said firmly. "You did what a responsible leader would have done." He maneuvered David back a few paces so that Jenna could work without obstructions.

The leader of the Dragons shook his head. "Amy knew something was wrong and I talked her out of it. Amy knew Kathryn better than anyone. I should have trusted her instincts."

"Kathryn is a very resourceful Guardian," Luke replied steadily. "Something she was always reminding us of. How could you have known that she was in over her head?"

David couldn't think of a viable reason. Instead he turned his attention to the dead man, "What are we going to do with him?" He didn't bother to hide the contempt in his voice.

Luke made a face. "As far as I'm concerned we can feed him to the rats, but we should probably bury him."

"Send Daniel and Tyler to dig a grave out in the cliffs, we'll bring out the body when they're done." Turning to Jenna, David asked, "Can we move her?"

"Kathryn!" Amy's anguished cry echoed through the room before the healer could answer. Amy raced to her friend and knelt beside her. "Is she going to be okay?" she asked hoarsely.

David moved to kneel beside her. "We don't know," he said quietly. He paused, not wanting to alarm her, but decided that she deserved to know the truth. "Her injuries are severe." For the first time, he allowed himself to actually look at their fallen comrade. The blade's hilt immediately grabbed his attention, the silver and gold glinting in the light; the bright red of blood staining the steel blade before it disappeared into a very jagged and torn looking wound. Jenna had already cut away a section of the dress Kathryn was wearing and what he could see of her torso was stained with blood, rivulets dripping down her sides and pooling on the floor. Despite the horror her injury appeared to be, her face was serene. Peaceful. Pale. Deathly pale.

"She has to be okay... she can't leave me..." Amy whispered brokenly.

"Jenna will do everything in her power to help Kathryn, but we need to let her work." He pulled Amy to her feet and turned to face the rest of the team that had slowly filed into the room after Amy.

"I take it you took care of the rest of the guards, Tyler."

"Like swatting flies," Tyler grunted. "We now control the castle."

Jenna's voice spoke up from behind them. "Tyler, you have a healing gift. I need your help."

"What do you need me to do?" Tyler hurried over, his normally dour expression replaced by one of a concerned healer.

"I need you to pull the knife out...slowly."

Tyler and nodded and gripped the hilt of the weapon. David wrapped his arms around a tearful Amy and held her head against his shoulder, not wanting her to watch, but unable to prevent himself from doing so.

"Now!"

Slowly Tyler dislodged the weapon. The image of the long blade being slowly pulled from Kathryn's body, covered with her bright blood, would never leave David's memories for the rest of his life. Jenna quickly began to work to stop the bleeding that was seeping from within the wound.

David had seen enough. "Cass, Leia, and Rachel, I want you to go down to the kitchens and let the servants know that there's been a change in management. Also tell them to ready a room, we're going to bring Kathryn down."

Jenna's head shot up. "I don't know if we can move her yet without killing her."

"As soon as you can, you move her," he ordered. "Amy, Daniel, and Elizabeth, I want you to go through the castle and make sure that there are no surprises waiting for us. Also see if you can get a message to the Guardian council. They need to know what happened here, ask if they know anything about this supposed Brotherhood."

Just before they disappeared around a corner a sudden thought occurred to him. "Wait!" Elizabeth halted and stepped backed into his view. David continued, "while you're at it question the servants maybe they know something.

"Matt, Luke, find some shovels and go out to the cliffs. Daniel, as soon as you've cleared the castle I want you to join them. You get to dig graves for the dead." Quickly he added, "and grab as many able bodied servants as you can find to help you"

David turned to face the two remaining Guardians. "Natalie, Lindsey I need you to stay here and help Jenna and Tyler in any way you can."

Natalie nodded, her face pale as she watched the two healers work on Kathryn.

"What are you going to do?" Luke asked as the rest of the Dragons hurried to fulfill their assignments.

"I'm going to invade the library and the study. I want to know what this Brotherhood is that Tanner spoke of and I'm going to see if he was careless enough to leave some information around." He turned back to Jenna. "Let me know when you can move her and I'll help."

She nodded but didn't look up. "Natalie I'll need a needle and some thread."

Reluctantly David left the healers and their assistants to their job and prepared to do his. He retrieved Tanner's sword from the floor and attached it to the extra loop on his belt. He was determined it would remain there until he reported to the Guardian council. There were four studies and one large library in the castle and he intended to tear them all apart.

The first study he came to was bare of any personal effects or writings. David doubted that this was the study that Lord Tanner had used but he didn't care. He needed something to focus all his energy on and tearing apart a study seemed like a good use of it.

He started on the desk, going through every drawer, examining for false bottoms or compartments. Methodically, he looked closely for any hidden designs or writing etched into the wood. Once he had torn apart the desk to his satisfaction he turned his attention to the chairs. The wooden ones were easy to examine, but the padded ones created a mess.

Tyler and Daniel appeared at some point and told him that they'd completed the task he had originally given them. He sent them each to another study to tear it apart. After the furniture he turned to the tapestries that lined the walls. There was nothing special about them other than the price Lord Tanner would have had to pay to obtain them. Too bad they would be nothing but thread by the time he finished with them.

"Sir?"

David turned from the tapestry he had been studying and found Lea standing in the doorway.

"The healers say they can move Lady Kathryn now."

He nodded a thank you and hurried out of the room. As he passed through the corridors he noticed that the wall lamps had been extinguished and briefly wondered what time it was. When he reached the tower room he saw faint rays of sunlight through the window on the west side. Sunrise.

A stretcher had been brought up and David and Tyler carefully lifted Kathryn onto it and carried her downstairs. Lea stood before a room and motioned them forward. "Here," she said waving them inside.

Gently the two boys eased Kathryn onto the bed and then stepped back to let Jenna take over.

While Jenna worked to get Kathryn comfortable, David, desperately needing a diversion since the healer had gently refused his help, pulled Tanner's sword from his belt.

There were no marks along the blade, nothing to ever indicate that this sword had been in battle. But it had and David had a wound on his arm to prove it. With a start, David realized he had seen this sword elsewhere. The thief from his first day on patrol with Kathryn had wielded this very same sword.

But how had Tanner gotten a hold of it? David had turned it over to the council during the Queen's birthday celebration. Was it merely a copy?

No.

He was sure this was no copy. It was the same sword he had faced all those months ago. But how had it gotten here? That was the question. That and who had forged it.

Looking closely, David noticed that the sword was very similar to the one he carried as a Guardian. Unlike a Guardian sword however, this one was completely straight and only had one edge. The material appeared to be the same but the blue-white crystalline structure famous on a Guardian's sword was blood red with bright yellow veins running through it. Also unlike a Guardian's sword there was wording on the blade:

Ai eis Paer, byli tal mal shaerysi ti

I am death, none can stand before me.

Interesting. There was also a symbol David had never seen before. A sword had been etched into the metal, two curls of flame running down the right side of its edge. To David's eye the sword and flame almost formed the capital letter B, but the hilt of the sword stretched out farther on the right than the left, distorting the image.

Even without his Guardian training, David would have known that the mark meant something important. But something deep in his bones told him that it was also extremely dangerous.

Chapter 39

David strode through the halls of the castle, pausing only when he passed a study or the library. So far the search had turned up nothing on the Brotherhood Lord Tanner had spoken of before he died, but David wasn't prepared to give up yet.

A message, containing a detailed account of all that had taken place, had been sent by way of a servant to the capital where it would be delivered to the Guardian council.

All the remaining guards that had been loyal to Lord Tanner were presently locked in the castle's dungeon with a Guardian driven fire barring every exit. The servants, rejoicing at being freed from Tanner, had thrown themselves into making their temporary masters comfortable ... not that the Guardians had time to be comfortable.

A quick midday meal had been served to the Guardians in the various rooms they presently occupied as they searched the castle. David had just left the study on the first floor where Amy and Luke were busy looking through books.

He opened the door to Kathryn's room and entered quickly. "How is she?" he asked as he drew closer.

Jenna shook her head sadly. "At this point it could easily go either way—but she lost so much blood during the time I took to sew up the internal wounds. It was nearly a radian before I could work on the entrance wound." She sighed. "You know, legends say that healers used to be able to heal with a touch. One touch and a wound like this would have been completely healed. No scars. Nothing. Now we're reduced to poultices, herbal concoctions, sewing skills, and luck," she commented derisively. "What's the point of being a healer, if I'm barely better than the local medicine woman?"

"Don't sell yourself short, Jen," he said quietly. "You can do more than you think. And you certainly know more than the local medicine woman."

The healer sighed and moved to stand next to the bed. "I just want her to wake up. I don't care if she goes back to being cold and unapproachable all the time, I just need her to wake up."

He took a deep, bracing breath before asking, "Do you think she'll make it?"

Jenna hesitated. "I honestly don't know. Kathryn's always been stubborn but with the events at Blackwood Manor being so recent and everything else that's happened," she sighed. "I really can't say. She's very weak, David."

"It's okay, Jenna. I know you've given your best."

"I just wish she'd wake up...or something," she whispered turning to look at the still form on the bed. "Give me some sign that she still has the will to live." They were silent for a long time before Jenna spoke again, "I wish..." she faltered.

When she didn't continue he prompted her. "What do you wish, Jen?" he asked gently.

"I wish that I'd had more experience with healing serious wounds," she whispered. "I'm good at sickness and simple cuts, but this?" She looked at David her face serious and worried, "I don't even know if I'm doing it right. I've never worked on a wound like this."

"You've done what you can," David replied. "That's all you could ever hope to do."

"But what if it isn't enough?" Jenna asked, her voice rising. "What if what I did isn't enough? What if she dies? She'll die because of me. Because my gift isn't enough to save her," she cried, tears running down her cheeks.

He turned to look at her. "Jenna, look at me." He waited until she faced him, tears in her blue eyes. "You've done your part. You stopped the bleeding and sewn up the wound." He turned to look at the bed, "It's Kathryn's turn now. You can't do any more. Like you said earlier, she has to have the will to live."

"And what if she doesn't?" Jenna asked quietly. Despairingly.

"She does," David replied firmly. "Somewhere, deep inside, Kathryn is a survivor," he looked back to Jenna. "She has the will to live," he promised. *She just has to find it*, he thought to himself.

Jenna looked at him, and then nodded. "Thanks, David." She didn't sound overly encouraged so he couldn't tell if she was taking any comfort from his words or not.

David squeezed her shoulder comfortingly. "I'll send Tyler up in a few radians to relieve you so that you can get some sleep."

"Thanks."

As he walked down the hallways away from Jenna and Kathryn, despite his strong words to Jenna, David felt a sense of defeat. They had defeated a tyrant, but at what cost? A life of one of their own? For a simple tyrant, he felt the cost too steep. He really wished that they could be back home in their glade, where the Dragons wouldn't have to hide the intensity of their prayers for Lady Kathryn's survival, nor where they would have to remain masked and in the bloodstained clothing they had worn throughout the battle. The only place they could remove their masks was in Kathryn's room, where Jenna only allowed the Dragons to enter.

He stepped out onto a balcony that overlooked the plains. "If we ever needed a miracle," he said to the air, "now is the time."

Thinking back on the siege he was relieved at the small number of injuries his family had accumulated. Tyler had a few bruises across his ribs where a mace had grazed him and Matt had a black eye that would cause everyone who saw him to wince for the next few weeks. His and Luke's injuries had been relatively minor. The scrape on Luke's forehead had been superficial and the cut to David's own arm had missed the vital muscles and tendons. Originally, Tyler had believed that Daniel had broken a leg when a guard had tackled him down the stairs, but it was only a pulled muscle and severe bruising. A few other knuckles had been scraped and a couple cheeks were missing a few layers of skin, but aside from that no one was seriously injured. It was as if Kathryn had taken the brunt of the consequences of storming the castle for them. No one else so much as sported a sprained finger, yet she was dying.

It wasn't fair.

He heard someone behind him and turned to see Lea standing in the archway, looking unsure of what she should do. He admired the young woman who had never been far from Kathryn's side, who in fact had risked her life to save the strange Lady. "Is there something I can help you with, Lea?"

The young woman hesitated and then asked, "Will Lady Kathryn live?"

David sighed. "That seems to be the question of the day—a question no one knows the answer to."

"She was so brave," Lea whispered, she lifted her head to look at David. "Did you know that she refused to back down to Lord Tanner? I'd never seen anyone do that before, at least not do it and live."

"What did she refuse Lord Tanner?" His mind immediately went to the more sordid possibilities and was immensely relieved at the young woman's reply.

"The truth," Lea said simply. "That she was a Guardian."

David studied the young woman, "What makes you think Lady Kathryn is a Guardian?"

Lea twisted her hands in her skirt, "I...uh...I have a gift. It's not strong enough to qualify me into the Guardians," she added hurriedly. "But strong enough to tell me when another gifted person is nearby."

"That is a gift," David commented, and a rare one. The ability to determine whether another person was gifted or not was a trait that the Guardian council guarded jealously.

"Of course, if Lady Kathryn was anything other than a Guardian you would have sent for a village healer once your healer had stopped the bleeding...and you wouldn't be pacing the floors with worry."

"Lady Kathryn is Dowager Princess Jasmine's ward and she would have our heads if we didn't do everything in our power to save her," he told her, knowing it was the truth. His aunt would *kill* him if he ever let something happen to Kathryn.

"Really?" Lea said in surprise. "I thought she'd made that up."

David shook his head. "No, she really is the ward of the princess." After a moment he asked, "Did Lord Tanner know of your ability?"

"I don't believe so, like I said, it isn't very strong."

"You were very strong and brave to risk your life to help Kathryn," David told her.

Lea blushed. "Do you think so?"

"Yes. Most servants would have cowered before their master, refusing to defy him in anything."

"I couldn't let Lord Tanner turn Lady Kathryn over to the Brotherhood. She was too special."

"She is special," David agreed.

"How did you know to come here?" Lea asked curiously.

He smiled. Lea's attempt at an interrogation was almost funny and while he understood it he couldn't disclose the truth. "Lady Kathryn sent a message to the Guardian Council. It was a cryptic message but they figured it out."

Lea frowned at him. "But how?"

David shook his head. "That, I'm afraid, I can't reveal."

℘·℃

That night David stayed in Kathryn's room with Jenna and Tyler. He stood near a window, the stars occasionally marking the cloudy sky and the moons casting their weak light into the room. Jenna was sleeping on the couch and Tyler had gone to the kitchens to fetch something, David wasn't entirely sure what. He honestly wasn't sure he cared.

The sound of Kathryn's labored breathing filled the room ominously, overshadowing Jenna's calm and regular breaths. Destiny had entered the room earlier, circled it twice and then perched herself above on a ceiling rafter. There she sat, still and solemn with eyes fixed on her companion, occasionally drowsing as fatigue from the long battle overtook her.

Suddenly he was aware that he wasn't the only one awake in the room. His eyes flew to Jenna who still slept calmly, when his eyes rested on Kathryn he knew immediately that there had been no change with her. Quickly he scanned the rest of the room, his eyes coming to rest on a shadow near the door.

"Who's there?" he called softly, drawing his sword.

"Put away the weapon, David. You need not fear me," the voice that spoke was calm, but firm.

"Who are you and how do you know my name?"

"I know everyone's name," the figure told him.

David frowned in the darkness. "That's impossible."

The shadow laughed softly. "Not for me."

"Step into the light," David ordered, still refusing to lower his sword.

The stranger complied and David took an involuntary step back. The man was tall, broad shouldered, and dressed like he was about to step onto a battlefield. His armor was a style unfamiliar to David. His tunic was fitted but the cut was unlike anything David had ever seen or studied. Around the man's back and to his knees the tunic had been cut to knee-length but from the knees it had been given a diagonal cut until reaching a point at his navel. It vaguely reminded David of the petals of a flower. The stranger's feet were clad in boots and ranging all the way to his mid-calf David could see white chainmail hanging down his legs. His elbow-length tunic was covered with a brigandine that was completely unadorned, lacking the usual straps or buckles, and along his forearms David spotted more of the white chainmail. A sword hung at his waist. Whoever this stranger was, he was a warrior.

"Who are you?" David demanded, glancing briefly at Jenna's still sleeping form.

"I come in peace, David," the warrior replied. "Do you not recognize me?"

David thought a moment, focusing on the stranger's face. Recognition finally dawned. "I briefly saw you talking to Kathryn weeks ago near the waterfall."

The warrior nodded. "I am Elyon."

David lowered his sword, but remained cautious. "How did you get in here?"

374

Humor laced his reply. "Locked doors present no challenge to me."

"Who are you?"

"I am a Dūta."

"A Dūta," David echoed doubtfully. "What in the kingdom's name is a Dūta?"

"It is many things, but mostly a leader and protector of people."

David understood that vague reference all too well. "A king," he said flatly.

"Maybe in the sense of your people, but not of mine."

"And just who are your *people*."

Elyon smiled. "My people are the Dikaios."

David searched his memory for any recollection of a people known by that name. He came up empty. "I have never heard of your people."

"Very few have."

"Is your kingdom large?" *Are they all warriors like you?*

Elyon canted his head to the side. "And just what is the definition of large?" he inquired. "We have families, towns, villages, and cities. Warriors, craftsmen, and farmers alike. It is a growing kingdom."

He was beginning to understand why Kathryn had had a hard time pinning down an explanation of the man. He certainly didn't answer questions without confusing you along the way. "Where?"

Elyon smiled. "The Dikaios are not restricted by the boundaries others create," he informed the young Guardian.

David stared at him. "I do not understand. What are you saying?"

"My people do not reside in one place, they wander and live wherever they choose."

So not a warrior culture then... Abruptly David's mind made a connection and he fought the urge to stiffen, raise his sword, and run the man through. *They wander and live where they choose.* Wanderers. Outcasts. "Sounds like an ineffective way to rule a kingdom."

"There are many kingdoms throughout this realm and across the great waters. The Dikaios are the greatest of them all."

"How can a kingdom be great when its people are scattered and the king cannot call upon them to defend it?" *Thank the stars. Whether or not the legend of the Great War with the Wanderers is true, the last thing this kingdom needs is a war.*

"Because the people call upon their *King* to defend them," his companion replied calmly.

David frowned. "That is not the way it is supposed to be."

"Maybe not in Archaea," Elyon said mildly. "But it is so with the Dikaios, and it is why they are the greatest."

Every kingdom that has ever existed has claimed to be the best," David returned.

"And yet they all end."

"All things come to an end," David argued.

"Really? Does love ever truly end?"

"It ends with death."

Elyon studied David for a few minutes longer. "Perhaps it does. But who is it that brings death? Kings and their wars for power and prestige claim more deaths than any sickness."

David was becoming frustrated. "Your point?"

"With war comes destruction and with destruction comes death. Every leader must define himself in some way and most choose to do it through the number of lives they've taken. But you do not."

"I take no pleasure in killing."

"Yet it is your job."

"Killing is only part of my job," David corrected. "And only when necessary."

"So you claim. Yet you were prepared to take this castle by force, which would have resulted in much greater bloodshed, had Kathryn not shown you a different way."

Warning bells went off in David's head. *How could Elyon know that Kathryn had opened the front gates for us via Lea?* "Only if there had been no other way and besides Kathryn is different. She's family."

"Could not many kings throughout history claim the same? How often did they use the murder of a family member as an excuse to go to war?"

David didn't want to think about it. "What's the point of all this?"

"There will come a time in the future when you must decide whether supporting your family is worth the destruction that would follow."

"The Dragons have pledged themselves to my leadership and I to their guidance and wellbeing. If one of us goes astray, it is because we all have."

"It is not the Dragons of whom I speak."

David was rendered utterly speechless. How could this Elyon possibly know who he truly was? He settled with asking. "What is your true design in being here?"

For a moment it seemed like the older man would continue on with his subject of war and family but finally Elyon nodded to where Kathryn lay. "I promised her I would never abandon her if she had faith in me."

"What has that got to do with anything?"

"She called out to me several times and I have come to help her. But more importantly, because I am her Guardian-Father."

"Her *what?*"

"Kathryn knew me as an infant. Her parents are of the Dikaios. So is she, if she so chooses. Until she rejects me, I am her Guardian-Father."

David's head spun, trying to understand what Elyon was saying. "Are you saying that Kathryn is *Dikaios?*" Could this be the key to Kathryn's origins? Stars above, could Kathryn truly be a descendant of the Wanderers? Was that why the Council kept such a close eye on her and her abilities?

"If she so chooses."

"If she chooses? One does not choose one's people."

"I am giving her that choice. She can be Dikaios or she can be of your people. I offer you the same choice, David."

The Guardian jerked in surprise. "You would ask me to betray my King and his people?" he asked angry disbelief. "You do not know me, or Kathryn, if you think that our loyalties are so easily swayed." *And if you think that I will throw aside everything I have ever worked for to become an Outcast you are gravely mistaken.*

Elyon smiled. "It is because I know that your loyalty is absolute that I offer you the choice."

"That makes no sense."

"As a Guardian, the people and the King both call upon you to fight their battles for them. Who can *you* call upon when you're overwhelmed?"

"My family, the King, and the people," David replied immediately. "The protection offered by the Guardians is reciprocated by the people to the Guardians."

"Then why did you not call upon the King or the people for this mission?"

"There wasn't time to get a message to the King." David wasn't entirely sure why he was defending his mission choices to a stranger, but after working for a year to earn the respect of the Dragons as their leader, he wasn't about to let this foreigner destroy the confidence he'd built up.

"And the people? Surely they would have helped if the Guardians had asked."

Truth be told, David didn't believe that the people would help a Guardian unless it helped them in some way. But that wasn't the main reason he hadn't included them in this fight. "The people are not fighters, if I had involved them in the battle, blood would have been spilt on both sides instead of just one."

Elyon nodded sagely. "So again I ask: who do you rely on when you are overwhelmed?"

"We are trained to face overwhelming odds," David said after a few moments of silence.

"Ah, yes," Elyon said sarcastically. "The famous Guardian notion of 'my sacrifice will preserve others'."

David let his tone cool. "Sacrifice has always been a part of service. No matter who it is to."

"True," Elyon agreed. "Great sacrifices and absolute loyalty are required from those I protect and guide. But in return I give them my sacrifice and my loyalty. I do not see that here."

"It is the King's way of showing his loyalty and sacrifice to his people. It always has been."

"Your Kings are brave indeed to risk the lives of other men and women to prove their loyalty to their people."

"Do you simply enjoy arguing philosophies or is there a reason you're here?" David asked irritably.

"I already told you my purpose, David," Elyon said softly, admonishment in his tone. "I came to help Kathryn."

"You're too late," David said firmly. "She doesn't need your help."

Elyon looked at him steadily. "Am I too late, David?"

"Yes, we already defeated Lord Tanner."

"Then why are you not at home celebrating your victory?"

David glared at him. "Kathryn was badly injured, but you already know that."

Again Elyon nodded. "Yes I know." He paused and then asked, "Did she tell you about our meeting those few weeks ago?"

"A little."

"Did she tell you that I had healed her?"

David hesitated. "Yes."

"If you will allow me, I can do it again."

David looked back to where his second-in-command lay still. He would do anything to preserve his family and he suspected that Elyon knew it. "Fine, help her if you can," he said roughly. "But if you do anything suspicious, I will kill you."

Elyon looked into David's eyes and the young commander found himself unspeakably unsettled by his gaze. Fires suddenly burned in the man's eyes and they flashed like lightning. Faint thunder rolled through the room and David swore that the floor shook. Suddenly overwhelmed with a dread that paralyzed, realization hit David. Elyon may or may not have been a king, may or not may not be an Outcast or a Wanderer, but he was definitely a sorcerer. An extremely powerful sorcerer. He possessed secrets of enormous power long thought lost. Magic that went beyond the gifts of the Guardians and into another realm entirely.

In other words, he was not a man to cross.

Finally, Elyon nodded and moved to the bed. Gently he put his hand on Kathryn's forehead for a few moments and as his hand lay there her breathing evened out and became less labored. When Elyon took his hand away she was breathing normally. "She will live," Elyon stated quietly as he moved away.

"There are many healers, many of whom are extraordinarily gifted. Yet I know of none who could heal with a simple touch," David commented warily.

"Scrolls of knowledge have been lost over the eons," Elyon said easily. "Still, you are correct. There are very few known to have such an ability. If you were to become a Dikaios, become one of my protected, the lost knowledge would be made available to you."

"You ask the impossible. My loyalty is to my King, my people. I cannot abandon them."

"And who will you turn to when *they* abandon *you*?"

David froze. "What are you saying?"

Elyon was silent for a moment before speaking. "The choice to join me will always be open, I will never rescind it. However you will soon face a trial that will challenge everything you know and believe in. When you face it, know that I never change and will never abandon my people who call upon my protection." His eyes turned to the bed and he spoke gently, "David, when she wakes she will need water and something to eat."

And then he was gone. As quickly as he had appeared he disappeared. David was stunned and not altogether sure of what he had just seen—or not seen. Quickly he hurried over to Kathryn's side—her breathing remained steady and unlabored. "Jenna!"

Jenna woke quickly. "What is it?"

"Tell me what's happened!" Despite all evidence that Kathryn had improved, David was not a healer and he wanted a healer's second opinion.

Jenna hurried over and checked Kathryn's vitals. After a moment she turned a relieved face to David's. "She pulled through! David, she's going to make it!" Jenna was crying with relief.

David hugged her, his heart overflowing with relief.

Word spread quickly and within half a radian the entire castle knew that Kathryn would live. All the Dragons came to the room, reassuring themselves that what they'd heard hadn't been a rumor. They didn't stay long, but each went to find a bed and relieve their exhaustion after a long two nights.

As the early morning rays of dawn were beginning to show themselves over the horizon, Kathryn began to stir. The noise woke David out of a fitful sleep and he quickly woke Jenna. Together they watched as Kathryn slowly came to consciousness.

David left to allow Jenna to care and explain everything to Kathryn while he went to fetch some hot broth. By the time he returned, Kathryn was fully awake and talking with Jenna, Destiny perched on her lap.

"You know," Jenna joked as she took the broth from David. "If you hadn't starved yourself, you wouldn't have nearly died on us."

Kathryn gave Jenna a weak grin. "Sorry." Her voice was hoarse and scratchy, but David was relieved to hear it.

"You're forgiven—so long as you don't ever do it again."

"Yes, Ma'am," she coughed and then turned her attention to David. "You sure took your time getting here." Jenna helped her into a sitting position and convinced her to take a few sips of the hot broth. Destiny watched her human sip at the bowl like a cat watching a mouse but refused to budge from her position, even when Jenna tried to shoo her away. She merely hissed irritably and settled herself more comfortably on Kathryn's lap. With an eyeroll, Jenna left the bird alone.

David smiled at her as he leaned against the bedframe. "Well the note we received was a bit cryptic. We had to do some thinking."

"Does your head still hurt from the effort?"

"No, but my ear hasn't stopped ringing," he told her. "Destiny has the voice of a court trumpeter."

Kathryn grinned at him. "I figured that would get your attention."

"It startled him off his chair, he nearly fell to the floor," Jenna told her with a smile.

Kathryn laughed, it was a little weak, but it was a laugh. "Are you serious? Our strong, brave leader fell off his chair at the sound of a bird call?" Jenna persuaded Kathryn to take a few more sips of the broth.

David raised an eyebrow. Was Kathryn *teasing* him? "Well the bird did happen to land on my shoulder and put her beak in my ear before shouting."

His lieutenant smirked.

"You trained her to do that on purpose didn't you?" he asked, comprehension dawning.

"I have no idea what you're talking about," she replied innocently.

When she finished the broth, Jenna replaced the bowl with a goblet of water. "I'll let the others know that you're awake," she said as she headed toward the door, pausing and turning around to say, "You know, Destiny spent most of yesterday and all of last night right above you. Kind of reminded me of a hen guarding her chicks." She gave a quick smile and hurried out of the room, leaving Kathryn and David alone.

"So Destiny sees you as her baby chick?"

Kathryn ignored his playful jab glanced down at the water Jenna had forced into her hands and frowned. "I don't suppose you'd be willing to sneak me some real food from the kitchens, would you?" she asked looking up, a wry expression on her face.

"And face Jenna's wrath?" he asked with a chuckle. "Sorry, you're stuck with broth until she decides otherwise."

Kathryn grimaced and sipped at the water. "Why are you looking at me like that?" She asked David.

"What do you mean?"

"You're studying me like I'm a creature from the stars, is something wrong?"

David shook his head quickly. "Nothing's wrong," he assured her. "I'm just trying to figure out what has caused this change in you. You just took a blade to the stomach in the worst way possible. I was ready to forgive you any grouchiness or irritability since you almost died on us. Instead, you're happier...less guarded."

She looked down at her glass for a moment, but then she looked up and spoke. "While I was locked away here, I had a lot of time to think," she said slowly. "I came to the conclusion that while I may not have had a family when I was younger, I wanted one now. I often watched the rest of the Dragons laugh and talk amongst each other like family members, but I felt at odds, like I didn't belong. Spending time here made me realize how much I really want to belong. How much I was missing."

David couldn't stop the smile that covered his face. "We've been waiting for you to say those words."

"Mind you," Kathryn warned. "I won't change overnight. Silence is a hard habit to break. You'll need to keep reminding me."

"I'll keep reminding you if you give me sparring lessons."

She laughed. "Deal."

Then the rest of the Dragons then flooded the room, ending the moment. Amy practically threw herself onto her friend, crying with relief. Destiny squawked in irritation, but refused to move even as Amy's bulk threatened to squish her. They shared an embrace before the rest of the family pushed forward. Natalie and Lindsey were teary eyed as they congratulated Kathryn on being stubborn enough to beat death back. Kathryn actually laughed at their words.

The rest of the boys hugged her without shame, welcoming her back. Cass and Elizabeth couldn't stop crying, while Leia, Rachel, and Jenna couldn't stop smiling. Destiny remained on the bed beside Kathryn and let out a victory call. After everyone had hugged Kathryn once, the eagle became protective, nipping at people who got too close to her human until Kathryn repositioned Destiny near her head so Amy and Natalie could curl up on the bed without needing a healer's attention.

Lindsey stepped forward and handed Kathryn a small wrapped package. "What is it?" Kathryn asked.

"Open it and see," Lindsey said, blushing. "I wanted something to remember you by in case you didn't make it. But since you did, I want you to have them."

When she tore the paper away, Kathryn found herself looking at two elegantly drawn pictures. The first was a portrait of herself in the white dress she had worn to the final ball at the Queen's birthday celebration. The second was a group portrait of all the dragons, each focusing on their own projects. Lindsey had drawn her sitting on Lerina with Destiny swooping over her shoulder. Beneath all the portraits Lindsey had written, *Family.*

Kathryn turned to look at David, who winked at her, "Welcome to the family."

℁·ℂ

Several days later the castle received some visitors. Dowager Princess Jasmine arrived with all the fanfare due to her station and her worry. Trailed by Lord Jasse and the faithful Arianna, she marched straight into the castle, bypassing the servants who attempted to take cloaks and offer refreshments, and made her way to Kathryn's room immediately. Her own guards and retinue made themselves comfortable as they scattered discreetly throughout the castle.

David wanted to chuckle at the disaster his aunt had left in her wake. The servants were racing around the castle, preparing meals and rooms and generally acting as if the king himself had stopped in for a visit.

Lord Jasse shooed the Dragons out of the room so that Jasmine and Kathryn could have a few moments alone. "Well done, David," he said quietly as they stood guard outside the room.

"Thank you, sir."

The door opened and Jasmine stepped out into the hallway. Both men came to attention and David could see the worry in the older man's face. "She'll make it," Jasmine reassured Jasse who then quickly slipped inside the room to see for himself.

And no doubt deliver a lecture.

The dowager turned to her nephew. "As soon as she's strong enough, I'm relocating her to my palace where she can rest and heal. I'd also like to bring your healer with me." Her tone abided absolutely no argument and David agreed with her. If Kathryn went back to the Dragon's glade to heal, he had a nagging suspicion that she'd try to get herself back onto patrols before she was ready.

He bowed. "As you wish, Your Highness."

His aunt glanced up and down the hallway before pulling him into a quick hug. "Feel free to visit," she whispered in his ear. "I never get to see you enough."

℁·ℂ

Two days later, despite Kathryn's protest that she was perfectly fit and ready to return to her duties, David saw Kathryn and Jenna tucked into the Dowager Princess's carriage. Lord Jasse promised to send daily updates and even suggested that the Dragons take turns visiting so that Kathryn didn't feel left out of their day to day lives.

David promised to send the others regularly, already reworking some of the patrols in his mind to make it work. After the progress Kathryn had made in becoming one of the family, he wasn't about to give her time to rethink and regret that decision.

Chapter 40

David stepped out onto the back porch, watching the early fall morning mist rise from the smooth, gently flowing river before him. His cup of hot tea defended his hands against the morning chill. Letting out a contented sigh he leaned against the railing, enjoying the quiet and peace. It felt strange to be up before Kathryn and Destiny, but in the week that they'd been home and back on duty neither had been as early of risers as before. The stillness of the morning and the fact that he had no pressing duties allowed his mind to wander.

It was hard to believe, but in a few short weeks, the Dragons would complete a full year of patrols. Their accomplishments weren't exactly worthy of the song writers at the Royal Court, but all else considered, he believed that they had done an excellent job. They had caught a band of roving thieves and returned their plunder back to the rightful owners, hunted down several outlaw bands, restored several farms that were salted, rescued the Princess Roseanna and Kathryn, and had managed to scare off the troublemakers who had been plaguing their region when the Dragons had first arrived.

But more importantly, at least in David's mind, they had become a family. Fourteen strangers had learned to live, work, and fight alongside each other. Kathryn had been spending much of her time of late getting to know the rest of them, even opening up a little about her own experiences and past. Natalie had even stopped pestering Matt about Lacey. A year ago he hadn't believed it possible, but Kathryn's brush with death had pulled the family together in a way that not even six decades of close quarter living could have.

His second in command had made a full recovery in just days, surprising Jenna with the speed of her recovery and eventually prompting the healer to quietly ask him during one of his visits if there was anything special about her.

Wide eyed she proclaimed, "There isn't even a scar, it's amazing, it's...it's impossible."

David had been honest, saying that there was speculation but nothing solid, and that even after all the time spent together in the same family, David still couldn't confirm or deny any of the theories regarding her...abilities. Then he'd confided to her just how Kathryn had made such a speedy recovery. The healer had been horrified at the idea of him allowing a stranger to "heal" one of their family, but even she couldn't deny the results. Whatever Elyon had done, David would always consider it a miracle. So far, Kathryn hadn't asked about her speedy recovery and he sure wasn't going to volunteer that information. Until Elyon mentioned it to her or she asked him, it would remain his secret.

Jasmine however hadn't been as convinced of her ward's recovery and had kept Kathryn at her palace for an extra three weeks, just to reassure herself that Kathryn wouldn't suffer a relapse upon her return to duty. The inactivity had driven Kathryn insane, and she had appealed to him several times by message bird to bring her back to the glade.

"What can I do?" he'd asked her during one of his visits. "She's the Dowager Princess. She outranks me. Hey," he'd added as Kathryn had begun to get exasperated with him. "You're the closest thing to a daughter that she has and you almost died. Let her process what happened and move past that in her own way." Reluctantly Kathryn had agreed and resigned herself to a few more weeks of boredom.

Overall he was pleased, and apparently so was the Guardian Council for just two weeks after their successful return to their glade he had received a very heartening letter of commendation. Their consent to his request that had followed had been received with less enthusiasm.

Upon returning home, he had spoken privately with each of the Dragons, receiving their honest opinions about the siege of Lord Tanner's castle. Most of the feedback had been positive, bolstering David's wavering confidence as their leader, but many had said that it was hard to work together with someone other than their shift teammates. Living and completing chores with friends was easy, learning to fight alongside one another was much more difficult. Kathryn's training sessions had helped, but not enough.

As such, David had written to the Council informing them of his decision to withhold his team from day to day patrols for one week to allow for team training sessions. After reviewing his very logical arguments, expertly prepared by Rachel, the council had granted his request with their blessing. Even if they hadn't given their approval, David had been prepared to go ahead with his plan and risk their anger. It was more important that his family was able to comfortably fight beside each other than bow to the wishes of the council for fear of their reprisals. Thankfully they had agreed with his assessment, even if it was a bit grudgingly. Lord Jasse had even included his own sealed letter with combat situation suggestions, suggestions that David fully planned on using...starting today.

The high-pitched creak behind him alerted him to another's presence. Was it Luke or Amy? Over the last two months, they had risen to the challenge of easing the burdens of Kathryn's duties so that her return to patrol was easier. She complained and griped about it, but not hard enough to convince anyone that she was really that upset about it. Today, she was the only one who knew what was really going on. The rest of the family believed it was simply a one day group training session.

"You're up awfully early."

He turned, surprised to find the object of his thoughts standing behind him, her own cup of tea warming her hands. "It's not that early." He nodded towards the already rising sun.

She joined him at the railing and cocked an eyebrow at him. "You only rise this early when something's bothering you."

"No I don't."

She eyed him carefully. "Seeing as you are the leader and are in a particularly stubborn mood I won't argue the point, but yes, you do."

David opened his mouth to retaliate but the sudden flutter of wings announcing Destiny's arrival saved him from having to come up with something.

Reaching into her sleeve, Kathryn pulled out a piece of oven dried jerky and tossed it to the bird.

"Matt won't be thrilled to know that his dinner is being used as a treat to tempt birds," David said wryly.

"She deserves it," his companion replied quietly.

David silently agreed as he reached up his own sleeve and pulled out a slightly larger piece of jerky and tossed it to Destiny.

Kathryn tossed him an amused look. "You're going to spoil her worse than I do, aren't you?"

"Like you said," he replied calmly. "She deserves it."

Destiny let out a squawk and flew across to the training wall and barreled back at them. She landed on the railing, looked at Kathryn, and let out another squawk.

"Do you understand her?" David asked laughing. For as long as he lived, he doubted he would ever truly understand the eccentric bird.

"She wants to climb."

David looked up at the one hundred foot wall standing firm against the swirling mists at its base and the swiftly moving clouds above. "Well, who are we to disappoint her?" he asked.

Kathryn's right eyebrow jerked upward. "We?"

"Sure. You climb and I'll watch safely from the ground to make sure you don't kill yourself."

She rolled her eyes at him, but began walking toward the stone barrier, David followed.

As they walked the path that paralleled the river he asked "Have you ever climbed this before?"

"A few times."

"Will you go blindfolded?" he asked, slightly hopeful to see that particularly impressive feat demonstrated once more.

They were on the bridge now and she paused, studying the structure. "Not this time."

"Any particular reason?" He asked, squelching the disappointment he suddenly felt.

"I train blindfolded to prepare myself for missions at night," she explained as they reached the wall. "Today I simply want to climb. Destiny still guides me; it's just that I can pick my own handholds as well."

Before he could reply she reached upward and pulled herself up, her feet seemingly able to find a steady foothold without fail on the first try.

Up.

Up.

And Up.

David shook his head in bewilderment and wonder as Kathryn scaled the thirty meter wall in just a few minutes. She waved from high above him and Destiny swooped down with a loud call.

Summoning up his courage, David began to attempt to climb the wall freestyle, something he had never done before. He'd climbed at the school, but as a student he'd been taught to use his two daggers and to dig them into the wall or rock. For those students who had wished to learn to scale a wall without any assistance there had been freestyle climbing lessons, but David had preferred to climb with something solid to hang onto.

His lack of experience and skill was showing now as he was barely eight meters up and already stuck. Hesitant to let go of the solid wall, he was unable to find a crevice to dig his toe into and push himself further up. Something prickly brushed against his cheek and he jerked, one of his feet slipping out of the crag it had lodged itself in.

Calming his startled heart, David relocated his foothold and glanced at what had startled him. A vine as thick around as his upper arm dangled next to his head. He grabbed it and began to pull himself up the rest of the way, as he did the vine seemed to grow shorter with him almost as if not wanting to leave a path for anyone else to follow.

When he finally reached the top, he gingerly made himself comfortable. The full meter thickness at the apex that had seemed so substantial from the ground suddenly seemed paper thin thirty meters up in the air.

"Nice view."

And a nice view it was. Rising behind them, the sun cast its warm rays across the drowsy landscape, slowly awakening the creatures and brightening the colors for the new day. Looking down, David felt his stomach suddenly drop and he grasped the wall for support.

"You know," Kathryn commented casually beside him, Destiny perched beside her. "I would have never pegged you as someone who couldn't handle heights."

"It's not the heights I'm worried about...or the falling from the heights," he told her.

"What is it then?"

"It's the sudden stop at the end that has me worried."

She laughed.

They both went quiet as lights began to appear in their house. Two figures appeared on the porch, but quickly went back inside.

"Think they're looking for us?" David asked.

"Probably."

"Should we go back down?"

"And miss this sunrise?" Kathryn asked indigently. "No way. They can come to us." She stroked Destiny and said, "Show Amy."

Destiny leapt off her perch and took off like a shot towards the house.

They didn't have to wait long. After about a minute, figures began pouring from the house. Destiny circled them once and returned to her perch on the top of the wall. Kathryn and David waved.

The Dragons below congregated and one broke from the party and ran back into the house.

"Matt must have left some biscuits on the stove," Kathryn laughed.

"You know who that was?" He asked in astonishment.

"Of course, can't you tell?"

"My eyesight's good, but not that good." He looked at her for a moment. "Are you sure you aren't part hawk or something?"

"Well since I'm not sporting any feathers or a beak..." She let the sentence hang, eliciting a chuckle from him. He was impressed with the strides Kathryn had made in becoming one of the family. Two months ago she'd never smiled and rarely laughed. Now she'd developed a familiarity around them that gave her the ease to crack jokes.

Matt, if Kathryn's eyesight was to believed, returned from the house carrying a bow, even David could recognize the distinctive shape.

"Think he's going to try and shoot us off," he asked.

"He could try," she replied with a sniff.

They waited, both interested to see what Matt was doing. Their companion took aim and shot an arrow into the wall, then another, and another.

"Ah," Kathryn said with a smile. "Very smart. I honestly didn't think anyone would think of it that soon."

"If I ask what, will that make me look stupid?" David asked in mock seriousness.

"Not really—

"Good to hear—

"Especially since I've already made up my mind on that point."

"Nice to know you have such a high opinion of me," he replied sardonically.

She turned to look at him, "I never said what my opinion was, you rockhead."

He blinked. Rockhead? Where in the kingdom had she gotten that particular...Luke, it could only be Luke.

Glancing down again he saw what she had already seen. Matt was climbing up the arrows while somebody, probably Leia, continued to shoot bolts all the way up the wall. Matt reached the top just as the last arrow dug itself solidly into the stone.

"Good morning!" The cook's bright red hair was made even more eye stunning with the sun glistening off the water droplets still in his hair from his morning wash.

"That's cheating," Kathryn protested, even as she scooted over to make room for Matt.

"If there are no rules against it," Matt replied as he sat down and watched the rest of the Dragons make their way up the wall, "then it's not cheating."

"He has a point," David agreed.

"Who has a point?" Tyler grunted as he pulled himself up beside Matt.

"Never mind," David replied.

"Never mind what?" Cass asked as Tyler helped her up.

"Who cares?" Elizabeth groaned as she pulled herself up onto the wall, "Ooh, what are we doing up here so early in the morning?? And whose bright idea was it to have a family meeting thirty meters up in the air??"

David grinned in sympathy, "Sorry, Elizabeth. I forgot you don't like heights."

"So can I blame you for this?"

"Sorry, Destiny's your target."

"Good luck on that," Amy laughed as she pulled herself up between Kathryn and David. "I've had better luck catching ghosts than that bird."

"You catch ghosts?" Cass looked at her doubtfully.

"Ghosts?" Natalie shrieked as her head came into view. "What about ghosts?"

Lindsey's head followed Natalie's feet as she echoed Natalie's cry, "Who's seen a ghost?"

"Amy, you handle this," David laughed.

As Amy proceeded to explain to the two girls that there were really no such things as ghosts or spirits and that she had merely been using it as an illustration, Luke's head popped up next to David. "Hey, scoot down make some room!"

Everyone who was perched on the wall cautiously shuffled over a meter or so.

"Wow, nice view!"

"We've covered that already," Kathryn told him.

Leia and Daniel appeared next, followed by Rachel with Jenna bringing up the rear. The fourteen sat in contented silence as the sun rose, appreciating the quiet and peace of the early morning. Each grateful for their own reasons.

Finally Luke asked, "What's on the agenda today, O Great Leader?"

"Getting down for one," he began resisting the sudden urge to look down. "And sparring."

"That should be fun," Tyler said.

"The sparring or getting down?" Elizabeth asked.

"I'll help you down Elizabeth," Kathryn offered.

"How?"

"I'll wrap a vine around you and lower you to the ground."

Elizabeth looked terrified at the idea. "Lower me to the ground? Um...I think I'll take my chances on the arrows."

"It's not that bad," David assured her. "She used it to haul me up this morning—

"And you claim I cheated!" Matt exclaimed.

℘·℃

Thirty minutes later they were all on the ground and the breaching arrows had been plucked from the stone.

"Now what?" Matt asked brightly, shifting lightly from foot to foot in eager anticipation of what might occur next.

"Can we eat?" Tyler groused.

"Great idea!" Matt dashed into the house, pulling a startled Cass with him, before David could reply.

Half of the remaining Dragons turned to David in anticipation. Shaking his head in amusement, David laughed. "Well he is right. It is a good idea." A moment later Cass poked her head out the door and yelled out for Daniel to fetch a ham hock from the smoke house.

Matt and Cass cooked up a delicious breakfast and the group enjoyed a rare family breakfast filled with friendliness and ease, without any false pretenses or stress.

"Here's the plan," David began after all the dishes had been cleared. "It's been brought to my attention that, while we've all learned to work with our shift members, we are having a much harder time working with anyone else. It's time to rectify that."

"By one mass training day?" Tyler asked doubtfully.

David shook his head. "Not one, but seven. We're taking the week off to train."

Elizabeth frowned. "Are you sure the Council will approve? They frown on families taking such a long absence from the people."

"I've already written my intent to them and they have responded favorably," David assured her. He didn't feel it would be wise to admit to her that he would have done it with or without their permission.

"So what's up first?"

"We spar. Everyone get your training weapons."

A little while later, David led the way to the sparring ground and watched as his teammates formed a circle around him. Daniel, Luke, and Natalie set up the training weapons trestle and each Guardian set down their weapons until they each held their sword and a pair of daggers. He motioned Kathryn to join him in the center. She did, looking slightly apprehensive.

Jenna must have been feeling similarly because she asked, "Kathryn, are you sure you're strong enough for a full week of training?"

"You did clear me for a full return to duties."

"For *light* duties," Jenna clarified.

"Training is light. Besides, it's David I'm worried about. I don't want to break him."

David sent her a mock glare. "Thank you for your concern. Okay. Kathryn, you and I have never fought each other. We're going to today." He turned and looked at the rest of his family. "Matt," he singled out their cook who couldn't quite keep still. "Who haven't you fought yet?"

Matt looked around. "I've trained with most everybody here," he finally admitted.

David felt some surprise when the rest of the group voiced the same opinion. "So are Kathryn and I the only pair who haven't sparred?"

"Go get the dessert, Matt," Luke laughed. "This should be good."

Kathryn pointed her sword at him. "You're next."

"Excuse me while I start running now."

David rolled his eyes. *What have I gotten myself into?* "Well pair up with someone you haven't sparred with…or who you don't usually spar with. I want everyone to do the same. I want you to fight three times and then find someone else until you've fought everyone."

After the initial confusion of finding someone they hadn't sparred with in a while and finding someone who wasn't already paired up with someone else, the Dragons were ready.

David held his sword at the ready and was surprised when Kathryn dropped her sword and grabbed her knives.

Matt chuckled from behind him. "I hope you enjoy eating grass."

Ignoring his friend, David lunged forward and prepared for a vicious cut across the abdomen.

Suddenly, Kathryn was beside him, close enough to touch, and his blade was swiping empty air. The impact of her practice weapon hitting his Cirin armor knocked the breath from his lungs. An instant later her hilt slammed into his hand, which opened reflexively, and his sword dropped from his hand. A powerful backhand swing caught him once in the chest and he dropped like a stone.

"How did you do that?" He asked between gulps of air, he still hadn't regained his breath from her initial strike.

"Practice." She held out her hand and helped him up.

This time, he attacked more cautiously...a tactic which didn't end up doing him any good. She blocked his side thrust with ease and spun out of range. He strode forward with a devastating downward strike—

She parried upward, bringing one of her knives up and around her head, and smoothly began a strike at his ear. As he moved to block, her other knife whipped down and caught him across the thigh, distracting him enough to get her ear strike in. A sudden jerk of her foot around his ankle and he was sitting on the grass again.

He rubbed his stinging ear, grateful that she had at least slowed down the momentum of her weapon at the last second to a sharp tap instead of a killing blow. He could no longer doubt Matt's earlier words.

Kathryn was good.

Really good.

Her hand appeared in his line of vision and he gracefully accepted.

This time he would wait for her to strike first. She didn't disappoint him. She lunged at him, a powerful downward strike which he evaded. He aimed a side strike at her that she easily parried. Then she reached over his hilt to cover his hand with her own and yanked towards her, David stumbled forward, and felt his sword forced from his grasp as she twisted to the right, leaving him an arm lock.

"I surrender!"

She released him immediately and he retrieved his sword. "Where did you learn to fight like that?" He asked in disbelief. The ease and swiftness with which she had disarmed him was frightening, even for a Guardian.

"Same place you did, at school."

Before David could continue his line of questioning, Tyler came up and claimed Kathryn for his next partner.

Putting his questions aside, David focused on his new partner, Daniel. His technique was subtler than Kathryn's but no less devastating, just in a different way. Carefully David mapped out his plan. Daniel was nowhere near as powerful as David when it came to brute strength, but he had an agile-ness to his fighting style that reminded David of a wolf.

Suddenly, Daniel smiled.

"What?" David asked cautiously.

His opponent shook his head. "Nothing. Are you ready?"

In answer, David lunged at him, but to his surprise, Daniel was already moving and deftly avoided his strike, landing one of his own. Astonished, David studied Daniel carefully. The younger man had moved as fast as Kathryn had...and with the same effectiveness and ease. Suspicious David ran through all of his memories of watching Daniel fight. Before he could even go through half of them, Daniel attacked with a high strike aimed at David's temple. David blocked but Daniel used the momentum from the collision to bounce his blade off of David's and whip it around for a strike at his midsection.

Moving to the right, David brought his own sword down in a sweeping block, moving their swords over their heads and to the left. Daniel brought up his elbow in a strike at David's nose. David ducked and, balancing on one leg, struck out at one of Daniel's legs. Amazingly, Daniel moved aside and brought his elbow down on David's shoulder. David let the elbow hit and then used the added momentum to roll out of Daniel's reach. Deciding that finesse was not going to win him this battle, David abandoned all subtlety and attacked with all of his energy.

Impressively, Daniel managed to block all of his moves and David disengaged, moving back a few feet. "How did you get this good?" He panted. "You didn't fight like this before."

Daniel grinned at him. "You make it easy."

I make it easy? David pondered his words. As if lightning had struck him, Daniel's words suddenly made sense. "You're reading my mind." It wasn't a question.

Daniel's grin widened. "I really remind you of a wolf?"

David shook his head in disbelief. "Alright, you've made your point. So teach me, how do I fight a mind reader?"

Daniel paused a moment, finally he said, "By emptying your mind."

David frowned. "How?"

For a minute that actually seemed to stump Daniel. "I don't know," he finally admitted. "Ask Kathryn, I can't glean anything from her mind when I fight her."

"Of course you can't," David muttered. Seeing that Tyler was waiting, David released Daniel as his partner and sought out Amy.

From the moment they began to spar he could see Kathryn's influence over her fighting. Like Kathryn, Amy fought with a single minded determination that David found disconcerting. Kathryn must have drilled Amy in speed and reflex drills because she was faster than he had expected. However, unlike Kathryn, Amy fought with a fiery ferocity that was exactly opposite of Kathryn's icy intensity. Amy came at him like a whirlwind, her sword flashing whereas Kathryn came at him like a predator who had cut off all avenues of escape. He wasn't sure which technique scared him more.

After two more radians of continuous sparing, David finally called a halt.

"Finally!" Matt groaned as he sank to the ground and rubbed his sore forearms. "I thought you'd have us sparring all day."

Natalie laughed. "Come on, Matt. It isn't that bad!"

He glared at her. "This from the girl who's started using her knives rather than her sword."

Natalie shrugged. "They're lighter and faster," she said with a wicked gleam in her eye.

David looked at Kathryn. "You're a bad influence, you know that right?"

Before she could answer, Matt spoke up mournfully. "Has anyone seen Lacey? I haven't been able to find her for the last two days."

One by one all of the Dragons voiced negative answers. "Where is she?" Matt groaned. "I'm worried sick!"

Destiny swooped down and landed on the grass beside him.

Matt eyed her apprehensively. "You wouldn't."

Destiny stared back at him.

Matt's expression became sorrowful. "You couldn't!"

Destiny opened her beak and belched.

"She did!" Natalie chirped cheerfully.

"Kathryn, I'm going to kill your bird."

"Before the feathers start flying," Jenna spoke up. "You might want to eat lunch first."

The redhead eyed Destiny with malicious intent. "You're right," he agreed. "She's easier to catch when she's full." He led the group back to the house and together, he and Cass, served lunch, which consisted of cold sandwiches, fruit, and cold water. Matt picked up and tilted a large stein. As he took a long swallow of his drink, Matt became aware that there was something big moving in his mouth.

Gagging, he threw his cup and spewed liquid all over the table, drawing shrieks from several of the girls and sounds of disgust from Luke and Daniel. But he ignored them for in the middle of the table, covered in water and his saliva, sat Lacey. His family erupted into laughter.

"If only you could see your face right now!" Luke laughed.

"B...but, how?" Matt asked flabbergasted.

"Gotcha!" Natalie crowed from several seats down.

Epilogue

Two Months Later

Generations of planning, destroyed. He hoped that whatever grave had been dug for the idiot Tanner had been shallow and ravaged by wild animals. Lord Tanner should never have been recruited into the Brotherhood of Fire. His dying words to the Guardians when they had rescued Lady Kathryn had alerted the Guardians to the presence of his previously invisible society. And on top of all that the idiot had let another of the swords fall into their hands, letting the Guardians know that they weren't the only ones with unstoppable weapons.

He hoped Lord Tanner burned forever in some fiery pit with no mercy.

Events that weren't supposed to happen for years, events that had been planned for almost a score of years, refined countless times and worked out to the minutest detail, he had been forced to reevaluate and reorganize. His spy on the Guardian Council had kept him abreast of the developments of their investigation into his organization, including the ruling that had ordered all inquiries into the matter over. However, his spy had warned him that there were certain parties within the Council who didn't agree with the ruling and were quietly continuing the investigation. He needed them distracted.

He hated the Guardians with every fiber of his being. They had taken everything from him and given him nothing in return. His life was nothing to him, the Brotherhood was everything. The Guardians needed to be destroyed and this was the first step.

Crawling slowly he made his way to the top of the ridge. When he reached the trees he stood slowly, blending in with the forest. This was the first execution he had scheduled for today. Tonight there would be one more. He waited patiently.

There! His target was walking with his wife through the royal gardens, no doubt celebrating something. The Queen always liked to celebrate something.

Taking a deep breath he pulled an arrow from his quiver and notched it. Slowly he pulled the bowstring back and took aim—

ℹ·℺

That night, Selvin slowly picked his way along the narrow path. To his back, sharp stone ripped into his skin as he kept his body pressed tightly against the cliff wall. It was pain he was willing to endure considering the alternative. The path was barely half a meter wide and wound along the side of the sea cliff with an ancient shoreline high above. Below he could hear the sharp slapping of the waves as they hit the base of the cliff, but even more ominous he could hear the roaring crashes of the waves breaking over the multitude of rocks and sea stacks jutting up from beneath the tumultuous water. The pain in his back was a small price to pay to avoid being broken on the rocks below.

He felt his way along the cliff, darkness hid the path and neither of the moons were visible through the heavy cloud cover cloaking the landscape in blackness. Finally his searching fingers felt a hole in the cliff. Pulling himself inside, he breathed a sigh of relief. He hated the trip necessary to reach the Brotherhood's gathering place.

More confident now that he wasn't a heartbeat away from falling to his death, Selvin moved quickly through the tunnel his footfalls falling dully on the damp rock. During his initial visits he had broken his nose several times before he had learned when the tunnel changed directions. Now, he easily navigated the dark path until, after turning a corner, his eyes were blinded by the sudden appearance of torches along the walls.

He had never learned how their leader kept the light of the torches from spilling around the corner, but he had also learned not to ask insignificant questions. Shivers ran up his spine just thinking about it. He vowed he would never make the same mistake that Talbor made. The dolt couldn't keep his mouth shut. Resisting the urge to cover his nose to block the stench of rotting sea life and dank mold, he hurried forward. To be late would be to forfeit his life.

Three more turns and a long hallway found him standing before an intricately carved wooden door. While the craftsmanship was breathtaking, the scenes depicted on the door would have unnerved even the most experienced of campaigners. There were images of men and women being tortured in various ways. Vines that had the heads of snakes curled around victims, their fangs a heartbeat away from the fatal bite. There were other images of creatures and tortures that Selvin had not recognized, but just looking at them made his skin crawl.

He opened the door and stepped into the room beyond. It was a circular room with blood red curtains hanging on the wall every four meters. In the center of the room a stone fire pit had been dug out. As near as Selvin knew, the fire that burned within the pit never went out. The flames licked out of the pit and reached upward several meters, illuminating the room.

Directly across from the door was a raised platform, upon which one lone throne stood. The stone the chair had been hewn from was as black as the tunnels had been, but it was covered in blood and fire jewels. Blood jewels, deep red with black veins running through them, were highly prized by the noble class, but fire jewels were forbidden to all but the king. At first glance, fire jewels appeared to be nothing more than a clear crystal, but when one looked closer, the observer would see a raging fire contained within the crystal. The flames ranged from red to white to blue. The black background of the chair enhanced the flames of the gems and made them normally visible, even from across the room.

But tonight he couldn't see the gems, he couldn't even see the chair. Instead, his attention was drawn to the three cloaked figures, standing on the dais, obscuring his view of the throne. He knew these men, they were the leaders of the Brotherhood. Their cloaks were black but were covered in flames that refused to burn through the cloth they covered. As he approached, Selvin could feel the heat from the fire pit on his back and the heat from the cloaks on his face.

Selvin knelt and touched his forehead to the cold, wet stone beneath his feet. "My Liege."

"I am disappointed in you."

Selvin winced. The cultured voice was carefully controlled, not allowing him to glimpse just how disappointed his master was.

He opted for the ignorant approach. "My Liege?"

The voiced hissed, "You have failed me."

"Please, My Liege..." Selvin started to protest but cut off his protest when fire coursed through his body in waves.

"Your assignment was simple, destroy the Dragons and keep Lord Tanner under control," The voice said harshly. "Instead the Dragons are stronger than ever and Lord Tanner's actions have cost this Brotherhood dearly. And you have lost your sword...again."

"I found it the first time," Selvin protested weakly.

"I found it," his master corrected. "And I gave it back to you without requiring blood payment."

Selvin winced. To create the magical swords that could withstand the attack of a Guardian sword, the Brotherhood had resorted to old magic thought to have been lost for centuries. It required the new sword's owner to sacrifice part of his body during the smelting process. It was the blood of the owner that gave the sword the red veins and only lived as long as the one who donated the blood. Once the owner died, the sword would dissolve into blood. Selvin had given the tip of his little finger and at his master's reminder the phantom tip began to throb as it had the day it came off.

"I will not fail you again, master," Selvin promised. He waited in silence for several long moments before his master uttered two slow words.

"I know."

Two simple words. From a teacher to a student they could have been seen as words of encouragement, but from master to servant, they were deadly ominous.

Before Selvin could reply he heard the flap of heavy fabric and the room was suddenly filled with the strong scent of Gredenia flowers. A low growl sounded from behind him and he couldn't help himself. Selvin turned to look.

His blood froze in his veins and all the strength fled from his body. "Wh—wha—what...?!"

"Do you like my new pet?" His master asked softly. "It has taken me years to find it. All but the Brotherhood believed it to be a myth, but we knew better."

Selvin felt terror unlike anything he'd ever imagined. "Tha— that's...impossible!" He turned to face the hooded figures on the dais in time to see his master nod.

In the space of a heartbeat the nightmare was on him and its claws were wrapped around his body. "Master, please!" Selvin begged as he desperately struggled.

Pain blossomed in his lower back and then nothing. A glance down showed that despite Selvin's mental commands, his legs remained as limp and unmoving as a doll's. More pain, just below his neck and Selvin found himself paralyzed from the neck down.

Helpless he could only watch in horror as the creature unhooked its massive jaws and force them over his head. Selvin could feel the hot wet sticky salvia as his body— no, its body was pulled over him. The curved needle-like teeth dug deep furrows into his scalp. The pain flared once more, and then darkness

℥·℣

The Master watched silently as his new weapon finished with his worthless servant. Satisfied with the display he ordered it back to the holding pen.

"You have come a long way with it," one of his companions observed.

"With it at our side, we cannot lose," the second said confidently.

"Now that my earlier mission has been completed, we are ready to begin the next phase," The Master agreed. "It is time to unleash our new weapon."

Glossary

Radian—A unit of time similar to an earth hour

There are 26 radians in one day

The calendar is comprised of thirteen months, each with twenty-eight days. Once every four years there is an extra day added at the beginning of each year. It is considered a free day and not a part of the yearly day count. The twenty-eight days are divided into four weeks.

Two moons are visible in the sky. Firea is the smaller of the moons, purple in hue, with a three week cycle. Niea is the larger of the moons, red in color, with a six week cycle.

Days of the week: Lumbar, Nénar, Ambar, Tancol, Carnil, Elemmírë, Luinil

The months of the year and the seven major holidays:

Spring:
Narvinyë—Dark Moon (New Year's Day: 01 Narvinyë)
Nárië—Growing Moon
Cermië—Flower Moon (Festival of the Moons: 03 Cermië)

Summer:
Urimë—Mead Moon
Lótessë—Lightning Moon (Girl's Day: 05 Lótessë)
Víressë—Honey Moon

Fall:
Hísimë—Storm Moon (Boy's Day: 07 Hísimë)
Narquelië—Blood Moon
Súlimë—Harvest Moon (Festival of Stars: 09 Súlimë)

Winter:
Nénimë—Winter Moon
Yavannië—Frost Moon
Nénarë—Old Moon
Airë—New Moon (Festival of the Solstice: 13 Airë.
            Day of Cleansing: 28 Airë.)